# Fate of the Five
## Veil of Vasara
## Niamh Rose

Niamh Rose

Copyright © [2024] by (Niamh Rose)

All rights reserved.

No portion of this book may be reproduced in any form without written permission from the publisher or author, except as permitted by U.K. copyright law.

For the people who were saved by stories.
For the people whose comfort characters carried them through.
I'm glad you're here.
This is for you.

# Trigger Warnings

*F*ate of the Five is an epic fantasy with several dark themes. Please be aware of the trigger warnings below.

Involvement (on page) of: violence, blood, captivity, imprisonment, torture, death, poverty, hate crimes, riots, animal cruelty/abuse, scars, nightmares, mental health issues, (including a panic attack scene and a derealisation scene), infant harm, alcohol abuse, substance abuse, PTSD, loss of a limb, chronic pain, ableism (towards a disabled main character that is not romanticised), sexual assault (not romanticised, including one scene of attempted rape that is thwarted).

Mention (off page): domestic abuse, child abuse, paedophilia, suicide.

*"The integration of magic wielders into society is mandatory and enforceable by law. All magic wielders across Vasara, Jurasa, Kalnasa, Audra, and Zeima will be allocated designated living quarters. These quarters will be located within the established draining centre of each Kingdom, where magic wielders will voluntarily partake in the periodic draining of their magical cores into the earth, as Vessels, to ensure Athlion's survival. Any non-magic wielder who shows signs of the development of a magical core, be it Darean or Acciperean in nature, must report this to the authorities immediately, so that they may be integrated. Any magic wielder attempting to avoid integration, and any non-magic wielder harbouring such sorcerers, will be tried and executed under Vasara's, the ruling Kingdom's, law."*

*- The Thirty Second Tenant of Vasara's Justice Treaty*

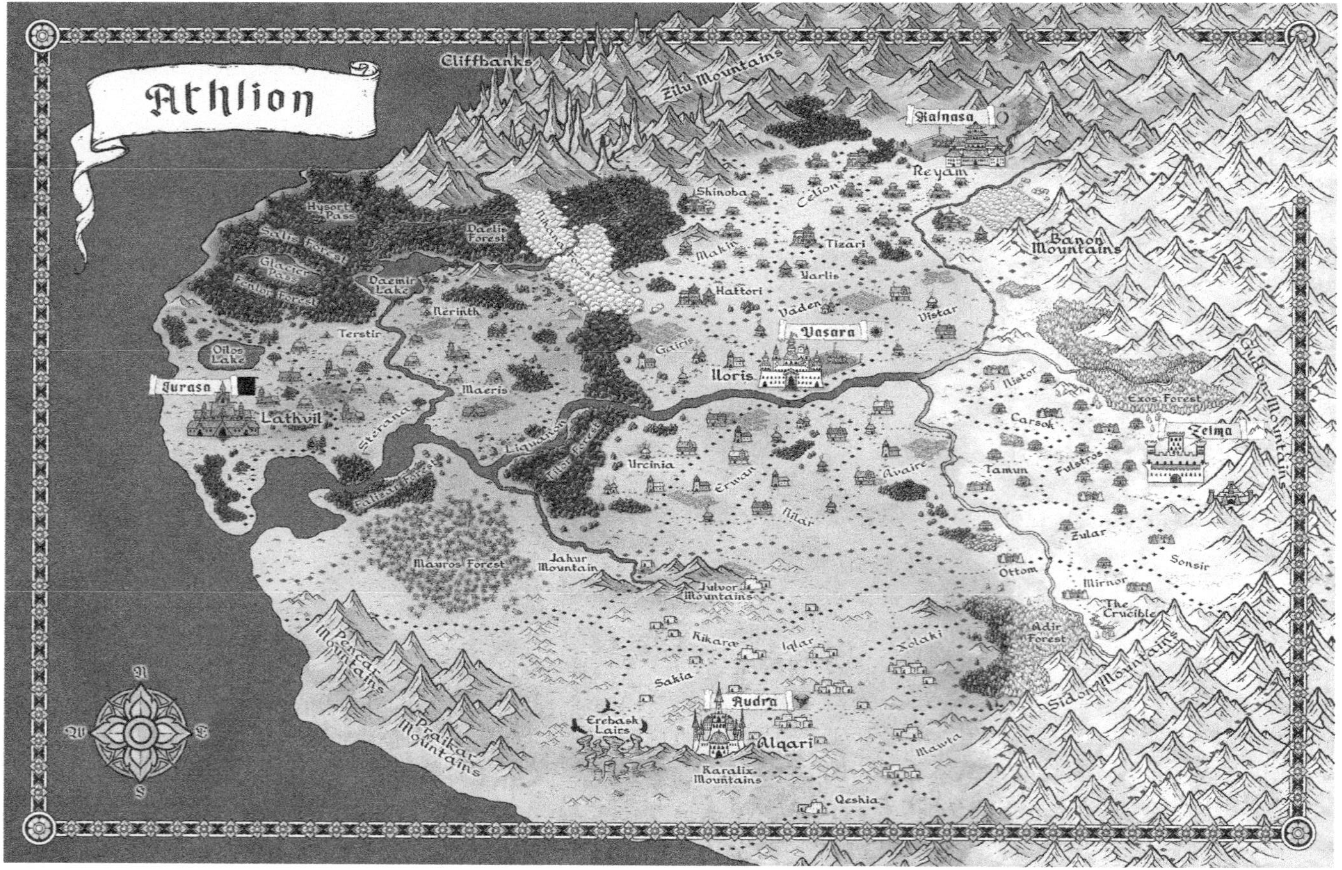
Athlion
Cliffbanks
Zilu Mountains
Rainasa
Reyam
Shinoba
Celion
Makir
Tizari
Yarlis
Haftori
Vaden
Vistar
Vasara
Banon Mountains
Hysort Pass
Salis Forest
Glacier Pass
Fenlor Forest
Daelis Forest
Daemir Lake
Nerinth
Terstir
Oilos Lake
Jurasa
Lathvil
Maeris
Sterana
Gairis
Iloris
Nistor
Exos Forest
Carsok
Zeima
Tamun
Fulstros
Urcinia
Erwan
Avaire
Nilar
Zular
Sonsir
Mauros Forest
Jahur Mountain
Julvor Mountains
Ottom
Mirnor
The Crucible
Adir Forest
Kikara
Iqlar
Xolaki
Sakia
Sidon Mountains
Pencar Mountains
Praikar Mountains
Erebask Lairs
Audra
Alqari
Mawta
Karalix Mountains
Qeshia
N
W
E
S

# Athlion

Athlion is made up of Five Kingdoms. Each Kingdom has its own Royal Family. Vasara is the ruling Kingdom and its monarch therefore, rules Athlion. Each Kingdom is known for its distinct weather conditions, architecture, and the physical characteristics of its inhabitants.

## Vasara (Va-sarr-uh) – Vasarans, known as "The Leaders"

**Hair:** red, auburn, brown, coppery blonde, straight mostly, slightly waved

**Eyes**: varying shades of brown or red, rarely blue

**Skin**: white or slightly tanned white

**Colours**: Reds, golds, oranges, white, and pale blue

**Attire**: Extravagant, expensive, sharply cut, often modern and regal

**Weapons of choice (with specialities in italics):** *Swords, whips, bayonets*, daggers, crossbow, bow and arrows

**Main magical creature native to Vasara**: Chimera

**Emblem**: The Sun on a red flag

**Weather conditions**: Sunny, warm

**Patron Gods**:

- Furos (Few-ros): Male, God of Fire and Perseverance

- Terros (Tair-os): Female, Goddess of Earth, and Wisdom

**People of note**:

- Eliel Solisan (Eh-lee-al Sor-liss-un): King, 26

- Elias Solisan (Eh-lee-as Sor-liss-un): A Lord, the King's cousin, 28

- Jarian: Captain of Vasara's King's guard, 42

- Trenton: Councilman, 37

- Wayman: Councilman, 67

- Raynard: Councilman, head, 61

- Fargreaves: Councilman, 35

- Gwin: Chambermaid, 18

- Narvo: Curser/Curse user who works for Vasara, 45

- Tarren Lestor: Noblewoman, Vasara's candidate for the Courting Season, 22

- Parthias: (Parthee-as): overseer of drainage at Vasara, 46

- Faina: (Fae-na): Vessel from Vasara, 24

- Vale: Vessel from Vasara, 20

- Orlis: Vessel from Vasara, 19

- Erilia (Air-ril-ee-ah): Elias' mother, sister to Elion, 49

- Harlin: Erilia's sister-in-law, 42

- Agnesa: servant of Elias' family, previously of Elia's father Gillion, 52

- Gendall: Blacksmith and Jewellery merchant, 45

- Elion Solisan: dead but mentioned, Eliel's father, died aged 47

- Celise Solisan: dead but mentioned, Eliel's mother, died aged 45

- Malia Solisan: dead but mentioned, Eliel's younger sister, died aged 9

- Gillion (Gill-ee-on): dead but mentioned, Elias' father, died aged 39

## Trackers (a regiment of Vasara)

The trackers are a unit that consist of former Vessels (captured sorcerers who drain magic back into Athlion's earth). The trackers are cursed and bound (by the Curse of Servitude) to hunt down other sorcerers in exchange for small partial freedoms.

**Weapons of choice (speciality in italics)**: *Crossbows, bow and arrows*, swords, whips
**People of note**:

- Shadae (Sha-day): new recruit, originally from Zeima, Darean class four, Navigator, 25

- Cheadd (Chee-ad): Commander of trackers, originally from Jurasa, Darean class three, Elementalist, Lightening and Fire, 48

- Vykros, (Vick-ros): originally from Vasara, Darean, class four, Teleporter and Navigator, 26

- Lideus (Lid-ee-us): originally from Jurasa, Darean, class four, Teleporter and Nourisher, 29

- Ava: originally from Jurasa, Darean, class four, Shielder, 18

## Audra (Or-dra) – Audrans known as "The Warriors"

**Hair**: Almost always black, sometimes dark brown, silky straight, tousled, curled
**Eyes:** black, brown, gold, or hazel
**Skin:** Golden skin tone, pale to moderate tan
**Colours:** Gold, black, purple, navy, and silver
**Attire:** Dark, elaborate, jewelled, transparent, sheer, thicker in colder weather, and for their warriors - dark, sharp, and supple
**Weapons of choice (with specialities in italics)**: *Daggers, shakens (throwing stars), dual swords, brass knuckles,* swords, sabres
**Main magical creature native to Audra:** Erebasks (see glossary for description)
**Emblem:** Tornado on golden flag
**Weather conditions**: Sandy, dry thunderstorms, humid
**Patron Gods:**

- Tundros (Tun-dros): Male, God of Thunder, and Courage

- Ventos: Female, Goddess of Air and Freedom

**People of note:**

- Nathon Albarsan (Nay-then Al-bur-sun): Prince, 24

- Loria (Lore-ee-ah Al-bur-sun) Albarsan: Princess, 21

- Sarlan (Sar-lun) Albarsan: King, 49

- Strava (Strah-va) Albarsan: Queen, 41

- Kazal (Ku-zal): Nathon's Erebask

- Mathias: Sarlan's right hand man, 50

- Silus (Sigh-las): an agent that works for Sarlan, 28

- Ruban (Rue-ban): an agent that works for Sarlan, 27

- Alijah: an agent works for Sarlan, 22

- Julios: an agent that works for Sarlan, 24

- Rina: an agent that works for Sarlan, 23

- Marco: overseer at Audra's draining centres, 42

- Arton: former overseer at Audra's draining centre, died aged 34.

- Karll: former overseer at Audra's draining centre, died aged 31

## Kalnasa (Cal-nass-uh) – Kalnasans known as "The Rangers"

**Hair:** brown, silver, white, black, often braided or straight
**Eyes:** lilac, dark blue, silver, grey
**Skin:** beige, sandy, white
**Colours:** mint green, pale blue, purple, peach-pink, silver
**Attire:** Robes, fluid, elegant, ethereal like
**Weapons of choice (with specialities in italics):** *Spears, lances, staffs,* swords, bows and arrows, crossbows
**Main magical creature native to Kalnasa:** Pegasus
**Emblem:** The moon on a blue flag
**Weather conditions:** Cool, airy, rainy, windy, often rains, early spring like
**Patron Gods:**

- Terros: Female, Goddess of Earth, and Wisdom

- Ventos: Female, Goddess of Air and Freedom

**People of note:**

- Hestan Hikari (Hess-tun Hick-arr-ee): Captain of Kalnasa's Hunt, 30
- Dyna Kumosan (Deena Coo-mo-sun): The King's Niece, 16
- Dunlan Kumosan: King, 45
- Dryselle (Dri-sell) Kumosan: King's Sister, 43
- Lyra (Lie-ra) Kumosan: Queen, 37
- Purcell: Member of the Hunt, 23
- Zain: Member of the Hunt, 38
- Kaspian: Member of the Hunt, 33
- Mulani (Moo-larn-ee): Captain of Kalnasa's King's guard, 34
- Amdir (Am-dear): Smith and weapon's expert, 59
- Xora (Zo-ra): Member of the Hunt, 28

## Jurasa (Juw-ra-suh) – Jurasans known as "The Scholars"

**Eyes:** Aqua, green, or blue
**Hair:** golden blonde, ash blonde or dark blonde, often slightly curled or wavy, sometimes straight
**Skin:** white, pale, or rosy, can be freckled
**Colours:** green, blue, aqua, olive, brown, bright gold
**Attire:** Comfortable, folk and village like
**Weapons of choice (with specialities in italics):** *Bow and arrows, crossbows, long swords, tridents,* swords, nets
**Main magical creatures native to Jurasa:** Larlynx's (see glossary for description)
**Emblem:** Sea waves on a green flag
**Weather conditions:** Autumnal, cooler towards the coast/Kalnasa, warmer and more humid at the border of Vasara
**Patron Gods:**

- Aquos: Female, Goddess of Water and Emotions
- Arkos: Male, God of Wood, and Tranquillity

**People of note:**

- (First name unknown) Orthisan (Or-thee-sun): Jurasan King, 27

- Maiwen Orthisan (May-win, Or-thee-sun): Princess, 19

- Lord Beckett: Maiwen's escort and a member of Jurasa's King's guard, 33

- Lord Parlin: Maiwen's escort/member of Jurasa's King's guard, 26

## Zeima (Zee-ma) – Zeimans, known as "The Strategists"

**Hair:** dark brown, black, usually textured, thick, or curly for example. This is also the only Kingdom that uses herbs and plants to 'dye' their hair a variety of bold colours (usually strands of it)

**Eyes:** blue grey, brown, dark brown

**Skin:** Dark brown/black

**Colours:** Blue, pale blue, brown, white, grey,

**Attire:** Cloaked, patterned, sturdy, bold

**Weapons of choice (with specialities in italics):** *Axes, hammers, boomerangs, blowpipes,* swords, bow, and arrows

**Main magical creatures native to Zeima:** Vilkan Wolves (see glossary for description)

**Emblem:** Snowy mountains on a silver flag

**Weather conditions:** Cold, snowy, icy, bitter

**Patron Gods:**

- Glacios (Glass-ee-os): Male, God of Ice and Intelligence

- Aquos; Female, Goddess of Water and Emotions

**People of note:**
- Xena Thelusan (Zee-na Thair-lew-sun): Queen, 53

- Rhana Thelusan (Rain-ah Thair-lew-sun): Princess: 26

- Ako Thelusan: Rhana's older brother and Prince, 34

- Koro Thelusan: Rhana's older brother and Prince, 32

- Hakim Thelusan: Rhana's older brother and Prince, 30

- Tylil Thelusan: Rhana's older brother and Prince, 28

- Jayli (Jay-lee): Guard/escort of Rhana, 24

## Main rebel sorcerer group

There are many groups of surviving and rebel sorcerers throughout Athlion. Many work together. The largest group is at the focus of *Fate of the Five, Veil of Vasara's* events.

**People of note:**

- Nemina (Na-mee-na): origins not fully known, Acciperean, abilities not fully known, 24

- Baz Nahar: originally from Audra, Acciperean, abilities not yet fully known, 21

- Yaseer (Ya-sear): originally from Zeima, leader and founding member of rebel sorcerer group, Darean, class two, Sense Transformer, 46

- Nyla: originally from Kalnasa, Darean, class three, Elementalist, Earth and Fire, 29

- Ullna: originally from Jurasa, second leader and founder of rebel sorcerer group, Darean, class two, Telekinetic, 58

- Riece: originally from Vasara, Darean class four, Navigator, 28

- Fasal: originally from Audra, Darean class four, Nourisher, 31

- Aeesha (Aye-ee-sha): originally from Audra, Darean, class four, Teleporter, 30

# Contents

1. CHAPTER 1 - NATHON — 1
2. CHAPTER 2 – THE ACCIPEREAN — 7
3. CHAPTER 3 - LORIA — 14
4. CHAPTER 4 - ELIEL — 19
5. CHAPTER 5 - NATHON — 29
6. CHAPTER 6 - HESTAN — 42
7. CHAPTER 7 - LORIA — 51
8. CHAPTER 8 - ELIEL — 63
9. CHAPTER 9 - HESTAN — 71
10. CHAPTER 10 – NATHON — 78
11. CHAPTER 11 - HESTAN — 85
12. CHAPTER 12 - LORIA — 94
13. CHAPTER 13 - LORIA — 100
14. CHAPTER 14 - NATHON — 106
15. CHAPTER 15 - THE ACCIPEREAN — 116
16. CHAPTER 16 - ELIAS — 122
17. CHAPTER 17 – NEMINA — 127
18. CHAPTER 18 - LORIA — 140
19. CHAPTER 19 - NATHON — 148
20. CHAPTER 20 - NATHON — 158
21. CHAPTER 21 - ELIEL — 167

| | | |
|---|---|---|
| 22. | CHAPTER 22- ELIAS | 175 |
| 23. | CHAPTER 23- ELIEL | 184 |
| 24. | CHAPTER 24- SHADAE | 191 |
| 25. | CHAPTER 25 - LORIA | 199 |
| 26. | CHAPTER 26 - NATHON | 205 |
| 27. | CHAPTER 27 – ELIEL | 212 |
| 28. | CHAPTER 28 – ELIAS | 218 |
| 29. | CHAPTER 29 – NATHON | 221 |
| 30. | CHAPTER 30- HESTAN | 224 |
| 31. | CHAPTER 31- LORIA | 230 |
| 32. | CHAPTER 32 – BAZ | 236 |
| 33. | CHAPTER 33– SHADAE | 240 |
| 34. | CHAPTER 34 – ELIAS | 249 |
| 35. | CHAPTER 35 – NATHON | 255 |
| 36. | CHAPTER 36 - HESTAN | 258 |
| 37. | CHAPTER 37- BAZ | 267 |
| 38. | CHAPTER 38 – LORIA | 274 |
| 39. | CHAPTER 39- NATHON | 283 |
| 40. | CHAPTER 40 – LORIA | 291 |
| 41. | CHAPTER 41- NATHON | 305 |
| 42. | CHAPTER 42 - HESTAN | 310 |
| 43. | CHAPTER 43- SHADAE | 316 |
| 44. | CHAPTER 44- BAZ | 332 |
| 45. | CHAPTER 45- ELIAS | 340 |
| 46. | CHAPTER 46- SHADAE | 349 |
| 47. | CHAPTER 47– NATHON | 367 |
| 48. | CHAPTER 48 – HESTAN | 375 |
| 49. | CHAPTER 49 – NEMINA | 378 |

50. CHAPTER 50- NATHON — 381
51. CHAPTER 51- HESTAN — 391
52. CHAPTER 52- NEMINA — 401
53. CHAPTER 53- NEMINA — 411
54. CHAPTER 54- SHADAE — 421
55. CHAPTER 55 – HESTAN — 437
56. CHAPTER 56- NEMINA — 458
57. CHAPTER 57- NEMINA — 465
58. CHAPTER 58 – HESTAN — 474
59. CHAPTER 59- BAZ — 479
60. CHAPTER 60 - NEMINA — 485
61. CHAPTER 61- ELIEL — 495
62. CHAPTER 62- SHADAE — 504
63. CHAPTER 63- HESTAN — 516
64. CHAPTER 64- NATHON — 532
65. CHAPTER 65 - NATHON — 537
66. CHAPTER 66 – THE HEALER — 546
67. CHAPTER 67- SHADAE — 548
68. CHAPTER 68 – LORIA — 556
69. CHAPTER 69 - HESTAN — 561
70. CHAPTER 70 -SHADAE — 574
71. CHAPTER 71 – BAZ — 586
72. CHAPTER 72- ELIEL — 592
73. CHAPTER 73- NATHON — 598
74. CHAPTER 74 - SHADAE — 604
75. CHAPTER 75 – HESTAN — 612
76. CHAPTER 76 – NATHON — 622
77. CHAPTER 77- LORIA — 627

| 78. | CHAPTER 78- HESTAN | 632 |
| 79. | CHAPTER 79- NEMINA | 637 |
| 80. | CHAPTER 80- HESTAN | 644 |
| 81. | CHAPTER 81- HESTAN | 648 |
| 82. | CHAPTER 82- ELIAS | 653 |
| 83. | CHAPTER 83- NATHON | 656 |
| 84. | THE END... | 660 |
| 85. | GLOSSARY OF LORE | 661 |
| 86. | ACKNOWLEDGEMENTS | 670 |
| 87. | ABOUT THE AUTHOR | 672 |

# CHAPTER 1- NATHON

I should have brought a thicker rag to gag him with.

His screams were far louder than I had anticipated. They continued to crackle against the cloth, weaving through the forest around us.

I winced. His voice box should have given out by now. I peered at him more closely, wondering about his vocal capacity as I leant against a tree by the lake. The dark of the night coloured the water black, shrouded the man and I in shadow.

I always made sure to conduct my work in those shadows, away from the prying eyes of other people and the sun.

After all, if anyone stumbled across my path, I would be ordered to kill them.

And I preferred to keep the killing by his orders to a minimum.

In truth, I would have preferred to avoid it all together, but I had been afforded little choice when it came to the matter, since I was a child.

Perhaps that was a lie. Perhaps I did have a choice, then and now. Perhaps I had simply become very, very good at telling myself very convincing lies.

The man's wheezes of exhaustion drew me from my speculations. I pushed myself off the bark, spinning the dagger I'd just used to pull off his seventh fingernail between my thumb and forefinger. I crouched in front of him. Tears were in his eyes, and dark strands of hair clung to his forehead, slick with the sweat pain had drawn from his pores.

He made several noises which sounded like grunts of anger and whimpers of desperation. Still, he made no indication he would talk, no sign that he wished for me to stop.

I wished he would talk. I wished this could stop.

My assignment was to discover the names of all those who had been involved in this getaway and, of course…to end all their lives.

So far, I had discovered nothing from this man.

I sighed, and with a mask of indifference looked directly at him. He was older than I had anticipated, I guessed around forty-three, forty-four. I had become good at estimating ages, at estimating most things.

I started talking, the man's gaze, clouded by fatigue, found its way to my face. "I must admit that I'm rather thankful to you."

He looked confused and furrowed his brows.

"Most of the people I have the pleasure of speaking with give up so quickly. It doesn't afford me much time to practice new techniques. I've been dying for an opportunity to experiment on someone with more...stamina, shall we say?"

My speech of falsehoods had worked. He looked terrified, but also...repulsed. He looked at me in a way that told me, without a gag, he would have spat the blood he had accumulated in his mouth at my face.

I can't say that I would have blamed him.

I sighed, glad my performance was achieving its desired effect. "So, tonight is going to be rather enjoyable. For me, of course, I should add...most certainly not for you."

I forced a laugh, intending to unnerve him as I put the dagger back inside my belt. I took out another. This one was waved, jagged at the sides, utterly useless during combat but for these purposes, ideal.

Sarlan had given it to me as a gift when I was eleven.

I ran the dagger along the man's exposed upper chest. He tensed up, his breathing quickened. I dragged the blade down his torso.

The next instant, I was in. The man yelled, yelled with such ferocity that I had to place my other hand over his mouth, causing him to fall backwards from his knees and onto the grass below us. I hovered over him, kneeling by his side. His face had grown significantly paler, from panic and blood loss, I assumed.

I stopped, just before I would have punctured a vital organ. That would have resulted in his immediate death. I still needed some more time.

"Now, as much as I'd like to see how long you'll last, I am here for a reason. So...I suppose that means I'll offer you a choice. You can answer my question, or I can indulge my curiosity. Which would you prefer?"

I begged whatever powers may be to loosen this man's lips.

This was not a curiosity that I wanted indulged. This was no curiosity at all.

But the man did not answer.

I slid the blade upwards. He cried out again and coughed, choking on the gag.

Gods, this gag really was terrible.

I used my free hand to yank the gag out, which had been half protruding from his mouth. As swiftly as I had done so, I positioned my hand back over his face to stop pleas for help escaping from his lips.

"Here's what I'll do," I suggested. "In a moment, I'll remove my hand. If you scream, I'll take that as a sign you're willing to take part in my experiments, if not, then the blade will move no further. Understood?"

The man nodded underneath my hand. I removed it.

He did not scream, but he did say, "There was no one else."

Relief flooded my chest. He was finally talking.

I placed my blade down, the grass tickling at my knuckles. I gave him an incredulous look. "You mean to tell me you were able to flee without any assistance whatsoever?"

"Yes," he gasped, rather than said. His body was beginning to fail him.

"You're not lying to me, are you?" I leant a little closer.

"No. No. I'm not."

That made two dishonest men, submerged in this grass.

He was so willing to protect the others. They had certainly not shared his sense of loyalty.

"You see, before I found you here," I addressed him, "I came across several individuals who all told me a rather different story. What were the names? Iavan, yes that was one of them. Remind me, was he the younger or elderly one, I can't recall?

"I don't...I don't know an Iavan," he said hesitantly.

"He seemed to know rather a lot about you. How would that be possible, without your mutual acquaintance? Unless he was some sort of secret, extremely resourceful admirer of yours...Arton?"

Arton's eyelids flickered with fear at the sound of his name falling from my lips.

"Let's try that again." I pressed my hand against his open wound to induce discomfort and stress my impatience. "Who organised your little escapade?"

He let out a wail of pain before answering, "We.... we all did." His voice was little more than a whisper now.

They all did? This was not a case then, of one man's gold buying the silence of others, of a man buying his way out.

To find the escapees, to end their lives, that was my assignment.

It was not part of my assignment to ask the next question I found myself putting to him.

"Why?"

Arton's eyelids fluttered closed. I compressed his wound. It would be better if he didn't bleed out before our conversation was over. Sensing the pressure, he craned his neck down, then back up at me.

"Answer me."

"Why? I'm...I'm dead anyway."

"Yes, Arton, you are," I nodded. "But your child is not."

Arton did not know, of course, that I would never take the life of a child. That was the one thing I had refused to do, and I had suffered for it.

But my reputation preceded me. There were whispers of all kinds, that I had murdered babies in their cribs, and slaughtered flocks of toddlers. That I had danced on the bones of infants and cackled at their cries.

I only needed Arton to believe I would kill his child, and I could tell by the look in his eyes that he did. That, and his surprise.

Arton had made great efforts to hide the existence of his son, even when he had lived among us, but his attempts at discretion were easily overturned by the same currencies I'd found usually worked on everyone...money, threats, and bribes.

"You really don't know? You...of all people." Arton sounded genuinely surprised.

"Evidently," I bit.

Arton took in a few more heaving breaths, looking up at the night sky with resignation.

"The things they're doing there...it's...they..." he drifted off again.

"They what?"

Arton's eyes closed over. I shook him. He jolted back to a barely perceptible level of consciousness.

"Arton. If you do not finish your sentence before you draw your last breath, I will send your son into the afterlife to meet you. You know I will," I insisted, pushing down the personal revulsion at my own sentence.

Much to my astonishment, Arton lifted his right hand and grabbed my forearm.

"They are lying. They are...dying."

I was starting to think Arton had become delirious from the loss of his blood volume, until he whispered. "Mar..."

But the remnants of his promised words dissolved into the darkness.

His arm fell to the ground with a thud.

Arton was dead.

I looked at Arton for a moment. He had passed sooner than I expected. But there were times I knew, when a man's spirit waned long before his body did, making that slip into death far faster, far sweeter.

A twinge of remorse suddenly played at my gut over his son. It wasn't the first time I had taken someone's father from them, someone's husband, friend, mother, daughter. It was only that I never usually had the time or the information to think too deeply on it. I didn't allow myself to either. I knew the alternative, for her and for me.

I was a liar, yes, and I was selfish as well.

It was a cruel truth of the world, that men like Arton died, while men like me lived.

There was movement in the trees behind me.

I didn't move. I waited. I pretended to be unaware.

"Get anything out of this one then?" A smug voice emerged from the darkness.

Silus.

I let out the tension I'd been holding in my core, preparing for an attack.

Occasionally, Sarlan would send others to check on my progress, my results, ever since I'd refused to complete the task he had set for me, all those years ago.

Far behind Silus, watching in the shade cast by the branches, was Ruban.

He'd sent two of them. I had to suppress a laugh.

"Nothing," I lied to Silus. "The same as all the others."

I debated the probability of my lie being discovered. Knowing Silus, it was relatively high. I knew when I was suffering the consequences of this lie, I may regret my decision, but that was a problem for days away. Weeks, if I was fortunate.

Silus peered over my shoulder to examine the body. His long dark hair swept over his face. He whistled in admiration after examining Arton's wounds. "You gave it your best. He'll be pleased about that."

As Silus laughed, I grabbed Arton by the ankles. "Take his shoulders," I instructed.

Silus did as I asked. The soil squelched beneath our boots as we moved towards the lake. Ruban watched us from a distance, eating something.

"It doesn't make sense," Silus mused. "Nobody runs for nothing. People don't risk their lives, fleeing in the middle of the night for no reason."

"No," I agreed. "They don't."

"What do you think happened?" Silus raised a brow.

I couldn't trust Silus with any information. Silus worshipped the man who gave us orders as if he were one of the Nine Gods themselves.

The Nine. If they were real, and as benevolent as many claimed, then it would have been my dead body being dragged across this plane.

"I think their death has mitigated the need for that question," I lied. Again. If anything, their death only made its answering more urgent.

But I preferred to work alone, and not with the tendrils of Silus's breath creeping down my neck. Or Ruban's, who I trusted even less.

"Always the pessimist, Prince," Silus grinned.

"Do you have any theories?" I asked, ignoring his attempt at camaraderie.

Silus shrugged and the shoulders of Arton's body moved up and down. "He did something which made someone angry. He tried to flee. He didn't get far."

I suppose I was foolish to expect a deeper insight from him.

Arton's escape plan had been terrible. He had been a terrible planner and a poor strategist who had trusted the wrong people.

But he had also been brave.

Anyone who would attempt to run from them, from me, possessed a certain level of bravery. A naïve, ignorant, desperate sort of bravery.

I couldn't decide whether I admired it or found it utterly ridiculous.

It was clear that Arton had carried secrets, secrets they were desperate to conceal.

How fortunate then, that extracting secrets was my speciality.

Arton's body sank into the water, enveloping his limbs one by one. The chill night air slapped against my face as I turned away from the sight.

"Leaving so soon?" Silus called out.

I looked over my shoulder. "Would you like to hold hands perhaps? Say a prayer to Noxos for his soul together?"

Silus tutted, tilting his head to the side.
I had no time for him, or to pay my respects.
No ability to dwell on his death for too long.
I had somewhere to be.
It was time to return to Audra.
It was time to pay Marco a visit.

# CHAPTER 2 – THE ACCIPEREAN

Four days had passed since I'd eaten.

Two nearly since I'd had water.

Today was the first I'd been allowed to wash myself in a week.

Earlier than usual.

Strange.

The water was cold enough to feel as if it were stripping the skin off my starved frame. I shuddered as I attempted to wipe the grime from my limbs.

A thud, loud and impatient, sounded to my left. I winced, fixing my gaze upwards, clutching at the sharp shard of soap I'd been given.

"You've got one more minute. We're not letting you try again," a voice hollered from around the corner.

*Try again.*

I scrubbed at my palms faster.

It wouldn't work.

I had tried to die many times before.

But I could never die fast enough, they always caught me before I could slip into that oblivion.

Because they needed my power. I was one of the few Accipereans left.

I grabbed the rag hanging on the wall, placing it over my body moments before the guard emerged.

Marco. I knew this one's name, unlike most the others, to whom I gave numbers. He looked as he always did, a pale tan made even cooler by the black of his short hair and uniform.

His dark gaze was trained on me suspiciously. "You took too long."

I said nothing.

If he was hoping for an apology, some profuse admittance of wrongdoing, he was hoping in vain.

He strode forwards, I stalked behind him.

I wanted to die, yes, but I did not want to grovel.

Grovelling seemed worse than death to me.

I shook my head at the absurdity of the thought. I didn't understand that part of me, thrashing around, fighting to live. The taste of resignation on my tongue always seemed so sweet but the words 'I'm not done' dripped from them each time I opened my mouth.

Or in this instance, kept it closed.

I was shoved onto the floor of my cell.

It was hardly difficult to ascertain why I was in despair, but harder to understand why I insisted on maintaining any shred of dignity I'd been afforded.

They took it away, after the Wielders' War. I had been five when that had started, decades ago. The Five Kingdoms had united to eliminate sorcery from our lands.

Both kinds of sorcerers, Accipereans and Dareans drew power from the earth. They drew power from the air, the water, the soil, and the sun to use their magic. But for Dareans, their magic gave back to the world in kind. They were the healers, elementalists, protectors, transporters. But for Accipereans like me, their magic took a little more, from the land and, they said, from the self.

There used to be so many of us, illusionists, enchanters, necromancers, divinators.

Destroyers.

But there had been Accipereans who craved domination. Accipereans who would have bled the world dry to obtain it, had they not been defeated.

Now, we were paying for their mistakes, for their greed.

We were paying and they were gone.

We were told we should be grateful for our half-lives. After all, Vasara, Kalnasa, Zeima, Audra, and Jurasa, had planned to wipe out sorcery completely, to kill all sorcerers, to crush us. They pointed at the crumbs of the feasts they had barred us from, chanting 'look how we feed you.' They liked to think themselves generous. They cast themselves as saviours in Athlion's story.

But I had heard the real stories, carried by hushed voices of guards and overseers, or from fellow captives, during those rare moments we were able to utter words to one another. I had heard many things, before they put me down here, deep in the underbelly of Audra's lands.

I had heard that the Five Kingdoms did, at first, crush us. That it was only after doing so, that they discovered sorcery was necessary for our world. Without it, foul things festered, crops died, the seasons stopped changing, the rain stopped falling.

They believed, foolishly, that they could undo what they had done. They captured Dareans and creatures of sorcery, hoping to use them and their abilities to remedy their mistakes.

Not Accipereans though, they did not think there was any use for those whose magic took from the world. They slaughtered every Accipereans they could find.

They devised a way to harness the magic of Dareans, to mine it and pour it back into our lands unnaturally, through a variety of instruments, devices, and torturous procedures.

And it worked.

For a little while.

Until the roots of trees grew so deep, they ripped through the earth. The days grew too long and the nights too short. The rivers overran and the seas rose, threatening to swallow everything whole.

Until they realised, they needed us, they needed Accipereans too.

They hunted down every Acciperean still breathing.

They needed balance, but they had murdered so many of us that there were practically none of us left. The few who had escaped were hiding and running. Some were still out there now, living a life in vacant, overlooked spaces.

I could barely remember my parents, or my life before this place. I'd spent practically every waking moment as a captive. They'd taken me from whatever home I'd had. They took all the Accipereans away from their families, their houses, their hideouts. But still, I knew as surely as the beat of my heart, that they were no saviours. Some desperate cry from my chest called out, that I had not deserved this. That no sorcerer had.

They didn't call it enslavement, of course. They called it 'the integration of magic wielders into society' and they called those they drained 'Vessels' as if it were some sort of honorary title. But we weren't integrated into anything. We were only allowed to breathe, move, eat, bathe, and blink within the quarters they allocated to us.

Vessels weren't allowed to step outside of these quarters. Vessels were discouraged from speaking to one another too often, for fear of inciting rebellion. We were assigned to groups that changed every few months, never allowing us a chance to get too close to anyone. Vessels and non-Vessels were not allowed to converse with one another, to have any kind of relationship or reproduce together.

That didn't stop the guards from trying to force themselves upon some of the women though, and the men.

That's how I ended up deep underground.

Nobody would have believed us about their attempts, if we had told them the guards were violating the codes Vasara had established after the War, as the ruling Kingdom.

That's why I didn't regret killing the guard who had forced himself onto a girl, a few years ago. The chains around our limbs drained us of our powers, so I didn't kill him with sorcery. I couldn't. I killed him with his own sword instead, the sword that had been attached to his discarded belt.

Piercing his flesh had been easy, far easier than I had anticipated.

I had thought they would execute me after that. I had hoped for it. But being an Acciperean, death was not an option for me.

This was.

This isolation, starvation, humiliation. These beatings and burns. Whatever they could come up with that was enough to hurt me, but not enough to kill me.

A balance, they were all about balance. At least they were consistent in their cruelty.

A voice emerged in the distance.

*Marco…again.*

I could tell, not only by the sound of his voice, but by his steps. They were heavy, dragging across the ground. They were heading in my direction.

There was someone with him. I didn't recognise their voice.

"…Many left." I caught the end of Marco's sentence. "How many do Kalnasa need?"

"As many as we are willing to give them. For a price of course," the voice answered. It was a woman's voice, devoid of emotion, indifferent, bored almost.

This happened regularly. Vessels were transferred and moved between the Five Kingdoms often. This was the third I had been dragged to. I had not seen any of their renowned landscapes or architecture though, only bars, barricades, and cells.

"And how many are we willing to give them?" Marco asked.

"How many do we have?"

"Sixteen."

The woman's steps froze. Marco stopped with her.

"That is…troubling. I thought we had more." Her tone was accusatory.

"We did, but not all of them can take the drainings. We need to drain them harder than the Dareans."

Accipereans, they were talking about Accipereans. Were there really only sixteen of us left here?

The woman tutted. "Who is responsible for their draining?"

"Tristan."

"I should like to know what methods this…Tristan is employing."

"Shall I send for him?"

"Afterwards."

Their voices were growing louder.

"You said you'd selected suitable Vessels?"

"Yes, I've left five of them in the draining chamber for your inspection, but there's another here I thought you'd want to take a look at."

The woman sounded as if she were smiling. "Why is it down here?"

*It.*

"She's the one that killed Karll," Marco explained.

Now I knew two of their names. Many sorcerers forgot their own during the drainings. Though that was not the reason I did not know mine.

The woman and Marco reached my cell and were standing in front of it now.

My eyes widened. There was no doubting it. The woman was Royalty, or nobility at least.

Her dark dress covered her shoulders like pads of armour. On top of those pads were silver ornaments, shaped like bird feathers. Its neckline revealed her brown skin, and a set of pale jewels that sat against her collarbones.

Her black eyes were slitted into a squint as she studied me. She laughed, the sound was clipped and without any real amusement. I snarled involuntarily at the sound.

"Yes, that one will do. Choose the three weakest from the others to send with it. We need the stronger ones for ourselves."

"We're truly sending them? But I thought—"

"You thought correctly, the plan has not changed."

"I see," Marco nodded.

"And Marco?"

"Yes?"

"I heard" – she stopped, placing a hand on his shoulder – "that you were speaking with my son."

Marco blinked hard. His gaze shifted around as if searching for an answer in the air. "He asked some questions. I answered them. Should I not have? I thought he was aware."

"You tell him nothing. Do not tell him of this either." Her voice was sharp.

"Understood." Marco nodded but appeared perplexed by the instruction.

"I'll be waiting for Tristan. Get this done," she said, casting me one final glance before walking away.

Marco, however, entered my cell.

"Get up," he commanded, not aggressively like many of the guards here, but with no sympathy either.

I didn't get up.

"Trust me," his voice became softer, "doing as I say will be better for you."

"Being free would be better for me," I snapped as he forced me to stand.

"Not anymore," he mumbled, dragging me out of the cell.

"Who else is being sent there?"

Marco didn't answer.

"Is Amali?"

Marco didn't take a second to respond, "Who?"

Of course, they didn't know our names and not because, like us, we had never learnt them, but because they had never bothered to learn ours.

"She has a birthmark on her—" I began explaining.

"Dead," he declared without feeling.

I could barely feel the sensation of my feet moving, or of getting closer to the dreaded light.

*Amali is dead.*

"How?"

He didn't respond. He didn't care. Of course he didn't. Our value was in our utility, losing one of us was like losing an object, not a person.

A short time later, I was shoved into the back of a cramped shuttle. I was thankful for the darkness it shrouded me in, my eyes were not used to the light yet.

Three other Accipereans were staring back at me. I recognised one of them. A man about my age, brown olive skin, dark eyes, black hair that had grown to his shoulders, an unshaved face. He looked much thinner than when I had last seen him.

But then again, that had been years ago.

I didn't know how many. There was no way I could measure time accurately underground. Had it been two? Three? Five? I wasn't sure.

The other two Accipereans were a woman and child. The woman was shaking. The girl stared at me wide eyed. She appeared about six.

None of us said anything to each other. What could we say? What words would be worth it? None of us wanted empty platitudes and comfort. We had all gotten used to our own company, we had all gotten used to living in our own minds.

I supposed that was how we preferred it now.

We had never been given the chance to prefer anything else.

There were no windows. We couldn't see where we were going, or at what point of the journey we were on. I lost count of the days we had been moving. It was only the erratic distribution of small quantities of food that gave us any sense of time passing.

At least I had eaten.

It was because of the lack of windows though, that I didn't know where we were when it happened.

Our shuttle tipped over to the side.

The child was crying, the mother was trying to calm her down. The man and I looked at each other with alarm, fear, and that distinct emotion I had seen in the eyes of many Vessels.

Bitter determination.

This was our chance, this was our one, and likely, only chance to be free.

We didn't know who had attacked the shuttle or why, we didn't know what awaited us. Perhaps we would be shot, cut down, killed as soon as we attempted to escape. Perhaps this was a test.

But this was it. In all the years of my life I had never had a chance like this. By the look in the man's eyes, neither had he.

I nodded. He nodded back at me. We looked at the woman and the child, silently communicating our intentions.

Outside, the sound of people dying.

Inside, the silence of people determined to live.

For the first time in years, I was adamant about the fact I would live.

The man spoke, looking at the mother.

"Are you coming with us?"

She nodded. *Yes.*

"Fuck it." The young man kicked at the side of the cart, trying with all his might to break it down.

I joined him. We struck it again and again, but the casing was far stronger than it looked, while we, chained and bound, were still weak.

"It's not going to work," the woman wailed.

"It has to work. It has to fucking work!" the man shouted. The chaotic sound of battle surrounded us from all sides, seeping through the slats of the wood we were encased in. The child's shrill cries sounded louder than before. The man started screaming, his shouts laced with sobs and quivering with despair.

I put my hand on the man's shoulder. "Stop."

He didn't listen to me. He kept hitting and hitting and hitting and hitting until his hands were raw and bloody.

"You're hurting yourself. It's pointless!" I yelled trying to get through to him.

"No, this" - he lifted his wrists, nodding at his chain - "this is hurting me!"

There were tears in his eyes. We looked at each other, he with tears in his eyes and mine dry from all the tears I had shed over the years.

"I know," I whispered.

He sank back to the wall.

"Maybe we should..."

I halted.

Nothing. Silence. The commotion outside had stopped.

All the sounds that had dissolved into the air before now sounded so loud. Our breathing, our gulping, the sound of the footsteps approaching us. We all looked at each other.

*These could be the last faces I see.*

*These could be the people my dead body lies by in some ditch.*

With one swift movement, the side of the shuttle was torn off.

There was only one thing that could do that in this world.

One thing.

# CHAPTER 3 - LORIA

"Loria, please, just come with me," Nathon grunted, attempting to drag me along.

Nathon's hand was around my wrist. I yanked my arm from his grasp, but he only gripped it tighter. I bit back a whimper of pain, determined not to show my discomfort, but he noticed the tightening of my lips.

Of course he did.

He let go. "Sorry. Does it hurt?"

"It would hurt anyone to be this close to you," I replied.

He tutted, smiling at me with such arrogance that it took everything I had not to slap him in the face with my free hand.

But that would only make things worse.

"Are you going to come with me?" he asked, his voice vibrating in the air like thunder.

"Do I really have a choice?" I bit back.

"Of course you do. But not all choices are wise choices," he grinned.

Sorcery had long been shunned, its activities banned, but if someone had told me a drop had been involved in the creation of my brother's face, I would have believed them. His brilliant white smile was the perfect contrast to his bronze skin, to his short hair, the same shade as the dark mountains that shrouded our home.

Being in his presence was always utterly confusing, for me, and for everyone else. He carried an ethereal air, not one of light, but one of freedom, as if he flung about the world fleetingly as a breeze.

But it was an air, nothing more. The truth was Nathon's soul was the most revolting thing I had ever come across. He was not that playful, carefree wind, but a stifling smog come to suffocate the masses. To choke them with smoke and blood.

I went to move. He blocked my path.

"I thought this was urgent," I attempted to use the reason he had approached me against him.

"Ahhh, now you're suddenly bothered about the summons. You didn't seem so worried a few minutes ago."

"That was before you threatened me."

He scoffed. "When did I do that? Besides, how could you think I would ever hurt my own sister?"

"I'm confident you're capable of far worse than that."

"It warms my heart to hear you have such confidence in me." He bowed deeply, watching me from under his brows as he straightened to his full height.

Nathon was disgustingly good at this. So good at taunting, at getting under people's skin. He could somehow both charm and disarm anyone into doing whatever he wanted. It was a wonderful trait for politics, or the most dangerous one. I shuddered to think what he would become, when he was crowned King of Audra himself one day.

"You would need to have a heart for that to happen," I answered.

He laughed again, crossing his arms over his chest. He was about to say something when a flash of lightning rippled across the sky above us, reflecting in his golden eyes. A foreboding roar of thunder followed.

Nathon turned towards the sound, looking thoughtful. "We need to go. They say this storm is going to be one of the worst we've had for years."

He was distracted. I could use this moment to get away, to get out of whatever this summons was. I turned on my heels and ran. I knew this terrain like the back of my hand, if I could just make it to the top of that slope then...

Something cold smacked against my face so forcefully that my ears rang as I fell to the ground. Nathon hovered over me, his right arm outstretched, connected to his rounded black and gold shield.

"Bastard!" I shouted.

"I didn't expect you to run straight into it." He set the bottom of his shield on the ground, still holding it at the top. He looked at it with confusion now.

"Did you really think I wouldn't try to..." I stopped talking as something watery trickled across my lips. I lifted my fingers to touch them. They came away stained with blood.

I looked up at Nathon, expecting him to appear proud or smug. Instead, he appeared absolutely mortified.

He crouched beside me, letting go of his shield.

"Loria," he sighed. "Why did you have to be so stubborn?" He reached out to touch my nose, where the blood was coming from.

"Get your hands off me," I hit his forearm.

"We've got to stop the bleeding before you see him." His mouth twisted painfully at the blood running down my face.

"Or maybe, I could avoid seeing him altogether."

"That's not an option." He flicked his brows up and down.

"Why would the sight of my bleeding nose phase father of all people? It's never bothered him before," I spat.

Nathon looked down, quickly running his hands through his hair. "Pinch your nose and tilt your head forwards. Hopefully, it stops before we get there."

A sound of protest escaped my throat, but before I could speak, Nathon whistled. Within seconds, the silhouette of his Erebask -Kazal, emerged from the dense clouds.

Kazal was the largest Erebask in Audra. A creature of magic native to our Kingdom. Birds far more magnificent than any other, able to discharge lightning powerful enough to tear debris from mountains. Kazal's feathers were like gazing into oblivion itself. A dark and inky blue, blended with an unrelenting black. His eyes, a stunning mix of green and gold, now pierced through the dark fog like arrows. Many had competed, had fought over the right to claim Kazal as their own, but Nathon had outsmarted, outmanoeuvred, or killed anyone who had tried to take Kazal from him.

I had always wondered how Nathon treated the creature, considering how poorly he treated people. But from what I had seen, Nathon treated Kazal with respect...perhaps even love, if he was even capable of such an emotion.

"Get on," he ordered me, strapping his shield to Kazal.

"But I—"

"I know you don't like to ride, but I'm not quite sure you'd enjoy dying in a storm either." He turned up his palms in a questioning gesture.

"I can find my own way back."

"He's summoned you. He sent me to fetch you. It has already taken far longer than I would have liked to find you, since you're always hiding in some hole or crevice. Now, we are far later than we should be, one of the worst storms that the Kingdom has ever seen is on the horizon and you're bleeding. You are coming with me. Now."

Kazal looked at me from behind Nathon, having landed while he was speaking. The Erebask squinted as if to tell me, *"Do as he says."*

There was a small chance I could escape Nathon, but both Nathon and Kazal? That was impossible. Seeing no other alternative, I reluctantly stepped onto the Erebask, seating myself behind Nathon.

An unease spread throughout my core, clutching at it like talons.

"Hold onto me," he glanced over his shoulder.

I, even more reluctantly, put my arms around his torso. My nose was still bleeding.

Eventually, after a short flight, the Citadel's domed roofs came into view. Nathon remained silent as he dismounted and helped me down. The storm was beginning to grow angrier now. The wind was battering our bodies. My hair flew in all directions.

I followed Nathon inside. We began making our way to the throne room. A meeting in the throne room was highly unusual. Waves of anxiety swam through my stomach at the thought of its purpose.

Just before we stepped inside, through thick, dark doors, Nathon stopped walking, and grabbed my chin.

"You look horrendous," he made it sound more like concern than an insult somehow.

"No thanks to you," my voice was bitter.

He pointed at me. "Wipe your face, there's still some blood on it."

I did as he said.

"Fix your hair."

"What is this? Is someone important inside?"

Nathon didn't say anything. Normally he would have replied with some distasteful comment.

"Stop asking questions Loria. Just get on with it," he commanded in a clipped tone.

I patted my hair down, trying my best to detangle it, but the dark silky strands had already become a matted mess.

Nathon sighed, clearly exasperated. "Gods help us."

He pushed open the doors.

Behind them, our father sat on the throne. Beside him was our mother. They were whispering and smiling at one another.

"Your—"" Nathon started, but was interrupted by our father, who raised his hand to silence him. He didn't even look in Nathon's direction, he was still looking at our mother. He brushed his thumb against her knuckles, kissed them, and murmured something in her ear.

Nathon and I glanced sideways at each other. Our mother was like a ghost of a person, she always had been. The only thing she could acknowledge, could see, could truly interact with was our father. She worshipped him, adored him, made herself into whatever he wanted. She carried out his every demand, his every order, his every request without question.

Finally, after some more hushed words were exchanged between them, our father turned to us.

"Nathon," his ominous voice echoed through the room. "You found her."

Nathon only nodded in reply, standing a little straighter under our father's gaze.

That gaze darted towards me.

"What happened to her face?"

I was standing right there, he could have asked me, but he didn't. He barely ever addressed me in these situations, always referring to, or asking Nathon questions on my behalf.

Nathon looked uncomfortable, speechless even. It was unsettling seeing him so...unsettled.

Father stood now. I flinched. Nathon however, remained utterly still. Our father walked towards us in measured, drawn out steps.

I could have answered. I could have told him Nathon had smashed my face in with his shield, but for some reason, I didn't want to. I didn't want to speak at all. Words retreated from my lips, as if afraid of the air my father breathed.

"I told you to find her, not to damage her. We need her to look presentable."

"It was a mistake, I—" Nathon protested.

"Yes. It was. You know how much I dislike those."

The look he gave Nathon promised he would pay for that mistake, very soon.

"You summoned me father," I finally mustered the courage to say.

"Yes." His voice was soft, but his moments of tenderness had always been infinitely more frightening.

"I need you to do something for me."

"Of course." I bowed my head, feigning obedience.

He came very close to me. I was forced to look at him. Both his dark short beard and hair were braided, skimming the shoulders of his tunic. The tunic was golden, the same shade as his own, as Nathon's, as my eyes. They sparkled against his tan, brown skin. I could see my own reflection in his pupils. I looked so small, so fragile.

"What is it you want me to do, father?"

"Not want...*need*." His gritty emphasis on the word sent a shiver skittering down my spine.

Nathon appeared wary, his gaze darting between our two faces.

But my father didn't notice, he kept staring at me. The corner of his mouth slowly twitched upward before he spoke again.

"You...my girl, are going to kill the King."

# CHAPTER 4 - ELIEL

I had always liked it when someone died.

Not because of the death itself, but because of this sight, a sight that only ever happened when someone of import had passed. People strolled down the streets, shrouded in deep wine red, near black, the colour of mourning in Vasara. They were weaving through the roads, pooling together at the Palace gates.

They looked like a puddle of blood, spreading outwards in different directions.

I used to watch this as a child, when the life of a monarch, someone of Royal birth, or even a notable warrior had ended. I would sit by the windows and watch. I used to watch the red swarm, utterly mesmerised.

Now, I stood in the King's chambers, soon to be my own, and looked down at the sight again.

The people were waiting, waiting for me.

I was waiting too. Waiting for the moment someone would inform me this had all been a misunderstanding, that my parents were still alive, that I was still a Prince, and not a King.

There was a knock at my door.

"Your Highness." A muffled voice travelled through the wood.

"Come in," I replied.

Jarian. He was the Captain of Vasara's Royal guard. His armour was gold, his cape was wine red, as opposed to its usual amber orange, as a sign of mourning. Across his breastplate, in the centre of his chest, the symbol of a sun was carved, the real-life counterpart of which was reflected against Jarian's sword.

"Your Highness." He bowed.

"Please Jarian, there is no need for such formalities." I offered him a small smile.

Jarian looked as if I had mortally offended him. I tilted my head to the side, indicating I was curious about the purpose of his visit.

He cleared his throat. "The Council are waiting for you, Your...they're expecting your arrival this morning. I've come to escort you there."

I nodded to acknowledge that I had understood.

I couldn't stand most members of the Council. It largely consisted of cowardly, small-minded men whose riches were more often than not, unfairly earned. They were undoubtedly circling around me like vultures, planning their strike right at the moment they perceived me most vulnerable. My parents had just died, I was mourning, I was inexperienced, I was young. All these things made me a perfect target for their claws.

But I had learnt to fend off such claws when I was a boy. Their talons did not concern me, but they did need to be blunted. Soon.

"Very well. Although you do not need to escort me Jarian, I am perfectly capable of traversing these hallways alone."

"Yes, Your...Eliel, it is only that your life is vital to protect, now more than ever. The Council and the nobles think it would be wise to have guards with you at all times."

I chuckled. Of course, that is what the Council and the nobles would advise. I had been aware for a while that not everyone here worked directly for the Royal Family. There were some who had been bought by the nobility, from this Kingdom and likely from others. Who could say which of them were spies and which were not? I was more likely to be assassinated by one of my so-called protectors than any intruder.

"Something to be discussed at today's meeting," I raised my head to look Jarian directly in the eye. He looked away.

*"You have cold eyes,"* one of my childhood tutors had once told me.

How ironic, I remember thinking, that a child of the Kingdom perpetually illuminated by the sun, had eyes of ice. They were pale blue. Most people's eyes in this Kingdom were various shades of brown or red.

When Jarian did not move, still intent on accompanying me, I told him explicitly, "You are dismissed, Jarian."

"But –"

I looked at him again, this time raising my eyebrows.

"It suits you, Your Highness." He looked at my outfit. "The same shade as your hair."

I glanced at the cherry red doublet I was wearing.

I didn't respond. Jarian bowed and took his leave.

Why Jarian was ever appointed as Captain of our guard remained a mystery to me. He was a good man, yes. Good men commanded loyalty, but they did not command death. No matter how they were portrayed, the guards were meant to be a symbolic threat of death to anyone who would oppose us.

I wasn't even sure Jarian could kill a person.

I was sure, however, that the number of fighters who truly deserved a place in their ranks could be counted on one hand.

As I stepped through the hallways, people bowed, curtsied, murmured, or declared their condolences every other second. The passers-by all had red hair, auburn hair, golden hair, chestnut hair. It was as if a sunrise itself had scattered through these corridors.

If I could have travelled through the secret passages behind these walls, I would have. Alas, I had to be *"seen."* Athlion needed to know that I was alive, that I was ready and willing to take the throne, that our Kingdom was *"strong."*

A few of the more familiar faces, the cooks, the nurses, the servants approached me with tears in their eyes. They declared how sorry they were through trembling lips. I spent far too much time informing them it was not their fault, that I was alright, that they did not need to be sorry.

It was a special kind of torture.

People had loved my parents. They had respected them. They appreciated the stability they'd brought to our lands over the past few decades. They appreciated their part in the successful outlawing of sorcery, which all Five Kingdoms had instigated around twenty years ago, and the integration of Dareans and Accipereans into our world, as Vessels.

They valued the gifts my parents bestowed upon them, a life free from the dangers of sorcery but one that could thrive upon its powers and the magical creatures allocated to each Kingdom.

Far too many people delighted in the intimidation of sorcerers and magical creatures. They fed off that victory from decades ago like starved children. I had seen people beat their designated creatures for sport. I had heard of the creatures being forced to fight against one another in pits for entertainment.

Once, I had taken a whip against a man who'd been battering a Chimera with it. It was I that was punished rather than the man, and the next day, that Chimera was hanging outside the Palace gates.

It wasn't the only being of magic out there. Sometimes sirens, sorcerers, centaurs, pixies, banshees, and other creatures that had been caught were outside. Their heads were on spikes, their bodies hung by a rope that had broken their necks. This did not, however, bother the people. It did not frighten or sicken them. It made them feel safe. It shrouded them in a false sense of security.

But it sickened me.

It was obvious those who possessed sorcery would always be more powerful than us. It was obvious these sporadic massacres were futile. We could never truly know if we had escaped the dangers of sorcery completely, or at least crushed sorcerers enough to prevent such dangers from fully re-emerging. If they did, they would end us all. Easily, quickly, and painfully.

Some said we would deserve it. Their voices never rang aloud for long.

And I still valued the head on my shoulders. I would not speak my mind aloud.

For now, I would play this role, the subservient, obedient, and altruistic King. Becoming King, this was simply adding a few more gemstones to the ornate mask I was familiar with.

I wore it now, as I stepped into the Council chamber.

Everyone rose, crossing their right fists to their left shoulders. They bowed their heads as they spoke in unison.

"Your Highness."

"Please rise and sit gentlemen." I approached the head of the table, gracefully strolling past them. I had been taught how to walk, move, talk, breathe, and fight from a very early age. The sound of my footsteps was barely audible.

Councillor Wayman opened his mouth. I could tell what he intended to say by the forlorn look in his gaze.

I raised my hand before he could speak. "And please, no condolences. They are not necessary. I know how much my parents meant to you all."

I pondered which of them, in fact, rejoiced over their passing.

"I appreciate and know your sentiments. You need not voice them out loud. It would be better and more efficient if we began immediately. As you can imagine, I have many matters to attend to in light of recent events," I added. In truth I was keen for this meeting to be over as soon as possible.

I placed my hand back on the table. The dark red stone of my family ring knocked against the mahogany wood. A stunned silence followed, confirming my suspicions. Each of the men had planned a speech about how saddened they were by my mother and father's death and now, with such a disruption to their plans, they shifted uncomfortably in their seats.

I would not hear their attempts at grievance. It would only be insulting to my own.

It was Councillor Trenton who was the first to speak.

"Your Highness," he addressed me.

I debated telling him that he should call me by my birth name, but it would be of no use, not with these men.

Trenton continued, "You are your father's only heir."

"I'm very aware of that Trenton. What is your point?" I found it hard to hide the irritation in my voice. I had always noticed people spoke to those in power as if they were incompetent. It was likely due to some sort of fear, but it was incredibly frustrating and wasted untold amounts of time.

Councillor Raynard spoke up. "It is only to say...Your Highness, that in tumultuous times such as these, we think it would be wise to conduct your Coronation as soon as possible." Sweat beaded across Raynard's bald brow. He dabbed at it with a small handkerchief before resuming. "There is, of course, normally a two-month mourning period to pay our respects to the deceased, but we feel" -- he looked around the room, searching for the virtual support of the Councilmen -- "that it would be wise to shorten that...slightly, on this occasion."

This was curious. I knew there had been rising tensions between Vasara and some of the other Kingdoms, particularly Jurasa and Kalnasa. Although Jurasa's King was infamous for his prickly relationship with most rulers. I also knew, there had been reports of sorcerers organising small rebel groups, but these were issues our Kingdom had dealt with for many years.

For centuries, no matter the circumstances, no matter the strife, even when the Wielders' War had ensued, the mourning period had been respected and upheld by all Kingdoms.

"Please elaborate," my voice was dry as I met each of the Council members' eyes.

"Your Highness...I am not quite sure—" Raynard started.

"I would advise you become sure Raynard, and quickly. Your seat around this table is of no consequence to me, to see you replaced would mean nothing for myself, however I am sure it would be quite devastating for you and your prospects."

To even insinuate Raynard's prospects could be devastating when he likely possessed enough wealth to last him four lifetimes was ludicrous. But I needed him to believe that an end to his position would mean the effective end to his pathetic existence.

I continued to look at Raynard, expecting an answer, but it was only stuttering noises rather than words that came out of his mouth, like pathetic attempts at rainfall in a drought.

"Apparently Raynard has lost the ability to answer a simple question. Would someone kindly do it for him?" I asked.

The Council members cast wary glances at each other. I had sat on the Council a few times before but had often been discouraged by my father from doing so. He would proclaim it was tedious, filled with conversations centring around tiresome practicalities about taxes, shipping, and supplies. These were conversations, he said, I should be grateful to avoid until my time to rule came.

Only now my time had come, and nobody was speaking about anything.

"It is rather hard to have a productive conversation if my own Council will not participate in it." When nobody spoke again, I added, "The order to have guards accompany me everywhere I go is to be revoked. Now, if there is nothing else, I will take my leave."

I stood. Just as my chair had fully made its way back from the table, Councillor Trenton spoke.

"It's the sorcerers, Your Highness..."

I slowly turned to him. I sat back down in my chair, resting my right elbow on its arm, my hand hovering by my face.

"What about them?"

"They are...regrouping."

"They have been regrouping sporadically for a while. What are you insinuating?"

"We believe..." He paused as if debating how to word his statement. "We believe sorcerers killed your parents, Your Highness."

I gripped the side of my chair in one swift movement. "You believe... or you are certain?"

"We are...fairly certain of it, Your Highness," Councillor Wayman confirmed.

"Why?" I tried my best to hide the swirling pit of emotions raging through my mind. I was not sure if I was succeeding in doing so, but I was determined to get through this meeting as calmly as possible.

Councillor Trenton continued. "The Palace physicians who examined their bodies found marks on their chests. They were unmistakably marks of sorcery. They were" – he looked at me tentatively – "Your Highness I'm not sure if you should hear this."

I was not sure either, but I said, "I must know every detail Trenton, after all, this relates to matters of our security, to my own security."

Trenton nodded. "The marks were carved into their chests, presumably with some kind of blade or knife. There were smaller, similar marks engraved on their wrists and at the nape of their necks."

"I was told" – I took a deep breath – "I was told, they died of an illness. They had been sick for days and nobody noticed these marks. What fool of a physician diagnosed them?" I slammed my palm against the table, louder than I had intended.

"They were sick, Your Highness, the physician believed them to be inflicted with the Darts, their symptoms were identical." Wayman's tone was not entirely without fear.

I did not enjoy scaring people, but for some reason, most of them had been afraid of me, since I was a young man.

*"You have cold eyes."*

The Darts was an illness that had spread across all Five Kingdoms over the past few years. It had claimed many lives. It was mostly the poor who were affected, but some members of higher society had contracted it also.

"How did a Royal physician mistake the work of sorcery for the symptoms of Darts?" I looked at Wayman with as blank an expression as I could summon.

"It seems they were also poisoned, Your Highness," he answered. "After their deaths, the physicians, assuming that the Darts had cruelly taken their lives, did not immediately think to examine their bodies so...intimately. Not until this morning, when they were being prepared for the public funeral. It was then they found the marks Trenton speaks of and traces of the Tuspian Leaf inside their mouths. It is a rare and deadly poison. Its effects mimic that of the Darts in many ways."

I sighed. How could I be surrounded by such complacent fools?

"The Tuspian leaf?" That wasn't just rare, it was practically extinct. "Why not simply kill them?" I paused for a moment, processing how strangely the words sat in my mouth. "With the poison?"

"The Tuspian leaf is a slow acting poison, Your Highness. It can take many days, at times weeks to achieve its full effects. Presumably the" – Trenton side-eyed me before he continued – "assailants did not have the time or ability to wait, so they used a small dose to mimic the effects of Darts, waited but a few short days, then delivered the final blow using...sorcery."

I pressed my lips together, eyeing the table. I attempted to steady my breathing before I spoke again.

"So, what you're implying, is not only were my parents assassinated, but they were assassinated by sorcerers? That this information, which should have been known to all of us, to me, days ago, has only come to light now due to the obvious incompetence of several people both within the Palace and around this table?"

"We are very sorry, Your Highness. We are greatly distressed –"

"Your distress is useless to me, to all the people here. If what you say is true, we are in a graver danger than we previously anticipated."

The silence that followed my statement confirmed what I had already begun to suspect.

"You were already aware of this threat, weren't you gentlemen?" I leant back in my seat.

Councillor Fargreaves, who was sitting at the opposite end of the table, his auburn hair cast in the shade, replied. "Your father was aware, as were we. He...we were trying to find a way to deal with the situation. He thought he could find the origins of this group and wipe them out before you or your mother ever needed to know."

I placed my head in my hands for a moment, before realising it would be best not to demonstrate any level of exasperation or emotion in front of these men.

"Did you find this group?" I dropped my hands, returning them to the table.

"Unfortunately not, Your Highness. It is unlikely they have one set location." Councillor Trenton shook his head. "Either way, it is this threat, along with the rising tensions among the Kingdoms that has prompted our suggestion of expediting your Coronation."

"I see," I stated. It did not truly matter when I would be coronated, not to me. The result would be the same, I would be the King of Vasara, of every Kingdom, of every person in Athlion.

"We believe it would be a good idea to interrogate the Vessels, Your Highness," Wayman suggested.

"The Vessels aren't allowed out of the Northern Wing. Their powers are stripped by their chains. How would they have done this?" I squinted.

"They may not have committed the deed, but they may have information."

I sighed. "Arrange for them to be questioned."

"Do we have your permission to use more extreme methods, should they be necessary, Your Highness?" Trenton asked.

I thought about it for a moment. "No, we need the Vessels. If any of them seem suspicious, you will report it to me. I will deal with them myself."

Trenton and Wayman looked at each other in surprise.

"As you say, Your Highness," Trenton nodded.

Raynard started, "In light of the rather unique familial situation that Vasara faces –"

He had found a delicate way of revisiting the fact that Vasara was the only Kingdom with one heir. It used to be two, until Malia had died. There was also Elias, my cousin, but under no circumstances would any of the nobility support him as King for several unsavoury reasons, nor was there any possibility Elias would allow himself to be crowned.

"We also believe the Courting Season should be discussed," Raynard added.

"The Courting Season is not for many months." I abruptly faced him, furrowing my brow.

"Your Highness, we feel your need for a wife is also more pressing, in light of these threats." Trenton met my eyes. It was easy for me to notice that Trenton had assumed the role of leader amongst the Councilmen, being the one to take charge of topics the other members shied away from.

"How so?" My voice sounded flat with disapproval.

"It could strengthen our alliance with one of the other Kingdoms, should your chosen Queen originate from one of them," he replied. "Jurasa or Kalnasa would be a particularly good choice, Your Highness."

"I would rather not spend any more time than necessary in the Jurasan King's presence," I mumbled under my breath.

"He is a rather…unpleasant man." Fargreaves sounded pained. "But he is a powerful one."

Raynard scoffed. "He knows it too."

Being the ruler of Jurasa meant their King had control over the largest bodies of water that existed in Athlion. They were mostly located to the West, where Jurasa was situated. Therefore, good, or at least neutral relations with its monarch were vital if we were to survive. Not that he made such relations easy.

It was not the prospect of conversing with Jurasa's King that truly pained me but that of the Courting Season. The Season was a tradition all rulers of Vasara had upheld for centuries. At some point within the first year of a King's reign, five candidates, one from each Kingdom, were selected as candidate for the Season, where they would vie for the King or Queen's hand in marriage.

The Season filled me with more dread than the thought of any war, battle, or assassination attempt. It would require my undivided attention at several points. It was an outdated rite of passage, full of hypocrisy, backstabbing, and plots for power. There had been candidates sent to the Courting Season as young as sixteen, some as old as sixty. There had been candidates who had cried and begged to return home, and candidates who had plotted to murder each other. I had heard the stories. Had I the choice, I would have banned it, but there were too many powerful people involved in its creation and eliminating it would take many years. Time was not a luxury I had.

"Do you really believe we have time for this? You know full well how long and tedious the Season is. War is likely on the horizon, and you believe rather than planning for it, I should be attending balls and dinners, charming noble ladies?"

"Your Highness, it is precisely *because* war is coming that you need a wife as soon as possible, that our Kingdom needs a Queen, and heirs." Fargreaves creased his brow.

"In case it has escaped your notice, heirs cannot be produced over-night. By the time any Queen of mine gave birth to an heir, we could all be dead."

"Still…it is important, it is necessary for the stability of the Kingdom. Your safety is our priority." Trenton shifted in his seat.

"If only you had possessed such an attitude towards my father's safety Trenton."

"Your Highness," Trenton sounded angry, "I can assure you, your father's safety was something I took very seriously."

"Not seriously enough." We were staring at each other now. Trenton was the first to look away.

I turned to the side and looked out of the arched, tall windows lining the walls of the Council chamber. The room was elevated enough that dense clouds floated past them, giving the illusion of being far removed from the world. Ironic, since here, within these four walls, conversations were held that could, and would, change the course of history.

When I hadn't spoken for a few minutes Fargreaves declared, "We think the Coronation could be combined with the Season. We could implement it as part of the Season's activities and invite the candidates to participate."

I shook my head. "This haste will not solve our problems."

"It will not, Your Highness, but it does not need to solve them all, it simply needs to send out a message to the other Kingdoms, to the people and to these…*sorcerers*" – Wayman uttered the word with disgust, his jowls and grey hair wobbling from side to side – "that we are united, that we are ready, that we are –"

"Strong, yes. Only there was no reason for anyone to doubt that before the death of my parents and they died all the same. They were assassinated all the same," I stated.

Wayman's mouth was open in shock. He was gaping like a fish out of water.

"Do you think Wayman, do any of you *truly* think, that the sorcerers who murdered my parents will quiver in fear when they hear I have been *officially* crowned? That I now wear a larger headpiece, which weighs more in gold. That I have been married? Do you honestly believe that these" – I waved my hand in front of me – "empty gestures of power will convince them? Because I do not."

"It may not convince them, Your Highness," Trenton answered, "But it would certainly serve as a distraction to the people, both from the grief and the news of the assassination, should it be uncovered."

"Are you expecting it to be uncovered, Trenton? Is our Palace so rife with traitors?"

"I am afraid all centres of power are rife with such people, Your Highness," Trenton's tone was condemnatory.

It pained me to agree with him.

"It will also," Trenton continued, "possibly fool our enemies. If these sorcerers are not convinced we are strong, they will at least be convinced you are preoccupied."

"I will be preoccupied. That is the problem."

"We can work this to our advantage, Your Highness," Fargreaves added, not without a hint of patronisation to his tone.

"The question is whether there will be people roaming these walls capable of noticing our distraction for what it is," I looked back at Fargreaves.

"That is a risk we will have to take," Trenton stroked the brown hair of his moustache and beard, deep in thought.

Perhaps they were right. If we were to plan and strategize, it would be best to shroud those activities. Something as large and eventful as a Coronation and the Courting Season would provide ample distraction, especially if they were combined.

If we were to stand a chance against these sorcerers, we would have to think like them, operate like them.

"When?" I questioned.

"We could send out invitations this week, Your Highness, with the aim to begin the Season at the start of next month," Raynard suggested.

Three weeks away.

"Do it and start the interrogations today."

"Yes, Your Highness."

I stood, this time, fully drawing my chair back, and fully intent on leaving. "We did not have the courage to see what was right in front of our eyes," I addressed them, "to see what was happening before us, and these, gentlemen, these are the consequences. I will not suffer them. My people will not suffer them. You will ensure that, or you will suffer your own."

All the men looked at me in unison as I left, and not one of them uttered a word.

# CHAPTER 5 - NATHON

When I was a child, there was a time I believed I had died. Even years later, I still found myself wondering if I had. I would seek out whatever danger, feeling, pain, or part of this world that could anchor me to it, that could convince me I was in fact, still alive.

I remembered that feeling well.

Here it was, creeping back into every fibre of my body, that distinct sensation of not being here, of floating into the distance while a heavy weight crushed my chest. It was like I was dying all over again, only I wasn't. I was here, in the throne room, staring at my father with undisguised shock.

Loria wasn't speaking. She was simply looking at him, blinking hard and insistently, as if she were hoping in one of those instances, she would open her eyes to find she had been hallucinating, dreaming, or simply imagining everything.

Sarlan reached out to stroke her face with the back of his hand. It was strange to see such tenderness from him. Sickening.

I knew I should remain silent, but watching this false display of softness, after giving her such a command, was too much to bear.

I took a step towards them.

"You want her to kill the King? Have you completely lost –"

He dropped Loria's chin and within a second, with the same hand, shoved me to the floor before I could fully reach him.

He loomed over me as my back slammed into the black marble.

"Did you forget yourself so easily?"

I looked over his shoulder to find Loria staring at me. I could almost see the thoughts swirling around her mind, trying to make sense of the situation, trying to decide what to do. He was getting closer.

"Sarlan." Our mother strolled towards him, paying no attention to me. "We should return to the matter at hand."

It was tempting to persuade myself that her intervention had been a way of rescuing me, but I knew better. She simply saw this as a distraction, an inconvenience.

"Yes." Sarlan's gaze drilled into me. "*Without* interruption this time."

After hovering over me for a moment, he turned away. I shot up before he could change his mind. I could feel the throb of my hip bone as I rose, but it was of little consequence.

After all, I had sustained far worse injuries in the past.

He turned to Loria who was still standing, frozen in place, looking at me. Her facial expression indicated she wished to speak but thought better of it. Her lips tightened. Her fists were clenched tightly by her sides.

"Where were we?" Sarlan tilted his head, appraising her.

She didn't answer. I didn't blame her for it.

Our mother's bitter voice filled the silence. "You should speak when your King addresses you."

"I...I don't understand," Loria finally spoke.

"King Elion and Queen Celise are dead. Such a tragedy.... the Darts they say," Sarlan chuckled.

"They... say?" Loria asked.

I shot her a glance. What was she doing?

Although it was difficult to condemn her for opening her mouth at an inappropriate time, considering I had just done so myself.

Sarlan squinted. "If you are implying I had something to do with it, you are mistaken."

"You just... asked me to kill the King." She appeared confused.

Condemn her no, but her newfound bluntness was dangerous. She needed to stop talking.

"Yes, the soon to be King Eliel. I would never have been so foolish to do such a thing while Elion reigned."

"You have been planning to strike them then?" Loria's voice was quiet.

"Strike?" Sarlan's harsh laugh ran through the air. "No. Vasara's armies are strong, their warriors too well trained. There is no guarantee we would defeat them in the field."

Why was he entertaining her questions? He never normally spoke to Loria at all, let alone allow her to speak to, or challenge him.

The realisation dawned upon me. A sharp pang of understanding sliced through my gut.

"But now," Sarlan continued, "with a young, inexperienced, and if rumour is to be believed, conceited King... now is our chance."

Loria was trembling slightly, from fear or rage, I couldn't tell.

"Did you know," Sarlan ignored her question, "that Vasara is actually the smallest of the Five?"

Loria was quiet for a moment, then suddenly, as if remembering our mother's previous instruction, blurted out. "Yes. I do. I did know."

"It has the least resources. Its Royal Family is one of the youngest in existence and yet...Vasara possesses the power, the influence, the riches." Sarlan began pacing in front of us. "It takes from us and reaps the rewards."

"The Kingdoms are... living in peace," Loria protested.

Sarlan laughed, genuinely amused. "Peace? Peace, is it? This peace is simply a war waiting to happen. I am not the only person who thinks so. We are not the only Kingdom displeased with Vasara's reign."

During my time blending into different territories and listening to the rumours circulating around each Kingdom, I had heard complaints, discontent, and grumbles of frustration about each of the Royal households. But I had not judged them to be any more than the anticipated amount, normal for those subject to the rules and laws of others.

I would have known. If there had been discontent among the people strong enough to spread across the Kingdoms, to amount to war.

It was not truly the people then, but the nobility, the elite, the powerful, they were the discontented.

As if Loria had read my thoughts she said, "The people do not seem displeased. I thought that—"

Sarlan cut her off with a warning look. "This is our chance to take what Audra deserves. Eliel is Elion's only legitimate heir. His death would throw Vasara into complete disarray, without him, their Kingdom will be left without a King...without direction. An empty throne is much easier to take than an occupied one."

"But Elias—" Loria started.

"Is a drunken disgrace. He poses as much threat to us as a moth to a flame. It will be he that burns if he intervenes."

"I'm... I couldn't...I don't know how...I've never." The reality was engulfing Loria now.

She gave me a desperate look, one that pleaded for my intervention, one that said, *Why can't it be you? Why can't you do it?*

But the answer had struck me already, unforgivingly as a sharpened blade primed to kill. Loria was a pawn, a sacrificial piece on a board. Sarlan could not take the throne himself without being questioned, without being branded a usurper. He could not influence or rule from Vasara directly.

But Loria...Loria could do something the rest of us could not.

"I'll be killed, I—"" Loria sputtered.

"You will not be killed. You will be his wife." The volume of Sarlan's voice increased as he finally revealed his true intentions.

Loria looked as if she had been doused in ice cold water. She looked like a terrified little girl and not a young woman.

"No...no...I," she took a step back. Sarlan quickened his pace to close the distance between them, the shadow of his form swallowing her.

"This is not a request. You will do this. You will not disappoint me."

He turned to look at me now. "And you...you will go with her."

"Did you want me to marry him as well?" I asked.

That was a mistake.

The disturbing grin he gave me only confirmed it was.

"That's the third time today, Nathon."

I strained to remember if I'd ever made three 'mistakes' in one day before. I had, I thought. I'd survived those days, those punishments.

I wasn't keen to relive them, but for some reason, I couldn't stop myself from making such "mistakes" from time to time.

There would be consequences for them, after this meeting was over.

"I –" I attempted to speak.

"You will be silent." Our mother looked at me with disgust. I pressed my lips together, tightening them shut. I had long since learnt to hide the disdain I felt for her from my face.

"You will be accompanying Loria to Vasara, as her escort for the Courting Season," Sarlan explained.

"That's many months away is it not?" I made an effort to sound more passive rather than confrontational this time.

"It seems that Vasara is aware of the vulnerability a lack of heirs continues to create for them and is seeking to rectify the situation as soon as possible. Of course," – he turned to look at Loria, reaching out to remove an errant strand of hair from her face – "it will not be soon enough."

I continued to adopt a cautious tone. "Is it not usually a member of the Kingdom's guard or army that accompanies the candidates?"

"It is...but it will be you."

"Why?" Loria asked.

Sarlan thought about it for a moment, "Because, while you are taking part in the Season's activities, Nathon will be supplying us with information. It would not be possible for you to do both without arousing suspicion. A guard could do this, yes, but Nathon's...*reputation*, will allow him to spend more time outside the Palace walls without inviting unnecessary questions."

Sarlan glanced at me, a cold serpentine glint sifted in his gaze. I didn't react.

"But what if The King doesn't –" Loria implored.

"He must. You must make him choose you," Sarlan lowered his gaze to her. "If you do not, I will be very, *very* displeased. Do you understand?"

Loria's fists were clenched even harder now, her nails were likely digging into her palms hard enough to cut them.

"Once you are carrying his heir, only then will you kill him. Or get him to do it for you." He pointed in my direction without taking his gaze off Loria. "I do not care how it is done, stab him, poison him, strangle him, that is of no consequence. We can ensure the blame is laid at another's feet. Afterwards, with you as the rightful Queen, harbouring his unborn child, nobody will challenge us." Sarlan sounded pleased with himself.

At the realisation she was expected not only to win the Season and kill the King, but to bear his child as well, Loria's eyelids fluttered in an attempt to hold back tears.

I took a step towards them. My mother tutted so loudly, glaring in my direction, that Sarlan looked over his shoulder. A threat in his gaze pinned me in place.

I did not stop for my own sake, but for hers.

"Please...please," Loria begged. Fruitlessly, she must have known. Or perhaps she did not. Perhaps there was a part of her that believed she could appeal to his better nature.

A nature I knew did not exist.

Tears pooled at the corner of her bright golden eyes. They looked like lakes the sun was shining upon, rippling with gleaming light.

"Enough," Sarlan's tone cut through her whimpers. "This is what you were born for. You will kill, lay with, and speak to whomever I tell you to."

Without realising, my breath had begun to quicken. Seeing Loria like this was painful. This is what I had hoped to spare her from, to keep her from, all these years. It was infuriating to think my hopes may have been nothing more than whimsical delusion.

I approached him tentatively. "There must be another way."

Loria's gaze darted towards my face in what seemed like surprise.

Sarlan turned to me. "I had considered sending you to execute this order, but after the results of the last, I would rather not take any risks," Sarlan spat out in clear disappointment.

I held my breath.

The results of the last.

Silus had found out then.

"Besides, his death is not enough, we need a legitimate claim to power," Sarlan finished his explanation.

I took a step forwards. "This is also a risk. A massive risk."

"It is not for you to question my commands," Sarlan took a step towards me.

"She could end up dead," I pointed in Loria's direction.

"You will not let that happen. You will die if you must, but she is the key, if she dies and you live...then you will suffer for it."

My head jerked back. My arm dropped.

"You leave seven nights from now," our mother added.

I kept forgetting she was there. She was like a silent statue that only ever made its presence known to amplify our father's voice.

Loria didn't speak. I didn't speak. We had nothing to say, it seemed, nothing to add. I had believed myself incapable of being shocked by what my father or mother did anymore, but somehow, they always found a way to leave me stunned by their actions.

"Go Loria. Find Strella. She will prepare your outfits and the things you will need for the journey. She will need to fix... this." Our mother waved a hand over Loria's body, surveying her own daughter with disgust.

Loria glanced down at herself, then back up at our mother, then at me. I'd never seen her look so broken, so devastated before.

Her gaze was still fixed upon me when Sarlan spoke. "Leave Loria. Nathon, follow me."

After a few moments of glaring at each other, Loria tore her gaze away from me and shuffled towards the exit. The guards closed the heavy doors behind her.

"Come," Sarlan walked towards an alternative exit behind the throne, without checking to see if I was following him.

He didn't need to. I knew I had no choice.

As I followed, my heart thumped hard enough to cause a slight tremble of the daggers attached to the belt across my hip. Even after all this time, Sarlan's actions still unnerved me.

We kept walking. Not once did Sarlan stop, or pivot to face me.

I knew now where we were going.

We emerged into the Erebask pits, strolling through its main wide central, circular area, which was currently unoccupied. Normally, this was where Erebasks were trained, brought out to test their combat abilities, the projection of their lightning. Towering all around us were dark stone walls with large arched entrances, through which different Erebasks rested and lived.

I stood, rooted in place in the centre of the arena. Sarlan didn't bother to acknowledge my lack of movement. He walked towards a man who was standing at the corner of the space, removing the debris from earlier sessions. He bowed deeply as my father approached him. Their quiet conversation was inaudible to me. After they had finished speaking, the man departed from the central space, retreating into the narrow walkway which led to the Erebasks lairs.

Sarlan strode towards me, his dark pants tickling the sand we stood on. "You think yourself noble?"

My brows furrowed, confused at the question. I definitely did not think that.

I pondered whether it was worth replying to his statement but kept silent. I had known this was coming. The price for voicing my opinion was always...

"Silus came to see me this morning."

I let out an inadvertent huff of laughter and licked my lips. "Honestly, I'm surprised it took him so long."

"You do not deny it then." Sarlan's sounded agitated.

"Would there be a point in doing so?"

My father lifted his chin, sneering at me in anger.

"What did Arton tell you?"

I took a deep breath. I had known Silus would eventually uncover the fact I had been able to retrieve information from each of the escapees. He was good at his work, almost as good as I. But still, I had no intention of sharing the details of what that information was. It was far too intriguing. Far too suspicious.

I clasped my hands together, silently conveying I would not be answering Sarlan's question. He fiddled with a ring across his finger and came closer to me.

"You've always been a selfish boy, Nathon."

I scoffed.

"It's the truth. You were a selfish child and now you are a selfish man. You care only for yourself. You do only what is best for yourself. You do not let your emotions guide you. You feel little guilt or remorse when hurting others. I have seen it. In truth I wish Loria were more like you. It would make our task far easier."

*Our task?*

I wasn't entirely sure if he meant to insult or compliment me. Either way, the insinuation we were anything alike, made my insides twist in disgust.

He must have noticed the tension upon my face but continued. "Too many people allow themselves to be guided by their feelings, their beliefs about what is right and what is wrong. There is no such thing. There is no such line, not in our world.... but not you. You do what needs to be done, you are not sentimental. These are traits that keep someone alive. These are the traits that make someone strong. Your practicality is a weapon, it is a tool. You will need it, and you will use it when I tell you to, without question." He paused for a moment. "Have you forgotten that?"

"No," I groaned, barely able to restrain my loathing.

"I would attempt to force the information from you, but" – he looked me up and down – "I think that would prove unsuccessful. You have been too well trained."

He waved his hand. In an instant, our bodies were cast in shade by the towering creature that was being pulled towards us on chains.

*Kazal.*

I made a move to walk towards Kazal, but my father stopped me instantly, his sword outstretched towards my neck.

I scoffed. Fear was Sarlan's favourite tool. He knew the kiss of cold steel could make someone sicker than what it may actually do.

But I was no such person.

I met his eyes. "A corpse can't bring Loria to Vasara."

He was quiet. He wished to frighten me. To frighten others. He knew how people gave power to the one brandishing the blade.

The true cowards were the ones with their hands around the hilt.

*I suppose that includes me as well.*

Sarlan spoke, "Your nature is of great use to me. But it makes punishing you...difficult. The very same thing that makes you invulnerable to threat and manipulation from our enemies, makes getting you to fall into line a tiresome task."

He twisted the sword a little, it was cool against my throat. Almost soothing in its promise of pain.

"You need reminding of what is at stake when you disobey me. The scars on your skin clearly aren't enough."

Kazal was looking at me, struggling against his chains, there were multiple men holding him now. Those chains were designed to weaken his abilities and strength. They had been infused with magic, and while sorcery had been banned across our world for decades, creatures like Erebasks and devices capable of controlling them were still at each Kingdom's disposal, to ensure creatures of sorcery remained compliant.

Once I had claimed Kazal, I had removed those chains from him. I had hoped to spare him the feeling of helplessness, of captivity they inflicted.

But he was covered with them now.

"I have heard about your night visits here," Sarlan gave me a taunting smile. "I have heard about your dedication to this beast. How touching. How...useful."

My heart was pounding harder now, flapping around as wildly as Kazal's wings.

"Don't," I said.

"What did he tell you?"

My gaze flitted between Kazal and Sarlan. For the first time in a long while, I was unsure of what to do, which path to take.

"As I thought," Sarlan almost sounded pleased. He nodded towards the men surrounding Kazal.

One of them passed the chains to another and returned holding an axe. It was made from the same golden metal the chains were, covered in runes. Its sharp edge created a line across the sand as he dragged it towards Kazal.

"No!" I couldn't believe the sound of my own voice as I pleaded with Sarlan. My yelling sounded hoarse and desperate. It was an unfamiliar sound to my ears. The sound I had made as a child.

I had not been one for long.

Sarlan revelled in it. "Watch and remember."

The man drew closer to Kazal, who, sensing the axe, began screeching, twisting, and trying to free himself. With the chains weakening him, that was impossible.

"This attachment is useless. Erebasks are nothing but our weapons. One can easily be replaced with another." Sarlan gestured towards the caves around us, indicating the number of Erebasks we had at our disposal.

"Kazal is—"

He raised his eyebrows. "*Kazal,* is it?"

Most riders did not name their Erebasks at all. We were actively encouraged to view the creatures as our possessions rather than our companions.

He gripped my arm. "You must learn. This will teach you."

He faced the men. "Four times I think, for three mistakes, and... this instance of withholding information."

He looked at me and grinned, dropping his blade.

I ran toward Kazal but six other men, who had clearly been behind us the whole time, grabbed my arms and shoved me to the ground. I would normally have been able to rid myself of them within seconds. But Sarlan's sword returned to my neck.

Kazal's gaze was full of dread. I had never seen him frightened before. I hoped he could see his fear reflected in my own eyes. I hoped he knew I did not ask for this, that I would never have hurt him myself. That I would have taken countless beatings, lashings, or punches if it meant this noble creature could have avoided one.

Without warning, without any hesitation, the man holding the axe lifted it high above his head and swung it, plunging it deep into the flesh of Kazal's right wing.

The growl of pain that erupted from his throat was so loud, it caused a cascade of sand to swirl around us. It entered my mouth, my eyes.

Again.

Kazal's dark blue blood pooled underneath his wing, sinking into the sand below. His wailing grew louder by the second. The men holding his chains looked concerned, they turned towards their King with a question in their eyes.

Sarlan stood there, smirking, surveying me with keen intensity.

The third time, then the fourth, it crunched through bone.

I glared at my father. The sand rushed around us, scratching at my face, my neck, my eyes, but I did not close them. Kazal's roar reached its peak intensity, blue lightning crackling within his eyes, radiating searing heat across the atmosphere.

I turned to look at each of the men yanking at his chains. I studied their faces, I memorised them. I did not care if they were afraid. I did not care if they were following orders. I did not care if they were men.

I would make sure one day, they paid for this.

Four times over.

Kazal sank with a weakness onto the sand. He looked at me with a weariness that tore at the inside of my chest.

Sarlan signalled to the men once more, who dragged the now bloodied Kazal back into the caves. The men behind me relaxed their grip, hastily retreating, as if they feared what I might do.

They were right to be afraid. I studied their faces too, before they sank into the shade.

I turned to Sarlan, seething with unbridled anger. Seconds passed before he spoke.

"You look at me this way, as if you can claim innocence." Sarlan withdrew the blade from my neck, returning it to his sheath. "But I know what you are. I know the things you have done in the twenty-four years of your life. Things … you, yourself Nathon, asked me to do. Imagine what you will do in the next."

I refrained from reminding him the reason for those exploits.

"Loria does not know the half of it, does she?" He smiled. "I'm sure you'd prefer I keep such information to myself."

Loria hated me. I already knew. But she could still look at me, still, albeit reluctantly, converse with me.

If she knew the half Sarlan was currently threatening to share with her, however, I was sure she would never utter a word to me again.

"I'd say that would hardly be in your best interests, considering you want me to escort her." I gave him a false smile.

"For now," Sarlan shrugged. "But that's the wonderful thing about knowledge, isn't it? As long as you have it, it will always be a weapon. Blades and arrows can fail or dull with time. They can be lost, and sorcery is all but reduced to nothing… but knowledge? Knowledge cannot die, not while someone holds it, and not, when there is always someone else it can be shared with."

"Unless it dies with the one who possessed it." I looked him directly in the eye.

"A pity for you then, that I am not the only one aware of your true nature."

Our mother was aware, so were several of my father's men, the other *"weapons"* that formed his unit of soldiers and spies. It was honestly surprising that Loria remained oblivious.

"You know how I disapprove of your…other nightly activities." He laughed, shaking his head. "I never thought I'd see the day where they became useful to me. Your reputation as a delinquent will work to our advantage. You will pass on information about what is going on at Vasara to our informant. They will meet you at the Solar Inn at night. They will approach you."

"I'll need gold then. To keep up my… *delinquency*." I smiled coldly, planning on all the other ways I could use that gold.

My 'reputation' was the product of the time I spent in such places. I was now branded, amongst other things, as a gross indulger in revelry.

It was not the revelry I sought. I did not care for that at all. It was the noise. The clamouring desperation of people lost in themselves, their desires, their lives.

No matter where I went, I was recognised. People watched me like an animal, as if they were waiting for me to tear their throats out with my teeth. But under the darkness of night, the shade of debauchery and drunkenness, people's gazes softened. It was the only time I felt a man and not a beast.

Yet the sun would always rise, hauling the truth with it over the horizon. I was a beast. I had been for years.

This element of my reputation was hardly the worst of the whisperings that carried my name. It was, however, the only one which Sarlan himself believed.

He knew the truth of the rest.

Only the world did not know the truth of him.

For as with most cruelty, his lived behind four walls, barricades, and locked doors. There it was safe. It did not have the bravery to face the world.

After a few moments of silence, Sarlan waved his hand in a gesture of dismissal. "Your Erebask's flight will be a problem for some time. You will travel there by horse," he added.

I could taste blood as I bit down on my cheek. "Send someone to treat Kazal's wounds."

"I will do no such thing," Sarlan raised his voice "Your *Kazal* will heal, I do not recall ever sending someone to treat your wounds. Why then, would I afford such a luxury to a slave creature?"

I opened my mouth to speak, but Sarlan continued, "The next time you disobey me, I will make sure your Erebask never flies again. Do you understand?"

I didn't respond.

"Do you understand?"

"Oh, I understand perfectly," I spat.

"Good," he smiled. "This Kazal will be further motivation for you. Fulfil this task and your Erebask lives. Fail and your Erebask dies."

My breathing was ragged, uneven, stuttering in and out of my chest.

"If we fail, and you kill him," I finally stood, "You better make sure you kill me too, because I will not rest until I've slit your throat."

Sarlan's expression was blank, unreadable. I was convinced he would strike me. There was perhaps a part of me that wanted him to hit me, to send me into that unawareness for a while.

But he didn't, instead he laughed. "Him?"

He tilted his head, peering at me with a cold curiosity. It was the kind of gaze that scraped against your bones, making you writhe. Like a drop of cold and piercing rain, sliding down your neck. It should not be there. It was somehow wrong.

I did not answer, but I did not look away. Sarlan smirked and strode to the exit, as Kazal's dark blue blood stretched towards my feet.

After he had left, I ran without hesitation towards Kazal's pit.

He was no longer conscious, strewn against the ground, eyes closed, his chest heaving with the effort of breathing.

A Keeper who was inside, straightened up as I entered.

"Your Highness, we—" he glanced between Kazal and I, a pained expression in his gaze. I held up my hand, nodding in understanding.

I entered the pen, and crouched by Kazal's side, I reached out to touch him, but withdrew, worried I might aggravate his wounds. I sighed and gradually stood once more.

"How long?" I asked.

The Keeper brows drew together. He was startled by the question. "Not...at least...for a month, Your Highness, most likely two."

*Two months.*

I rubbed my forehead, nodding, recalling the injuries of mine that had taken such a time to heal, or longer.

The pain of them was distant, like a reflection in the water, but it was something I could still hazily recall. To think Kazal suffered in a similar manner now...

"Your Highness, we will... care for him as best we can. He will be...he is strong." The Keeper smiled.

"Pain does not care how strong you are," I told him.

I hung back, standing in the shadows. The Keeper cast me awkward glances every few seconds.

"Why do you possess those weapons?" I asked. I knew cursed shackles existed, but the weapons, that axe, should long have been destroyed. They too were banned.

The Keeper's lashes quivered. He looked down, avoiding my eyes.

Which meant, I knew, it was on Sarlan's orders they were kept.

"How many do you have?" I inquired.

"I...truly do not know, Your Highness."

I frowned. That seemed unlikely.

The Keeper raised his gaze towards me, but hurriedly cast it back at the floor when he noticed my expression.

"Twenty?" I asked.

Silence.

"Fifty?"

Silence.

"One ...hundred?" I dragged out the words.

Silence.

"More than one hundred?"

The Keeper's breathing pace had increased.

"There's enough for an armoury," I stated to myself.

The Keeper didn't contradict me.

"*There is no guarantee we would defeat them in the field.*" Sarlan had declared, with an entire armoury of these devices at his disposal.

It did not surprise me. Sarlan would not lift a blade when he could wield his own children. For he knew that which could not be denied. That which the new King could not escape.

That a smile could cut sharper than a sword.

That words could corrupt faster than poison.

And that people were the most dangerous weapons of all.

# CHAPTER 6 - HESTAN

"I heard she was a Banshee."

"I heard any man who's ever been with her, is cursed with an insatiable desire for her."

"Didn't Barlan say he'd been with her?"

"Barlan says a lot of shit."

"So do you Kaspian."

"At least I don't fall for this nonsense. Banshees don't even exist anymore."

"I've heard some do. They've gone to the Cliffbanks," Purcell said.

"Nobody could live there," Zain chimed in.

"Maybe Banshees could."

"Banshees don't exist," Kaspian insisted.

"I've heard their ghosts can haunt mortal men."

"You've been hearing quite a lot." I cut the members of my unit off, approaching their campfire. They clutched onto their spears, and drew their swords, startled by my presence.

"Gods, Hestan, you scared us," Purcell sighed in relief.

"Xora is not a Banshee." I grabbed a piece of bread they had taken out over the campfire and settled down beside Zain.

"She could be!" Purcell asserted. "She's won every fight she's ever been in. She never seems to get tired. I don't even think I've ever seen her wounded."

"Maybe that's because she's a better fighter than you are." I glanced in his direction, as I freed my silver hair from the tie it had been in.

"That's hardly difficult to accomplish," Kaspian quipped. In response, Purcell flung an apple core in his direction, which he dodged.

"Like us, she's a member of the Hunt, and a good one at that. I won't have you spreading rumours about her." I pointed at them. "She's twice the fighter you all are, so if it came down to keeping her... or you, then it would be her," I declared.

"Come on, Hestan, don't be like that, we're friends, aren't we?" Purcell said, approaching me with his arms outstretched.

"Don't even think about—"

But then he was on me, his arm wrapped around the top of my chest. Zain followed his lead and wrapped his arm around my shoulders. I protested, freeing myself from their clutches. "Leave the woman alone," I said sternly.

"We meant nothing by it," Purcell said as he shrugged his shoulders.

I looked at them all in turn. "You all know the punishment for those who even speak of sorcery, let alone those who are accused of practising it. Your conversations are dangerous, both for yourselves and for those who you would cast under the shadow of doubt. Xora would not have a chance to defend herself, she would be dead within a day if certain people caught wind of what you were saying. Speak on this no more, that's an order."

The three men looked at each other, not entirely without guilt in their eyes. "Sorry Captain," Kaspian said, clearing his throat. "We will."

"Did you lay with her then? Charmed her with those pretty purple eyes of yours?" Purcell jested, nudging my elbow.

"You don't need to lie with a woman to see her value," I replied. "I just warned you about your jokes. Did you not hear me?"

Purcell's face flushed red from embarrassment. "I did, Captain. Sorry."

These men were my friends, yes, but I was also the leader of their unit. I was responsible for making sure they didn't get themselves, or anyone else killed. It mattered more that they respected rather than liked me. I could live without their friendship. I would prefer not to live with their deaths.

"What did we catch today?" I asked.

We began going through what we had obtained during the past few hours. The Hunt was crucial to the survival of Kalnasa, it had been for centuries. Food was scarce here, our diet mostly consisted of plants. The altitude of our Kingdom made it difficult for many species to survive and while our people had adapted to it, many animals could not. It hadn't been an issue decades ago, but now there was a lack of meat at all times. It was our job to traverse the difficult terrain required to catch plants, as well as the large birds, fish, mammals, and bears that could feed our people.

The task was gruelling, difficult, and harsh on our bodies. It was also dangerous. There were several members of the Hunt who had died after being attacked by animals or falling from high peaks. There were fifty members of it, and each year, around ten of them perished. I had been in charge of the Hunt for four years and each year, each death, only became more difficult.

After totalling up our catches, Zain sighed. His hands were resting on his hips. "It's getting worse each time. What are we going to tell the King?"

"The truth," I replied. "We tell him the truth. He is already aware of the situation."

"But what if he thinks it's us? That's what some of the villagers are saying now." Purcell sounded nervous. He fiddled with his chestnut curls.

"He knows it's not," I reassured him, placing a hand on his shoulder.

Kaspian's dark eyes squinted at me. "What do you mean?"

"I mean if you are concerned about facing blame then you need not be. King Dunlan has been trying to resolve the situation regarding our resources with Vasara for some-time." I questioned whether I should be telling them this information, but it seemed harmless to share it.

"You mean to say" – Zain peered at me under his dark brows – "that Vasara could be helping us, but they are not." He laughed. "That's hardly surprising. Asking the rich to protect those less fortunate is like asking the sun if it could stop drying up the rain."

"I have said nothing of the kind, and I'd suggest you refrain from claiming such things yourself," I said. I knew there was discontent about Dunlan's handling of our situation amongst the people. I could feel it festering like a disease. I was trying my best to stop its spread, its destruction.

Kaspian glanced up. "We should be marching on Vasara and—"

"That is not the answer," I interjected. "To fight another, thinking it will end a fight of your own, it is only a folly that will end in blood."

Kaspian scoffed. "Right because that's going to work isn't it." He stood, long dark hair slipping over his shoulders as he pierced the ground with his spear. "Let's all just keep quiet and pretend our bellies are full, and our children aren't starving. As long as Vasara is satisfied I suppose?" He sounded agitated.

I stood in kind and strode towards him. He inched back slightly in surprise. "You know it is not that simple. Innocent people dwell in Vasara, and we cannot make demands of our King or—"

"Demands?" Kaspian laughed. "To have access to food? To eat? It's not as if we're asking for riches Hestan."

"The King is dealing with it."

"Is he? How long has it been since you had a full meal? Any of you?" He looked at Zain and Purcell. "It's been seven months for me. But I can bet my right arm that The King, who's *'dealing with it,'* has been eating plenty. The Royals are probably responsible for consuming half the food we catch alone, while the rest of us beg for the scraps. He's not going to deal with it when it doesn't affect him is he? He's not going to barge down to Vasara and fight for us. Wake up, Hestan. You've always been naively loyal when it comes to our King."

"He is the King." I could feel myself growing frustrated.

"Yes. He is the King. Only he's doing a bad job at being one isn't he? When his people are struggling to survive, and he hides away in his Palace amongst the clouds."

"That's enough Kaspian." My voice dropped.

"I see. The King comes before your own men now does he?"

"I owe him my life. You know that."

"For how long?" Kaspian asked.

The confusion was visible on my face.

"So, he saved you once, years ago. Now you're going to kiss his feet for the rest of your life, even if he's in the wrong?" He persisted.

The King had saved me, many years ago, when I was but a child. Some sorcerers, rebels, they had said, slaughtered my entire village, my family. The King and his men arrived at my house, after it had been taken over by the intruders. The intruders who killed my parents, my older brothers before my eyes. I could still remember the sound their blades made as they forced their way into bone and flesh. I could still remember the sound of their screams, of all the screams of the innocent people, merging into one.

Kaspian waited for my answer. Zain and Purcell were watching us anxiously, looking at each other with a silent question in their eyes as to whether they should intervene.

"You are dismissed Hunter."

"Fine. I'm going home."

"You misunderstand me. You are dismissed from your duties until further notice. Give me your medallion."

Kaspian's face fell. "What?" he murmured.

"Give me your medallion. Now."

Purcell's voice came from behind my shoulder. "Hestan, don't –"

"You're going to kick me out because I spoke my mind? Do you want a unit that is afraid to voice their concerns around you?"

"I want a unit that will not talk of treason."

"Treason?" He grimaced.

"Give me your medallion."

After silently staring at me for a few more seconds, Kaspian, rather than handing me his medallion, ripped it off his neck and threw it to the ground. The silver tinted circle, engraved with the moon, Kalnasa's emblem, was now covered in dirt.

Kaspian scoffed. "Your loyalty to that man will be the death of you." He backed away from the group, still facing us until he reached his horse and retreated into the night.

The palpable tension that hung over the remaining three of us lasted until we had ridden back to the Celion, Kalnasa's Central City. We were to ride to the Palace to deliver our bounty, which would later be distributed amongst the people according to the Kingdom's laws and policies.

As we neared the Palace, several people stepped out of their houses to catch a glimpse of our stock. Their hungry eyes grew more and more ravenous the longer our journey continued. Zain and Purcell shifted in their seats, ill at ease.

It was growing worse, this desperation, this fragile unspoken peace between us and them. We were a symbol of authority, an authority they felt had let them down, had abandoned them. All the members of the Hunt were keenly aware of that, each time we travelled down this road. I looked around, keeping an eye out for any sign of ill intentions.

Rain began falling, sputtering against the ground, sliding off the curved roofs, drenching out clothes.

Through the downpour, I caught sight of a figure approaching our cart.

It was small, lithe, and clad in a cloak. We were used to thieves trying to steal from us on our return, we had been for a while now. But this figure, shrouded in shadow, was fast and quiet, unlike any of the thieves we had encountered before. They shuffled between the villagers on the road with precise and clean movements, weaving themselves through the denser parts of the crowd.

"Halt!" I shouted, clutching at my spear. Zain and Purcell stopped behind me, and catching wind of the situation, reached for their own weapons. The crowd grew nervous, and their murmurs grew louder the closer the figure approached.

"You there, stop!" Purcell shouted, but the figure paid no mind to his command. Now it was closer, I could tell it was a woman. The leather of her clothing was covered with a blue bodice and shoulder pads. A hood attached to the grey cloak she wore concealed her identity. Only her mouth was visible.

I dismounted from my horse in an effort to intercept her, but before I could, she had reached our cart. Zain took a swing at her from his horse, which she deftly avoided in one swift manoeuvre, but Purcell, who had been anticipating her move, knocked her exposed side with his spear, hard.

The woman fell on top of the cart and clutched at its contents. She grabbed some of the food we had managed to retrieve. She had no weapons on her, at least none which were visible. We tried our best not to kill or hurt those who attempted to steal from our cart, after all, we knew they were hungry, we knew they were struggling, but we also couldn't let such attempts be successful. So far, we had been able to stop the attempts in their tracks. Sometimes the King's guard killed the thieves, in an effort to deter others, a method I detested.

But I knew it was only a matter of time before a thief succeeded. Once that happened, other villagers would start planning their own raids on our crew.

If that happened, civil war would soon follow.

The woman leapt off the cart, skilfully avoiding another attack from Purcell, but her landing was awkward, slipping against the wet ground. The tightening of her lip revealed she had hurt herself in the process. It would be easy then, I calculated, to stop her now.

The crowd had begun cheering, some of them willing her victory, some protesting at her selfishness. Their hollers intertwined with the sputtering rainfall, a torrent of discontent swelling all around us. If food had not been scarce, there is no doubt in my mind they would have started throwing it at us, or her. She turned around abruptly, scanning the scene for a quick exit and found what she was looking for almost immediately. I followed her gaze but found nothing. She had likely planned her escape in advance.

She shifted away but I was upon her now. She shoved the stolen goods down the front of her clothing and grabbed at the inside of her cloak. She drew out a knife. It wasn't a dagger, or a sword, or any weapon of any craftsmanship, but it could cut me, and it could certainly kill me.

She crouched in front of me, her arms were outstretched, waiting for my next move. Her hands were gloved and gripped tighter around the knife.

"Put that down, give us back what you stole, and I promise we will not hurt you," I said.

The woman didn't move, didn't indicate in any way she had heard me or intended on doing as I asked.

I could hear horses approaching. "The King's guard aren't here yet, but once they are I won't be able to protect you. They will kill you." I spoke softly, attempting to get through to her.

It was louder now, the sound of the King's men approaching the street. As was the rain, which fell more ferociously. By the slight parting of her lip, it was clear she understood, but even this close, the skin of her chin was darkened by shadow. I couldn't tell her race, or what Kingdom she may be from.

I reached for her arm, but she dodged my hand and slit my bicep with her knife. I looked at her in disbelief. None of the people who had ever attempted to steal from us had ever actually tried to wound us before.

She looked more determined now, but her balance was off, likely from her painful dismount from our cart earlier. I stood forwards and moved my leg towards her feet, in an attempt to sweep her off her own, but she drew her knife across my outstretched thigh.

I hissed at the pain, losing my patience. I resolutely stepped towards her. Sensing my aggravation, she ran directly into the townspeople. Some made way for her, some were scratching at her clothing, trying to remove the hood from her face.

But there were equally as many people doing the same to me, angry at the Hunt's lack of service to the people. There were many who believed the Hunt took the food they acquired for themselves, only pretending there were shortages.

I greatly regretted the fact my hair remained loose. Its wet strands were now the perfect target for the civilian's clutches.

The King's guard were here now, likely alerted by all the commotion and noise. One of them approached me, pushing people off them like dirt.

"What happened?" she shouted.

"The woman in the hood there," I pointed in her direction, "She's taken from the cart."

"What did she take?" the King's guard asked.

"I don't know. I didn't have the time to check," I shouted, gesturing towards the scene going on around us.

As we were talking, three of the King's guard had begun to force their way through the crowds in her pursuit. But she was far ahead of them, even with her injury. She swam through the crowd like a fish in a stream.

I lost sight of her until, in the distance, her figure could be made out, climbing one of the houses. She scaled its sides until she reached the roof. She turned around to assess the situation, glancing at the King's guard, but they were no longer paying attention to her. They were dealing with the angry mob of villagers who were yelling, demanding answers, demanding the King do something about their hunger.

I looked back at the woman. She was still facing me. She ripped something off her clothing, held it up in the air as if to signal she had done so and threw it down on the roof.

She stared in my direction for a few more moments and then disappeared into the night.

Nobody else had noticed, they were all too distracted, too overwhelmed by the noise.

I stood in place for a few minutes, wondering if she would return, knowing she would not.

I walked back towards the cart to find an exasperated Zain and Purcell guarding it. There must have been several more attempts to steal from it during the uproar and distraction the woman provided.

Purcell's eyes widened when he saw me. "You're bleeding."

I'd honestly, forgotten. "It's nothing" I mumbled. She hadn't cut me deeply, whether that was deliberate or simply due to a lack of training, I couldn't say.

Before I could even catch my breath, another King's guard member was upon me, his beige skin was plastered with rainfall, the water glinting off his silver armour.

"What did she take then?" he asked gruffly.

I nodded at Zain and Purcell in a silent instruction to discover the answer to that question.

Zain lifted a cover off the cart, protecting its contents from the weather. He turned around looking bashful as he said, "Practically nothing."

"What do you mean practically, what did she take?" The King's guard demanded to know.

"She took some Riggon." Zain shrugged.

"Riggon?" I asked, narrowing my brows. Riggon was a plant, its nutritional value was almost next to nothing.

"Why by the Gods would she take that?" Purcell asked.

"Well, I don't give a shit as long as I don't have to report to the King we've got less food for this lot." The King's guard gestured to the townspeople behind him with his thumb.

"But isn't it just used for seasoning?" Purcell asked nobody in particular.

"Can be, but it's also used for tea," Zain said.

"Of course," Purcell chimed, "That must be it, she just wanted some tea."

"As opposed to your theory, where she would be using it to season the non-existent food, we all have." Zain leant against the cart with his arms crossed.

"Alright hilarious." Purcell's voice was flat.

"Maybe that's where all the meat is," Zain continued, enjoying taunting him, "With that woman, she's got the entire supply."

"Prick."

Then it dawned on me. "It can also be used as a medicine."

Purcell and Zain turned towards me at the same time. "Can it? I've never heard of that," Zain said.

"No, he's right," Purcell spoke up, gazing at his feet. "For...fever, is it? No...that's not right. Pain?"

"Yes, it can be used for pain," I confirmed. "But it can also be used to treat wounds, when it's ground into a paste."

"Well, with any luck, she'll perish from whatever injuries she's got, and we won't have to look for her," the guard stated.

"Captain Hestan." The first King's guard who had approached me earlier came towards us.

"Captain Mulani," I nodded in greeting.

"You're coming with us," she said, raising her chin.

"Nothing was taken, we defended—" Purcell began to protest.

"It's not about that," Mulani asserted.

"What is it about?" I asked, not expecting an answer.

"You will know soon," Mulani replied, as expected.

"My unit and I were just making our way to the Palace with this stock." I nodded at them.

"Don't worry about that. The guard will take care of it. Your men can go home." On hearing her command, members of the King's guard approached the cart, relieving Zain and Purcell of their duties.

"It's fine," I assured them, "Go."

"See you tomorrow," Zain said to me.

"No, you won't," Mulani replied on my behalf. Zain and Purcell's eyes darted towards each other, shocked.

"Am I to be reprimanded, Captain?" I would rather have known beforehand if I was about to be punished.

"I've already said this isn't about what just happened. No, you are not to be reprimanded, Captain."

"What then?"

"It's not to be discussed outside the Palace walls."

I nodded once more to Zain and Purcell. "You can go, and Zain, you're in charge for now." Zain nodded, with a tense expression on his face. The two men looked at each other and reluctantly walked away.

Mulani, sensing my restlessness over the situation, came closer towards me and whispered. "Everything will be explained once you arrive, but"— she looked around quickly to make sure nobody was within hearing distance— "you are to escort someone somewhere."

"Who?" I frowned.

"Enough." She silenced me with her decisive tone. "I can tell you no more."

She walked towards her horse. Her men gestured for me to do the same. As I waited on my saddle for the other men to join us, my gaze drifted towards the roof the woman had been standing upon, framed by a greying sky.

If I was about to be tasked with escorting someone, then I had very little time left in Kalnasa.

If I wanted to find out what she had left on the roof, I would have to go there.

And it would have to be tonight.

## CHAPTER 7 - LORIA

I had been washed, waxed, stripped, measured, clothed, squeezed, and wrapped up in this gown like a prized mare.

I had always known this day would come. The day when I would have to attend the banquets, smile, and shake hands with men who looked at me as if I were an ornament they could admire, touch, and play with. That I would be asked to please them, make them feel powerful, make them want for nothing. All so I could bear a useless title, so I could convince myself and others I had a place in this world.

But I would rather have had no place in it, than that place.

I had spent the whole week trying to devise a way to get myself out of the scheme my father had created. But every session of speculation ended in the same conclusion. There was nowhere I could go where my father would not find me. There was nowhere I could run where Nathon would not follow. There was, short of throwing myself off the side of the Citadel's highest floor, nothing I could do.

I had considered it. I had thought about merging myself with the thunderous sky and leaping to my death.

But I was not ready to die. Not yet.

And why should I die so Prince Eliel could live? I had no trust, no faith in my father except this – I trusted in his desire for power. As long as I was useful to him, and as long as he got what he wanted, I would live.

I owed Eliel nothing. I owed myself a chance to survive.

The only way to guarantee my own survival at this moment in time, was to go along with this plan. Perhaps, I hoped, I could figure out a way to sabotage it while I was in Vasara. But the likelihood of me being able to do that while remaining alive was extremely small.

I would need to become that toy, that plaything.

I would have to endure it.

I would endure it.

We had been waiting for Nathon for some time now. Our departure had been scheduled at dawn, but he was still nowhere to be found. The travelling party would consist of twenty, including Nathon and myself, to ensure we reached Vasara safely. All the guards had awoken early for the undertaking of our journey.

They were beginning to grow impatient.

I stood near the outer edges of the Citadel's front courtyard, looking out over the golden landscape of the villages below. I overheard them speaking.

"He should have been here at least an hour ago. That little shit."

"Keep your voice down." Without checking, I could tell the woman who replied was glaring at my back.

"It's freezing out here and he's probably got his head smack down on the table of some tavern."

"Who has?" a voice interceded.

I spun around. Nathon had just strolled out of the large archway leading into the Citadel. He was shrouded in a light cloak, outlined with dark fur. Though the weather in Audra was humid, it was cooler in the early hours, the wind leeching the air of its heat. Nathon skipped down the steps, approaching the man.

"Urrr...my brother. He's—"

Nathon laughed, placing his gloved hand over his mid torso. "You're a terrible liar."

I hadn't moved, I was watching the exchange from afar. I did not intend on approaching any closer. Nathon was wild and unpredictable. I had no idea what he would do at any given moment. I pitied the man, but not enough to help him.

The woman must have been thinking the same thing, for she did not rush to defend her comrade either, or confirm his story.

Nathon slapped the man on the top of his shoulder.

"Your Highness, I swear—" the man began.

Nathon rolled his eyes, removing his hand. The man's shoulders visibly relaxed, but before he could fully release his breath, Nathon yanked the man's sword from his belt, and pointed it at his chest.

The man widened his eyes, the entire party tensed. The air stretched and fissured with that tension, seemed to crackle with it.

Nathon turned the dark sword in his hand, observing it in the dull sunlight struggling to reach us. "These are reserved for the most prestigious soldiers in the King's infantry. That's because they're made from a special kind of mineral we mine from deep within our lands. Noxstone, they call it. They named it after that... God." Nathon smiled at that, as if it amused him. "It cut sharper than most blades, pierce deeper, but they're lighter to wield. You can't find that material anywhere else in the world. It's what my daggers are made from. Very few people possess a weapon like this. People will pay ridiculous amounts for them, both here and across the other Five Kingdoms." Nathon sighed. "Exquisite."

I didn't own a weapon of Noxstone myself. I had never felt quite comfortable with one in my hand, knowing the damage it could do.

The man, not sure whether he should speak, looked at the woman standing beside him. She, like all the other people present, was watching Nathon with a mixture of terror and curiosity.

The soldier turned back around and licked his lip. "I am honoured to own it, Your Highness."

Nathon scrunched up his face as if squinting, tilted his head to the side, and added the sword to his own weapons belt. "Only you don't anymore. I think I'll take this with me."

"But Your Highness... it's my only weapon."

"Such a shame. I sincerely hope you don't end up needing one then."

"But I am to journey with you... Your Highness."

"Yes. You are. Without a weapon, and *nobody* shall give one to him." He looked behind the two figures to the remaining soldiers. "If we are in a life-or-death scenario then I suppose you'll just have to improvise."

There was in fact a fairly moderate chance we would end up in a life-or-death scenario. Murdering a candidate would provide the others with a great advantage, and even with the Courting Season aside, we were never short on enemies, across the Five Kingdoms, and within our own lands as well.

"But, Your Highness, I—"

"What's wrong, soldier? You were perfectly happy to improvise just moments ago when I asked you who you were speaking about. I assume you will be able to do so on a battlefield as well." There was no logic to what Nathon was saying, he knew it, all the soldiers knew it, but nobody would dare inform him of it.

After a brief pause Nathon added, "If I catch anyone sneaking him a weapon or giving him one during a fight then I will take theirs too. Is that clear?"

Everyone mumbled their agreement. Nathon smiled widely, then turned to face me. The smile remained on his face but faded as he approached.

"What's wrong with you? You look miserable." He addressed me.

I turned away from him. "Your arrival probably has something to do with it."

"Of course, my apologies, it seemed you were all simply brimming with joy before I arrived."

"You're intolerable," I couldn't help but mumble under my breath.

"Trust me Loria, there are *many* escorts who would be far, far worse than me."

"Really? I can't think of anyone I'd prefer less than you," I rotated my body to face him.

"Does that matter? I'm not your escort so we can take midnight strolls and gossip about the colour of the King's eyes. I'm coming to make sure nobody tries to hurt you or kill you. I'm coming to make sure we see this task through, and we survive it. You may not like my company, but you can rest assured if anyone harbouring ill intentions towards you even blinks in your direction, they won't live to see the next sunrise."

I didn't know whether his speech comforted or petrified me.

I looked around. "Why are we here? I thought we would be riding."

Nathon's expression changed and he swallowed quickly. "There's been a change of plans. I'm sure you're pleased to hear it."

I was. I nearly died riding an Erebask when I was ten. At first, my flight had been blissful, almost calming. Then, without warning, the Erebask I was on suddenly stumbled and dropped, as if it had become incapable of carrying me. I was tumbling to my death, crying, and screaming, pleading with the creature to stop, to rise, but it seemed equally distressed. I had been moments away from becoming a fractured mess of blood and bones on the ground when Nathon, flying on Kazal's back, had saved my life.

That was back when he had a soul.

"I am," I admitted. "But I've never seen you go anywhere without your Erebask."

Nathon rubbed the side of his jaw and neck. I peered at him. He was acting strangely.

"Are you sure there's not something wrong *with you*?" I asked him.

Nathon's hand fell to his side, and he began peering at me. "Why are you asking me that?"

"You're...you seem distracted."

"Because I was scratching my neck?"

"No."

"What then?"

"Because you didn't kill that man."

"Sorry?" Nathon crossed his arms.

"That man, who said you were probably stuck in a tavern. You didn't kill him."

Nathon was regarding me the way one would a stranger. "So?"

"You would have killed him normally. Or hurt him at least."

Nathon stroked his chin quickly, still maintaining eye contact. "Are you quite sure I didn't?"

"What?"

"Now that man's long journey to Vasara will be plagued with fear, with the constant unease that comes with being on the open road unarmed. The trepidation and knowledge that should we be attacked, his death is guaranteed, is a much sweeter punishment for him...and for me. I'm going to thoroughly enjoy watching his facial expressions on the way. I need some form of entertainment, after all."

I sighed. He wasn't distracted. If anything, he was simply more unhinged.

"Get in the carriage and make sure you don't get your lovely dress dirty. We need the King to like you, don't we?"

Nathon made to get into the carriage himself.

"No," I said firmly.

He blinked hard, with one foot on the edge of the carriage.

"You're not sitting in the carriage with me," I declared.

"You expect me, the Crown Prince of Audra to ride on a horse outside, in the rain?" he said ironically.

"It doesn't bother you when you're riding your Erebask."

Again, his expression shifted, his eyes darted to this side. "I'm getting in that carriage with you Loria. Move."

He shoved past me and sat down inside. Some of the soldiers were watching us from afar, clearly waiting for me to join him so we could move out.

I would endure this.

I got into the carriage and sat next to the opposite window, as far away from Nathon as was possible in this cramped, dark black box.

The same look that had clouded his expression moments ago remained on his face. I don't know why I found myself curious about what had caused him such turmoil. He never showed any care towards anyone but himself, and should the situation have been reversed, I could guarantee my struggles would not have occupied his thoughts for a single moment. But still, I was curious, largely because Nathon was never phased by anything.

"There is something wrong with you," I stared at him. Now that he was trapped with me in this carriage, as I was with him, he had no way of escaping my statement.

He turned towards me and leant his head back against the wood. "I already told you there wasn't," he grumbled.

"I don't believe you." A violent nausea, born from nerves, ignited in me as I spoke.

Nathon quickly removed his head from the wood and leant forwards. "I've been roped into escorting you. I'm not entirely happy about it."

"That's not it."

"Yes, it is."

"Why are you lying?"

"Why are you asking?"

"Why can't I ask?"

"Why can't you remain silent?"

"If you wanted to be left alone why did you sit in this carriage with me?"

"I didn't think I'd be getting interrogated."

"I'm not interrogating you."

"Yes, you are, and it's starting to irritate me, so stop."

I contemplated it. I thought about stopping. But I had the upper hand now. For the first time in my life, I had the upper hand with my brother.

"Or what? You can't hurt me or kill me, you said so, not unless you want to die yourself."

He smirked at that. "Still tempting though."

A moment of silence passed between us. After our sharp and hurried exchange of words, it seemed to stretch out for an eternity.

Nathon huffed. "I'm not going to answer your questions, just because you want to be right about something, Loria." He leant back against the wood and closed his eyes.

"Am I right?"

"You're still asking questions."

"You're still pretending."

He looked me in the eye, grinned, and spoke. "Aren't we all?"

That ended our conversation.

It took us eight days to reach the outskirts of Vasara. The soldier whose weapon had been acquired by Nathon, did indeed look constantly alert and exhausted the entire journey. He hardly slept. Nathon would every so often, draw my attention to his wide, darting eyes and laugh, or give the soldiers orders about the watches they would take and the stations they would occupy.

The closer we got to Vasara, the warmer it became. The soldiers slowly discarded their cloaks and Nathon himself was eventually clad in a low-cut black vest, with wide pants to match. The gold and silver embroidery on his clothing made it clear to the Vasarans he was a person of importance as we dragged the horses down the smoothly paved streets.

Two nights previously, I had taken off my plum-coloured cloak, revealing the dress I had been hiding underneath its layers. The looks I had received from the three soldiers on duty made me far more uncomfortable than the heat, and although I knew they could not act on whatever foul intentions were swarming through their minds, I would rather have remained stifled by the warmth, than be subject to their leering.

Nathon, who now noticed me sweating, moved closer to me. "Why are you still wearing that? You'll boil to death before we've even arrived."

"Maybe I'm hoping that will happen," I replied.

A few minutes later, sentries from Vasara approached us. Their golden and amber uniforms glinted harshly in the bright sun. It made looking at them painful. They were here to escort us to the Palace, they told us, bowing in our direction as they did so.

"How far are we?" Nathon inquired.

"Another hour by carriage, Your Highness."

Nathon turned back to the soldiers who had been accompanying us on our journey. "You can return now. We won't be in need of your company anymore."

"But, Your Highness, we were instructed to escort you to the Palace Gates."

Nathon spun around in a circle. "I don't see anyone here who will inform my father you did otherwise. Do you?"

When nobody answered he dismissed them. "Please, leave."

The soldiers looked at one another and slowly shifted, turning around to depart.

"Thank you for your help," I said before they could make their way. Some of the soldiers nodded their heads in gratitude, others looked baffled. Nathon looked amused.

We walked towards the carriage the sentries had brought us. It was much larger than the one we had been travelling in, golden and embellished with symbols representing the sun, light, and radiance on its sides.

Nathon smirked at me with a sidelong glance, shaking his head.

"Somebody should thank them," I said.

"Somebody would have, had they actually been helpful."

Another guardsman approached us and bowed before he said. "Captain Jarian of the King's guard at your service. We are honoured to welcome you to Vasara."

Nathon beamed. "I'm sure you are."

Jarian gestured for us to enter the carriage. Inside, the seats were much further apart and cushioned with thick layers of red velvet. Nathon immediately sat on one side and lifted his legs to rest them on the other. The windows had curtains too, which Nathon shut on his side. I did the same, thankful for the fact the fabric managed to block out some of the sweltering heat.

An hour later, we were outside the Palace gates. Jarian, after letting us out, announced, "The Prince is currently detained but he, as per tradition, intends to welcome every candidate and their escort in person. If you would be so kind as to follow me, I will show you a comfortable place where you can rest until then."

I wasn't even looking at Jarian. I was in awe of the Palace. It towered so high above us I couldn't see the top of it. It was so wide I couldn't see either end of it. It was coloured cream, and all along the walls and sides, were several stained-glass windows rich in ruby, amber, golds, burnt oranges, scarlets, and yellows. Two large sculptures of Chimeras facing each other scaled the sides of the entrance. Their claws joined together above the high archway, cupping a golden sun in their paws.

Nathon didn't seem to care about the architecture at all. Instead, he was keenly focused on Jarian. "Are we the first to arrive?"

"You are the third. First to arrive was Zeima, then Jurasa. Kalnasa is due to arrive later today and of course the Vasaran candidate required no travel."

I managed to tear my eyes away from the building and look at Jarian, who noticed the wonder in my expression. "It still takes my breath away at times."

Nathon sighed impatiently. "I would rather like to see the inside of it and settle in that comfortable place you were mentioning."

"Of course," Jarian replied hastily.

Inside, the Palace was somehow even more magnificent. The sun that poured through the stained-glass windows left scattered pools of delightful warmth on the stone ground. Pillars of beige, cream, and white towered all around us. It felt like being inside the sun itself. A gentle breeze passed through the several open doorways and hallways, carrying with it the scent of the flowers planted in the Palace gardens.

"If the King is half as impressed with you as you are with some ceilings, then this will be easier than I thought," Nathon mumbled. His probing comment pulled me out of my haze.

"You aren't impressed?" I asked.

"It's a building. I'm far more interested in the people who occupy it."

Jarian led us into a large adjoining room that opened onto a courtyard adorned with several bushes and plants. It was furnished with large and comfortable chairs, honey and amber in colour, along with small mahogany tables upon a rust-coloured carpet. The sand-coloured walls were lined with books on one side and paintings on the other.

"I shall inform His Highness of your arrival." He bowed and left. Nathon immediately sank down onto one of the chairs.

"Alright, time for you to take off that cloak now." He waved in my direction.

I stubbornly clutched at it tighter.

Nathon sighed in irritation. "You're not going to be able to walk around in it forever."

"I know."

He stood and walked towards me. "It's going to look very bad for us if you greet the King in that."

"No, it won't." I knew that was a lie.

"Stop playing naïve with me. I know you're not that ignorant."

"I'm comfortable this way."

"I'm not comfortable in this heat and I'm wearing this." He gestured to himself.

"This doesn't concern you."

"Unfortunately, it does. Remember? Make the King fall desperately in love with you, or I die?"

"That's enough incentive for me to fail."

In response Nathon grabbed the edge of my cloak and began yanking at it. "I'm sorry but..." He grunted as he struggled to remove it from my shoulders.

"Get off me," I shoved him with one hand.

"I don't want to force you, Loria. It would be much more helpful if you just took it off yourself."

"I—"

The doors opened behind us. Nathon, who still had his hand gripped at my cloak, turned around swiftly. I followed his movement.

In front of us, stood the Prince.

He regarded us both with the blankest expression I had ever witnessed. His eyes roamed up and down both of our bodies almost too quickly to notice.

Remembering where we were, Nathon let go of my clothing and got down on one knee.

"Your Highness," he said.

I, still shocked the Prince had arrived so quickly, continued to stare at him for a moment. Nathon turned his head to the side and coughed, suggesting I replicate his action.

The Prince barely glanced at Nathon before returning his cold gaze to me.

"Your Highness," I said and got down on my knees as well.

The silence that followed was stretched out so far, I began to hear my own breathing like tumultuous waves crashing against a shore in my chest.

I looked up to find the Prince had shifted and was now standing directly in front of me. A small smile played across his closed lips.

"Princess Loria," he finally spoke. "You may rise."

In my attempt to rise with grace, I tripped over the cloak gathered around my feet. I was about to fall when a hand steadied me at the crook of my elbow.

The Prince had grabbed my arm.

The Prince wasn't supposed to touch any of the candidates, in any capacity until long into the Courting Season's activities. I stared at his hand like I had never seen one before. His fingers were long and elegant. His first was decorated with an ornate ring, his family ring I supposed.

Nathon, who had been watching us with much curiosity, widened his eyes at the touch. Jarian, who was standing behind the Prince, cleared his throat as if to alert the Prince of his error.

Gently, and painfully slowly, the Prince let go of my arm.

"Thank you, Your Highness," I said.

"You'll have to keep that a secret I'm afraid." He smiled, placing both his hands behind his back. Then he turned to face Nathon. "You may rise as well."

Nathon got up successfully, with the precision being a warrior afforded him.

"Are you well, Princess?" the Prince asked, eyeing Nathon as he did. He was referencing the situation he had walked in on, I realised.

"Yes, Your Highness. Sibling squabbles nothing more." I smiled politely.

"I see." He regarded Nathon once again. "Of course. You are Audra's Crown Prince. I have heard much about you."

Nathon raised his eyebrows at the remark, "What have you heard, Your Highness?"

The Prince didn't smile, but his eyes glimmered with something akin to delight. "Nothing worth mentioning. Nothing good at least."

Nathon smiled. It was always hard to know what he was thinking, whether he found the Prince's response humorous or offensive.

"I was simply suggesting Loria relieve herself from the heavy cloak she is wearing. We are not so climatised to Vasara's weather, you see."

I glared at him with as much anger as I could muster.

"Is that so?" The Prince turned back to look at me.

"I—" I found myself struggling to explain.

The Prince slightly tilted his head. I was looking at him more directly now. A strand of his cherry red hair crossed over his pale face. His features were cut as sharply as the shape of his clothing. Vasara had always been well known for the unusual cuts of their attire. His white tunic was neck high, but a triangle was cut out around his upper chest, surrounded by a scarlet red outline. It perfectly complemented the triangular angular shape of his face, his pale skin, and his high cheekbones.

His stare. It was like being caressed by a cool breeze. So crisp and sharp, yet refreshing and uplifting. It was like being hit with an arrow that numbed every part of your body. It was like feeling nothing and everything. It was unnerving.

"I...do not like what is underneath."

Nathon pressed both his lips together, widening his eyes at me in alarm.

"I can assure you, Your Highness, she is dressed befitting –" he began.

"Why is that?" The Prince looked at me, ignoring Nathon completely.

I was torn between the voice in my head telling me to be honest, and the one to be careful.

Nathon filled the silence, "Your Highness, I must apologise for my sister—"

"There is no need, Prince. If the Princess would prefer her cloak, that is her choice. Although, we have lighter ones available, should you prefer."

"She –" Nathon started.

"I should like" – the Prince turned to face Nathon – "to hear the Princess speak."

I looked at a surprised Nathon before saying, "I would be grateful for one, Your Highness."

The Prince turned around and nodded to Jarian, who left to inform a servant of the request, I assumed.

Then he turned back around to us. "I have some matters to attend to and we are still waiting for Kalnasa's candidate to arrive. We will convene later in the grand hall, for the formal opening of the season, with all five candidates present." The Prince's voice became detached, as if he had rehearsed this part of the conversation.

Nathon bowed, smiling widely. "Thank you, Your Highness. We are *honoured* to be your guests. Once again, I apologise for the misunderstanding."

"As I said, there is no need." The Prince looked at me. "No need at all."

After a brief pause, he took two steps towards me. "I'll have a servant bring you a choice of cloaks. Do you have a preference?"

"A preference, Your Highness?"

"A colour?"

"Oh, no, Your Highness. We only ever wear dark colours in Audra, I wouldn't know, that is to say" – I cleared my throat – "I will happily wear whichever colour you prefer."

The King looked at my cloak, confirming my statement about the shades we wore.

"My favourite colour is green," he said rather unexpectedly. He glanced over my shoulder to the plants outside. "Alas, we do not craft clothes of that colour here. Like Audra, we too, have dress codes."

I was not sure what he expected me to say.

"Perhaps you could have something made, since you are to be the King, Your Highness?"

He smiled tensely, still looking behind me. "That is precisely why I cannot." He was silent for a few moments and then said. "I will see you at the opening."

He was led by Jarian, who had just returned, out of the door.

After a few moments, Nathon broke the silence, turning towards me sharply.

"You're going to get us all killed before this has even started." He rubbed his face.

"It's not my fault you were grabbing me before he entered."

"You and your obsession with this cloak. You'd think you were naked under there," he said, staring at it again.

"Can you please refrain from speaking for a while?"

"If you could refrain from trying to have us disgraced."

"You could manage that on your own," I snapped.

"Stop Loria! I don't like this anymore than you."

"You're not the one who has to do this!" I lost control. Nathon looked at me bewildered.

"You're not the one who has to parade around and…and get someone to desire you, only to murder them. To have someone touch you, only to –"

He covered my mouth with his left hand. His right hand rested on the back of my head "Be quiet! Be quiet Loria!" He whispered harshly. "Maybe you don't care about your life, but I do. I don't want to die. Do you hear me?" He shook me slightly "I have things to do, things to finish, promises to keep. I will not have you be the death of me because you don't know when to keep your mouth shut!" His voice, although quiet, was clotted with such aggression that I froze. "We are in the Palace now. We are probably being watched, listened to, and observed at all times. You need to act as if someone is constantly breathing down your neck before someone snaps yours and mine."

I yelled against his hand, but it only came out as a muffled whimper. He pressed down harder on my face. Then, against my will, I started to cry, My tears spilt over his knuckles and swam into his palm. Instead of screams, I was sobbing now, sobbing into his hand.

Nathon loosened his grip on the back of my neck. After a moment's hesitation spent searching my face with his eyes, he pulled me to his chest and held me. I stiffened. My arms became rigid by my side. His left hand was still over my mouth and his right arm wrapped around my shoulders.

"Please stop crying." Though this was the closet in proximity Nathon and I had been for years, he sounded distant, lost.

I silently whimpered.

"Please, Loria, someone could walk in," he sighed.

I slowed my breathing and eventually stopped. I was still pressed unnaturally against his chest. Once he noticed my tears had stopped flowing, he let me go.

Then placing both of his arms on his shoulders he said, "I'm going out."

"What, why? For how long." My voice was raspy.

"I don't know. I'll be back before the opening."

"What is so important you need to leave right now? Of all times?" I didn't want to be left alone here, not when I had just arrived.

He made his way to the door backwards and winked at me.

"Something green Loria. I'm going to find you something green."

## CHAPTER 8 - ELIEL

"Did you find Gwin?"

"Yes, Your Highness," Jarian said, as we turned the corner, where Gwin was standing, her head meekly bowed.

"Gwin," I started. "Please can you find some cloaks, or a similar garment that can cover a person's whole body and bring them to Princess Loria when you have found them. Give her a few to choose from." I turned away from her.

"Her size, Your Highness?" she called out after me.

I stopped, startled, and threw her a quizzical look. There was no way I could know such information.

Gwin's face turned red, "I'm sorry, Your Highness. Of course, I will bring her different sizes and—"

"She's rather short," I added, trying to ease the dread I had unintentionally filled the serving girl with.

"Thank you, Your Highness." She curtsied and hurried down the hall.

Jarian and I continued walking. He looked at me with an unmistakable question as to whether he could speak.

"Yes Jarian."

"Your Highness if I may. The Albarsans of Audra, they seem rather—" he faltered.

"Go on," I said, as I walked in front of him.

"Impudent," he finished.

"And?"

Jarian became flustered. "And, Your Highness, I do not believe they respect the traditions here, nor the ceremony itself. It has long been rumoured the Prince is a –"

"Yes, I have heard the rumours, Jarian. I prefer to decide about people for myself, rather than let the distorted rumours of others do so for me."

"Of course, Your Highness. One should not believe everything one hears. It is only that they seem…troublesome."

I paused to face him. "I am quite aware of their nature since I am perfectly capable of observation."

"I never meant to suggest otherwise, Your Highness."

I sighed. I knew Jarian was only doing what he felt was best, warning me about people he perceived to be dangerous.

Still, I said, "I know that, Jarian. I am thankful for your dedication to my safety. But I prefer to judge a person based on their actions and not their reputation. It is often those who hide behind smiles, platitudes and prestige that have the darkest secrets to hide, in fact."

Jarian, silent in thought for a moment, said, "Indeed, you are wise beyond your years, Your Highness."

And yet, despite his many, he was still oblivious. True evil was not ugly, but a beautiful smile when light was shed upon its face, disappearing in the dark.

Nevertheless, I could not say I wholly disagreed with Jarian's assessment. The presence of Audra's Prince puzzled me. It irked me that I was unaware of the reasoning behind it.

"Have they been gathered?"

"Yes, Your Highness."

"Let us do this now," I said.

Jarian made a noise that indicated he agreed with me.

We were on our way to speak to the Vessels. The Vessels Palace Security had deemed suspicious enough to be brought to my attention, to be questioned more thoroughly in relation to the death of my parents.

I had no plan as we strolled towards the Northern Wing and up to the quarters where the Vessels were kept. I did not know how I would seek to retrieve information from them. I was in essence, completely unprepared for what I might face.

The Northern Wing was large, but the heavy presence of its overseers left it feeling much smaller. The Vessels that walked past us did not hide the disdain in their eyes as they glanced in our direction. Each of them wore a chain, fashioned as an ornate choker, anklet, or bracelet, which prevented them from using their powers to escape.

We allowed the Vessels to traverse the whole of the Northern Wing, both what was in and around it, but it was an illusionary freedom. If they ventured even one metre away from these designated areas, they were captured or executed on site.

We were getting closer to the transfer chamber, where the Vessels were drained of their magical cores on a daily basis. It was located to the left of the main walkway, which we were currently strolling down, to the right of which was a small, and modest courtyard. A small fountain and some benches were deposited throughout its cobblestoned paths. Several Vessels were currently undergoing a transfer, their sorcery seeping into the manacles and devices they were attached or strapped to. Some stared into the distance with a blank expression, some winced uncomfortably. I had heard that depending on the ability of the wielder, the transfer could range from painless to excruciating.

We eventually made our way to the chamber room, which was at the end of the walkway. The wooden floors and panelled walls were a pale, sand colour. The furnishings that had been inside had been removed for the purposes of our visit, leaving only two wooden chairs by the far-right window, and a small table, with a vase on it.

Standing in the centre of the room, cuffed, and surrounded by several overseers, were three wielders. A man, and two women.

The man's eyes burnt with an expression that told me he was determined to approach me before he even took his first step. Jarian, of course, did not notice.

The man took several broad strides in my direction, and before Jarian could draw his blade, the man spat at me. Several of the Palace workers, and overseers of the Wing grabbed him, drawing him away. His saliva had landed on the bottom of my chin, I had my height to thank for the fact it had not landed in my eyes.

He must have been around my age, I noticed, as I peered at the young man it had taken four others to subdue.

I stepped closer to him.

"Your Highness, I –" Jarian intervened.

I lifted my hand to indicate he should remain behind me.

"What is your name?" I asked the man.

He looked at me as if I had asked him which way he would prefer to be executed.

"They took my name. You took my name."

I furrowed my brows slightly, baffled by his statement.

The man laughed, but it was a rueful laugh, full of sorrow.

I squinted to indicate I was waiting for him to explain.

"Our powers are tied to us. Once we start to lose them, we start to lose ourselves. We forget things, we –"

"Stop," one of the women protested.

"No," the man argued, turning over his shoulder to look at her. "He should know. He should know what he does. What his *kind* do." There was so much resentment in his tone, so much hatred.

"Your Highness…please spare him." The woman got on her knees. Despair coloured her voice with a quiver. She was clutching her hands together. "He is…we had nothing to do with the King and Queen. We would never do such a thing."

"Silence woman!" one of the overseers heaved her up, gripping at her forearm forcefully.

I looked at the overseer. He was like many other people in this Palace, enamoured by their position, believing it gave them the right to act in whichever way they saw fit.

"Why have you brought me these three?" I asked him.

"They were sick, Your Highness, or so they say, at the time of your parents' deaths. They were excused from their duties and confined to their rooms. Nobody saw them for days."

"Nobody?" I asked, "Did they not receive food and water?"

"Yes, Your Highness, but we leave their meals at the door when they are unwell and possibly...infected."

"And did their food and water remain untouched?"

"At times, Your Highness."

"And the other times?"

The overseer looked uneasy. "It was simply a strange coincidence to me, Your Highness."

"It wasn't a coincidence," the male wielder argued. "We *were* sick, the drainings make it easier for us to fall ill." He looked at me directly. Even people who were my supposed allies did not do that, they actively avoided my eyes. I almost admired him.

I walked towards one of the overseers, and swiftly drew a silk handkerchief from his tunic, using it to wipe the saliva off my chin.

"How are you now?" I asked the man.

He seemed to grow increasingly confused each time I spoke.

"Don't pretend you care about our welfare."

"I do, our Vessels are vital."

"Of course," he scoffed. "Dead slaves aren't as useful as live ones."

The second woman was silent, her dark amber hair had fallen over her face, which was directed towards the ground.

"We are well, Your Highness," the first woman said.

"I am glad." I was.

The man shook his head, clearly indicating he disbelieved me.

"You've heard of the resistance, I assume?" I looked at the three wielders.

"Yes...yes, Your Highness but we know nothing of them. We have only heard some stories," the first woman replied.

"Which stories?"

"Faina," the man warned her, glaring at her with frustration.

"Is there someone you are protecting young man?" I asked.

He looked me in the eyes again. "If there's even the slightest chance there are people like us in the world, living without a chain around their necks, then I want no part in bringing them to heel."

I took a step towards him. "A noble sentiment. Not one that will save your life, however." Then after a few seconds of contemplating, I asked, "Are these rebels aware of your existence?"

"No," he reluctantly admitted. Whether it was true, it did not matter, it allowed me to elaborate in the way I had intended.

"Your death, therefore, will mean nothing to them, as your life means nothing to them. It would not advance their efforts or cause."

"But it will protect their freedom." The man's jaw was firmly clenched.

"Not for long. But here's something you can protect." I pointed towards the two women. "Tell me what you know, let your companions tell me what they know, or they will be punished. And you will watch."

The second woman still hadn't moved. The sound of her shackles shook at her slight trembling. It was the only indication she was still breathing.

The man shook his head, obviously agitated.

"Faina is right, we had nothing to do with the death of your parents," he said.

"That remains to be determined," I said calmly.

"You're here because you suspect sorcery, aren't you? Do the people know that?"

"Do you intend to inform them?" I raised my eyebrows in question.

He laughed. "How exactly do you think my companions managed to murder your parents using sorcery when we have these life sucking necklaces wrapped around our throats?"

"It is unwise to eliminate possibilities simply because they are improbable," I replied.

"It's not improbable, it's impossible," he hissed.

"Perhaps. Perhaps not. Either way, you will tell me what you know," I asserted.

The man gave a pained look to the two women. It had worked to our advantage that he had been brought here with them. There was no doubt in my mind that had he been alone, he would have died before even contemplating sharing the knowledge he possessed.

Then resolutely, and much to my surprise he said, "No. I will not."

"Your Highness, I will tell you," Faina shouted. "I will tell you everything, please."

I was still looking at the man. I was wrong. He would sacrifice the life of these two women for the lives of sorcerers he did not know.

Then I understood. To him, the lives of those strangers were more valuable, not only in their number, but in their essence. The rebels were free, they were a threat, they were a symbol. The two women beside him were none of these things.

"You will," I looked at Faina. Her face relaxed a little, relieved I had accepted her offer. I looked at the man. "You, however, will die today."

"No!" The second woman unexpectedly raised her head and tried to run towards the man. She was abruptly stopped by the overseer behind her. "No, no, no, no, no," she continued to repeat.

"Orlis!" The man called out to her.

"No!" Orlis wailed and scratched at the overseer's arms. He swore and let her go. She charged towards me, looking like a wild animal that had just been set free. Jarian once again, was far too slow to react.

When she was within arms distance, I grabbed her wrists with one of my hands and held her in place. "Kill me," she sobbed "Kill me, kill me please."

I blinked hard, startled by this change in events.

"What are you doing?" the male Vessel exclaimed, sounding terrified for the first time.

The woman sank to my feet, sliding down my lower legs. "Kill me, kill me, kill me, kill me, kill me," she kept whispering.

Nobody moved, the overseers and Jarian were unsure of what to do. Orlis was not attacking me. She was pleading with me. To kill her.

I wondered how old she was. She looked younger than the man.

"As you wish," I said coldly. "Take them both away," I directed the overseers.

Faina looked exasperated as she watched the man and Orlis be dragged out of the door. Orlis was limp in the overseer's grip, but the man continued to struggle. His eyes remained fixed upon me until the moment the door closed.

"So, tell me," I turned to Faina.

"Your Highness...will I be spared?"

"That depends on what you say."

She hesitated and looked around the room.

"And how fast you say it," I added.

"I know little, Your Highness."

"Where are the rebels located?"

"A few say Kalnasa, most say Jurasa."

Jarian looked at me. I could tell he also found this information alarming.

"Who leads them?"

"I don't...I don't know, Your Highness. But they say many sorcerers lead them, not just one."

"What is their purpose?"

"I am not sure, Your Highness, I only hear rumours."

"What do these rumours involve?"

She bit her lip and looked up at me with consideration.

"Do you wish to join your companions?" I asked her, gesturing towards the door.

"No, Your Highness."

"Then what have you heard?"

"They say they wish to free us, Your Highness. To free all sorcerers, and creatures of sorcery...to change the way of things."

"How long have they been planning this?"

"I first heard the rumours about them a few years ago."

"How many?"

"Of them are there?" she asked.

"How many years ago?"

"Five, perhaps six."

Jarian shuffled on his feet. Five years. If the sorcerers had been planning this for five years, and we had only just been made aware of their plans, then we were at a catastrophic disadvantage. Who knew what they had learnt about each Kingdom in that time, what they had learnt about their own abilities, their own potential, what other powers they had uncovered?

I hid my dread as best as I could. I suppressed it, contained it deep within my chest before I continued.

"You will find out more," I instructed her. "You will ask everyone and anyone you know. You will gather every scrap of information you can on this topic and report it back to me. If you do not, you will join your companions outside the Palace gates. Remember you are still a suspect in my parents' deaths, I am granting you a great leniency."

"But Your Highness," she gulped, "I do not know if the others have any more to share."

"Find out. That is the purpose of your task."

"What if they do not?" Her voice shook.

"I find that difficult to believe. You may go now." The overseer took her outside. She did not resist, she simply walked away quietly.

Once Jarian and I were alone, he stood in front of me.

"Your Highness, I apologise for not acting swiftly enough when you were—"

"Do not dwell upon it, Jarian. I remain unscathed."

"But Your Highness, I should have—"

"Be at ease, Jarian."

The truth was I did not trust Jarian to save my life, or to keep me from harm at all, but it did not matter to me. It did not matter because I could defend myself and while I did not trust Jarian as a bodyguard, I did trust Jarian to do one thing, which was more important.

To remain loyal. To remain silent. To obey.

The same could not be said for the majority of the other people who worked for me. I valued his loyalty more than anything else.

"We will have to speak with the Jurasan King," I declared.

"Yes," Jarian agreed. "The rumours all point to the West."

"I will write to him today, after the opening. You will personally deliver the letter to the outgoing carts yourself."

"Your Highness, would it not be best to delegate this task to someone else? You have many responsibilities on your shoulders of late."

"No. I do not trust anyone else to do this. For now, you will speak of this to no one."

"But the Council –"

"No one, Jarian."

He nodded. "I should escort you through the Wing back to your bedchambers, Your Highness."

For once, I did not protest his company. I knew Jarian was a hopeless guard, but the magic wielders did not.

The walk to my bedchambers was lengthy, but I did not allow myself to dwell upon what had just occurred. It was only when Jarian closed the doors behind me that I did. I strolled into the washroom and began to clean my face. I could still feel the film of the Vessel's saliva stuck to the bottom of my chin.

It was only then that I allowed myself to consider the indignation and the loathing that had permeated the features of the man as he looked upon me. That I thought about his face, his age. He can't have been older than my twenty-six years.

That I thought about Orlis' screams, and her hair like a dark flame searing at my feet and she begged.

*"Kill me, kill me, kill me, kill me, kill me."*

A wave of sheer revulsion, of earth-shattering detestation came over me.

I clenched the edge of the basin so hard I thought it might crack.

And vomited.

# CHAPTER 9- HESTAN

I was not entirely sure what I had been expecting from my conversation with Dunlan. Some part of me had hoped the food shortages would be the topic of our meeting, but I suppose, in some ways, it was.

For if his niece Dyna could secure the King's hand in marriage, it would strengthen our alliance with Vasara, which would mean access to their wealth and resources, which would mean more food.

I was right about one thing, the task at hand required urgency. We would be leaving tomorrow morning. It was my job, my sole priority, to secure Lady Dyna's welfare. For that, I would need to be well rested before tomorrow's ride. Especially since it had been years since I'd ridden a Pegasus. The Hunt weren't granted access to the animals, only the King's guard and Army. It would be difficult to hunt anything, to get close enough to catch any food, with a Pegasus around.

I highly doubted we'd face any immediate danger on the journey to Vasara since most of it would be spent in the sky.

Normally, however, I wouldn't have been prepared to take that risk.

But now, I was standing by the house the woman had scaled.

I hesitated. I knew whatever I found up there would be important, relevant somehow. I also knew it would be my duty to report my findings to the King and his guards.

I could currently avoid informing them about what I had seen without breaking my oath, since the notion she had left something behind of import was only an assumption.

But if I did find something, then it would become truth, and I would be faced with a choice. Break my oath or break this woman's trust.

I had no reason to keep her trust, no logical reason anyhow. I had served the King for most of my life. He had saved my life, it was to him I owed my loyalty, and yet, I could not bear to hand this woman over to the authorities.

Just as I was trying to make sense of my strange pull towards protecting this person, the door of the house opened.

"What do you want? You've been hovering outside my house for ages now, begone will you!" An older man, his brown skin peppered with silver stubble, dismissed me with a gesture of his arm.

"Captain Hestan Hikari," I introduced myself.

The man's eyes widened in recognition as he took a closer look at my face. "Captain." He peered at me more closely. He didn't seem apologetic, if anything, that made me warm to the man.

"Can I help you with something?" he asked.

Telling the man the one thief who had managed to steal anything from our supplies had been standing on his house earlier, and had potentially left something behind, did not strike me as a good idea.

"Yes," I replied, deciding to try a different strategy. "Who lives here?"

"Just me," he answered, still sounding antagonistic.

His house was rather large. "Just you?" I questioned, catching a glimpse of its wide interior. Most of the people in Kalnasa lived in small houses, cottage type abodes or huts. But there were a few who could afford to live in larger houses, in Kalnasa's Central City Celion, and its Inner City, Reyaru, closer to the Palace.

"Yes, my wife died last month," he said. "Is there a problem?"

"May she rest with the Gods," I bowed my head slightly.

"Damn the Gods," the man muttered under his breath.

I raised my head and did not dispute his statement. I'd said it as a sign of respect, nothing more. "Sir, I was looking for someone who lives around here, but I cannot seem to find them."

"Hardly surprising, since you've been standing in the same place for the past half hour."

I blinked hard, and offered him a slight smile. "I've scaled the area already. I was thinking about where I might have failed to look."

"Who is it you're looking for?" he asked reluctantly.

"Sara Vaich." A woman I knew lived in a different village.

"Never heard of her."

"Do you know where I might ask?"

"If I've not heard of her, then nobody around here has."

"Still, I'd like to be sure."

The man glanced at my uniform quickly, the white and blue garments overlaid with silver armour, and then at the spear behind my back.

"Did this Sara do something?"

"If she did, would that be incentive enough for you to help me?"

"Would I receive an incentive?"

That made sense, times were tough here, if I were this man, I'd likely try a similar tactic on a wealthy looking warrior.

"Would you like one?"

The man crossed his arms. "I wouldn't say no."

"How's ten gold pieces to ask around for me now?"

"Now? In the middle of the night. Hah." He reflected for a moment "Forty gold pieces."

I internally groaned. "Fifteen"

"Thirty-five"

"Eighteen"

"Twenty-five."

"Twenty."

"Twenty-two."

Twenty-two gold pieces was a lot of money. Despite looking well dressed, and well paid, I wasn't actually well paid at all. Everyone's wages had been decreasing. These clothes and weapons were the only thing of value I owned.

Not only was I considering going against those I had spent my life serving for this woman, but now I was giving away my own money too.

She had somehow managed to steal far more from me than she had intended.

"Is it a deal or what?" the man asked impatiently.

In response, I opened a pouch hanging deep within my clothing. I gave the man eleven gold pieces.

"You will get the other eleven when you return, and not too quickly, otherwise I will know you haven't taken your time to do this properly."

"For you Captain"- he saluted me mockingly - "I will take all the time in the world."

"I'm very grateful." I smiled slightly. "I'll wait here."

"No, no, please, make yourself comfortable." The man opened the door more widely behind him.

Deciding not to arouse any further suspicion, I nodded quickly at the man and went inside his house. Shortly afterwards, his footsteps echoed down the street and his fist began thumping at nearby doors.

I didn't sit on any of the wooden chairs surrounding the small fireplace. I didn't move at all. I simply stood in place and waited. I closed my eyes and listened. Listened for the moment when I could no longer hear the man's voice, or the sound of his fist thumping insistently on wood.

The moment came, and I didn't hesitate. Within seconds I was out of the door and scaling the sides of the building. I was on the roof, right at the corner.

I crouched low, despite the fact the owner of the house was a few streets away, I could see him from the height I was at now. I bore witness to the several angry confrontations he had with his neighbours, who were furious about being awoken at such a late hour. I would have felt pity for him, only I knew I had paid him more than enough to face them.

Still remaining low on the roof, I slowly made my way towards the centre of it, where the woman had been standing. At first, I couldn't see anything. That was unusual, I had a sharp eye, but then, a slight movement, a lulling breeze created a shift in the fabric's position.

I was, I noticed, fearful. I was afraid of touching this object. I had no idea what it was, or why it had been left here in the first place. I didn't know if it was dangerous, poisonous, or a trap of some kind.

I ran my hands through my now tied back hair, shaking my head at the absurdity of my choice and lifted it up.

It was not a piece of fabric, but rather a piece of paper. Black, thick, gritty like sand.

I had seen this before, once, many years ago. I was with Dunlan, who at the time, was a much younger King, and I, barely a man.

*"It's beautiful isn't it,"* a voice from behind me had said as I peered at it across a desk in the library.

*"What is it?"* I'd asked the girl, a young child.

*"It's called Noxscroll. They make it from Noxstone."*

*"Is that why there's nothing on it?"* I'd asked touching the corners with my thumb and forefinger.

*"No. There's writing on it, you just can't see it."*

*"What do you mean?"*

*"You just can't. It's a secret."* The girl smiled at me, mischievously, clearly finding my ignorance amusing.

*"So how does someone see... the secret?"* I asked, raising the paper above my head.

She jumped to try and reach it, but her height made it impossible.

*"I'm trying to show you!"* she said, frustrated.

*"Oh."* I passed it to her, a challenging look in my eyes.

The girl walked across the room and said something to a man who I realised had been watching us. He handed her a dagger.

*"Don't tell me only blood can reveal the writing,"* I said, mentally preparing myself for a humble exit.

*"No, look, come."* She beckoned to me, guiding me towards the window where the light was entering the library. Then, she held the dagger just above the paper in a way that would allow the weapon to reflect the moonlight onto the page. The lines flickered and erupted onto the paper as if summoned against their slumber. It was no secret, just a symbol, the symbol of the Audra, a dark tornado, infinitely spinning on itself.

*"You can only read marks on Noxscroll by the light of Noxstone,"* she said proudly.

*"And what do you write with, a shadow quill?"* I asked sarcastically.

The girl looked confused. *"There's no such thing as a shadow quill. We use the steel...see?"* Using the dagger, she drew a line across the paper, then holding it to the light once again, smiled as the line showed up across its surface.

I had the feeling that whatever was on this piece of Noxscroll I now held, was more than an emblem.

Did the woman who left it here write on this? Or did someone else? Why did she want me to see it? Surely, she knew I would not be able to read it myself. Noxstone was rare, weapons of their making were mostly owned by a select few prestigious warriors in Audra, and an ever-fewer number of people from other Kingdoms, who had extravagant amounts of money to spend on such a purchase.

After the twenty-two gold pieces I had lost today, purchasing a Noxstone weapon was out of the question. There was no way I could visit Audra anytime soon either, since I was headed for Vasara tomorrow morning, or more precisely, later today.

There was one third and final option, which added to the list of poor choices I was making as a result of my unfathomable need to follow this woman's path.

That was stealing some.

This woman had made sure to draw my attention to this paper. Perhaps I was desperate to uncover her motives because I knew I was the only one who could.

No, that wasn't true. I could, I should inform Dunlan, then others could assist.

But I did not know what this Noxscroll was concealing. Its contents could be utterly useless, something I would be wasting the King's time with. To employ the assistance of several others, therefore, could be complete profligacy.

But the contents could also pertain to a threat to the King's safety.

A wise man would have shared it with the King, with his friends, his allies.

Or would he? I had no true notion of where wisdom lay. Trusting in others, or trusting in oneself?

The owner of the house was walking back towards it. Before I could come to a final decision, I pocketed the paper within my clothes, jumped off the building with a light landing, and slid back into the man's living room.

I hadn't noticed before, my eyes had been closed, focused on paying attention to the vicinity of the owner to his property, but now I had a spare moment to look around, I took in the wide variety of weapons stacked along shelves, mounted on the walls, and stuffed into corners.

This man was a smith, and well respected one at that, which explained his ability to live in this house.

He walked back in now, smiling widely. "Sorry Captain, nobody knows this Sara of yours, as I said."

I lowered my chin slightly, placing my hands over one another as I said. "Unfortunate."

"You promised me eleven more pieces."

Without replying, I placed the remaining eleven pieces in the man's outstretched palm.

"You're a smith," I said as a statement and not as a question.

"Was."

"What do you know of Noxstone?"

The man raised an eyebrow. "I know that I would never go near it, even if you gave me all the gold pieces in the world."

"Why?"

"Because it's lethal that's why."

"In battle, yes, but as a smith?"

"Never come across anything like it, in all my years. I've known smiths who've injured, damn near killed themselves just trying to handle that stuff," he elaborated.

"Do you know of any smiths who take the risk?"

"No," he said. "Not the sane ones anyway?"

"And those who are not?"

The man looked impatient. "Like I said, no. I told you nobody would know your Sara and you didn't believe me, and I'm telling you now, there is not one smith in this entire Kingdom that will forge a Noxstone weapon, for any price."

I remained deep in thought, my eyes fixated on the door behind the man.

"In other Kingdoms?" I inquired, slowly bringing my eyes back to his face.

"What are you up to Captain -ey?"

I mentally reprimanded myself. Revealing my interest in Noxstone to this man was dangerous, both for him and myself.

"Nothing. At least that's what you will tell people, should they ask why I was here."

"And will there be an incentive for my silence as well?" he eyed me greedily.

"Staying alive should be incentive enough," I retorted.

He clenched his jaw. "I see."

I reached for the door.

"Gendal," he blurted out, as I did.

I looked over my shoulder.

"He's a smith, used to make Noxstone weapons, other tools, jewellery of rare gems and the like. Stopped all his work a few years ago. Nobody knows why."

"I thought you said nobody in this Kingdom would touch the metal."

"I didn't say Gendal was from Kalnasa."

"Then where?"

He shrugged his shoulders. "I don't know. He moved around a lot, went wherever business was good."

"Certainly not here then," I muttered. The man grunted in agreement.

"Last I heard, he was in Vasara."

"What does he look like?" I asked.

The man outstretched his palm in an expectant gesture. I sighed heavily.

He smirked. "I don't think you'll actually kill me so…let's say five, shall we?"

I walked over to the man, and reluctantly placed another three, rather than five gold pieces into his rough, calloused hands. His fingers grasped over them immediately.

"What do you want to know?"

# CHAPTER 10 – NATHON

Well, the King hadn't been lying. There really was not one piece of green fabric anywhere in this place. Not even a dishcloth, or a handkerchief, let alone a piece of clothing. It was strange that something as simple as a garment, coloured differently to a Kingdom's dress codes, was such a luxury in this world, such a rarity.

I'd never really cared much about what we wore in Audra. Swaths of vibrant gold, plum and dark sheer fabrics, adorned with tassels, coins and gems. I preferred the armour. It suited me, the black and the silver. The buckles and the buttons. The belts, the high collars, and supple boots. It was practical and efficient. It gave me enough space to carry a variety of weapons.

And enough fabric to cover up every inch of my skin.

But then again, I wasn't trying to impress the King. If I had been, I would have failed miserably at that task. I could tell he despised me already.

Even I was beginning to wonder what Loria was wearing underneath that cloak. At first, I had thought she was simply being stubborn, that she was angry about being here at all, which I could understand. But Loria was more intelligent than she let people believe. That was proof of her intelligence in and of itself. To let people buy into an image of you, all the while concealing your true heart, your true self, was a great tool.

And she had cried. I hadn't seen Loria cry in years. I don't think she had seen me cry at all.

Although come to think of it, I couldn't remember the last time I had cried.

Gods knew what they'd dressed her up in.

The streets of Vasara were lively, bustling, and full of chatter. People were basking in the heat, their sharp and strangely cut clothing revealing pieces of their pale, and rosy skin. They were touching one another, laughing, arguing, and hustling. The narrow pathways were surrounded by rust, sand, and beige coloured brick buildings, short and square. Stone steps sprouted from everywhere, and winding rivers, trickling between cobblestoned walkways and paths.

I stopped by the bank of the largest and main river now, peering into it. The current was chaotic, unsteady, ungrounded, reflecting my inner state.

A man had just approached me. He wasn't saying anything, he was looking at my crotch?

No, my waist.

No, my hips.

No, my sword. Rather, the sword I had recently acquired from that miserable excuse for a liar that had accompanied us.

I was fascinated and taken aback by the man's brazenness. His glare was open, undisguised, daring almost. It wasn't hard to recognise where I was from based on my features. It was also obvious; the man was not from here either.

His light skin tone, suffused with a hint of beige. His long silver hair. His violet eyes. This man was from Kalnasa.

After a long moment of silence and unrestricted glaring, I spoke.

"Is it customary where you're from, to stare so much before introducing yourself?"

The man's eyelids shot up. At first, he looked embarrassed, then surprised, then serious, all within the space of a second. His ability to conceal his emotions so quickly was worthy of praise, but it wasn't quick enough for me.

"Apologies. I was admiring your sword." He pointed at it.

"Yes, many have admired it during my walk, just from a much greater distance," I replied.

"Then they have not admired it at all," he asserted, looking at me directly.

The corner of my mouth slid up into a slight smile. "Indeed. I suppose most people would rather not risk approaching me for the sight."

"Are you that dangerous?" The man looked unconvinced.

"Of course." I smiled widely. "Don't you believe the stories?"

"I can't say I've heard them all."

"Or bothered to listen?"

"Or that."

As if he had only just realised who he was speaking to, a flicker of recollection spread across his face, and he bowed abruptly. Once he rose, he met my eyes again, this time with more wariness and interest.

"Prince," he addressed me. "I haven't seen you for a long time, Your Highness."

"I wasn't aware we had met before," I looked him over, trying to recall our previous meeting.

"We were children then, Your Highness."

"You'll have to forgive me." I pressed my palm to my chest. "I have little memory of that time."

Most of the memories I did have were horrendous.

"There is nothing to forgive, Your Highness. I am glad to meet you once more."

I laughed out loud at that. "Well, that's something I don't hear too often."

He looked baffled.

I gestured to the people walking as far away as possible from me, shifting to take different routes, darting their gazes between me and their feet. I smirked at the man. "Very few are glad to meet me."

"Then you may count me as one of them," he said confidently.

There was something about the man, a severity and tranquillity that was compelling yet alarming. Restraint made someone a far greater threat than impulsiveness, I had always found.

"Then I shall need your name, to add it to that short list." I outstretched my hand. "Nathon." I introduced myself informally, curious about his reaction.

He did the same, stepping closer to me, his face becoming clearer. He was slightly taller than me and older, perhaps about thirty. His hand was adorned with several rings, silver, lilac, and peach in colouring. Some were large and sat just above his knuckle, others were winding, in the shape of a spiral, such as that above his right thumb.

"Hestan Hikari. Captain of the Hunt."

I shook his hand, his grip was strong, but just like his manner, restrained. I had no doubt, however, he could have crushed all the bones in my hand if he had wanted to.

"Ahhh, yes. I have heard of the Hunt, and its…perils." I chose my words carefully. I knew being a member of Kalnasa's Hunt was viewed as tantamount to a death sentence by many. Several people did not survive a decade, let alone a year in its ranks.

A thankless job, not one I myself would have signed up for willingly.

We separated our hands. "I am sure being a Prince is perilous in and of itself," he said.

"Oh no. It's all bowing, smiling, and shaking hands." I shrugged, feigning nonchalance.

The Captain looked at the people, still intent on avoiding us. "I do not think people would be so afraid of you, if that were the case."

"What makes you think they are afraid of me?"

"You said so yourself, Your Highness."

"I did not. I simply said people were not glad to meet me, but there could be a number of reasons for that."

For some reason, I was intent on drawing emotion from this man. It seemed impossible to me that anyone could be as controlled as this, as composed.

"Perhaps they dislike me. Perhaps they are jealous of me. Some may even be hopelessly in love with me. So many possibilities." I outstretched my palms casually.

"Forgive me, it was merely an assumption." He sounded unimpressed.

Such self-control. How intriguing.

"All is forgiven. After all, you are probably right, Captain, I was just curious as to why you thought so."

"It is simply a matter of observation, Your Highness."

"Something you are good at?"

"I believe so."

"Good for you," I said. The Captain still looked thoroughly unaffected. "What a rare breed you are then Captain. Unafraid of *and* glad to meet me."

The Captain smiled tightly.

"So, what is it you want?" I asked. I could feel the conversation shifting and by the deep breath the Captain took, I knew he could too.

The Captain opened his mouth, about to, no doubt, feign innocence and simple curiosity. Then decided against it. "Do people only approach you when they want something from you, Your Highness?"

A cunning response, neither denying nor confirming his need. "Do you always avoid questions so tactfully?"

This man was intelligent and assuming he had heard at least some of the rumours about me, either very reckless or very confident in his own abilities.

"A death wish, then?" I tilted my chin down slightly.

"Pardon?"

"Is that what you want? For me to fulfil it?"

I could sense the cogs in the Captain's mind turning, and yet his face remained completely calm save for the slight furrowing of his brow.

"I have no death wish," he decided to reply. A safe response.

"Are you sure?" I tilted my head back and up, still looking at him curiously. "It would certainly seem that way at present."

"I am sure," the Captain didn't sound nervous at all.

I scratched behind my ear, thinking.

He glanced at my belt again.

"You're going to make me blush, Captain," I raised a brow.

His face became a stout hardened picture of gravity. "Your blade," he decided to admit. "I wondered if you would be willing to let me hold it, Your Highness."

I tilted my head to the right. This was a highly unusual request. I had expected him to ask for a favour, or try to kill me but...this?

"I think it would be unwise for me to draw my weapon in public."

"You were willing to fulfil my hypothetical death wish just moments ago...Your Highness." His voice deepened.

"Well, I never said I'd fulfil it here. Did I?"

The Captain remained silent.

"Drawing the sword here might give these fragile people the wrong impression." I faked a sympathetic glance at the passers-by.

"It seems they may already have the wrong impression of you."

I couldn't help but raise my eyebrows. "How sure you seem."

"Am I wrong?" he asked.

A moment of silence stretched out between us. I saw no reason to confirm or deny his highly unusual level of insight.

"Why do you wish to hold it?" I asked, eventually.

"I have heard many rumours about these blades, and how it feels to hold one. I would like to know if they are true."

"I thought you didn't pay attention to rumours."

"I do, to those that interest me."

I chuckled. "It is true that rumours of the blades are far more interesting than those regarding myself." I patted the hilt of my sword with my hand.

"I have heard they can cut a man clean in half."

"Have you really? What else have you heard?"

The Captain cleared his throat, eyeing my sword again. "That they are lighter than any weapon, but much stronger. That it takes little force to pierce a person with one. That they can tear through the flesh of any creature, human, or sorcerer, and through any material."

"Mmmmm. Not all rumours are lies, Captain," I said, confirming his statements.

He placed his hands over one another. It was amusing, I thought, that in doing so, he looked far more regal than myself, or most of the Royals I had met.

"Fascinating," he whispered.

I weighed my options, of course I could give him the sword to hold but what did he intend to do with it? He could slice my head off in one clean stroke, with little effort or force. Of course, he could have attempted that prior to holding the sword, but with it currently at my hip, it would be him that ended up dead. Despite the fact I had two daggers of the same material hidden in my clothing, if I gave him the sword, and he tried to murder me, my chances of death would be much higher.

But this man seemed far too measured to assassinate someone as well-known as myself in a public place. Many people had already seen and noticed us talking, it would be easy for them to describe such a slaughter in vivid detail. Besides, his features stood out enough that it would be easy for people to identify him as the killer.

But I found it hard, no impossible, to believe that the Captain simply wanted to hold the sword for the pleasure of doing so. There was no doubt he was a capable man, but most people would never dare to touch a weapon of Noxstone, had they never handled it before.

The Captain could clearly see I was debating my course of action and decided to interject. "Your Highness?"

I thought about that offer. What could the Captain of Kalnasa's Hunt do for me?

There was one thing I needed and had failed pathetically at acquiring. It was worth asking, I supposed.

"Do you own anything green?"

The Captain looked at me as if he were concerned for my sanity. "Pardon?"

"Do you own anything, anything at all that is green?"

"You mean...the colour?"

"What else would I mean?"

"It's a rather...unusual request."

"So is yours."

The Captain nodded, clearly deciding not to dig deeper into my comment, for the desire, I guessed, to keep his true motivation for his interest in my blade hidden.

"No. I do not. Green is not a colour we wear in Kalnasa."

"I know, but there's always a chance you own something rare."

"Why do you need something green?" he asked.

"Why do you need to hold my sword?" I replied in kind. I had thought he would have been astute enough to avoid that question.

He didn't respond. "I do not own anything green, but I know someone who may."

"Is this someone nearby?"

The Captain sighed. "I'm not sure."

"A shame. It was nice to meet you, Captain." I moved to leave.

"Wait," he called out, with my back to him. Then remembering who he was addressing. "Your Highness, please, if you'll allow me, I can find them for you," he added in haste.

"And how long will that take?" I turned back around, spinning on my heel.

The Captain's gaze shifted to the side and up, then back to my face. "Less than an hour."

I was intrigued. "We'll meet here in an hour. If I like what you bring, you can hold the sword."

The Captain cleared his throat, then placed one hand over the other. "I should like to borrow it."

"Borrow it?" I said dryly, raising my eyebrows. This was becoming concerning. "No, Captain, that will not be possible."

"It would only be for a short while," the Captain said calmly.

"How reassuring. Only a short while is plenty of time to murder a person with a blade I own and have been seen to possess."

"I do not intend to murder anyone."

"Again, that does little to reassure me." I placed both my palms on my upper chest.

The Captain looked ever so slightly exasperated beneath his composed exterior. "What would reassure you?" It sounded as if he was squeezing out the words, as if each and every one was painful to him.

"People do not ask to touch a blade of Noxstone, let alone borrow it. Your request is no longer unusual Captain it is suspicious," I said bluntly.

The Captain looked past my shoulder to the streets behind us, deep in thought. I could tell he was deciding whether to share his reasoning with me.

"Very well. I will bring you something green at the hour. If you should be so kind as to let me hold the sword, that will suffice, Your Highness."

I tapped my fingers rapidly against my thigh. "You are a very dubious character, Captain. It is not in my nature to deal with such people."

"It is up to you, Your Highness."

I thought of Loria, and everything riding on this forced mission of ours. Something green could make no difference, or it could make all the difference. I didn't know Vasara's Prince well enough to be sure.

But I knew Loria well enough to hope.

"At the hour, Captain."

He nodded, bowed, and walked away. His silver hair fluttered in the wind as he went.

An interesting person indeed.

It would be a shame if I had to kill the Captain. As per my father's orders, I was to kill anyone who got in the way of his goal. The Captain may very well do that.

I admired inquisitiveness and curiosity in a person, but it was also a trait that got people killed. For as long as I was a designated assassin, the inquisitiveness of others would remain an inconvenience to me, rather than something that I could, that I wanted to appreciate. The more questions someone asked, the more murdering I would have to do.

I was truly hoping to keep the murdering to a minimum this time.

But I couldn't shake the feeling that no matter what happened, no matter how careful we were, this Captain would be a problem.

And worse, that he would not, by any means, be an easy person to kill.

# CHAPTER 11- HESTAN

What had I been thinking?

What had I been thinking when I climbed onto that roof? My life would have been far easier had I avoided the temptation to give into curiosity. I would have been at the Palace right now, where I was supposed to be, with Dyna. She had assured me she was happy to be left alone for a while, that she felt safe surrounded by Vasara's guardsman. That was incredibly naïve of her. Normally I would have informed her of that, but instead, I was doing the dishonourable thing of using her naivety against her, in order to fulfil my own plans.

Her lessons on trust would have to be postponed. I could only hope Dunlan would never hear of this, of any of this.

Audra's Prince was completely insufferable, as everyone had said he was. His sly grins, crude comments, and endless questions had made me want to shove him into the river we had been standing beside.

Especially his, *"Good for you."* It took everything I had not to do so right there and then.

My intuition told me, however, he was far wiser than people had suggested.

As for his renowned cruelty, that was something which could only be confirmed or refuted by time.

Yet I couldn't help but notice he had found the fear he invoked in others amusing rather than satisfying.

He had found everything amusing, on second thought.

And what to make of his request for a green item? I didn't know whether he needed it for himself, or for someone else, or why a green item would even be important. But I could not afford to ask such questions. Not now.

The man whose house I had unceremoniously invaded back in Kalnasa, Amdir, had told me all about Gendall in the end. He'd told me Gendall had not only sold Noxstone weapons, but rare gems and jewels, some which were almost impossible to find in certain parts of the world.

If anyone had anything green in Vasara, it would be him.

I was walking towards the North of Vasara's capital city now, Iloris, where Amdir had told me Gendall was last seen. In the *"avenues with the steep steps,"* he had explained. I was scaling them now, avenues squeezed narrowly between rows of brick houses, inns, shops, and bars. I stopped at the end of one avenue and turned right. I strolled carefully down an even tighter stretch of walkway, and then left.

In front of me, stood three small buildings at a dead end. The one in the centre was Gendall's workshop if I had followed the instructions correctly.

I looked around me cautiously, nobody was in sight. This part of Vasara was one of the poorest. Some mice scurried past my feet, the only onlookers to my visit. I jumped, gritting my teeth in discomfort as they brushed past my boots.

I had grown up in poverty, surrounded by mice and rats, and yet the creatures made me shudder, even now.

The door to Gendall's workshop was partially open. I carefully and quietly placed my palm on its yellow painted surface and eased it forwards.

A loud thud and clatter resounded from behind me. An arrow had flown right past my neck, from inside the workshop. It found itself stuck on a sign stretching from one of the buildings lined down the alley.

I very subtly reached behind my head and pulled the spear off my back.

"I'm not here to hurt you," I declared to the possible assailant inside. "Amdir sent me."

There was no answer.

"I'm going to enter now. I am not here to hurt you, I have no intention of harming you. I am a friend of Amdir's."

A lie yes, but one that would hopefully stop my lungs from being the next target of this person's arrows.

I tenderly touched the door once again, but before I could apply any force beneath my fingertips, someone grabbed me by the shoulder and pulled me inside, slamming the tattered door behind us.

He had a blade pressed to my chest. "Who are you?"

Before me, I assumed, stood Gendall. He was very short, as was his dark brown hair. He looked like he hadn't washed in weeks, or changed his clothes for longer. I quickly scanned the room behind him, a workshop yes, but it was in a state of total disarray, as if someone had desperately been trying to find something amongst all the items, or stolen something from them.

"You listening to me, Kalnasan?" He drew my attention back to his bearded face.

I raised my arms up. "Like I said, I'm a friend of Amdir's. Gendall, I presume?"

"Amdir friends with the likes of you? I find that hard to believe." He sneered at my clothes, which looked expensive and clearly implied authority.

"Let us say that Amdir and I... have a mutual understanding."

"Yeah? And let's say I cut you open, right here, right now."

Two death threats in one day. How delightful.

"That would be incredibly unwise, since my absence will be noted very quickly."

"Someone important, are you?"

"You could say that."

"What do you want?"

"I only want to ask you some questions."

"That's what they said," he sneered.

"Who said?"

As if being shaken from a stupor, the man turned back to me, aggressively pressing the blade harder against my sternum. I was thankful this was not a weapon of Noxstone. If it had been, my heart would already have been removed from my body.

"You're one of them," he hissed.

"Sir, I am one of nothing, I am simply myself."

"Lies," he said through his teeth, but I could see the doubt in his eyes.

"Amdir told me you closed your workshop and stopped your business five months ago, why?"

"I didn't stop you fool. They stopped me."

"Who are *they*?"

"I'm not telling you shit."

I held my palms up higher. "I can help you."

"Nobody can help me."

"How will you know that, unless you hear what I have to say?" I kept my hands raised, on either side of my head.

Gendall looked at me curiously. He took what felt like several minutes to ponder whether he would listen to me. "Go on," he finally prompted.

"Someone forced you to stop your business. Did it have something to do with the Noxstone?"

"It did," he groaned.

I had suspected, but I had hoped I might be wrong.

"An unknown individual or group, with access to the blades has become a threat to my security." I decided to tell a partial, rather than whole truth. "I need to know more about them, and about who was interested in the weapons. Amdir told me you could help."

"Did he now?" he sounded irritated.

"Let me finish," I interrupted him. "You tell me who did this" – I glanced at the state of his workshop— "You tell me more about Noxstone, and I'll make sure you're escorted back to Kalnasa safely."

This would cost more money. Wonderful.

"How can I be sure you'll keep your word?"

"You can't, but it doesn't appear as if you have any other options."

"At least my other options guarantee my heart will stay beating."

"For how long?"

"Is that a threat pretty eyes?"

"No…" I sighed at his comment. "It's a warning. The people who did this to you do not care for your life. I would not rely on their generosity forever if I were in your position."

After a few moments of contemplation, Gendall removed the blade.

"They took all of them."

"The weapons of Noxstone?"

He nodded. "Told me if I ever forged another Noxstone blade again, they'd find out about it and kill me, real slow, with those weapons, they said. Noxstone can inflict such pain you'll wish you were never born. It was easier to close up shop all together, than to explain to the customers why I'd stopped selling those weapons."

"How many of them were there?"

"It was dark when they came. They took me into the back." He pointed behind him. "I didn't see them all, but I think about three, maybe four."

A discreet operation then. "What did they look like?"

"It was dark, like I just said. They all had their faces covered with some kind of metal masks and they were in dark clothing too. I couldn't tell if they were men or women neither."

"How many people bought weapons of Noxstone from you? Did you have any regular customers?"

"A few. But they never gave their names. They usually covered their faces too, but with hoods, cloaks, a scarf, or something."

Noxstone was hard to acquire, It was no wonder those who managed to do so wished for their possession of such a weapon to remain a secret.

"Can you describe them?"

"How are you going to get me out?" He changed the topic.

I straightened up. "A group I was travelling with is still in the city. We arrived this morning. They are resting now before returning to Kalnasa later. I trust those people implicitly and they trust me. They will take you with them."

He remained still for a few moments and then nodded in agreement.

"So, these customers?"

"The first was an older, middle-aged man, I think. Tall, pale, auburn, maybe brown hair that I could tell. Another was younger, just grown into manhood, muscular, well built, tanned. I couldn't see the colour of his hair underneath his hood though. The rest were just occasional buyers."

"Do you know if there is anywhere you can purchase Noxstone weaponry now? Outside of Audra?"

"As far as I'm aware, no. There were reports of someone in Jurasa selling it around a year ago, but they vanished."

"The reports or—"

"The seller."

Troubling. Somebody was trying to either get rid of or acquire all the Noxstone weapons across the Five Kingdoms. Most would assume the obvious culprit to be Audra, in order to ensure they would be the sole owner of the material. But Audra already owned it in such high quantities that removing what little there was across the other Kingdoms would be a pointless task.

"Is that all they said to you?"

"Yes...well, no, they also said they would be watching. They could be watching us right now."

I groaned. He could have told me that much earlier.

"Do you think they are?" He eyed me worriedly.

"I couldn't say."

Yes, I thought, yes, I did think they were watching, which meant I was now a target of theirs.

"But we have little time if they are. Come with me now." I walked towards the door with Gendall at my heels and suddenly remembered.

"Jewels."

"What?" Gendall looked baffled.

"You'll need to take something with you, to sell once you get to Kalnasa, for money. I assume you're running low. Weapons will be too heavy. Jewels are easy to carry."

"I...yes, yes," Gendall stuttered.

"Where are they? Let me acquire some for you quickly."

Gendall, clearly too perturbed and overwhelmed by the whole situation, agreed almost immediately. He pointed me in the direction of the gems, in the back room.

I stopped abruptly on seeing the collection. There were gems here I'd never seen before. I had seen sapphires, pearls, moonstones, and amethysts in Kalnasa, but I had never seen some of the others. There were those Vasarans wore frequently such as rubies, ambers, and garnets, and those the other Kingdoms adorned like diamonds, aquamarines, topazes, and there...emeralds.

An emerald necklace. It was so simple, one circular ring of emerald upon emerald with small diamonds in between. I lifted it. It was so radiant, so bright, I almost forgot for a moment we were likely being watched by deadly assailants.

I took it and placed it in the pouch by my hips, the one which carried my constantly dwindling gold pieces. I would like to have added more jewels to my own pouch to make up for my losses, but we didn't have the time, and I didn't have the heart to steal from this man, even if he had tried to kill me.

I grabbed him by the wrist and led him towards the door, throwing the small bag of jewels I had gathered into his arms.

"Stay here, let me check outside first."

Gendall remained frozen in place. I stepped outside with a growing sense of unease. I knew how to scout an area. I did so all the time on the Hunt. I couldn't see anything, but there was a chance someone was out there, and was extremely well hidden.

Still, we would have to take the risk.

I waved Gendall towards me. He didn't move.

"I can't stay long. I'm honouring my word. Either I help you now, or not at all."

Gendall dipped his head and followed me out of his workshop.

The walk back to the Palace was intense and filled with the constant threat of an arrow piercing through our skulls. On it, I realised reluctantly and with great dread, that I would have to get used to such a feeling. Even if nobody had been watching us just now, the people watching Gendall would undoubtedly find out about his escape, and possibly about my association with him, since the people in Vasara had eyes to see with and tongues to speak with.

I was always on my guard, especially in Kingdoms other than Kalnasa, but it seemed I would have to be on it tenfold this time, if I wanted to return to Kalnasa alive.

I left Gendall with two of the guards I had arrived with. One was Captain Mulani. I told them he was a dear friend of a friend, who required safe transport back to Kalnasa. I had done all I could, what he did once he arrived at Kalnasa was up to him.

"A friend of a friend you say?" Mulani regarded me with suspicion.

"That's right. I hope this will not cause you too much trouble?"

"It won't, Captain," she said.

Gendall's eyes shot up in alarm when he heard my title.

"Good luck," I said to him quietly.

"Thank you," he replied "Captain?"

"Yes?"

"Be careful."

Mulani and the other guard were glancing between us with confusion.

"I will." I smiled tightly and made my way to the river, where the Prince would be.

He was already there. I had assumed he would be late, but he was sitting on the side of the riverbank with one arm resting on his right knee. It was unnerving to see the effect he had on people. It was as if he were the centre of a large circle people dared not cross the boundaries of.

His golden eyes flicked towards my direction as he heard me approach, even from afar. His hearing must have been particularly keen, to detect my footsteps so easily.

He didn't get up, he patted beside him, suggesting I sit down.

I bent my head down to face him. "Your Highness."

"Won't you sit, Captain? I'd imagine your legs are tired after running around on my errand this past hour."

"I'm a member of the Hunt, Your Highness. If my legs became tired after an hour, I would have succumbed to its 'perils' long ago."

He tilted his neck up, smirking again, most likely at my choice of words, borrowed from his earlier ones. "I understand. You're a strong warrior etcetera, etcetera." He swayed his hands in front of him.

He jolted up quickly. His movements were very fast and clean. "Was it successful?"

That is not the word I would have used to describe my encounter with Gendall.

Without answering, I drew the necklace from my pouch. The Prince placed his hand over his mouth, quickly stroking the sides of his face. He laughed, but with his mouth closed, so it appeared more like a vibration in his chest and throat.

"Very good, Captain." He caressed the gems tenderly, as if afraid to break them.

Then, as swiftly as he had stood, he placed the necklace around his own neck.

"Suits me nicely, don't you think?" He pointed at his neck.

This man was utterly confusing. "It's... a beautiful piece," I said carefully.

"As is this." Contradicting his earlier concerns, the Prince pulled the sword out from his belt and placed it delicately across one of his palms, grasping its hilt in the other.

Gasps could be heard from around us, as the Prince sliced the air with it. "Here." He walked towards me, holding the end of the hilt, leaving me just enough room to grip the top of it. "Quickly, before I scandalise the whole town."

I reached for it.

"Don't" – he placed his hand on top of my arm and drew the blade back towards him – "touch the blade itself. You're not used to handling this metal, It will slice right through your bone."

His voice had suddenly changed, taking on a much more serious quality.

I nodded in confirmation of my understanding. I very warily, placed my fingers around the hilt.

The rumours had not been a lie. Holding the sword was almost like holding air itself. It was practically weightless. I could only imagine how hard it would be to train and fight with these weapons. I had trained all my life to move with and wield a blade or spear of some weight in my hand, to balance with it. Going from that, to holding this, being able to interchange between the two weapons and fight with the same level of skill, must have been an incredibly difficult task.

The Prince noticed my stunned silence.

"So? What do you think?" He sounded genuinely curious.

"It's...How do you wield this, Your Highness?"

The Prince shrugged, "It takes time. I've been learning since I was young."

"Is it easier or harder?"

"Oh, much harder. It requires more focus, more concentration, much more precision."

"Have you ever taken a life with one?"

The Prince looked confused by the question. "It would make little sense to possess a weapon you had no intent on using, would it, Captain?"

"Not all weapons are used to kill."

He chuckled "For what then? Polishing?"

There it was, the streak of cruelty people had mentioned, I assumed.

"To defend, to disarm, to protect," I said dryly.

He closed his eyes and smiled, speaking as he did. "To defend someone from death, to disarm someone to prevent them from killing you, to protect yourself from being mortally wounded... by another weapon." He opened one eye, looking at me with interest.

"A cynical view," I replied, dropping my voice.

"Is it?" he asked confidently. I could tell the question was rhetorical.

I was still holding the blade. "Could I come to look at it, from time to time, Your Highness?"

I had to find a way to access this blade again. It was hardly as if I could pull the Noxscroll out in front of the Prince and begin to read it. After all, Noxscroll originated from his Kingdom. It could have been written by someone who knew him, or by the Prince himself.

"You plan on staying in Vasara?" he asked.

"Yes. For the Courting Season."

Understanding spread across his facial features. "You must be the escort for Kalnasa."

"Yes."

"As am I, for Audra."

The Prince noticed my confusion. Candidates were escorted by members of a King's army, guards, or warrior personnel, but not a member of the Royal Family or nobility.

"Yes, yes, I know what you're thinking, but I volunteered. I haven't been here for a while and wanted an excuse to take a trip away."

"I thought being a Prince wasn't so challenging," I probed him, raising my brows.

Why I had done so, did not make any sense even to myself.

"What happened to *'Your Highness'*?" The Prince chuckled, noticing the absence of my formal address.

"Your Highness," I added flatly.

"Not all my decisions are related to being a Prince." His voice softened. "You are more than welcome to visit me, Captain. You are by far the least tedious person I have met at one of these Royal events for some time."

"Thank you, Your Highness, you honour me," I lied.

"No, I don't." He smiled again and outstretched his hand to take his sword back. I passed it to him.

He placed it back in his belt. "I'll see you at the opening, I take it?"

"You will, Your Highness."

"Well, at least that means there'll be somebody I know present."

I wouldn't exactly say we knew each other. If anything, I knew him less than when I had only heard rumours of him.

"Do we... know each other, Your Highness?" I asked.

The Prince looked impressed. "We know more than we did yesterday." He gestured at his sword, then at the necklace around his neck. "And as someone I know and despise has always said, knowledge is a weapon is it not?"

I frowned. He raised his eyebrows, his hand still rested on the gems around his neck.

"Do you intend to use it?" I asked, tensing my fingers behind my back.

"Not unless I have to, Captain." His voice had taken on that serious quality once more.

This, this was a warning. The Prince knew I wanted the sword for something other than my own personal interest. He had offered to let me see it in the future, but he had also let me know that should the need arise, he would find out what I wanted it for, and he would use that information against me. He would let me see the sword, not out of generosity, but because it would benefit him.

"You will not have to, Your Highness." I lifted my chin up.

"I very much hope that is true. For your sake." He looked at me one final time. He began walking backwards at first, then he strolled away, a path cleared for him as he did.

And just like that, the Prince became another person added to the list of those who would watch my every moment.

Just like that, I had gone from being free to having multiple targets on my back.

Which one, I wondered, would be struck first.

# CHAPTER 12- LORIA

Nathon had been gone for four hours. It had been the only time in my life when I'd actually wished for his presence.

Despite the undeniable beauty of this building, it was still unsettling to be here. I wish I had come here under different circumstances. I wish I could have had the time and ability to admire the paintings, the walls, the plants, the ceilings, and windows properly.

Instead, my thoughts were solely preoccupied with this ceremony, and what I was supposed to do while I was there.

What I had been instructed to do after it.

Sickness swam inside my stomach. I hadn't eaten anything since the morning. I couldn't bear the thought of eating, or of hundreds of gazes fixed my way as I was introduced as the candidate of Audra later. I shuddered involuntarily as I imagined it and closed my eyes.

A while after Nathon had left, a servant had shown me to this room. She had said little, but the words she did utter sounded stifled and fuelled with nervous anxiety. I almost wished I could reach out and hold her hand, to tell her I was just as scared as she was, but she darted away like a startled mouse as soon as she had shown me in.

The room was very different to the ones at Audra. The ceilings were lower, the walls were white, the bed frame was white, the floors were tiled. The bed sheets and furniture were an amalgamation of rust, amber, and ruby.

There was a very large set of double doors leading out onto a balcony. I'd stepped onto it the first second I had arrived here, trying to escape from the stifling heat. It hadn't worked. I had stayed there anyway, before being ambushed by a large pigeon. It had been peering at me with an almost sympathetic gaze, as if it could sense my distress. My experience with the Erebask as a child had made me uncomfortable around all birds in general, and so, I had spent far too much time trying to chase it away.

The cloaks arrived next, one was scarlet, another was amber, and another was gold. I bathed as soon as they did, without calling upon any assistance. I did not wish to be scrubbed at like a mare. Again. Let me feel a woman a while longer. Before this all began.

The hot water stripped me of the sweat and soil I had picked up on the road. Stepping out of it, I strode towards the dress. I considered asking for different one, but I knew it would be viewed as a liberty here. All the candidates were dressed in garments from their home Kingdom, specifically for the Opening Ceremony. A cloak was one thing, I could make excuses for that. I was too hot for my former, and too cool to do without one, but to change my dress altogether, there would be no explanation for that. My father and mother would hear of it.

An unease rose in my chest, that familiar feeling of nervousness fraying at my composure. Always they chipped away at it, like I was wood, and they the flame come to waste me away. I loathed it, and still, I could not douse that fire.

I placed the dress on again, and opted for the gold, and largest cloak I'd been sent. Unlike the thick hooded cloak I had been wearing from Audra, this was light, and made from a fluid, near transparent material. It hung over my shoulders in a straight line, with an ornate clasp in the shape of the sun fastening its two sides together. From there it spilt to the floor.

I was admiring the garment when a knock sounded at the door.

"Some food for you, Princess." The serving girl's voice was quivering. She held a plate of fruit and appetisers with her shaking hands.

"Thank you." I went to take the plate from the girl's hands. She stared at me wide eyed.

"It's alright, you can go." I smiled softly as I gently eased the plate from her tight grip. I had forgotten most Princesses were served more directly across the Kingdoms, and that a noble taking food from a servant's hands was highly peculiar.

I was very rarely at the Citadel's grounds in Audra, which meant I usually avoided the servants and did things for myself. That was a small price to pay for being as far away from my family as possible, as often as possible.

"Your Highness, they told me to inform you the ceremony will start in an hour."

I smiled again, mentally panicking about the fact Nathon was not here. Part of me was beginning to wonder if he had intentionally left me alone for this event. It was something he would do, I thought.

"Thank you for the message," I said. The girl curtsied and left.

I placed the plate on the nearest table and sighed. As I scratched my temple, I noticed the pigeon at the double doors again. I strode across the room and opened them, attempting to rid myself of this feathered creature's company permanently.

Laughter reached my ears.

I turned to my left. There on the balcony protruding from the room next to me, was a woman. Another candidate, I presumed.

Her brown curls bounced from side to side as she shook her head. "Very ladylike." She chuckled.

I didn't know what to say. I hadn't yet prepared myself for a formal conversation. I thought I'd have another hour at least.

"Relax... Gods," she held up her hands.

"You're from Zeima," was all I could think to reply. A Kingdom perpetually dusted in snow.

"Yes, so being here is like walking straight into an inferno," she said, fanning herself with her hand.

*Even without the heat.*

"It must be hard for you too. Although maybe not…" She corrected herself as she took in my cloak. "Audra is humid after all."

She, on the other hand, was wearing a grey dress that shone against her dark skin. Its transparent sleeves ended with cuffs of bright blue gems. Flowers of similar colours were placed in a band across the bed of her thick curls.

"Yes," I said. "It is not so difficult an adjustment as would be for you," I smiled.

"Or the Kalnasans," she mused. "I've heard it often rains there."

She was ready for the ceremony, and we were engaged in stilted conversation about the weather. This was it. This ridiculous terrifying game had begun.

Perhaps I would actually be sick.

"I'm Rhana," she declared. Rhana was the Crown Princess of Zeima. She was the youngest of the four heirs there, the other three being men.

I cleared my throat, dry from the heat and anxiety. "I'm Loria."

"The Princess then."

"As are you," I replied.

"Aren't we fortunate?"

"Of course."

"A true honour."

"It is."

We were saying all the right things, the right words, but it felt as if a thousand others existed between those lines. Words which were equivalent to something like, *"If only we were our brothers."*

"Who's your escort?" She asked. I could tell she wasn't truly interested by the tone of her voice. She was simply trying to find a way to maintain dignified conversation.

I regretted the fact I could not avoid answering, and that my answer was, "My brother."

I would have assumed that Rhana, like many Royals, had been trained in some way to hide her emotions. But the shock and fear that spread across her face at my answer was as clear to me as the cloudless sky above us. She looked as if she had involuntarily held her breath.

"Who is yours?" I said, trying to divert her attention elsewhere.

"Your brother is your escort?" she asked slowly.

"He is." My hand was clutching the front of the cloak so hard I thought I might tear through the fabric.

"How..." She cut herself off. "Then it will be an honour to meet him." She raised her chin, looking at me directly with her grey blue eyes.

"He will be glad to hear that," I nodded.

From the weather to blatant lies. This is precisely how I had anticipated such interactions to go.

"A member of our guard, Jayli."

"A woman?" The pitch of my voice rose.

Female guards and army members did exist, but they were few in number, and still often perceived to be lesser warriors than the men. I was surprised then, they had sent a female as an escort with the Princess.

"She's equally as skilled as any man. If not more so."

"Apologies. I never meant to imply otherwise." My palms were sweating. The words between her lines were clear. *My escort could kill you, or anyone else easily.*

"I know," she smiled. "We women know our strength is often ignored."

I wasn't sure I cared about being ignored. I'd happily be underestimated, a second thought, left in peace. I didn't want to be something. I didn't want to prove anything. Be beholden to another's expectations or desires.

There was the faint sound of a knock at Rhana's door. She looked into her room, then back at me. "I will see you there, Princess." She took her hands off the railing and slid into her chambers.

I enjoyed some time in silence on the balcony, perhaps twenty minutes, maybe thirty, before Nathon came barging into mine.

He whistled in approval as he looked around, slamming the door behind him. He meandered towards me with his usual imperious step.

"Fit for a Queen." He wriggled his eyebrows suggestively.

"That is the point," I said without turning around.

"Welcome back Nathon, oh Nathon, I've missed you, I was so worried Nathon." He raised his voice to a high pitch, clearly meant to imitate my own.

He flanked me. He too had clearly bathed, having changed out of his former attire. He was now wearing a dark silken chemise, small golden gems at its cuffs and waistline.

I stared at him with disdain, I didn't even try to hide it. I did not have the energy for his antics.

"You know, we should probably devise some kind of system." He placed his hands behind his back, looking down at the streets below.

"What kind of system?" I followed his eyes to the ground.

"A way we'll know if one of us is in danger. Say... we meet every day, or every few, at a certain time in a certain place, and if we're not there, then we'll know."

"You're my escort, won't you be around me all the time?" I asked, irritated.

"Most of the time yes, but unfortunately for you, no. I have things to do, remember?" He outstretched his arms across the railings.

"Fine," I agreed reluctantly. "Where and when?"

"I don't know yet. I'll need to look around, find somewhere that's private enough, but easy enough for us to get to quickly."

"So, we don't have a system then."

"Patience Loria, we will and…" he paused, "I have a feeling we will need it."

I grimaced at his words. He noticed. We stood there unmoving, not speaking for a few minutes.

"Do you think we'll die?" I asked him suddenly, unemotionally.

I could hardly believe I had. I could hardly believe I had just asked Nathon a question so revealing of my fears and thoughts.

He didn't say anything for a few moments, but I could feel him looking at me with an expression that showed he was just as surprised as I was at my question.

"I think it would be a waste," he answered quietly.

"What would?"

"For us to die."

I rolled my eyes. "Of course, because you're such a blessing to the world."

"No." He shook his head, chuckling to himself. "It would be a waste for us to have survived what we did, only to die now."

I turned my whole body to him. He wasn't facing me anymore, he was just facing forwards, not really focusing on anything.

"Don't you think?" He tilted his head towards me.

I was stunned and confused. He was looking at me with such sincerity I was completely thrown off guard. I felt as if I was looking at someone I didn't even know. A stranger.

"I think it doesn't work that way," I said carefully. "I think nothing works that way," my voice trailed off.

"But still. It would be, wouldn't it?"

Why was he so concerned about my answer? Why was he looking at me with such pity…*pity* in his eyes?

"Maybe. Maybe not. But that's not what I meant. I meant—"

"I know what you meant. And I meant what I said. It would be a waste. I don't like waste. So, I'm going to do everything possible to make sure our lives are not wasted…or lost," he spat out quickly and aggressively.

I rubbed my hand against my forehead. "I hope it works."

"So do I." Then laughing again, he said, "After all, I *am* a blessing to this world, it would be such a shame for it to lose me."

"I think you're more of a curse."

"Perhaps a bit of both." He winked, digging into the pocket of his black loose pants, and pulling out some jewellery.

Some green jewellery.

It was simple, understated, but it was very beautiful. Nathon's smug facial expression made it clear he expected a response.

"Oh well, our task has been accomplished, we can go back to Audra now," I said dryly.

He clasped his hands over the jewels in surprise. "You *can* make a joke after all."

"Only if it's at your expense," I mumbled.

"Just wear it, will you? You're already at a disadvantage wearing that cloak. Are you sure you can't just take it off?" His face looked contorted with awkward confusion, as if he wished he didn't have to ask.

"I am sure."

He sighed in resignation and dropped the necklace into my hands. I clasped it around my neck, it was high enough to be a choker of sorts.

Nathon nodded in something akin to approval.

"How did you find this?" I asked.

"I have my ways."

"Did they involve danger of some kind?"

Nathon looked as if he was genuinely considering his answer. "Time will tell."

"What does that mean?" I scowled.

"It means exactly what it means. I do not know yet." He leant on the railing with his right elbow.

"We're in enough danger as it is Nathon," I said, distressed.

"Trust me Loria I—"

"That's the last thing I can do."

He closed his eyes slowly and then opened them. "Well, you don't really have a choice, do you?"

He glared at me meaningfully for a few moments, obviously vexed. I gritted my teeth, bit at my lip, and turned away from him, walking back into the room.

He was right. I didn't have a choice, and my life was largely in his hands. My life had always been in someone else's hands, never my own.

Another knock at the door. "It's time Princess," the same girl said.

Nathon had come into the room, after hearing the girl speak. We looked at each other.

"No wasting," he said to me.

I nodded and we opened the door out into the halls.

# CHAPTER 13- LORIA

I had expected to be escorted straight to the throne room, but the guards lead us away from it. Nathon's sidelong glance at me revealed he was curious about our route as well.

"Where are we going?" I decided to speak up.

Before the guard could answer me, a man appeared. He was tall, his hair a burnt amber, specks of which adorned his jawline. His hand was placed horizontally over his golden vest. He approached us with a confident gait.

"Princess," he addressed me, bowing slightly. "Prince." He repeated the action in Nathon's direction. "We are escorting you to an adjoining room. Each of the Kingdom's candidates and escorts will enter the ceremony when called upon. You will walk down the centre of the hall. Once you reach His Highness, you will curtsey" – he glanced at me – "and you will bow," he said to Nathon. "You will wait until he acknowledges you, at which point you will join the other candidates at a table adjacent to His Highness's throne. Where you should sit will be indicated by the presence of a guard holding your Kingdom's flag."

He looked at us both, flitting his eyes between us, searching for any confusion on our faces. "Any questions?"

I looked at Nathon, he remained staring at the middle-aged gentleman. I turned back to him myself.

"What after that?" I spoke.

The man looked at me and sighed. I raised my brow, confused by his clear annoyance.

"Is something troubling you, Sir...?" Nathon asked, who had clearly caught the sigh as well.

The man's upper lip twitched slightly in surprise. "No, Your Highness. It has simply been a tiresome and long day. The preparations have been extensive." He smiled, forcefully.

Nathon smiled with his teeth. "I'm sure, I'm sure."

I cleared my throat. "What comes after the introductions?"

"Food and drink will be served. The other candidates will be there, as well as the most important members of Vasara's Court. It is a wonderful opportunity to improve relations with them and learn more about our Kingdom."

"Not much of an opportunity for the Vasaran candidate," Nathon couldn't help but add.

The man shrugged. "A chance to meet the other candidates is useful for all."

Useful. This was not anything other than a chance to scout out the competition, to try and outmanoeuvre everybody else. I never thought I'd want to go back to Audra. But I did now. At least I could hide there. Here, I was like a rabbit in a forest, with an arrow pointed at its throat.

"Of course," I said, grateful I had spoken just as Nathon opened his mouth to interrupt. "Thank you for the information. Will you be at the table Sir?"

"I will, Your Highness." He placed his hand on his chest. "Lord Fargreaves."

Nathon's eyes darted to the floor. He squinted as if in deep thought but recovered almost instantly.

"A pleasure, Fargreaves," I said, by way of distraction.

"Please, follow me." He walked ahead, leading us to the adjoining room. I lagged a little, slowing our pace so I could whisper to Nathon.

"What is it?" I asked, my curiosity defeating any sense of composure.

His hands were behind his back. He didn't even look at me as he breathed out. "I don't know."

"Do you know this man?" I tried to make my lips move as little as possible.

"Possibly."

I fiddled with my clasped hands. "Possibly?"

"He's familiar. I don't know why." Nathon's clipped sentences stirred my chest with tension.

"Maybe you've simply heard of him before?" Even as I said the words, I didn't believe them myself.

"It's not that."

I didn't like this. Nathon was always so sure about everything. I hated to admit it, but if he said this man was familiar to him, then he was. I dreaded to think of the reason why.

"I suggest you find out what *it is*." We couldn't afford any further complications. This situation was already wildly complex and dangerous.

I expected him to make a joke or a sarcastic remark about my uncharacteristically commanding tone. Instead, he just said, his eyes focused on the back of Fargreaves' head, "Don't worry, I will."

With each step we took towards the room, nervousness blazed brighter inside me. The corridors grew increasingly quiet, indicating we were heading into more exclusive areas of the Palace. We eventually reached a set of brown square doors, which Fargreaves shoved open roughly, gesturing with his hand for us to enter.

Inside were the other four candidates and their escorts. My eyes darted around the room and their faces. Rhana smiled at me warmly and nodded slightly. Her escort straightened up as we walked in, and her gaze fixed on Nathon with a predatory intensity. I had no doubt Nathon had noticed, but he didn't acknowledge it. He, like me, was busy surveying the faces of the others present.

On their left and sitting down was a young woman whose face had been turned to the window behind her. Jurasa's candidate. Her long thick golden locks obscured the side of her face as she turned to the sound of us entering. She surveyed us cursorily for the briefest moment and turned away as if uninterested. Her escort did the same.

To their left stood a lean pale woman, whose slick cherry red hair ran all the way down a sun-coloured gown to her waist. Her escort muttered something in her ear, eyeing us with a look that made me feel uneasy. He looked as if he were informing her of who we were. Her eyes widened in surprise at something he said.

In the very far corner of the room sat a man. He seemed familiar to me, but I couldn't ascertain how. His silver hair reached the leg that was bent up to support the spear he was sharpening across his knee with a stone. Next to him was a young girl, certainly the youngest candidate here. Her light brown skin appeared golden in the light that struck her from the window. She was chatting to the man fervently.

But he, he was distracted by our presence. He turned towards us and met our eyes. His stare lingered on both Nathon and I's faces for far longer than any of the others had looked at us. The woman he was with, Kalnasa's candidate, tugged on his sleeve and whispered something in his ear. Without taking his eyes off us, he shook his head, indicating *no* to whatever she had asked.

Clearly ignoring his advice, the woman walked, practically skipped towards us, and curtsied, spreading out the bottom of her silver dress. The light silk rippled through the air, danced as she moved. Kalnasa's nobles and Royals possessed, by far, the most luxurious clothing of all Five Kingdoms.

"Your Highnesses. I've heard much about you. I'm Dyna Kumosan." She stood slowly, smiling innocently.

I mentally reviewed my Royal History, and all the books I had read on family dynasties at Audra. "King Dunlan's niece," I said, as I remembered. Nathon smiled slightly, seemingly glad I had remembered her, for both our sakes.

"Yes...urrr yes!" She looked utterly shocked I would recognise her name and turned behind her left shoulder to look at her escort in surprise.

"This is my escort... Captain Hestan Hikari." Dyna gestured to him.

Hestan nodded tensely. He pocketed the stone in his pale blue robe, placed the spear on his back, and stood to shadow her. It seemed he'd rather be anywhere but here.

"You look familiar, Captain, have I seen you somewhere before?" Nathon said. He drew out every word in a provoking manner, tilting his head to one side, slightly rubbing the side of his temple.

The Captain looked thoroughly irked by Nathon's question, which made me unintentionally smile in his direction. He caught my eye and immediately corrected his expression once he saw my own.

A strange man I thought, brave enough to make his irritation at my brother clear. Perhaps the only man here with a shred of honesty running through his veins.

Although even I was not courageous enough to face Nathon. Was I no different from the vapid liars here then?

I found myself genuinely interested in what the Captain's answer would be, and I could tell by the expression on Nathon's face, that he was delightfully curious about it. But there was a knowing glint in Nathon's eyes as he looked at the Captain that confused me, and Dyna as well.

"Answer him," she hissed innocently in the Captain's direction. I was beginning to think the Kalnasans had a very different approach to etiquette than the rest of us. I wouldn't have minded growing up there, I thought.

The Captain cleared his throat. "No, Your Highness, I don't believe so. You must be mistaken."

"Mmmmmmm," Nathon hummed. "Perhaps."

Perhaps it was the Kalnasans attitude that had put me at ease enough to say, "I confess, I thought the same thing of you, Captain. I feel I've seen you somewhere before."

Nathon looked at me confused. The Captain too, seemed startled.

"I didn't realise my escort was so well known. What have you been doing these past few years to be recognised by such prestigious people, Hestan?" Dyna giggled and placed her hand on his shoulder. Their familiarity was unusual, but Hestan seemed unperturbed by it.

"Forgive me, it might just be my imagination." I decided it best to drop the subject for now, since the Captain seemed uncomfortable.

For now.

"No, I..." The Captain cleared his throat. "That is to say, there is nothing to forgive, Your Highness."

Nathon chuckled slightly. The other candidates had, I noticed, been watching our exchange with disguised interest, although they could not hear it. All but the golden-haired woman, who was still staring out of the window, her eyes glazed over.

"Still, we didn't mean to unsettle you. This atmosphere is already unsettling enough," I murmured.

Nathon gave me a warning look. The Captain's expression remained blank, while Dyna's looked almost pained.

"Yes," the Captain said, glancing at Nathon briefly.

An attendant walked into the room. "Lady Tarren of Vasara, please, follow me." The slim red-haired woman trailed behind the attendant out of the room, along with her escort.

It was starting then. We were being called into the ceremony. As if by some invisible force, each candidate and their escort separated to the farthest corners of the room, conversing with one another.

Strategizing, more accurately.

"That was foolish," Nathon muttered through gritted teeth.

"It was true."

"I didn't say it wasn't true, I said it was foolish." Nathon looked down at me.

I smacked my lips together in frustration, glancing to the side.

"Can you please refrain from your noble desire to be honest while we are here?" he whispered.

"And what of you and that Captain? You were clearly probing him."

"The Captain won't get us killed, foolishness might."

"You don't know that."

"Stop it Loria, please." His voice became quieter. "You know full well what I mean."

We pretended to be waiting patiently, admiring the architecture of the room.

"How do you know him?" I said after a few moments.

"Who?"

"The Captain."

"I don't."

"You're lying."

"You said you recognised him as well, Loria."

"Yes, but I don't remember how."

"Well, I suggest you remember then," he said, visibly pleased with himself he had echoed my earlier words about Fargreaves.

"Why won't you tell me?"

"There's nothing to tell."

"You're full of shit," I whispered, smiling for the sake of any curious onlookers.

Nathon smiled back, so warmly it almost made me believe in it for a second. "Maybe when you learn to keep your mouth shut, I'll share some of my shit with you."

"So, you do know him."

"I didn't say that."

"It's what you're not saying that's more revealing."

"Drop it Loria, you know—"

I hadn't noticed that one by one, the other candidates had been called into the throne room, until an attendant stopped right in front of us, and bowed. "Your Highness, it's time."

I looked up and realised we were the last ones to leave.

Nathon held up his arm for me. "Shall we?"

I warily grabbed onto it. My fingers were trembling. It didn't go unnoticed by Nathon. He glanced down at his arm and back up at my face as we got closer and closer to the entrance. He placed his hand over mine.

"Loria," he said. I looked at him, swallowing nervously. "I've got you, alright?"

"Unfortunately," I said.

Nathon laughed. I couldn't remember the last time I'd heard him laugh like that. Genuinely, warmly, with real amusement. Not the fake, restrained, and carefully constructed laugh he employed around other people. One that I had similarly perfected myself.

"Unfortunately," he repeated, without moving his hand.

The doors opened, and hundreds of faces turned in our direction.

# CHAPTER 14- NATHON

She was shaking like a leaf desperately clutching to a branch in a storm. I had a feeling if I had taken my hands off her, she would have fallen to the ground as easily as one from a dying tree.

We stepped slowly into the room. We had clearly been cast in shadow by the doorframe, for once we stepped into the well-lit central walkway, the silence that had settled like a soft blanket over the magnificent space was shattered.

Gasps shred the silence in the space apart. People darted their eyes between Loria and me, muttering amongst themselves. Loria gripped my arm even harder. I in turn, gripped her hand tighter, and smiled as we grew closer to the throne, and Vasara's Prince.

I had to admit it, the man looked reverential.

His blood red tunic perfectly matched the shade of his hair, which was slicked back and resting just below his ears. Its high neck rested just above his collarbones, bleeding against his pale skin. The crown he wore was partially fashioned in the shape of the sun's rays. It made the sharp cuts of his face look even more regal somehow.

I could hear Loria stop breathing as she fixed her eyes on him. He was staring at her now, not in the way I had seen men stare at women in bars, pleasure houses, or similar establishments. He was looking at her with an unrestrained curiosity.

Their eye contact was prolonged enough for a flourish of further whispers to hum behind us as we stopped at the established line in front of his throne. Loria curtsied and I bowed.

A man to our right held out a scroll and in a booming voice, far too loud for the hall shouted, "Princess Loria Albarsan and Prince Nathon Albarsan of Audra."

The muttering that had slithered between the crowd like a silent snake became an uproar of shock. I smirked, Prince Eliel noticed, and slid his gaze away from Loria to look at me. I could feel Loria's eyes on me too, as well as every other human being's in this hall.

The rumours about me had their advantages, sometimes.

Prince Eliel raised his hand in a casual, graceful gesture. His jaw clenched as he did. The muttering quieted down almost immediately, but stubbornly persisted in certain corners of the room. In response, Prince Eliel stood, slowly and deliberately, his blizzard blue eyes scanning the crowd for moving lips. The room became utterly still.

I turned around to look at the crowd and then back at him. He clearly commanded much authority here and... even fear perhaps. Something he and I had in common, it seemed.

If he did in fact command fear, I had to figure out why, and quickly. I had to figure out his strengths and his skills, so we could do what we were here to. I'd have to gather as much information as possible while Loria batted her eyelashes at him for weeks.

I didn't envy her in the slightest. I'd much rather assassinate than seduce people.

Although, I would have been equally skilled at both, and I'd truly have preferred the option of doing neither.

"Welcome to Vasara," Prince Eliel said, lowering his hand, but remaining standing. "It is an honour to have not one, but *two* members of Audra's Royal Family here." His voice was low but relaxed, like a stream from a hot spring. His emphasis on *two* made clear he was aware of the strange nature of my escorting Loria and would not soon forget it.

Loria lifted her chin proudly, but I could tell she was nervous when directly addressing the Prince. "The honour is all ours, Your Highness. My brother couldn't refuse the opportunity to visit your Kingdom and witness such a historic event. He is rather restless, as I'm sure you may have heard." She finished with a smile.

The look on the Prince's face told me he was thinking almost, if not the exact same thing as I. Loria's response had been unexpected, and incredibly intelligent. She had in a few sentences, accepted his welcome, complimented him, complimented his Kingdom, expressed our 'delight' at being here, and explained my presence away with a light-hearted remark.

Loria squeezed my arm gently under my hand. Her way of saying, *"Let me do the talking."* I squeezed her hand back, my way of saying, *"He's all yours."*

Prince Eliel smiled slowly, staring at Loria in that same way again. "Yes. I feel I know much about your brother and very little about you."

*I feel.* This man did not take rumour for fact then. Frustrating. Had he done so, that would have worked to our advantage.

"I look forward to correcting that, Prince," Loria said confidently.

The Prince's closed smile grew very slightly wider. "As do I, Princess."

The silence now felt even thicker after their exchange. They kept their eyes on each other. I turned to notice several of the escorts whispering into the ears of the candidates they accompanied. I found myself wishing I could just kill the Prince right here and now and be done with it, simply to put an end to this grotesquely ridiculous farce.

The Prince slowly backed away and sat down on his throne.

"Let the festivities begin," he declared.

He never took his eyes off Loria's face.

We turned and walked towards the table and sat down in our allocated seats. It was only after Loria removed her hand from my arm that I could see how white her knuckles had turned from gripping it so tightly. I had barely felt it. That was hardly surprising, I'd developed a high pain tolerance over the years.

Sitting across from us was Vasara's candidate and her escort. They were seated next to Dyna and the Captain. We were seated next to Jurasa's candidate, and at the short end of the table, on two seats, sat Zeima's candidate and her escort. The one who had informed me with her eyes she would gut me the second I so much as blinked in her charge's direction.

At the other end of the table sat a few noblemen. Fargreaves was amongst them. There was one unoccupied Councilman's seat and by the looks on the faces of Vasara's Council, they were extremely displeased at the mystery individual's absence.

"Nicely done," I muttered into Loria's ear. She jumped, visibly startled, which drew the attention of the others.

I remained indifferent for the sake of our fellow dinner guests, but I was concerned by her sudden outburst of fright.

"Are you quite alright Princess?" Zeima's candidate said.

"Of course, thank you. I was just lost in thought," Loria replied.

The Zeiman Candidate sipped her goblet of wine. "There is much to think about." She looked at me briefly and then looked away.

"Who are you, may I ask?" I held her scuttling gaze. "Since we entered last, we are at a disadvantage. We didn't learn your names." I grabbed a goblet of wine and began to drink.

"I'm Rhana."

"Ahhh, the Princess."

"Yes."

"And who's your lovely friend?" I pointed at her escort.

Rhana nodded at her escort, giving her permission to answer herself. "I am Jayli, Your Highness." She sounded starved of air.

"Are *you* quite alright Jayli?"

Jayli's dark brown eyes narrowed. Rhana, who had been pleasantly polite up until that point, looked at me coldly.

"She's probably afraid of you." I turned to find Dyna speaking as she popped a grape into her mouth. "Did you hear them all when you walked in? They were all talking about you, Prince."

"Are you... afraid of me Jayli?" I turned back to her curious.

"No, Your Highness." She flicked her braided hair behind her shoulder.

"See...she's not afraid of me," I said, raising my glass in Dyna's direction.

"She wouldn't say yes if she were afraid of you, would she?" Dyna said teasingly, as if she had provided the most insightful comment of the century.

The Captain looked at Dyna, silently suggesting she stop talking.

"I, for one, was excited to meet you Prince." Vasara's candidate gave me a cloying smile. "Tarren Lestor," she introduced herself.

Loria could barely suppress a snorting sound under her breath.

"Were you? Isn't that nice." I smiled back, beginning to place food onto my plate.

"I think many are excited to have you here," she continued.

"You've asked them, have you?" I raised an eyebrow, sceptical of her inane friendliness.

"There is no need. A handsome and famous warrior such as yourself, and Royalty no less." She leant further into the table, deliberately.

Loria jolted up suddenly, Tarren looked mortified.

"My Lady." Loria sounded angry. I'd very rarely heard that. "I'm assuming your footwork was meant for my brother."

"I...I... I don't know what you mean, Your Highness."

"I think you've got your Princes confused. I would suggest you save your manoeuvres and flattery for the one whose hand we are competing for."

Tarren feigned outrage. "I would never...I...you are misunderstanding—"

"It would be hard for me to misunderstand your foot on my thigh," Loria bit.

Rhana was smiling behind her goblet. Dyna's mouth was gaping wide open. I held Tarren's mortified gaze, raising one eyebrow.

"Apologies, it was not intentional." She looked at me and Loria apologetically, but also with a newfound respect.

It would be all too easy to underestimate Lady Tarren as a jealous, ambitious young woman, but there was always more to someone than the obvious, than the easy conclusion of their personhood.

"It was," Loria said, looking down at the plate she had now begun to fill herself.

"Was your outfit?" Tarren added.

Loria's head spun back up.

"Intentional? It's only...as you say, we are competing for Prince Eliel's hand, and are you sure this is the best way to do it?" She looked at Loria's cloak up and down.

"Thank you for your concern, My Lady," Loria replied. "But I would prefer to keep my tactics a secret."

"Of course, of course." She smiled, feeling victorious at having shamed Loria so openly.

Tarren's escort yanked on her sleeve and muttered something into her ear. If he had half a brain, he would be telling her to use the few brain cells she was clearly utilising at this moment to keep silent.

I glanced up at Prince Eliel. Somebody was bending behind his throne, having hurried to it with great haste. He was informing him of something, moving his hands in a way that indicated distress. I nudged Loria's arm with my elbow and gestured with my chin at the scene. Her gaze followed mine.

The Prince furrowed his brow and pinched the bridge of his nose, casting his head downwards. He turned around to reply to the man, and just as he did, the doors of the throne room burst open with a loud thud.

A man walked in, completely underdressed for the occasion, in nothing but a thin white, crumpled tunic and dark red loose pants. He looked as if he had awoken less than an hour earlier. His hair was the same colour as Prince Eliel's, only part of it was tied back at the top in a small bun, and the rest was longer, sitting just past his shoulders. He scratched his broad, stubbled jaw without reserve, and strolled down the centre of the aisle, winking at several of the ladies at the tables. He lifted his arms out in a warm gesture, then struck his own chest with a slap.

"Cousin. Pardon my lateness. I was busy." He looked puzzled for a moment and then continued "Well, I wasn't busy actually but..." He lowered his voice for dramatic effect, since everyone else could clearly still hear him, "You have to admit these things are fucking boring."

He went on, "I wouldn't have come, only this time, I heard some beautiful women would be here, from all across the world. All for...you." He pointed at the Prince, who looked so furious, I thought he might spontaneously combust.

"Elias." Prince Eliel greeted the man, a hostile edge to his tone.

Elias...this was the Prince's cousin.

"What do you look so angry for, c'mon, c'mon, I came dinn... I?" He was slurring his words. He was drunk.

Elias paused for a moment in thought, and looked over at our table, surveying each of the women at it with a curious glare. "You only need one, right? You could leave me the others?" He pointed at us laughing and turned back to the Prince, who remained staring at him as if promising death itself.

"Why's that one wearing a fucking cloak?" Elias blurted out, glaring at Loria with amusement. "What's she got under there that's so interesting? Maybe I could look for you and—"

The Prince rose from his throne so quickly, that by the time he appeared in front of his cousin, I'd barely had the time to blink. He grabbed him by the collar of his flimsy clothing, almost gently, then suddenly yanked him forwards, placing the other hand behind his cousin's head. He said something directly into his ear that nobody could make out.

Prince Eliel pulled back carefully, Elias looked at him and grinned, clicking his tongue.

"Mmmmm... your wish is my command." He stumbled towards the table. He was clearly extremely inebriated. He made his way towards the unoccupied Council chair and gradually, quiet conversation started up around the room again, most likely about him. Prince Eliel followed his cousin's movements all the way to the table before turning back to talk to the man who had approached him just moments before.

Before Elias reached his chair however, he took a long and hard look at everyone seated at our end of the table.

His searching glances stopped at me.

"You?" He came closer. "What are *you* doing here?" He leant on the corner of the table, his arms crossed over his chest. His breath smelt of alcohol, in fact his whole body reeked of it.

"You should address him as 'Your Highness'," Tarren said.

I internally groaned at her comment.

"Or what?" Elias laughed, training his dark red eyes on me. "What's he going to do? Kill me right here and now in front of all these guests?"

I smiled back slowly, "Don't tempt me, My Lord."

"No, no, no, that's not your style though, is it?" He poked my shoulder.

I was beginning to wonder if my 'style' was worth changing.

"You'd kill me in the middle of the night or something. Or...or make me wait for months, thinking I was safe and sound. Then one evening, I'd be balls deep in some woman and you'd barge into my bed chambers and slit my throat, right?"

"No."

"No?"

"No. That's far too messy," I smiled.

He looked at me with a mixture of delight and bemusement. "Is it true you killed forty men at once, all by yourself at the Hysort Pass during those riots?" He leant forwards, closer to my face.

That wasn't true, it had been more like ninety.

I didn't say anything at first, momentarily distracted by the memory of that night.

"It's not a hard question, is it?" His warm breath struck my face.

"Nor was it a hard task," I lied. It was a scourge on my memory, on my soul, a stain that I would never get out.

"So, it *is* true." The man covered his mouth with his hand "Shit, you really are a psychopath, aren't you? Just like they say."

"And you are...what exactly, a drunk, a circus act?" I clipped back.

Elias laughed heartily at that. "Look around you, *Your Highness*." He used air quotation marks for my title. "All this, these people." He made a circling motion with his finger. "This is the real fucking circus."

"Maybe." I glanced up at him. "But you're either part of the show or you're a prop. I'd rather have a leading role myself."

He grimaced. "Would you really? Enjoying the show, are you?"

I remained silent.

"And what about your pretty companion here?" he said, looking at Loria.

Loria observed him with something akin to morbid fascination. She thought for a moment and spoke. "Props get used by those who have a leading role. I don't want to be used."

"What would you call your father sending you here to make lovely little babies with my cousin then?"

Loria's mouth twitched slightly at the corner. The thought she would have to carry Eliel's child against her own will as part of my father's plan made me physically ill.

And I could tell she was thinking. *Only that's not what I was sent here for at all.*

"An audition," she replied. "For the leading part."

"Fuckkkk." Elias straightened up. "Please tell me the rest of you aren't as strange as these two."

Nobody replied to his question.

"What about you?" He pointed at Dyna. She looked up at him, her dark blue eyes the same colour as the details in her silver dress.

"What about me?" she asked him, searching his face.

"Are you...enjoying the show?" He gestured around the room again, this time placing one arm on the back of my chair.

I thought about all the ways I could and would remove his arm for him if he didn't do so soon.

"Of course," Dyna said.

"So well trained. You're obviously fucking miserable."

Suddenly the Captain spoke. "I think it is you, My Lord, who is the most miserable of us all."

I couldn't help but smile. The Captain had actually broken his stone-cold façade for this man.

Elias went quiet, looking at the Captain as if he had just pulled out his guts and laid them on the table in front of him. They continued to stare at one another. He dropped his hand from my chair.

"I think you should leave now... Lord Elias," the Captain said. Dyna was obviously anxious, avoiding making eye contact with the man.

"I was just about to, don't worry." He gagged for a second and placed his fingers over his mouth. After regaining his composure, and presumably swallowing his sick, he added, "I won't devour your maiden there, Kalnasan, rest assured."

He looked at Dyna some more, then exclaimed, "Fuck how old is she?" He tilted his head down, as if trying to look at her from under her chestnut hair.

"Sixteen, My Lord," Dyna replied, without meeting his eyes.

Unexpectedly, the man shook his head in disapproval. "Too young for this shit." He huffed out a laugh. "Guess I better go, before my dear cousin strangles me."

He sauntered over to his seat, dragging it across the floor before settling into it. He exchanged what sounded like barbed words with the fellow Councilmen.

"Delightful man," Rhana said.

"It's a shame we can't marry *him*," Loria added.

I tensed up but was put back at ease when Rhana replied, chuckling, "I'm not even sure he'd be able to stay conscious during the nuptials."

"Or what came afterwards," Loria mumbled.

"That might be a good thing," Rhana said.

They both laughed, as did Jayli, and even a frightened Dyna smiled slightly. Tarren watched the exchange between the two with what seemed like jealousy and disgust. I watched it with interest. It was good Loria was making an ally. We could use that later. We would.

I peered around the room and table for a few moments and noticed Jurasa's candidate was still quiet. Loria noticed me watching and turned to the woman, who was sitting next to her.

"I like your ring, My Lady," she said, referring to a turquoise gem that sat across the woman's index finger.

The woman looked up at her slowly, as if in a trance. "Thank you," then abruptly added, as if suddenly realising she was meant to speak to others at this event, "My brother gave it to me."

"It's... a very generous gift. I've never seen anything like it." Loria said, staring at the woman's hand.

"Neither have I. He's very kind to me. He..." She tugged at the end of her hair nervously. "He was worried about sending me here."

"He sounds...wise," Loria said carefully.

The woman looked at the ceiling, avoiding eye contact with her the whole time. "He is."

"What's the stone?" Loria pointed at it again.

"I...I don't know. I never thought to ask."

"Well, maybe we could find out. We could ask a jeweller here. They may have seen it before."

"Oh no, Your Highness. I wouldn't wish to trouble you."

"It's no trouble, I'm curious myself." I didn't detect any dishonesty in Loria's statement.

The woman looked at Loria directly for the first time, and then at her neck, her necklace. "It's like the ones we have at home."

"Yes, I noticed that, how *did* you get emeralds in Audra?" Tarren piped up again.

I glanced at the Captain who seemed to have only just noticed Loria was wearing the necklace he sourced for me. It had been partially covered by her cloak. He squinted subtly at Loria's throat and then fixed his eyes on me, clearly trying to figure out why I had gone to such trouble to get it for her.

I could only hope he thought me a doting brother, rather than a would-be King Killer.

"It was something I received a long time ago. I don't remember how," Loria fibbed.

This was not good. It would have been one thing for the Captain to know I was lying about where the necklace was from, but now he knew without a doubt, that Loria was lying too, and was likely trying to figure out why we would both bother to hide so much about a piece of jewellery.

"How unfortunate," the Captain said. "It would have been interesting to know."

I cut into my steak with my knife, looking at the Captain intently.

*This will be me at your throat if you keep talking Captain.*

He threw a surreptitious glance at the Noxstone attached to my torso, then looked at me.

*I'll keep your secret if you keep mine, Your Highness.*

The rest of the evening passed quickly, with cordial, forced, and quiet conversation stirring amongst the hall. Prince Eliel remained a stoic picture of leadership the whole time. Elias drank enough wine to empty two whole jugs alone and Dyna continued to remain silent after his arrival. Towards the end of the meal, one of the Councilmen rose. He was old, short, bald, and sweaty, dabbing his neck with a handkerchief. He licked his lips before raising his goblet, and struck it with a spoon, announcing his speech.

"Thank you all, for coming to the opening ceremony of the ninety-eighth Courting Season."

"Ninety-eighth?" Dyna said surprised, as a round of applause sounded across the hall.

"As per tradition, the Prince will now have a private audience with all five candidates and their escorts. Please follow the guards to leave the hall one table at a time."

The Candidate from Jurasa turned to Loria and smiled nervously.

"What's your name?" Loria asked her.

"Maiwen, Your Highness."

"Your brother...is the Jurasan King?" Dyna asked, having overheard their exchange.

"Yes, he is."

Next to myself, the Jurasan King was probably the most spoken about individual across the Five Kingdoms, but for a very different reason. Rumours surrounding me were based on my deeds, my skills, and my cruelty. Some of them were true, most of them were lies. But the rumours about the Jurasan King were based around the fact nobody really knew him at all.

He barely left his Castle, it was said. There had only ever been vague reports about his appearance, and they changed every few months. Those who had met him had nothing good to say about him, and he was known for being difficult to negotiate with, and speak to. Despite that, he had held the throne since he was very young, having been crowned at the age of thirteen, apparently. Many had predicted his failure, but under his leadership, Jurasa had become more powerful than it had ever been before.

I respected him. Strange I knew, considering I had never met him, but to keep your own secrets as one of the greatest and most successful rulers in the history of Athlion, was no small feat.

"Are his eyes actually green or are they blue? Some say one thing, some say another," Dyna asked joyfully.

That question reminded me of her age. If I'd had one chance to ask a question about the Jurasan King, it certainly wouldn't have been something as utterly useless as the colour of his eyes.

"They're...it's hard to say." Maiwen sounded perplexed.

"But what would *you* say?" Dyna asked, her childish curiosity was so out of place in this hall.

"I'd say you can't describe them with one colour."

"How mysterious." Dyna rested her hands on her chin. Her face fell as the Councilmen stood to leave.

Elias walked past us, winking as he did, "Good luck flirting, ladies." He knocked against a table on his way out, lumbering towards the exit off balance.

The guards who had been standing behind us, holding our Kingdom's flags, directed us one by one to a spot in front of Prince Eliel's throne. Eventually, all candidates and their escorts stood in front of him in a line.

Fargreaves, the short sweaty man, and another middle-aged man with dark facial hair, remained at the King's side.

"The King will now appraise you one at a time. Candidates, please step forwards and escorts, please step back."

Tarren bounded forwards immediately, Dyna did so soon afterwards, then Rhana. Maiwen and Loria lagged behind. Loria took a deep breath.

"Don't worry, you've covered everything up anyway." I gave her a side glance.

She shot me a bitter look. I backed away with my hands up, and then put them behind my back. She stepped forwards, as did Maiwen.

My eyes found themselves on Fargreaves, I was still trying to remember where it was I had encountered him before.

I noticed the Captain watching me, staring at Fargreaves. I raised my eyebrows questioningly. Rather than looking irritated or deterred by my inquisition, he turned to squint at the auburn-haired man himself inquiringly, then looked back at me again in a similar manner.

Unusual.

Prince Eliel stood and made his way to the first candidate.

Time for the auditions to begin.

# CHAPTER 15- THE ACCIPEREAN

We'd had hoods on our heads for fifteen hours now, I guessed. I'd become slowly used to tracking time roughly, based on changes in light intensity and temperature. My thighs were chaffed from sitting on the saddle of a horse all this time without any riding gear.

Not that I'd ever worn any riding gear, I just knew it was something you were supposed to wear.

I sat back-to-back with the man who had been trapped with me in the cart earlier. While I was on the saddle, he was not. We'd barely had the time to glimpse a fraction of our saviour's face, before they had concealed our sight, and bound our hands.

*Some saviour.*

I smirked under my hood at the foolish hopefulness I had felt in that moment.

*More like captor.*

Someone was dragging our horse along, and somewhere nearby, there must have been a separate horse carrying the woman and child who had been trapped with us. I could still hear the girl's cries, growing weaker by the hour. At one point they had been so loud the man whose back I was sitting against inadvertently gripped my hand. I had gripped it back. We had been holding each other's hands since.

It was disconcerting, to touch someone. I had forgotten what it had felt like. I had only ever known someone's touch when it had been intended to hurt me, beat me, grab me, slap me, kick me, or shove me. Those or accidental touches, like the passing of an object, or the strapping to a chair to be drained.

A touch like this, holding someone's hand, it felt so new to me. Both comforting and uncomfortable. In truth, I had only continued to grip his hand because of my twisted curiosity over the sensation.

It was growing darker; day was turning into night. The temperature was dropping. We were only wearing the rags given to us in the chambers far below Audra, so the wind felt as if it were laughing at our excuse for clothing. I started shivering violently. In response, the man squeezed my hand tighter. Soon, he was shivering too.

About an hour after that, our horses came to a sudden stop. Someone very roughly grabbed me by the waist and shoved me off the horse and onto the ground. I could hear the same thing happening to my companions. I was still barefoot. The ground felt...wet? Earthy? We were in some sort of woodland. That much was already obvious based on the smells surrounding us, but not many places had this level of vegetation or rich...

Jurasa. Jurasa did, or so I'd heard.

We were pushed forwards in a certain direction, with no consideration for our frozen, confused state. I debated asking where we were going but didn't see the point. I knew I would find out soon enough.

The girl started crying again.

"Shut her up!" a male voice said to someone.

"What do you expect me to do?" another male voice replied defensively.

"I don't care, whatever you need to do. We didn't come all this way for this brat to finish us off."

"Alright, alright, let me deal with it."

We all stopped. Footsteps sounded to our left, growing more distant as they approached the girl. The woman, her mother, perhaps, was begging for mercy. My breathing rate increased. It hit me then how exhausted I was. Each breath felt like a monumental effort for my intercostal muscles. All my muscles were weak, after all, I'd been stuck underground for years. Vessels were able to exercise, it was encouraged, to keep us 'healthy' and 'drainable.'

But there was only so much exercise you could do, after killing one of the guards.

Eventually, by way of a cloth in her mouth I assumed, the girl's crying became muffled and then stopped.

The man returned behind us. "Done, are you happy?"

"Thank you."

Thank you? These two men must be friends, or friendly at least. They didn't sound the type of men who would sell people as captives. Then again, I hardly knew how that type would sound. I was only familiar with the kind who would.

After walking for some time, my legs began to tremble incessantly, which only got worse as we made our way uphill. At the top, we arrived at what seemed like a campsite. I could make out the sounds of a tent flapping open and closed and the smell of campfires being lit and burning.

We were dragged into one of the tents. I could tell because the wind had stopped snapping at my skin so harshly and the lighting changed from that of a silver glow to candles and flamed torches.

Without meaning to, I fell to the ground, my legs gave out on me almost instantly.

The man I had been travelling with heard my fall. He reached out with his bound hands, trying to find me, patting at my shoulders.

But before he could go further, someone yanked my hood off, and his, and the woman's, and the child's.

I was right, we were inside a tent, a spacious one. A large table sat at its centre, surrounded by a few chairs and a large bed to the left. Maps, scrolls, weapons, and clothing were strewn about the place in a non-orderly fashion.

Someone stepped inside from behind us.

"This is them?"

"Yes," one of the possibly non-captive selling men replied.

A large boot stopped next to me. I barely had the strength to look up.

"How long have you been a Vessel?" He didn't sound interrogatory, but he didn't sound patient about my answer either.

I was still looking at his feet. I debated saying nothing. I didn't know who these people were or what they would do with such information, but the thought about what they might do if I remained silent was enough for me to sigh out.

"What year is it?"

"1118," he replied.

I swallowed, hiding the shock tearing at my chest.

"Nineteen years," I half whispered, processing it myself as I spoke.

"Shit," one of the men said. "That's…they don't usually survive that long."

"No," the man who had asked me added. "They don't."

I didn't know that. I didn't know I was meant to be dead already.

I wondered if that might have been better.

The man crouched and lifted my chin. I knew my tired eyes could barely stay open, that my mouth was cracked and my face ashen, but I didn't care. He examined my facial features with great curiosity and confusion.

"Your hair is coppery but…" He squinted and went mute for a few seconds. "Where are you from?"

"I don't know," I replied.

I took in his facial features. He was older, his dark brown skin indicating he was from Zeima. His long braided hair was dark, but laced grey with age, and his face was decorated with slight wrinkles. One of his thick eyebrows had a deep scar across it.

He closed his eyes for a moment as he pressed two fingers to my forehead.

He stood so quickly I almost fell to the ground as he let go of my face.

"She's an Acciperean," he said to the men who had brought us here.

"Oh…well, that's a good thing, isn't it?" one remarked casually. The Zeiman didn't answer him.

"What about you, young man?" he asked my travelling companion.

Clearly seeing no reason to put himself through possible punishment either, he responded, "I am too. So are they." He nodded to the mother and child, sparing them the same questioning.

"How did you find them?" the Zeiman asked the two men behind us.

"The same way we always find them."

"Bring Nyla here, now," the man said commandingly. "And Riece."

"Yes?" Riece said.

"Bring them some clothes and get them some food. And bring the blades for the shackles"

"Alright, but we don't have much…err… women's clothing."

"We don't have much clothing," I muttered under my breath, still shivering in my thin rags.

"What the lady said," the Zeiman responded to Riece, smiling.

Once Riece and his possible friend left the tent, the Zeiman spoke.

"I'm Yaseer. A Darean."

"Lucky you," I muttered again. I'm not quite sure where my audacity came from. Exhaustion, hunger, and pain, I supposed.

"Luck, is it? Acciperean or Darean's, we are all slaves. None of us are free."

Embarrassment clutched my chest. I sighed heavily. "Sorry," I said. It was all I had the energy to say.

"There is no need for apologies. I know what you allude to. Accipereans are hunted far more forcefully. You are drained more often and more harshly. You are fewer in number."

"Yes," I groaned, wondering why he had bothered to refute my statement if he agreed with it.

"What are your names?"

"Baz," the man next to me said.

"Prya," the woman said, "This is my daughter Enala."

"And you?" the man asked me.

"I don't know," I admitted, swallowing to try and regain some moisture in my throat between words.

"The drainings?"

"No, I just…don't know it."

I could feel Baz looking down at me with sympathy. I still didn't have the energy to raise my head up or stand.

"Choose one then," Yaseer instructed.

I laughed. It was the kind of laugh that made me sound insane and ended with a loud sigh.

I'm not sure I wanted a name. There was something about having no name that made some of the pain easier. I didn't know who I was, but I didn't remember who I was beforehand either. I'm not sure I wanted to start discovering myself. I'm not sure I'd like what I'd find or be able to bear the fact that person was lost.

"It doesn't matter," I spoke.

"A name is everything…you are nobody without a name." Yaseer proclaimed.

"Then I am nobody."

"Nobody is nobody."

"Well, I have no name so that must make me nobody," I mumbled at the floor.

Yaseer fell silent for a few seconds then said.

"Nemina."

I found the strength to raise my eyes up at him.

"Nemina. It means Nobody. That is what we will call you." He sounded pleased with himself.

I knew my upper lip was raised in a scowl at his suggestion, but I was too tired to hide it.

"So Nemina…tell me, what can you do?"

"What do…" I caught my breath "What do you mean?"

"What are your abilities?"

Baz, as if sensing my struggle intervened. "Not everyone has fully manifested theirs before they're…taken. We don't get to find out. There's no way for us to truly experiment with them. We might find out by mistake, but we don't really know."

It dawned on me then. "You…you've never been a Vessel?" I asked Yaseer.

Yaseer looked almost guilty as he replied, "I have not."

Baz and I looked at each other in surprise.

"So, you are lucky then," I retorted.

Yaseer laughed. "If you can call running for your life luck."

"I would, in comparison," I said, with a clear and loud voice, for the first time during the conversation.

"And I am sorry you have endured it. Truly."

I sighed, embarrassed again. This man had a way of making me feel like an impudent child. Even though everything I had said had been fair. Mostly.

Yaseer continued. "I want to help you. I want to help the others."

"Why did you drag us here like captives then?" Baz asked, sounding doubtful.

"We always do that. To protect our location."

"Who do you think we would tell?" Prya spoke up.

"Nobody in particular." He smirked in my direction, clearly thinking about the name he had given me. "But I would rather be safe."

It was hard to argue with his logic, but it still felt…flawed somehow.

Riece and his possible friend returned, carrying an eclectic mix of clothing that had clearly come from each of the Five Kingdoms.

"This is all we had."

"This is fine," Yaseer confirmed. "Where's—"

"She's still in Kalnasa."

Yaseer nodded. "Of course." He spun his head in our direction. "Riece will bring you some food and water. In the morning, we will talk."

"Talk about what?" Baz asked.

Yaseer looked over his shoulder as he left the tent.

"About war."

# CHAPTER 16- ELIAS

"Get me more wine," I barked at the serving boy standing outside my chambers. He looked at me as if a Chimera had entered the hallway, rather than a person.

"What is wrong with you boy? Wine. Get. Me. Some. Wine."

"Yes, My Lord." He scurried down the hallway like a field mouse.

I sighed and groaned as I lay back on my bed.

"Fuck!" I yelled as my leg was pierced with a knife-like pain again.

I sat up sharply and immediately sent the room spinning.

"Back down, back down, back down," I chanted to myself as I braced one hand on my forehead and another on my thigh.

There was a knock on the door.

"Why are you knocking? Just bring it here," I shouted at the ceiling.

The clipped measured steps that circled around my bed were not of the shivering servant boy.

"My Lord."

I scowled into my arm. "What is it, Trenton? Aren't you meant to be scoring potential brides on a scale from 'too opinionated' to 'perfectly docile'?"

"I left that to the hands of the other Councilmen... as did you."

"I make no secret of my feelings about the Council's activities. You on the other hand..." I dropped my arm to look at him.

"I do what I must."

"*Must* you visit me now?"

"I needed to speak with you, My Lord."

"About what?"

"About your responsibilities." Trenton sounded as if he was approaching a child.

"What responsibilities?" I sat up more slowly this time. Trenton's face was slightly blurry, but he wasn't moving in front of me, which was a marked improvement from my last attempt at being upright.

"You and I both know my responsibility is for show, it's non-existent and I have never minded that at all. You're the military man, Fargreaves kisses the arse of the other Kingdom's ambassadors to maintain alliances and trade. Raynard upholds the law...most likely while breaking it himself and Wayman, is it? What does he do again? Other than marry girls young enough to be his fucking granddaughter every two years."

"He handles finances," Trenton reminded me.

"That's it," I clicked my fingers. "So, you see Trenton, there's nothing left for me to be responsible for is there?" I shrugged, "What a shame."

"We have discussed it with His Highness, and he agrees."

I closed my eyes and shook my head. "I don't care what you bloody agreed."

"We would like you to lead our armies."

I was so stunned by his statement, I forgot about how drunk I was, swivelling my head in Trenton's direction far too fast.

"This is low, even for you," I enunciated slowly.

"You have much fighting experience. You are one of the finest swordsmen this Kingdom has ever seen."

"Yes, and as well as my supreme experience I also have…one leg. One. Not two. In case you had forgotten." I patted my prosthetic. "People usually have two and that helps quite a bit when they're in the middle of a battle and trying to maintain things like balance and well…their fucking lives."

"I had not forgotten, My Lord."

"Well then, maybe you had forgotten how I lost it in the first place."

"I have not."

"You can see my reluctance then surely?" I smiled sarcastically at him. "I was done with fighting years ago. I told you and I told him that. I won't be killing any more men and I'd quite like to keep my other leg actually."

Trenton took a deep breath in. "We need you to train the soldiers."

I stood suddenly. Fuck, the room started to spin again. I steadied myself against the edge of the bed.

"I said *no* Trenton. Do not ask me again. I have said no many times before. I'm not quite sure why an intelligent man such as yourself is finding *one* simple word so difficult to understand. I will *not* be training soldiers, I will *not* be joining an army, I will *not* be fighting in an army. If that means my place on the Council is forfeit, then so be it. You and I both know I couldn't give a fuck."

"Come to Council this Friday…Eliel will explain." He spoke softly, like he was trying to tame a wild animal.

"Eliel is…" I cleared my throat trying to calm down. I started my sentence again. "You've fought before, haven't you, Trenton?"

"Yes, My Lord."

"Eliel hasn't. He doesn't know what he's asking of me. You do… and yet you are asking."

"That is because we are facing a far greater threat than any of us have ever encountered in our lifetimes. Nobody wants to fight, My Lord, but we do not have a choice."

I peered at him. "What threat?"

"Come to Council, we will explain then."

"Council is far too early in the morning. I will not wake up at first light to hear something you could easily tell me now."

Trenton silently looked at the door, then back at me.

"You know I won't come, Trenton, so it's now or never. I haven't had any alcohol in about..." I stopped and pointed upwards, calculating, "An hour, so my patience is running out."

Trenton opened his mouth to speak, when a knock at the door, and a frightened boy's voice travelled through the door. "Your wine, My Lord."

Trenton looked at me.

"Bring me the wine, will you?" I asked him.

Trenton narrowed his eyes at me, unhappy with my order.

"Oh, and give him the empty one back." I waved in a perfunctory manner towards the table.

Trenton yanked the door open with such force, I was surprised it didn't come off its hinges. He grabbed the jug of wine from the boy's hand with equal impatience, then shoved the empty one into his arms.

He outstretched his arm towards me.

"I can't drink it from a jug, can I?" In truth I would happily have taken it straight out of the jug, but seeing Trenton's perfected role crumble at the hands of simple instructions was entertaining. A man who dedicated himself to the service of others, or so he said, was finding it impeccably difficult to pour me a drink.

Trenton walked over to my desk, took one of the unwashed glasses from it, and threw it on my bed.

"Come, Trenton," I mocked him, "I thought we were friends."

"Must you always act this way?"

"And which way is that exactly?"

"Like an impudent adolescent, My Lord," he droned. "You are twenty-eight."

"Act this way as opposed to what way exactly?" I poured some of the wine into the glass and began to drink. "How everybody else acts? Acts. You're all acting." I waved my hands theatrically. "You're all pretending. You're all snakes, shedding different skin, taking on new patterns around different people. You're all poisonous... fucking... snakes."

The alcohol was as usual, loosening my tongue far too much. I, as usual, didn't give a shit.

"Like I said, I do what I must, so does everyone else."

"Only that's not actually true is it, Trenton?" I swallowed another glass. "Not everyone does this to survive, some people do it because they actually like it. They enjoy it. They feed off it like a disease that spreads to the minds of others. They crave it like...well like wine." I tapped the side of my glass. "I'd much rather crave this, than power."

"Power can protect you. Alcohol will only kill you."

I scoffed into my third glass. "It didn't protect my dear aunt and uncle, did it?"

Trenton stiffened up.

"So, you're wrong. That's..." I sniffed. "That's what's so fucked about it don't you see? You all convince yourselves you're going to be untouchable if you can *justtt* get your hands on that piece of land, that mount of gold, that...bride." I thought about the sixteen-year-old girl who had been at the ceremony earlier and grimaced.

"But you're not untouchable Trenton, nobody is," I finished.

"Wielders killed your aunt and uncle," Trenton replied.

I stopped pouring my wine. "What?"

"It was sorcery. That is how they died."

I stared at the wall. My mind gifted me with flashbacks to the day I lost my leg. Not even the wine could stop those glimpses now, only dull them. But I remembered. I remembered the way the earth had moved, the way the branches had circled around my thigh and broken my bone and...

I swallowed a fourth glass.

"Shit," is all I could say.

"We anticipate more attacks. We assume they are regrouping, in much larger numbers this time."

"Well, we're all fucked then."

Trenton grabbed the glass out of my hand before I could drink a fifth.

"Is this your plan? Drink yourself into oblivion until the sorcerers are knocking down our doors, killing innocent men, women, and children?"

"It's quite hard to have a plan of any kind, when you've only just told me about the sorcerers less than a minute ago."

Trenton went to reply but I continued. "Buuut...I do like the sound of tha...particular plan." My speech was beginning to slur.

"Your adamance at drowning in self-pity serves no purpose, and it most certainly does not garner the sympathy you expect," Trenton said with contempt.

"Ha," I bit out a laugh, raising a brow. "Is that what you think it is? You think I want your sympathy?"

Their sympathy, their sorrow, their remorse. I wanted no part in it.

Trenton ground his jaw. "You could be the difference between us having armies that could win this war or armies that don't stand a chance."

"Trenton...we don't stand a fucking chance anyway. We don't stand the tiniest, teeniest flicker ova shance." My speech continued to become more incoherent.

"I know what happened there but—"

"You know, yessss. But you were not there." My teeth were gritted now. "Were you?"

I stood very close to him, slightly towering over him. "Why... would I spend... the final few months of my life... sweating... and, and listening to the sound of dying men's screams? When I could be listening to... altogether different screams and sweating for an... altogether different reason, right here." I pointed at my bed, "In the comfort of my own bed...with wine."

"Does it work?" Trenton asked, looking at me with disapproval.

I grabbed the glass from his hands and took a sip from it.

"Does it matter?" I mumbled, after swallowing.

"I should think so?"

"No Trenton, it doesn't work. But..." I tapped my eyelids. "It stops me from dreaming." Then I tapped my thigh. "And this from hurting." I sighed, looking behind his shoulder. "Which... is reason enough."

"What a sorry figure you have become," he said quietly.

"Would you look at that?" I threw him a false grin. "I garnered your sympathy after all. Feel free to feel sorry for me... as long as you never disturb me again."

"Do you have no honour? No sense of duty? Of loyalty?" Trenton hissed.

"Not anymore," I grumbled.

"Then did you ever have it in the first place?" Trenton sounded disappointed.

I stepped closer to Trenton again. He flinched. "I should think my lack of a limb would answer that question, wouldn't you?" I didn't hide my anger at his ridiculous question.

Trenton backed away. "Your Council seat remains yours, Lord Elias, should you change your mind."

"I won't. You can fuck off now."

"My Lord," he groaned and walked out.

As soon as he did, I roared and threw my glass at the wall. It smashed and sank to the ground in pieces. I rubbed both my hands over my face and stared at the shards.

Well, that had done it. I had tried my best to not think about that day, every waking second for the past five years. And there had been Trenton, who had become a walking, talking reminder of it just now.

Fucking prick.

I wouldn't sleep tonight. There was no point in even trying. There was only one reasonable solution to this utter travesty of a day. A place where I could forget about everything for a short while.

I grabbed my coat and coins and headed to the Solar Inn.

# CHAPTER 17 – NEMINA

I didn't know what to make of the clothes Riece had brought me. I'd never seen so many colours. I didn't even know how the majority of them were worn. They looked like intricate contraptions designed to trap your limbs.

There were some pants. I recognised pants. They were deep red in colour, almost black. They were tight. That felt unusual. I'd only ever worn loose clothing. I'd only ever been given loose clothing. Wearing these was like wearing a second skin. They were supple, flexible. I liked them.

I didn't have any undergarments. I had no desire to reveal my starved frame's more filled out areas to these strangers or to anyone. I glanced at the shirts, searching for one with longer sleeves. I picked up a white one. It was clearly intended for a male body, but that made it perfect for this occasion. It had laces near the top and slightly ruffled sleeves at the end. I ran my finger along those ruffles, their texture was delicate and soft. There were patterns running through the shirt, so intricate and fine they looked as if they had been woven into the garment by light itself.

My gaze was drawn to a black jacket with silver buttons, buckles, and a silver lining. It was exactly like the one the guards had worn at Audra, but longer, more magnificent even. I approached it and rubbed the edge of a sleeve between my fingers.

I put it on.

There was something so disgusting and yet tantalising about wearing it, about wearing the uniform I had only ever seen as a source of brutality and pain. This jacket had been discarded amongst a pile of more discarded clothing, forgotten, left to gather dust in a corner. Once, it had been a symbol, and now it was nothing.

Now, it was mine.

I hoped one day I could return to that place. I'd like to kill some of those guards wearing this.

Kill them with their own swords, in their own clothes. A pattern seemed to be emerging. I chuckled quietly then stopped suddenly.

*I'm going insane.*

I sighed.

*Hardly surprising.*

I was about to take it off, shaking my head, when somebody stepped into the tent.

"Please tell me you're not wearing that." Baz sounded displeased.

I took a moment to process his presence.

"There's not exactly much to choose from, is there?" I snapped back.

"What are you talking about? This is more choice than we've had in years." He put his hands on his hips, glancing at the pile of clothes with the same awe in his eyes as I had, just minutes earlier.

"And yet you chose that." I pointed at his attire. He was wearing a pale, mint green tunic. It was high necked and covered in iridescent floral golden patterns. His pants were an equally fluorescent gold, and were partially see through, like curtains. "You look…" I tilted my head to the side, trying to find the words. "Colourful."

He shrugged, "I like it." He fiddled with the waistband of his trousers. "Why would I want a reminder of that?" He pointed back at my outfit. "Why would you?"

"I like the idea of murdering them in it."

Baz snorted out a laugh, but when he realised I wasn't joking, he looked startled. I thought about how my words must have sounded, but I didn't care much for platitudes and conjectures, and I was far too exhausted for them.

"Murdering who?"

"The people who wear these things."

"Right." Baz looked uncomfortable. "They're not here though so…."

I laughed at his expression. "Don't worry. I'm not planning on murdering anyone at the moment."

"At… the moment?" His voice was drawn out and thin.

I took off the jacket and put on another, similar one that was dark brown and leathery. "Better?"

He nodded. "You looked like Gina in the other one."

"Gina?" I asked.

"You know, very short, dark, black eyes. She used brass knuckles to—"

"Oh, guard number eight."

"I didn't know they had numbers."

"They didn't. I just gave them numbers."

Baz was looking at me with increasing concern. "Why?"

"I never learnt most of their names after I was sent…below."

"I see," Baz said, now looking at me with pity.

I crossed my arms. "What are you doing here?"

"I just thought that we should talk about…all of this."

"What is there to talk about?"

Baz looked dejected at my tone. I suddenly realised this was probably the longest conversation both he and I had with anyone for years. He was probably hoping for it to be warmer.

He stepped closer to me, lowering his voice. "Everything. Like why we were being sent to Kalnasa in the first place?"

"That doesn't matter now."

"Yes, it does. The transfers, they've been doing them more frequently. Why?"

"I don't know."

"I'm not saying that you know. I'm saying that it doesn't make sense. And why did these people free us? What do they want? What do they mean by help and by... *war*?"

I sighed and looked at the ground. I knew I was probably coming across as an imperturbable, inhumane person, but the truth was I just didn't care.

"Nemina? Are you even listening to me."

"Don't call me that," I said bluntly.

"I don't have anything else to call you. Unless you want me to call you by your captive code?"

"I don't want to speak to you at all." I was being rude. I knew I was. Still, I couldn't muster the ability to care, or to feel guilty about it. My mind was riddled with far too much information, too many memories, too many possibilities.

Baz jerked his head back as if offended. "Look. I get it. You don't want to talk to me, or anyone. But we're here now and we've got to figure out what to do."

"There is no we. I don't even know you."

"Out of everyone here, you know me the most."

"That's not a reason to trust you or talk to you."

"I'm not asking you to trust me, I'm asking you to be on my side, and I'll be on yours."

"I don't need you on my side." This discussion was becoming more tiring by the second. I wasn't sure how much more clearly I could indicate I didn't want him here.

Baz walked to the precipice of the bed and sat down. "You know, I heard about what you did."

I debated dragging him out of the tent but the deep fatigue setting in my bones throbbed in protest.

"Everyone heard about what I did." I sighed.

"I hated Karll. He was a pervert. Just" — he scoffed— "The worst kind of human being."

"What are you getting at?" I asked, impatiently.

He licked his lips and spoke. "Did you know that after you killed him, after you were sent down there, that we all protested... for days? Did you know that?" He looked me in the eye. His eyes were dark, but warm. A rich brown. It was the first time I'd really focused on their colour, or the colour of anyone's eyes.

"Yes."

He seemed taken aback by my answer. "How did you know that?" He put both his arms behind him and leant back on the bed, half sat up.

"People died in those riots, and every time someone died, they came to tell me about it. They'd sit there and tell me their name, what they looked like, where they'd been from."

He looked horrified. "Oh."

"The first time, the first few times I screamed at them to stop. I'd tried to drown out their voices by bashing my fists against the floor, yelling, covering my ears, whatever." My voice sounded detached. "Then I gave up. It just kept happening for weeks. The irony is that I knew far more about them in their death than I would ever have been permitted to during their life. But they died because of my decisions."

Baz shook his head. "No. They made their own decisions. They fought because they wanted to. They knew the risks. We all did."

I understood then. "You fought in them too." I stated it as a fact, not a question.

"You became a bit of a symbol there, actually." He shrugged. The gesture sweeping truth beneath a veneer of indifference. I recognised it instantly. I had practiced such a thing myself. Many times.

I laughed wearily. "Sorry to disappoint you."

Baz opened his mouth, probably attempting to say he wasn't disappointed in me. But before he could, I raised my eyebrows in his direction, indicating I already knew it would be a lie.

"My point is that those people, they didn't know you, but they fought for you anyway, of their own free will. We don't know each other. But we could. We could know each other, and we could fight together. I have a feeling we'll need someone in our corner if we're going to get through this...whatever this is."

I thought about it. I would be better off alone. I didn't need to be worrying about someone else's welfare. I didn't want that. I trusted myself, at least enough to know my actions would be based on what I thought was best for myself, and my chances at survival.

And yet, I might need help at some point. I was aware of all the possibilities that could arise, the different things which could go wrong. In a large proportion of them, being alone would save me, but in an even larger number, being alone might be the reason I die.

I leant against the bed frame and put one leg over the other. I was still barefoot.

"To answer your burning questions," I started, and Baz smiled slightly, sitting up. "I couldn't care less about the intentions of these people because I don't plan to stay here for any longer than necessary. Do you have a problem with that? Because if so, our partnership isn't going to last more than a few hours."

Baz took a second to think. "No... I don't have a problem with that. But we can't leave tonight, they're expecting us to talk to them tomorrow, and we haven't even figured out how to get out of here yet."

"I know that." I nodded. "We stay here until we gain enough of their trust to formulate an escape plan. Then we're gone."

"What if they do really want to help other people like us though? Shouldn't we help them do that?"

"Like I said," I repeated, "I'm leaving. You decide what you're going to do and let me know."

"I already said that I'd come with you."

"Great," I said, sounding less than enthusiastic. "Oh, and don't ever burst into my tent again. I could have been naked."

Baz laughed. I was so confused by the sound that I uncrossed my arms and turned to face him. His laugh was high pitched, light, almost like a giggle. He waved his hand around in the air in front of him.

"You don't need to worry about that. I don't..." He cleared his throat "Women don't interest me."

"That's wonderful. I'm so happy for you," I said flatly. "My privacy does interest me though."

The amused look on Baz's face slowly dissipated. "Fine, fine."

I had an idea.

"Sleep here."

"Did you not hear what I just said?" Baz looked genuinely bewildered.

"Don't be ridiculous." I threw him a reproachful look. "We'll take turns sleeping, the other person will keep watch."

"I thought you didn't trust me two minutes ago."

"I still don't. But I trust these people even less."

"What are we going to say if someone asks why—"

"We'll say we were making passionate love all night. That against all odds, we formed a bond during captivity as Vessels. Something heart wrenching and emotional. That should embarrass them enough to avoid any follow up questions."

Baz's jaw dropped. He couldn't seem to get his head around my sharp way of speaking.

I made my way to the bed and grabbed a blanket from it.

"So, what, now we've got to act like we're in love? This partnership is moving very quickly." He raised his palms into the air.

"I'm sure you'll manage."

Noticing I was placing the blanket on the floor in front of the bed. Baz said, "It's fine you can sleep first."

"I know, I was going to do that."

"The bed is here," Baz gestured to it, behind him.

I pointed at it. "I haven't slept in a bed like that since I killed Karll. I'm used to sleeping on the floor." I settled down on the blanket and lay down, looking up at the ceiling.

Baz's arm slowly dropped. I could feel his eyes on me from across the room.

I turned my head to the side. "What is it?"

"You didn't eat the food they left there." He pointed at the table.

"Again, I wasn't exactly fed much as a convicted murderer. I could only eat some of it before I felt sick."

Baz silently glanced at me for longer than was comfortable, then walked towards the bed.

"Wake me in a few hours."

"I'm still calling you Nemina."

"No, you're not."

"Do you have a better alternative?"

"You don't need to call me anything."

"That would be a bit strange don't you think. Considering how madly in love we are?"

I made a grunting noise of displeasure and lay on my side.

"How about Nemi?"

"Stop talking."

"Nem?"

"Please be quiet."

"Mina?"

I was about to tell Baz that if he suggested a name for me one more time, I would personally tape his mouth shut.

"Nemina it is then."

I gave up.

"Goodnight, Nemina."

I thought he had finally stopped talking until he said, "That's unusual isn't it."

"What is?" I asked reluctantly.

"Saying goodnight to someone." He sounded as if he was on the verge of crying.

He was right. It was. It rang like some unfamiliar entity in my ears.

"Not as unusual as your outfit is," I said after a moment's silence.

He chuckled softly.

We both said nothing after that. I didn't sleep at all. I still didn't trust Baz wouldn't slit my throat in my slumber. I wanted to see if he would do anything while he thought I was unconscious.

He didn't.

He lightly tapped my shoulder around four hours later to *"wake me up."* I sat up and leant against the foot of the bed. I found myself lost in thought, taking in each and every detail of the tent's interior. My eyes found their way back to the coat from Audra.

I smiled to myself. Yes, that coat was mine.

\*\*\*

The next morning crept upon me like a silent predator. The lighting gradually dissolved from a silver-streaked indigo into a warm orange as the sun rose. I still wasn't used to that, to sunlight. It felt painful. I covered my eyes with my hand and looked down at the ground. Maybe if I squeezed them hard enough, I could shut the light out, shut it all out.

"Keeping watch, I see," Baz's sleep lulled voice sounded from behind me.

"The night is over," I grumbled.

"Since when has that ever stopped anybody?" Baz scoffed. He was right about that.

"You can eat some of this." I walked over to the table of the food I hadn't much touched, and handed him the platter, sitting on the edge of the bed.

"Thanks." He sat up, grabbing some fruit off the plate. I did the same.

"So," he said between mouthfuls. "Do we wait for them here? Or do we try to find them ourselves?"

"I need more time," I declared flatly, looking at my distorted reflection in the silver of the plate.

"Time to do what?"

I sighed. "My eyes. I'm not used to the light. I don't think I can...go looking," I said bitterly. It irritated me beyond belief. I felt powerless. I was sick of that feeling.

"Fuck. Not used to a bed. Not used to food. Not used to the light. They really punished you."

"They'll get what's coming."

Baz raised an eyebrow.

"Once I can see, that is," I scoffed under my breath.

"Urrr, lady, can I come in?" Riece's silhouette was outside.

Baz looked panicked.

"Yes, come in," I answered before Baz could try to hide.

"We're having breakfast and.... oh... urrrr." Riece scratched the back of his head, looking around the room awkwardly once he noticed Baz in the bed. "That saves me the walk to his tent at least, ha."

"You were saying?" I urged him to continue.

"Yes, I was. Yaseer wants you to join us. For breakfast, that is."

"We'll be there soon," I said, nodding.

"Alright, ummm...alright." He hurried out.

Once he was gone, Baz turned to me.

"What are you going to do?" he sounded wary.

"We have to go. I'll bear it." I stood and lifted the hood of the brown leather jacket over my head, so that it partially covered my eyes.

"Here we go then." He pulled the tent's flaps open.

Baz and I walked outside.

The sun was much, much worse than I had anticipated.

I had forgotten how bright it was. Everything looked so white and reflective. Everything gleamed so unnaturally. Everything was attacking my sight with colour and brightness. I couldn't take it all in fast enough. It reminded me of the stories people had shared on how the world had appeared, when Acciperean sorcery was lost. There was too much life, too much light. I sucked in a sharp breath and involuntarily groaned at the pain the sun had caused, not only in my eyes, but throughout my entire body. It was so hot too. It burnt, caressed my skin like a blistering flame.

"Nemina?" Baz whispered, gently grabbing my elbow.

"It's...fine."

"It's clearly not. Maybe you should wait inside and—"

"No," I cut him off.

"You can barely walk out here."

"That's not true."

Baz sighed, clearly not wanting to attend the meeting alone.

"Just close your eyes and look down, I'll lead you there."

Before I had time to protest, Baz started dragging me along, and I, not being foolish enough to refuse the opportunity to spare my eyes, closed them.

I was used to that. I was used to having to accept things I didn't like. I was used to making decisions with my head and not my heart.

I used to imagine things. I used to imagine a life where I was free, or at least not underground. I used to imagine a life where I made decisions based on what I wanted, what I desired. I created scenarios and people. I dreamt up love, friendship, sorrow, travels, because it was the only way I could live. Inside my own head.

But it was also the worst place to live. There were so many things lurking there, much darker than my imagination.

Baz stopped and I opened my eyes slowly. From the bottom half of my vision, I could make out a small group of people sitting around a scant fire and eating what smelt like bread of some kind.

"Aaaahh here they are, care for some?" someone offered.

"We'll pass, thank you," Baz answered for us.

"Really? You both look like you haven't eaten in weeks," he insisted.

"Almost as if we've been prisoners or something," I said, my face and eyes still locked at my feet.

I couldn't see their reactions, but I could hear teasing laughter directed at the man. Baz gripped my arm slightly harder.

So much for making decisions with my head.

Someone stepped into the left side of my view. I recognised the dark thick boots from the day before. "Leave them be."

"We were only offering them some food," a female voice protested.

"Come with me," Yaseer commanded in our direction.

Baz led me inside the same tent we had been brought to yesterday. Cautiously, slowly, I raised my head but left my hood up.

There were more people here this time.

Yaseer stood at the edge of the large table. Surrounding its other edges were Riece and Fasal, but there were new faces as well.

A woman with light brown skin and short silver hair peered at us curiously, her arms crossed. Next to her, a young man sat, one of his brown eyes was surrounded by purple swelling. Opposite them were two women. One tall, lean, her features sharp, and her brown hair the same shade as my jacket.

The other was an older woman. Her face was hard and cold, but her green eyes were luminous. Her dark blond hair was tied up, coiled around a golden pin. She looked Baz and I up and down with dissatisfaction.

As her eyes rested on me, her lips grew noticeably tighter. She took in a deep breath, jerking her head away from us.

"They're nothing but skin and bone, Yaseer," she said, still appraising us.

"Do not be fooled by their current state Ullna. You know what they harbour."

"Are you sure about this?" She spoke to Yaseer with far more confidence than Riece and Fasal had.

"Do you doubt me? After all this time?"

"It is not you I doubt." Her gaze slid over to us again.

"I think we need them," the battered man spoke up. "We haven't freed an Acciperean for years, let alone two."

"Four," I corrected them.

The bruised man looked at me, and then stole nervous glances at both Yaseer and Ullna.

"Alas. Not anymore," Yaseer said softly.

"Not anymore? What did you do to them?" Baz flared up immediately.

"*We* didn't do anything, boy, other than save your lives in case you had forgotten?" Ullna spoke.

"Where are they?" I asked, avoiding the implication of murder.

"The child is alive, but the mother..." Yaseer trailed off.

"Prya," Baz interjected.

"Prya...did not make it through the night. She had a deep wound hidden behind her rags. It had become infected."

"And we're just supposed to believe that?" Baz sounded furious.

"Trust me young man, we value your lives, we value your gifts. We would not wish to see any sorcerer leave this world, especially not an Acciperean."

This was beginning to feel familiar. Our value was tied to our abilities. Yet again.

"I am sorry," Yaseer spoke carefully.

"Her child? What will happen to Enala?" Baz asked.

"Her child will stay with us. We will look after her."

"Until she's older, and she can fight in your...war?" I spoke up.

Ullna tutted. The silver haired woman smirked. Yaseer gave me that same disappointed, burrowing glare.

"We will be done with the war long before that child is grown," he asserted.

"She will have no chance to grow, should you lose," I replied.

"And what will she grow into should we do nothing? We are fighting for children like her, and for all the children that will come after," the woman with brown hair spoke up.

"And when do you expect they'll be arriving?" I said to her. "Since repopulating sorcerers is so strictly regulated. Or is that you expect the members of your troupe to handle the task?"

Yaseer straightened up, taking the fists he had been leaning on the table off it. "I understand your scepticism. I do. But you and I both know that no future is better than a future where nothing changes, Nemina. We have been collating a network for years now, liberating sorcerers from their captivity all across Athlion, as often as possible. Soon, we will have enough to strike back, and fight for the future we deserve."

"It sounds as if you've already decided what I know, for me, and for everyone else."

"This is the only option we have."

"Dying?" I asked.

"I told you, we're wasting our time on these two," Ullna said proudly, her green eyes glinting with disdain.

"Oh no," the silver haired woman disagreed. "I think they're perfect."

"Of course you do, Nyla," Ullna rolled her eyes. "They have no desire to help us. They've made themselves clear. You heard them."

"We don't even know what you want our help with," Baz refuted.

Silence fell for a few seconds.

"Do either of you recognise... this?" Yaseer pulled something out of his pocket and pressed it to the table with an outstretched hand.

Baz and I looked at each other, deeply confused.

"Are we supposed to?" Baz said.

"Do you?" Yaseer reiterated.

"No," Baz answered. Yaseer turned to me.

"No. I don't," I replied cautiously.

"This was found on one of the guards accompanying you to Kalnasa."

"I...don't...what is it?" Baz's upper lip rose in irritation.

"It's Noxscroll," Fasal spoke up.

"I've never heard of it," Baz said.

"It's extremely rare. Made in Audra, where you and I are from." He looked at Baz. "You can't read what's written on it without Noxstone," Fasal said.

"Also, extremely rare," Nyla added.

"Right," Fasal nodded in confirmation.

"What does this have to do with us?" I asked.

"Everything." Nyla leant against the table with one hand. "You should not have been travelling there in such a large number. Four transitions at once is almost unheard of. Four Accipereans being transferred, that's..." She struggled to find the words.

"A sign that something greater is at play," Yaseer finished her sentence.

"There are things we cannot do. Things you can. We need your skills," Nyla explained.

"To do what... exactly?" Baz asked before I could.

"To make sure we win," the bruised man said.

"We told you yesterday," Baz started, "We don't know how to use our powers. We weren't allowed to understand them."

"Yes...Yaseer told me that." Nyla looked at him. "But you can learn. I will teach you. You are not the first to arrive here without such knowledge. Besides" — she shrugged — "you are naturally stronger and swifter than non-magic wielders. That's a good start."

"We haven't agreed to anything yet," I reminded them.

Ullna stepped forwards. "Where else do you have to go, girl? We are giving you a chance. A chance to learn what you are and what you're capable of. A chance to have somewhere to sleep, to eat, to bathe. A chance to make something of your life. A chance to fight. That is more than you could ever have dreamed of a few nights ago."

I stepped forwards, closer to her. The bruised man stood. I looked at him and furrowed my brow. Did he think I was going to attack her?

I looked back at Ullna. "Don't try to frame this as a chance for me, when we both know that this is a chance for *you*."

"It's a chance for us all. This isn't just about you. Or is that you're simply too selfish to see that?"

"*Selfish?*" I sneered and stepped closer to her again. She didn't react at all, but her eyes betrayed surprise at the movement.

"I've had people make decisions for me all my life. I've had people control my life for as long as I can remember. I was never, not at any point, allowed to decide for myself. I was never allowed to be selfish. How can I be something I've never had the opportunity to be? You say that this is a chance to make something of my life. It's not. It's a chance to make my life yours. It's a chance to be your captive, rather than theirs. I've earned my right to make a choice for myself, even if that choice is at the expense of others. I've earned my right to rest. I've earned my right to say no. You, and nobody else here" — I pointed around me — "will convince me otherwise."

Ullna's facial expression was contorted with a mixture of anger, shock, and disgust. "I knew he was wrong about you," she murmured to herself.

Yaseer, I assumed. It was his fault for placing me on a pedestal.

"As I said," Nyla broke the silence. "Perfect." She shrugged with her hands in the air.

I was aware the plan Baz and I had formulated the night before was falling apart. How would we gain the trust of these people when I was unable to bite my tongue? I was used to not having a voice. I was so used to suppressing my true feelings and thoughts, that I had assumed doing so would come naturally. But now, I couldn't stop speaking.

"Nineteen, near twenty years," Ullna stated. "You've survived as a Vessel far longer than anyone else ever has. Why do you think that is?"

I squinted at her, trying to understand the motive, or meaning behind her question. "I don't know."

"That's one of the reasons they move you around, didn't you realise? So that you never noticed when somebody died from the drainings, or...other circumstances. It's clever. It prevents any stories or rumours spreading about those deaths. It prevents people from grieving anyone."

*Amali.*

A deep pang blasted through my gut. That's how she had died, in all likelihood.

Ullna observed the look on my face. "You didn't realise," she said.

My silence confirmed I didn't.

"The fact remains. Nobody, I mean nobody since the Wielders' War has survived the drainings for that long."

I was still staring off to the side, through and not at the table.

"I have a theory," Ullna restarted. "I have many theories as to why, but they all have one thing in common. And that is your abilities...are different somehow. They are unique."

"How long before—"

"Before you? No longer than seven years had been recorded," her eyes drifted over my shoulder to look at Baz. "That's about as long as you were there young man. I'd say you had months left to live."

Baz gulped at the revelation.

Ullna focused back on my face. "You make your choice, and you make it your own. But do not convince yourself that running away from this, from this war, from yourself, is the only autonomous one. If anything, it is only fuelled by those who placed chains around you in the first place," she snapped.

Nyla added in a calmer voice. "Choose this. Choose to help us, and we can stop it."

I stepped backwards so that I was standing side by side with Baz again. I turned to meet his eye. I abruptly remembered his desperate punches against the side of the cart, his bloody knuckles, his voice cracking as he raised his chained hands and spoke.

*"This is killing me."*

And it literally had been. Baz would have been dead in another few months. Prya was dead. Amali was dead.

A part of my soul was dead too.

He had agreed. He had agreed to come with me. To leave this all behind, but I knew at this moment, that was not what he wanted. He wanted to fight. He wanted to try. For whatever reason, he believed in a better world.

I didn't.

I either lived in this one, running, or I died in the hope of never running again. Both options were terrible. But Baz had made up his mind and to my absolute horror with a resolute lift of his chin, he asked.

"What do you need us to do?"

# CHAPTER 18- LORIA

I couldn't do this. I couldn't. I didn't know what I was going to say to the Prince at this 'presentation' or what I was meant to say.

This is where it would begin. This is where I would need to start coaxing him towards the trap we were laying.

But laying traps was something Nathon was adept at, not me. Nathon, who seemed to have found getting through this whole ceremony as easy and naturally as breathing.

"It's an honour, Your Highness," Tarren said, as she curtsied low in front of him. Rhana made eye contact with me and made an ever so subtle expression of mocking disgust.

The Prince smiled subtly and nodded his head in acceptance of her greeting.

"My father respects you and your family to the highest degree. It would be the greatest honour for me to serve you, as he has served your family for generations," Tarren declared.

"Maybe not in *quite* the same way," Nathon muttered behind me, grinning. Rhana and Jayli, who were standing to our left, were the only ones to hear him. Rhana held back a smile.

There it was. Nathon could charm someone in one breath and choke them with another.

"Indeed, your father is a great ally to me," Prince Eliel responded courteously.

I wondered who her father was. Since she was his offspring, I found it highly unlikely her father could be a great ally to anyone, rather a great thorn in their side.

"I was humbled to have been chosen." She placed her hand on her chest.

I knew Tarren was playing her part well. I knew she was only following the script we were all expected to follow, but I couldn't help but feel disgusted at the complete and utter contrast between her real life and constructed persona.

I would have to build my own, and swiftly. That was the true reason for my revulsion. I was not revulsed at Tarren, but at the inevitability I would turn into her.

Prince Eliel stood in front of her like a statue, patient and serene. "I am pleased to hear it."

"*Elated, I'm sure,*" Nathon quipped again, more quietly this time.

"If you'll allow me, Your Highness, you look wonderful this evening," she added eagerly.

"You yourself, have been hard to ignore all evening, My Lady."

I squinted, ascertaining the hidden meaning behind the Prince's double-edged words.

Tarren displayed some more forced humility and curtseyed again. "You are too kind, Your Highness."

"I speak only the truth." Prince Eliel nodded very slightly and moved onto Dyna.

Dyna curtseyed and rose shakily. "Your Highness." She sounded both overjoyed and petrified.

"My Lady. Thank you for being here."

"I...You need not thank me, Your Highness, I am happy to be here."

"Of course, but still. I know things are difficult for Kalnasa as of late." The Prince gave the Captain behind her a long look. "I hope you know we will do everything we can to help."

The Captain nodded curtly. It seemed he was unsure of whether he could speak.

"That's very generous of you, Your Highness." She stared at him wide eyed.

Watching Dyna talk to the Prince was physically uncomfortable. There was no missing the fact she worshipped, admired, and revered him. Neither her age nor life experiences had afforded her enough to be able to look past his overwhelmingly majestic exterior. Her joy over what the rest of us knew to be a heavy task, felt like watching someone laugh throughout a funeral. It was so misplaced that I wanted nothing more than to drag Dyna away by the wrist, and tell her to go back home, to live, to be a child a while longer.

But I couldn't do any of those things. So, I stood there, a mirror of Prince Eliel's perfect statue.

He moved onto Maiwen next, who seemed to look into everyone she met rather than at them.

"Princess. I am pleased you are here, and even more so that your brother, the King, sees me as worthy of you."

Maiwen looked utterly startled at the implication he should be the one honoured to marry her, and not the other way around. Her gaze shifted across his face, as if searching for some kind of trap.

"You are the future King, Your Highness, you would be worthy of anyone," she replied carefully.

"How is your brother?" the Prince asked. I could sympathise with Maiwen. I, too, was questioned about my sibling on far too frequent a basis.

"He is well, Your Highness. He would be glad to know you asked after his welfare."

"You may inform him I did then, if it will please him."

"It will."

The exchange continued for another minute or so, and then Prince Eliel strolled to Rhana, who was certainly the calmest of the five of us.

No, that wasn't it. She only seemed the least concerned about the outcome.

"I was sorry to hear about your father, Princess. The Prince sounded remorseful. "I met him a few times. He was a very kind person, from what I could ascertain of his character."

Rhana smiled warmly. "He was. Thank you, Your Highness. I was sorry to hear about the late King and Queen. Their death was a sudden shock for us all."

She was brave, I thought, to bring up his parents.

"They were. I thank you for your condolences. They mean a great deal."

"I hope you will find a worthy Queen, Your Highness, to sit on the throne your mother once did."

It was an odd remark, I thought. There was the sense, at least to me, that Rhana was implying Prince Eliel's parents had never been worthy of the throne in the first place.

The Prince's tense silence made me suspect that he too, had felt strangely about her comment.

"I am sure she will be even more worthy, considering the candidates." He smiled tightly.

"Of course, Your Highness," she looked at him with sadness in her eyes, attempting to convey some sense of shared grief, I guessed.

"Your escort is the first female in the history of this event," Prince Eliel stated.

"Yes, Your Highness. That is permitted, is it not?"

"Of course. In fact, I am glad to see her here." He cast his eyes over Rhana's head and at Jayli. "I have always said myself that we should allow more female warriors into our ranks."

"An excellent proposition, Your Highness," Rhana confirmed.

"I believe so as well. Unfortunately, not everybody agrees. It is something I hope to change."

Behind him, Fargreaves and the two members of the Council who had remained behind, glanced at each other with an understanding.

"I look forward to witnessing that, as well as the many other things I am sure you will achieve as King."

This was the first of the four encounters that had felt like an actual conversation. Rhana was far more natural at this than any of us could hope to be. But it was disconcerting, to see her speak to the Prince in such a relaxed manner.

"Thank you, Princess Rhana." He smiled. He turned around.

Those blue eyes again. They were staring at me now, as Prince Eliel leisurely walked in my direction. I looked away. I couldn't bear the intensity of his gaze. Of him. If Maiwen looked into everyone she met, Prince Eliel looked through them. It was if he could see everything you ever wanted to hide about yourself. As if truth, your truth, was his right to know.

He stood in front of me. I had noticed it before, but now, his height felt even more impressive. More intimidating. I summoned up the courage to raise my head, to look into his eyes. His lips were slightly parted, his bottom dark red eyelashes brushing against his upper cheek. My heart was thumping so quickly in my chest, I was starting to think I would lose consciousness before I could even introduce myself.

We stood there, I had realised, in silence for too long. I opened my mouth to speak. He closed his and squinted, anticipating my first words.

Once I had come to my senses slightly, I curtseyed and rose, having to bend my neck up to fully take him in.

"The cloak becomes you, Princess," he remarked, speaking first after all.

"I thank you for it, Your Highness."

He smiled slightly. "Thanks are not necessary. It is of little use to me. I am sure whoever it belonged to can live without it."

"No, Your Highness, I insist I return it."

"As you wish."

His face relaxed and he tilted his head. He had noticed the necklace.

He moved his hand and quickly stopped himself. I followed the movement and caught his eye, indicating I had seen it.

"Your necklace," was all he said.

"Yes, Your Highness?" I asked.

"I didn't notice it before." His eyes travelled its shape, the way it curved around the sides of my neck and rested slightly above my collarbones.

"It was a last-minute addition, Your Highness. I wanted to…" I hesitated.

"Yes?" he urged me on.

"Wear something green." I looked at his chest as I was saying it, the deep cherry red of the fabric that covered his torso. My veins were flooded with fear, such intense fear that I couldn't stand to watch his reaction.

"Green… why?" he asked.

I slowly made eye contact with him again. His lips were slightly parted, in a faint grin this time.

"It's my favourite colour."

"I see." He looked at my neck again, then back up at my face. Slowly, so agonisingly slowly, as if time was his to stretch and break.

It was an unusual feeling. No information of any consequence had been exchanged between us, and yet, we had acted as if the revelation of his favourite colour had been a secret only we would keep. As if it was the most valuable piece of knowledge, held only by us.

How many more secrets would I keep? I was already holding enough within my heart to last me a lifetime. I was already filled to the brim with them, that I was, at any time, moments away from spilling them all in one horrifying scream.

And here I was, staring at him, in a way that felt far too intimate and far too distant all at once, with the most dangerous secret on the tip of my tongue.

*I'm here to kill you.*

"I hope you've enjoyed the evening," he continued on my behalf.

"Very much, Your Highness. Thank you for the warm welcome."

Prince Eliel replied instantly. "It was the least I could do for you, for you all."

He walked back towards the Councilmen.

"As you all know, the Season comprises of a variety of stages, activities and events, which will be used as a way for me and my most trusted advisors" – he gestured towards them with his left hand – "to evaluate your candidacy. This Season will be unique, in that you will be invited to attend my Coronation as part of it. At the end of the Season, after five weeks, I will ask one of you to be my Queen." His eyes travelled along the line, from Tarren, to Dyna, to Maiwen, to Rhana, and rested on me.

"Whatever the outcome, you will all be welcome back here at any time, and we will always remain most grateful for your participation. It has been a long day, and many of you have travelled far. Please rest. Should you need anything, our servants are at your disposal."

All the candidates curtseyed in response. The escorts bowed.

Tarren moved with her escort to walk out of the hall, followed by the others. I turned to Nathon, who appeared lost in thought. I walked over to him, ready to depart.

"Princess Loria," a voice called out from behind me.

Nathon and I spun around. The other candidates who were closer to the door, did the same.

"Would you stay for a moment?" Prince Eliel said.

I turned to Nathon, who was looking at Eliel with a suspicious glare. Despite our clear discomfort with the situation, both he and I knew what I must do.

"Of course, Your Highness," I tentatively answered. I moved forwards. Nathon grabbed my hand, more gently this time, probably thinking of the way in which the Prince had first found us.

"It's alright," I muttered to him.

He looked at me doubtfully, but took a deep breath in, and let go of my hand. "I'll find you later," he whispered.

I nodded in response. Nathon made to leave. The other candidates were still frozen in place.

"He said *Loria*," Nathon spoke to them all, in an equally lightheaded and menacing tone.

Tarren opened her mouth to object but halted after her escort whispered urgently in her ear. Nobody would dare defy Nathon. Nobody was strong enough.

Nathon took several quick and wide paces past them all and opened the doors.

"Ladies first." He smiled at the candidates. Tarren scowled back. Rhana looked amused. The Captain was the last to reach the door, looking at Nathon blankly, after which Nathon, with a wink in my direction, closed it behind him.

I focused on the door for a few more seconds. Once I turned around to face him, then it would begin.

I did turn, at the sound of other doors opening and closing behind me.

Fargreaves and his two companions were gone. There was nobody left in the hall but Prince Eliel and I. Alone.

Neither of us said anything. He was still standing on the raised platform next to his throne. The one he had been on when he had dismissed us, making our height difference even more stark.

I didn't move. He didn't move. We were at an impasse.

I knew I should move. He was the future King. I was meant to be doing everything I could do to make him want me as his Queen. But I couldn't.

Slowly, painfully slowly, Prince Eliel walked towards me. Each step echoed in the hall like a large drop of water splashing against a pool in a cavern. Each reverberation prickled against my skin like warm sunlight, burning me more and more the closer he came.

He stopped. He was so unnaturally still.

"Take off the cloak," he said.

My eyes widened in alarm and confusion. Did he have the right to demand something of me so soon? Would I be wrong to refuse him this request? Why had he gone to all the trouble of honouring and respecting my wishes, only to disregard them now?

Sensing my inner turmoil, he spoke again. "Let me see." His voice was so soothing. So deceptively soothing.

"Why?" The hint of despair in my voice was impossible to disguise. "Your Highness?" I quickly added.

Prince Eliel lowered his brows in a sympathetic way. He looked as if he pitied me.

"I will not force you to do anything. Unlike some." He smiled knowingly, clearly thinking of Nathon. "But I am curious."

"About what, Your Highness?" I dreaded his reply.

"Princess. I can imagine how this may seem. But I assure you, this request is not fuelled by... personal interest."

"I..." I cleared my throat. "I don't understand, Your Highness."

Prince Eliel closed his eyes fully and exhaled for a fraction of a second. He opened them suddenly and took another step towards me.

"Do not be afraid. I am not trying to..." He seemed at a loss for words. I was so stunned by his uncharacteristic uneasiness that I took a step backwards.

What was I doing?

"Are you... afraid?" Prince Eliel asked, straightening up. He sounded faintly disappointed.

"No, Your Highness." It was true. I wasn't afraid of the Prince, rather what our interactions would inevitably lead to.

"Then what is it you are uneasy about?"

He stepped back slightly. It seemed an effort to make me less uncomfortable.

"If you would oblige me?" he prompted.

I pondered on the benefits and consequences of doing so, and finally decided to say.

"Of everyone. Of everything."

Prince Eliel peered at me, a deep pondering in his eyes. They were only the icy surface of a vast ocean, rippling with thoughts.

"Then you will endure far longer than those who are not."

He turned around and began striding towards the doors Fargreaves had exited from. "You may go, Princess," he declared with his back to me. "As I said, I will not force anything upon you."

I wanted to let him leave. But I couldn't bear the thought of informing Nathon I had refused the Prince a request. I couldn't stand to imagine the look on his face, what he would say, what he would do when I told him.

"Your Highness."

Prince Eliel stopped walking and slightly turned his head over his left shoulder.

I walked towards him this time, as he fully pivoted. I stopped a few steps away, keeping a distance that didn't feel so entirely suffocating, but felt close enough to indicate I was, indeed, not afraid of him.

My shaking hands rose to undo the golden clasps of the cloak. Prince Eliel was watching me, undoubtedly able to notice my tremor, but he was either indifferent towards it, or polite enough to keep silent.

As I loosened the final clasp, I looked down, embarrassed and quickly, before I could change my mind, removed the cloak.

There was no sound or indication from the Prince he was even there. Just silence, silence as he took in what I was wearing.

Thin black strips of a transparent material started at my shoulders, fastened with a silver clasp in the shape of bird feathers. They cut down across either side of my torso so low that my skin was visible from my neck to just above my belly button. My back was completely bare save for a single black thread joining the two sides together. A similar thread held the two front sides across my breasts, which were only just covered. The remainder of the gown was just as fine, with only a slightly thicker part cutting across my hips at the junction between each thigh. Those pieces of fabric, affording me the slightest piece of modesty, dropped to the floor, trailing against it.

I winced involuntarily at the silence. The Prince took a few steps forwards.

"You do not want to be here, do you?" the Prince asked.

Of all the things he could have said, of all the reactions to my attire, this was the worst possibility.

I tried to look away unconsciously, hoping it would be easier to fabricate a lie if I could just tear myself away from his gaze, but it was impossible.

"Do you?" he repeated.

"Do you, Your Highness?" I asked timidly.

"I live here" he responded coolly.

"As do I...now."

Prince Eliel's eyes fell down my body and back up again, purposefully, but there was no satisfaction in his gaze, no enjoyment.

"This tells me much."

I didn't reply.

"As does this." His delicate, long fingers touched the necklace, careful to avoid the bare skin of my neck and collarbones. His touches felt so light, so considerate.

"What does it tell you?" My voice was barely audible now.

Prince Eliel withdrew his hand. He smiled, his lips closed, but there was an authenticity to it that felt different to any of his previous smiles I had witnessed.

He took a step back. A tense quiet hung in the air, an uninvited companion to our strange conversation. An unwilling one.

"Thank you, Princess. For indulging my curiosity." His eyes lingered on me a few moments longer.

Before I could respond, he turned around and briskly left, leaving me standing in what was likely the grandest and largest room in the world, half naked, and alone.

# CHAPTER 19- NATHON

I closed the doors before any of our dinner companions could weasel their way into the private audience Loria had somehow managed to secure with the Prince.

But a conversation wasn't necessarily a good thing. I could not yet say whether the nature of it would assist us or become another problem.

I sighed and moved to walk down the corridor, towards the exit.

"Your Highness," Rhana stopped me.

"Princess." I spun around "What can I do for you?"

"Would you join us, sometime, you and the Princess, for dinner?"

"Wasn't one evening in our company enough for you?" It had certainly been enough for me.

She laughed, feigning amusement. "I suppose not."

"Are you quite sure Jayli there will survive such an affair?" I pointed behind Rhana's back at the escort. "Between you and I, I think she might choke on her own breath if she spends another minute in my presence."

"Jayli is within her rights to be cautious. That is her task, after all."

"Is it also her task to inform me of all the ways in which she'd like to kill me with her eyes?"

Rhana and Jayli were stunned. "No, it's not, is it?" I confirmed for them.

"But…if you can promise to withhold the deathly glares, then I can promise we will be there."

Rhana responded, "I am glad. I like your sister. I should like to get to know her better, and you, of course."

"Naturally," I grinned.

Jayli tensed up. Gods it was so easy. I despised myself for how easy I found it, and the events that had created a version of myself so well versed in manipulating the emotions of others.

Emotions were always so easy to manipulate, to turn on, to turn off, to use against your adversary, against anyone.

For when people were angry, they were irrational, when they were sad, their will was weak, when they were jealous, they were foolish.

I let out a light laugh at the realisation. Rhana and Jayli glanced at each other.

It was not a tool I would employ, had I not the necessity for it, but it was most useful for situations like this when it could be the difference between my life and death.

I feigned a smile and swallowed before speaking. "Oh, Princess...It's good to know that *one* competitor is out of the running."

"What are you implying, Prince?" Jayli spoke up, viciously.

"I'm not implying anything. I'm *saying* that my sister and I would be glad to chaperone you during your little evening together."

"How dare you—" Jayli started. Rhana shot her a look that silenced her instantly.

"Who said, Your Highness, I was out of the running?" Rhana said quietly.

I raised my hands in the air and shrugged. "It tends to be hard to produce heirs without engaging in...certain activities. I have an inkling that might affect your *suitability*, as these people like to put it... to be Queen."

Rhana and Jayli looked furious. I wondered, I was waiting, to see if they would say anything.

I knew people feared me, but I couldn't comprehend the level at which they did at times. They feared me based on stories, stories they had only heard of in passing, never truly read.

"Something to discuss over dinner perhaps?" I tilted my head in question. Rhana gulped. "Don't tell me you want to revoke your offer now?"

"No, Your Highness. We will arrange something and let you know."

"Wonderful. I very much look forward to it. Now, if you'll excuse me."

"Of course," Rhana said tersely.

Rhana brought her lover here. That was a poor decision.

Love. That was the most dangerous emotion of them all. An affliction that could make people do all sorts of ridiculous things.

But I could not deny that it would make Jayli a truly dedicated escort, someone who was willing and ready to sacrifice her life for the Princess.

Love made people foolish, but it made them brave as well.

It was no matter. This would work to our advantage. We needed more of those.

It was growing darker. If they weren't already, then the Prince's men would, by my estimates, begin watching and tailing our every move very soon. Not that it would stop me from completing our task, only make it more tedious.

Tonight, I would exploit the lack of guards at my back, and the lack of sober guards around the Palace after tonight's festivities. This was the best night to visit and familiarise myself with this...Solar Inn. I doubted my contact would be there so soon, after all, Sarlan wouldn't ask for a report until at least a few days had passed. Still, I needed to gather all the information I could about the place. The visitors, the entrances, the exits, escape routes, the different rooms, the tables, down to each and every single scratch mark on the bar stools. I needed to know everything. Be prepared for anything.

I considered wearing my own hooded coat to hide my face, but realised its very colour acted as a way of identifying me. It was inevitable that eventually, I would be noticed at the Inn. That wasn't a concern of mine. I had my reputation to act as a cover for that.

But I preferred to go unnoticed the first time.

I walked back to my room and noticed a servant hurrying away as I approached.

"You," I said to him.

He stopped and turned around "Yes…Yo…Your…Your Highness." He was clutching an empty jug of what smelt like wine.

"Fetch me a light coat, mine's too heavy for this weather."

"Yes Your…Your Highness."

"Forget about this," I grabbed the empty jug from his hands. "Get the coat."

The boy stared at the jug in my hands with so much bewilderment. I felt as if I'd just ripped his heart out of his chest.

"Go now, please," I snapped him out of his trance.

It was definitely wine, and strong wine at that. The pungent smell of the remnants in the jug travelled up my nostrils.

*Ardica Wine?*

Who in this Palace was drinking Ardica?

I largely pretended to drink. It was much easier than you would think to fake drunkenness. To pour the liquid from your mug on the floor, or into an adjacent cup, or swap it with that of an inebriated person's. Being drunk was too dangerous. Especially for me. But pretending to be drunk, that was highly useful.

But Ardica. That wine was possibly the strongest I'd ever encountered. The fateful day I had consumed it, in an effort to blend in with other locals present, I ended up sweating and profusely vomiting in a backstreet, rather than fulfilling my task.

I remembered the punishment for that one. Ah yes. One of his finest, and most unique. If I wanted to be a drunken fool, he'd said, then that is what I'd be. I was force-fed the beverage for a whole week. I purged my guts up so much, I was convinced I might actually die. I never touched the stuff again, to blend in or no.

But this was a whole jug. Completely empty.

The boy returned with a coat less than perfect for the occasion. It was far too small and bright gold, but I didn't have the time to be captious.

"Perfect. Now, you can bring this back to wherever you got it from. Where was that by the way?" I held out the jug to him.

The boy was clearly trying to decide whether revealing or concealing the information would cause him more trouble.

"Come on. Where?"

He gulped and blinked several times. "I'm n...n...not sure that I can s...say, Your Highness."

I wouldn't threaten a child. I would do plenty, but I would not do that.

"Fine. Go then."

The boy walked off, looking behind him as he did, as if expecting one of my daggers to be launched into his back at any moment.

I placed the glaring coat around my shoulders. It was certainly a lighter material than the ones I had brought with me and was lined with dark golden thread around the edges, the same colour as its clasps, in the shape of a leaping Chimera. I lifted up the hood.

Hideous.

It served its purpose. My pants were largely covered by it. However, my boots were still visible. That certainly granted me the luxury of some unusual glances, but I arrived at the Inn undetected.

It was riddled with people. I could immediately see why this place had been chosen to exchange delicate information. It was hard to hear your own thoughts in here, let alone the sound of people speaking to one another.

Music was sounding from the furthest corner of the ground floor, near the bar. Four men, two playing stringed instruments, one playing a flute and another singing with an accordion, were joined by several of the Inn's visitors. Moaning and giggling could be heard from several corners, as people embraced, fondled, and I was quite sure, even had sex out in the open. Almost all the tables were occupied, surrounded by people talking, laughing, teasing, mocking, flirting, and shouting. The raucous space carried the scents of sweat, alcohol, and...yes, that was Papaver. The smoke of which clung to the air as tightly as the lovers clang to each other. Here, a blatant truth swam through the air, stuck to the walls, and clung to the tables. That many would drown in something sour for the search of something sweet.

I walked up to the bar.

"What will you have?"

Avoiding eye contact with the man I replied, "Whatever you recommend."

"Not fussy huh? I get it...all does the same thing anyway."

I thought about Ardica.

*No. It doesn't.*

I turned around and leant against the counter, taking in the whole room. The upper floor seemed just as lively. The far side of which was visible through the flimsy railings framing it, leaving a large square space, from which either floor could be viewed from the other.

My eyes rested on a man, chugging mug after mug of liquid, dripping down his chin, through his sparse facial hair and onto his clothes. Several people cheered him on.

I grabbed the unidentified alcohol laid at my back, quickly thanked the bartender, and made my way up to the commotion. The man had sunk back onto the table, barely conscious.

"I bet he can," one of his encouragers said.

"No bloody way, he's not got it in him."

"Two rays says he does."

"Five says he doesn't."

"Ten for each of you to leave us alone," I spoke up.

They all turned to me.

"Leave you alone, ey?" one of the men said. "He must be good if you're willing to pay that much for him."

The others burst out laughing.

"Fifteen sunshine...since you're so desperate," a woman propositioned.

"It's five now. That's my final offer. The next will involve less money and more...violence," I replied.

The eight or so individuals looked at each other and laughed again.

"Nice try, Mister, but you're messing with the wrong crowd."

"Ahhh...but that's my favourite kind of crowd to mess with."

"What are you on?" another man laughed heartily.

"I'm telling you, that Pap fucks with the head, just like it does with you, Roni."

"I'm not on anything actually," I interrupted their dawdling. "You're beginning to waste my time. I don't like waste."

"Yeah, he's definitely high," the first man said.

"Time you fucked off now," Roni made a move to hit me. I placed my mug down on the table behind me.

With little effort, I grabbed his outstretched fist, pulled his arm towards me, and smashed my own fist into his shoulder socket.

A loud thud confirmed I'd dislocated it, as intended.

Roni started screaming and fell to his knees.

But that was the great thing about a place like the Solar Inn, nobody could hear him.

"You fucking bastard...I'll...ahhhhhhhh. Fuck! You broke it...You've fucking broken my arm."

"Relax, *Roni.*" I leant forwards. "It's not broken, it's dislocated. Get one of your lovely friends to reset it for you."

"You think we're healers or something?" the woman said.

"I think you could have afforded a healer if you'd spent less on alcohol, and bets."

"Fine, give us the five each that you promised. For the healer."

I highly doubted those forty rays would be used for a healer.

"No, I don't think so. My new offer is this." I clasped my hands together. "You leave with intact joints, how does that sound?"

The first man went to speak, the woman stopped him, dragging Roni along with her.

"Leave it, this guy's fucked in the head."

I laughed to myself. She wasn't exactly wrong about that.

Once they'd slank down the stairs, I picked up my mug and slid into the seat across from him. His head was thrown back, leaning against the wood panelled wall. His eyes were half open, half closed. He didn't seem to be aware of anything that had just happened.

"You never told me there was a post-ceremony celebration," I said.

His dark red hair was stuck to his sweaty face. "Who the fuck are you?" he barely got out.

"I'm hurt. After all, you recognised me so easily earlier."

Elias turned his head indolently and snarled, his upper lip rising as his left eyebrow sank downwards. Then he rolled his eyes so far back into his head, I thought for a moment he was about to pass out.

"What do you want?" he said, confirming he was still conscious.

"Isn't the pleasure of your company enough?"

"It's not even enough for me, for fucks sake."

"Well, it must at least be an improvement from your previous companions. Nothing quite like crushing loneliness to lure in the snakes."

Elias guffawed into his mug. "Yes. And here you are."

I took a fake sip. "He was right then."

"Who?" He sounded lethargic.

"That Captain. You are the saddest man I've ever seen."

He laughed. One harsh crisp laugh. "Better sad than a maniac."

"Is it?" I raised my brows.

"What are you doing here?"

"You're the only person I recognise here. I didn't feel like drinking alone."

"Really? All you'd need to do is remove that hood of yours and you'd have" – he paused to swallow – "people begging for your attention."

"Yes... but you're far more intriguing."

He turned his body fully around and placed his arms flat on the table, one on top of the other. "What is it that you want to hear mmm? What, you want to talk about my tragic past? You want to know my darkest secrets? Think you can use them against me? Is that it? Let me tell you something, *Vulture*."

I winced at the pseudonym. Fortunately, he couldn't see that as I looked down.

The Vulture, the Bird of Death. People referred to me by that alias far more often than my actual name or title.

"You can't," Elias continued, his surly expression unyielding. "Because for that to happen, I'd have to give a shit about people finding out about my secrets. I don't."

"You won't mind sharing them with me then, will you?" I looked up. My hood still covered the sides of my face. Anyone who walked by wouldn't be able to recognise me, but Elias had a full view of it.

"Here's the short version. I was born a Duke, and I was good at it. I was the perfect little Duke. Yes, Your Highness. No, Your Majesty. If it pleases you, My Lady, and do you know what?" He pointed at me. "I fucking loved it. Gods, I loved it." He slammed his fist down onto the table.

"I did everything they wanted. Everything they asked. If they'd ordered me to cut off my own finger, I would have asked, at which knuckle? I was even engaged to a noblewoman. She was from one of the highest-ranking families here. Then one day…" He interlaced his fingers and squeezed his hands as if making two fists.

He leant back suddenly, shaking his head.

"You know, I must say, I'm impressed with your ability to remain so cognizant and bite your tongue while you're this intoxicated," I said.

Elias chuckled, "I did that too."

"Did what?"

"Lied. All the time. I spoke bullshit fluently. You're clearly a fucking expert at it."

"Why thank you," I smiled. "One day what?"

"One day." He paused and looked past me as if remembering those events. "One day it all went to shit, they all died, and you know what they did? Nothing. Absolutely fucking nothing."

"Who died?"

Completely ignoring my question Elias continued, "You know, you said you wanted a leading role, didn't you? Or was that the woman with you? It doesn't matter because it won't last. You'll have it, sure, you'll hold it for a while and then." He slammed his fist on the table again. I wasn't sure if he intended to startle me or was just incapable of controlling his emotions.

Either way, the sound was far too familiar for me to flinch.

"Somebody takes your place. Could be anyone. Your best friend, your family, your lover, someone you fought alongside, fought for. It's all the same…the point is…you'll lose your role, and that's if you don't lose your head first." And Elias had lost his. Once a Duke, now a Lord. I wondered if he cared. Despite how fervently he was speaking, it didn't seem the loss of his title was the cause of his anger.

"I will say, I'm very surprised yours is still attached to your body," I couldn't help but admit.

"That's the first honest thing you've said all evening."

The fact he was actually correct was unnerving.

"I'll drink to that," he added, grabbing the wine in front of him. Ardica wine.

I was now also surprised his heart was still beating.

"Why is that?" I asked him.

"Why is what?" Elias asked, losing trail of the conversation.

"Why *is* your head still attached to your body?"

"They're waiting for me to be useful, aren't they?" he murmured into his cup.

"Something you intend on being anytime soon?"

"Fuck no." He wiped the back of his mouth with his forearm.

"How long do you think you'll last?"

"I doubt any of us have long left."

I frowned and moved closer to the table "What do you mean?"

Elias seemed dazed. "Mean by what?"

He'd be unconscious within minutes now. "That we all don't have long left."

"Did I say that?" Elias asked.

It was difficult to tell if he was using his drunkenness as an excuse to avoid the question, or if he had genuinely forgotten his own words, but still I answered, "Yes, you did. You're far too expert a drunk to have alcohol affect your memory."

"I don't know what you're talking about," he grumbled.

"I thought you said you used to lie, not that you still do."

Elias didn't seem to care enough about his own life for a threat against it to work.

"You shouldn't listen to the ramblings of a drunk man."

"Only they're not ramblings, are they?"

Elias, shockingly, managed to stand up. "I'm leaving. I'm far too drunk to deal with you for a minute longer."

"You mean you're far too drunk to keep your mouth shut for a minute longer?" I glanced up at him.

He leant on the edge of the table as he stumbled past me towards the exit. "Listen, Vulture. That's all you need to do here…listen." His breath smelt so strongly of alcohol it felt I was drowning in it.

"Ingenious advice," I replied.

"It really is." He threw me a broad smile, then stumbled off, out of the Inn, and into the night.

The fact that man was still breathing was proof anything was possible.

I found myself wondering who the contact would be, what they'd look like, if I'd know them. I often did. Sarlan always sent his trusted advisors and spies to do these sorts of jobs for him, all of whom I was familiar with. But occasionally, there would be someone unsuspecting. A young boy, a woman or an elderly man sent to do the task. I had a feeling it would be the latter this time, since we were in Vasara, which meant the risk of recognition was too high. But I could never be sure.

I listened. I moved around and listened. I heard nothing of consequence. There were many nights like that in places like these. Sometimes you could spend forty nights in one and hear nothing. This was a waiting game. It always was.

Because on the forty first night, you might overhear something, even for the briefest moment, that could afford you with vital information. Information that might just save your life, that might just change everything.

I had automatically assumed, for some time now, that everyone was lying. Lying about everything. They lied about how their day was, who they loved, who they hated. They lied about their ambitions, their fears, their desires, their woes. They lied about their intentions, their feelings, their thoughts. In this world, people treated truth as they treated sorcery, a substance to be afraid of, to be wary of, to shun.

I wouldn't have said that Elias was being entirely truthful either, both with those around him and with himself. I also didn't consider anything anyone said under the influence of alcohol to be a true honesty, but an accidental one.

Was his reference to our ephemeral state due to his disdain with this place, this city, its game players, or was it something more?

My gut told me the latter, and if Elias was keeping it a secret, and able to keep it, then it must truly be concerning.

I pondered all of this on my way back to the Palace. There were many things I had to inform Loria of. Elias' words, Rhana's impromptu dinner invitation, and I had to find out what the Prince had said to her, what he had wanted.

The darkness shrouding the streets told me we were deep into the night now. I'd have to wait until morning to discuss it with her.

But I was restless, I was not quite ready to sleep yet. I needed to think. I needed to understand. There was something I was missing, and it was gnawing at me like an itch I couldn't scratch.

We were staying as guests in the West Wing of the Palace, where the majority of chambers were situated. The South Wing was where the throne room had been, as well as rooms, from what I could gather, for official business and meetings. The East Wing was littered with chamber rooms, rooms designed to entertain, to host, as well as the gardens. And then there was the North Wing.

The hallways were still. I had been right, the Palace's security was rather lackadaisical tonight, but there were still several guards with keen eyes glancing in my direction.

Putting on my best impression of an intoxicated person I asked, "Sir, would you -elp me please?"

The guard, covered in golden armour and an amber cape recognised me instantly.

"Certainly, Your Highness."

"Thank you. Thank you." I put my hand on his shoulder. "I'd like…a stroll. Yes. Mmmm. A stroll… in the Palace gardens. Where are…they, ex…exactly?"

"Let me show you." The guard walked towards the East Wing and led me through a series of corridors to one which ended in an open archway.

Without saying anything, the guard bowed and left. I waited until he had disappeared completely both from my sight and hearing range, and went outside.

# CHAPTER 20- NATHON

I was completely unused to plants. In Audra, the climate prevented the majority of them from growing. Our trees almost always appeared dead, only sparse silver leaves adorned their thin white branches. There were so many flowers here, their pungent scent bleeding through the air. I wondered what these flowers could do, if any of them could be mixed into a concoction to put someone to sleep, to soothe an ache, to stop someone breathing.

I was well versed in the art of poisons. I had learnt all about them as a child. But poisonous plants were difficult to grow and hardly an inconspicuous feature of any public garden.

I moved Northward, around the building, further and further ahead.

At some point, the gardens stopped at a large golden fence with several spikes at the top.

Yes, that fence would be highly difficult to scale.

But I was the Bird of Death. I could fly.

I discarded the golden monstrosity around my shoulders, it would attract far too much attention. I scaled the wall adjacent to the fence, it was largely flat, but there were enough small indentations in it for me to climb. Once I was high enough, I perched one foot in between two spiked fence railings and did the same with the other. Then quickly, while my delicate balance remained, jumped down, silently.

I had heard rumours about these places. I had even asked one of the guards in Audra's draining centre about it once. But before he had been able to go into too much detail, another man had stopped him, called him away on some task.

Task. It was no task. It was an attempt to silence him.

I wanted to see for myself.

Vasara's drainage centre was the largest in Athlion. After all, they were the ruling Kingdom, but this was also where the drainings had started, where they had been invented. If Loria had done something like this, gone to a restricted area of the Palace, I would have intimidated her into never doing it again. But Loria was not used to this, the shadows were still a source of darkness for her, not a familiar ally.

I stayed crouched for a few seconds, before rising, and slowly, keeping to those shadows and moved further into the wing. The closer I got, the more I could make out the faint sounds of crying. I was on a walkway, the right of which was a courtyard and to the left, the room where the crying was coming from.

A hand yanked me backward, throwing me off balance. My eyes widened at the realisation someone had managed to approach me. They pulled me into a crevice, a smaller walkway off to the side of the main one. Their gloved hand was over my mouth, a dagger pressed against my left jugular vein. Their hand was small, not wide enough to cover my jaw, and their frame was short. Their voice only just reached my ear.

"Don't move."

Killing someone here would be far from ideal. My presence here was supposed to have gone unnoticed. I'd have to turn the tide. Easy enough.

"Please, please don't." I decided to feign distress. Perhaps she'd feel inclined to release me out of pity. That would be useful.

At that, the figure slammed their other hand against my lower abdomen.

"What are you doi—" I said, genuinely confused.

The hand travelled down to my hips and gripped around the hilt of one of my daggers. They swiftly drew it from my belt and directed the sharp end at my lower stomach.

"I know...what this is."

Yes, I'd been right about my suspicions. It was a woman.

"You have far too many of these to be the kind of man who begs for your life in these situations."

I gritted my teeth in irritation. I had miscalculated. But more than that, a Noxstone blade was now poised at my abdomen. All it would take was one wrong breath for my guts to be all over the floor.

But this woman, she was holding the blade with a steady hand, she had enough control to stop it from shredding my skin.

She had held one of these before.

"And yet..." I said, noticing the vexation in my tone. "You still decided to put me in it."

"I didn't really have a choice, since you're drawing so much attention to yourself."

"Get these weapons away from me, now, or you won't like what I do next."

In response she pressed both weapons against me harder.

"No. What you will do, is leave. Your visit can be arranged for another day."

"Oh no. I'm not going anywhere."

"You know." She tapped the hilt of the Noxstone dagger with her finger. "I've killed someone with one of these before. I hadn't really planned on doing it again, but if I have to, I will."

I'd been right about that too.

"Congratulations, but I agree it doesn't feel very pleasant, does it?"

"Why are you making this difficult?" She leant in closer to my face. "Just go. I have no desire to kill you, but you are in my way."

"Yes, and you're in mine."

"I was here first."

"Really?" I said sarcastically. I went to tilt my head, which caused the blade to nick at my neck, a small drop of blood spilling from the cut.

"It's only polite for you to leave, isn't it," she sounded angry.

"Ahhh yes. Spying, the number one tenet of which is...politeness."

"I'm getting tired of this."

"Agreed."

With both blades in a lethal position at my body, preventing me from moving forwards or backwards, I grabbed both of the woman's wrists, and with as much force as I could, crouched, and flipped her over my right shoulder. The Noxstone blade cut up and through my clothing, leaving a line of my torso exposed. I was just able to back away before that became my own flesh.

The woman rolled forwards and landed in a crouched position with her back towards me. She stood, her fists clenched by her side. She turned to face me.

Only I couldn't see her.

A dark red cloak, almost black, covered the top half of her face. It trailed down to her calves, which were covered in brown pants, the same shade as her boots, and the waistcoat covering her white blouse. The only part of her I could see, was the bottom half of her pale face, and her mouth, which was parted, and open, letting out deep breaths.

"So that's how it is," she whispered.

"How it was always going to be. I did warn you."

"And I you." She raised her right hand, which had somehow managed to keep a hold of my Noxstone blade.

"That's mine. I'm going to need it back."

"I think you have enough, don't you?" She used the dagger to point to my collection.

"Tsk, aren't you afraid?"

"I'm afraid that you might never stop talking."

I couldn't help but smile.

"You're right. That's truly a horrifying concept."

"Are you trying to get us both killed?" she hissed quietly.

"No, no, just you."

I lunged forwards, closing the distance between us, drawing two of my own daggers out as I did. I threw one at her, she dodged it. By the time she had regained her balance, I was next to her.

I directed the other at her neck. She used mine to block its path. I pulled another out with my left hand and made a swipe for her stomach. She jumped back and spun around with her leg raised, striking me in the face with her boot.

I tasted blood in my mouth.

I grabbed her leg before she could withdraw it and lifted it, shoving her to the ground. I crouched over her, raising my dagger over her face, but she shifted to the side and wrapped her leg around my torso, flipping me over.

She was on top of my thighs. I abruptly sat up and aimed again. She grabbed my arm with both her hands and pressed her foot against my torso, using the momentum to get up and distance herself from me.

She raised her own hand and attacked me again. I undercut her movement and wrapped the whole of my right arm around her neck, squeezing tightly. Her body grew more limp. I could hear her wheezing, just a few more seconds and...

She grabbed another knife from under her cloak and swung it at my ribcage with her left hand. I had no choice but to dodge, and as I did, she spun out of my chokehold.

I swung, she ducked. As she came back up, I elbowed her in the throat. She staggered back, choking. I took advantage of her state and attacked again. She clutched my wrist, lifted it up, and spun underneath my arm to the side.

"It's hardly a fight if you keep dodging."

"Do you expe..." She coughed, her voice still strained.

"What? I can't quite hear you?" I held my hand to my ear.

She scowled and ran towards me, going for my face with her blade. I crossed my arms in front of me and blocked the movement, staring down at her, or her upturned lip, at least.

She used her other hand to punch my diaphragm. That was uncomfortable. My breath caught in my throat. She used the momentary distraction to strike again, swinging from my right to left, trying to slit my throat. I ducked, and on getting up, shoved into her side, disarming her.

She raised her fist to hit me in the jaw, I gripped it and squeezed hard. I could hear a grunt of pain escape her lips. She pushed at my right shoulder with her left hand, trying to get away, but it didn't work.

I squeezed harder, her bones made a cracking sound. She fell to her knees, a strangled yell escaping her lips. I kneed her in the face. She dropped to the ground, her hands behind her, gasping as her weight was taken on her right one.

She kicked out again. I caught her foot and pulled her closer and wrapped my hands around her neck.

"If you could die quietly, I'd be most grateful."

Her left hand grabbed my own, trying to remove them from her throat. Her right, suddenly slashed down, into my left arm. She had picked her knife off the floor.

She had cut my bicep deeply. I squeezed her throat tighter with my right hand while grabbing her wrist with my left.

"Now that wasn't very…polite.""

She headbutted me, hard. My grip loosened ever so slightly, but it was enough for her to pull away from it.

She crawled backwards and stood unsteadily, the knife in her hands. While I was still on the ground she came for me. I stood quickly and grabbed her outstretched arm, pulling her down and behind me, as I turned and kneed her in the face again.

She landed on the ground, flat on her stomach. I pinned her down with my knees on her back before she could get up.

"Regretting anything now?"

"Do you ever… shut up?" She managed to say against the paving stones.

She reached behind her and for my hips again, grabbing one of my daggers, and slitting across the thigh pinning her down.

As I was distracted, she rolled out from under me, lying on her back to my side. She struck still lying flat. I gripped her arm.

"Give up. You won't win this fight."

"So, it's…" She coughed again "A fight now, is it?" Blood that had come from my blows to her face trickled down her chin.

It was actually the closest thing I'd had to a fair fight for years.

But still nowhere near close enough.

"What is it you're willing to die for? Mmmm?" I leant in closer to her.

She got up and pressed her thumb deep into my left eyeball.

"Agh." I jerked my head back, clutching my face. She released her arm and stood. I followed. Now we were facing each other, blood trickling from several areas, bruised ribs, jaws, limbs, and tracheas.

But she was still alive. I hadn't expected that. This was becoming infuriating.

"Listen. I don't have the time for this. I did want to avoid cleaning up your blood, but at this rate the time it will take me to do that will be shorter than the time it takes to kill you."

"Is that…" Her voice was barely understandable, raspy with the damage near choking her to death twice had done. "Is that…a com…pliment?"

"It's meant to be a threat."

"Well, come on then." She raised her hands defiantly. "At least I know that…. if…I…." Her voice continued to crack. "Lose…you'll." She coughed. "Have…to get away wi…with…cleaning u…up the mess." She gestured all around us. "With…them here…good luck wi…" She gasped for air. "With…that."

"Oh, trust me, I've cleaned up far more disgusting and inconvenient messes."

"Prou…d…of that…huh?"

No, not proud.

Good at it though.

I hadn't planned on killing anyone tonight, but since this woman was intent on my own demise, I had to retaliate.

I drew my sword out this time. This would cut right through her neck in...

"No...no please." An unrecognisable voice was coming down the hallway.

I looked at the woman. Although I couldn't see her eyes, I knew she was looking directly at me too.

"Please...I...I can't, not tonight," the voice pleaded again.

"Stop whining," another man said, gripping tightly onto the slim arm of the Vessel, I presumed.

"No...no...I'm too tired, I won't be...I can't."

They were drawing closer. Before I could truly understand or fathom what I was seeing, fingers clasped around my wrist, drawing me deeper into the crevice.

The woman yanked me towards her and pushed me behind her, pressing her entire right arm across my torso.

"What do you—"

"Please be quiet," she whispered. There was something in her voice, an insistent desperation, that actually made me stop talking.

"No...I...I..." The voice of the man grew weaker. The woman slightly turned her head around the corner to watch what was going on, I did the same.

The man was barely walking, more like being dragged along by the other. His feet scraped against the stones.

The cloaked woman's breathing quickened. Her chest rose and fell rapidly next to mine.

"Parthias...oi, Parthias," the overseer shouted. "Help me out here, will you. This one's being a pain in my ass."

Another overseer emerged from the large room I had been looking at before being ambushed. "That hardly narrows this lot down," Parthias laughed at his own joke.

"Hurry up seven-eight-five, we don't have all night. I need my beauty sleep." He laughed at his own joke again.

"I can't...I..." the Vessel protested.

The woman's hand curled into a fist over my torso.

The Vessel collapsed to the ground, blood leaking from his ears.

"Oh, for God's sake," Parthias said, kicking him with his boot.

"Another one? That's five this week," the other overseer said.

"Yeah...we really need a new batch. The current one is starting to run its course."

Five. Five Vessels dead in a week. What were they doing to these people?

"What are we going to tell the Prince?"

"Nothing, for now. We'll tell the other one."

"Huh?"

"You know who I mean."

"Oh right. Yeah. Sounds good. I don't fancy getting blamed for this."

"Nothing to blame us for. This ain't our fault, Gidos."

"What do I do with him?" Gidos awaited instruction.

"The same you do with the rest and hurry up about it."

"Someone needs to take his place."

"Oh...oh yeah. Ummm, take fifty-four."

"The ginger?"

"Got lots of them."

"The pretty one?"

"Yeah, her," Parthias confirmed.

The woman next to me made a quiet noise of disgust. I couldn't say I disagreed with her reaction.

"Ohhhh yeah. Ha, shame she's one of them."

"Yeah, I wouldn't mind draining her in a different way, if you know what I mean."

They both laughed.

They were standing there, laughing, making crude jokes about a woman, over a dead man's body.

I was hardly the person to preach about morality and ethics, but even to me, this was revolting.

"Alright, I'll do it now."

Gidos lifted up the man's limp body. "Good thing he doesn't weigh anything."

"You've always liked them skinny," Parthias remarked.

"Oh, fuck off."

Parthias laughed and stepped back into the room, while Gidos walked away, whistling.

The woman immediately tried to move away from me, but before she could, I pulled her clenched fist, still resting on my chest, towards me.

"You know about these places?" I asked her.

"Get off me." She shoved me hard. I didn't move much. "What, you don't?" Her voice was monotonous with sceptical disbelief.

It was highly disconcerting to have a conversation with someone whose face was not visible. I reached for her hood. She gripped my hand with hers.

"Stop."

"How do you even see through that?"

She didn't answer.

"Look." She began coughing again, her damaged vocal cords fading in and out of use. She clutched at her throat. I crossed my arms across my chest, impatiently.

She pressed her other hand against the wall, which was bruised and bloodied at my having crushed it earlier. She sounded breathless. I'd been so close. So damn close.

I could get rid of her now. Easily. She was wounded, she was tired. But her reaction to the scene we had just witnessed had been far too interesting.

And I wasn't entirely sure I wanted her blood on my hands.

I waited for her to speak.

After taking a few deep breaths and clearing her throat she said, "We need to leave now. They're going to be back with the other Vessel within minutes. These drainings occur." She swallowed, trying to regain her voice again. "All day and all night. The guards will probably change" – another cough– "at the hour, and it will be much harder for us to get out while that's happening."

"How do you know all of this?"

"It doesn't matter."

"I beg to differ."

"You can beg all you like. I'm not telling you." Her head was down, looking to the side. "I'm coming back here, the night after next. You come back another time," she commanded.

"What if I feel like showing up that night?"

She huffed out a bitter laugh, which sounded more like a wheeze. "Desperate for a second round, are you?"

"The first was rather fun, don't you think?"

Ignoring my comment, she stepped closer, pointing at my chest and spoke. "If you tell anyone, or even hint to anybody you saw me here, I will kill you."

"Will you now? And how do you plan on doing that?"

"As quickly as possible."

"I think you'll find that rather difficult. I'm not someone who can just disappear without people noticing." I gestured to myself.

She looked at me up and down. "Noticing is far less dangerous to me than you running your mouth, which you clearly enjoy doing far too much."

This woman was testing my patience. I moved closer to her. "Nobody...and I mean *nobody*, threatens me, and there's a good reason for that. What I do, and what I say about what I've seen will not depend in any way, on your welfare, or your ultimatums."

"Nobody huh?" She quietly laughed under her breath. "So be it."

She pressed something to my chest. It was the Noxstone dagger she had stolen from me earlier.

"Perhaps you could educate me as to what goes on in these places?" I said as she pulled her hand away.

"I'm sure you're fully capable of doing that yourself."

She stood back.

"Who –" I began to ask.

"No." She stopped me "No questions." Her voice cracked again. "N...no answers either. I wasn't here, you weren't here. I don't know you. You don't know me. That's the way it stays."

I squinted. "I will find out anyway."

She smiled, but it wasn't a genuine smile, more one of disgust. The blood from our fight was smeared across her pale round lips.

"I don't think so." Her lips went back into a straight line.

Then without warning, she turned and disappeared into the darkness. Into the shadows.

I waited for a few minutes and left, finding my way back to the fence and scaling the wall, which was now considerably harder to do with my wounds. I mentally thanked myself for not getting rid of the golden abomination that was my newly acquired coat as soon as I entered the Palace gates. It now concealed my wounds and torn clothing.

I stumbled back into the Palace. If anyone asked, my cover for my gait would be having spent the night at the Solar Inn, and returning here drunk.

On returning to my room, I removed my coat and clothing. The cut on my thigh was deep, but the gash on my arm was much deeper, and was still bleeding. I was used to treating my own wounds. Still, I hadn't anticipated I would have to tend to some so early during my stay here.

I could feel a bruise forming across my jaw already. Brilliant. Her kick had been hard. But that would be easy enough to cover up.

Fortunately, a full jug of wine lay in my room. I tore at the fabric of my pants which were no longer usable, and doused them in the alcohol, pressing them to my thigh and arm. I bit down hard on my lip at the pain. I had to press down on the wound on my bicep for a good while before the bleeding stopped.

I'd have to stitch this one.

I took the bandages, thread and needle, out of the packs I had brought with me, and began to sew through the wound, taking a few gulps of the wine before I started.

"Fuck!" I silently exclaimed. This was considerably uncomfortable. I had long since grown accustomed to pain of this level, and worse.

But still, though no tears formed in my eyes, sweat beaded at my temples, and the muscles in my core shuddered each time the needle was inserted into my skin.

After thirty minutes or so it was done.

And as the first few hours of the next day were already underway, I drifted off in my seat, dreaming of a red cloak, men with red hair, and red blood dripping out of people's ears.

# CHAPTER 21- ELIEL

The High Priest had been delivering his sermon for near an hour. I sat at the front of the Church, as always, paying dutiful attention to his words. He spoke at length about the gifts of the Gods and the wisdom that comes with trusting in their teachings.

There was, I could admit, power in the unity that came with our Church, just as there was in any form of unity at all. I had long since disregarded any personal belief in such systems, but to all those around me, I was a devout follower of Elemantas and a firm believer in the elemental Gods.

Nine statues, three on the left side, three behind, and three on the right of our altar, depicted the elemental Gods those across Athlion worshipped. Fire, Ice, Air, Water, Earth, Light, Darkness, Thunder, and Wood, or as they were better known by their names in the Elementas texts; Furos, Glacios, Ventos, Aquos, Terros, Luxos, Noxos, Tundros, and Arkos.

We stood and finished the ceremony with our usual words of prayer.

*Elementas, Elementas*
*Guide our waking hours*
*Bestow on us*
*Your humble servants*
*Your divine powers*
*The strength of Furos*
*The will of such flame*
*The courage of Tundros*
*The way of the brave*
*The justice of Glacios*
*Of clear and sharp mind*
*The freedom of Ventos*
*To create and decide*
*The wisdom of Terros*
*Of perspective true honed*
*The spirit of Aquos*
*Those emotions we own*

*The tranquillity of Arkos*
*A transcendent peace*
*For Luxos, our life*
*Our health and vitality*
*And for Noxos*
*A way through the darkest of deeds*
*A righteous end*
*Of honour*
*Of glory*
*Elementas, Elementas*

Most of the Gods were gendered in their depiction. Ventos, Terros, and Aquos were female. Tundros, Arkos, Furos, and Glacios were male. But the remaining two – Luxos and Noxos, their depiction was constantly changing. After all, no-one had reportedly seen them, or been able to ascertain their appearance.

I did not believe anyone had seen the Gods at all, only used such stories to claim the attention of others.

I glanced up at the statue of Noxos as we recited the words. If I were a pious man, it would be Noxos I prayed to now. Noxos, I prayed to for a righteous end to the maelstrom fast approaching us. Noxos, who I would pray to for an end to those sorcerers who were once again, preparing to drown our Kingdoms in blood.

I did not think Noxos would listen. He was the God of Darkness, would it not delight him to watch such affairs unfold?

Perhaps the best I could do was pray to him for a quick death.

Better still, not to waste my time on prayer. I would not wait for a mythical being to provide me with a solution. It was my task, and my task alone, to find one.

This evening, I was to meet with the Jurasan King.

I had been surprised to learn from Jarian, that my letter had not only been received, but that the King had also written us a reply. There was, however, no text included, simply a date, a time, and a place. A point where the borders of Vasara and Jurasa met, along a river called Liquanon.

It was, however, better known by its alias – River of Blood. It had been a place of much conflict and battle during the Wielders' War, and since. Several people, humans and sorcerers, had met their end there, and it was said the river ran dark red for weeks after each fight.

Jarian had argued and pleaded his case substantially for near an hour regarding my going there. The Councilmen had been no better. All but Trenton had expressed a great reluctance at my attendance, who had suggested I should attend only on the condition that a full armed guard accompany me.

I was, of course, not oblivious to the dangers of an audience with the Jurasan King, nor was I keen to allow myself to be exposed so easily. However, the nature of our conversation was discreet, and bringing a fully armed guard which consisted of twenty or more men, would not facilitate such a discussion. It was well known and documented, that dealing with the Jurasan King, via letters, his emissaries, and staff, was an unpleasant experience, and that gathering information from him was near impossible. It was unlikely, therefore, that such an extensive and obvious show of force would encourage him to loosen his lips.

On the way out of the Church, Fargreaves approached me.

"Your Highness, are you still intent on travelling as we discussed?"

I glanced at him and quickened my pace. "Yes, Fargreaves, I am."

"He will not agree, Sir."

I stood still in the centre of the hallway and took a deep breath. "He can be persuaded."

Another voice from behind me, Trenton's voice. "I would not be so confident of that, Your Highness. His cantankerous nature is...overwhelming. We have little time remaining to find others to accompany you and—"

I turned around. Trenton stopped speaking the moment I looked at him.

"He will be coming."

Trenton and Fargreaves glanced at one another, silently communicating their doubts about my statement.

Trenton smiled, more grimaced as he replied. "Your Highness, I do not think he is in a fit state to come...to go, anywhere."

"I will be the judge of that." Trenton's insistence was beginning to drain me.

Trenton licked his lips slightly. "He..." He stopped to think and resumed. "It requires little more than a glance at the man to come to that conclusion."

Fargreaves added. "He cannot protect you, Your Highness."

"It is not his protection I am in need of. That will be all gentlemen."

I continued down the hallway, my shoes striking the marbled white floor, without waiting for their answers. I had little care for them anyhow.

I was on my way to see the man who I was intent on being my companion.

Elias.

My cousin was currently, indeed, a terrible choice of companion when it came to my personal safety and security. He was, however, without a doubt, the best choice for one particular reason. That his presence would be entirely and wholly unexpected. His temperament and inability to filter the words he spoke ran the risk of being offensive, but they could also be disarming and unsettling. Elias' attendance would give us the upper hand simply due to the fact that he, for a while now, had been universally viewed as a useless fool who posed no danger to anybody, and one who could grate on even the most composed of individuals.

He was not truly a fool. I knew that to be the case, yet I saw no reason to defend him. It had been Elias' choice to act and present himself to others in such a manner. It was not my responsibility to inform him of the consequences. I was in fact sure, he was aware, and likely glad of them.

If I could not change Elias, then I would utilise him, and even trust him somewhat.

I burst into his room. The two guards who had been accompanying me remained outside Elias' door. He was sprawled across the bed, entirely naked, save for a rope around his neck with a key attached. I walked over to his curtains and drew them back sharply. He groaned and rolled over to his side, propping himself up on his right elbow holding up his left palm in front of his face. His dark red eyes squinted at me, no doubt struggling to focus. With the amount and quality of alcohol he drank, it was a wonder he was not yet blind.

"Ohhhh. Oh Gods. What...What the fuck," Elias half mumbled, half spoke to nobody in particular.

"Get dressed," I said, regarding him with disinterest.

"Eliel?" He dropped his hand and winced as the sunlight struck his face more viciously. His face was contorted in confusion. "What...why are you in my room?"

"You are needed today."

With great effort, Elias dragged himself up to a seated position, holding his right hand in front of him and wagging his index finger from left to right, in a gesture of refusal.

"No. No Eliel. I am not involved in this Kingly shit. That's the way we both like it, isn't it?" He leant over to his bedside table and began pouring himself a drink.

"I need you today," I said, more truthfully.

Elias chuckled into his glass. "What could I possibly be useful for?" He shook his head. "Oh, I know, would you like my opinion on your potential wives? That" — he swallowed some alcohol— "I can do. Just don't marry the fucking child. Please."

I sighed. It was unlike me to do so in front of others, but it was precisely this effect of Elias' presence I knew would be helpful.

"It has nothing to do with my upcoming marriage. I need you to accompany me somewhere."

"Me?" He laughed again. "Won't your advisors spontaneously combust over that suggestion?"

I stepped closer to his wardrobe and began choosing an outfit for him to wear, an outfit that differed from his usual choice of a sparse shirt and loose-fitting pants.

Still facing his poor selection, I replied, "Since when have you concerned yourself with their opinion?"

"I don't care what they think. But you do." He answered from behind me.

I pulled out a dark red jacket and threw it at him. "Do I?"

Elias narrowed his eyes on me. They were almost as red as the wine in his glass.

"This. This is why you're good at this King business."

"Why is that?" I turned back to his wardrobe.

"You're a good liar."

"Am I?"

"Yes Eliel, you are. And you answer every question with a question. Very Kingly of you."

I selected a pair of dark red pants, the same shade as the jacket, and walked towards him, holding them across my arm.

"I will not lie to you, Elias."

Elias raised an eyebrow at me. "Like I said, it's a skill."

"What could I say to persuade you?"

"Absolutely nothing." Elias got up and threw the bedsheets off his legs, covering the jacket I had thrown on his bed in the same movement. He strutted past me and walked towards a large chair in the corner of the room, which was straddled with a pile of discarded clothing. He was limping slightly. His pale golden artificial leg shone in the morning light like armour. It was of the finest artisanry. Metal pads the shade of the early morning sun formed a shin, a calf, the front, and back of a thigh. An amber one glistened as a knee, the same hue as the components resting in-between those pieces. I had heard the components provided near identical manoeuvrability as an ordinary leg.

My gaze trained on the contraption as Elias picked up a shirt. At certain angles, the leg glinted silver. In others, pale blue. In some, the ambers bled to red, the gold to bronze. It was a mechanical mirage of ever-shifting colour, intricate and flexible.

He put the shirt on and turned towards me as it went over his neck. "You've got plenty of people who would give their right arm for a chance to accompany you." Elias chuckled at his own choice of words. "Although I think they'd regret offering it so freely."

"I am aware. But it is you I wish to accompany me."

"Why, Eliel?" Elias buckled a belt over the waistband of his trousers. "What's your plan here? And don't try and tell me that there is no plan, because I know there's no other reason you'd stoop so low as to come and ask for my assistance."

Seeing no reason to disguise my intentions, I drew in a breath and spoke. "Yes. There is a plan. But I have not yet disclosed it in its entirety to the others."

"Seems a bit unwise, doesn't it?"

"On the contrary, it's the only thing I am sure of."

Elias placed his hands on his hips, his back to the window. "What's the plan then?"

"I'm meeting the Jurasan King."

Elias raised his eyebrows and was silent for a few moments. "Does the Jurasan King know about that?"

"Yes. In fact, he sent the invitation."

"The Jurasan King? The Jurasan King personally invited you to visit him? We're talking about the King, who by all accounts, doesn't utter a word to anybody. You're telling me he actually asked to meet you? Of his own free will?"

"He did."

Elias sank onto the chair, which still had clothes adorning it. "This is about your parents, isn't it." His face was turned towards the window. He looked thoughtful, which was a rare expression for him to wear.

"How—"

"Trenton."

"Of course."

"He's a prick that one."

"He's a smart man," I countered.

Elias looked back at me. "Doesn't make him a good man."

"Do you believe there are any?"

"Any what?"

"Good men?"

"You don't?" Elias sounded wary.

"I only know that good men are rarely powerful men."

"Do you count yourself as an exception then?" He grinned.

"Not necessarily."

Elias looked startled once more. "Oh, come on. You're nothing like those men."

"I never said I was."

Elias went quiet again.

"Do you?" I asked.

"Do I what?" Elias said.

"Believe there are good men?"

Elias leant forwards in his chair, his elbows resting across his knees as he looked at the ground. "I knew many. So yes, I do."

"Knew?"

"I suppose the good ones die first," Elias raised his head.

"Which only leaves the evil."

"They die as well, Eliel. We all die." Elias was looking at me intently. "Far too many powerful men use power as an excuse to corrupt them. And they will say they had no choice, that to survive and rule, they had to be cruel. But I think those who are so easily corrupted, who so easily let themselves be cruel, were never really willing to try and be anything other than that. Power is an agent through which the worst of us can reveal our true nature without anyone batting a fucking eyelid."

Elias stood and placed his boots on. "That's what I think."

I was astonished by his sudden philosophical outburst. He walked towards me and slapped me on the shoulder, slightly towering over me. "Good luck with the Jurasan King. I've heard he's an arsehole." He moved to leave.

"Yes. It's a wonder he sent his sister here," I muttered absentmindedly.

Elias stopped near the doorway and turned back around. "His sister?"

"For the Courting Season." I was perplexed by Elias' confusion with the subject. "Were you unaware he had one?"

"No. I mean. I knew he had siblings I just didn't realise..."

"Realise what?"

Elias took a step towards me, his eyes searching the floor. "It doesn't make sense. After everything we've heard about him. His sister, and now this invitation."

"Does that mean you're interested in accompanying me?" I crossed my arms, playing with the fabric at my elbow.

Elias tapped his finger against his artificial leg repeatedly in thought. "It's probably an alliance he wants...what with the sorcerers coming to blow us all to smithereens."

I tutted and looked to the side. "Trenton, I assume."

"He told me what you had planned for me, Eliel." He sounded displeased.

"Is there anything he didn't tell you?"

"Well, he didn't tell me about this Jurasan King shit."

I looked to the floor as I spoke, "I will not force you Elias, either to come with me today, or lead our armies. These are my hopes, not my orders."

He nodded slowly and sincerely. "Good. Because I'm not going to be your General. I'm not."

"Understood."

"But..." Elias walked over to his bed and shook his sheets forcefully, re-exposing the jacket I had placed on its edge.

He lifted it up and held it against himself. "I'll meet this King with you."

I had saved the worst piece of information until last. "It will be at Liquanon."

Elias froze and his breathing changed. It brought me no pleasure to remind Elias of anything related to that fateful day, but alas, it had to be done.

"And you... agreed?" His voice had become strained.

"I was unable to disagree."

"Unable? Write to him for fuck's sake and tell him you will not go there."

"But I will."

Elias pursed his lips together and threw the jacket onto the bed. "He knows Eliel. He knows what that River meant for us, for our people and still he suggested you meet him there. Do you not see?"

"I do. But it will not alter the outcome of the discussion."

"That couldn't be further from the truth. He is asking to meet you on what is historically, losing turf for us. It's a clear insult."

"Let him believe it matters. It does not matter to me. History can be rewritten."

"No Eliel, you cannot erase the past as if it never happened. As if this"— he pointed to his leg, his voice had grown darker— "never happened."

I tilted my head and looked at his leg, then back up. "No. But we can make sure that Liquanon is a place of our victory, as well as our defeat. Starting today."

Elias rubbed his face with both of his hands. "You know, for somebody who doesn't believe there are any good men in the world, that's a ridiculously idealistic way of looking at things."

"And for someone who believes there are, you seem very ready to give up on them all."

Elias huffed and regarded me with a weary resignation. "Glacios gifted you with a silver tongue, as well as those eyes huh?"

"Again, I will not order you, it is—"

"No," Elias interrupted me. "No. I should go back. I always knew one day I'd go back." He shrugged. "I suppose I thought if I drank enough, and slept enough, I'd make myself forget I ever intended to. But...ha...it seems like life is intent on making me remember recently."

I waited. I let him have his time to think, to process his upcoming return. I had heard much about that day at Liquanon. Elias and one other man from his troop had been the sole survivors. The other had taken his own life just months after his return. Elias spoke little of it, both of his death, and of that battle. But people knew, people knew what had happened there, what destructive force had shredded apart the skin, bones, and flesh of those present as if it were nothing but the wind.

Elias smacked his lips together in a decisive gesture. "When do we leave?"

I smiled, slowly and unintentionally. "At midday, it will take us hours to ride, and we will be disguised."

"What's this for then?" Elias pointed at the dark crimson jacket on his bed.

"For when we arrive."

"Seems a hassle to me."

"Be ready and dressed by midday."

But Elias didn't even acknowledge I'd spoken. He just turned around, walked over to the bathroom, and shut the door behind him.

# CHAPTER 22- ELIAS

I couldn't breathe.

I came in here when it got like this. There was something about how cold these tiles were that helped. My body was shaking, uncontrollably twitching. My heart was apparently undecided between beating so fast it felt as if it were about to explode and so slowly it felt as if it might stop. I had turned on the bath faucet before settling against the tiles, to drown out the sound of my gasping for air, and chattering teeth.

I was personally going to rip this Jurasan King's fucking throat out.

Wait. No. That was a bad idea.

So was going to meet him. On that riverbank.

On that riverbank.

On that riverbank.

On that riverbank.

*The blood, the smell, the screaming, the mist, the impossibly foul-smelling dark mist. The earth cracking in half. The sky. The sky turning red, raining blood, roaring so loudly my skull almost burst, burning through us like a dark rippling flame.*

*Shit.*

*Breathe, fucking breathe.*

*In and out*

*In and in.*

*No, in and out.*

How the hell was I supposed to sit there and look at the Jurasan King, talk to him, stay focused on whatever he bothered to say, if I couldn't even think straight? If I couldn't even think of anything other than…than Milos.

The way he had begged me, begged me to make it stop. The way his eyes had turned black, his veins had rippled with a poison so viscous it made his skin…

*Stop. Fucking Stop.*

I leant over the sink and splashed cold water across my face. It didn't help much, but it grounded me, it placed me back here.

Not a tactic I'd be able to use later.

What the fuck was I going to do later?

Who knew, maybe Aquos would find it in her heart to make it rain?

Not that she'd found it in her heart to stop the sorcerers from lifting up her precious water and drowning us with it that day.

I laughed into the sink. "Some help you are, Goddess," I said to myself.

A few hours more passed, and eventually, after dressing myself in-between waves of unbridled panic, midday arrived. I always hated the coming back from one, the slow descent into reality. It tasted like adrenaline and salt.

I considered washing my hair for the first time in a while, but decided against it, instead, gathering part of it back in a messy knot held in place by a strip of leather. The rest fell down my neck.

Eliel arrived at my chambers as agreed and led me out towards the stables. He mounted a brown steed, different to his usual one, and handed me a black horse to ride. I had, at one point, owned my own horse, but he too, had perished. I couldn't bear to take another after that.

Before setting off, Eliel offered me a large dark brown cloak and adorned himself with a similar one of a maroon shade. Unlike most of the clothing he possessed, these cloaks were of a much worse quality, designed no doubt, to make us appear much poorer, and more inconspicuous.

We said little on the ride towards the river, Eliel was clearly far too concerned with the passing looks of the pedestrians and townspeople we rode past, while I was doing my best to calm the raging fire of panic from emptying my stomach contents.

I had already thrown up twice before Eliel had arrived, which I knew to be from the anticipation of this visit, rather than the alcohol, which no longer affected my stomach at all.

They said that meant I could 'hold my liquor.'

It only meant I couldn't drown in it anymore.

After about two hours, as we were approaching the outskirts of Vasara, Eliel dismounted.

"Taking a shit?" I asked.

Eliel, without turning away from me, drew his sword from where he had attached it to his saddle and spoke.

"We walk from here."

*Walk? Fucking walk.*

If I'd known a large portion of the journey would be spent walking, then I would have outright refused.

"That's information I'd liked to have possessed before you asked me to come with you," I said, still seated on my horse.

Eliel spun around and glanced up at me. "Will it be a problem?"

*Will it be a problem?*

For someone as intelligent as him, what a fucking stupid question. I knew I hid the impact of living with an artificial leg, and the constant pain well, but it still baffled me completely that everyone was willing to assume it had no bearing on my life whatsoever.

An excellent design, they would say. As if I gave a shit, as if its monetary value could replace the value of what I had lost. Some even quipped it was an improvement, that it appeared a limb of armour, a replacement fit for a warrior.

It didn't feel like a replacement. It felt like a foreign intruder, crushing a limb I no longer had. As if the leg that had been torn from my bone still lingered like a ghost, invisibly asserting its place, fighting for dominance with the metal. Their battles riddled me with agony that only the alcohol had managed to touch. None of the tame herbs the healers offered had even come close.

The pain would disappear, for certain, they'd told me. They'd been lying. Even the healers amongst the Palace walls were fabricators and preachers of falsehood. I shouldn't have been surprised.

I supposed they had been desperate to offer me some hope. Harder to treat a sick man with no desire to get better. Easier for them to make such promises. Easier for everyone else to ignore the leg, to avoid the uncomfortable lack of certainty over what to say about it. I couldn't decide if I loathed them or forgave them all for it.

I grunted and dismounted, clumsily, as I always had done since my sense of balance had changed. "No Eliel. It's perfect."

"We need to—"

"Don't bother explaining yourself. I'm walking with you anyway."

Eliel clutched tighter at his cloak as a soft breeze played with the fabric. "Very well."

Walking was anything but perfect.

I had brought some alcohol with me in a pouch underneath my cloak, but even that could not dull the sharp and throbbing ache clawing through my upper leg, and down towards my non-existent calf. There were moments the pain was so excruciating I felt like sitting down, or passing out, or both, but I just kept walking. I knew if I sat down, I would not get up again. I was barely finding the will to drag myself along to this wretched place as it was.

I swigged some of the alcohol back.

"Hide that when we get there."

I gave Eliel a sidelong glance. "As if the almighty Jurasan King will be concerned about my drinking habits."

"This is serious Elias."

"Yes. This is seriously the worst idea you've ever had."

Eliel was about to speak when we saw it. The River of Blood.

My heart rate sped up instantly. I could feel my palms clamming up as if fire were caressing them.

"It…" I swallowed, unable to finish my sentence.

Eliel turned to me slowly, clearly waiting for me to finish.

"It…it looks the same," I said quietly. "I don't know if that makes it better or worse."

"Go on," Eliel said, turning back to the water.

After a moment processing, I spoke. "Oh, I see. You want me to go first in case there are any lethal traps."

Eliel laughed. I hardly ever heard him laugh. It was light, pleasant, the exact kind of laugh you would expect to hear from him. Everything he did, said, the way he moved, spoke, and laughed…were all full of grace.

It was a gift to behold, and a horror.

"Drink some more, before you can no longer do so."

"How kind of you, my liege. Let me kiss your arse while I'm at it as well."

Eliel suppressed another laugh. "Save that for the King."

I drank and we walked on.

Every step I took felt so much infinitely slower than it should have. Time slowed down. Every patch of grass, every crevice, every twist and turn at the river's bend was a place, a moment etched in my memory. An area where a man's face had lain as it was drained of life. A square where arrows had protruded from the ground, and from another warrior's stomach.

I had thought being here would have been exactly like being in my washroom this morning, but this…this mental clouding, this distance, this feeling of floating, suffocating slowly, rather than drowning at a speed, I hated this even more.

It was also far more inconvenient, considering what we were here for.

Eliel stopped so suddenly I bumped into his back. He outstretched his hand and placed it on my elbow. I followed his eyes to their destination.

There was one horse, just one on the other side of the river. On its white hide sat a man, or at least what appeared to be a man from a distance. He was shrouded in a dark green cloak, the colour of the deepest trees surrounding us. His face was entirely hidden. His whole body was entirely hidden. He seemed to be more a wraith than a person.

"Is that… him?" I whispered to Eliel. I don't know why I had whispered, it wasn't as if he could hear us from that distance.

Eliel however, whispered back. "Who else could it be?"

"But he would come here? Alone?"

"We are alone."

"You are an ambitious fool, and I have no regard for my own safety. The Jurasan King, however—"

"You may call it foolishness, but it is clear he shares the same thoughts as I."

"This is—"

"Leave if you must." Eliel could sense the unease in my voice.

"We've been over this. I don't wish to leave but you have to admit this is highly strange."

"Yes. But it is also our only opportunity to get the answers we need."

"Answers to what exactly?" We were growing closer to the man now.

"You will see."

"Very Kingly," I muttered.

The figure shifted slightly, and although we could see nothing, we had the distinct impression he had turned our way. He remained impassive, still, waiting.

"Do we cross?" I asked Eliel.

"There is a passage...where the river run's thinnest, we must walk there. He will follow."

I knew the passage of which he spoke. In fact, I knew this whole river better than I knew my own ass from my elbow most days.

Eliel, without waiting for my agreement, walked onwards. I followed him, careful not to look at anything, at any part of the whole scene, for too long.

It wasn't working.

This place was making me physically unwell, but I kept putting one foot in front of the other, and for once, was thankful for the agony in my leg. It served as a twisted kind of distraction for the agony in my mind.

The figure on the horse moved as well, so silently, as if he were a spirit. In the same direction, on opposite sides of the river, we moved. Two sides, two Kingdoms, merging into one.

We reached it. Here the river was about as narrow as thirty hands side by side. The King reached it after us, despite the fact his horse would easily have allowed him to arrive first.

He trotted up to the edge and dismounted, facing towards us the whole time. His cloak was so thick its passage off his horse, and onto the ground by his feet, was audible.

We stood there in silence. Eliel removed his cloak. I did the same.

The Jurasan King did not.

If this even *was* the Jurasa King.

"How do we know it's you?" I raised my voice to ask.

Eliel didn't react. He made no visible indication my question had irritated him, but I knew from the way he gripped the tips of his forefinger and thumb together that it had.

The Jurasan King...or not the Jurasan King, didn't answer.

Definitely an arsehole.

"You...the Jurasan King is a man of mystery. You could be anybody," I added.

The man's chest rose and fell in calm and precise movements. Although Eliel had obviously disliked the way I had asked the question, he was clearly wondering the same, since he had not intervened, or tried to shut me up, as he often did.

Seconds passed.

Then more.

Nothing.

"You have five minutes," the man suddenly said.

His voice was deeper than any I had ever heard before. He sounded completely calm and infuriated at the same time. We still could not see his face.

"We've travelled for three hours and you're giving us five minutes?" I couldn't hide my irritation.

The man didn't answer again. It was as if talking was something that repulsed him.

Eliel's silence though, was encouragement enough for me to continue.

"Aren't you at least going to prove you are who you say you are. I doubt you'd want us being so careless with the information we intend to share with His Majesty."

"Four minutes," he said.

I looked at Eliel, unable to hide the expression on my face displaying how much I wished to leap over the river, and smack this possible Jurasan King in the face.

Eliel did not return my glance and instead said, "Thank you for agreeing to meet with us. Since you are so pressed for time, I will skip the formalities. You are already aware of what I want to know. Indeed, if you are the Jurasan King, there will be no need to explain what that is, since it was he, I have been informed, that received my letter and request."

"Seriously?" I murmured under my breath. What had been the point in wasting that first precious minute of the Jurasan King's time if Eliel had known how to prove his identity all along? The way his mind worked was so frustratingly complicated.

Eliel ignored me, but the Jurasan King did not.

"You were here that day," he said unexpectedly, looking up as he did. His cloak cast his face in darkness, only the vague sharpness of his long face and the extensive length of hair was visible.

The slight flicker of tension across Eliel's jaw was the only sign he was shocked by the Jurasan King's statement. I unconsciously gripped my hand tighter around my sword, which it had been resting on.

"I'm not here to reminisce," I said, trying to stop myself from shaking as I did.

"But you are here," the King replied.

"I thought that time was of the essence, Your possible Majesty?" I felt sweaty.

Ignoring my remark, the man stated, "You answer one question, and I will answer yours."

His head turned between Eliel and I, his face still completely covered by shadow.

"As you wish," Eliel said.

"What are you doing?" I snapped.

"Obtaining answers."

"And giving them," I reminded him.

Eliel, still facing towards the King and not me, said, "What is it you wish to know?"

The King took one step forwards. His long dark boot caught the sunlight for a brief moment. He turned to me.

"How did you survive?"

A soul crushing weight of fire inside my chest burned again. It rose, threatening to escape my lips in a burning cry I would not be able to silence. Ever.

I shifted my weight onto my left, artificial leg, hoping the pain would draw me out of the spiral.

It didn't.

Eliel glared at the King with an icy intent but seemed completely unbothered by this turn of events. He only seemed to care about receiving his answers, and not how he did so.

I knew I had been an instrument in his plans, but I did not think I would be a topic of interest to the Jurasan King. To converse with him like this would have been a great honour for many. Many grovelers and how was it the Vulture had put it? 'Circus leaders.'

"Three minutes," the Jurasan King said, breaking the silence.

I still didn't speak after that. Eliel's fingers were dancing around each other now, in an anxious manner.

"I don't know," I replied eventually. The truth. But one I knew, the Jurasan King would not be satisfied with.

I added. "I hope you won't hold that against my cousin here." I pointed at Eliel. "If you know the answer to his question, do not withhold it because I did not know the answer to yours."

The man was still, so utterly still. It was if he blended in with the forest behind him somehow.

"The sorcery did not affect you?" he asked.

"That's two questions, isn't it?" I said, frustrated.

"Two then," his deep voice declared insistently.

"It did." I practically had to heave the words through my teeth. Now talking was repugnant to me, as well as the Jurasan King.

"Then how?"

"Three? They won't believe us back at Vasara when we tell them how talkative you actually are."

The Jurasan King didn't respond. He was so tall, I'd only just noticed. Taller than Eliel and I. Taller than Kalnasa's escort who had told me politely, to fuck off at that opening ceremony, who had towered over the others at that table. The Jurasan King didn't seem entirely human.

"Very well," the Jurasan King said. He inclined his head in Eliel's direction and continued, "Yes. They have been here."

"When?" Eliel asked.

"Weeks ago."

"And you did not know?" Distrust coloured Eliel's voice.

"No," he replied.

"How is that possible?"

"Three," the King said, turning back to me.

The third question from both parties was the same.

*How.*

Eliel looked at me with a silent command to answer the Jurasan King's third question. I was never helping this little shit again.

I closed my eyes for a few moments, as if the blanket of black replacing the trees would help me understand, but it couldn't, it never had.

"I don't understand it myself. It's not as if I was immune." I pointed to my leg, opening my eyes. I sighed, trying to find the most evasive words, "It was as if the sorcerer…"

The Jurasan King lowered his chin, looking at my leg as he waited. "Yes?"

"As if it…took its time on me. Purposefully. As if it was…enjoying it. I…" I cleared my throat. Eliel was looking at me incredulously. It was a horrific feeling. I had never really spoken of that day, or of my thoughts on it. I had asked myself the same question the Jurasan King put to me several times now, but I had never voiced my suspicions about the answer out loud. I was the only survivor. It sounded utterly ridiculous.

The Jurasan King tilted his head slightly to the left and looked at the river.

"They use sorcery to hide their location, it seems," he answered Eliel's question.

"Why would they do that?" Eliel asked himself rather than the King, clearly done, thankfully, with offering up my memories as trade for his answers.

"Don't the others?" I asked him.

"No. That much sorcery, to conceal that many people for that long is…"

"Difficult?" I guessed.

"Unheard of," he replied. "Whoever is with them, whoever is leading them, is very powerful."

The Jurasan King, without offering a farewell or acknowledging our conversation, turned back to his horse. As he re-mounted, I could see the slightest strand of hair escape from his cloak, the end of it almost at his knees.

Ash blonde. Not golden like some had said, not honey, not dark…Ash.

"Once again, Your Highness, I am grateful. I am in your debt," Eliel said, bowing.

"Would you repay it?" The Jurasan King said, grasping at the reins of his horse, who remained as still as his owner.

"Would you seek repayment?" Eliel sounded wary.

"If I agree to meet with you here, as, and when you wish. If I agree to share what I know, then would you?" His deep voice had become slightly louder.

"What do you seek in return?"

"You will not take my sister as Queen."

Eliel looked thoughtful. He asked the very question I myself was thinking.

"Forgive me, Your Highness, why send her as a candidate at all?"

"That is the law," the Jurasan King replied dryly.

"It is the law to send a suitable candidate, it need not have been your sister."

"Do you agree?" the King pressed, clearly growing impatient.

"I—"

But before Eliel could declare his answer, an arrow flew through the forest and sank deep into the eye of the Jurasan King's horse.

# CHAPTER 23- ELIEL

The Jurasan King drew his sword as his horse plunged to the ground.

Another arrow, this time straight for the King's chest. He deflected it with his sword as if it were nothing more than a fly. He turned towards us as the arrow smacked against the soil, and although his face was shrouded in darkness, I could sense the accusation in his hidden glare.

I knew how this appeared. It appeared as if we had planned this. The very thought of such unavoidable suspicion gripped at my throat with a tightness I could not release.

"Get down! Eliel!" Elias yelled from my right side. He shoved into me with the full weight of his body. I fell on my back, my elbows behind me.

Another arrow, again for the Jurasan King. He dodged it and rolled forwards in a perfunctory manner, edging closer to its source. There was a fury emanating from him more insistent and calmer than the river flowing between us.

Elias was still standing, his head swivelling frantically in all directions, trying to ascertain where the arrows were coming from.

I jumped up towards my horse, who was kicking up and panicking at the scene. I grabbed the shield I had brought with me, resting on its hind. I just managed to withdraw it from its fastening when the steed buckled off into the forest.

"Shit!" Elias tried to grab onto it, but the animal slipped from his grasp like the wind.

I turned to face the Jurasan King "This isn't us!" I asserted loudly.

He ignored me completely, clearly doubting my words. Another arrow, and another, the Jurasan King spun around them all, some even tore through the dark green cloak he bore, but none through his flesh. I couldn't help but admire his skill.

I rushed towards him, intent on assisting him in his defence, but Elias grabbed my clothes from behind me, and pulled me back.

"Are you trying to get yourself killed?"

"We cannot do nothing," I spat.

"That is *exactly* what we are going to do." Elias tugged me back more insistently.

"And if he dies, what then?" I edged closer to his face.

"You said it yourself…nobody knows about this meeting. We were never here."

"Nobody?" I asked him rhetorically. "Other than the owners of those arrows." I pointed into the distance.

"They want him dead! Why should we bother them?" More arrows kept coming.

"We are a perfect alibi. We will become the culprits. We will become their cover."

I knew, because that is exactly how I might have planned it, had I planned it myself.

But how did they know? How did they know we would be here? There was always the possibility that it was from the Jurasan King's end that information had escaped. But given his history of secrecy, I doubted it very strongly.

"It behoves us to do something," I beseeched Elias.

Without waiting for a reply, and with a break in the downpour of arrows. I crossed the river, having to soak my clothes in water to do so.

"This isn't us," I repeated to the Jurasan King, this time standing directly in front of him, as to be sure he would not misunderstand, or mishear me.

The Jurasan King was hardly paying attention to me. His eyes, like Elias,' were scanning the surroundings for oncoming threats and arrows.

"Who then?" the Jurasan King said. "The arrows are falling at my feet." He stated it simply and calmly as a fact, with no trace of distress in his voice.

Footsteps sounded from behind me. Elias had crossed the river.

"If this had been by our design, we would have left as soon as they began falling," I protested.

"What would be the need? If you were not the target?" the Jurasan King replied sedately, still facing away from me.

More footsteps now, only this time they were coming from in front of, and behind us. Figures stepped into our view. They wore dark masks and dark clothing. Some were running, others raising bows as they moved.

"Eight," Elias counted instantly.

"No," the Jurasan King said, looking up. "More."

There were another few, leaping through the trees.

"Get out of here!" Elias implored me. "Leave!"

"There is only one way of achieving that now," I said, taking in our adversaries.

But each and every one of them was focused on the Jurasan King.

He could not die. We needed him for the information he could provide.

At the head of the group was a short woman with braided hair. She raised her hand. She bore no weapons and carried no steel.

"Oh Gods." Elias gasped. "These are—"

"Sorcerers." The Jurasan King finished his statement for him.

Elias had turned completely pale. This place again. These foes. I could only imagine his torment. I was beginning to think bringing him here had been a poor decision and a cruel one on my part. I glanced at him cautiously, his gaze remained fixed ahead.

My attention was turned back to the woman as she brought her hand down through the air and smashed her fist into the ground. It cracked, the earth shattering towards us at a rapid pace. Another man to her left did the same, and the crack tore deeper through the soil, slithering towards us like a snake, intent on poisoning us.

We all braced ourselves. The Jurasan King traced the curvature of the line, his chin following its movements. We stumbled backwards, our footing became more unsure by the second, and the crack deepened.

The others who had arrived with the earth-shattering duo watched from behind them, appearing utterly unphased.

The earth opened from under my feet. I attempted to jump to the left, but the hole had already begun to swallow me, throwing me off balance. I tilted forwards with my arms outstretched. Elias grabbed onto my hand, gritting his teeth with the effort of supporting my weight on such unsteady ground.

"Just hold on and—"

There would be no point in dragging him down with me.

I let go of his hand.

Falling into the underground, I caught jagged shards of rock, earth, and stone as I passed further down and landed on my front.

A crack snapped through the air. There was no change at first, only the unwelcome presence of dirt in my mouth and scent of wet soil, tinged with a hint of burning...the sorcery, I assumed.

But then, like a fire seething across my bones, a searing agony swept across my forearm and down into my wrist. There was no doubting it was broken. I could feel a scream clutching at my throat and yet my mouth remained agape.

That was until the earth shook once more and Elias landed next to me, a few steps to my right. He had used his blade to slow his fall and remained uninjured. Clever.

The impact of the second wave of motion allowed the yell of pain to escape my lips. I rolled over on my back and crossed the broken arm, my left, across my chest, squinting my eyes shut. All around us the earth was still trembling, rumbling, shivering, threatening to crush us under its weight at any moment. The intensity of the noise it created almost shrouded my cry of pain, but not enough for Elias to remain ignorant to it.

"El...w.... stay....and...." I could only make out snippets of his words.

He found his way beside me and looked me up and down, finding the cause of my distress within a fraction of a second. He tore a fragment of the bottom of his tunic off and wrapped it around my upper torso and arm, creating a makeshift sling. He must have made many of these during his time in our army, I thought.

"The King—" I started.

"He's still up there," Elias said, sounding as unphased as the other sorcerers had looked.

"He'll die," I said.

"We could die," Elias said, glaring at me.

I used my other arm to force myself into a seated position. Elias and I peered up at the sky. It was overcast with a thick fog, dense, and dark.

Elias' eyes remained fixated on the matter, but I could tell from his facial expression that here, and now, were not where his mind remained.

I knew more about sorcery than it was deemed necessary or appropriate. Humans had convinced themselves that if they understood less about a threat, or an enemy, that enemy would become less dangerous. It was a strange fact of the world, of humanity, that we would mistake ignorance for truth, when it was only ever an illusion. And so, I had studied the topic in as much detail as possible. My father had ordered several texts around sorcery to be destroyed, but some remained, and I had scouted out rarer editions in secret. I had asked whoever was capable and willing to converse on the matter and acquired all the information about sorcery I possibly could.

It was simply for this reason, that I knew this dense cloud was the work of an Accipere-an.

I thought about suggesting an ascent, but I could see no means or method to undertake that task. Nor could I see any way to convince my cousin to step into that darkness intentionally.

Using my other hand, I pressed myself up off the ground, as if that would somehow allow me to bring myself closer to the strange substance floating above us, allowing me to understand it better. The smoke carried with it a deadly silence that blended with the wind seamlessly, drifting above and around us. Such a contrast to the roaring of the quake just moments before.

I waited for a few moments, minutes, but there was no further sound, no sign of any movement or activity. I turned to look at Elias, his head was now bent, he was staring at the ground, utterly lost, utterly transfixed in his own memories.

"Elias," I said, as authoritatively as I could manage, through gritted teeth.

He didn't respond.

I crouched beside him. He was clearly unaware of my presence. I placed my hand on his shoulder. The touch awoke him, he shoved me aside and drew his sword.

I jumped back, startled. Elias' eyes were wide, focused, yet not. His dark red irises were like droplets of blood growing ever smaller as his pupils widened.

I raised my right hand. "Elias," I started, carefully, as if speaking to a child. "You are not yourself."

His arm remained outstretched. His sword remained firmly in his grasp. His face was twisted in an expression of contempt.

"Elias...put the sword down. I am not your enemy. It's me, it's—"

"I know who it is," Elias said, disproving my former theories about his state of mind.

"Then what...what are you doing?" I asked, trying to remain calm. I could feel my outstretched hand shaking slightly. There was little that brought me fear but I was not immune to the feeling. This scenario however, dying here, by Elias's hand, was not acceptable or desirable.

"We're not going up there," Elias asserted. His grip, his glare were steady and sharp as his blade.

"We must," I said.

"I'll cut both your calves if it means you won't. And you're in no state to fight me."

Elias' voice was full of something I had never detected in him before. An insistence. An aggression. A powerful force that was daunting.

"I understand your concerns but this decision—"

"No, you do not. You read about sorcery, you talk about it, you study it..."

My eyes widened. My lips parted slowly. I was unaware Elias was so attuned to my interest in the topic. I thought my concealment of it had been sufficient.

"...But you do not understand it, and you do not know it as I do."

"We have no choice," I tried to persuade him.

Elias smiled slightly, but it was full of bitterness and melancholy. "Yes, I remember hearing those words from your father's lips, before he sent all those people to their deaths."

I was suddenly overcome with a wave of seething irritation. It was not as if I did not comprehend Elias' feelings or thoughts, but they bore little relevance to our current situation.

I strode towards him confidently, letting his sword rest at my breastbone.

"Do you propose we stay down here then? For how long? Hours? A day? Multiple? We are wounded and we have lost our supplies and horses. We cannot hide here and wait to die. If you are so determined for us to face such a fate then by all means, cut me down here and now."

Elias and I stared at each other for seconds, each passed by between us like an eternity, hanging heavily in the clouded silence.

He lowered his sword slowly. "We stay here for a short while, then we find a way out, but the Jurasan is on his own."

I nodded curtly to confirm the plan. Elias was right, he was stronger than me, and not only when I was wounded. It would be foolish to test his patience, especially now.

His blade remained in his hand unsheathed. I sank back down to the floor.

Elias looked down at me. "You're not completely sane, Eliel."

My head spun towards him, I was dizzied by the movement, from the pain. "What?"

"No sane person would ask another to kill them over such a small disagreement." Elias looked amused.

"Small? You threatened to slice my legs open," I could feel myself losing composure around Elias again.

"That threat still stands. Stay where you are." He waved his sword at me elaborately.

"Who could be?" I mused. "Sane and survive in this world?"

"Absolutely nobody." Elias sat down next to me. "Especially not a King."

"So, the Jurasan King is unsound of mind?" I asked.

Elias shuffled, turning in my direction. "You're telling me you thought he wasn't?"

"He was—" I searched for the word, but my mind was clouded by pain, "Extremely skilled," I eventually said.

"Yes," Elias confirmed, looking at his feet. "Do you believe he was being truthful?" he asked.

"I believe what he said is true, it is what he has omitted that concerns me more."

"Will you do as he asks?"

"I see no reason not to. His sister is of no interest to me."

Elias sighed, relieved, and nodded.

"Although all of this means very little if he is dead or has been captured. We will have to ascertain whether or not that is the case before we proceed."

"And if he is?"

"I don't..." I leant my head back, a sudden wave of throbbing in my arm gripping me. Elias furrowed his brow in concern.

"Just a little while, Eliel. Just a little while."

I lost consciousness.

***

Sometime later, when the sky was considerably darker, and night had already begun, Elias' voice woke me up.

"Eliel." His hand gently shook my other arm. "Let's leave."

I looked around, confused, and perplexed.

"You've been passing in and out of consciousness for about five hours now. I thought it best to just let it happen, considering well..." He gestured at my broken arm with his chin.

Elias, it seemed, had spent the last few hours climbing and slicing groves into the rock surrounding us, enough for us to slowly, exhaustingly, heave ourselves up to the surface.

Around an hour after, we both stood on that shattered ground, cracks running across it like veins.

There were dead bodies everywhere.

Their faces were frozen in screams, their bodies twisted at awkward angles.

But the Jurasan King was not one of them.

"Well," Elias said morosely, "I think that answers our question."

An icy chill swept across the forest and caressed the river. The river that once again, ran red with blood.

# CHAPTER 24- SHADAE

"Don't say anything," he grumbled. "And by the Gods, don't ask any questions. Just nod your head, kiss his ass, all that shit."

I glanced sideways at the man, slowly. The scepticism on my face must have been painfully clear.

"What were you expecting, girl? A badge of honour?"

*Obviously not. I'm not delusional.*

I remained scowling at him.

"Wipe that expression off your face, right now, before we go in there. Do you want to lose this post after you were just appointed?"

I turned away from him. I had hardly expected this endeavour to be simple, but it would have been preferable had the Commander been tolerable.

I had been recruited as a tracker just days ago. They had come to inspect the Vessels, the ones who had passed the 'health checks.'

*Ha. Checks which translated to 'those not on the brink of death' more like.*

I had volunteered myself for consideration, almost immediately after my brothers and I had been transported to Vasara's draining chamber, eighteen months ago. I had been waiting since then, hoping I would be chosen.

A tracker meant freedom from being a Vessel, an income, and a warm bed to sleep in. In exchange, we were bound by a Curse that forever tied us to the role, the role that required us to hunt down other sorcerers. The Curse ensured we would not, that we could not run from it. Applied by a Curser, a class four Acciperean, working for the Crown.

*Likely by force as well.*

The Curse of Servitude. One of the strongest, and hardest to break.

Still, I had no intention of running.

My two younger brothers had despised me for it, yes, but it was the only way. The only way I could think of, to get them out.

I would get them out.

I lowered my head, avoiding the Commander's gaze and glancing at my hands. The brash white of the uniform struck harshly against my dark skin. This long white coat. These golden buttons and shoulder panels, framed by crimson. These slight and small intricate chains hanging down the shoulders like tear drops. These pants, as dark red as blood. The illusion of purity. The illusion of purification.

I swallowed uncomfortably.

The Commander turned behind him as another woman approached. Another tracker. She shook her head no. He closed his eyes for a second and turned back to speak to those gathered.

"I don't want to hear a single word from any of you. If you even think about talking, just think about my foot shoved up your ass and that should bring you to your senses."

I couldn't hide the look of bafflement on my face.

"You." He glared at me. "One more look like that and I'll personally ensure you are escorted back to your charming quarters, permanently."

I nodded in confirmation, reluctantly resetting my facial expression, something I often found difficult to do.

The doors opened in front of us, and we, a band of around fifteen people were led into the Council chamber. Someone strolled by us, having just been dismissed. An apothecary it seemed, clutching at a vial.

The room was as vast and spacious as I had heard. I couldn't help but marvel at the openness of it, the amount of distance between everyone within it. I managed to do it with a straight face this time, however.

We all bowed, as we had been instructed to.

"Your Highness," the Commander said.

In front of us sat the Prince, at the head of the table. He looked pale, sickly almost. His arm was hung in a sling. He leant forwards against the table in a way that meant he was looking at us from under his brows rather than directly at us. Other men were seated around him, Members of the Council, I presumed.

I drew my gaze back to the Prince.

*It must be nice, to have such injuries treated by an apothecary.*

I couldn't say I felt any pity for him, despite how unwell he appeared.

"Commander," the Prince said quietly. At his acknowledgment, the Commander rose, and we followed.

"We have an urgent mission for you, Commander Cheadd," another man said. He was seated nearest to the Prince, his dark hair like the night against the Commander's bright gold.

"We are at your service, Sir."

"A group of sorcerers attacked His Highness yesterday," he explained.

I took all the strength I had not to react to that.

"May I offer my sincerest condolences," the Commander said, "I hope His Highness recovers quickly. Rest assured we will do everything we can to capture the culprits."

*Kiss his ass indeed. Just follow your lead, you could have said.*

"We expect swift results, Commander, this was a direct attempt on the Prince's life, it cannot go unanswered or unpunished," the dark-haired man stated.

"Where was His Highness attacked?" the Commander asked.

Another man interjected, "You are not privy to that information, Commander. We can tell you what we know of their abilities and appearance but—"

The Prince raised his hand, silencing the second man. "Fargreaves, it will be rather difficult for the Commander to do his job without such information."

"But, Your Highness, we cannot risk—"

"You said it yourself," the Prince sounded exhausted, "the risk has already reached unprecedented levels."

The Prince turned to face the Commander. "At Jurasa's border," he answered.

The Commander straightened up. There were even a few murmurs of surprise from the others who had accompanied us. The Prince travelling that far out was definitely unusual, I gathered, not from my own limited knowledge, but from their reactions.

If the Commander was perturbed at the location being so close to his home Kingdom, he did not show it.

"And their appearance? Their abilities?" he asked, curtly.

"Accipereans. Several are dead, several of them escaped, including a woman who was leading them, short, dark haired. I did not see their faces, they were all dressed in black, masked," the Prince said sedately.

Accipereans? That there were enough of them both free and alive to band together to launch such an attack, it seemed impossible.

"We will begin the search right away, Your Highness."

"You have two weeks," Fargreaves said, "We want a full report afterwards, and we expect results."

The Commander nodded but did not move.

The Prince stood slowly. Even in his wounded and withdrawn state, there was a presence about him that could not be denied. He looked like a pale ghostly God. I supposed that was apt considering he was worshipped as one by the large majority of people.

"The matter that we discussed last month, Commander, do you have an update?" the Prince asked him.

The Commander cleared his throat and for the first time appeared phased.

"Apologies, Your Highness, the tracker we sent out to retrieve the information...did not return."

Ahhh, I understood. The message that had been delivered to the Commander just moments before this meeting, the nod of no, was about this tracker.

"I see," the Prince said wearily. "I take it you have found a suitable replacement for your ranks."

The Commander turned towards me and beckoned me forwards with his hand. I gave him a quizzical look. He gave me one that instantly reminded me of the promise he'd given in the hallway.

I resumed a neutral facial expression, to the best of my ability and stepped forwards.

"Recruit seventy-eight. Shadae Warlow. Twenty-five years of age. Darean. Navigator. Originally from Zeima. Vessel for eighteen months. Passed all the health and physical requirements necessary."

"Has she been initiated?" the Prince asked, still looking at the Commander.

The Commander nodded in the direction of my wrist. Understanding his silent instruction, I shifted the sleeve of my clothing up to reveal the mark of the Curse of Servitude all trackers were branded with.

The Prince looked at me briefly, as if I were no more or less interesting than the clouds passing by the window.

"You understand what this mark means?" he said to me.

*That I am forever bound to your ugly soul.*

"Yes, Your Highness."

"And what will happen if you dishonour your oath?"

*There's nothing honourable about it.*

"Yes, Your Highness," I dipped my chin in false acquiescence.

"Good."

I was suddenly overcome with the realisation that any one of us could possibly kill him. Yes, it would mean our certain death, and likely the death of every tracker in this room, but still, it was possible, and it would be so quick. He looked like an injured bird. A beautiful, small, fragile thing one of us could so easily snap in an instant.

I mentally shook myself from the thought.

*I can't die yet. I have people to protect.*

I placed my arm back into position.

"Why her?" the Prince asked the Commander.

The Commander answered instantly. "She is weak, her reserve is low. She has enough power that she will be helpful to us, but she is of little use to you as a Vessel, Your Highness."

*Are you trying to make sure I get sent back there!? Weak? Reserve is low? What a wonderful way to convince the Prince of my suitability.*

But it was true that my ability – a Navigator, was one of the most common, and least powerful of all Darean abilities. I had never been superiorly skilled at commanding my sorcery, and of course, had never really seen a need to improve my skills, since doing so only made my capture more likely.

*So much for that, remaining weak to remain safe didn't work at all.*

I silently chuckled to myself at the thought.

"Is something amusing, recruit seventy-eight?" the dark-haired Councilman asked.

*Fuck.*

The Prince looked at me with the same disinterest as before. The Commander with the promise that his foot would most certainly be up my ass after this meeting was finished.

"Do you disagree with the Commander's assessment?" the Prince asked.

"No, Your Highness. He is correct, I am not" – I cleared my throat –"overly skilled."

"Are you sure she is the right choice, Commander?" Fargreaves sounded suspicious.

"I am, Sir."

The Prince looked at me for a few more moments. I wondered what he was thinking. I wondered what he was planning. His stare was so convincingly penetrative I could have believed he'd discovered I'd been considering murdering him just minutes before.

"Then you are dismissed," the Prince said.

The Commander bowed, we did the same and followed him out of the doors.

Once they were closed behind us, and we were left alone in the equally spacious hallway, one of the trackers spoke.

"Accipereans," they said, an air of disbelief evident in their tone.

"That many?" the woman who had approached the Commander beforehand added.

"It doesn't matter. We do what we have always done. We find them, and we bring them here," the Commander replied.

"But...Accipereans are far more powerful than we are."

"Do you have an alternative plan? By all means...why don't you stroll in there and tell His Highness you don't think you're fit for the task? Fancy going back to your cell?"

"No but—"

"But nothing, you follow my orders, you do as I tell you and you remember"– he pointed to his own wrist– "what the consequences are if you do not."

A solemn silence filled the air.

"We will discuss our plans at noon in the usual place, until then, do as you please, you," – he poked my shoulder unceremoniously – "come with me."

He walked off and the others dispersed. I contemplated ignoring his request but thought better of it.

After following him for a while, we entered a room, a room that appeared to be a base of some sorts for him.

He shut the door, walked around me, and slapped me in the face.

I clasped the side of my cheek in shock. It was by far the first time I had been hit, but it was the least expected of all the blows I had received since arriving at this dreaded Palace.

"Are you dense?" he asked me.

"I—"

"You are lucky, extremely fucking fortunate that the Prince was clearly exhausted today. Because I am telling you." He pointed at me. "If he hadn't been, you would have been interrogated for far longer on your little fit of laughter."

"It was—"

"Fucking ridiculous, that's what it was. Childish and arrogant. You won't last two days in this role if you carry on acting impetuously. This isn't even the difficult part. You're going to have to fight other sorcerers, kill them, even as they beg for their life. You're going to have to do whatever the fuck they ask you to, and *all of it* with a straight face, not even a twitch, do you hear me? A straight face. Are you ready for that? Because it doesn't seem like you are to me."

I removed my hand from my cheek, still reeling in confusion, still able to feel the prickling burn of where his hand had struck my skin.

"I..." I cut myself off. It suddenly felt wrong, and incredibly futile to try and lie in front of this man.

I swallowed. "I will do what I'm instructed to."

"Will you? You don't fill me with much confidence."

*Do I need to?*

But still, I tried to reassure him.

"I will," I said, more assertively this time.

"Why did you volunteer?" He crossed his arms.

The question confused me. "For the same reason everybody does?"

"You think everybody has the same reason for volunteering?" He raised an eyebrow.

"Being a tracker is the only way out of being a Vessel."

He didn't say anything, just stood there, clearly unsatisfied with my answer.

"I have a reason," I finally said.

He squinted. "Everyone says that, but sometimes, their reasons aren't enough. I've seen plenty of recruits come and go over the years. I've been a recruit for thirty-two now, Commander for eight of those. I've seen people die on the job within weeks, go mad, try to escape, do all sorts of shit. They thought they had their reasons too, and they thought they were enough. Enough to do what needed to be done. Enough to train as hard as possible, to fight sorcerers far more powerful than themselves. Enough to ward the guilt and the fear away."

My face fell. "Is this the motivational speech you give to everyone once they start their role?" I asked him.

"Only the ones I think need to hear it."

*Nobody needs to hear this.*

"It won't happen again," I reassured him, unsure if I was correct. In fact, I was now unsure of everything. Unsure as to whether or not I was even up for this task.

"You're right, because His Highness won't be so distracted again. You better hope he doesn't reflect too hard upon your behaviour and decide to punish you anyway."

I creased my brows in confusion…would the Prince do that? I suppose it seemed possible.

"Now get out, come back here at noon."

I stood there for a few moments, internally debating whether I should ask the question hovering in my mind.

"What is it?" He sounded impatient.

"The other matter… that the Prince discussed, the one the other tracker didn't return from. Is there a way I could help with that?"

The sooner I advanced the ranks of the trackers, the more I would earn, and the more I earnt, the faster I could acquire the amount of money necessary to bribe some of the overseers into letting my brothers escape.

I had heard rare instances of this happening, most of the time, of course, the overseers responsible were caught and killed, but on the rare occasion, they were not. If I had enough money, I could find out which of them had successfully conducted these underhanded deals, and hopefully make the risk to their life seem insignificant in proportion to the sum I offered them.

The Commander scoffed. "You're very keen to die quickly, aren't you? You have a lot to learn and a lot more to prove before you can be involved in missions like that."

I raised my head. "Then I will. I will learn. I will prove myself and I will do what I need to do." I paused and added. "With a straight face, of course."

The Commander looked me in the eye. "You need to kill that part of you that wants to fight back, not fully, but just enough you don't fight back at inappropriate moments, do you understand?"

I nodded yes.

The Commander was silent in thought for a moment.

His face resumed its usual hardness "Do something like that again and I will happily kill you. I've ended the lives of many sorcerers, yours will be no different, and if your death means protecting the lives of the other far more reasonable and level-headed trackers here, then I won't think twice about it."

"Understood," I said flatly. "If I do anything wrong either you, the Prince, another sorcerer, or this curse will kill me."

He shook his head in disapproval at my reply. "That's exactly what I'm talking about, and that's the very last time you will act that way around me, or the others. I mean it. Kill that part of you, or someone else will kill all of you."

I ground my jaw in annoyance and turned around to leave. I deliberately slammed the door on my way out in anger.

I grimaced at my own action. Yes, that was rather childish, but I couldn't stomach the thought.

I'd already been forced to mellow, make myself meek and quiet for the sake of the ban on sorcery, then again as a Vessel, and now again as a tracker. I could never truly be anything other than docile. It was like being unable to tap into a part of your soul, unable to scratch an itch, and the longer it went unscratched, the more it demanded to be, the more it built up like an inferno I could not douse with water.

I sighed in the hallway. I tried to calm down. I knew this was the price for living in this world as a sorcerer. To never truly know yourself, never truly be yourself.

It's only that I didn't know if I could bear to pay it forever.

But for my brothers, and for now, I would.

For them, I would pay that price, and a thousand others.

For them, I would become a murderer.

# CHAPTER 25 - LORIA

I hadn't seen Nathon for two days.

He had informed me to stay away from his room. He told me I shouldn't approach him and only ever wait for him to approach me.

But tomorrow, it would have been three days, and I was growing increasingly anxious. I knew the most likely reason for his absence was to do with the gathering of information but still, I was growing tired of being left in the dark. And truthfully, I wanted to speak to him, I needed his advice on recent events.

As much as I loathed the side to Nathon that could plan, manipulate, and deceive, I needed it now, I needed to learn from him.

I stood and resolutely walked to my door, crossing the hall to his room. I was the key to this plan, and the key I thought, should know which doors to open, not be stranded in the hallway, alone.

I knocked.

There was no sound.

I knocked again, this time, I said "Nathon?"

Nothing.

I was in a nightgown, but I had covered myself with one of the cloaks that had been provided for me when I first arrived here. I shook my head. This tradition of being barely clothed within these Palace walls was becoming almost comical.

So was my decision, I realised, this was a mistake.

A hand grabbed my wrist and pulled me inside the room.

Nathon shut the door quietly and sighed. He sounded exasperated and turned towards me slowly.

He didn't say anything, only looked at me with a silent reproach.

I ran my fingers through my hair. "Where have you been?" I whispered as loudly as possible.

Nathon's hand slid down the door. He straightened up and looked at me as if glancing at a crushed insect, or a piece of rotten food.

"It's been days, Nathon. We aren't in a position to go days at a time without speaking to each other. I need to know what you know, and you need to know what I know."

Nathon slowly smiled, then slowly blinked. What was wrong with him?

"Why aren't you speaking? Did the Nine Gods finally grant me my most desired wish of removing your ability to talk?"

"You're still just as foolish as ever, Loria," he finally spoke. "The Nine Gods would never be so generous."

His face fell after his quip. "You don't come to my room, I told you that."

"You haven't given me much of a choice. Do you expect me to sit around and wait for you all day and all night?"

"Do you have anything better to do?"

"I would, if we could actually converse and decide what those things should be."

Nathon widened his eyes. "Are you asking me to dictate your every action?"

"Stop it," I bit.

Nathon raised a brow as if to ask - *Stop what?* As he did, he strolled past me towards a table, opposite the door.

"Being intentionally obtuse," I clarified.

"Unfortunately, you're going to have to use something called initiative and figure out certain parts..." Nathon paused for a moment, swallowing, and seemingly taking a deep breath, "Figure out certain parts for yourself," he finished.

I looked to the side. "I want to make sure I'm not doing anything...wrong."

"Oh, it's almost guaranteed you will do something wrong, and I will do something wrong. But that doesn't matter... as long as we make it out in the end."

"How can you be so calm?" I asked him. "You heard what he said, if we fail, your life is effectively finished."

Nathon chuckled at that. His laugh tolled through the dark like an ode to the stars, to the night.

"Is it?" he mused. He turned around, crossing his arms. "The Zeimans want us to dine with them."

"What? When? This is why you should have come to visit me," I reminded him, pointing at the floor as I spoke.

"It's hardly an urgent matter, but I'll make the arrangements and inform you of them soon."

"Anything else?" I asked him, knowing full well the likelihood of him answering that question truthfully was miniscule.

Nathon's eyes searched my face, and I could tell he was aware of my distrust.

"No. But the King's recent injury is rather interesting and probably not the fall from his horse he claims it to be."

"You don't believe him?"

Nathon looked, once again, appalled by my existence. "He's an expert rider by reputation. It's true there are very few potential plausible causes for such an injury, but the fact he resorted to such a lousy lie, only makes it more obvious that whatever he is hiding, is something extremely important."

"Do you think it will be relevant to us?"

"Well, I hear he's left-handed, meaning that if it isn't fully healed by the time the Courting Season is over, killing him will be much easier." He grinned, ironically, the smile falling from his face almost instantly.

"But if it wasn't a fall then it might mean—" I began.

"That another person made an attempt on his life. That our father isn't the only one making a move to seize power here." Nathon's fingers tapped against his upper arms.

"So, we are not only trying to kill him, but we are trying to make sure we kill him first," I said, despondently, looking at my feet.

"Precisely," Nathon said, with irritation.

"What do we do?"

"You do nothing. I will find out whoever is making the attempt on his life and kill them." He said it so easily, as softly as wind moving through air.

My gaze fell over him with undisguised confusion, perhaps admiration as well. I was unsure.

"How will you find them?" I asked meekly.

"Would you like a detailed lesson on tracking, following, watching, drawing out, and eliminating targets Loria?"

I scowled.

"Don't ask such questions. I will do as I always do. You should leave now." Nathon suddenly became colder.

Suddenly? I caught myself surprised at my own thoughts. Nathon had always been cold.

These past few days, these flickers, and fleeting moments of warmth from him should not have been enough to convince me otherwise.

"Did you find out who Fargreaves was?" I asked.

"Not yet," he turned away from me.

"But you expect to find the elusive assassins who tried to kill the Prince?" I replied sneeringly.

"Would you like to ask someone else to try and gather this information? I'm sure father would be happy to send out Giro perhaps. Or Mathias?"

"Why are you always so cold?" I asked bitterly.

Nathon leant forwards, smiling serenely as he answered.

"Because the world is a raging inferno, and it's the only thing that stops me from being consumed by the flames."

Silence.

We both stood there, so close together, and yet it felt as if there was an ocean between us, an ocean no ship could cross, no bridge, no tunnel. Just water, ready to swallow and fill the lungs of anyone who dared to walk across its waves.

"He asked to see what I...was wearing," I said, timidly.

Nathon turned around, leaning against the table now. "Interesting."

"He thought so too...about my attire, I mean."

"Not in the way we might wish him to find you interesting, I assume."

"No."

I noticed it then, a dark stain on his upper arm, he had been concealing it...intentionally with the hands of his crossed arms.

I took a step towards him, staring at the patch.

Nathon turned back around. I walked faster, reaching his side.

"What's wrong with your arm?"

"Go back to sleep, Loria."

I don't know what made me think I could swim in the ocean I was now stuck in. I grabbed his arm hard. Nathon was good at hiding his pain, which did not surprise me, but even he could not conceal the spasm that spread across his jaw.

He slapped my hand away instantly.

"You're wounded," I stated.

"Was there a need to confirm that?" Nathon said, his lip upturned in a scowl.

"Why isn't it closing?"

Nathon rubbed his hands over his face quickly. "Loria. Leave."

"What happened? Why are you keeping so much from me?"

"Because it's safer that way!" His voice rose slightly, he stepped towards me as he said it.

"For whom?" I asked. "I am already unsafe, I am already at risk, we both are. What use is keeping me in the dark?"

"I don't trust you," he snapped.

Those four words. I had told Nathon the same ones many times. But for some unknown reason to me, hearing them from his lips was hurtful.

"Why? I have never given you a reason to doubt me."

"Or one to confide in you," he said.

"You don't confide in anyone."

"Do you?"

"If given the opportunity, I would."

"Then you are as foolish as I said you were. Do not come to my room again. I will find a place for us to meet, and I will tell you when to meet me there. I will tell you what you need to know. No more. No less. If you listen to me, we will have a much better chance of fulfilling this task."

"Are they dead?"

Nathon appeared confused.

"The person who did that," I looked at his wound. "Did you kill them?"

Nathon took a few steps back. "What do you think?"

"I think...that you should use the Glavdian plant, create a poultice from it, mix it with honey and Riggon, and cover the wound with it. It should...help it close. I can make it for you."

"How charming. Do you have a recipe for a broken clavicle you might like to share with His Highness? Perhaps you could wander to his chambers in the middle of the night and deliver it to him?"

"I'm leaving now," I grumbled discontentedly.

I turned around and walked towards the door. My hand was outstretched, hovering over the handle.

A thought struck me, as sharply and quickly as a slash of a blade, as bright and reflective as one, as if this very conclusion should have been obvious some time ago.

"What if they're the same?" I murmured. "The people who attacked you...and him."

Nathon's silence rather than immediate dismissal was telling.

"They're not dead, are they?" I asked. "You didn't kill them. You would have just dismissed my idea otherwise."

Nathon rubbed his eyebrow with his thumb. "You know I'm starting to think I prefer it when you act oblivious."

"Nathon—"

"They could have been working together. Or it could be a complete coincidence. Like I said, I will find out."

"Are they dead?"

A long stretch of silence.

"Yes," he finally said.

I shook my head in disappointment. "If you couldn't kill them, and they attacked the Prince. I think we'll all be burning in those flames before too long."

Nathon didn't bother to deny their death for a third time.

"No need to worry, Loria. I've got enough ice to stave them off."

I gripped the door handle and bent my chin slightly over my shoulder. "If you get Mathias to come here, I will personally ensure the flames consume you first."

"If Mathias is sent here, I'll jump into them before you can even think to push me," Nathon replied with a slight laugh.

A hint of a smile played at the corner of my lips, and his.

And just as swiftly as it had appeared, it died, drowned in the ocean between us, scorched by the flames enveloping us.

We could never be anything other than two strangers who trusted each other little and trusted the world even less so. We could never know one another in the way perhaps, some small part of us yearned too, and some larger part of us feared to.

We could only ever be this, I realised, in order to be at all.

## CHAPTER 26 - NATHON

"Come on, pretty." One of the women working at the Solar Inn placed her hand on my upper arm. "Don't you want to play with me? We'd have so much fun." She bit her lip, blinking at me incessantly.

"I'm not interested." I removed her hand.

She came closer and pressed both her palms to the table I was sitting at. "Sure I can't do anything to change your mind? Someone like you shouldn't be sitting here all alone."

This was a nuisance, but it was to be expected, after all, the last time I had visited the Solar Inn, there had been no shortage of individuals engaging in intimate activities, or of people propositioning others to join them. Still, this woman's insistence was beginning to test even my patience.

"For the seventh time…Tabatha. I am perfectly happy to sit here by myself. You're wasting your time and skills on me, I'm afraid." I grinned.

"Don't like the ladies huh? We've got plenty of men…pretty like you, perhaps you'd like one of them?"

"Have I made any indication I would?" I leant further back into my chair, trying to distance myself from her clutches.

"Perhaps you like to keep it a secret."

"What I would like… is to be left alone."

"Picked a bad location for that handsome. Someone with a face like yours couldn't hope to be left alone in a place like this." She giggled, falsely and twirled a part of her brown hair around her finger, her hand reached for my leg.

This was growing more difficult. I couldn't draw attention to myself here, and so, I could not refuse her as harshly as I would have wished. While it would hardly have been the first time I partook in such activities against my desire to obtain knowledge or reach a target, I was here for a purpose.

I grabbed her hand and took it in mine with both palms. From the outside, it would simply appear to be a tender and gentle gesture.

"I won't be repeating this again. I am waiting for someone. I have not the time or money to test out your services, nor am I particularly inclined to. Leave this table now. If you attempt to touch me once more, I doubt you'll be able to make any money for the remainder of the evening. Or the month."

Tabatha quickly withdrew her hand from mine and tutted.

"Vile man," she murmured to herself as she hurried away, bumping into others as she did.

"Now, now, Nathon, didn't your father teach you better manners than that?"

I knew I should look up, meet the eyes of the person whose voice had just demanded my attention. But this voice, his voice, was enough to make me freeze. Enough to impede my ability to think, to reason, to process information.

I lifted the mug of alcohol to my mouth and took a sip. This was one occasion where I did require alcohol. I laughed into the drink, at the realisation Sarlan had deliberately sent him here.

"I should have known it would be you," I said as I placed the mug back down.

Mathias, who was also disguised somewhat, sat down in front of me with his own drink. "Don't sound so disappointed. We work well together, don't we?"

Mathias had wanted to fuck me since I was old enough to be taller than him, which, wasn't very old at all. He was the worst of all my father's advisors. Cruel, completely depraved, and perverted. Of course, my father didn't care about his nature, his activities, or his advances, since he was willing to do whatever my father asked of him, relished it even.

"She seemed to like you," he continued.

"She touched me without my permission. Something I don't take very kindly to," I took another sip of my drink.

Mathias laughed salaciously. "That's not what I remember."

I swallowed air. "I think we remember certain events of the past differently."

"I remember them fondly."

He was trying to unsettle me. I loathed to admit his presence alone was rather effective at the task. I decided to remain silent. That was possible, in fact, in this instance, it was preferable.

Mathias looked from side to side, ensuring nobody was listening as he asked, "How is she?"

I involuntarily held my breath for a moment. "She's well."

"Let's hope she stays that way, mmm?" Matthias took a sip of his drink.

I peered at him. "Your concern is touching, but there's no need to worry, I'll make sure she does."

"I have no doubt," Mathias replied. "After all, it affects you as well."

"Exactly," I said, forcing a close-lipped smile, and forcing myself to look into his dark, small eyes.

"How do you find Vasara?" he asked. *How far have you progressed with your task?*

"It's crowded but it has its charms." *Slower than I would have liked, but progress has been made.*

"You really think so? Name a few." *Really? What have you discovered?*

"There is much to do, and see, plenty to grab your attention, and hold it." *She's got his attention, and I've got my ideas about the motivations of the others.*

"All things become boring after a while. Don't you think so?" *Will she hold it?*

"Not all things." *I believe she will.*

"I'm not a fan of crowds myself. Although I can hardly think of a place where Vasara isn't teeming with people." *What is the nature of your setbacks?*

"You're right, even in the quieter areas, rabble are everywhere." *People operating from the shadows.*

For a brief moment, Mathias could not hide the concern from his face.

"It's a shame what happened to His Highness." *Is it related to his injury?*

"He'll recover, I'm sure. He has plenty of time for peace and quiet." *I suspect so.*

"Let's hope he does so soon." *Deal with them. Quickly.*

"He has the finest physicians at his disposal." *I'm already working on it.*

Mathias hummed thoughtfully, a trickle of liquid from his mug slipping into his facial hair.

"Yes, that's true, all Princes do." *End them, or it will be your end.*

"I'm fortunate I've never required one." Nor was I ever offered one, even after my worst injuries.

"Have you heard about what's happening at Kalnasa?" he asked.

I frowned for a moment. I couldn't decipher the meaning behind this question.

"No..." I replied, tentatively.

"Riots, everywhere. The people have been looting, stealing, and trying to flood the gates of King Dunlan's Palace." He sounded disgusted.

"They're starving. It's hardly surprising," I mumbled.

Mathias laughed. "Starving? They're greedy, that's what they are. Not one report of anyone dying from starvation there at all."

I contemplated if there was a specific reason as to why Mathias would bring up this topic. Did my father instruct him to inform me? Or was he actually trying to make conversation? It wouldn't have been the first time his twisted way of thinking convinced him we were colleagues, or even...friends.

"When did you hear?" I asked, curious.

"Just yesterday, gossip, whispers, the usual ways, but it will be common knowledge in a day or two."

Meaning he had discovered this several days ago at least, through his 'usual ways.'

My thoughts turned to the Captain and that girl who was Kalnasa's candidate. This would only make them more determined than ever to succeed, I assumed. I wondered if the Captain knew about these events himself, how he would react. That would be interesting to witness.

"Trade to and from there has been blocked as well."

"By whom?"

"By the commoners. Uninformed sordid scum. Squabbling like fractious children. How do they help themselves by cutting themselves off from the rest of the world?"

"Kalnasa possesses certain resources no other Kingdom can mine," I reminded him.

"Let them get on with it. They'll destroy themselves."

"Weren't you the one lecturing me on manners just moments ago? But here you are, reeling off invectives, ready to condemn a myriad of civilians to death." I smiled, my lips parting slightly in amusement.

Mathias smirked. "Manners are for high society, civilised people. They aren't civilians, they're nothing more than filth."

He was the real filth. The real scourge and scum of this world.

But I smiled again and said, "You know best," while sipping my drink. I placed it down.

"Someone's going to need to retrieve their merchandise though, Athlion won't survive without one Kingdom's draining for long."

"Their drainings have stopped?"

"So, they say."

Merchandise? As far as I was aware, Vessels were not bought or sold, simply confined to the Kingdoms of their origins. In truth, I'd had little time or initiative to investigate the possibility. I wasn't sure whether the slip had been intentional or unintentional on Mathias' part, but I wasn't about to inform him of it.

"I saw Jezil last week." *Your father wants to pass a message onto you.*

"Ah Jezil. How is he?" *What is it?*

"Troubled." *Angry.*

"About?"

"Someone is stealing from his pantry." *Someone has taken something from us.*

"You'd have thought he would have learnt how to better seal his store by now."

Mathias's face fell in irritation. "Alas, thieves are ubiquitous."

"Well, as you said yourself, they're nothing more than filth. I'm sure the Gods, or the universe, or what was it you implied... self-destruction? Will take care of it."

Mathias looked unamused. "He'd like to hire someone to catch them." *He wants you to deal with it.*

"Good luck to him. I doubt many people will be willing." *I'm too busy.*

"I'm sure there are ways they can be persuaded." *Must I remind you of what is at stake?*

"Does he suspect anyone in particular? Maybe his neighbour? A business rival? A jaded lover?"

"A rival most likely." *Someone from another Kingdom. Someone powerful.*

"How much have they stolen?" *What have they stolen?*

"Significant amounts." *Information.*

"Of what?"

"Vital ingredients, recipes, things he would need to make his product."

Even I was baffled by that answer. When it came to information, that could mean anything.

"Well, he has several products, doesn't he? Can't he live without selling one?"

"Yes, but there's one patisserie, he's famous for it, it's the thing that keeps his business running. Nobody else makes another like it. They've stolen items related to that." *Something no other Kingdom is aware of or was meant to be made aware of.*

"When was the last break in?"

"Four weeks ago."

"Nothing since?"

"Nothing needed since. He can't make them without those ingredients."

"Can't he get them back?"

"It's not a matter of getting them back, but a matter of them being gone in the first place."

I rubbed my eyes briefly. "He must think himself rather important, if he believes an investigator is going to help him over some stolen flour. They have more important things to look into here, don't they...what with all the rabble and the crowds." *I have enough to do here as it is. Send someone else.*

"They're the only ones who can do anything about it, what choice does he have?" *You need to do it. You are in a position to do it.* "He has people to provide for," Mathias said. "People who are counting on him." *Don't forget what we'll do to your sister, to Kazal, if you disobey us.*

I peered at Mathias, my face from the outside would have seemed calm, soft, but my eyes betrayed my frustration at this request, which I did not try to hide for his sake.

"I see." *Fine.*

"You know...it's impolite to refuse such a fine lady's attention." He pointed to Tabatha who was now on the far side of the room. "It's unfair, isn't it? To deprive them of affection. Of their... desire?" He looked me up and down. His gaze was a slick poison, running over my skin.

"I'm sure they'll manage," I said tersely.

"Manage? Yes... but you might find them to be rather persistent."

"They might find that to be rather unpleasant." My hand gripped tighter around the mug's handle. I smiled at him. We were both smiling, sitting naturally, casually, always aware of our surroundings, of our appearance.

"Still...you can't say no forever." *Remember you need to blend in here.*

But I also felt an unspoken *to me,* hanging at the end of his sentence.

"I can do whatever I want." I knew that was a lie. It tasted sour on my tongue as I said it.

"A caged bird can fly, but it's still in a cage." Mathias took great pleasure in reminding me, lingering on every word.

"As long as it has wings, it can always escape."

"Not if those wings are clipped."

"Perhaps even then," I met his eyes, smiling. "Even birds with broken wings still look to the sky."

Mathias frowned. He leant in closer, so as to speak more freely. "A little bird shouldn't get any ideas about being anything other than that. It's not an Erebask, or a lion, or a wolf, it's just...a little bird. Ready to sing and look pretty for passersby."

I leant in as well. "Tell me. Have you heard of Pitho?"

Mathias didn't answer.

"I thought not. It's a small bird, black, with a bright golden breast. It looks rather beautiful." I held out my hands a short distance away from each other to indicate its height.

"But it's one of the deadliest and most toxic animals in Athlion." I lifted my finger. "That's because...their bodies and feathers produce a deadly toxin which can kill people within a day. It's a very slow and painful death. At first, you might not notice. Your fingertips turn a little cold, and then numb, and then your lips. Your muscles begin to ache, and your gums begin to bleed. But soon you're in searing agony and begging for death. And all you have to do is" –I flicked my own hand – "touch them. Just once. Isn't that fascinating?"

Mathias looked anything but fascinated.

"You shouldn't underestimate little birds...old friend. Some wolves will wander away from you, some lions will pay you no heed, but some little birds, some little birds can do the greatest damage of all."

Mathias didn't say anything, he simply glared at me now, with a mixture of both predatory and aggressive intent.

"Still perhaps you're right...it wouldn't do me any harm to relax."

I stood, beginning to make my way towards the score of women. It was time after all, to put on the facade, to make my reasons for being here seem reasonable, and unquestionable.

Mathias looked up at me and whispered through gritted teeth, "You'll always belong to him."

I stopped and turned around. "You pretend that pleases you, but we both know you wish to own me yourself." I leant towards him. "And I'd clip my own wings to avoid that fate, but...not without letting you touch them first... of course."

I faced away from Mathias and strode over to the Inn's counter, flashing my brightest smile. I let the people touch my arms, my body, my face. I laughed at their jokes. I complimented their appearances, entertained their advances.

I was singing yes, singing for them all.

And all the while, Mathias was watching.

# CHAPTER 27 – ELIEL

Three hours passed until my audience was finished. Until I had heard, observed, been inundated by, and given my solutions to those who presented me with problems which required solving, or propositions which required my approval.

I could feel myself waning, the pain in my arm grew steadily worse as time went on, and voices droned away. If Elias lived this way on a daily basis, I could only say my respect for him had increased immensely, and that it was no wonder he avoided contact with these people by any means possible.

Fagreaves turned to me once the audience was over. "Your Highness, the final matter is that of your Coronation."

"Mmmm," I replied.

"The preparations have been made. It will take place tomorrow eve."

I sighed. "I see."

"Should Your Highness wish to depart from the ceremony at an earlier time, that can be arranged."

*How generous.*

"Should I need to depart, I will depart, there will be no arrangements necessary," I replied.

"Of course, Your Highness." He bowed his head slightly.

Trenton approached me, bowing before he did. "Your Highness, here is the order of events as they will take place." He handed me a piece of thick white card, outlined with golden symbols of Vasara's emblem, the sun, at each corner.

*Arrival of the guests*
*Procession*
*King's Greeting*
*Oaths*
*Divine Sacrifice*
*Crowning*
*Audience with the King*
*Grand Feast*

"Has His Highness decided what he will offer for the Divine Sacrifice?" Trenton asked.

The Divine Sacrifice was a tradition upheld by every ruling monarch of every Kingdom. Once crowned, they would kneel before the altar of the Gods, giving up something important in return for a bestowal of blessings for their reign. Vasara's ruler, however, was expected to offer the largest sacrifice of all at this event, considering it was the ruling Kingdom, and its monarch was therefore granted power over the others. Previous rulers it was claimed, had sacrificed a beloved animal, a weapon they had wielded for decades, years off their life, their looks, their knowledge, one of their five senses.

"Yes," I stated.

The members of my Council looked at each other cautiously. "May I ask what His Highness has decided upon?"

I knew if I informed them of my sacrifice they would protest to a great degree, and so, my answer was, "You'll find out soon enough."

Trenton nodded in a restrained manner, deciding that probing me further would be futile. He was right.

Jarian approached me from my right. "Your Highness, he has arrived."

"Bring him in," I instructed.

The doors before us opened, and with long, purposeful strides, the Vessel entered the room. The same one I had interrogated just days before.

I had not killed him, or Orlis. In the end it had been he, who had offered his services, in exchange for Orlis' life. In the end, he had changed his mind.

"Kneel before His Highness," Wayman spat.

"No need." I raised my hand to stop him from speaking.

Wayman glared at me utterly confused.

"Where is she?" the young man asked.

"She is being looked after—"

He interrupted me, "Where?"

Wayman looked as if he might faint at the sight of someone interrupting me if it continued for much longer.

I licked my lips and replied, "She is no longer in the Northern Wing, if that is what you are asking." I knew that it was.

The young man nodded, satisfied with my response.

I stood, mentally berating myself for forgetting about the dizziness that had set in just an hour prior.

I remained in place for a second, then approached the man. My guards stepped in beside me, the young man looked at them, then back at me.

"What have you discovered?" I asked him.

"They were there."

I had asked him to track the sorcerers from Liquanon, to the best of his ability. I had debated asking the trackers, but I could not say how adept the sorcerers who had attacked us were at scouting out, and expecting pursuit from that unit.

"And did you follow the trail?"

"Yes."

He was clearly reluctant to expand upon anything. I said nothing, waiting for him to do so.

He remained silent.

"Did it lead anywhere?" I spoke. I was exhausted, I had no time for these long pauses.

"It did."

Fargreaves tutted. "Do not play games, boy. This is no time to prevaricate. You are fully aware of what His Highness wishes to know."

The man didn't even look at Fargreaves, his gaze remained fixed on me.

"What will you do to them?" the young man put to me.

"It is not your place..." Wayman started.

"Nothing, for now," I told him. It was true.

The young man contemplated his words for a brief moment, then answered. "The trail leads to the Glacier Pass, it stops there."

The Glacier Pass was an area just North of Jurasa. It was deeply embedded within woodland and at its centre was a large lake, often frozen over.

"A good place to hide," Trenton observed.

He was right, the Glacier Pass was difficult and dangerous terrain to cross, making it an ideal area to evade pursuit.

"How is it possible the trail stopped there?" Fargreaves glared at the young man.

"I'm not lying," he insisted, glaring back at him.

It was as the Jurasan King had said. "It is possible, if the sorcerers are powerful enough," I interjected.

"Which implies that these powerful sorcerers joined the others at Glacier Pass and were not at Liquanon. They must have colluded on this together and arranged to meet up at Jurasa's Northern point afterwards," Fargreaves said.

"Possibly," I replied.

Fargreaves made his displeasure evident, looking at me sharply. "What other possibilities are there, Your Highness?"

"Many," I stated. "The first group of sorcerers could have been acting alone. They could have deviated from the group and re-joined later, without the more powerful sorcerers being aware of their actions. After all, if the plan were to kill the Jurasan King, why not send the most powerful sorcerers to Liquanon to do so? There would be no benefit in waiting at the pass since they could have cleared their traces of sorcery at the river itself."

I was met with silence.

"There is also the possibility they were the sorcerers we speak of, that one of them had the capability to remove traces of their sorcery but chose to lead us to the Glacier Pass before they erased it. In this scenario, they may have split into groups after Liquanon, with the more powerful sorcerers heading to Glacier, and the rest wandering, possibly alone, or in much smaller numbers towards another direction. Travelling in smaller groups would make it much harder for people to trace their energy, and so, anyone searching for them would follow the path to Glacier. It could have been a deliberate diversion. We do not know whether there is one group acting to deceive us, whether there are two groups working together, or two groups working alone."

Fargreaves tutted. Trenton nodded in assent. The young man looked at me thoughtfully.

"You are to find them," I said to the young man.

"Your Highness, we already have the Commander—" Wayman began.

"The Commander's job is to apprehend them. Your job" — I looked at the young man — "will be to infiltrate them."

The young man's jaw clenched. "You want me to be your spy?"

"Yes," I confirmed.

"I'd rather continue being a Vessel for the rest of my days," he said vehemently.

"That is no longer an option."

"You really are scum," he scowled.

"You are speaking to Royalty, boy, have some respect," Wayman rebuked him.

"I'm quite sure that earning this man's respect will be impossible," I said, "But that is no matter. What matters is that you uphold your side of the arrangement."

"This is no arrangement," the young man grunted.

"Do as I ask, and I promise, Orlis will be safe. I will allow you to live your lives freely and—"

The young man laughed at the word 'freely,' loudly, and openly.

"Do you think you're some kind of saviour? Some kind of God?" He made a move to step towards me. All my guards placed their hands on the hilt of their swords.

The young man assessed the situation, and stepped back, clenching his fists.

"I think nothing of the sort," I told him. "But it is my duty to protect my people."

"And what about sorcerers? Do they not count as people too? The children who learn they can grow food when they are five, or the ones who learn they can hear their neighbour's thoughts when they are ten. What are they, *Your Highness?*"

He was right. They were people. They were people with whom we had coexisted, whom we had deemed a threat, who had proven us right all those decades ago. And now, we could not afford to wait and see if they proved us right again. Those who did not possess such gifts, such abilities, they could not protect themselves. If those who did possess them decided to act, those who did not would all fall, all perish, they would have no chance at survival. It was not that I did not view the sorcerers as people, but that I viewed them as dangerous people. It was not that they did not have the right to exist in this world, or that I wished harm upon them, but that I wished no harm to come to the defenceless. It was that this world had become a battlefield for the prize of living.

And that I intended to win.

I realised I had been silent for a few moments, contemplating these facts, leaving the young man unanswered.

"They are cut from the same cloth as those who lined these streets with blood decades ago. Some of them may even be the same individuals. They are a memory, and they are a reminder of the mistakes we made, of the lives we lost."

The young man huffed in disappointment at my answer, but he did not reply.

"You will set out tomorrow morning."

"And how exactly do you expect me to get away, to pass on…information."

"You'll find a way, I'm sure. Your sister's comfort depends on it."

"And if I die…will she be kept so comfortably then?"

"You have my word that she will. Leave with Jarian, he will give you what you need for your journey."

I nodded towards Jarian. He walked towards the man, intending to escort him out. The sorcerer remained in place for a few moments, as if debating whether or not to speak, then he turned around, and left.

Fargreaves spoke up immediately "Your Highness, this boy—"

"I have made my decision. It is final. That will be all." I had no patience for these men for the remainder of this day.

I leant into the high-backed chair that had been left in the hall. It wasn't the King's throne, which I would only have the right to sit on after tomorrow, but it was equally as uncomfortable.

Once all the men, bar my guards, had left the room, I eventually made my way to my chambers, accompanied by a few of them.

Elias was waiting for me there.

"Ahhh you're back." He straightened up, having been leaning against the doorframe.

"Elias?" I said to him questioningly.

Elias raised an eyebrow. "I came to check in on you, but they said you were busy nodding your head, and signing your contracts."

"I'm well," I said, reaching for the door handle, with my free hand.

Elias placed a hand in front of it. "You look like shit."

"Elias," my voice carried a warning tone this time, urging him to move.

"Decided to sacrifice your good looks tomorrow. Didn't you do it a little early?"

"Elias," I repeated, not having the strength to say anything else.

He was in appropriate attire, for the first time in years, I realised.

"What is it...that you've chosen to sacrifice?" Elias asked carefully, craning his neck around to try and find my face,

"Something inconsequential to me."

Elias huffed. "That doesn't exactly narrow it down."

"Something important to others."

"Neither...does that," Elias spoke slowly.

I turned to him. "And you? How do you fare...after being there once more?"

Elias sighed and waved his hand casually through the air. "No different."

That seemed improbable.

"Terrible," he admitted after a few moments of silence.

"I will not ask such things of you again," I asserted, placing my own hand on the handle now that Elias had removed his.

"You will," Elias stated, so fervently that I couldn't help but look up. "And I won't refuse you."

"You...will not?" I asked doubtfully.

"No. Someone's got to stop you from breaking the other arm, after all."

# CHAPTER 28 – ELIAS

The music rang through the hall as if floating in the air. The guests to Eliel's Coronation were utterly still, entranced by his walk towards the King's Throne. His cloak, the brightest and most luminous gold trailed behind him, far enough to leave at least five steps between us. I couldn't see his face from here, but I could see the faces of the crowd, those who caught a glimpse of him, their eyes wide in admiration, awe, and reverence.

His steps were in perfect time with the melody, his movements as fluid as it. He went on as we, those who had accompanied him on his arrival, branched out and took our place at the front of the hall, next to the candidates here from each of the Five Kingdoms. To my left was Jurasa's escort, to his, Maiwen, to hers Vasara's entourage. To my right was Fargreaves, to his, Wayman. An aisle separated the remaining guests who were seated at the front, including the Albarsans from Audra as well as the representatives from Zeima and Kalnasa.

I took a look at their faces, at their reactions to Eliel. The girl from Kalnasa appeared utterly enamoured, her escort entirely emotionless. Princess Rhana smiled slightly, as if she were proud of him. The Albarsans however, the woman, Audra's Princess I'd since discovered, looked nervous, sick almost. Her brother's eyes roamed over Eliel's attire multiple times as well as his sister's obviously anxious disposition.

Eliel knelt before the High Priest, who brought the sacred text before him. He placed his hand on the paper, after which the High Priest spoke.

"Do you, Prince Eliel Arcon Solisan, son of King Elion Larius Solisan, the ninety-eighth Heir to Vasara's throne vow, that you will dedicate your life in honour and service to the people of Athlion?"

"I will," Eliel raised his voice to respond.

"And do you vow, that you shall uphold the teaching of both the Gods and your ancestors, that you will live by the tenets of divinity, sacrifice, justice, and virtue?"

"I will."

Of all the people I knew, Eliel was the least devout, the least inclined to believe there were any Gods watching over us. These divine sacrifices always came to pass. That should have been enough evidence to convince him the Gods existed, but to Eliel, it wasn't 'a clear enough explanation to justify the existence of nine distinct celestial beings.' I smiled a little to myself as I remembered the explanation he had offered a High Priest who'd been instructing us both as young men.

*"Faith is the absence of proof,"* the High Priest had said.

*"Then it is not faith,"* Eliel had replied, *"But hope."*

*"Hope and faith are similar,"* the High Priest had protested.

*"Your Gods don't ask for hope,"* Eliel had answered. *"They feed off its absence."*

He had been fifteen then.

It was not that I agreed with him. I believed the Gods existed. Only that I thought them all to be selfish fucking sadists. That they not only fed off the absence of our hope but revelled in our anguish.

But then so too, did Kings.

Eliel removed his hand from the book. The High Priest was passed a small bowl, by another shepherd of the Church. In it were the dark golden ashes of a Chimera. Their ashes were kept specifically for this purpose, for noble ceremonies. They smelt rich, like the fumes after a small flame combined with fresh grass. The Priest drew the symbol of Vasara on Eliel's forehead with the substance.

Audra's Prince whispered something into his sister's ear. She didn't react. As he raised himself back up to his full height, his eyes caught mine for a brief moment.

The man to my left raised a hand to his mouth and swallowed. I had forgotten the smell of the ashes might be nauseating for those who hadn't come across it before. Saying that, I had smelt far worse in battle. It seemed as if this man hadn't. A wonderful choice of escort for Jurasa's Princess.

I turned my attention back to the spectacle. A tension swarmed my body, encroaching on the entire space. This was the moment I had been dreading. Eliel's plans grew ever more mysterious to me, and delirious altogether. I wished he would discuss these things with someone before he decided upon them.

It struck me then, that such a person should have been me. It was my own fault I had not been there for him. It was my own fault I had strayed so far, he felt I could not be trusted.

I should, I wanted to rectify that now but...it could be too late.

Although it was hard to say if Eliel would trust anyone.

I certainly didn't.

I certainly didn't trust this sacrifice was going to be anything minor. Eliel liked making statements. This was the perfect opportunity to do that, before all the Lords and Ladies and Gods knew what other titles were stacked like ants around the room, crushed into a tiny space, waiting with bated breath for their King to rise.

Why he had to sacrifice anything at all was beyond me. Whoever had come up with that idea I decided, was a fucking fool.

It certainly hadn't worked for Elion, and he'd sacrificed a whole year of his memories.

Now that I thought about it, that didn't sound too terrible. There were things I would have been desperate to forget. The year selected was random of course, but still, there was a good chance that whatever year the Gods selected, if such a sacrifice had been applied to me, some hideous memories would have been eliminated.

The music faded out, the choir and the instrumentalists slowly reducing their volume.

"Your Highness, have you decided upon your divine sacrifice?"

Eliel stood and turned around. Clad in his golden cloak, in his long, white and golden embroidered tunic, the high collar of which curled around his neckline, his dark red hair partially tied at the top, in golden thread that weaved throughout the rest of his strands...he truly did look like the King of all people.

He addressed those people now.

"For the blessing of the Gods upon my reign, and all the people under it, I, Prince Eliel Arcon Solisan, have chosen to sacrifice..."

He paused.

"My fertility."

The hall, although silent before, felt as if death itself had come to watch. Not a single soul moved, or spoke, or drew breath, it felt.

Well.

He really should have discussed this with someone first.

# CHAPTER 29 – NATHON

This was monumentally, devastatingly, bad.

No fertility, no child. No child, no way our father's plan could come to fruition. Not in the way he had intended.

Which only meant he would seek an alternative means of its success.

I didn't believe in the Gods, and hence the sacrifices, and hence...the Prince's true lack of fertility. But I did believe the Prince would now go to great lengths to ensure he did not bear an heir, with anyone, after declaring this his divine sacrifice.

A discomforting sickness, a tension, clawed at my gut. I could only imagine what Loria was feeling. But we couldn't move, couldn't react. Nobody else in this entire hall was doing so. We couldn't show any sign this meant something to us at all. Theoretically, yes, this would mean something for each of the five candidates, but for us, it was something entirely different.

Why had this Prince chosen to sacrifice his fertility? What Prince, what noble in the whole of Athlion, would do such a thing? It would guarantee no heir, which for many, equated to their notion of no legacy. It would increase the fragility of their position. It would make them a far less...

It would make them a far less desirable candidate for marriage.

It couldn't be. We were already here. The Prince had already agreed to this Courting Season, it would have to be seen through until the end, one of the women standing at these front benches would become his Queen. That was already predetermined.

At least, I believed so. Was it? For once in my life, I could not anticipate the actions of my target.

*"But no, with a young, inexperienced, and if rumour is to be believed conceited King... now is our chance."*

I recalled my father's words to Loria. Young, yes? Inexperienced, naturally. But conceited? No, this King was not conceited. He was simply certain of his own mind, his own strategy.

The High Priest's face, his lackeys, the members of the Prince's Council, their faces left no room for doubt, they had not known about this either.

"Is Your Highness..." the High Priest started. "Sure?"

The Prince, without moving his head, glanced at him, moving his eyes to the side. I had never heard of someone being asked if they were sure about their divine sacrifices before. If my life hadn't just been thrown into imminent danger with this Prince's decision, I would have found the entire scene enthralling. In fact, despite the threat to my existence, there was still a part of me that did.

He had managed to complete a manoeuvre that had taken everyone by surprise, one that by their own laws and faith they could not reverse.

It was almost enough to make me consider taking him as the King seriously.

"It...it shall be done. Let the Gods witness it. Let the King honour it. Let the people reap from it." The High Priest sounded unsure and utterly dispassionate.

A tall auburn-haired man made a move to step forwards, presumably to stop the sacrifice. The movement was slight, but I caught it just in time to see a large hand grip him around his bicep and hold him in place with little difficulty. The drunken cousin had stopped Fargreaves just in time. Fargreaves stared at him, trying to shake him off, but Elias' grip only tightened, to the point of evident pain for the Councilman.

Perhaps the cousin had known. Perhaps.

The High Priest brought forwards a larger bowl, containing a liquid, and a small blade, which Eliel used to draw across his hand, the one still hung in a sling. He dropped his own blood into the mixture. He then drank it and turned, kneeling to the position he had started in.

"By the divine energy that flows through me, by the will of the Gods, I crown thee, Eliel Arcon Solisan, King of Vasara and of Athlion."

The High Priest placed a large crown on his head, fashioned in the shape of the sun's rays, it had been similar to his crown as a Prince, but larger, and adorned with dark ruby, amber and golden gems.

Eliel turned, and at once the crowd roared.

"All hail the King! All hail the King! All hail the King!"

The High Priest spoke to the crowd. "His Majesty will now hold his audience, for those who have not been permitted, please enter the adjoining banquet hall, where the Grand Feast will—"

The doors swung open. The mass sound of the entire crowd turning around sounded like a strong gust of wind. Hundreds of eyes were met with the sight of a young man, dragging a woman in by the wrists. Her shackled wrists.

A Vessel.

I couldn't help but think of that night, that woman.

The man was carrying a sword, which he pointed directly at the King. He let go of the woman, and raised his other hand, seemingly stretched out towards nothing. But his eyes...they glinted with the unmistakable surge of sorcery.

He dropped his free hand.

The hand he had used to freeze us all in place.

A Telepath.

None of the guards were moving in to apprehend him.

Nobody was doing anything at all.

I wasn't doing anything at all.

We couldn't move.

The man's grip on the sword never wavered as he moved further down the aisle. As he came closer, I could see the scars adorning his arms.

He was a Vessel too.

And now, he was free.

# CHAPTER 30- HESTAN

I had managed, just before we had been forcibly planted in place, to grab Dyna's hand. I could sense, as soon as these Vessels had entered the hall, her instant overwhelming fear, and although we could not move, she was still trembling in my grip.

Unlike the large majority of guests, I saw no use in trying to break the sorcery this Acciperean had cast. He was obviously a Telepath, and so any attempts would only be in vain. I could only plan what I might do once it was lifted, and even that was proving difficult. There was a chance, I knew, we may not live to act at all. The other Vessel's shackles were still firmly planted around her wrists, but there was no saying whether or not this man had the ability to remove them, or what her abilities might be.

My own death here, I could accept if absolutely necessary, but Dyna's, she was just a child. Dunlan's niece, I could not.

My eyes followed the path of the young man as he approached the King, each step closer, each step louder. His eyes were full of rage, of chaos. I doubted he had planned his actions thoroughly at all, but his intentions were clear.

I opened my mouth, but no, it did not surprise me, I could not speak.

But the King could.

His eyes were cold as he regarded the incoming guest. He appeared utterly unafraid, as if he were glancing at a child.

"What do you hope this will achieve? I can assure it will not be the result you hoped for."

It seemed his main hope was the King's death, so I couldn't help but disagree.

"It certainly won't be the one you did, *Your Majesty.*"

"You are powerful, but you are not powerful enough to end the lives of everyone here."

The King spoke this as if it were fact, rather than a bluff. It wouldn't surprise me if he were that knowledgeable, but on the topic of sorcery…that was surprising.

"Therefore, there will be at least one hundred people who have seen your face before you flee. You won't get far," the King warned.

The man laughed. "It doesn't matter. It doesn't matter if I live. All that matters is that you don't."

"And what about her?" The King's eyes moved to the woman the man had dragged in. "Do you not care for her welfare?"

The man was now close enough to raise the blade to the King's neck. "Don't you dare speak of her welfare, you, who placed chains around her hands and feet."

"You know I speak the truth, kill me now and you condemn her to death." He had spoken to them before, I realised. He had spoken to these Vessels. He knew this man, and he knew who this woman was to him.

Whatever the subject of their conversation had been, it had clearly not been something the young man had appreciated.

"You speak as if she is ALIVE," he screamed in his face, moving in so close they could embrace now. The yell of this one man was so stark against the induced silence of an entire crowd.

"What life is this for her? What life is this for us? It's not a life at all. Death would be a release for her." The man was speaking through heaving breaths, his voice was shaking, cracking with every word.

The young woman squirmed under the man's grip, physically showing her disagreement with the statement. The King noticed too.

"It doesn't seem... that she agrees with you."

"She is not in her right mind. And it's no wonder, after what you've done to her."

The woman continued to struggle, glancing wearily at the man.

The King persisted. "She is frightened of you."

The man looked down at the woman, confirming the King's statement. He gritted his teeth. "She's not well."

"Then allow our doctors to see her."

"That's fucking ENOUGH."

The King lost his ability to speak.

He strained to talk and as he did, blood began to escape his lips. He sank to the floor on his knees.

At his own Coronation, the King was kneeling before another man. The blood dripped from his lip, the only sound in the room, like hailstones smacking against the marble white floor.

The man placed the blade above the King's neck, as if he were about to behead him. The King couldn't move, he remained fixed in place, his eyes locked onto the man who was standing at his side.

She shrieked. The pitch was so high it tore at the air. The auburn-haired woman ripped away from the man, wailing, falling onto her elbows, and backing away.

"Orlis," he said gently.

Orlis was sobbing, dragging herself across the floor.

The young man grabbed her hand, she had barely moved away from him at all. His blade was still at the King's neckline.

"Let me go," she said, whimpering.

The young man's face fell.

For the briefest second, I felt it. Dyna's hand squeezed mine tighter, ever so slightly. I had barely been able to perceive the feeling, I had barely been able to notice that for a fraction of a moment, a slither of time, the sorcery had lifted.

Nobody had. The moment had come and gone in the same tiny fragment.

Nobody but him.

His hand remained outstretched, now frozen in the air. His palm faced the ceiling, his fingers were slightly curled, his index finger was pointing forwards.

Audra's Prince was smiling.

We had been stripped of all our weapons. Unlike the other events we had attended, this one was highly public, and not even the Courting Season's escorts had been permitted to bring any weapons into the Ceremony, to avoid any accusations of bias. Only Vasara's King's guard, currently immobilised around the space, had been allowed to hold them.

We had been checked thrice over before we had been permitted to enter this hall and yet...

A dagger was now lodged in the young man's throat.

Within that miniscule piece of time, Audra's Prince had withdrawn the weapon from its hiding place and aimed with enough precision to avoid injuring the King and to strike a lethal point on the Vessel's body.

The Bird of Death. His alias was not an exaggeration. It was a perfect analogy.

Slowly, little by little the sorcery lifted from our bodies. As the life was drained from the young man, so too was his hold on our minds. Within minutes, he no longer had the energy to maintain it.

Orlis was screaming now. The young man had sunk to the floor, kneeling in a near identical position to the King. Her hands slipped across the slick blood trailing down his neck and onto his upper chest. The young man was choking on his own blood, staring at Orlis wide eyed.

Audra's Prince leapt up the stairs in a few movements and reached his target. He stood there for a moment observing the scene. Orlis turned around and threw herself at him, weakly trying to scratch his face, his throat. Audra's Prince easily lifted her off himself and shoved her to the side.

The King's guard who had finally become free of the sorcery stepped in to apprehend the woman. A panic seized the crowd, waves of cries and hollers mingling to form the indescribable sound of fear. People were rushing to leave. The King's men and his guards were trying their best to allow for an orderly exit, but it was nearly impossible.

I squeezed Dyna's hand and approached the altar.

Audra's Prince strode over to the young man.

"I need that back." He pulled the dagger out from the man's neck, after which he fell on his back to the floor.

I stepped in beside him. We both watched as the man's blood spread across the blanket of white ground as if searching for something to hold onto.

"Unfortunately for you, the King's guards do a thoroughly unthorough job at searching for weapons," Audra's Prince put to the half alive man.

"It had nothing to do with the weapon," I mumbled under my breath, loud enough for Audra's Prince to hear.

"It's hardly as if I could have cut him open with the air, is it, Captain?" He smiled at me knowingly.

"It's hardly possible anyone could have done that at all."

"Is this your way of saying thank you…I—"

The King who had now stood, approached us. "You have my thanks, Your Highness." He bowed to Audra's Prince. *Bowed* to him.

The Prince and I glanced at one another in surprise.

"I was only doing my duty. After all, saving the King's life is a great honour." He gave a restrained smile.

"Was it his life you were saving?" I found myself mumbling.

The King glanced at me confusedly, as if he was surprised I had spoken. As he did, he used his thumb to wipe errant blood away from his mouth. It was still smeared slightly across his pale lips and chin.

Audra's Prince, however, laughed. "Don't be jealous, Captain. But you are right, I had my neck in a terribly awkward position when he froze us all in place." He pointed back at the young man, who was now dead. "It was horrendous having to wait for the moment I could end his life and stretch it out."

I wasn't sure if anything he was saying bore any actual truth.

I was inclined to believe not.

"Do not diminish your deed. I owe you a great deal," the King stated.

"It's nothing. Besides, I broke your rule of no weapons in the hall, so if you can let that go, then I can promise to seek no reward."

"Very well," the King replied.

Audra's Princess approached us. The King glanced at her in surprise. A woman coming so close to the sight of a dead body and this much blood wasn't customary or common, particularly in Vasara.

"Your Majesty, are you…unharmed?"

The King's face softened slightly. "I am, thank you Princess. Do not trouble yourself."

"It is no trouble," the Princess replied confidently. "I am only sorry that you had to face such an ordeal."

"The fault does not lie with you."

"But still, your life was in danger. I am glad you are safe."

"You need not be concerned for her, Your *Majesty*," Audra's Prince made sure to emphasis his new title. "The sight of blood isn't enough to make her faint."

"Still. It is not a pleasant sight," the King responded.

"Seeing the dead body of someone who wished you dead just moments before is hardly an unpleasant sight, is it?" Audra's Prince argued.

I let out a small sigh at his statement and looked to the ground. Why was he so insistent on making these comments?

"He had his reasons to despise me," the King said, his gaze resting on the dead body.

We were all stunned by that statement. Even Audra's Prince was silent for a moment before he said, "If everyone who had their reasons to hate me was afforded the same level of sympathy, you'd be dead now...Your Majesty."

"It is not sympathy. Only understanding."

Something only the King could understand, what had transpired, between him and this man, now lifeless on the ground.

"You will make a great King, Your Majesty," I found myself saying. It was no fabrication. I believed it to be true.

"I hope you are right, Captain."

The King's Cousin approached him and pulled him to one side, leaving me standing with the Albarsans.

"So, Captain, will I be getting my thanks anytime soon? Or should I wait for a grander gesture from you at a later date?"

The Princess looked impatiently at her brother.

"Apologies Captain, he speaks too freely." She smiled.

"And too often," I added coolly.

The Prince laughed. "You might be one of the only people I've met who's not terrified of me, Captain. No...perhaps the only person."

I looked him in the eye. "Who says I'm not, Your Highness?"

It wasn't fear I felt for the Prince however, only wariness.

The Prince almost looked disappointed as he placed his dagger back within a deep fold in the clothing at his ribs.

It was as if the Vessel had come back to life, and I was frozen in place once more.

There was no mistaking it. The dagger was Noxstone. That explained why a throw from such a far distance was able to penetrate this man's flesh with ease and tear through most of the arteries in his neck. It was jagged, small, its hilt was fashioned into the shape of a bird's wing.

And there was no mistaking the fact I had seen that dagger before.

I had seen that dagger years ago.

In my older brother's back.

# CHAPTER 31- LORIA

The Captain had been staring into space for the last minute. Nathon and I had been glancing around the hall, examining the frenzy that had ensued shortly after he had ended this young man's life.

In less than a second, as if it were nothing.

The King on the other hand looked infinitely calm, despite the fact it was he who had suffered an attempt on his life.

The Captain was still lost in thought.

"Are you…" I began, looking at the Captain cautiously.

Nathon's attention was drawn back to him as I spoke.

"Are you alright Captain?" I finished asking.

The Captain, who was shaken from his stupor, looked up at me, then at Nathon. "Forgive me, I must accompany the Lady back to her room."

"Of course," I said. "I hope that she does not suffer too much from this ordeal." The words felt foolish as they left my lips. It was obvious this event would have shaken her. It had shaken me, and I was five years her senior.

"Thank you for your concern, Princess." The Captain bowed, glancing at us both one last time, before making his way towards Lady Dyna.

Nathon and I stood there in silence. I knew the same thoughts were swirling around both of our minds, the same hopelessness. I still hadn't processed the King's announcement of his sacrifice before our movements had been taken under the sorcerer's control.

We were both lost, like two leaves from a tree, flying through a raging storm, with nothing to latch onto.

"We should leave as well," Nathon said.

Just as we were about to do so, Elias, who had been standing by the King, turned away and left.

Nathon caught me examining them.

"Not now, let's just go."

I ignored him and walked over towards the King. He was clearly startled at my approach but walked towards me in kind.

"I never had the chance to express my sorrow about your injury, Your Majesty. I hope you recover well and soon."

The King smiled slightly and looked at my face from side to side before he spoke. "Thank you, but you need not fear Princess. I have the best healers one could hope for."

Apart from those Dareans who had been Healers, I thought, the rarest ability of the type. They were almost extinct now it was said. In fact some declared they already were.

The King noticed my silence. "What are you thinking about?" His voice dropped in volume, it almost sounded as if he were asking the question to himself.

"Apologies, Your Majesty, nothing of importance."

"Indulge me. It has been a trying day."

I couldn't help but feel suddenly aware of the strangeness of this scene. The noise from the crowd still hadn't dissipated, all around us were signs of death, fear, and panic. I was still standing on the altar where blood was spreading at an ever-increasing rate.

And yet here I was, exchanging conversation with the now King, as if we were strolling through the Palace Gardens.

It was absurd. I knew.

I tried to invent an alternate thought. I wasn't sure my original one would be appreciated.

"Princess?" he interrupted my attempts.

I looked at his feet as I replied. "I was thinking about those who can heal with sorcery, Your Majesty, when you mentioned your healers. About how it is said there are almost no sorcerers left alive with that ability now."

There was a pause. I waited in anticipation.

"You were thinking about sorcerers?" he said quietly.

My stomach sank. I knew about this Kingdom's stance on sorcery, on the King's.

"I...it was only..." I could hear the anxiety laced in my tone. I was still looking at the King's legs.

"True," he finished my sentence. "It is true there are hardly any Darean Healers left in Athlion. It is said they could heal almost any ailment of the body or mind."

"It seems a shame," I said quietly, as if I was afraid of my own thoughts. "They could have saved a great many people."

"Sorcerers have also ended the lives of a great many people."

I looked at him then, not because I wanted to, but because I could hear him approaching me more closely.

"So have humans, it...can be said, in truth..." I spoke more quietly.

My answer was clumsy, tripping on my tongue. To have grown so long, stifling thoughts that slipped into my mind, only to say them aloud in Eliel's presence now. It felt like falling. The words I uttered were feeble and weak, as if their edges were jagged, not ready for speech. As if they were withered and dusted from having been suppressed in the corners of my mind too many times. How to articulate my true thoughts, how to indulge Eliel in them, was a mystery to me. And yet, with him, I was compelled to try. I didn't know what it was, what came over me when he was close. Of all the people I should filter my thoughts and words around, it should be him. But it was that gaze, and his presence, it was as if they lured honesty from my mouth.

I'd been seized so long by an urgent terror. One of my own voice.

But another slumbered underneath. Quieter, yet more insidious.

The one of remaining silent.

And Eliel drew it from the depths of my chest, brought it to the surface like a bone breaking through flesh.

Let him hear my distorted attempts. Perhaps he would be able to decipher the meaning in them, with that gaze. A gaze that was not jagged, or rough. Not ugly or dark. But radiant, practiced and assured. Ready to draw the hideous from anyone. Ready to see it whole. Devour it. Indulge in it.

Were there really people who could not only see such parts in someone, but delight in them as well?

"Humans like your brother?" Eliel's hushed voice drew me back to the present.

I looked over his shoulder, unable to meet his eyes. "I...Yes. Like him."

"You do not seem to mind when he kills." I could feel him looking at me, demanding I look at him.

I didn't reply.

"Would you forgive the sorcerers for their crimes, the way that you forgive him?"

I couldn't tell him I did not forgive my brother, that I couldn't stand to think of his deeds, that I loathed the very thought of his actions.

*Would you condemn him the way you condemn the sorcerers?* Was what I wanted to say.

And what was he implying? That the sorcerers should be forgiven? That Nathon should be condemned? Every word that came out of his lips was like a puzzle I could not solve.

"Do you believe that I should?" I asked.

"I am more interested in what you believe."

I turned to him. "I believe that you accuse me of something all Five Kingdoms are guilty of, Your Majesty. For better... or for worse."

"Which is it?" He moved in slightly closer. "Better or worse?"

"I—"

Nathon's palm was on my upper back.

"Excuse us, Your Majesty. Congratulations on your coronation and surviving such a horrifying assassination attempt."

The King backed away from me slightly and peered at my brother.

"It will be the first of many, I'm sure," he replied.

"If you need my services to end any of their lives, please send word."

"Thank you." The King tilted his head forwards. "I will be sure to remember that."

Nathon bowed, I curtsied, and he led me out of the hall.

I had expected we would walk to our chambers, instead, Nathon led me to the West Wing, through various floors, corridors, and walkways until we reached an alcove, on a high floor. It was overlooking Iloris, Vasara's capital, and supported by white pillars. It was simply a fairly small semi – circle overhanging off the side of the Palace. There were no railings or gates preventing someone from falling to their death. The floor was marble and painted with golden and amber symbols of the sun, fire, chimeras, and the stars.

"Think you'll be able to remember the way?" Nathon asked me, his arms crossed.

"I...this is the place you've chosen?"

"It's perfect, there are only two of these in the whole Palace, one is here, next to the library. The other is also in the West Wing, but that's next to the weapons hall, which is far more heavily guarded. Nobody likes to come here since it's awkward and difficult to access and far too many people have fallen from this height." Nathon looked at the ground. "It's no wonder, it's tiny."

"I'll...remember." I wasn't even sure it was true.

I didn't even know what to say, or where to begin.

"What will we do now?" I muttered.

"I'll have to let Mathias know and—"

"Mathias? Mathias is here?"

Nathon grimaced and squeezed his eyes shut. He had obviously intended to keep that information from me.

"You won't need to deal with him, don't worry."

"But you will."

"I can handle him."

I hadn't been around the Citadel very much as a child, I had tried my best to stay away. As much as that had made me unaware of certain events, and a target of great scrutiny, it hadn't made me oblivious. I had seen and heard Mathias' attitude towards my brother, towards the other young men and boys who had been around the Citadel, working within its walls, or for my father's armies.

Nathon interrupted my thoughts. "I'll let him know and I'm sure we'll receive word about any changes to the plan quickly."

"How? How can this plan be changed?" I protested.

"Just proceed with what you're doing for now. Asking the King if he was well was a good idea." He smiled at me slightly.

"You were the one who saved his life."

"Which may turn out, was a complete waste of my time, if I'm about to be instructed to end it."

"But it helps us, doesn't it? For now. He may be inclined to trust us more."

Nathon let out a tired chuckle and shook his head. "No, that man isn't the trusting kind."

"How did you even do that?" I said, a touch of melancholy to my tone.

"Do what? You mean kill him?"

"You only had the shortest amount of time to—"

"Does it matter how?" he asked.

"I suppose not." My fingers found their way through the ends of my hair.

"I'm going to find the cousin."

"What? Why?"

"I want to get closer to him. I think he knew about this sacrifice."

"Why do you think that?"

"Many reasons. But if I'm right, I might be able to get it out of him since he's drunk most of the time."

Although he was indeed drunk for a large amount of time, the King's cousin didn't strike me as someone who was easy to manipulate. If that was my assumption, then Nathon surely had already come to the same conclusion.

Which meant that once again, he was hiding his true intentions.

"Is that what you're doing with the Captain too?"

Nathon looked confused, spinning his head around from the view to my face. "What?"

"You seem...close to him as well."

Nathon sighed. "The Captain and I have an understanding."

"About what?"

Nathon was silent.

"You never tell me anything."

"There are some things you are better off not knowing."

"Is this one of them?"

"The Captain wants something from me. I've agreed to give it to him, but... I'm still deciding on what I'll ask for in return."

Nathon sounded completely relaxed about this agreement, but I couldn't fathom how the Captain wanting something from him meant anything good.

"What is it he wants?"

"Something trivial. It's not going to affect us in any way."

"Are you sure?"

"Yes. But the Captain himself...I'm not so sure of."

"In what sense?" I moved slightly closer to the view, to Nathon.

"In the sense that, out of everyone in that hall, he was the only person who came over to examine that body. As well as you, of course." He pointed at me. "He's curious, he's wary. Jurasa's escort looked as if he were about to empty his stomach contents. Vasara's was utterly useless, and Zeima's was too busy comforting her lover."

"Lover?"

"Ahh yes, I forgot to mention that."

*Zeima's escort is Rhana's lover? Her partner?*

"How did you find out?"

"I used my eyes."

I rolled mine. "How's your wound?" I had given Nathon the balm I'd spoken of yesterday morning.

"It's healed."

I scoffed. "It's not possible a wound like that could heal so fast."

"By my standards, it's healed."

This was a pointless topic of conversation to pursue.

"You're getting close to the cousin, the Captain, and you're conferring with Mathias, there must be something else I can do."

"No, Loria. That's the whole purpose of my accompanying you here." He took a step closer towards me. "It's your job to remain unsuspicious. If you really want to help, then just be that."

A scream scratched at my brain, inside my chest, inside my limbs. I was not doing my part. Sarlan would not be pleased. Then another thought pierced through my fragmented mind. Is that what Nathon wanted? To take the credit for our possible victory here himself? I didn't want such credit, but I wanted...no, *needed* to know I could account for my role here. That I could prove my utility to my father. That I could say for sure I had carefully considered every step. That I had done enough.

After waiting for a reply I did not provide, Nathon took several steps back.

And with one hand on the left outer wall, he jumped off the edge of the alcove.

I ran to its edge, glancing down. He had landed on a jutted-out window ledge below us. He leapt to another, then another. Further down, down, and down.

And though I was the one of us standing still.

It felt I was the one sinking.

# CHAPTER 32 – BAZ

"It's been three weeks Yaseer, and we haven't heard a single thing."

Yaseer sighed wearily, leaning further back into his chair. The air in the tent was musty, suffused with the scent of leather and parchment. The same tent Nemina and I had been brought to on our arrival here, weeks ago.

"What is it that you want me to do, young man? We knew this might take some time," Yaseer glanced up.

"What if something has happened to her?"

"Nemina is perfectly capable of handling herself."

I closed my eyes, trying to convince myself Yaseer was right. I knew Nemina was powerful, but still, she wasn't fully trained. How could he have asked her to do this so early? No, how could Nemina have agreed? Why was I surprised, of course Nemina had agreed. Nemina would have done anything to get away from this group of people.

For all I knew she had gone on her own way, using this mission as an excuse to leave and never return. I hoped that wasn't true.

I knew wanting her to return didn't make any sense, but still, I wanted her to.

I supposed I was just that lonely, that the first person I had spoken to properly after years had automatically become dear to me in my mind.

It was highly unlikely Nemina felt the same.

"Couldn't we at least send someone to find out?"

"It's too dangerous. Risking the life of one sorcerer is something I am already displeased about."

That didn't strike me as the truth.

"War will inevitably mean all their lives are at risk," I reminded him.

"There will be no war, no chance at salvation, if there is nobody left to fight in it."

He was being rather dramatic. As if sending one person to see if Nemina was still breathing was a monumental sacrifice.

"Let me go," I suggested, clasping my hands behind my back.

"Your training isn't finished." Yaseer insisted.

"Neither was hers."

"She possesses more raw power than you do, more energy. Besides, we need you here. You are good for the people."

What was that supposed to mean?

"They like you," Yaseer clarified.

It was true that over the past few weeks I had been learning more about the people here, speaking with them, and growing closer to them. I had laughed for the first time in years, I had smiled.

But Nemina. Gods, she hadn't smiled once. She hadn't done anything other than keep to herself. The light still hurt her eyes, I knew. I visited her as often as I could, but she hardly seemed glad to see me the majority of the time.

I shook my head. It wasn't my job to save her.

But who would. Could she do that for herself?

It didn't seem so, at least not to me.

"Nemina will survive. She will do what she has set out to do. She will come back."

"How can you be so sure?"

"She likes you too," Yaseer answered, his voice tinted with pride.

"You have a very high opinion of me," I awkwardly turned away.

"It's true." Yaseer leant back into his chair. "The second week after your arrival, one of the newcomers tried to take some of the clothes you had set aside for yourself. It was..." Yaseer thought for a moment. "A garment from Kalnasa I believe, lilac in colour. Nemina snatched it from his hands and told him that it, as well as other specified items were not to be touched." Yaseer chuckled. "She hadn't meant to threaten him, I believe, but still, the young man certainly perceived it to be a threat. Nobody has touched those clothes since."

I looked down at my tunic. Lilac.

So, she wasn't completely intolerant of my company. I knew it. I smiled to myself.

Still, "I'm not sure that's substantial evidence," I countered.

"I understand your concerns. But the plan was thorough, and well thought through, and I have faith in Nemina's capabilities."

"She isn't the only one with capabilities. There are very powerful, influential people there at the moment."

"Yes. But there isn't one living creature that could pose a threat to her there."

"What if they catch her?"

Yaseer walked over towards me and placed his hands on my shoulders. "They won't. Please, unburden your mind of these thoughts and relax, rest. You have earned it."

"So has she."

A woman walked into the tent.

"Ahhh, Faina," Yaseer greeted her. "What is it?"

"There's been a troupe of trackers spotted," Faina replied. Her long dark hair was ruffled, as if she had run here. She sounded out of breath.

Yaseer's voice dropped as did his arms from my shoulders. "Where?"

"Three miles east."

"How did they get this close?" Yaseer asked himself.

"What shall we do?" She probed him.

"We need to leave now. Find Nyla, she can cover our tracks."

"Nyla returned to Kalnasa," Faina reminded him.

"Let me try," I found myself saying.

Yaseer thought for a moment. "Very well, you should be capable. Come."

Faina, Yaseer, and I left the tent. Within minutes, Yaseer had gathered everyone and informed them of the situation. We had, by his estimates, less than an hour before the trackers found us. We had to pack any essential belongings, destroy the rest, and then I would remove the traces of our energy behind.

I immediately felt regretful. What if I wasn't strong enough to do this? What if I lead the trackers right to us? What was I thinking? Nemina's poor decision making and impulsiveness must have started to rub off on me.

Ullna approached us. "Where is Nyla?"

"She isn't here, Baz will do it for us," Yaseer told her.

"The boy?" Ullna looked at me as if I were a stranger.

"We have nobody else."

"You have me, why didn't you ask?"

"I need you to ride out now. Go to him and let him know, Ullna. This is the fourth time this has happened in the space of a month, they're getting closer."

"That can wait, Yaseer—"

"No," Yaseer bellowed. "Go now."

Ullna seethed at him, then tutted. She looked at me. "Don't fail, boy."

"I—"

But before I could finish, she turned around and left.

"Who is she going to see?" I asked.

"An ally of ours," Yaseer answered, as he moved. I followed him.

"Why aren't they helping us now?"

"He's not in a position to do so."

He...so this ally was a man.

"Is he a sorcerer?"

Yaseer didn't answer as he walked towards the horses.

Faina looked sick. She was a relatively new addition here, and had arrived after Nemina and I.

"They've gone through this before," I said, trying to comfort her. "I'm sure we'll escape in one piece."

Faina swallowed and nodded. "I...I don't want to go back."

I gripped her hand. "You won't"

I'd personally make sure of that. If they even considered taking her back as a Vessel, I would kill her before they could get the chance.

There wasn't one former Vessel alive who would prefer going back to death.

Although, in all honesty, I couldn't be entirely sure about what Nemina's decision would be. Her mind worked entirely differently to anyone else's.

"Young man," Yaseer said to me, "You must begin now."

I had only learnt the concealing spell a short amount of time ago. It was a form of one of the five basic castings any Acciperean or Darean could conduct with time- translucency. Translucency could be applied to the self or extended to an entire group if the sorcerer was powerful enough. The other four were strength enhancement, speed enhancement, enhanced healing, and levitation. Enhanced healing was largely unconscious. Of the others, I had managed to succeed in applying speed, and strength enhancement, but I found levitation and translucency more difficult.

The people rushed around, but in an orderly manner. It was clear they had undergone this routine several times before. I closed my eyes and concentrated. I thought about what Nyla had taught me. To let this world's energy flow through me like a conduit, I had to empty my mind, I had to let it in.

That was far easier said than done. After all, I was petrified too. I was petrified of getting this wrong, of getting captured, of dying.

Slowly, I could feel it. The warmth of the source flowing through my limbs, my chest, I redirected it. I focused on my intention. I focused on my task.

The world's sounds became quieter, the movements of others muted. The sound of Enala crying was the only thing that subtly pierced through the fog. I could distantly hear Yaseer giving orders and instructing others to leave me alone.

In order for Nemina to return, I had to make sure there was somewhere for her to return to.

Just as I had finished, a hand rested on my shoulder. Faina's.

"We need to go."

# CHAPTER 33– SHADAE

The food tasted like shit.

But still, it was far better than what I had eaten in the draining centres. I supposed anything would have tasted divine in comparison to that.

One of the other trackers, who'd been sent out on this expedition, sat down beside me. We were in Vasara's outskirts, some trees the onlookers to our sorry meal.

"You'll get used to it," she spoke.

"Mmmmm," I simply murmured in reply.

"This is the best it's going to get food wise." She chewed in-between speaking. "They give us these rations for the jobs. It's always the same stuff though. You'd think they could add some variety."

"You're right, we should go and ask the King for a more enriching menu," I replied.

"Are you being sarcastic?" She said, confused. She was young, probably around eighteen, and at that moment, she looked even younger.

"What do you think?" I huffed, placing another spoon of the vegetable slosh into my mouth.

"I think I'd like to know what real meat tastes like... and candies."

"Yeah?" I looked at her. "Which flavour?"

"Fruit."

"Good choice," I spoke. I wish I knew what they tasted like myself.

"What about you? If you could eat one thing, what would it be?" she said.

I placed the small portion down. "Back where I'm from, there used to be this dish my mother would make. It was spicy, it had...some rice I think, some beans. I don't know what it was, but that."

I thought back on the taste, I couldn't really recall it now. All I remembered was that it had been wonderful. She had been wonderful, beautiful.

And then she had died, and our father had left us alone.

I had always wondered whether or not he had evaded capture. Despite his negligence, I wouldn't have wished being a Vessel upon anyone, not even him.

"Sounds good," the girl said. "I'm Ava, by the way." She held out her hand.

"Shadae." I shook hers.

"Zeima?" she asked.

"Yeah." I took in her features, her bright blonde hair, blue eyes. "Jurasa?"

"That obvious?"

"It's usually obvious for everyone isn't it." I pointed at some of the others. "He's from Kalnasa, you can tell from his eyes, that dark blue. He's from Vasara, the red hair. She's from Audra, so is she." My eyes landed on the Commander. "And he's Jurasa as well."

"I suppose you're right." Ava clasped her hands over her knees.

Her youth led me to ask the next question.

"How long have you been—" I started asking her.

"A year," she answered.

"How did you become—"

She pointed at the Commander. "He got me out."

I looked at him in surprise.

*Him?*

"How?" I asked.

She shrugged. "Don't know. Never asked why."

"Aren't you curious?"

Ava laughed, it was light and quick. "Of course, but anytime I hinted at it, he'd look at me like." She made a face to imitate his glare.

"Sounds about right." I nodded and chuckled.

"What's your class?"

"Oh, class four." The lowest class of the Dareans. "I'm a Navigator." Meaning that my sense of direction was almost impeccable. It was easy for me to scout terrain, follow trails, and find my way through difficult landscapes. There were quite a few Navigators on the team, I had heard, which made sense, it was an ideal ability for the task.

"You?"

"Class four Darean too, only I'm a Shielder."

"Protective abilities. Must be useful."

She shrugged again. "It's alright."

Footsteps approached us. The Commander's.

"What are you both sitting here blathering on about? Can't you see the rest of the group have gathered just two feet ahead of you?" He pointed at the gathering. "Did they take your sight as well as your energy during the drainings?"

*Did they take your ability to speak normally?*

I couldn't help but tut.

Cheadd raised his brows. "Something wrong?"

*Other than the fact that you permanently act like someone shoved a foot up your ass and never took it out, no.*

I stood. Ava did the same. "No Sir, apologies," she responded for us.

We followed him to the circle.

"Right," Cheadd spoke up. "Our scouts have found a group of sorcerers West of here. It's possible that they have their own scouts and are aware of our location too, so we need to move in now. We'll split into two groups of ten. One group will approach from the North, the other group from the South. It's likely that they'll try and escape further West to avoid running into us."

Cheadd then dictated who those two teams would consist of. He, I and Ava all belonging to the team that would attack from the South.

"Remember. These sorcerers are not your kin. They will kill you instantly without hesitation. Your life means nothing to them. To them you are the enemy. If you want to survive and they attempt to kill you, make sure you complete the kill first."

Weapons were handed out and distributed between us. The large majority of them were bows and arrows capable of firing at both short and long distances. Some of the arrows were designed to kill, others were only designed to strike the target bluntly, coated with an elixir which acted as a sedative if it touched their skin. All the arrows were infused with curse marks that could nullify a sorcerer's abilities. After I had been initiated, I had received basic training in their use, as well as swords. I was hardly an expert, but I knew how to fire an arrow with relative accuracy.

"The aim is to take these sorcerers alive. Each one will be valuable to the King, but if they attack, and you have no other option, you are sanctioned to end their lives."

I swallowed. It was one thing to convince myself that I could do this, for my brothers, but another to actually end the life of another person, another sorcerer.

Ava's hand covered my own. "Don't worry. I'll use my shielding abilities on you, that way you won't have to kill anyone." She smiled softly.

*That's lovely, but it won't last for long.*

"You should focus on using them on yourself," I told her.

"That would make me completely useless!" she protested.

"Move out," Cheadd directed. Ava, I, and the other seven trackers followed him.

After a few minutes, one of them asked, "How many are there?"

"The scouts said around forty, perhaps fifty."

*Fifty? How are a group of twenty meant to take on fifty sorcerers?*

"Not as many as the last time then," another one said.

I looked at them in disbelief. The first man caught my glance.

"Most of them can't fight anyway. Their abilities are usually on par with ours and we have more weapons." He tapped the bow he was holding.

"And what happens if they are more powerful?" I spoke.

"I mean, usually we don't have to worry about that," the second man said. "They tend to scatter before we even arrive."

"So, you've never fought someone, a sorcerer, more powerful than yourself?"

"We have," Cheadd replied for them.

"And?" I asked.

"And stop asking questions. Do your job."

Being a class four Darean meant it was almost guaranteed that the majority of sorcerers would be more powerful than I was. That didn't place me in a good position. Not that I was in a good position to begin with, or that any of us were.

Around thirty minutes later, we reached the spot where a scout was still remaining.

"Down there." She pointed.

We followed her down to the area in question.

It was utterly deserted.

"Shit," Cheadd blurted out. "As I suspected, they caught wind of us." He turned around to face the scout. "Didn't I tell you to look out for any scouts of their own?"

"I didn't see anyone," she protested.

"They could have used concealing sorcery. Translucency for the whole group." For some reason, I felt the need to defend this stranger.

The Commander turned to me sharply. "You're a Navigator aren't you? Search around for traces now. Of energy or anything else."

I nodded and began traversing the area. Ava followed me without being instructed to.

The team who had approached from the North eventually met us in the centre of the space. We were spread out, although it was only I, and the two other Navigators who had been sent out on this patrol, that were actively doing anything.

I could hear the other two a short distance away from me. "There'll be nothing here. There never is when the group is this large."

"Yeah, this is pointless," the second one agreed.

I turned away from them and sat on the ground. I closed my eyes and placed my fingers at my temples. Some Navigators found it easier to get their sense of direction through observation, touch. But for me, I always found it easier to sense direction from my surroundings, as if it were a call that I could only hear in my soul, through the air, and the earth.

I took some deep breaths, and reached out, I reached out to latch onto any sign of...

That.

I stood abruptly and looked around, I found Cheadd within an instant. Ava had been hovering behind me silently, not saying a word.

"What is it?" she asked.

I didn't answer her and strode towards the Commander.

"There's nothing—" one of the Navigators who had reached the Commander at the same time started.

"I found something," I cut him off.

The Commander looked between us several times. The other Navigator glanced at me confused and let out a grunt. "That's not possible."

*I suppose it wouldn't be for someone who hadn't even bothered to look.*

The Commander looked at the man. "She seems to think that it is."

"She must be mistaken."

"I'm not mistaken," I asserted.

"What did you find?" Cheadd asked.

"There are traces of energy, I can feel them...they're leading East."

"East?" the other Navigator laughed. "You think they'd walk right into the direction that we were heading from?"

*You think I'd lie about this? Unlike you, I actually want to make sure I do this job properly to avoid being executed.*

I stepped towards him. "It's possible, isn't it? If their scouts discovered us, they would know we would come to find them, and so, we wouldn't be East anymore, would we?"

"They can't have known that for sure," he argued.

"We're wasting time." The Commander silenced us. "We'll head East."

"But—" the other Navigator protested.

"I'm not asking for your permission cadet." The Commander looked at me. "Lead the way."

The Commander called the others to our location. I turned, closed my eyes once more to make sure my bearings were correct, and moved. I was leading the group. Everyone was following me.

I hoped I was right about this. If I failed the first task assigned to me, then that might mean I would be removed from the squad, and that couldn't happen. I had to do this for my brothers. Even if they couldn't understand, couldn't see that now.

I quickened my pace, the others behind me followed suit.

It was less than a half an hour later when we came across the sorcerers.

We halted. Cheadd placed a finger to his mouth, signalling for us all to be silent.

But it didn't matter, one of the sorcerers had sensed us immediately.

"THEY'RE HERE!" he shouted.

"GO!" Cheadd shouted too.

All the trackers rushed forwards, and I was rushing with them. I wasn't even sure how I would force someone into captivity. I would have to fire as many of these blunt arrows as possible, and hope they found their mark.

I could taste sick in my mouth.

Ava's hands were illuminated with a warm blue glow. She was preparing to cast shields around us if necessary.

The other trackers began firing. The group of sorcerers, which had previously been tightly stacked together, scattered, as they ran to evade the shots, as they screamed in fright.

I aimed and struck the back of the neck of a sorcerer. They fell to the ground instantly. I reached for the next arrow behind me, and aimed for another, but he had seen me and evaded the shot by levitating quickly.

Behind me, one of the trackers fell to the ground, yelling. There was a hole in his side, and a sorcerer stood above him, a ball of flame having just left her palm.

We met each other's eyes. She ran towards me, preparing to strike. I fumbled around for another arrow, one that would kill, but my hands were shaking. I couldn't grip the wood. The sorcerer gritted her teeth and flung a swirl of fire directly at my chest.

The flame was deflected, scattering into sparks, careening to the side. Ava was standing beside me. She had shielded us both.

The sorcerer grunted in irritation and levitated. Within an instant she was behind us. Ava didn't have time to form a new shield before she flung a series of fireballs our way.

I shot an arrow at her, but missed, miserably. I could barely see anything. The smoke from the fires she was casting was clouding my vision. In fact, all my senses were distorted, the shouting, the smell of fumes, the pounding of people running, was completely obscuring them all.

Ava and I lurched to the side, somehow managing to evade the strikes. The sorcerer landed between us smiling.

Then, an arrow landed between her eyes, which rolled to the back of her head. She fell to her knees, and then on top of Ava, who began screaming.

One of the trackers was standing in front of us. "Get up!" he screamed impatiently.

As fast as he had arrived, he was gone.

I made my way towards Ava and shoved the dead body off her. It was heavier than I had thought it would be. "Are you—"

"Look out!" she screamed. I turned around to face a sorcerer, who was standing in front of several pieces of scrap metal, floating behind him. Telekinetic. He smiled and closed his eyes, firing out several of the pieces in all directions, including towards us. Ava formed a shield just on time around us, but the fierce yells of several trackers hit by the shards exploded through the air. Behind the right shoulder of the sorcerer, the first Navigator who had argued with us was wailing, as a piece of glass lodged into his eye.

Within an instant, another sorcerer approached the Navigator as he was distracted and cut his head clean off with a blade.

Ava began screaming again. Her screaming was borderline a cry. It was like the shriek of a new-born child, terrified by the world. I was still shaking, shaking so hard and so much I couldn't think, I couldn't move.

The Telekinetic came towards us.

*What good is navigating when metal is flying at your throat? What the fuck am I supposed to do?*

I tried to steady myself and silence my thoughts. I grabbed an arrow, blunted, and aimed it at him. His eyes widened in recognition.

But my hands were still shaking. The arrow managed to strike him, but not his skin. He paused for a moment as the impact of the shot halted his path.

The sound of thunder appeared, to my left, the Commander was conjuring lightning to cut off the paths of sorcerers towards escape.

Someone grabbed the collar of the Telekinetic and dragged him away. It was a woman, she was tall, her long brown hair was matted with blood.

"We need to go!" she told him.

I could hear a baby crying. She was holding a baby in her arms. It didn't look like her child.

I lifted an arrow. I raised it and aimed it at the Telekinetic. This time, my hands were steadier. The woman met my eyes. The baby was wailing, wailing so loudly.

Cheadd's yell reached me from the left, "What are you waiting for?!"

I fired, but the arrow never met the man. Someone else, another sorcerer had intercepted it on time, appearing as if from nowhere, grabbing the arrow in his hand. His lilac tunic was torn, and he was already wounded, a deep gash at his upper arm.

Speed enhancement.

He turned around and looked at me. I raised another arrow again. I hardly had any of the blunt ones left. "Faina, leave now. You too Claus," the man in lilac said.

Claus screamed. "You're the one who got us into this mess. You think you can give us orders now, you flagrant fuck!"

Ava's hands were on my shoulders, she was trembling behind me, examining the scene with confusion.

*Should I fire this arrow? Who at? There are three of them in front of me now, I can't fire three arrows at once.*

But none of them were attacking.

*That isn't the point. It's my job to catch them. It's my job to sedate them.*

But if I fired this arrow at one of them, the other two might strike back, and I didn't even know what abilities they possessed.

*A Telekinetic is bad enough, Gods know what the other two can do.*

Before I could make up my mind, another arrow flew past us, and struck Faina bluntly in the throat. She fell unconscious and the baby that had been in her arms slowly dropped from her grip. The man in lilac swept the baby up in his arms and looked behind us in the direction of the arrow.

It was that archer again, the one who had struck the Elementalist between her eyes.

Claus yelled and, in an instant, shot a sharp object in the archer's direction.

"Eiro!" Ava screamed what must have been his name. She lurched from behind me and thrust out her hand, trying to shield him.

But Claus, Claus had anticipated that.

She didn't see, and I didn't see the sharp object he had discharged, just a second later in her direction.

It went clean through her stomach.

"No!" I yelled and fell beside her. Ava's eyes widened as she fell flat on the ground, blood was spilling from her core so fast, so fast, it was everywhere.

I tried to stop it with my hands, but it was like trying to stop the rain falling from the sky.

*It's so much warmer than I thought it would be. There's so much. It...it won't stop.*

*And it smells. Like metal burning. Like liquid gold.*

The archer sank to the ground as well, with no shield, the sharp object had struck him straight in the chest.

He died instantly.

"Claus!" The man in lilac scolded him.

Ava was coughing up blood, looking at me with a plea in her eyes, begging for me to save her. "I...don't..." She tried to get the words out, but she couldn't, blood was coming out of her nose.

"What?" Claus said. "You think they'd just let us go, you fucking—"

Claus stopped speaking, his hand clutching at his chest.

Right where I had just sent a sharp arrow straight through it.

The man in lilac turned around to face me. I looked down at him, at the baby in his arms. The baby that was sobbing, shrieking. Ava's blood was on my hands, it was on my clothes. My lips were quivering. I lifted an arrow and pointed it at his skull.

The man wasn't doing anything.

*Why? Why aren't you moving? Why aren't you using your ability on me? You're just going to let me kill you? Like that? You aren't even going to fight?*

It didn't matter. It didn't matter.

He watched me with such exhaustion in eyes. He held up one hand, the hand he wasn't cradling the baby with.

"Please," he whispered softly. "You can take me...but let her go." He pointed at the brown-haired woman on the ground.

"I can't...I can't do that." I still had the arrow pointed at his head.

"Please," he whispered again.

*I should take him out, before he kills someone. I should do it.*

*Now. Now. Do it. Now.*

But I couldn't.

A searing pain shred my wrist, like a thousand needles of an icy flame, digging into my arm, clawing its way up and around.

I winced out loud and couldn't help but drop the bow from my hands. The man was looking at me bewildered. I grabbed my wrist, it was glowing slightly, where I had been marked. Branded.

I was disobeying my purpose by hesitating, and the curse knew, it knew.

I looked up to find the man staring at me, at my arm.

Another sorcerer approached, lifting the woman off the floor. He peered at me suspiciously.

"She's hurt, Fasal," the man in lilac said.

"She should be dead," Fasal replied, his golden skin turned red with blood.

"We don't have the time."

I stared at them, still grabbing my wrist. The pain was growing worse by the second. My vision started blurring.

Fasal grabbed the woman and hurried away. The man with the baby turned around before he left. His eyes fell on Ava's body.

"I'm…I'm sorry," he said, stumbling around his apology, looking at her.

He was blurry now. I couldn't make out his facial expression. He began to walk away. His silhouette grew fainter by the second. In the distance, I could hear the Commander hounding orders, and wails tolling like bells. I could smell rain, electricity, fire, and smoke. I could see a large white glow. Someone must have been teleporting the sorcerers away. I could taste blood, and feel it stuck to my palms. I was swathed in that liquid gold, being swallowed by darkness.

And before my vision fully blackened, I could see Claus' cold dead eyes, staring at my own.

# CHAPTER 34 – ELIAS

"How could this have happened?" I stared at Trenton.

He sighed and glanced at Raynard who was shaking his head. The two men had ushered me here, an adjoining room to the throne's, within minutes of blood being spilt before its seat.

Within minutes of Eliel's life nearly having ended.

"The King had ordered that Vessel to undertake a mission on his behalf. He was meant to have set out hours before the ceremony. We've sent out scouts to search for the guard who was accompanying him when he departed. We anticipate that he will be found…dead," Trenton explained.

A Vessel conducting a mission? This was monumentally, unfathomably absurd.

"Why wasn't I informed of this?" I asked.

Fargreaves crossed his arms. "With all due respect, My Lord, you were not present when it was discussed, and decided upon."

I couldn't believe that Eliel would have made a decision this reckless. His Councilmen of course…but him?

But Eliel still didn't understand what sorcerers were capable of.

I took a deep breath. "You collectively decided that it would be a good idea, to send a Vessel on a sensitive mission, I assume, without him having been branded or marked. Presumably, his chains would have to be removed at some point during the journey. So, he would have been free to do whatever he wished."

The four men looked at each other warily. "The King provided incentive enough for him to fulfil the task," Trenton said.

That woman. It must have been.

"Even so, that incentive was something he managed to obtain himself. I'm assuming those who were guarding that woman are dead as well?"

"Yes," Fargreaves confirmed dryly. "We have already found them dead. They stabbed themselves with their own swords."

I winced at those words, at the memories they ignited. It wouldn't have been difficult for that Telepath to manipulate them into ending their own lives. He had stopped a whole hall of people from moving without a hitch of breath.

"This is a disaster." I placed my hand over my face.

Trenton spoke up. "If it hadn't been for Audra's Prince, our King would likely be dead."

"And he wasn't even supposed to be an escort," Fargreaves added.

Yes, the Vulture had saved my cousin's life. Of all people. I suppose I'd have to thank him for that at some point.

"And with Noxstone, of all things." Raynard's voice was thick with horror. "I've never seen its...effects, up close."

I had. Many times. Noxstone was the only kind of blade that could prevent a sorcerer from healing themselves and so, Eliel's father had made efforts to arm Vasara's soldiers with it.

He didn't know the cost...none of them knew...

*Yes, it stops sorcerers from healing themselves, but that's not all it can do...*

"Did you know about his choice, My Lord?" Fargreaves interrupted my thoughts.

I sighed. "No. I didn't. But stopping the ceremony was out of the question. Weren't you made aware of his decision?"

Nobody responded.

Trenton stroked the stubble on his chin. "I can't fathom what his reasoning might have been."

"And what of the Courting Season. Will the candidates remain? What if they withdraw?" Raynard asked.

"Is that his plan then? To eliminate any possibility of taking a wife?" Fargreaves said despondently.

"He *was* opposed to this Season in the first place," Raynard added.

"Either way, the Season would have come around eventually," Fargreaves reminded him.

Wayman rubbed his forehead. "Now that the King has sacrificed his chance at having an heir, this won't be the last time something like this happens. What are we to do? Who knew the young Prince would turn out to be such a reckless man?"

"Eliel is anything but reckless," I spoke. "Whatever his motivations, they will have a purpose. Even if we cannot see it."

Fagreaves huffed. "What would you know about such affairs? Your participation in them is conveniently elective, *My Lord*."

"You know almost nothing about Vessels, Fargreaves, or at least, far less than you think you do, and yet you underestimate them, time and time again. Today was the result."

"I know far more about them than you assume, My Lord," Fagreaves spat.

"Really?" My voice was flat with disbelief, as were my brows.

Fargreaves stepped towards me aggressively. "It is easy to criticise the decisions of others, when you dedicate your life to the absolution of them."

I turned to Trenton, who was examining the scene with interest. "Does your offer still stand?"

Fargreaves turned around to look over his shoulder. "What is he talking about?"

Trenton, ignoring him, replied. "Yes. It does."

"Then I will be happy to accept." I turned to Fargreaves, who was still looking at Trenton bewilderedly.

I took his hand in mine, which made him turn around abruptly. I shook it. "Looking forward to working with you, on a non-elective basis."

Fargreaves snapped his hand from my grasp. "What is this, Trenton? This man" —he pointed at me without looking— "doesn't take anything seriously."

"I take an assassination attempt on my cousin *very* seriously."

Fargreaves laughed and dropped his arm. "But not a successful one on your aunt and uncle. That... you are decidedly lackadaisical about."

I scoffed, but I couldn't deny there was some truth in what he had said. I hadn't pursued their killers thoroughly enough. I'd had complicated feelings when I had heard they'd passed.

Wayman added. "It's well known that Lord Elias and his former Majesty did not see eye to eye."

Wayman was right, Elion and I had never agreed upon most things. Upon his strategies, upon his obsession with eliminating sorcerers, upon his disregard for his own men.

But Gods was I really that kind of person? The kind of person who only cared when the people close to me were hurt, and not when others were?

"I hope that will not be the case for us, Sir," I said to Fargreaves.

Fargreaves tutted, and just as he did, a servant approached him, whispering something in his ear. Without saying anything, he turned around and left with him.

The rest of the Council dispersed, and I made my way back to my chambers. The buckles and straps of my overly ornate tunic smacked against my hip painfully. I closed my eyes and imagined the bliss that would be the wine slipping down my throat as I took this thing off and...

My door was open.

There were no guards in the hallway. They must have been called to cover the stations those who had died had occupied.

It didn't shock me. I'd been dismissing the guards shadowing me for years. They were only ever at my door as a formality, and only when I lacked the energy to tell them to fuck off.

But it was amusing how quick they were to drop that formality. To remind me, they placed as much value on my life as the pigs slaughtered for their feasts. They'd sooner place a crown on one's head than mine.

As would I. It would fit in well with the rest of the Nobility, at least.

I stood still and listened. I looked down at where the floor of my room was just about visible. Shadows were cast across the slither I could see, and a man's voice sounded from inside.

"I know what you're doing. Do you think you can fool me? I saw you…"

I squinted, the gritty voice was faintly recognizable, but I couldn't quite place it.

"Do you?" he said again.

"Get off me."

I recognised that voice.

As quietly as my movements would allow, I slid inside the gap, and closed the door behind me.

Maiwen's escort had her backed against the wall. She was in a pale blue nightgown, her left hand clenched tightly around a darker blue shawl she had wrapped around herself. His right hand was on her wrist.

Both looked at me as soon as I entered.

"Why do you look so surprised, Sir? This is *my* room, isn't it?" I spoke slowly, trying to assess the situation.

He didn't move. Maiwen glanced down, as if she were embarrassed.

"I think you should comply with the Princess' request." I pointed at his hands.

He stood back slightly but did not let go of the Princess. He turned towards me.

"My Lord, there has been a misunderstanding. The Princess is distressed from today's most troubling events. She has been quite hysterical, I'm afraid, and ended up fleeing around the Palace. I can assure you, it wasn't my intention to end up inviting myself here."

"No…no, I," the Princess started. She looked at me pleadingly, "That's not true."

"Sir," I faced him. "Remove your hand from the Lady's wrist."

He brought her hand down by his side but didn't let go of it. The Princess struggled to free herself from his grip.

"This is for her own safety, you understand." He made a move for the door, dragging the Princess with him.

I blocked his way, pressing my hand against his upper chest to stop him.

"My Lord, I would never—"

"Harm the Princess? Why are you gripping her wrist so tightly then?"

"So that she will not get lost." He tried to move around me. It didn't work.

"I'm not quite sure she was lost in the first place."

He breathed through his nostrils. "My Lord, it is with the greatest respect that I say this, but you do not know the Princess, she is not quite…well."

"Will removing your fucking hand from her worsen her health significantly?" I snapped.

The man was clearly startled by my change in tone.

"My Lord," he said reproachfully, as if he intended to reprimand me for my outburst. "Are you drunk?"

I surprisingly wasn't.

I kicked him in the kneecap. He fell to the floor and the Princess began to fall with him. I caught her before she did and stepped back immediately.

"There, look, the Princess is still alive. What a fucking surprise."

The Princess was rubbing her wrist with her other hand and looking at the man.

"How dare you—" The man stood, facing us both.

"How dare I? What? Stop you from attacking the Princess here. You're fucking pathetic."

"I...My Lord...I was not attacking her!" His eyes were wide with alarm. "These accusations—"

"Accusations? Do you think I'm a complete fool?"

The man sputtered and stuttered, looking at the Princess.

"Don't look at her. Look at me. She isn't going to save you. Nobody is going to save you. This time tomorrow you'll be crawling back to wherever you came from. Actually no... I think I'll let the Jurasan King know about this, let's see what he has to say about your behaviour."

"No!" Maiwen said, much to both of our surprise.

I turned to face her. My brows furrowed in confusion.

"See, My Lord! She knows the truth." He pointed a stubby finger at her face. "I was simply asking her—"

I smacked his finger away.

Maiwen stood behind me.

"Jurasan King or no, you will no longer be escorting the Princess. I'm sure we can come up with another reason to strip you of your title if the Princess doesn't wish to share this one."

"I will not have this!" he exclaimed.

"Get out, I will—"

Before I could tell him that I would escort the Princess back myself, he lunged for me, with his sword.

I jumped back, bumping into the Princess. Her hands grabbed the tops of my arms as she steadied herself, to stop herself from falling over.

"I won't have an excuse for a Lord like you ruin my reputation! You don't even know what's going on here! You're nothing more than a...than...than a...drunkard!"

He lunged at me again. I wasn't carrying any weapons, as we had been instructed to remove them for the ceremony.

Still his attack was clumsy, and anger fuelled, I dodged it easily. He went for me again, I tried to jump back, but the Princess' presence behind me stopped me from doing so. I had no choice but to stop the clumsy strike of the blade with my hand, wincing as it cut deep into my palm. Maiwen gasped.

"Fuck!" I said out loud. "You're making a big mistake, Sir. Back away and leave, now."

He ignored me, and with a grunt of fury, went for me again.

This was going to be a terrible fucking way to die.

Then there was blood, on my tunic, on my overly ornate straps and buckles, casting dark shades across the embroidery and the silk.

The man had fallen on top of me.

My sword was in his chest.

I turned around. Standing there, with both her hands shaking around the hilt, and her shawl fallen to the floor, was Maiwen.

She placed one hand over her mouth, staring at me wide eyed in shock.

I was staring back at her in kind.

The man sank down my clothes and to the ground. I leant over his body, pressing my ear to his chest.

I raised my head. Maiwen was looking at me with a silent question in her eyes.

"He's dead," I whispered.

"My, my!" a voice came from behind us. "This day is just getting more and more interesting."

I stood instantly and turned around. He was standing in front of the closed door, his golden eyes gleaming like a cat's on a dark night.

"Looks like I'm not the only one who took a life today."

# CHAPTER 35 – NATHON

This was the last thing that I expected to see when I went to visit Lord Elias. One unusual death within these Palace walls per year would have been strange. But two, two in one day?

I took in the scene, the wide eyes of the dead man fixed upon the ceiling.

"Isn't that her escort?" I pointed at the Princess standing behind him.

Elias didn't respond. He and the Princess looked at each other tensely.

I walked over to the body and looked down at it. The sword was sticking out of his chest. The angle, the position of it, the point of entry. It was utterly clear.

"Why has the Princess killed her own escort in your room?" I put to Elias, resting my hands on my elbows.

The Princess wrapped her arms around herself. "I—"

"It wasn't her," Elias lied.

I looked back down at the body. It was definitely her.

But, if the Lord insisted that he had done it, then I could play along.

"I see. Your swordsmanship really has suffered after all these years away from fighting."

Elias's golden outfit was stained in blood. To any other individual that had stumbled across this scene, it would certainly seem that he had been the one to kill this man.

"What are you going to do? Elias asked. His gaze was fixed upon me resolutely.

"I don't see how it would benefit me in any way to reveal your murderous activities. Or her little night visit." I pointed at the Princess. She looked completely lost.

"I don't believe that." He looked at me with suspicion.

He was right, to some extent. I could imagine certain benefits in revealing them. Elias would be out of the way, and he was clearly protective of the King. The Jurasan Princess would be eliminated from the Courting Season, which would improve Loria's chances.

But, having Lord Elias owe me, was far better than having him gone.

"If that's the case, what do you intend to do?" I asked him.

Elias laughed. "I'm not a fucking fool. If I fight you, I'll die."

"Well, you certainly would if you fought like that…" I pointed at the dead man.

"Exactly." He was admirably consistent in his façade.

"So, what do you propose?" I asked.

"I'll...I'll drop out of the season," the Princess blurted out.

We both turned to her. She stepped forwards slightly.

No. Absolutely not. The Princess dropping out of the season wasn't anywhere near useful enough.

"It seems like that's something that would benefit you more than me, Princess. That's just not how this works." Her face clouded over in disappointment.

Elias scowled. "Aren't you pleased with yourself? You've backed us into a corner and can demand whatever you want in exchange for your silence."

"You have to admit, it's hardly something to be displeased about." I outstretched my palms and shrugged.

"Leave her out of it." Elias slightly nodded behind him, at the Princess.

"But I—" the Princess started.

"Done," I cut her off.

Elias let out a breath. He turned around and approached her, picking up a dark shawl from the floor, and handing it to her.

"Here, you should go back."

"I...but you—"

"Go back," Elias repeated, waving the shawl in the air.

"I didn't mean to come here, I just...I didn't know where to go, and this door was open, and I was—"

"Stop," Elias cut her off. "You don't have to explain."

She looked up at him and gulped. Then suddenly her facial expression changed. "I'll find a way to thank you." She placed the shawl around her shoulders and made her way towards the door, she glanced at me wearily as she walked past.

"I am grateful," she said to me. I raised my eyebrows in surprise. She scurried out of the door.

After it was closed, I turned to Elias. We stared at each other for a few moments.

"You need to move this body now," I told him.

"I thought I'd wait two to three hours for it to grow heavier and more bloated before I tried, actually," Elias said, his face straight.

I laughed. "Well, I suppose anyone would be angry if they completed a murder this poorly. Look at your clothes after all, and they're probably the only decent set that you own."

"I'll handle it." Elias walked over to a drinks cabinet and poured himself some wine.

"How? You can't wander around wearing that."

"Then I'll change."

"Ahhh, but you need to get rid of those clothes as soon as possible. Not wait for two to three hours for the blood to marinate into the fabric."

Elias slammed his drink down. "If it weren't for the fact you'd saved my cousin's life, I think that I'd truly hate you."

He and everyone else. I was used to being hated. I was used to the feeling. There was a part of me that had even grown comfortable with it. Who would I be if I wasn't hated? I didn't know. I didn't even know if I wanted to know.

"Does that mean you hated me before I saved his life?" I asked.

"I didn't give a fuck about you beforehand." He poured another drink.

After swallowing some, Elias spoke again. "Look, Vulture, go and think hard about what you want from me because I won't be doing you two favours. Let me handle this myself."

I stepped towards him, pointed two fingers in the air.

"You *will* do me two favours, and in return, I will handle the body."

"Two favours for you? Ha. I'd be better off taking the risk."

"Are you sure about that? Someone just tried to kill your cousin. You can't exactly prevent further assassination attempts from a prison cell."

I refrained from telling him that if I were to be ordered to end his life, there was no way he could prevent the King's death. At all.

Elias sighed deeply. "In fact, I think I fucking hate you anyway."

He approached the body. "How are you going to handle this by yourself?"

"I've done it plenty of times before."

Elias smiled sarcastically. "I'm sure you have, but not here, not within unfamiliar territory and—"

"Unfamiliar?" I raised an eyebrow at him. I'd already spent the first few days here traversing and memorising the entirety of the Palace's layout. Besides, I had disposed of plenty of bodies in unfamiliar territory before.

"*And...*" Elias stressed the word, irritated by my interruption, "He's too heavy."

I stroked the corner of my lips. That was true. This ridiculous outfit the man was wearing added several extra pounds to him. Stripping him would take too long, and if anyone did notice anything from a far distance, seeing one man carrying another would be far more noticeable and alarming if one of them were naked.

Loria wouldn't be strong enough to lift him...besides, I didn't want her involved.

The Jurasan Princess looked even more frail than Loria did, acquiring her help would be tantamount to asking a child to help carry him with me.

I smiled to myself.

Of course.

I strode towards the door.

"I thought you said—" Elias began.

"Sssh. I have an idea."

# CHAPTER 36 - HESTAN

Dyna had fallen asleep an hour ago.

I had been sitting by the windowsill in her room ever since.

She'd asked me to stay and keep watch, terrified there would be another Vessel wandering around, trying to hurt other members of nobility and of Royalty.

There was no doubt in my mind that the Vessel had been acting alone and had only intended to punish the King, but still, to a child, to Dyna, such things were irrelevant. There was only a possibility of harm, and a memory of feeling as if it were about to befall you, without anything you could do to stop it.

I knew that feeling well. I remembered the attack on my village with the same vividness and emotions as I had experienced at the time. I remembered the feeling of helplessness, of having nowhere to run, no one to turn to, no way to save those you cared for, or yourself.

An image flashed before my eyes, my brother's body, face down on the floor, and the man who had pulled a dagger from his back.

The same dagger that was in the hands of Audra's Prince.

I knew I could not and should not draw conclusions too swiftly. It was possible that two such daggers existed, or even more than that. Of course, I knew Audra's Prince himself was not responsible, but there was a chance he knew who was, who owned that dagger before him, or owned one identical to it.

My older brothers, my parents were dead. Several members of the Hunt had died over the years. The people from my home Kingdom were dying, starving.

And yet, I remained. I watched as people came and went. For someone who knew the powerlessness of being unprotected, I was, it seemed, very bad at protecting people.

There was a knock at the door. I looked at Dyna, she remained undisturbed.

I found it unlikely a Vessel would need to knock. They would have simply torn the door of its hinges.

But still, it was late, and Dyna wasn't expecting anybody to arrive.

I slowly made my way towards it, not before, I drew my spear from my back and pointed it forwards.

I opened it.

"Captain!" The long sleeves of his dark shirt were folded up, and before I could close the door, he pressed his palm against it.

This was the last thing I needed.

"Prince," I replied, lowering my spear.

"I thought that you might be here. Fulfilling your duties day and night."

The Prince was dressed sparsely, his shirt half open, his brown skin partially exposed. I looked away and over his shoulder.

"Let us speak outside, Your Highness, the Lady is sleeping."

"Wonderful. So, you can come with me after all."

I furrowed my brows, my lips twitched in a silent question.

"I need your help."

I dreaded asking.

"With?" I met his eyes.

"A delicate matter," the Prince smiled warmly, and tilted his head, exploring my face with his eyes keenly.

"Your Highness, I'm sure there are people far more equipped to assist you."

Helping Audra's Prince with a 'delicate matter' seemed the very definition of foolishness.

"But you are the only person I can trust with the task."

I sighed and turned to look at Dyna one last time. Although I had the illusion of a choice, I could sense that refusing the Prince was impossible.

"Lead the way, Your Highness."

The Prince finally took his palm off the door. "I knew you'd agree. You can put the spear away now." He waved his hand in the direction of my weapon.

I placed it in the straps at my back and followed him through the Palace. He managed to avoid all the areas which were heavily guarded and led us both through the path with least visibility.

He had certainly been utilising his time wisely. It was chilling, to think of how much he already knew about this place, and its secrets. How many secrets he had of his own.

We stopped outside a large room.

I looked at him confused. "Who resides here, Your—"

"You'll see." His voice had dropped to a whisper.

He knocked the door, in what seemed like a patterned or coded manner.

It opened slightly, the Prince stepped inside, and I followed.

Lord Elias was standing at the front of the room.

I looked at Audra's Prince from the side. He gestured at me with both his hands.

"I've brought the help."

Lord Elias looked at me and then at Audra's Prince, seemingly very irritated.

"Are you fucking serious?" he addressed Audra's Prince.

My mouth opened slightly and closed in the same instant. Had he really just addressed him in that way? I knew that Lord Elias had little regard for such things, but still, any sane person would have bitten their tongue around the Prince, surely.

I recalled the words that escaped my lips earlier in the day, as I stood beside him, next to the Vessel he had killed. It seemed even I was not immune to such recklessness.

Audra's Prince, however, didn't seem to care at all. "What are you complaining about? Do you have any other alternatives?" He placed his hands on his hips.

"You may as well have brought the Grand Prosecutor himself."

"Oh, come on…he's not that rigid." Audra's Prince winked at me. I peered at him, confused. He was clearly some kind of interlocutor in this situation.

Lord Elias looked at me. "He's—"

"My Lord," I spoke up. It was uncomfortable to hear them both speak about me as if I weren't even present. "I am willing to help you, and I am able to be discreet about the matter," I confirmed the Prince's statement.

"For fucks sake." Lord Elias spoke into his hands. He looked up at me. "If you speak a word of this to anyone, I don't need to tell you what will happen."

Another threat to my life to add to the ever-increasing tally.

"No, My Lord, I am quite clear about that."

"Stop calling me My Lord," Elias groaned.

"Yes," Audra's Prince chimed in. "Instead, you should refer to him as the murderer of… this man." The Prince shoved past Elias, who until now had been standing in front of…

A dead body.

I drew in a sharp breath, as cutting as the feeling of shock that seized me. I recognised the man instantly.

"How did this happen?" My voice was strained as I looked at them both.

Audra's Prince shrugged. "I have no idea. Would you like to share?" he asked Elias.

"Just get rid of him." Elias walked away and grabbed a sack full of something as he left the room.

Now I understood. I turned to Audra's Prince after Elias had left and licked my lips before I spoke.

"You've called me here to help you dispose of a dead body."

He squinted at me. "Very observant."

I pressed my lips together. "Your Highness, this situation could place me in great danger, as well as the Lady I am escorting."

Audra's Prince placed his hands behind his back and leant forwards. "I think this is the first time I've seen you display any sort of emotion, Captain. You seem" —he narrowed his eyes further— "angry?"

"I am not pleased," I said tersely.

"Well, you'll have to remind me to make it up to you sometime."

I would much rather he didn't.

Audra's Prince lifted the man's arm around his shoulders. "We don't have much time, and you're here now. We're leaving out of that window and going around." He pointed at the window in question. A small window.

"But Your Highness, the window is very—"

"One of us will climb down, the other will drop the body to them, and climb down afterwards. Then we will proceed." He nodded to himself at his plan, then after a pause said, "You go down first."

I was trying to process everything that had occurred within the last few minutes. I stared at the window, my mouth falling open slightly.

"Are you waiting for something?" the Prince asked.

I sighed. The Prince was right. Unfortunately, I had been complicit in these events the moment I had stepped out of Dyna's room.

I deftly leapt from the window to the ground, which was a few feet below. I turned around, I barely had any time to do so before the dead body was flung at me by the Prince. I tried to catch it, but in vain, ended up crashing to the ground. He landed in front of me, crouching.

"I thought members of the Hunt were supposed to be agile."

I pushed the dead man off me. "We don't usually have dead bodies thrown at us, Your Highness."

"Sounds rather dull," he said as he stood. He grabbed the man by the arms again and placed one around his neck, he nodded at me to do the same. I did.

"Where are we... going?" I asked.

"Normally, I'd try to make this look like an accident, or a suicide, but the wound makes that impossible. So, we will find a body of water."

He spoke of these things so casually. I truly wondered how he did.

"There aren't any close by, Your Highness."

"There's one South of here, a mile or so."

"A mile?" I couldn't hide the surprise in my voice.

"You're strong." He poked my upper arm with one hand quickly. "It won't be a problem."

I looked down at where he had touched and then back up. "I'm more concerned about being discovered."

"You worry too much, Captain."

"I think this scenario warrants a certain level of anxiety."

"Perhaps you're right. I wouldn't know," he said softly.

I glanced at him over the dropped head of the dead man.

"He was escorting the Princess. What will she do?"

"The Princess killed him," the Prince said bluntly.

"What?" My voice was sharp. How was it that I had been roped into assisting Audra's Prince, in hiding the body of someone who the Jurasan Princess had murdered, in a member of Vasara's Court's chambers.

"The King's cousin denies it, he's protecting her for some reason, I can't say why."

"But how do you know that—"

"I know, Captain. I thought you didn't want to be involved in this. Why are you asking so many questions, then?" He looked at me, amused, a half open smile forming on his face.

"I'm involved now, Your Highness. I'd like to know in what exactly."

The Prince, taking that as the required explanation, fell silent.

"Why are you helping him?" I asked, although I already suspected the answer.

"Why do you think?"

"How did you find out about—"

"Chance."

Chance. I didn't think so.

I stopped moving.

"What are you doing, Captain?" Audra's Prince sounded impatient.

I removed the dead man's arm from my shoulder.

"Give me the Noxstone blade and I'll help you."

Audra's Prince shoved the dead man's body onto the floor. We stared at each other over it.

"I see," he said flatly.

"I only want to borrow it for a short time. Then I will return it to you."

"We've been over this, Captain. I don't like repeating myself."

"Then, Your Highness, I will be returning to my room."

Audra's Prince drew out the dagger.

Exactly what I had wanted him to do.

I knew he wouldn't have agreed to my offer. But I wanted to see this dagger, and I knew that it was hidden on his person.

I looked at it intently. "Do you intend to use that?"

"Maybe. Maybe not." He shrugged. "It's up to you to take the risk."

"I don't believe you would. Two escorts in one night would prove too suspicious."

"Would it?" He raised his brows. "And how would *I* fall under that suspicion?"

"A risk," I replied immediately. "It is up to you if you take it, Your Highness."

The Prince wore a knowing smile, one tinged with a strange kind of ecstasy. "Well, perhaps two escorts battled to the death. Perhaps... they had a disagreement of principles. A convincing story given your" – he eyed me up and down – "personality."

"It is not a convincing story," I replied bluntly.

"No?...Isn't it?"

"This man would not have been able to kill me," I stated. If Jurasa's Candidate herself had been able to kill him, then his skills would have been far inferior to my own.

The Prince laughed quietly. The sound rustled through the air lightly like leaves skipping down a path. "No... I suppose not." His eyes roamed over me, focusing on nowhere in particular as he put the dagger back into a sheath at his belt. "I knew I was right about you, Captain."

I wasn't entirely sure what he meant.

"But you heard the Lord's word of warning. I can't say that he's someone who will follow through on his threats, but I can assure you I do. As well as my promises. I promised you would be able to look at the blade, but under circumstances of my choosing, not yours. So, you won't be going anywhere."

I decided to see if I could convince him.

"The dagger then." I nodded to it.

"I'm quite attached to this one, I'm afraid. So, no."

"Then, I must also decline, Your Highness."

I shifted to the right to return to the Palace. But the Prince placed both his hands around his mouth, opened it, and yelled. "SOMEBODY HELP, HELLLLLP..."

I stared at him in shock. This man was truly unhinged.

"What are you doing?" I hissed at him.

"ANYBODY PLEEEASEEEE..."

I waved my hands in the air. "Stop!"

But the Prince continued. "HEEELPP PLEAA—"

Without thinking about what I was doing, I grabbed the Prince by his shirt, pulled him towards me and placed my right hand over his mouth.

The Prince's eyes went wide, his two hands were resting on the arm I had used to pull him towards me.

What was I doing? This was a Prince and not just any Prince, Audra's Prince. The kind of man that would have someone killed for doing what I had just done.

But the Prince didn't make any effort to move. He just stood there, looking bewildered.

I dropped my hand from his mouth and let go of him.

"My apologies, Your Highness." I averted my eyes.

Audra's Prince said nothing.

"I agree. I'll help you." I bent down to lift the man's arms around my neck. Soon afterwards, the Prince crouched to do the same thing.

"I knew you would."

"That was dangerous, Your Highness."

"That was the point, Captain."

He liked to be in control. No. He liked to remind others that he was.

No. He was adaptable. Whether he was in control or not, the Prince could manipulate the circumstances to make sure that he was holding the reins.

Which is why he had helped Elias.

Which is why, in all likelihood he had saved the King's life.

"Then, in return for my help, will you answer me a question, Your Highness?"

The Prince knitted his brows together, as if contemplating the risk. "I can't promise I will answer, but you can ask it."

We were a fair distance away from the Palace now, having just got out of its grounds. We were both breathing more heavily against the humid night air.

"Your dagger—"

"I've already told you—"

"No, I'm not asking you for it."

"What then?" The Prince adjusted the man's arm around his neck.

"Is there another like it? Or is that the only one in existence?"

Although it was dark, I could see the Prince squinting at the question, trying to figure out the nature of its origins.

"What an unusual question. Your fascination with Noxstone is...strange."

I knew that asking him was a risk, but I was currently hauling the dead body of a nobleman with him, so the risk seemed small in comparison.

"Will you answer it?"

The Prince sighed. "Why do you want to know?"

"Will you answer me if I tell you?" I kept watching his face as we moved, tracking the changes in its demeanour, its expression.

"It depends on what you tell me." He side-eyed me, smirking.

Everything depended on something else with this man. There was a clause, a condition, a consequence to everything.

I cleared my throat. "I have seen one like it before...many years ago..."

"Now that *is* interesting."

"You may not believe me, Your Highness, but it is the truth."

"No, no...I believe you Captain." He sounded genuine.

A few people came down the street.

"Here." The Prince pulled my arm, directing me down a side alley. In doing so, he lost his grip on the dead escort between us, who lurched forwards towards him. In a quick reflex like movement, I reached out and grabbed the bodies' torso harder, so that it wouldn't fall.

"Your...Highness," I struggled between words. "If you...would."

The Prince, noticing what was happening, let go of my arm and returned it to the normal position.

"You *are* strong." He let out a light laugh, escaping through his heavier breaths, propelling his chest up and down in steady movements.

I refrained from commenting.

"When?" he asked.

I was silent for a moment as I adjusted my position. The Prince, assuming I had misheard, repeated, "When did you see it?"

"When I was a child."

"An eon ago, then."

I closed my eyes, trying to compose myself. I was barely any older than him. This man's insolence knew no bounds. I wondered how his sister even stood to be around him for longer than an hour at a time.

The Prince spoke again "In that case…it may have been the same one, or it could have been another. From what I know, there are three of these. They each have subtle differences in crafts…" —the Prince paused as he stepped over some trash— "…manship…but they would appear similar to you."

I wanted to ask who possessed the others, but I knew he would not reply.

"You want to know who owns the others, don't you?" The Prince glanced at me.

I opened my mouth slightly in surprise at his insight.

"You will not tell me, and I would rather not risk the condition your answer came with."

"Who said there would be a condition?"

I gave him a side long glance, one that carried my answer.

*I am no fool.*

"As I said…I was right about you." He grinned.

"Right about what, Your Highness?"

"I think I'll keep that to myself as well."

I suppose I should have anticipated that.

In time, we reached the body of water the Prince had mentioned. It was a large river, similar to the one we had met at, but much wider, and with a faster current.

And unlike the one we had met at, it was deserted.

The Prince lowered the body down to the ground. I did the same. Then, he kicked it in.

The body flew away in a matter of seconds. I stared in the direction it had disappeared in.

"Don't pity him. He was a terrible person," the Prince said.

I turned to face him. "Some may say the same of you, Your Highness."

The Prince clicked his tongue. "I wouldn't expect them to feel sad about my passing though." He smiled thoughtfully.

Unsure of what to respond, I turned my eyes back to the river.

"Have you heard yet?" he asked me.

"Heard what, Your Highness?"

"So, you haven't."

"I suppose that you'll be keeping that to yourself as well?" My face was impassive.

"No need, most will know in a sunrise or two." He wiped his hands on his shirt. "There have been riots in Kalnasa."

"Riots?" I knew why, without even needing to ask. I knew, I understood, but in the moment, I was overcome with a desire to repudiate reality.

"For how long?" I asked.

"That...I don't know."

I wondered about the other members of the Hunt. They no doubt would be one of the first to bear the brunt of the people's anger. I wondered how they were faring, if any of them had been injured, or if any of them had joined the people in their fight.

"Will you stay here?" the Prince asked. "Or return?"

"Unless instructed otherwise, we will stay."

"Even with a barren King as the prize?" He watched me with interest.

The King's sacrifice. I had almost forgotten amid the events that ensued. But of all the things that had occurred, it was perhaps the most significant.

"It is not for me to decide."

"You have more power than you think, Captain. You need not wait for others to decide for you."

It made sense that he would believe and live by such a statement. A man who did whatever he wished.

I glanced pointedly at the river. "Recent events would suggest otherwise."

"Recent events would only make it more important you remember." The Prince looked at the water. "We'll go back separately. You go first. Again."

I refrained from commenting that he had just decided this for me.

I bowed. "Your Highness."

"Be safe, Captain."

I made a move to walk away, but before I did, the Prince called out.

"Three days from now. You can come to examine the steel three days from now." He held three fingers in the air.

"Are you leaving, Your—"

"No. Three days. I'll look forward to your visit."

Which meant I had three days to come up with a plan.

To read this message directly in front of the Prince.

## CHAPTER 37- BAZ

"It's not your fault," one of the women from the camp tried to reassure me. The same camp that was now in tears, having just fled from the tracker's attack. Having just watched people they knew, and love die before them.

Because of me.

I hung my head forwards between my legs. "Whose then?"

"You just weren't ready."

"I said that I was. I let them trust me. I—"

"YOU!" a woman came for me. Screaming, sobbing. Like the rest of us, her clothes were ruined. Her hair was matted with blood and dirt. We had been running for hours now. Half of us were wounded, some of us severely. Faina still hadn't regained consciousness.

"You...you did this!" Her voice was shaking, her breathing was jagged, interrupting her speech. "Y...you...let them find us! And he's dead," she wailed. "He...h...he's dead because of you."

She sank to the ground, vibrating with the force of her sobs. Others surrounded her to comfort her, including the girl who had just tried to reassure me that his death, that all the others who had died, had not done so because of my failure.

"Claus was here for years." She looked at me, and pushing the others away, strode towards me purposefully. I made no effort to back away. I deserved whatever she had to say, or whatever she would do.

"And you...you're here for a few months and this. What gives you the right?" She jabbed me hard in the shoulder, causing me to lose balance slightly. "To live, to live instead of him?"

Nothing. Absolutely nothing.

Especially not now.

She jabbed me again and this time, I didn't try to steady myself and fell to the ground. It felt better down there, it was impossible to meet her eyes that way.

"Enough." Ullna stepped out of the shadows. "Contain yourself. Your husband is gone. Killing him changes nothing."

The woman screamed furiously at her, while others pulled her away.

Ullna approached me. She stood above me, barely glancing down to acknowledge my presence.

"Get up, boy."

I pressed my palm into the earth and rose, facing her.

"You'll have to work five times harder to prove their lives were worth your own," she snapped. "In all the years I have known Yaseer, I have trusted him. I can't say we have always agreed, but I have trusted him. You and your friend might be the first thing that's ever given me cause not to do so."

What was I supposed to say? That I was deeply sorry about being the reason she doubted her long-term ally? That I would work ten, one hundred times harder to make sure I earned these people's forgiveness? That I was wrong? Incompetent? That she was right, and I wasn't worth the gamble?

But that would mean Nemina wasn't.

And I had a feeling that no matter what I said, Ullna wouldn't have cared anyway.

"Nothing to say for yourself?" she probed me.

Apparently saying nothing was also wrong.

"Nothing I think you'd appreciate."

"Tsk."

In the distance, behind us, I could see a man, a figure, dressed similarly to Ullna, swathed in dark brown and green travelling clothes. He dismounted from a horse and walked towards Yaseer, who was at the far side of the temporary camp we had set up here. We hadn't been able to bring the large majority of the things we had taken here, so now, we were short on food, tents, supplies, medicine.

And people.

Ullna noticed me watching. "Stay here."

She walked towards the two of them.

I sank into the ground and crossed my legs. I wondered what Nemina would say if she were here, what she would have done. I could only hope her mission was going far better than ours was.

I closed my eyes and practiced, mentally practiced starting the concealing spell again. Where had I gone wrong? Somewhere, at some juncture, I had faltered, the flow of my energy or sorcery was interrupted. I channelled it incorrectly but when? I had been so sure I had succeeded. So sure.

"Acciperean."

I opened my eyes. The man who had dismounted his horse was standing in front of me now. I wasn't sure whether I should rise. I couldn't see any of him, his cloak was completely covering his body, his hood, his eyes, and he was wearing a mask that covered the bottom half of his face.

"You are the Acciperean, yes?" His voice was deep, sonorous, yet severe.

"Yes," I replied, realising how parched I sounded.

The man looked up, far over my head, thinking to himself.

"Perform the spell," he said.

"The...spell?" I asked.

"The concealment spell. I'd like you to perform it again. Here. Now."

"But...what am I supposed to conceal?"

The man turned and pointed at Yaseer. He was watching us curiously. Ullna was standing by his side, scowling. "Conceal his energy."

The man returned his gaze to me and pointed at my shoulder. "Do you need someone to treat your wound before you try?"

I shook my head. "No, leave it. We need the medicine, and I've survived far worse than this... as a Vessel."

The man nodded. "Then proceed."

"Now?"

"Please. I have little time."

I didn't even know who this man was, but the glares of Yaseer and Ullna told me that I was expected to fulfil his request.

And so, I did. I closed my eyes, I repeated the steps, exactly as I had done, hours ago, focusing my channelling on Yaseer. He was a good choice for this test, he was powerful. I had never seen which class, which ability Yaseer possessed, but I could sense his power. He was a class two at least, perhaps even one.

A few minutes later, I opened my eyes and stood. "It's done."

The man turned around and faced Yaseer. I didn't know what he was doing. If he, too, were closing his eyes, I wouldn't have been able to tell.

It was only a few seconds after, when he turned back around. "Follow me."

He walked towards Yaseer and Ullna. I walked behind him.

"Well?" Ullna asked him, raising her eyebrows expectantly.

"It worked. The Acciperean can perform the spell successfully."

Ullna tutted. "On occasion, it would seem."

"I..." I hesitated as all three of them looked in my direction. "I performed it in the exact same way earlier. There were no changes. I'm sure."

"Just how sure can you be? That was only your second time casting the spell," Ullna responded.

"Ullna," Yaseer cut her off.

"She is right," I spoke. "It is only my second time. I cannot be completely certain, but I am...confident."

"That means little to us," Ullna stated.

The cloaked man spoke. "You must consider the possibility. I have tried to warn you before. You have not listened."

"It's impossible," Ullna slashed her hands through the air.

"It is worth considering," Yaseer said.

"Considering what?" I dared to ask.

"This does not concern you," Ullna said to me.

"Of everyone here, he is the only one we can be certain to trust with this information," the cloaked man told Yaseer and Ullna.

Ullna huffed. "Is he? If he were the one, it would make sense for him to sabotage his own spell, and lead them right to us, only to demonstrate later that he could perform it."

"You discovered him, did you not? That is what you told me Yaseer," the man asked him.

"We did, however, we have discovered and rescued several of these people."

"How can he be the one, if he had not approached you himself?" the man asked.

"Then by your very logic, anyone who has not done so is not the culprit. Why then do you say he is the only one?"

Culprit?

"Do you believe there is a traitor here?" All three of them looked at me at once.

"No."

"Yes."

Ullna and the cloaked man both spoke at the same time.

"These attacks occurred long before the Acciperean arrived," the man pointed out.

"And before many others," Ullna retorted.

"Of those, only a handful were discovered by you, yes?"

"Seven or so," Ullna confirmed.

"Then surely, they too, are free from suspicion?" Yaseer asked.

"But he is the only Acciperean," the man pointed a gloved hand at me. "They are far too valuable, too sought after, to use in this manner."

"That could be the exact reason he is perfect for the task. Nobody would suspect someone to give up an Acciperean so freely." Ullna looked me up and down.

I thought about waving my hands in protest, exclaiming 'I am not a traitor!' but it seemed utterly pointless, and I couldn't help but feel it would only make me appear more guilty, especially to Ullna.

"It would not happen. Trust me on this," the man sounded assured.

Ha. There was no reason for me to defend myself when this mysterious figure was doing a perfect job of it.

The man turned to me.

"Give me your hand."

I glanced sideways at Ullna and Yaseer, who nodded at me. I held out my hand, unsure of the position I was meant to place it in, my palm facing the air.

The man took my hand in both of his gloved ones. He didn't make a sound, he just stood there.

The wound in my shoulder began to ache less and less, until it was no longer there.

The man let go of my hand, hissing in what seemed like pain as he did.

I couldn't believe it. I had thought they were all dead. I had thought perhaps they were a myth.

Healers, the only ability ranked class one for Dareans.

I let out a delighted laugh. "You actually exist," I said to the man, unable to stop myself from smiling.

The man ignored me completely. "It is not him."

"You didn't have to do that to confirm this..." Ullna's voice became softer. I'd never heard her speak that way before. She was worried about this man.

"It was necessary and now we can be sure." He addressed Yaseer. "Where is his companion?"

"She is...not here," Yaseer met my eyes briefly.

"And that is for the best, especially now. That girl is like an arrow, drawn in a bow, waiting to be shot at any moment." Ullna shook her head in displeasure.

"She sounds like you," Yaseer said to Ullna. I could hear the smile in his voice.

This was unusual. These three individuals had probably known each other and been friends for many years. Watching them was a reminder of all the things that I, that Nemina, that anyone who was ever a Vessel had been deprived of. It was also a reminder of how long they had been planning this, of hoping for something more.

Ullna tutted again. "Nonsense."

Yaseer smiled. "There are similarities."

I was beginning to feel I should leave.

"Is she?" the man asked me. "Your companion?"

"Is she what?" I asked, momentarily distracted.

"Like an arrow, waiting to be fired?" He sounded genuinely curious.

"She's..." I thought hard. "No. She's more like an arrow that an archer shot from a bow, only to be picked back up by that archer, and then fired again and again, against her will. And now, she doesn't know how to do anything other than be that arrow."

I had been looking at the soil, and shook my head in surprise at my sentence, clearing my throat.

"And what about you?" the cloaked man asked.

"Can anybody ever answer such a question about themselves? Could you?" I asked him.

He was silent.

"Well, I can't," I mumbled.

I was tired, and this day had truly been awful. I didn't feel like answering any more questions that related to me possibly being a traitor or the nature of my soul.

"Where did you come from?" he continued his line of questioning.

"Audra," I replied.

"It's the worst of them, I've heard," he said.

"Are there any which are good?" I huffed.

Ullna and Yaseer were watching us both thoughtfully.

"And originally?" He was asking about my birth Kingdom.

"Audra," I said again.

"And your companion?"

"I don't know. But she came from Audra as well. She'd been transferred beforehand, several...times." I paused as I took in a breath. I truly needed some sleep.

The man looked to the side as if thinking again.

"They were being transferred from Audra to Kalnasa," Yaseer mentioned, obviously something he had not had the opportunity to share with the man until now.

"Back there?" the cloaked man said to himself.

Yaseer frowned as if he did not understand the nature of his comment, Ullna however didn't seem surprised.

"It's troubling," the cloaked man stated.

"Yes, we think so as well," Ullna confirmed. "We've sent someone to investigate."

"I will do the same."

"It's too risky for you," Ullna said.

This man must have been someone with eyes upon him, I concluded, with visibility, and a reputation to maintain.

Although, I thought, it was hardly as if that made him heroic. Most sorcerers were born villagers, poor, townspeople, merchants, ordinary people. They could not avoid detection. They did not have the ability or power to do so. If any of them had been born into power, then assisting others like them was the least they could do in such circumstances.

But still, it was a risk. A sorcerer born into power or position could have avoided doing anything at all, and lived a comfortable life, hiding their abilities.

The man placed his gloved hand on Ullna's upper arm. "Do not think of me. Think of yourself, and those you are protecting here."

He removed his hand then said to me. "I am sure we will meet again."

"I don't even know who you are," I remarked.

"You do not need to know. Only that I am on your side."

I wanted to know, however. Regardless of whether I needed to.

"What should I call you then?"

"They call me the Healer here."

"They must be upset that you're not around more often." I thought of all the wounded, and pointed to my shoulder.

Ullna took great offence at my words once again. "They are grateful. He has done far more for us than you can comprehend."

"What do I call you?" the man asked me.

"Baz."

"And your companion?"

I glanced at Yaseer furtively before answering.

"Nemina."

The cloaked man nodded slowly.

"I will remember that. Good luck."

"And to you, and thank you for." I gestured to my shoulder for the second time.

"Farewell," he said to Yaseer and me. He walked away, Ullna followed him.

When they were several steps away from us, I asked Yaseer, "Do you know who he is?"

"No, only Ullna knows."

"Only Ullna?" I said, surprised. "How does she know him?"

"I am not sure."

Wasn't he supposed to be the leader of this group?

"How long have you known him? How long has he been urrr...?"

"Around four years now."

"I can't believe it. A Healer." I shook my head.

"Yes. It's quite miraculous." We both stood quietly watching him depart, as Ullna said her goodbyes.

"Do you think he's right, about a traitor?"

"I think so," Yaseer sounded exhausted.

"How will we find them?"

"There is only one way that we can do it, with great assuredness."

"Which?"

Yaseer sighed.

"We need a Telepath."

# CHAPTER 38 – LORIA

"Come in," Princess Rhana said, opening the door to the dining hall. It was far too large for the four of us, but the Princess had set two chairs at the table's rear end, and on either side of it.

She sat next to her escort at the rear. Nathon and I sat opposite one another.

I had resisted attending this dinner. Nathon had argued with me about it for hours earlier this morning. He had said this was the perfect opportunity to learn more about them. I argued it was simply an opportunity for them to learn more about us. Nathon still hadn't heard from Mathias, or our father, and it had been two days since the Coronation.

There was nothing we could do he had said, but proceed with the plan as initially intended. Part of that plan, he reminded me, would involve blending in, and appearing amenable to these invites, and social occasions.

There was a plate in front of each of us, served by Palace Staff. It was some kind of fish, served on a bed of plants, and drizzled in a light sauce. Nathon hated fish, I remembered that from our childhood.

Nathon grabbed a fork and placed a large portion into his mouth.

"Divine." He swallowed, smiling.

I supposed he'd done far worse than eat odious food to meet his ends. This was nothing to him. This whole meal was child's play.

Princess Rhana smiled softly. "I wasn't sure what you both enjoyed, so I've asked that several dishes be prepared."

"Thank you, that's very thoughtful." I smiled at her. Rhana's escort remained silent.

"I thought it might be good to get to know each other a little better," Rhana said calmly.

"Just us?" Nathon asked, placing another portion into his mouth.

"No, in fact. Kalnasa's candidate rejected my request, as did Vasara's. I never received an answer from Jurasa's."

"How impolite," Nathon remarked light-heartedly.

"I suppose that everyone is wary in light of recent events," I murmured, picking up the cutlery.

Nathon and Rhana both looked at me. Jayli looked at Rhana. "Yes, you are right. But not you, it seems." Rhana smiled, now eating herself.

"We already agreed to dine with you, it would be discourteous to refuse now, and I too...would enjoy getting to know you both," I said.

"And who could refuse a free meal?" Nathon gave his reason, continuing to indulge in the free meal that he in fact, despised.

"So." I thought that it would make sense to ask a question. "Do you miss home?"

"Very much so," Rhana chuckled. "The atmosphere is very different here."

"You dislike it?" I asked.

"I am...not accustomed to it," Rhana answered. "I prefer the quiet, the mountains, the trees."

"You can always go back to them," Nathon probed.

Rhana swallowed some of her drink, placing it down with a soft smile. "I could become accustomed to it though...eventually."

"What about you?" she asked me. "Is Audra in your thoughts?"

"Of course," I replied. "But I am glad to have the opportunity to explore Vasara. I would like to visit Zeima one day as well."

Yes, Audra was in my thoughts, but not in the way Rhana had implied.

"And I Audra, I have never been," she said.

"I'm not sure you'd enjoy a visit to Audra's very much." Nathon leant back into his chair, finishing the plate.

"How so?"

"It's quiet like in Zeima, yes, but it also possesses a certain...roughness to it."

"Mmmm," I agreed. "The people are rather...lively."

"How interesting," Rhana said, raising her brows.

I wasn't sure that I believed she was unaware of Audra's nature, or the nature of its people. But Audra was something that could only be truly understood if one saw it and experienced it themselves.

"And you will rule it one day, Prince." She looked at Nathon.

Nathon smiled and quickly flicked his eyebrows up and down. "A perfect candidate for the role, wouldn't you say?"

"Psst." Jayli made a sound under her breath. Nathon ignored it.

A few minutes passed by in silence as we ate.

What were we doing here? So far, this dinner had amounted to nothing more than pleasantries, and polite conversation. I remembered and knew that Nathon had said such things were my responsibility, my contribution to this scheme. But since we were here now, impatience and frustration simmered within me. This meal could, and should, be a means for us to make progress. I had to ensure I did everything right. I had to do more.

I could do more.

"Do you truly wish to be the Queen?" I asked.

Nathon, whose arm had been hanging over his chair, dropped it, and turned to me, Rhana and Jayli did the same. Rhana peered at me, as if she were searching for a trick behind the question.

"Do you?" she said.

Perhaps Nathon was right, I should have avoided an attempt to gather further information, that was his forte not mine. His facial expression hadn't changed, after all, we were in the presence of guests, but I could feel, I could tell that he wasn't enthralled about my having asked.

Still, I had to pursue it now.

"I...believe it would benefit my people. I suppose the same could be said for you. As to whether I desire to rule, I am unsure. But perhaps that is better than seeking power for power's sake," I speculated, looking at my food.

"I do wish to rule," Rhana said, straightening up. "Power is the only way that someone can implement their ideals and make a change in the world."

"What ideals are those?" I asked.

"A world which is fairer, safer, that protects those who cannot protect themselves. That would see an end to poverty, to disease, that would allow the poor to learn, to grow, and thrive. That would spread wealth with equity, that would distribute goods evenly, that would not neglect the people."

"I truly hope such a world can exist," I said to her. I admired her enthusiasm.

"Yes. It sounds wonderful," Nathon added, squinting.

Rhana faced Nathon. "You don't sound convinced, Prince. It is your destiny to rule too, is it not? What do you wish to do with such power?"

Another dish was placed in front of us, meat and vegetable based.

Nathon leant forwards. "I haven't decided yet. There's still much that I have left to do first."

"Such as?" Rhana inquired.

Nathon didn't say anything, he simply smirked and began eating again. Rhana and Jayli glanced at each other. Jayli was like a statue, a shadow, her very presence at this meal felt simply for her own reassurance. She was barely eating or drinking anything.

"Perhaps travelling? Visiting each Kingdom's local attractions, for instance?" Rhana peered at him. Nathon's hand grasped harder around the flute of the wine glass he was holding. He set it down.

"Are there any you would recommend?" He smiled at her.

"I know little of Iloris, I'm afraid. But... the Solar Inn seems to be quite the bright spot."

Nathon's face fell slightly. I could tell without needing to ask, needing to speak, that Nathon, for whatever reason knew of this place, that he had in all likelihood already been there, and that somehow, Rhana had found out about it.

"That's interesting. I've not heard of it, how did you?" I asked her.

The Princess slowly turned to me. Nathon's eyes flitted in my direction. There was a glint of approval in them.

One thing I had learnt from my time growing up at the Citadel, from my childhood, was that if you didn't want to answer a question, asking an equally uncomfortable one tended to work well. Then, you would leave the other person no choice but to avoid probing you further in order to avoid answering themselves.

I am sure Nathon had learnt similar tactics himself, as well as more refined ones.

"From the maids, the servants here, I hear them talk," Rhana explained.

"They must have granted you the only talkative servants in the whole Palace, how fortunate. Mine are rather quiet. Aren't yours, sister?" Nathon responded.

*Sister.*

Inexplicably, a lump formed in my throat and my flesh crawled with a chill. Nathon rarely addressed me as his sister. I couldn't remember the last time he had done so in the presence of others.

Everyone was waiting for my answer.

I composed myself. "Mine seem afraid to speak to me at all." I chuckled lightly.

"Have you heard of it, Prince?" Rhana asked. "The Inn?"

"I have. In fact, I've even been there."

I was right. Knowing Nathon, the Inn was a place he frequented for his own pleasure or gratification. It was beyond me why Rhana would even wish to know more about it. She, in all likelihood, simply wished to inform him that she knew of his activities, but Nathon's reputation was hardly a secret.

Perhaps she was trying to shame him. But that wouldn't work on Nathon.

Not that she was aware.

"Ahhh. Well, I have little else to offer in the way of recommendations. Besides if the Inn sufficiently meets your desires and needs, why look elsewhere?" Rhana put to him.

His needs. Gods. This was beginning to become uncomfortable.

"Precisely," Nathon agreed. "And if a current lover or partner already meets your needs, why look elsewhere for another?" He looked at Jayli pointedly.

I tried my best to hide my glare at Nathon. He never could help but try and get the upper hand. If he saw an opening or a chance to attack, he always took it.

But this did not feel like the time or place to do so. Not to me.

Rhana laughed, airily, brightly. "Is that a logic you apply to your own nightly activities, Prince?"

Not the Inn again. I hadn't been able to anticipate where this conversation would lead, but Nathon's 'nightly activities' were not one of the possibilities I had considered or wanted to discuss.

"I make no false claims about my needs. Why are you so curious about them?"

Rhana waved her hand dismissively in the air from side to side. "Pay me no mind Prince. It was only idle chatter and curiosity. What you do in your spare time is your business...and who."

"I do not think that any curiosity is idle," I said, hoping to put an end to this conversation.

"Really?" Rhana's voice was warm. "What if I was curious about your favourite meal, for instance?"

"It wouldn't be idle, since you could attempt to impress me with such a dish," I replied.

Rhana shifted in her seat. "What if I was curious about your favourite...animal?"

I chuckled and thought. "Perhaps then."

"Well, which is it? I assume it is not an Erebask?"

I had been cutting my food but stopped abruptly. "Why would you assume that?" I asked carefully.

"They say of all the nobility in Audra, you are the only person who does not ride one."

"It is not the animal, but the ride I dislike."

"I had always thought it must be rather exhilarating. I envy those in Audra and Kalnasa for being able to take their creatures to the skies."

"Your Vilkan are said to be rather magnificent as well," I spoke. Vilkan were wolves born of sorcery, far larger, and more dangerous than ordinary wolves.

"They are beautiful beasts. Truly. I feel very lucky to know them. Do you feel that way as well, Prince, for your Erebask?"

Nathon took a deep breath in and out. "Very much so."

"Have you seen any of the Chimera's here?"

"No, we have not," I answered.

"I have heard that they will be present at the great festival in a few weeks' time, as part of this Season. To lay eyes on them will be a...wonder," Rhana sighed.

"Yes, it will be," I agreed.

A few more minutes passed as we ate.

"Ahhh, bring the dessert please," Rhana said to one of the servants.

In walked one of the servants, holding a large tray. Just one dish, on one platter, rather than multiple dishes for each person.

The servant was dressed differently.

No.

He wasn't just dressed differently. He was dressed in Audra's attire. Dark purple fabric covering his arms. Thick dark trousers lined with golden thread caressing the ground as he entered.

I looked at Nathon who was staring at the man, his eyes growing wider, his hand edging closer to his belt, where his daggers lay.

I recognised this person. I had seen him around the Citadel. I had spoken with him. I had spent time with him. He had guarded and accompanied both Nathon and I in the past.

"This is Ruban," Rhana said, smiling. Ruban edged closer to the table and placed the dish in front of her.

"He works for me."

In an instant Nathon shot up, standing at his full height, his nostrils flaring. His jaw was clenched so tightly as he glared at Ruban that he could have cracked his own teeth.

I couldn't understand. I didn't understand what was happening. I knew little of the activities of Audra's unit, but I knew that Audra was known to be far superior to other Kingdoms when it came to spy craft, intelligence, and undercover operations. How was it possible that this man had slipped through our nets? Besides, he appeared to be from Audra.

As I struggled to comprehend this, I looked at Nathon and Ruban again.

Ruban was smiling knowingly. Nathon was shaking his head slowly.

Rhana stood. Jayli did as well. "Ruban is of mixed heritage. He is Jayli's half-brother. He was born in Zeima and has been working for my family ever since."

As Rhana was speaking, Nathon lowered his head, closing his eyes, laughing to himself. "Well played... Princess." Then he looked at Ruban. "Do you truly believe you can evade his wrath?"

"There are places in Zeima not even your father knows of, Prince," Rhana's voice had become far more assertive, cold.

"Are there?" Nathon quirked a brow. "I'd love to visit one sometime."

Rhana was brave, bold, to confront us, to confront Nathon in this way, to place a spy within Audra's Kingdom. Of course, it was understood that all Kingdoms planted agents in the others, but the identity of the spies was not usually revealed to those who had been spied upon.

"Why have you told us this?" I asked, becoming the last person to stand. "Ruban could have remained your spy for many more years without detection, yet you have revealed his identity to us. You would not do so without reason."

Rhana addressed us both as she answered. "I have long suspected you had ascertained the nature of my relationship with my escort before you even clarified it yourself. You and I both know such information could be used, not only to force me to withdraw from the Courting Season, but to bring great ruin to myself and my family. I have no guarantees you will not use this information to your advantage and so, I feel it is necessary to inform you that I know far more about you" —she looked at Nathon — "than you realised. Ruban can worry about himself. All you need to be concerned with is this... you tell no-one of what you know, and I can assure you I will do the same. Ruban reports directly to me and to nobody else. He will not disobey my orders to remain silent. If, however, you try and use this information against me, then I will make sure that every trace of your dark past is cast under a light so bright that the glare will destroy you."

Again, she was looking at Nathon.

But Nathon only laughed sedately. "You place a very high estimate on the amount I value my reputation, Princess."

"Do you dare to play this game, Prince? I know there are things that even you wish to remain concealed. Things that even your sister" — she gracefully lifted a hand and gestured towards me — "remains unaware of. Things that pertain to yourself...and to her and—"

*To me?*

"That's enough," Nathon's voice was monotonous.

"What does she mean?" I asked Nathon. I mentally berated myself for asking him in public, for admitting that there was information I did not know, despite Rhana clearly being aware of it already.

Nathon said nothing.

Ruban turned to me, the sunlight striking his closely cropped hair. "The Prince is keeping things from you."

That wasn't surprising at all. I had always assumed Nathon kept things from me, but the 'things' that Ruban and Rhana were alluding to now, felt different in nature.

"You know, who's to say that I won't kill you myself before you get a chance to return to your hideout?" Nathon's squinted at Ruban.

"You won't do that. I know how you operate well enough," Ruban replied smugly.

"Isn't that wonderful. And would you like a more physical demonstration?"

"Nathon," I said quietly. Jayli looked as if she were ready to jump on him at any second.

Nathon turned to Rhana, taking one step towards her. "I understand. I must remind you though, that if you break your end of this bargain, that it won't just be your lover's brother I eradicate from this world. After all, if you *do* break your end of it, then I will have no honourable elements to my reputation whatsoever. My heinous deeds will become common knowledge to all, and there will be absolutely no reason for me to maintain any air of decency, or refrain from committing more. *Think about that.*" He spat the last three words.

Rhana looked a little unsettled. It made sense, for the possibility of Nathon's vengeance was considerably more frightening than hers or Ruban's was.

"I think I'm full. Thank you so much for the meal... and the threat." Nathon walked past Ruban as he made for the door, patting his shoulder overly hard.

I was left alone with the others.

I looked at the tray. "Is there even a dessert under there?"

"Of course," Rhana answered. She lifted the cover to reveal an intricate and exquisite looking fruit-based pastry, dusted with sugar and cream.

I sank down into my seat. "I'll have some. If you please."

Rhana and Ruban looked at each other. "You can go," she said to him.

Ruban bowed at her, then faced me. "You should stay away from him, Princess, if you can, when you can. You don't know a fraction of the things that man has done. I've worked beside him...I've seen it. He is pure evil."

I gulped. My blood iced at his words. It was as if a skeletal bony hand seized my chest, its joints a ruinous deliverance of the truth.

I hadn't dared to think about it. There were times I had considered, I had imagined the things Nathon might have been responsible for, but I had convinced myself not knowing them was better. To see him as a blade, forged from cold hard steel. Metal could not feel as it took lives. Neither could he. That was all I needed to know.

Now, reality was staring me in the face, weighing down on every limb like lead.

Yet still, I replied, "Then I hope for your sake, that you remain faithful to your word."

The corner of his lips twitched up, and he let out an amused sound. "You'll see, Princess, one day... you will know."

I shuddered inside. I wasn't sure I wanted that day to come.

After Ruban had left, some of the other servants entered and dished out the dessert. I began to eat it, half present, half in my own mind.

"You know more about my own brother than I do, it seems," I said, still staring blankly at where he had been sitting.

"Are you saddened by that?" Rhana said.

"I admire you for it." I was still in a trance, glaring at the table. "Not many people would dare to confront my brother in that manner."

"He left me with little choice."

"Did he?" I looked at her now. "Was it him? Or was it this place? This world. This life that we lead?"

It felt ridiculous to maintain such a strong air of pretence around Rhana. She already knew so much about my brother and his life. She had openly threatened us. There was no use pretending we were allies when we were in fact, rivals.

"Are you angry, Princess?"

"I am tired, and I am...not like you, or my brother. I am not good at this game, these tactics."

"You are better than you think, Princess, else you'd be dead already."

"How... reassuring."

"You know, I much prefer this version of you."

"It would only be a disrespect to you, to continue with the farce this meal had started with," I said.

"I agree." Rhana raised a glass to suggest a toast. "To our newfound understanding, and to the end of our farce."

I raised my glass to hers, reluctantly.

"So that Fargreaves is a bastard, don't you think?" Rhana said. Jayli looked at her in shock.

"The farce is over," Rhana said, shrugging.

"Between us," I said slowly.

"Exactly."

We looked at each other for a few more seconds.

I sighed. "He is a bastard."

Rhana's face lit up in genuine amusement. She laughed so much that her body shook with the force of it, placing her hand on her stomach.

And I, against my own will, found myself laughing too.

# CHAPTER 39- NATHON

If Zeima's Princess wanted to believe she possessed vital information, then that was absolutely fine by me.

What did she think? That Ruban and I braided each other's hair, held hands, and embraced, shared stories of our heinous deeds and missions around hearty meals? That we, and all the people who worked for my father in this manner, had group meetings where we would unveil all our actions and plans?

It was Ruban, however, who was the greater fool. He had no excuse. He had worked under my father for four years. He had very quickly proven his skills to become one of his agents, and he had barely associated with anybody. It was precisely for those reasons that I distrusted him in the first place, as well as all the other people who worked for Sarlan. At most, any one of them knew twenty percent of what went on with my work.

For Ruban, that percentage was probably closer to five.

But that was five more percent than the rest of the world knew.

Than Loria knew.

And that five percent would contain the one thing that I never wanted her to know.

That Sarlan had wanted to shape us both from blood-stained clay. Work on us like monuments he'd unleash against the world.

And so I had agreed with him, when I was fifteen, to work twice as hard, endure twice as much, indulge in twice as much bloodshed, as long as Loria would never do, work for, endure, or indulge in anything.

I had decided it would be better if she hated me and was free, than cared for me and was trapped.

And now, if she ever found out, she would only hate herself, and her freedom would have been for nothing, and she would only hate me more, for having made that choice for her.

It was selfish of me to want such information to remain concealed, but I didn't feel any guilt about it. It wasn't as if I made decisions based on my own desires and wants at any other time.

If this was the only one, then so be it. It would be worth it.

I hadn't even meant to leave the dinner so abruptly. But Loria had been looking at me with such confusion, such pleading, I couldn't risk staying there for a second longer without risking murdering Ruban on site.

I walked inside my chambers and removed my jacket and tunic, leaving the thin undershirt on.

It was only then that I noticed.

I had been agitated when I entered this room. My guard had been down.

I turned to the figure perching in my window. Her cloak just reached over the frame.

"It's rather impolite to watch a man get undressed like that... isn't it?" I grumbled.

It was the same woman who had been at the draining centre that night.

She pivoted slightly, still perching in the window frame.

"I had no doubt you'd notice me before your virtue was at stake," she said.

Her voice box had healed from before. I tried to place her accent, but like last time, I couldn't. Her voice was only slightly deep, but smooth, calm.

And laced with derision.

"Still hiding, I see. Won't you come a little closer?" I asked.

"So that you can try to kill me? I think I'll pass." She laughed under her breath.

"You're so sure I would attack you."

"Wouldn't you?"

She was right. I would absolutely have attacked her and tried to remove her mask.

She lifted a dagger and pointed it in my direction. "It hasn't healed."

I looked down at my shoulder. "Are you here to tend to my wounds?"

She removed her hand, perching her wrist on her bent knee. "I'm quite sure that you could send for your own healer...*Prince*."

So, she knew who I was.

At least, she did as of this moment. She hadn't seemed to be aware of my identity when we had met, despite the fact that my appearance was widely known, as were the nature of my clothing, and weapons.

"It hardly seems fair you know who I am, and yet I do not know who you are."

"I thought you had sworn to find out."

"I've been rather busy."

"So I've heard."

I wondered exactly what it was she had heard about.

"What's your name?"

"No."

I took a few steps towards the window. The woman stiffened up. I could tell she was preparing for me to attack her, but I stopped, just close enough that my boots touched the edge of the shadow her body was casting on the wooden floor.

My voice dropped. "What are you doing in my room?"

She put the dagger away. I assumed she meant to indicate that her plan was not to injure, attack, or kill me.

"Why were you at the draining centres that night?" she asked.

"Why were you?" I raised a brow.

"I am not a Prince. It would not be dangerous for me to be there."

"It would be dangerous for anyone to be there."

"Not for me." She smiled, just as before, I could see the bottom half of her face, but not the top.

I took another step closer. "What does that mean?"

She didn't answer.

"You know. This is how a conversation works. I won't answer any of your questions, unless you answer mine," I told her.

"Do you want something from me?" she asked.

I was startled by the question. Why would she assume that?

"What made you think so?"

"You didn't tell anyone about what you saw, about my presence. There are only two explanations for that. The first is that you have your own reasons for investigating the draining centres which you don't want brought to light, hence my first question. The second is that you planned to use this against me, knowing I would invariably return to the centre at some point. Which is it?"

"I want nothing from you. Sorry to disappoint," I waved my hand in a dismissive gesture.

"So, it's the first one."

I crossed my arms. "Even if that is the case, I see no reason for us to interfere in each other's plans."

"You are already interfering." She sounded frustrated.

"How? It is you who has invited yourself into my chambers."

She jumped through the window and took a few steps towards me. We were no more than an arm's length away from one another. No, less than that. I hadn't expected her to enter, or to come so close.

"Your knowledge of my existence is interference enough." Each word she spoke was sharp, purposeful.

"Your...existence? All I know is that you are a woman of a fair complexion. I would hardly call that incriminating evidence."

"Do not make yourself out to be a fool. I have heard enough about you to know that you can gather my meaning easily. The existence of an individual who is neither a Vessel, nor someone who works for the Palace's draining centre...can only be one thing, can't they?"

"You think that a spy in this Palace is such a rare occurrence?" I tilted my head and raised my eyebrows. "You think that is enough to warrant my attention. It is as commonplace as the clouds in the sky and the leaves on the trees here. You're not as important as you think you are."

"Until you decide otherwise?"

"You're not very trusting, are you?"

She let out a quick laugh. "Do you consider yourself a trustworthy person?"

"I keep my word," I said tentatively. It was probably because this woman had been the first person to actually wound me in years, but an uneasiness grew in me the closer she came. I was not accustomed to the feeling.

"And what is your word, *Your Highness*?"

"I will tell no-one of your existence. You have...my word." I bowed before her, reaching for my dagger as I did.

Before I could straighten up, she came closer to me. Her hand found its way to my arm, my wounded arm.

She squeezed it hard. I fell to my knees.

"You're lying." She looked down at me. "I can tell, especially since you *clearly* just tried to attack me."

"You—" I reached for a dagger at my belt, but she grabbed my other hand before I could. I still had my left hand free, but it was almost impossible to use with her fingers pressing harder and harder into the wound on that side.

"What do you want me to say? I just told you I would keep your secret, and you don't seem very pleased about it," I said through gritted teeth.

"That's because I don't believe you." She bent forwards so that our faces were level, if she hadn't had a hood over her face, I'd be looking at her directly in the eyes.

"What could I do... to convince you?"

She paused, and didn't say anything, then suddenly let go of my shoulder.

"I don't want to hurt you. Do you understand?"

The infinitely increased level of pain in my arm said otherwise.

"No, I'm afraid that I don't. I don't understand what you want at all, or what you're doing here."

She sighed, and then let go of my wrist. "I don't know you and so I don't trust you, and even if I did know you, I'd be unlikely to trust you anyway. If our situations were reversed, you would have killed me by now, but I can't do that since you're a Prince, and even if I could, that doesn't mean I'd want to." Unlike her previous sentences, these words came out hurried.

"You're not a very good spy." I couldn't help but smile. "Telling someone you don't trust so much."

She huffed. "It's no more than what you already know."

"Honestly?" I stood again with my right hand on my left shoulder. "This knowledge matters little to me. I don't care about it, or you."

"You mean that I'm not a threat to you."

"Are you?"

"I could be."

I didn't doubt that. I caught myself being surprised at my own thoughts.

I didn't doubt that this woman could indeed be a threat to me.

I had never met someone who had genuinely believed that. That they could defeat me in combat. Only complete fools. This woman seemed anything but one.

Which could only mean that she had good reason to believe she could, which did nothing to ease my growing concern in her presence.

I wasn't used to fearing for my life or placing much value on it at all.

But I had to live.

Or Loria would not.

"I think you may have forgotten the outcome of our last encounter," I said.

"I suppose it would be easier for you to remember, since I left such a permanent reminder." She pointed to where my hand sat.

"Perhaps one day, I'll return the favour."

"You *see*..." She sounded impressed with herself. "How can I trust this disregard you have for my existence won't suddenly disappear?"

"It won't."

"Would you trust you, if you were me?"

I smiled "Most definitely not. But as you've already said, you can't kill me and according to your own predictions, killing you would be impossible, so what is it that you are so concerned about?"

"Even if you cannot kill me, you could reveal my activities to any of the relevant authorities at any time, and that would effectively mean I cannot complete what I came here to do. I wouldn't be able to tell anyone about your presence at the centre without revealing my own, so...as you can see, you have the upper hand. I don't like that."

"And yet...that is the situation. You cannot change it."

"I would like to change it," the woman said.

"That's not my problem," I said, backing away from the woman slightly.

She noticed and took a step forwards. "We're not done talking."

"Could we be?"

The woman crossed her arms and then unfolded them again. She was apprehensive.

"If you tell me why you were there...I can help you, and in return you can help me."

So many deals. With this woman, with Sarlan, with Elias, with the Captain, with Rhana.

It was give and take in this world. Always.

And the take was usually far more merciless, more powerful.

I wondered what it must be like, to know someone who came to expect nothing of you.

"What makes you think that I need your help?"

"Don't you?"

I grimaced. "No. Not really. I work alone."

The woman looked at the ground. "And have you found what you were looking for?"

"I will. In time." I dropped my hand from my shoulder, rolling it slightly.

"Do you have time?" she asked, her head following the movement of my arm.

"I have more than enough."

"Really?" She leant against my bed frame, crossing her arms once again and tilting her head back, to glance at the ceiling. "Then why is it your drinking companion follows you around like a hawk?"

My face fell.

"Watches you like one too." Her head dropped as she turned to look at me.

She'd been following me?

But how? I always knew, I always could sense when I was being followed, being watched.

"He's certainly not protecting you. I've heard you can protect yourself...most of the time." She gestured at my wound.

"He's looking out for me." I leant back against the wall.

"Is *that* what it is?" She sounded doubtful.

"How long have you been following me?" I asked, irritated at my lack of ability to detect her having done so.

"Who says I'm following you? Perhaps I'm just...*looking out for you*."

"I'm not working with you."

"Are you working with your friend? I can't report your activities at the draining centre, but I can report him."

I was almost tempted to let her do it. Mathias behind bars would be a pleasant sight.

But that would inevitably put Loria and I in great danger.

This is how they must have felt. The Captain and Elias. When I backed them into a corner. When I demanded their help in exchange for silence. And not only them, but all the people I'd done so to in the past.

But if anyone were to find out about my true motivations for being here, for Loria's, the King would not be so forgiving, and if he didn't execute us, then Sarlan had already promised to do so, or at least, make us infinitely suffer.

Still, I had no intention of being manipulated.

"Be my guest," I told her.

"Such loyalty to your *friends*."

"What exactly is it you can report? That a friend of mine visits the Inn and watches me. Suspicious? Yes. Incriminating? No. The members of this Court are already suspicious of me. This friend of mine won't change that."

Calling Mathias my friend, even under these circumstances, made me feel physically ill.

"Besides, I already have the means to discover what it is I need to know," I declared.

The day after the Captain and I had removed the escort's body from his chambers, I informed Elias of the first favour I wanted from him.

To visit the draining centres and find out as much information about them as possible. He, I could tell, had been startled by my request, and not at all glad to fulfil it. But, as a self-proclaimed murderer of a noble, he really had little choice but to agree.

We had managed to keep the escort's disappearance hidden for now, since it had only been two days since the incident, and there had been no events which had required his involvement or accompanying of the Jurasan Princess. But it would only be a few more days before people realised that he was missing. Until then, the Jurasan Princess was remaining in her quarters.

The woman shook her head. "If you want to know anything about those places, you won't find anything useful by yourself, even if it *is* you."

The woman walked towards me and since my back was already against the wall, I had nowhere to go, apart from to the sides, which in this moment, felt wrong.

She held up a key. It was small and golden. She placed it in the upper pocket of the light shirt I was wearing.

It was the window key to this room.

Her voice became quieter. "You'll need my help. I guarantee it. I'll come back in a few days, and we can talk."

She took a few steps back and hopped onto the window again. She turned her head to the side slightly, and with a smile still on her face said, "You can get undressed now."

She left.

I instantly walked towards the window. I looked out, down, and around, but there was no trace of her anywhere, no footprints on the grass below. There were no signs she had been here at all.

I placed my hand in the pocket of my pants.

As the woman had given me my window key, I had also taken something from her, since she had been so close.

I opened my palm, and my breath faltered.

An enolith stone.

There was only one kind of person who could use an enolith.

The kind that could remain unseen, that could avoid my detection, that could leave no traces behind.

I had never spoken with one. I had only ever been sent to kill them when they lay sleeping in their beds. Unaware and unthreatening.

I had killed one, just two days ago.

I laughed. She hadn't been bluffing. She hadn't been wrong.

This woman really could, if she so desired, kill me.

Because this woman was a sorcerer.

# CHAPTER 40 – LORIA

The numbers on the boards before us were in my favour. For now. The ones containing the total score to the games.

The games were the third event of the Courting Season. The winner was often greatly favoured by the nobles, to which it gave an excuse to gamble and place bets, to line their pockets with further gold.

Horse riding, colf, batting, archery, and bowling. We had already played the first three, and as of now, myself, and both the Zeiman and Kalnasan candidates – Rhana and Dyna, were all close in scores. Jurasa's candidate, Maiwen, had fallen behind drastically, her eyes glazed over more than usual.

Archery was next. I'd been taught to throw daggers and shoot weapons since the age of five. My training had come to a sudden halt once I'd reached adolescence, but I'd still kept up my skills in private, somewhat.

"Confident about your chances?" Zeima's Princess asked me.

"Not so much," I replied.

Rhana laughed under her breath. Since our recent dinner, she had been acting very differently. Although, I thought, it was likely this was a better reflection of her true self. Not that there was anything wrong with that, only that it was an infinitely more treacherous version.

We were in an open field, wide and relatively plain. Short swathes of golden grass lay beneath us, dancing in the wind that weaved through it, carrying the smell of the city, full of meat, spices, and flowers. The thin transparent blouse that hung around my shoulders was similar to those hanging around the other candidate's, only that mine was purple, Rhana's was silver, Dyna's was blue, Tarren's was red, and Maiwen's was green. We each wore a dress of similar material underneath it. The fabric was itchy and scratched at my skin with every rustle. It almost made the thick cloak I had worn on arriving here seem comfortable. The only one unbothered by both our attire, and the event, was Princess Maiwen.

Rhana noticed me staring at her. "Her escort has been missing since this morning."

"That's...unusual." I unconsciously turned behind me to look at Nathon, who like all the escorts, remained a few steps behind us. He wasn't even paying attention, his brows furrowed in thoughts known only to himself. I did, however, catch eyes with the King, who was sitting behind us, under a canopy, shielding him from the heat. He smiled slightly as I noticed him watching.

I stood there, blinking, unsure of what to do. It would be presumptuous to return the gesture but cold to ignore him. As if sensing my internal dilemma, the King smiled even more, completely ignoring the man who was trying to speak to him on his right.

"Your Highness? Your Highness?" one of the attendants had come up to me.

"It's your round, Your Highness." He bowed as he told me.

"Ah. Thank you."

Nathon fell in step beside me as we walked towards the platform. Dyna had just shot. She looked thoroughly displeased with herself, lamenting to the Captain about her attempt.

As we moved, Nathon whispered in my ear, "You'd better win. I put a bet on you."

I suppressed the urge to roll my eyes in public.

"No, you didn't," I murmured.

He drew back quickly. "How do you know?"

"You'd never do anything that frivolous."

"Mmmm." He smiled to himself.

Now that we were at the platform, we were much closer to the King than before. His men were whispering amongst themselves looking at Dyna and I. Dyna was still hovering nearby.

The King and I locked eyes again, only this time, he wasn't smiling. He only tilted his head downwards slightly, in encouragement.

I turned around and drew my bow. We had three shots. Three. I could see from the board with its colour coded arrows that Dyna had landed two strong shots, but one poor one, Maiwen had unexpectedly hit near the centre each time, one average, and two strong shots. Tarren had failed miserably, two average, and one weak shot.

I took in a deep breath and focused, trying to pay attention to the direction of the wind. The string dug deeper and deeper into my flesh. I could feel people's attention on me, hear their voices, their quips.

My hand trembled slightly. It had been a long time since I'd practiced, and I was used to firing arrows in completely different weather conditions.

I fired.

"Ooohh," the crowd let out, painfully.

The shot had made Tarren's seem impeccable.

I let the bow down and closed my eyes. I drew a breath in and out. I could hear people laughing. Such a ridiculous way to be entertained.

My shot had barely made it to the edge of the board. I waited for Nathon to speak, to make some mumbled crude remark, but there was nothing, only the incessant chortling of those under the canopy. That and the thundering of my heart, thrashing against my ribs like a quake in the earth. I imagined my father's face, his eyes slit with disapproval. I imagined my mother's lips, stretching into a thin line of disgust. It was as if they were there, in the crowd, phantom observers to my failure. They were always there somehow, at the back of my mind, casting judgement upon all I did. I could never escape their shadow. Even when I had roamed through Audra's mountains, when I had stepped away from the Citadel for days at a time, they haunted me. That feeling, of inadequacy, of smothering futility had hunted me. And it had always struck true.

As the laughter bounced around me, the knowledge of it sunk inside my chest. That distance could not destroy it. That not every haunting could be outrun. That not every prison had a lock and key, barring out the pain. Some had doors wide open, letting in a gentle breeze, for there would always be a jailor waiting at the end of a paved street, and a million different ways their chains would stay on your wrists. No matter where you went. No matter what you did.

Was I doomed to live with this suffocating feeling till death? Was I fated to never feel anything but insufficient?

The laughing stopped as the King stood, holding his token. Each noble had a token, that was a sign of their bet, if they decided to place one. Just in front of the canopy was a large series of boxes, each one colour coordinated to the candidates, and inside them were the tokens, inscribed in ink with the bet that the noble wished to place on that individual.

The King grabbed his token and glided over to the boxes. He took the quill from the servant who was supervising it, wrote an unknown figure on his token's surface, and dropped it.

Into the purple container.

The people in the canopy gasped, some of them huffed, or whispered under their breaths.

I was stunned. I gripped my bow harder, trying to bring myself back to a sense of calm, but utterly failed. The King's gesture was a gesture of goodwill, I guessed, but if anything, it had only made me far more restless.

Nathon whose arms were crossed, raised his brows, and glanced at me from the side. The King spun around, his loose red blouse beating against his skin in the gentle breeze. He returned to his seat, looking at me directly as he sat down.

In the peak of the daylight's sun, his eyes looked even brighter, and paler than usual, as did his skin. He appeared like a glass sculpture of ice the sun could melt at any moment.

Nobody was saying anything. Tarren, who was still nearby the platform after her attempt, looked furious. Dyna's mouth was wide open. Lord Elias who was seated near Eliel was chuckling to himself, shaking his head. Everyone was simply waiting for me to fire my next arrow.

In a sudden motion and wave of seething rage, I turned around, drew my bow, and without giving myself time to think, or feel, fired again.

It struck the centre of the golden sun, painted deep inside the board.

The corner of my lips twitched up. Those who had been laughing before were now silent. Some of them approached the betting boxes, I could tell from the shuffling of feet behind me, but I didn't turn around.

I didn't give myself time to doubt, or dwell upon the stakes, or the meaning behind these shots, the consequences, the fate that awaited Nathon and I if we failed here, and failed again.

I shot once more.

"Impossible!" Tarren moaned. Dyna let out a little shriek.

The sound of faint applause rang from behind me, as had been customary after each candidate shot their three arrows.

I turned to face them and curtsied.

"Looks like you'll be even richer than you were this morning," Elias said to the King, pointing at where my third arrow had landed, just a whisker away from the second.

The King said nothing, only slid his index finger further up the side of his jaw, leaning further into his hand.

A few more nobles stood and placed their bets on me. I couldn't help but watch them hobble over in a rush, and smile at them as they made their way back to their seats.

It wasn't that proving them wrong made me feel anything in particular or gave me any sense of satisfaction. It was making them feel uncomfortable that was at least slightly enjoyable.

Still, my act of confidence and pride was impeded by the steady and persistent shaking of my hands, which had not yet faded.

I moved towards the candidates who had already shot. Nathon followed like a dark cloud. Even though Vasara had provided him with alternative clothing, he only ever wore the dark clothes we were used to in Audra.

Dyna approached me as I came closer. "That was magnificent! How did you do that? Can you teach me sometime! I tried my best to hit the centre, but I just couldn't do it. Wait, is it my bow hold? Let me show you." She lifted her bow up, about to draw the string back.

"My Lady, I'm sure that the Princess wishes to rest." The Captain approached from behind her. He gently placed his hand over her bow to lower it before an arrow could inadvertently be fired from its string.

"No, it's quite alright." I smiled, "But truthfully, I haven't used a bow and arrow for some time, I'm sure that it was simply good fortune, or the will of the Gods. I wouldn't be able to advise you." I looked down at her, despite my short height, Dyna was still shorter.

"You're being too modest! We all saw you, didn't we?" She turned to the Captain.

"It was an excellent performance, Your Highness," he agreed.

"Thank you, Captain."

"You must have done it somehow! Did you imagine something? I've heard that some people envisage a place, or pay attention to certain sounds?" Dyna's eagerness to learn was touching.

"Yes, I imagined that I was firing at him," I quipped, smiling as I pointed behind me towards Nathon.

"You? What?" Dyna seemed genuinely perplexed. "What does she mean? How would that help? He's your brother, isn't he?"

"Exactly." I nodded my head, my lips curling up, "That's exactly why it works."

"I don't understand. Do you understand?" she asked the Captain.

The Captain who was looking at Nathon now, said curtly, "I understand."

Nathon's eyebrows sank slightly. He smirked a little.

I cast my gaze between them both and made sure Nathon noticed my quizzical look. *Why is he looking at you like that? What did you do?*

Behind us, Rhana was making her way to the platform, and had already begun to lift her bow, to fire her first arrow. The crowd waited silently. Rhana's arrow struck true, similar to Dyna's first two. An auspicious start.

"She's good too," a voice from behind us spoke. Vasara's candidate approached with her escort.

"Not as good as you"— she looked at me — "or her." She cast a glance at Maiwen.

Dyna began trying to console her, "Archery is hard, you shouldn't be upset that—"

"I'm not upset. I was a slight bit frustrated at myself, but I knew that these games and athletics were never going to play to my strengths."

"Oh. What are your strengths?" Dyna asked curiously. It was difficult to watch her entertain Tarren with conversation. The rest of us were clearly wary of her, waiting for the bite to her honeyed words.

"Things which are more...refined?"

Nathon tilted his head to the side. "You don't think the art of being able to handle a weapon is refined, My Lady?"

"Not at all, it is a brutal and vicious thing, Your Highness."

Nathon pointed at the Captain, who looked slightly taken aback by the attention being brought to himself. "I was in Kalnasa once, a long time ago. I was about your age then." He looked at Dyna. "But while I was there, I snuck away. I'd heard about the training their soldiers undertake, the way in which they are taught to move, to fight, to wield their weapons as if they were a very extension of themselves. They train their soldiers from adolescence into adulthood, to prepare them to join one of their five regiments. The Army, the Cavalry, the King's guard, the Law Invokers, and the Hunt, but they're all trained in a similar manner."

Rhana fired her second arrow, another good shot.

Nathon continued. "I found their training grounds. Of course, nobody is supposed to find them undetected but..." Nathon shrugged, nonchalant about the fact he was openly admitting to infiltrating a highly secure location. I watched him startled, I had never heard this story before, this fabrication. He was always inventing new ones to adapt to whatever situation he was in. This was hardly a surprise. But there was a glint, a gleam in his eye that made me think that perhaps this time, it was true.

He smiled to himself before he finished the sentence. "I sat there and watched. For hours. I went back there a few times to watch while I was there. Because you see" — he looked at Tarren — "it was the most beautiful thing I had ever witnessed. It was like...they were dancing. I've even tried to practice or teach myself such things since then, but I can never quite find the fluidity of motion. The art of it. The...refinement." He grinned. Then he looked at the Captain, who was listening to him, a look of slight surprise on his face.

"I didn't see you there though, Captain. I supposed you'd finished your training by then."

The Captain furrowed his brows before he spoke. "What year was it, Your Highness?"

"1112," Nathon replied. Eight years ago.

"Then yes, I was finished, Your Highness," the Captain was regarding Nathon curiously.

"But what was so beautiful about it? I've always found such things rather tedious, if you'll pardon me, Your Highness," Tarren asked.

Nathon drew his gaze away from the Captain and back to her.

"You'd have to witness it to know." Nathon seemed like a completely different person at this moment in time. His face seemed to glow. I could tell that the others had noticed it as well.

Then suddenly, as if someone had shaken him from his dreamlike state, he pointed at Hestan and said, "Perhaps the Captain can give you a private show."

The Captain looked unperturbed.

Tarren stuttered. "I... that won't be necessary."

"Or the Captain can teach you, Prince?" Dyna said to Nathon.

The Captain and Nathon stared at each other for a few seconds before Nathon said, "No need. Although... I would like to see how the Captain moves one day myself."

"He's the best soldier Kalnasa has!" Dyna said enthusiastically.

"I do not doubt it." Nathon smiled at the Captain.

"He was taught by the very best himself...he..." Dyna's voice grew timid suddenly, as if she regretted her words.

"Really? By whom?" Tarren asked.

Hestan smiled sadly and looked up at her. "He was a great man, My Lady."

"Was?" Tarren asked, sounding shocked, but mostly, greatly excited, as if the story of this man's passing was a piece of treasured gossip.

"He was killed, My Lady," Hestan confirmed, his voice detached.

"Killed? When? Why?" Tarren asked.

Hestan seemed uncomfortable answering the question. "Before he was our mentor, he was a soldier, a warrior, a politician of sorts. He had no shortage of enemies, My Lady."

"That's dreadful." The insincerity of her tone was obvious.

A strange silence hung over the air, even Nathon, who was normally able to fill any, seemed disconcerted, looking down at his feet.

"You're very fortunate to have the Captain by your side with his skills, My Lady," I said to Dyna.

"Yes, that's true." She smiled brightly.

"But aren't you worried?" Tarren said.

Dyna looked confused. "About what?"

"About the riots in Kalnasa. Isn't the Captain better suited to dealing with the situation there?"

The riots? What riots? I glanced at Nathon's facial expression. He already knew, I could tell, but the Captain and Dyna seemed equally unsurprised.

They all knew.

Tarren's bait had not been taken, but there was still time for the hook to wander in the water.

Let her think we were flapping around, hungry for her lies. It would be better if she believed that.

"What riots?" I asked, feigning interest.

"Oh, they say it's awful, that the people are hungry, and the King is being brutally attacked for it. Who knows if any harm will come to the Royals there? It's terrible…just terrible." She placed a hand over her mouth.

She was trying to make Dyna angry, I realised. If Dyna acted aggressively in public, it would greatly discredit her image in front of all of these prominent people, improving Tarren's chances.

"I am sure Kalnasa are dealing with the situation as best they can," I said as confidently as possible.

"But who knows if it will be enough? What if the worst should happen and the King himself is injured?"

"My uncle is a capable and strong man. He will be safe," Dyna said quietly, as if she didn't believe it herself.

"Captain, you must be greatly worried. They say you've been by his side for years, his greatest confidant. It must pain you so that you cannot be by his side now. I hope you are able to return to his aid soon."

The Captain straightened up and tried his best to remain impartial, but the tension that hung over his brows betrayed his annoyance and anxiety.

Tarren noticed, and blinked softly, smiling equally so, clearly satisfied with herself.

Rhana fired her third shot, three solidly good shots.

"Ahh, looks like you won, Princess," Tarren said to me.

*And you as well.*

Hestan and Dyna's pained expressions were evidence of that.

Nathon noticed them too.

"And you...lost, most egregiously," Nathon said to her, pointing at Tarren's shots on the board.

"All is still to play for, Your Highness. Life is so unpredictable. Don't you think so?" she said to the Captain. "After all, who could have anticipated such a turn of events in your Kingdom?"

"The food shortage has troubled our people for some time, My Lady," Hestan said flatly.

"But you look quite well, Captain?" Tarren probed him. "It cannot be that bad surely."

"That's not true!" Dyna wailed.

Some of the nobles at the table turned to look at her.

The Captain tried to calm her down. "My Lady, it's—"

"No." Dyna lowered her voice but remained angry. "She's saying that you—"

"You're right, I am quite well, My Lady," Hestan said to Tarren, cutting Dyna off.

"Why are you letting her—" Dyna started again.

"Let people think what they will," I said to Dyna. "It doesn't make it true." I was trying my best to calm her. Tarren scowled at me. The thought that she hoped her look of disapproval would affect me in some way was almost amusing.

"It is not only me, Captain," Tarren continued. "There are many who wonder about this 'food shortage' you speak of, and they cannot help but question why, if it is so severe, and these riots are truly something to be concerned of, you do not rush to your King's side, and how you yourself look so well fed. Surely you can understand their misgivings?"

Hestan seemed torn between defending himself and remaining silent, pressing his lips together slightly.

"I have an idea," Nathon said, stepping closer to Tarren. "If you are so concerned about it, why don't you go and pay them a visit? That way you can verify the truth and relieve all these poor people of their... *misgivings.*"

Hestan and Dyna looked at Nathon with confusion. Nathon's words confused me less, however. He was probably trying to make sure that everyone but us walked away from this conversation appearing weaker.

"Of course, I can do no such thing, Your Highness, but that does not mean these questions are without merit, don't you agree?"

"No. I don't agree," Nathon replied assuredly. "You could in theory, go to Kalnasa, so could any of these people you mention that create such theories about the state of the situation there, but they do not. So, their concern, and your concern does not strike me as true."

"I forget, Your Highness, that you are so well travelled, so used to visiting different places. Alas, most of us cannot abandon our responsibilities and lives, to verify such information."

Tarren was very well spoken, and much more intelligent than she had previously seemed.

"So, if you cannot verify it, then surely, you cannot definitely refute it either, isn't that correct?" Nathon put to her.

"I suppose but—"

"But you enjoy the version which casts another Kingdom in the worst light."

"It is not that—"

"It is understandable," Nathon said.

Now I was completely confused as to his motives.

He continued, "If your rival looks poorer, then you look greater, isn't that true?"

"Your Highness, I can assure you this has nothing to do with—"

"Are you saying then, that you believe the words of these random individuals, over the words of the Captain and the Lady here?" Nathon added, an obviously feigned pain to his voice.

"I...of course not...I—"

"Excellent. So we can all agree the Captain is a semi-starved man riddled by the guilt of being torn between conflicting loyalties, and the Lady a dutiful young woman, who at this time, is doing what she believes is best for her people?" He smiled at Hestan. Hestan looked at him warily, the only sign of his bewilderment the fluttering of his silver eyelashes.

As intelligent as Tarren might have been, she couldn't outwit Nathon when it came to poisonous charms. He had orchestrated this whole conversation to arrive at this conclusion, as if he anticipated every answer she would give correctly.

This, this was like watching dancing.

"Indeed, Your Highness," Tarren reluctantly agreed.

"Ahh, excuse me," Nathon looked at the betting station and strolled towards it. Rhana, Tarren, and Dyna all made way to return their bows and arrows. Hestan was a few steps behind Dyna, having stood still for a few seconds, with his eyes closed.

Before he could walk past me, I spoke. "What do you want from him?" I said it quietly, my voice blended in with the chatter surrounding us.

The Captain came to an abrupt stop and looked at me sharply.

Nathon wouldn't inform me, and so trying to pry the information out of the tight-lipped Captain, while difficult, seemed the only alternative.

"Your...Highness?" He sounded hesitant.

"I know you want something from my brother." I fiddled with my bow, looking down, avoiding eye contact with him. "What is it?"

I could feel the Captain's gaze on me, his face still tilted at an awkward angle. He seemed unsure as to whether he should confirm or deny the implication my question had made.

"There's no need to deny it. I already know you have some kind of...preestablished arrangement. I just want to be sure it's nothing that will—"

"I have no intention of harming your brother, Your Highness," he said suddenly, taking one step backwards, to look at my face more clearly.

"Of course not." Who would even make such an attempt? "But...if your arrangement will endanger him in some way, please... withdraw from it."

Hestan was silent for a few seconds. "Your brother is safe, Your Highness. In any case, it is hard for me to imagine he would agree to something he believed too dangerous, or a risk."

I thought about the threats my father had made against us before coming here. How could a sentence be both so true and utterly false at once?

"It may be hard to imagine but...my brother is not..." I was trying to choose my words carefully. This dance of words was just as complicated, if not more so than the Kalnasan training. I sighed.

"A simple person to make dealings with," I finished my sentence.

"Are you...warning me, Your Highness?"

"It is not a warning." I chuckled slightly, trying to prove those words. "I just wonder if what you ask of him will be worth the cost...and if you will be willing to pay it."

Hestan furrowed his eyebrows. "I will, Your Highness."

I sighed. It stuttered as it left my lips.

"I will," he repeated again, glancing at my face caringly.

I looked up and turned to walk with him. "It's rather late for that I'm afraid, and it's hard for me not to be troubled when you...look at each other so...glaringly. As if you despise each other."

"I do not despise him, Your Highness," Hestan said coolly.

"I hope that is true," I said.

I returned my bow to the attendant. Nathon approached, waving a pouch back and forth in front of my face. He looked puzzled for a moment when he saw the Captain standing next to me.

"You're escorting the wrong one, Captain."

"I was only congratulating her on her victory, Your Highness."

"What about me?" Nathon pointed to the pouch he had brought over. "I won lots of lovely gold thanks to my intuition."

He had actually placed a bet on me. I stared at him, raising my eyebrows.

Nathon let out a light laugh. "I told you I'd bet on you, didn't I?"

"Congratulations, Your Highness." Hestan bowed and made to move away, but Nathon stopped him. He lightly lifted up the Captain's hand with the palm of his own and placed the pouch into his grip.

Hestan looked down at the pouch confused.

"Your Highness... what are—"

"Take it...after all, you're light on your belongings, aren't you?"

*Is he?*

Nathon's hand was still lightly touching the Captain's knuckles. His eyes searched the Captain's face from side to side. The Captain tipped his palm over, placing the pouch back into Nathon's hand.

"Your Highness, I cannot accept this."

Nathon repeated the action, returning the pouch to Hestan's hand. "Stop being so humble, Captain. I do not expect anything in return."

Hestan quickly glanced at me.

"Neither does she," Nathon said.

But Hestan's pride would not allow him to take it. "I am—"

"What's that?" Dyna asked, approaching us after having returned her bow.

"I'm trying to give your Captain a gift so that he can treat you to a meal, or whatever it is young ladies want. But he refuses... isn't that frustrating?" Nathon crossed his arms.

"Captain?" Dyna said, gripping Hestan's forearm slightly. "Please...I desperately want that... urrr dress. You remember the one! In the shop window from Roart Street?"

She didn't need the dress. She needed the money, just as the Captain did, but she was giving him an out, a reason to accept it that would not wound his pride. Dyna was too young to avoid making such things obvious.

Hestan grasped the pouch tensely. He appeared as if it took every fibre of his will not to throw it fifty feet away from him. "Thank you, Your Highness."

Nathon smiled widely. "It's a pleasure as always, Captain."

Dyna grabbed Hestan's arm and pulled him along. He glanced back at us once last time before they left.

I decided to try this again.

"What does the Captain want from you?" I whispered.

"My soul," Nathon replied teasingly.

I rolled my eyes this time, unable to stop myself. "Who would want that?"

"You're right. It would be a terrible reward."

We started making our way to the next station. The spaces between us, and the other candidates, and nobles widened, leaving us more room to speak.

"You did well. Even the King set his sights on you." Nathon nudged me with his elbow.

"You're avoiding my question."

"I've already answered it before."

"Then why do you look at each other with such...malice?" I thought to see Nathon's reaction to the same question.

He chuckled. "Do we? I hold no malice towards the Captain, perhaps he does towards me but..." He trailed off.

"Then why did you speak up for him?"

"Isn't it obvious? Letting Dyna be disgraced does nothing for us. She is a child, and the King will not select a child to be his wife, not this one. She is not a threat to us, but Tarren might be, so, exposing her schemes is more beneficial."

"Does she scheme?" I squinted ahead. "Or is she one of those, who likes to make others feel small, so that they can feel larger?"

Nathon threw me a sidelong glance, smiling slowly. "Both. Perhaps."

He seemed more talkative than usual today.

"Why give him the money?" I side eyed him cautiously.

Nathon was silent for a few seconds. "There's a message inside."

*Ah.*

"Any news?"

"I'll find out tonight. Just win this round for now."

"So that you can give the Captain more messages?"

"Tsk. Your obsession with the Captain is frightening."

"It is not me who is obsessed," I retorted.

"No, you're right, it is the King... with you."

"He is not obsessed with me."

"He likes you. That's good for us."

"Who knows what he thinks? You know that better than anyone. Perhaps he feels a need to repay a debt to Audra after you saved his life."

"He doesn't strike me as the debt paying kind."

"What does he strike you as?"

At that moment, I remembered Nathon's words before we left Audra.

*Does that matter? I'm not your escort so that we can take midnight strolls and gossip about the colour of the King's eyes. I'm coming to make sure that nobody tries to hurt you or kill you. I'm coming to make sure that we see this task through, and that we survive it.*

And I couldn't help but laugh a little.

"What's so amusing?"

"I...nothing."

Nathon squinted at me in disbelief before he said, "He strikes me as a debtor."

"What does that make you?"

"A debt collector."

"And me?"

Nathon said nothing.

"And the Captain?" I couldn't help but smile as I asked.

Nathon closed his eyes and smiled, shaking his head. "Stop meddling."

"Isn't that what you do constantly?"

"Yes, but I'm good at it."

It felt strange. We were speaking so easily, almost, so calmly, as if it were the most natural thing in the world.

A despair came over me as I realised how temporary this was, how meaningless in truth.

"What...do you think will happen?" My voice had dropped.

"I don't know, Loria."

I looked in front of us to find Dyna and the Captain whispering to one another.

Dyna stopped and ran towards us suddenly. Holding one of the coins from the pouch in her hand.

"This is for you!" She cleared her throat of her excitement. "Your Highness."

Nathon glanced at the lunar coin confused, then at me, then Dyna. "Whatever for?"

"Please take it! You defended us, you defended our honour and we...we owe you something!"

Hestan stood a good few steps away, looking utterly embarrassed.

"Ignore him! He's obstinate, but he is thankful too, he said so himself!"

"Did he?" Nathon sounded amused. "YOU'RE WELCOME, CAPTAIN!" He shouted, then pocketed the coin in his upper vest.

Hestan let out an exasperated sigh.

"He...He really hasn't." Dyna stopped herself suddenly.

"Hasn't...what?" Nathon asked.

She appeared ashamed and looked down. "He really hasn't eaten the same...since...for months now. He let his men have some of his rations. He told me he didn't, but I heard from them he did, and...he's lost weight I know, everyone knows. Well, he was always urrrrm slender, but now, he's even more so, and...when we go out, he won't spend the gold on himself, he only spends it on food for me, and he refuses to spend more than necessary, and... he's hungry I think, but of course, he won't admit it, because there are people starving back home, and here as well...and he would never claim to suffer while they suffer, and—"

Hestan, who had caught wind of Dyna's rambling, strode towards us briskly.

I waited for Nathon to tease him, but he only stood there quietly, saying nothing, looking at the Captain expressionlessly.

"My Lady, we are falling behind."

"Of course, sorry. I lost track of time and…gave the Prince the gold."

"It was His Highnesses' in the first place." He glanced at us cautiously, clearly wondering what Dyna had just told us.

"Let us go, My Lady." Hestan gently led Dyna away.

Once they were a fair distance away from us, I said, "He must hide it under his clothing, his armour. He doesn't appear slender."

"You'd like to get a closer look, would you?" Nathon said, grinning.

"Wouldn't you have a better idea of his physique? Since you 'watched their soldiers training'… of course," I replied mockingly.

"I did… you know."

"That…that was true?" My eyes widened.

"Most of it."

"Most of it?"

"There were some omittances. Like what happened when I was discovered." Nathon's voice was now subdued.

No words were needed between us for that, whatever it was that happened when our father, or someone in a similar position, had discovered that a young Nathon had been sneaking off to fulfil his own curiosity, rather than his duties, can't have been a story fit for public ears.

"Was it worth it?"

Nathon smiled softly, glancing at the grass, "Yes."

"Would you do it again? For the same result?"

"Yes."

"It must truly have been a sight then," I said incredulously.

"It was. If I am ever offered the chance to see it again for a price then…"

"Then what?"

"Then I'll pay it. I will."

*I will.*

# CHAPTER 41- NATHON

I fiddled with the gold coin between my fingers while I waited. Loria and Rhana had been dual winners of the games. That was good, but it wasn't ideal. Still, we had fulfilled our end of the bargain for now. That was all we could have done.

The side alleys that circled around the Solar Inn were revolting, but it was nothing I hadn't seen, sat, or even immersed myself in before. The streets were lined with filth, trash, wanderers finding their pleasure in sex with strangers, or drugs in alcoves.

I thought about that sorcerer, about if she was watching me right now, but I made no efforts to find her. If I hadn't detected her already, there was no way she could be detected at all.

"That's a lot of money, where did you get that?" Mathias approached.

"I won it. A bet." I told him.

"What did you bet on?"

I twisted the coin some more, moving it quickly between the spaces that separated my fingers and thumb. It was cold, hard, shining in the low light of the night's near full moon.

"On a certain semi-starved individual."

Mathias scoffed. "Delightful."

"Yes. They are." An image of the Captain apparated before my eyes.

"Did you look into the stolen goods of our dear friend?" he sneered.

*Have you found the information that was stolen?*

"Not yet but I will," I told him.

"One of his cooks recently abandoned him as well."

This must have been Ruban. Did he expect me to deal with him as well?

"He's looking for him though."

"What will he do once he finds him?"

"Make sure he never works again, most likely."

"He sounds like a wonderful employer," I replied sarcastically.

If Ruban died, then Rhana would need to find some other way to hold Loria and I to account, which I'd prefer she didn't search for.

Mathias leant against the wall next to me. "Why are we...here?" He looked around him in pure disgust.

Other than the fact I knew this setting would make Mathias deeply uncomfortable. "There are too many inside tonight. The games attracted attention."

"The crowds act as a dispeller of suspicion."

"Not when there are so many recognisable faces amongst them. The risk must be evaluated accordingly."

"Anyone could be listening."

"I've already assessed, nobody is listening."

Apart from the sorcerer perhaps.

"Ahh well outside, inside. It's all the same," Mathias said quietly.

*Kill the King straight after the marriage. The plan remains unchanged.*

It was what I had expected, but still.

"The men and women are different outside and inside too."

*Who kills him? Me or Loria?*

"I'm more partial to the men...as you know."

*You kill him, not Loria.*

"Yes, I know, I'm sure they do as well."

*The King will be suspecting something like that.*

"Then it is best not to give them time to think, before they are in your arms."

*Then do it quickly.*

Somehow Mathias was managing to convey my instructions and his thoughts on sexual consent at the same time.

"Nothing needs to be said."

*That's all.*

"You simply take them," he spat.

He grabbed my chin, turning it to face him. My face was hidden somewhat with a hooded cloak, red this time, but it was directly in his line of sight now. The feeling of his calloused hands on my jaw made me want to peel my own skin off, made me want to slither away into nonexistence.

His warm breath was tickling my cheeks, burning my flesh. It reeked of alcohol and the faint traces of his last meal. He licked his lips as he looked at mine.

He lifted his right arm and placed it around my shoulders so that he could press himself against me.

If this had been anyone else, anywhere else, I would have killed them instantly. If anyone else had even looked at me with such intention, I would have ended them before they could see it through.

But him, I could not kill. I loathed it with every bone in my body. My blood screamed, bashed around inside my heart and veins, around my limbs. A tumult of fury, begging to get out. But Mathias was the only person I was powerless to stop. His death would mean my punishment, and Loria's. His death would not be forgiven. His life was worth too much to my father. Worth more than my own, most likely. In Audra, I could escape his clutches, I could evade him, I could remove myself from the scene. But here, I couldn't attract attention, I couldn't be detected.

I had trapped myself in this alleyway.

As much as I had been aware of Mathias' perversion, I would never have believed that he would be stupid enough to try and act upon it so openly here.

Yet his breath betrayed his inebriation, not enough to weaken him, but enough to cloud his judgement.

"What's the matter? Not running away this time?" He leant in closer and sniffed me, his nose pressing itself into my hair. He let out a long sigh afterwards.

I backed away, grimacing in internal agony.

"Could it be... that you like it when I touch you?" he grumbled.

My lips quivered, with rage, or repulsion, or even fear, I wasn't even sure.

"It's like getting touched by a corpse, who could enjoy it?" I spat. My voice curdled with disgust.

Mathias gripped my face slightly harder. "A vulture might mmm? To a bird of death, the touch of a corpse is like the Divine Halls. Don't you want to know what they feel like?"

"Remove... your... hand."

"And what if I don't? What if I fuck you... right here, right now, in the dark, where nobody...is listening, where nobody can see?"

My legs shook slightly. I knew now, I was afraid.

I was afraid.

I was never afraid, but this man, this threat, this frightened me still. I'd already used my body for Sarlan. I had already sacrificed enough of my autonomy to wither it down to one single thing...that I had not been forced so violently or viciously in this way against my will.

That was what remained. That is what I had left.

Mathias spoke again, emboldened by my silence. "Not so snappy today, little boy."

I shifted in his grip and kneed him in the groin. He doubled over but remained standing and pushed my head against the wall. A wave of impact reverberated up through the back of my skull.

"My father might not be too pleased if he hears you fucked me in an alleyway," I hissed.

Mathias laughed slowly, as if he were savouring it. "Your father won't give a shit."

I swallowed down that bitter truth, gulping in hopelessness.

"So, I can do... whatever I want to you now."

"Careful Mathias...I might not be able to kill you just now, but I will make sure you suffer excruciating pain for a *long* time, slowly, before you die, if you touch me once more," I seethed.

"You know. It's hard to take you seriously when you're trembling like a little lamb. I like seeing you frightened." He used one finger to stroke my cheek. "Everyone's so afraid of you. I must be the only person that the Vulture himself is afraid of...how"— he sniffed me again— "fucking exciting."

He placed the hand that had been around my shoulders on my waist. I squirmed in his grip.

"Think about what you're doing." I reached for my weapons. I couldn't kill Mathias, but I could wound him enough to escape. I would suffer for it, yes.

But I would not suffer this.

"I am thinking...I've been thinking about you for a very, very long time." His hand slid lower, and lower. Now it was on my hip.

I couldn't stand it any longer. I pushed him off me, holding my weapon at him, but he had clearly anticipated my half-hearted attempt at resistance. He had clearly known I couldn't use my full strength against him. He grabbed both my wrists and slammed me back.

Mathias was perhaps the only one of my father's cadre that was more proficient than I at hand-to-hand combat. After all, he had been trained in the same manner, and had been practicing his craft for far longer.

He moved his hands further along. Now one was on my thigh.

I hit my head back against the wall and looked up at the sky.

Maybe, if I looked up at the sky, I could endure it. If I looked at the stars. I could count them. He wouldn't last that long anyway.

I could do it for Loria.

I could. I would.

But still, my body resisted against his fingers around my leg, gripping forcefully, his other hand sliding down my neck.

"Stop squirming so much," he whispered in my ear.

I turned around and spat in his face.

He used one finger to wipe it off.

Then he stuck that finger in his mouth.

And licked it.

I watched him mortified.

Mathias lifted up a blade and held it against my neck.

"Don't get any ideas now. Be good and do what you're told. Like you always do."

I struggled, but there were little manoeuvres I could attempt that wouldn't open my jugular vein. Mathias' hand moved deeper into my thigh as I tried to kick my way out from under him.

As if by an invisible force, Mathias fell forwards, and slammed fully on top of me. I pushed him off. Mathias rubbed the back of his skull and turned around.

Someone had attacked him.

"Who the fuck are you?" he yelled into the shadows.

A slap resounded against the ground. A hollow, tapping sound.

The individual didn't answer. Mathias stepped forwards. I remained against the wall, trying to assess the situation. I could run now, I could escape, but I didn't yet know who had attacked Mathias, or why.

Having caught sight of the individual Mathias scoffed. "Mind your own business. If you want one like him that bad, there's plenty inside."

"He's the one I want," a smooth voice replied.

I stiffened up, dread spread through my body.

Now I had no choice but to escape.

Because I recognised that voice.

"Too bad Kalnasan…he's mine."

## CHAPTER 42 - HESTAN

"Didn't you hear me? He's taken. So, fuck off," the man spat.

He pointed downwards towards the street. His voice was raised but subdued, the lines of his face furrowing deeper as he scowled at me. There was a faint sheen of something on one of his jowls.

I glanced at the figure huddled behind him against the wall. A red hood hid their face, but I could faintly make out the rest of their body. It was a man.

"He doesn't appear to be taken just yet."

"That's because you interrupted me, isn't it?"

"He also doesn't appear to be willing," I remarked.

"What... and you think he'll open his pretty little legs for you?"

The figure wasn't moving, but his posture, the tilt of his head towards the right, I could tell he was listening to everything with the utmost attention.

"Perhaps we should let him choose?" I watched the man in front of me cautiously. His light brown skin was tinted red with rage, or it might have been arousal. It was impossible to hide the scowl of disdain that formed against my lips.

He noticed it and laughed, cackled. "Let him choose? Since when do whores get a choice?"

"It'll make it more interesting," I said while looking at the man against the wall. Why hadn't he run? It didn't make any sense.

"Alright, I'm getting tired of this." The man walked towards me, a weapon outstretched in his hand.

A weapon so dark it absorbed the night sky, so opaque that even the moonlight was partially swallowed by it.

I lifted my spear off the ground, eyes widening. The inspiration to save this individual instantly seemed to have been a poor idea.

But if by some small chance I could render him unconscious, I could take his weapon. I could take the Noxstone.

The man in red pressed his fingertips against the wall, and sprung forwards slightly when he saw the blade, but he didn't move any further, crouching like a cat, waiting, watching.

The man in front of him lunged at me. I dodged to the side and spun, twisting my spear to slam into his left side. It hit its mark. The man gripped his ribcage.

"You cunt!" he yelled.

He went for me again, this time with far more skill. He feigned a left sweep, suddenly changing to a central one. I jumped back and used my spear to send his wrist off course. I spun around again, gripping the spear by its head and flipping it forwards to hit the man in the neck. He grabbed the spear and went to hack it with his blade. Although Kalnasan spears were stronger than most materials, the Noxstone would likely cut my weapon in half, if it were applied with such force.

I slid to the ground, and the man who was grabbing my spear had no choice but to fall with me. I yanked my spear from his grip upwards and flicked it behind me, back flipping as I did to fall into a crouched position.

The man grew more agitated and took out another dagger. Two of them...he had two of them.

For someone to have this many, there was no doubt he was from Audra. This, I had already guessed because of his features, his black eyes, his black hair, but only individuals of great importance were afforded so many weapons of this kind.

Fighting with this man was not bound to end well, but I was already in the midst of combat, and I had not been able to predict his identity before I had decided to intervene. Even if I had been, I was not sure I would have been able to walk past as he took the figure in red by force. He clearly wasn't someone who worked for the Solar Inn, despite the man's insistence that he was.

He came at me with the two daggers, slicing towards my top and bottom halves simultaneously. He was skilled, and fast. I blocked both of the attacks with the sides of my spear, being careful to only strike the flats of the blade as before. If my spear hit the sharp ends of the weapons, I couldn't say if it would survive the blow.

One of the weapons flew from his hand as I whacked against his wrist.

He ran towards me, then lurched to my side, making to stab me in the neck. I ducked, twisted, and slammed my spear into his back. He stumbled forwards and then, turned around again. Now our positions were reversed. I was standing in front of the individual in the shadows.

"Who are you?" the man pressed.

I could sense it was in my best interests to avoid answering that question.

"It doesn't matter. Whoever you are...you're a dead man anyway," he stated.

He grabbed a third dagger from somewhere in his clothing. This one was ordinary steel but curved. He aimed for my shins this time. I jumped upwards so he would stab at air. As I came back down, I kicked him in the chest. He fell to the ground, but got back up immediately, aiming for my leg once more. I sprung back, but the curve of the blade meant that he successfully hacked into my shin.

The pain was searing, clawing at my bones like a ravenous beast, starving for my screams. I used my other foot to step on his wrist and in doing so, disarmed him, but caused the blade to drag further down into my muscle.

I couldn't help but let out a grunt of pain. The blade had hacked at several layers of my tissue. It was only my dodge that had managed to prevent it from hitting bone.

"Look at what you've done," he spoke to the man behind me. "This innocent man is about to die because of you."

I kept my eyes on the man in front of me.

"Who says I'm going to die?"

"The blood loss is rather fast from this blade."

"If you had struck true, possibly."

He laughed patronisingly. "He doesn't know…How endearing."

Just as he spoke, a surge of blood spurted out of my leg, colouring the pale fabric of my pants like wine. I looked down in disbelief.

"You know," the man said, straightening up. "You're not half bad looking. Older than I usually go for…but that face of yours…it's really quite beautiful. Maybe I'll take you as you're bleeding out, and you can watch." He pointed to the man behind me.

I calculated I had about twenty minutes at most before I passed out.

And today was the third day, the day I had meant to visit Audra's Prince for the Noxstone. The Prince's coin pouch had contained a message, stating a time to come to his chambers.

There was no way that would be possible now.

I'd be fortunate if I could get back to the Palace alive.

I gripped my spear and twisted it in my arm. I approached the man. He used his dagger to lunge for my chest. I dodged and twisted around him, smacking the spear against the back of his shoulders. Before he could regain his balance, I spun around and slammed it into his diaphragm. I used the momentum to flip him over it. His face slammed into the pavement.

He bounced back up and threw his dagger. In response, I bent completely backwards, facing the sky to dodge it, and pressed my spear against the ground as I did. I gripped it as I came back up, facing the man again. Another weapon was in his hand. As he tried to strike, I sprung off the ground and flipped forwards in the air over his arm.

I landed crouched. The impact sent a wave of agony up my leg. I swallowed a yell then spun around on one foot. I flipped the spear forwards again to swipe at the man's legs. He fell forwards again, and this time, his skull crashed harder against the ground, and his eyes closed over. He was unconscious. Hopefully.

I pressed my fingertips against the pavement, heaving in and out, the blood was continuing to spill out of my leg.

I used my spear to help me up.

I looked into the shadows. The individual was still standing against the wall, regarding the scene with what could only be described by his body language, as calm surprise.

"Are...you...are you well?" I asked the man, struggling to get my words out.

He didn't answer. I took a few steps towards him.

He outstretched his hand in a 'stop' signal. It was gloved. He pointed down at my leg.

"I'm...alright," I said through gritted teeth. "Are...you?"

The man pointed more insistently at my leg again, and then towards the end of the street where the city was.

He was telling me to get help.

"I know. I...know." My mouth felt dry. I began to feel dizzy.

I took another step towards him. I stretched out my hand towards his. "Come...with me, I'll take you somewhere safer."

The man quickly withdrew his hand as if he were afraid I would touch it.

"I...you don't have to touch me...just...let me help you..." I had come this far to help this man already, making sure he was safe made sense to do.

The man waved his palm in a 'no' motion.

"Alright...but you should leave as well. You should get away from here."

The man shook his head slowly. His body was still cast in the darkness.

"Do you...Do you know this man?" I pointed at the unconscious Audran.

He shook his head no again.

"Go.... that's good," I spoke. "I—"

A rustling sound came from behind me. I turned around to see the Audran, with his Noxstone dagger, plunging for the back of my skull. The man in the shadows stepped forwards, gripping my left shoulder, and punched the Audran in the face, who fell to the ground instantly.

I tried to turn around, but the man from the shadows gripped my shoulder even harder, and I was growing weaker. I sank to the ground instead, on one knee. My grip on my spear was growing worse.

The man sank down in front of me, looking at the ground so that his face was still hidden. He reached for my leg, slowly.

"No...no, you should go, before he...before he awakens." I gently pushed his hand away.

He smacked my hand back. I looked at his figure. There was something familiar about it, but I couldn't think clearly, and my vision was starting to blur. I could only let him touch my shin.

I faintly saw him remove one of his gloves.

"What...what...are you...doing?"

I was growing sleepier, gradually slipping into unconsciousness.

He didn't answer. It struck me he may have been unable to speak at all.

The clothing on the lower half of my leg was already torn. The man placed his hand against my wound. I hissed. It stung.

He hesitated for a moment as he heard me wince in pain. But then continued, even more slowly.

It was only then I realised he had torn off some of his clothing and was bandaging my wound. His hands were cold. His fingers moved softly and carefully, as if he was trying not to exacerbate the pain.

"Have you...done this...before?"

The man nodded.

The bleeding slowed down considerably.

I looked down, blinking hard at my leg. "Thank...thank you." My breaths were becoming heavier each time I spoke.

The man made a 'no' gesture with his hands again, placed a palm against his chest and pointed at me.

*No, thank you.*

The man stood. He stared at me saying nothing. I knew if I looked up at this moment, from this angle, I would see his face, but I could barely find the energy. Slowly, I began to try.

But as I did, the man turned around, and slipped away into the darkness.

I hadn't meant to end up on this street. Roart street was fairly close by, but on my way back from there, to buy the dress Dyna had wanted, I had grown increasingly confused with Iloris' city scape. Unlike the time I had visited Gendall, I'd had no directions.

I hadn't even needed to buy the dress. I knew Dyna had only said she wanted it as a cover for my pride. But the gold that Audra's Prince had given us was plentiful, and ever since she had heard of the riots, she had been deeply upset. When we first arrived here, earlier in the month, Dyna and I had taken a walk around the city, along with some of Vasara's guards, who had volunteered to show us around. On Roart street, she had stared for a long while at a dark wine dress in a shop window. The one now packed and folded in a small pouch at my back.

I certainly hadn't anticipated bringing back a wound as well.

My strength, although compromised, was now slightly improved. I gripped the spear and stood. The man's body was still unconscious before me, and his Noxstone weapon lay next to him.

I didn't think too hard on my decision.

I bent down and lifted it up, carefully, by the handle. I was fortunate I had gripped the Prince's sword that day, so that I was used to the weight of these weapons somewhat. There was a sheath for it, attached to the man's torso. I gently pulled it from him. He remained unconscious.

Although stealing a weapon from this man was dangerous, there was no way I would make it in time to visit Audra's Prince now, and I preferred not to be beholden to him. Yes, I had already helped him move that escort's body, but who knew what else he may ask of me, if I was granted my wish.

I would in general, have preferred to avoid Audra's Prince as much as possible, and although tonight had gone remarkably awfully, it had not involved his presence, which was at least, something.

As I made my way back up, I stopped. Something reflecting the moonlight caught my vision, to the right, nearby the wall the individual had been standing at.

Ordinarily, I would have ignored it, but I could tell even from here what it was.

It was money. It was gold.

Identical to the coins I had in my pouch.

Identical.

Just one lunar.

One.

# CHAPTER 43- SHADAE

I placed Ava's body on the ground, as gently as possible. Those around me did the same. We had lost eight trackers in that fight. We had captured four sorcerers. I didn't know how many of them we had killed.

I opened my palm to look at the talisman. It was small, rectangular, attached to a rope Claus had been wearing around his neck. It was soaked in blood. The engravings in the wood were filled with crimson now.

I don't know why I had taken it. But leaving his body there, leaving all of their bodies there felt wrong. I had asked to bury them, when another tracker from Vasara, whose name I learnt was Vykros, had laughed in my face.

"*Do you think they'd bury us?*" he had said.

"*It's hardly as if they'd have the time,*" I'd replied.

"*Careful. We have our orders. Don't push it, cadet.*" Cheadd had overheard us.

So, I had taken it. As if it could absolve me of the guilt of leaving him to rot in the soil somehow. As if I had earned it. I could imagine him thrashing around in the afterlife, sick to think his killer was holding it.

But maybe, I thought, I had taken it because I hadn't felt guilty, not in the way I thought I would have. When Ava had choked on her own blood, I hadn't felt any remorse as I watched him do the same.

But still, he didn't deserve to die. Not for any reason I could think of. Nobody had.

"Bitch!" someone shouted at me from the left. It was one of the sorcerers, bound by an immortal coil, infused with the same Curse they used on Vessel's shackles. One of the three minor ones, the Curse of subjugation.

It was deliberate, it felt, that something as significant as the robbing of someone's freedom was branded as a 'minor' thing. As if the label might convince those it stole from they'd been deprived of something trivial.

And it was easier for them to do it now that generations were growing in chains.

*They can't miss something they've never tasted. You've never let them eat.*

*But I remember.*

*And I'll get it back. I'll get theirs back.*

I turned my head slowly to face them, my palm still open, the rope still woven between my fingers.

"That's not yours," the man said, nodding at the necklace.

"Riece, leave it, shut up," another man next to him said.

"You fucking killed him. You're nothing more than a dog!" he shouted.

I knew that my face remained impassive. I couldn't bring myself to feel anything. After the adrenaline and fear had coursed through my veins hours ago, now, I felt flat.

"Look at her, she doesn't even care!" Riece yelled.

The night was fading, and the early hours of the morning were beginning to make themselves apparent, a light layer of sun sifted amongst the clouds.

I walked towards the man.

"Look, you twat! Couldn't you have kept your mouth shut?" the man who had scolded Riece whispered.

"What's she going to do huh? Kill me. LIKE SHE KILLED HIM. COME ON, FUCKING KILL ME THEN!" Riece was screaming.

I stopped in front of him, looking down. "This isn't going to work," I said bluntly.

"What are you—"

"I know you want me to kill you, and I'm sorry, but I can't." My voice was tired, uncaring.

"Didn't seem to be an issue with him...did it?" Riece nodded at my fist, clenched around Claus' talisman.

*He would have killed me first*, was on the tip of my tongue but, what pathetic words they were to say, as if that would appease him, or make his death seem acceptable.

"No," I said, "Not really."

Riece shook his head in disbelief. "What are you doing with it anyway?"

"I'm..." I looked at it in my hand. "I'm not sure." I held it out towards him. "You...you should have it."

Riece huffed, his breath smacking against the cooler air of the morning. He looked at the man next to him. They both started laughing.

I withdrew my hand confused, looking at the ground.

"Nah...he was an arsehole," Riece mumbled his voice cracked slightly. "But still."

*But still.*

Cheadd approached me and the sorcerers. "What are you talking to them for?" he said through gritted teeth.

"He wanted me to kill him," I answered.

Cheadd looked at Riece. "Nice try. But no."

"Can you blame me?" Riece said, disdainfully.

"It's not about blame. Stop making noise. Your tongue isn't necessary for transport."

I was incapable of hiding the shocked side glance I gave to Cheadd.

I didn't know why I was surprised. It made sense. I didn't know, or understand the nature of Ava and Cheadd's relationship, but losing her had obviously affected him. If he had been aggressive before, he was even more so now.

"What are you looking at?" he said to me. "Watch them." He walked off.

I sat down on the grass, near the four of them.

"Oi, girl," Riece spoke again.

"Are you trying to have your tongue removed?" I asked.

Riece was quiet.

We sat in silence for a few minutes.

"He's right," I said, quietly, but loudly enough for Riece to hear. "Even if we wanted to kill you now, we couldn't anyway. You're asking us to kill you because you don't want to become a Vessel, but everyone you see here was a Vessel, and they were just as desperate as you to get out of those chains, enough to become a tracker. So, you ask if we can blame you for seeking death, can you blame us for doing this?"

"Yes. I'd rather die a Vessel, I don't know how you can live with yourself," Riece stated immediately.

I didn't know either. But somehow, I was doing it, and it didn't feel as painful as I thought it would have. What did that say about me?

"Maybe you're just a better man, a better person," I mumbled. "Or maybe, you have nothing to lose."

"Is there anything worse than losing your soul?" Riece scoffed.

"Yes." I thought of the faces of my brothers. "Yes, there is. So, we don't all get to keep our souls."

Later, as the morning fully bloomed, we made our way back to Vasara. At the gates, several guards arrived, to escort the sorcerers to the draining centres, to become Vessels. These sorcerers would probably never leave there. They would probably die there. I looked at each of their faces, their apprehension and rage were undisguised.

The guards approached us.

I quickly strode over to the captives.

"Cadet, what are you—" Cheadd called out after me.

But I reached them before he could stop me further.

"Don't talk back. Ever." I looked into the four sorcerer's eyes. "If it hurts, don't fight it, that makes it worse. If you can, lie down afterwards for at least thirty minutes. Don't eat or drink anything that Caden gives you. He drugs it. The bread is disgusting, it makes you sick, but the fruit is usually fine. Don't use the fourth shower room. Don't try to protect anyone. It's pointless."

I was speaking as quickly as possible, the words were rolling out of my mouth, running away with me, escaping in a way I could not. The four sorcerers watched me confused.

Some of them looked as if they had only started paying attention halfway through. Riece furrowed his brows concentrating.

"And if you have a chance to become a tracker, take it. You'll only get it once. If you can, try to volunteer in the kitchen, not the gardens. Avoid Parthias. If you're offered a choice, the shackle is best on your wrist. It's bearable on the ankle, but definitely do not get it on your neck, and—"

Cheadd grabbed me by the arm, pulling me away. "Get away from them. The guards are here."

The guards dragged the sorcerers off by their coils, which were dangling by their feet.

Riece turned around to look at me. "Looks like you've still got it. I hope you get to keep—"

A gag was shoved in his mouth.

*I hope you get to keep it.*

"*You too,*" I mouthed.

"What's he talking about?" Cheadd asked.

"I don't know," I lied.

*My soul.*

Cheadd sighed. He walked over to the guards. After a few moments of conversing with them, he rose his voice, and turned away. He came back over to the rest of us, agitated. He placed his hands on his hips.

"What happened?" one of them asked.

"They're saying...no," Cheadd replied.

"Again?"

"Are you really that surprised?"

"What are we going to do with them then?"

"They want to put them in with the Vessels," Cheadd said.

The mass graves. They were talking about the bodies.

"What?" Vykros said. He sounded crushed.

"It's like we never really got out," another woman added.

*Did you really think that you had? Take a look at your wrist.*

This was nothing more than a trade off from one prison to another.

As they were talking, I cast a glance towards the eight bodies. I could see them from here. I could see Ava's foot sticking out of one of the covers.

I marched towards the guards. This time, nobody called out after me.

"Sirs, can I ask you a question?"

They looked me up and down.

"What we going to get in return?" one of them said.

*Of course, even a question will cost me.*

I tried to think but couldn't come up with anything tempting.

"I'm afraid there's not much that I can...give you," I said.

"You get paid now, don't you?" the second guard stated.

"Well...actually I haven't been paid yet, I've only just started this position."

"Get lost then." One of them tried to push me away.

I stepped back before his hand could reach my shoulder. "Why are these bodies being taken to the draining centre? Where are they normally buried?" I took a chance, hoping that asking a question would naturally lead to an answer.

"Buried?" one of them asked.

"They don't get buried sorcerer, the trackers are incinerated," one of them said, laughing. He flicked all his fingers out of his palm at once in a 'poof' gesture.

"But...why?"

"The nobles are superstitious that's why," he continued. "Think the curses they've placed upon you lot are going to come back and haunt them."

"Load of bollocks," the other one said.

"The new King doesn't believe in any of that shit. Saves us the bother."

From what I knew, curses had no way of lingering after death, but then again, there had been all sorts of rumours about sorcery that had spun out of control for decades. In all likelihood, the other trackers and Cheadd, just used such superstitions as a way to lay trackers to rest in a better way. Incineration was better than a mass grave, I supposed.

*Look at me trying to decide which method of burial is preferable.*

Death had become so guaranteed, so assured, so unquestionable, that even I hadn't thought to hope for more.

"Now get lost. We've answered your questions and for *free*." Some other guards strolled past us, making their ways towards the bodies.

"Wait...How much do you want?" I asked the first one, who seemed more talkative.

"Huh...for what?"

"For...one of the bodies."

"Ha. We can't do that. No price is worth our heads."

I rubbed my forehead anxiously as I watched them approach the carts, and take them by the handles, to start leading them away.

"Isn't there anything, anything I could do to help... persuade you?"

The first one spoke up again. "Who do you take me for?"

*Someone who just a few minutes ago, offered information in exchange for money?*

But I said, "The King's not going to notice, is he? It's hardly as if he'll visit the mass graves to check."

The two men looked at each other.

"One hundred," the man said, "One hundred rays."

We only got one hundred and fifty rays each month as a tracker. I had inquired around and asked about it. Usually about eighty rays was enough to allow someone to scrape by each week. Even the humans with the least respected jobs got paid around two hundred and fifty rays a month.

"I..." I started. But they were dragging them away now. Within seconds they would pass through the gates.

"Yes...yes... one hundred rays. Once I'm paid."

"How can we tell if you're lying?" the second one said, raising one eyebrow.

I frantically searched for an answer. "I'll give you something of mine, something important to hold onto, and... I'll come back with the money."

The first guard grabbed the forearm of one of the others who was pulling the carts across. He beckoned me closer with his finger.

"Well, how are we supposed to know it's important to you?" the first man asked.

"Do you want one hundred rays or don't you?" I asked impatiently.

The man was teetering on the edge of reprimanding me for my tone, but time was running out, and the temptation was enough.

"Which one?"

"Her." I pointed to Ava.

"Alright, but we can't let you have her here. Meet us at the Northern gate in twenty minutes."

"Alright. Thank you."

*Thank you so much for letting me take the body of a dead girl, who died on your orders, so that I can bury her in a more dignified way, in exchange for the majority of my already completely insufficient wages. Thanks.*

The guards left. I stood by the gates, watching each of the tracker's bodies get pulled through, one by one. The archer's came last. He had saved my life. I hadn't even been able to ask for his body.

I bit my lip to try and distract myself from the sea of emotions flooding my chest, threatening to drown me.

Once I had slightly composed myself, I scratched my forehead and turned to see that the other trackers had dispersed. A few of them were walking in the same direction, towards the Iloris' centre, others towards the Palace. Cheadd was nowhere to be seen.

I walked up to one of them, who was just about to head into the Palace.

"Where's Ch...where's the Commander?"

"Don't know. He went somewhere east." He pointed in that direction.

*Very unhelpful*

"Thank you."

I waited twenty minutes and then walked inside to the Northern gate.

Standing there, with Ava's body, were the two guards.

"Told you she'd come," the first one said. "What's this special item you have then, sorcerer?"

I reached around my neck and pulled the talisman, Claus' necklace, over my head. I had cleaned it slightly while walking to the Northern gate, so that it was less clotted with dried blood.

I held my hand out. "Doesn't look like much," the guard said.

"It's important to me."

"Whatever you say." He grabbed it, then placed it in a pocket inside his pants.

"Take her. But you better come back with that money, else this piece of junk," he patted his hip, "Is going to disappear and then...so will you."

I couldn't help but look at him with disbelief. Even though I suspected he was telling the truth about his intentions, and that nobody would particularly care if a tracker died, something about the man struck me as unable to follow through on his threats.

"I'll find you, in a few days. I'm getting paid then," I told him, straightening up to my full height.

"See you then tracker." Both the guards walked past Ava's body and into the draining centres.

Just before they crossed the threshold of the gates, the first one turned around, looked at me, smiled, and spat on Ava's body.

The second one began laughing hysterically.

My lips parted and my brows dropped.

"Look at her. She looks so ferocious, like an angry little cat," the first one said.

"Better beware of her claws" the second one said, teasing the first.

"Oh, I'm terribly afraid. She'll raise a paw, and that mark will burn her."

They left, laughing to themselves. The first one waved goodbye.

I was unconsciously clutching at my wrist.

Once they were both a long distance off, I walked over to Ava's body and stood there. Her face was covered with an old, dark cloth, that lay over the rest of her as well.

I reached out. My hand was shaking as I drew the cloth back.

It had only been a few hours, but Ava's skin was already turning blue, her lips purple. The mottling of her face looked like thunder lacing through a cold sky. A few strands of her pale hair were stuck to the blood at the corner of her lips. She looked even younger in death somehow. And people lied. They lied when they said death made people look peaceful. It only made them look dead. Lifeless, and frozen, and no longer breathing.

How fleeting our existence. How ephemeral the light in our eyes. How easily we could forget that one day, they would no longer shine.

That one day they would close. They would dull. And our skin would colour like a bruise, battered by living.

I bit down hard on my bottom lip again, this time to the point of piercing pain, to stop the tears from flowing down my face. They simply hovered in the corners of my eyes, bubbling there.

I covered her face back up again, and bent forwards, with my hand on my knees. I took in a few deep breaths, but I was still trembling, from rage at those guards, from exhaustion, from despair. From it all.

I got up and reached for the handles.

"What are you doing here?" Someone's heavy footsteps were quickly approaching me. I couldn't decide what to do, or what was I going to say. I remained facing the body.

"Whose body is this?" The visitor stood beside me. I turned to the left slightly.

My throat closed over. I let out an inaudible gasp, gaping at the man without reserve.

He didn't notice, and only leant forwards, to remove the cover off Ava again.

"No! Don't…please, My Lord."

Lord Elias looked at me surprised. He examined my uniform up and down, which was stained with dirt and blood.

He sighed heavily and turned around to face me fully. "Why are you hovering here, tracker?"

I couldn't look at him directly. His eyebrows were furrowed, his bright red eyes regarding me with suspicion. I alternated between glancing at him furtively and at Ava's body. I didn't know which was worse. They were both torturous.

"She was…She saved my life. I'm…" Without knowing how else to explain, I stopped talking.

"That doesn't answer my question though, does it? Why are you here?"

"They were going to put her in the mass graves, with the others, but I managed to…get her body."

Elias squinted. "They don't put the trackers in mass graves."

"They do now, My Lord."

He waved his hands in the air. "Don't"

"Don't what, My—"

"Don't call me "My Lord," he said, sounding irritated.

*Huh?*

I didn't reply. I was stunned and confused. I was a tracker, a sorcerer. I had never once met a member of the human nobility that didn't demand we use proper titles in their presence, as if their very omission were some kind of sin.

"Since when?" he asked.

*Aren't you a Lord, despite not wanting to be addressed as such? You're related to the King, aren't you? How come you don't know?*

I looked at him bewildered. He and the King certainly shared similar features, only Elias was broader, stubbled, more unkempt. The King was almost his complete opposite in that regard.

"I don't know. I've only just started," I finally told him.

I didn't think it wise to tell him it seemed as if the King had ordered this himself, and that I currently knew more about his relative's decisions than he did.

Elias looked down, deep in thought to himself. "Mmmmm," he hummed.

*Should I go? No, but I need to take the body with me and… can I even leave without his permission now?*

"What happened? To your friend?" he said, breaking my trail of thought.

"We were…following a group of sorcerers who were near the borders between Vasara and Kalnasa, at Vaden. We found them, but…they were very powerful, and numerous, so…a few of us didn't survive."

Elias didn't say anything. He didn't offer his condolences, but he didn't taunt, spit at, or make jokes about Ava's death, which was more than I could say for the majority of human beings.

"Did you capture any?"

Capture. The word sounded so cruel and harsh.

"Yes. Four."

"How many were there? In the group?"

I thought about it, "Fifty or so."

"Do you think you could find this place again?" he asked me.

"I…yes, but they would have removed traces of their presence by now. They probably would have returned sometime after the fight to do so."

"If that's the case, then how did your unit find them in the first place?" He squinted at me.

"They hadn't hidden their tracks properly the first time, I don't…I hope you'll allow me the liberty of saying…" I tried to make my words sound as docile as possible. "That I don't think they would make the same mistake twice."

"The liberty of fucking saying," Elias repeated my words, with a slight amendment, chuckling. "You've learnt to speak well for a sorcerer."

*For a sorcerer.*

Although I supposed his sentence was founded. It wasn't as if any of us had a chance to increase our rank, or status, or education.

"Thank you?" I said questioningly.

"Who tracked them down, which of your unit?"

"I did."

"You?" he said, raising his eyebrows.

"Yes. I'm a Navigator." It was strange to defend myself in this way, as if I were trying to retain some credit for what I'd done. As if I was searching for some acknowledgement, some validation for it.

The realisation made me feel stifled. There was nothing good about what I'd done.

Nothing good, only necessary.

"What's your name?" he asked me.

*Don't call me 'My Lord,' what's your name? What is this?*

"Tracker? Tell me your name."

"Sorry it's just. We don't usually get asked that question," I admitted.

Elias sighed. "Will I ever learn it?"

"Shadae."

He nodded curtly. "I may need your assistance in the upcoming weeks to find any traces of these people. I'll send for you when it's time."

I nodded too. Agreeing verbally seemed pointless since I had no choice but to obey.

"Any Accipereans?" he said suddenly.

"I think…yes… there were a few, but it would be impossible to tell how many, or what their abilities were."

"You were there, weren't you? How could you have known there were Accipereans there if you didn't see them use their abilities?" He sounded sceptical.

"A few members of our unit reported seeing illusions during the fight, so—"

"Right." Elias looked at me, as if he were looking at something else, as if he were using my body as a focal point for his eyes while his mind wondered, like I wasn't even really there at all.

But then, his gaze found the scar around my neck, where my chain had been.

All sorcerers had the ability to heal faster than a human being, but the lower the class, the slower you were at healing, leaving you almost as prone to injury and scarring as a human.

He stared at it for a few moments, then looked up as he noticed me observing him.

"It's better when it's on the hands and feet, but…they know that so." I touched my scar fleetingly.

"Mmmmm," he hummed again.

*What does that even mean? Gosh this is uncomfortable.*

"How long were you a Vessel for?"

"Eighteen months."

"Did anyone die during that time?"

I twisted my face in confusion. Why was he asking me these questions? I couldn't help but think that this was some kind of trick.

"Some…yes. But it was difficult to be sure since we were rotated so often."

"How often?"

I looked straight at him.

*How come you know so little about this? Wouldn't you, as one of Vasara's leading nobles, know a lot about draining centres? Especially since Vasara's is the largest in Athlion? And what is this…a test? Are you trying to see how easily I would reveal information to someone?*

Sensing my anxiety, Elias said, "You're not being interrogated, and this isn't a trick. Just answer my questions." He sounded impatient and fatigued.

Seeing no other choice, I answered, "Every two weeks."

"How often were you drained?"

The memories of the drainings flooded my mind, I gulped.

"It varied and...I think it depended on the sorcerer as well, but roughly twice a day."

"How often do you get new Vessels?"

*We? We didn't 'get' them.*

It was an effort not to correct him. He noticed the slight look of irritation that waved across my face

"Something bothering you?"

I took a breath in. "No. I'm just..." I looked at Ava.

*I'm exhausted. I'm confused, I'm scared, and I don't understand what's going on. I'm tired of all of it. I want to rest. I want to go back home. I'm the reason Ava died. I'm the reason Claus died. I'm not sure what to make of you and these questions. I'm tired.*

I cleared my throat.

"You're what?"

"Nothing. To answer your question. New Vessels didn't arrive very often, but again, the rotation made it difficult for us to be sure of anything."

"How often were you fed?"

I hesitated, it almost sounded as if he was concerned about the Vessels, but that was very clearly not the motivation behind these questions. What the motivation actually was however...was beyond my speculation.

"Twice a day, sometimes it was once. If we were punished, we would be deprived of food for a while."

"For...how long?" He squinted as he asked.

"Two days, three."

"What were you given to eat?"

"Whatever you don't want." I raised my eyebrows, realising how bluntly my answer had come out, "That is...I mean—"

Elias raised his hand. "I understand." He didn't seem offended.

"Did anything strike you as unusual about the centre?" he asked.

*Apart from the fact that it was being used as a cover to torture people to death in the self-proclaimed service of humanity.*

I sighed as I thought that to myself.

"It's...what do you mean by unusual?" I looked at him cautiously.

"Did anything" — he looked up— "change while you were there? Did anything seem out of order to you."

*Order?*

"I was never...quite sure what that *order* was meant to look like."

Elias rubbed his eyebrows with his finger and his thumb. "Just think, and answer. Whatever comes to your mind."

"It would be like asking someone who had been to the Nevultus Pits what was so unusual about it," I said quietly.

The Nevultus Pits. It was said that was where those who had sinned so grievously and heinously were transported after they died. A domain of Noxos, pits of unrivalled despair, pain, and suffering.

I supposed there was a good chance I'd end up there now, if they existed.

Elias pulled his thumbs away from his brow and looked up at me quickly, clearly not expecting my answer.

"Well, what was?" he inquired.

I lowered my shoulders as I sighed. "All of it is strange."

"Can you elaborate?" Elias pressed.

*I don't like this. This feels...like a ruse. Yes, you said it wasn't, but I don't believe you.*

Elias insisted. "Can you hear me?"

*Unfortunately.*

I looked at my feet as I replied. "We had no idea what was going on the whole time. Everything was so highly regimented that it's as if we were completely isolated, even though we were around other people. Sometimes, someone would just disappear suddenly. Sometimes, someone would have new scars, and nobody knew where they had come from, or their wounds would stop healing altogether. I can't point out anything that was specifically strange, it was all strange."

I opened my eyes, having closed them towards the end as I spoke. Images flashed before me of the scenes my words were based on.

Elias walked past me and towards the gates. "You should get rid of the body quickly."

"Do...Do you know if there's somewhere where I can—"

"No, I don't," he said with his back to me.

*Polite.*

He vanished behind the gates.

I grabbed the handles of the cart and began dragging them out towards the south entrance of the Palace. I met a few confused glances as I made my way through the exterior paths, but nobody was bothered enough to inquire about my deeds.

Once outside, I dragged the body around Iloris, asking people if there was somewhere nearby one might be able to bury their dead. Some people ignored me, others spat at my feet, some told me to 'fuck off.'

Until one woman, with a small child said to me, "There's a field to the east."

I was in the West of the Iloris.

I hadn't slept throughout the night, which meant it had now been around thirty hours since I'd done so, and around the same time since I'd eaten.

But still, I continued the arduous journey with Ava's body across the city, trudging over cobblestoned streets. The decay of her corpse was likely getting worse in this heat.

She was only a child. She could have been either one of my brothers. She could have been alive if I had known how to protect her.

Eventually, after three hours, I found the field. I sank down into the grass, heaving, shaking from exhaustion. I sat for a few minutes to gain the smallest kernels of energy, before grabbing the side of the cart, and lifting Ava's body over my shoulder.

A shovel was sticking out from a heap in the soil. Someone else's body had recently been buried here. I placed Ava down on the ground, avoiding checking how far her body had begun to decompose now. I had dragged her for hours through the heat of the day, after all.

I placed the shovel in the soil next to her, pressed it into the ground, and dug.

But I was so weak, I could barely lift the shovel. I kept going, but after about five minutes, I had only dug a small and shallow hole, the length of Ava's body.

I leant forwards on the shovel. I didn't realise why my breath was shaking until the tears slid off my cheeks. I was too exhausted to even notice I had started crying.

I kept digging.

I would bury her. Even if I collapsed next to her immediately afterwards. I would survive. It hadn't been long enough to die of starvation yet, and I'd had some water on me which I had sparingly drank throughout the day. I would survive, because she had saved my life and as long as I was alive, it didn't matter how much I trembled from fatigue, or hunger, I would bury her.

My pathetic attempts at digging only seemed to get worse.

I screamed, my voice cracking, as if sharpened fingers were scratching at the inside of my throat. I yelled over and over again, and sank to my knees, pounding my fist into the dirt next to Ava's face. I looked at it now through my teary eyes. The sun had caught her blonde hair at the perfect angle. It shone so brightly against her ghostly appearance, as if it had come to illuminate her one last time.

I bent my head forwards into the soil and sobbed.

What was this world? Where a child, like Ava, would die, and have to be saved from being dumped into a mass grave, with children like her? What was this world, where people spat at my feet for asking to find a place for her to rest, because people I had never known, ancestors I had never met had killed their ancestors? What was this place, where the mark against my skin prickled more and more, the further away I got from the Palace? Where I could never be free except to kill, except to hunt others like myself, other people who shared the same dream of freedom, or peace? Where the only way I had found to survive was to deprive it of them. Where sorcerers killed sorcerers, and hated each other, as humans hated us. Where the actions of so few became branded as the future of so many. Where we had to work to prove our innocence to those who would never believe us, because once, long ago, we had given them reason to doubt. Where reason to doubt, no matter how far gone, no matter how long in the past, eliminated any reason to hope, or to strive for better. Where bloodshed felt comfortable for everyone. Where protecting those you cared about could only be done through that bloodshed.

Where Ava lay lifeless on the ground.

"How did you do it?"

I looked up through my tears. Cheadd was standing above me, looking at Ava's body. His face betrayed no emotion, but his fists were clenched at his sides.

I slowly looked at her, "I...I promised them money." My voice was strangled, from the screaming.

"You don't have any money," he said quietly. He had never spoken so quietly before.

"I know," I replied in a whisper.

Cheadd reached over and took the shovel from my hands, and began to dig where I had started.

There was nobody else around. It was only us, silent in the afternoon sun, only the sound of earth being torn from the ground to keep us company.

Once the hole was dug, Cheadd lifted Ava, and placed her inside, covering her body with the earth straight afterwards.

He took a step back.

"She was my daughter."

My heart fell into my stomach.

"She didn't know of course. Her mother was just...we made no promises to each other. But I'd gone back there once, years later as a tracker, back home, and found out they'd taken her, and that she'd had a child. I made enquiries, in the name of recruiting new trackers, and was told her mother was dead, but that she was still alive."

"I..." I choked.

At the sound of me struggling to speak, Cheadd continued, "She could have died any day. I knew that, and I still chose to recruit her. I could have tried to get her out, but I didn't want to take that risk, both for her, and for myself. I could have told her she was my daughter, but I didn't want anybody to find out, and use that information. You killed her killer, and then you got her body out of that mass grave. You did more for her than I ever did."

I stared up at him, bewildered by his sudden outpour, his confession.

"That's... not true," I managed to speak. "However, many years she did have, she had them because you got her out."

"She's probably better off dead anyway," he said sorrowfully.

My jaw opened and closed. Here he was, grieving, but grateful his daughter was no longer in this wretched place. The place I was trying so desperately to let my brothers have a chance to live in.

*Which of us is right?*

"Lord Elias wants me to help him," I spoke. I didn't know why I said it. Perhaps I just couldn't bear to speak about Ava anymore.

"That man hates sorcerers more than anyone else," Cheadd replied thoughtfully.

That hadn't been my impression, but it was clear he held no regard for us either.

"So, he'll get me to kill them?"

"No. He'd rather kill them himself. He'll only get you to find them for him."

I looked at my hands.

"Is he…he seemed…very—"

"He doesn't give a shit about anything, or at least, he gives a shit about very little. Killing sorcerers is probably one of the only things he has an interest in."

"If that's true, then why hasn't he been helping, or leading us?"

"Because he's…" Cheadd paused, clearly confounded. "I'm not sure. But he enjoys it one way or another." He looked up at me. "Be careful around that man. He's notoriously volatile."

*Is he? I supposed he seems slightly…impatient and…perhaps blunt, but volatile?*

"I'll try."

"Although…of all the people who look down on and hate us, he probably has the best cause to," Cheadd said dejectedly. "Sorcerers killed every person in his squad. He was one of only two survivors. The other died by suicide months later."

My eyes fell to the ground, I closed them, processing this revelation.

"Every person? How?"

"He won't talk, so nobody knows. But that level of devastation? It had to be Accipereans."

"Do you want to…say something?" I motioned to Ava's makeshift grave.

"No," he replied quickly.

I turned and looked at the grave. "Thank you for shielding me. Thank you for making me smile. I…" I swallowed back tears. "I won't let it go to waste."

Cheadd nodded at my words.

"Then you're going to have to do everything the Lord tells you for now." Then he added, "Can you?"

"You've already asked me something similar."

Cheadd grumbled. "I didn't believe you then."

"Do you believe me now?"

"No."

I couldn't help but smile a little. "Will you ever… believe me?"

"Probably not." He smiled slightly as well. "But I think you're most likely to change my mind."

The sun began to move, glinting against the soil that lay on Ava's body.

"Do you believe in the Divine Halls?" he asked, looking at me as he did.

The Divine Halls. The polar opposite of the Nevultus Pits. Where the souls of those who died by sacrificing their lives for others, or who had lived in the service of good, ascended. It was said they were able to rest in the Divine Halls of the Nine, and even acquire partial reverential status. Not all of them, but some.

"I'd like to."

"Then let's."

"Alright," I said, nodding.

I closed my eyes, and chose to believe, that Ava was watching us now, smiling, as vividly as she had done yesterday.

"They'd be fools not to take her. To choose her."

"That's good then," Cheadd said.

I looked at him questioningly.

"Because there's no doubt the Gods are fools."

I chuckled slightly. "They're meant to have created us after all."

"Terrible idea," Cheadd said regretfully, sorrowfully, despite the fact he was smiling.

I watched him smile. I watched him look at the ground with a mixture of tenderness and pain, of peace and regret.

*What a terrible idea. What a wonderfully, beautifully terrible idea.*

# CHAPTER 44- BAZ

Ullna, Yaseer, and Fasal were standing around a small table. In front of it, was a lacklustre and round object. They were staring at it with mute alertness, glaring at it as if they expected it to come to life and attack them.

Nyla, however, was sitting down, filing her nails with a small blade. She looked up at me as I entered.

"Nice," she gestured at my clothing.

I glanced down. I was wearing a shirt, rose coloured, and sheer, with embroidery throughout it. It was long and formed a jacket that matched pants of a similar material.

Ullna regarded me with a scowl.

"You're back," I smiled at Nyla, stating the obvious. "How was it?"

"Perfect." She grinned contentedly. "It all went according to plan."

"That's good. Better than here anyway." I immediately regretted my words. Ullna slid her gaze in my direction with a look that said, *No thanks to you.*

I cleared my throat. "What's that?" I pointed at the object and moved closer.

"This," Yaseer sighed, "Is what we wish to speak with you about."

I stood still, frowning, waiting for them to explain.

"This is an enolith," he stated.

I looked sideways at Nyla. I had no idea what that meant. They had stated it as if I did.

"You don't know what an enolith is?" Yaseer realised.

"No…"

"It's a communication stone. Only sorcerers can use it. One sorcerer can send messages to another from a long distance once they are trained in how to use one."

"So, you've received a message? Who from?" I asked.

"That's precisely the point," Ullna answered, "We haven't."

"The stone remains alight with a warm glow, as long as it is in the sorcerer's possession. But this…this stone has been dulled for days."

Yaseer looked at me with reproach, and… pity.

*No.*

"It's hers, isn't it?" My voice was thin with anxiety.

"Yes. It's Nemina's"

I let out a harsh laugh and stepped closer to the table. "I told you when we hadn't heard from her there was something wrong, but you assured me there wasn't!"

"It was not the lack of communication that concerned me," Yaseer was calm.

"It should have though...shouldn't it?" I outstretched my palms.

"How dare you—" Ullna started.

"You are new," Yaseer interrupted, sensing her anger. "A lack of communication is quite common when a sorcerer within our group leaves to undertake a task. That is why the stone's light is there to assure us of their safety."

I shook my head, frustrated. "In other circumstances, I'd understand why you would think that, but you sent her to *Vasara*. Her lack of communication should have been more...more...alarming!" I could feel myself getting flustered.

"Perhaps that is true." Yaseer let out a large breath. Fasal remained silent. He had been withdrawn since Riece had been taken. He couldn't meet my eyes. I assumed he blamed me for his capture.

"Let me—"

"We were about to ask you to go, to investigate," Yaseer cut me off.

I gathered myself. "Didn't you say it was too dangerous for me to go? Too dangerous to let two Accipereans walk away from here?"

"Yes, but you are the person most likely to find her. You are a Telepath."

I jerked my head back in confusion. "I'm not...I'm not anything yet."

"But you will be," Yaseer said, "I can tell."

"Sense transformation." Nyla pointed at Yaseer, answering my unspoken question. "It allows the user to enhance their own senses, and the senses of others, as well as take them away. They can sense the source of sorcery inside someone's core, and detect exactly what type, class, and ability a sorcerer has, or...will have, while other sorcerers can only guess."

Yaseer was a Sense Transformer.

I had been right, class two. He was powerful. Very powerful.

"But that man...he said we needed, *you* said we needed a Telepath." My thoughts were running away with me. I didn't say more. I didn't know if Nyla or Fasal had been informed about the suspicions of a traitor in our group.

"Do you want to leave or not?" Ullna crossed her arms.

"Yes. Of course, I do, but I don't understand."

"You are right, we do need a Telepath, for many reasons, but right now, finding Nemina is our priority," Yaseer told me.

A realisation dawned upon me.

"Does that mean...that you know what Nemina's ability is as well...what it will be?"

Yaseer and Ullna looked at each other. "I cannot tell," he said dejectedly.

"What? But you just said—"

"She is different." Yaseer raised his voice slightly.

I thought back to the way that he had reacted when he had approached Nemina, the first day we arrived, how quickly he had demanded Riece find Nyla.

He wanted her back.

He needed her back.

Why he did, I didn't feel particularly good about the possibilities. But either way, finding Nemina, and bringing her here, was surely safer than leaving her out there, alone.

"And you're taking Faina with you."

"Faina? But why?"

"She escaped from Vasara. She knows it better than anyone else here."

"Escaped? Nobody has ever escaped from a draining centre surely?" My voice flattened. Didn't this make Faina seem like the traitor?

"That's what we thought. But she wasn't in the draining centre. The King had taken her out, as well as two other Vessels. It seemed he intended to use them for his own plans, but in doing so, was careless. One of them managed to free the others and Faina escaped before they could catch up to her," Yaseer explained.

"How do you know? She could be lying."

"She isn't," Yaseer assured me. "The situation occurred during the King's Coronation, people have spoken of it since."

I raised my brows. During the Coronation? "And what happened to the others?"

"We don't know. We assume they were caught. Faina told us the Vessel who'd set her free refused to come with her. It seems his delay was a fatal error on his part."

"But don't you think…that she could…" I looked at Ullna and Yaseer meaningfully.

"It's unlikely," Yaseer smiled.

"It's possible, but I agree, otherwise why share that with us?" Ullna added.

I shook my head, unable to think of a logical reason.

"Alright…but why not leave now…Why tomorrow?" I pointed to the direction of Vasara, west of here.

"Because tonight…I'm going to help you access your powers," Nyla stood.

"In one night?" My voice lowered in scepticism.

"One night is a *very* long time…to do *a lot* of wonderful things." She winked.

I moved backwards. "I'm not…urrr… interested."

Nyla laughed lightly. "I know, I know, but watching you blush is so fun!"

"Isn't there anyone else who can train me?" I mumbled.

"Nyla is the best," Yaseer said softly. "Despite her…methods."

A few minutes later, after receiving further instructions and my own enolith, Nyla and I walked a fair distance from the camp, ready to train. This was a familiar routine by now. She had been helping both Nemina and I grow more in touch with the core and source of our sorcery since we had arrived.

She was playful and seemed as if she took nothing too seriously, that she worried about nothing. I knew it wasn't true but still, in ways, I envied her.

"What..." I began to ask then stopped myself. "No, you probably can't tell me." I looked to the side.

"What was my task?" Nyla said, raising her chin.

"I was only curious but—"

"I was in Kalnasa," Nyla answered to my surprise. "Which you already know. You also know that I was there a while ago, but what you *don't know*, is that I was there to deliver a message. I went back to see how things were progressing."

I waited for a few seconds before asking, "And?"

"And the recipient is no longer in Kalnasa."

I looked at her sharply. "I thought you said your task had gone well."

"That's precisely why it had," she wiggled her eyebrows.

"I heard...from the others there are riots there now."

"Yes." Nyla sounded mournful. She was from Kalnasa by birth after all. "It's...terrifying."

I could spend hours ruminating about the various things Nyla might have seen, or done, and probably still not come up with the full list of possibilities. If she said the situation was terrifying, then I could only imagine how brutal it was.

"I'm sorry."

"You're sorry?" She laughed. "Why?"

"It's your...well it was your home."

"It's no different to anywhere else. Conflict, fighting, that happens in every Kingdom."

"But we're trying to change that, right?"

"Yes. But what's happening there is beyond us."

"Is it? I mean if Nourishers were allowed to live in peace, they could grow the food."

Nyla furrowed her brows. "I had thought about that. Why haven't they used them?"

"Maybe...they already have," I said softly, trying to make the disgusting reality of the situation hit less harshly.

"You're right...of course you're right. That would have been the first thing that they did. The lives of sorcerers don't matter after all," she huffed.

"Who did you deliver the message to?"

"Mmmm. Not sure I can tell you *that*. But I knew him a long time ago. He always wanted to do the right thing. Seemed like a good choice."

"He sounds...urmmm...wonderful?" I said unsure.

She laughed again. "He was...is. That's why we chose him."

"What happened then? You said that you knew him."

"The war happened."

"So, you met him when you were a child?"

She nodded. "I met him when he was eight, and I was seven. The war started when I was nine. I managed to live in Kalnasa after that for a few years, right up until I was around sixteen, but then—"

"Your abilities emerged," I finished her sentence.

"Yes, quite late, wasn't it? But after that, I left. I didn't even get a chance to say goodbye to him properly."

She sat down on the grass, motioning for me to do the same.

"How can you be so sure he's as wonderful as he was back then?" I put to her.

"I hear things. I see things."

I raised my eyebrows quickly as if to verbalise, "*If you say so.*"

"He hates sorcerers though."

I frowned. "Well now I'm confused with your decision."

"They killed his family."

"That... isn't helping," I said carefully.

"Most people hate sorcerers, what's the difference?" She shrugged.

"You just said they killed his family. It sounds different enough to me."

Nyla looked me in the eyes suddenly. She didn't say anything, but for some reason her abrupt eye contact made me change my tone.

"Do you think he'll change his mind?"

"I think... that if he finds out what we want him to... then he won't be able to ignore it. He'll be forced to confront it, and he won't shy away from doing so. That's just who he was. Who he is."

"You sound like you're in love with him," I joked, raising an eyebrow.

She smiled sadly. "I confess, as a child, I thought he and I would get married. But...I was a child."

"That doesn't mean you can't love him now."

"How can you love someone you don't even know?"

I shrugged. "People hate others they don't even know. Emotions don't really make any sense."

Nyla tilted her head in thought. "I suppose. But... I don't love him." She looked up at the dark sky. "I care for him. He will always be a part of my past and my life. But he is not a part of my future."

"He might be...you don't know that."

"He might be a part of all of our future's, but not mine alone. Besides" — she chuckled — "you wouldn't believe the number of girls who threw themselves at him and he never even batted an eye. He didn't seem to care about anything like that at all."

I couldn't help but think of an obvious reason for that.

I decided to keep it to myself.

"What's his name?" I asked.

Nyla raised her eyebrows.

"Is that something I'm allowed to know?"

She let out a short chuckle. That was a no.

"So, this... man, you've gambled the uncovering of this information on his good will?" I looked at her tentatively.

She nodded slowly. "It sounds absurd, I know."

"No." I shook my head. "It's nice to believe that someone out there might have enough of a good will to take such a large risk on," I glanced at the ground, fiddling with the dry grass.

"What about you?" Nyla called out to me. "You and Nemina you're...aren't you?"

Ahhh, yes. The act that Nemina and I had agreed upon when we had arrived here, to be hopelessly in love, to be each other's partner. Although Nemina's self-isolation had certainly made that a difficult task, it was still one we had succeeded in overall, surprisingly. My concern for her was probably helping.

I tried to sound confident. "Yes, we're...together."

"Sure." She winked, making it clear she didn't believe me.

"Why ask if you know the answer?" I sighed.

"It's fun to watch you blush is why."

"I thought we were supposed to be training."

"We will, but who said that we can't talk too, about love, life, and everything else."

"We don't have much time."

"Oh, come on. It took minutes and look at what we've discovered. You and Nemina are destined to be together until the end of time, while I'm destined to die alone, obsessed with stalking a man who will never love me!" She pressed her palm to her chest in a mocking sob.

I couldn't help but laugh a little.

"You know they're only destroying the very world they live in," she stated suddenly. Coldly.

I paused for a moment before replying, startled by the abrupt shift in her tone.

"They think they're saving it," I whispered. It wasn't an attempt to defend them only... explain it to her. Not that she needed, or wanted me to try.

She scoffed, and began playing with blades of grass between her fingers. "The world is like a large basin of water. When a Darean uses sorcery, it fills up. When an Accipwerean uses it, it empties a little. They're both meant to exist. *We're* both meant to exist. But they think they can craft our lives carefully, control them, and the flow of sorcery. But what they're doing with the drainings, the way they're extracting it from us, and releasing it into the world unnaturally, it will never be the same. And without Accipereans living long enough to draw breath and bear children, this world won't last. But...it's...it's as if they don't care. Because they can't see the devastation it will cause after they're gone, only the problems they face now. Ones they helped create."

Everything she was saying rang true, but still, it settled in my chest uncomfortably like a blade between my lungs, or down my throat. A sharp reality to swallow.

"Do you think we can change that?" I whispered, my gaze drifting to the side.

Nyla's fingers stilled. "I don't know. But we have to try...right?" She glanced up at me, excepting a reply.

I nodded. "Right. If everyone gave up at the despair of the world, and never tried to change anything, even if they knew they wouldn't live to see that change become reality... we'd all have died... long ago," I said.

It seemed like she needed to hear those words. Or I did. Another reality to swallow. Not a harsh one however, but one full of agonising hope.

She smiled slowly, gently. Then she stood.

She lifted a dagger and aimed it at me.

I got up quickly. "What are you doing?!" I raised my hands, and the pitch of my voice increased.

"In a moment, I'm going to close my eyes and start throwing daggers at you. I've got a whole bag, see?" She pointed to the bag she had brought with her. I hadn't even thought to ask what the contents were.

Because I hadn't supposed it would be an endless supply of knives.

"Why?!" I said exasperated.

"I can't tell if one of them is going to hit you, can I? So...make me stop."

"You're...this...this is why that poor man didn't want you!"

She laughed and closed her eyes. "You and I both know that the best way for someone's abilities to emerge is under stress and pressure."

"This isn't stressful, it's life threatening!" I shouted.

"Keep your voice *downnnnnn*." She sounded perfectly calm, as if we were still discussing our falsified love affairs.

"I'm sorry but it's hard to remain calm when—"

I was interrupted by a knife flying in my direction. I ducked.

"Nyla, let's do this another—"

Another one. She had stated that she 'wasn't sure' if they would hit me, but even with her eyes closed, she could tell that I had ducked, and aimed the knife lower.

"Right...I don't even know how to do this—"

She threw another one. "Just reach inside yourself, tap into the source, and use that energy to bend your will into shape. Use it to bend mine, use it to reach into my mind. You can do it. Just get on with it!"

She kept throwing and throwing and throwing.

I dodged one blow after another. This continued for several minutes.

"How am I supposed to reach inside and tap into my source if I can barely catch my breath?"

"You're right, I'm sure the people in Vasara will let you take a rest, and give you plenty of time to reach inside your source to kill them."

I scowled. I began to try, but it was like stopping and starting a fire. Each time I was attacked, the flame died a little, and maintaining it was almost impossible.

The next dagger cut across my cheek.

"Tsssk."

"Ooooh did I hit your pretty face? I'm sure Nemina will still love you all the—"

Nyla froze, her arm mid-air.

She laughed.

"Now look at that. You might just be able to save your beauty after all."

## CHAPTER 45- ELIAS

"You're in my seat." I looked down at Audra's Prince, who was sprawled across a chair in my chambers. His legs hung over the handles on the left and his back leant against the handles on the right.

"You're back. Finally!" He turned slightly but made no movement that suggested he was going to stand.

"I didn't know you were waiting," I grumbled.

The Prince opened his mouth "I—"

"If I had, I would have made sure to prolong my stay out."

He scoffed then raised an eyebrow. "So?"

"So?" I repeated.

"Do I need to remind you? Would you like a reminder of the events that led me here?" He narrowed his eyes.

"It's been less than a week," I reminded him.

"That's plenty of time, after all, aren't you idle most hours of the day?"

I walked over to the chair, and reached out behind the Prince, making sure to keep my distance. I pulled the jacket he was sitting on out from behind his back.

"Not anymore."

"Really?" He leant back more insistently into the chair. "Why the sudden change?"

The man was like a scab that seemed to form over every wound in existence, yet refused to let it fully heal. His incessant questions were profoundly irritating.

"We're not discussing that," I insisted.

"How defensive you are," he mumbled.

"Are you capable of having a serious conversation?" I bit.

"Of course, aren't you capable of having a non-serious one?"

"Of course." I smiled falsely. "Just not with people like you?"

"People like me?" His voice protested innocence.

I didn't feel a need to reply and state the obvious.

"I've always felt that you and I are quite alike," the Prince said quietly, looking up at the ceiling of my chambers.

"Ha." I could only laugh at that ridiculous comparison.

"You don't think so?" He lowered his head again.

"I think you enjoy all of this. So... no."

He laughed softly. "You're in charge of their military now, aren't you?"

I rolled my eyes. As I suspected, the Prince was simply playing a game.

"You already knew."

"No!" Nathon's eyes lit up. He clicked his fingers. "But I guessed, and you've just confirmed it for me...so I'm much obliged to you."

I let out a large sigh. "Can you just get to the fucking point?"

"I was waiting for you to do that."

I crossed my arms. "I didn't find anything particularly useful. I even questioned a tracker about it, and still, nothing."

"That was a good idea." The Prince looked thoughtful, and for once, sounded sincere. "She didn't tell you anything remarkable?"

I thought back to the tracker's words, the way she had regarded me with fear and suspicion when answering my questions.

The scar on her neck.

"Nothing I wouldn't have already suspected. Only that some of the Vessels seemed unable to heal their wounds."

The Prince glanced out the window, a quizzical expression on his face.

"Is that...unusual?" Nathon said.

I see. He didn't know much, or perhaps anything about sorcery. I was surprised he had openly admitted it. But then again, he probably felt no need to hide it, since such a high level of knowledge on the topic was not expected of anyone. In fact, it was seen as highly strange and perverse.

"I don't know," I said truthfully. "Eliel—"

I stopped when I realised my mistake.

"What about the King?" The Prince tilted his head.

*"Eliel would know,"* I had been about to say. Eliel didn't care about how frowned upon a topic was, he would learn everything and anything he could about it. In fact, he was more likely to delve into its intricacies, and seek out information on it, when it was regarded with disdain. Knowledge attracted him the way sex, alcohol, love, food, and power attracted others. And the rarer its existence, the more Eliel craved it.

"Eliel's father would have known more about it," I said instead.

But by the look in the Prince's eyes, the slight smile on his face, I knew I hadn't rescued myself, not truly.

"All I know, is that Vessels heal their own wounds fairly well, and that even those with the least power can do so, usually. But still, the point is, they don't bleed, or bruise like us."

"Only some of them do...now," the Prince concluded.

Asking Audra's Prince a question related to his motives was by any standards, an awful fucking idea. But his inquiries directly involved Vasara, and so, they directly involved Eliel.

"What do you want to know? About this centre? Why are you investigating it?" I crossed my arms.

The Prince looked undisturbed. "If you're worried about your cousin's safety, I can assure you it has nothing to do with that at all. My interests in the centre are purely personal."

"Do you really expect me to believe that? What do you take me for, Prince?" I said, moving closer to him again.

When I had moved within an arm's, length I spoke again. "Why risk exposing yourself to me? You could have asked any favour, anything, but you asked me to do this. It's true that only members of the Council have access to the centres but still, I don't doubt you could have tried to investigate it yourself, that's if you haven't done so already. In fact..." I stopped myself and laughed.

"I'd be willing to bet that's exactly what you've done, only to realise that getting inside was almost impossible, and too dangerous for you. You. Even you. Fuck. Everyone speaks about you as if you're the most dangerous, venomous, calculating man in the world, but in asking me to do this, you've exposed yourself. I can't understand how you think that would benefit you, and why you're so willing to trust I'll keep my mouth shut about it. When it comes to choosing between the safety of the King or my reputation, I *will* choose the safety of the King." I lowered my voice, emphasising my intentions behind the last sentence.

The Prince finally stood. "Let's imagine for a moment you tell the King I've asked you to do this. What do you think will happen? Do you think he'll be particularly pleased you've fulfilled my request?"

"I could explain—"

"Ahhh, yes you could explain. 'Oh cousin, I apologise. I was responsible for the murder of an escort during this Season and allowed myself to be blackmailed by the Prince from Audra'," the Prince mocked.

"It's not—"

But he spoke over me, "The King I suspect, already distrusts you somewhat, and if you reveal this to him...I can't imagine his trust in you will ever be reborn. So, you will likely be banned from partaking in any political activities, and I will be locked up and interrogated. Unfortunately for you, I don't tend to succumb to interrogation." He picked up a grape from a bowl on the table next to him.

"I've had plen-y of pra-tice," he said with a mouthful.

He grinned. He was enjoying this.

"Now," He pointed a finger into the air. "You might say the King will lock up my sister and do the same to her, but she doesn't know anything. There's also Vasara's relationship with Audra to consider. If they hear that Vasara has locked up their two heirs over an accusation *Lord Elias* made…"

He emphasised my name. He and I both knew my reputation for being a drunken reprobate was firmly cemented into the hearts and minds of the majority of people.

"I think you'll find that public opinion works against you. So, let's conclude." He picked up another grape and threw it into his mouth. "You tell the King. He no longer trusts you. He confines Loria and I to absolutely no avail, placing a great strain on his relationship with Audra, and the public, and calling into question his aptitude for Kingship. This process will not uncover my motives, and will do more harm than good to His Majesty. Don't you think?"

I tutted. "You've thought through everything, haven't you?" I did not disguise the patronisation to my tone. It was true the Prince had planned and foreseen several possible outcomes. But not all.

Not that I was about to tell him.

"You should try that…thinking. It's quite helpful." The Prince tapped the side of his temple.

"I *think*…that I'll soon find out just exactly what your motivations are." I wasn't even sure that was true, but it currently felt as if I was being pushed into a deep well, and was desperately clutching at the stones, to avoid falling further.

"So, you're still not thinking then," he said. "You and I both know one thing, one indisputable fact. That if you want to protect the King, you need to be by his side, and to be by his side, you'll need to stay silent about this matter."

A wild frustration imploded within my mind. This man had manipulated me so easily. This man four years my junior.

"Do we understand each other?" he asked.

"Would I be telling the truth if I said that I truly understood you?"

"You're right…but we agree on this at least?"

"Agree? Fucking agree?" I laughed bitterly. "*We* aren't doing anything. *You* are playing a game and moving everyone across your board like little wooden figurines." I wiggled my fingers. "And you're right, I can't see your end goal, and I can't do anything about it for now. But I can see the set-up, and I can see the players. Don't make the mistake of thinking that won't be enough."

"I never underestimate anyone." The Prince's voice had deepened.

"Brilliant. I'm overjoyed. Now get the fuck out."

He motioned to my chair. "But I was only just beginning to get comfortable."

"What a shame. Leave."

The Prince shrugged. "I look forward to seeing your next move."

He walked backwards out of the door, closing it behind him while maintaining eye contact.

"Egotistical prick," I muttered to myself.

I poured myself a drink.

I looked into the glass, dark red, the aroma of the beverage wafted around me, drowning out everything else.

I shook my head and swallowed it whole, reflecting on the past few days.

Eliel wouldn't admit it, but he was still weak from his injury, and he'd probably not been too glad about his attempted assassination either. I knew that he was keeping these things to himself.

I set the drink down and made for the door. I was off to attend this morning's Council meeting, the first one that I had attended in years.

Too early. Too fucking early.

Not that it mattered. I hadn't been able to sleep the night before, and had wandered around the Palace grounds for a while.

Which is when I had returned to find the Prince entirely comfortable in my room.

I needed to start remembering to lock my door. I supposed beforehand, I hadn't really cared if someone had walked in and skewered me in my sleep. Maybe I'd even welcomed it.

But now, things were different.

As I walked into the Council room, Eliel was informed I'd been appointed to my new post. Fargreaves looked as if he'd been force fed horse shit when Trenton uttered those words aloud.

Since the trackers had returned empty handed, I had waited until the others had left, and the rest of the meeting had been concluded before I said to Eliel, "I'd like to look for them myself."

Eliel leant forwards, resting his chin on one hand. He looked so still, so calm.

But I knew that underneath that veneer, delicate, and made of glass, was a fire that could shatter everything around it, whenever it chose to do so.

"Are you sure?" he asked after a few moments of contemplation.

"I'm sure," I confirmed. "I've found the tracker who picked up their trail. I'll take her with me."

"Just one?" Eliel said. He sounded neither surprised, confused, or doubtful. He spoke like that often, with no emotion, no sign of judgement, or opinion.

"I don't need the others, and it will be easier to travel in smaller numbers."

The true reasons for my decision were first, that a class four Darean was the only kind of sorcerer I would ever accompany, for theirs was the only kind of sorcery that couldn't forcibly be used on, or against an individual. And second, that I preferred to travel with, and be in the presence of, as few sorcerers as possible. If the task truly warranted more assistance, then I would have accepted that, but taking more sorcerers on this journey wouldn't help me fulfil my task any faster, and would only make me feel uneasy.

"Very well. It is your decision how you conduct yourself in your new role." Eliel closed his eyes over, a slight dusting of purple circled them underneath.

"It's supposed to be your decision, isn't it, *Your Majesty*?"

"I'd not be foolish enough to think you were entirely within my control, Elias." His eyes were still closed.

I thought about the words that Audra's Prince had uttered.

"You don't trust me, do you?"

Eliel's eyelids slowly lifted. He looked at me for a long time. I was beginning to regret asking. What good could come of an answer, no matter what it was?

"I trust your intentions," he said softly.

"Just not my means of acquiring them. If that's true, then why are you giving me such free reign? Why let someone you cannot control, and do not fully trust, help you?"

Eliel frowned. "Are you upset?"

"Yes... But not with you," I replied, looking down at the table.

Eliel sighed. "I do not expect you to be anything other than you are. Nor do I wish it. You are reckless, and you can be unfocused, but you are loyal, and when the situation demands it, you are bold. You may not be able to plan and plant seeds with words and schemes, but that matters little to me. I have plenty of people who can fulfil such tasks, and none I trust with my life as much as you." He smiled at me slightly but genuinely, with meaning.

I nodded. "Then that is enough for me. That you trust me with your life."

"I do."

"Do you...trust anyone else with it?"

I didn't ask because I wanted him to say yes, but because I was afraid there was nobody else he felt assured would protect him. I was afraid the answer was no.

"What do you think?" He leant further into his hand.

"I think it's a shame that we do not have more allies," I groaned.

"It is the nature of things."

I thought for a moment. That didn't strike me as true. Yes, holding power naturally meant you would have enemies, that you would have no shortage of people who wished for your downfall, who tried to plot against you.

But why should that mean you had nobody who was loyal to you, who was willing to, and proud to work for you? Why should that mean you be deprived of those who would be glad to stand beside you, to help you rule, and achieve your goals, to advise you, to care for you?

"You're quiet. That's unusual."

I decided to keep my thoughts to myself.

"You will not marry the child, or Jurasa's heir," I stated instead.

Eliel blinked hard once to indicate, "I will not."

"So, which of the others are you considering?"

"I am considering them all."

"But you like Audra's Princess, don't you?"

"Do I?"

"You bet on her, didn't you?"

"That's because she was about to win."

"There's no fucking way you could be sure of that, and you don't even need the money."

"No. But I do need the Court to be talking, spending their time ruminating, and prattling on about the Courting Season, and who I am taking a favour to. The more I give them to speculate over, the less time they will have to speculate about other affairs."

I laughed. "There's nobody else here, cousin. You can just tell me if you'd like her to be your wife. Come on, tell me the real reason."

"Do you…" He paused. "Tell me the real reason for everything you do?" He looked down at my palm. "What happened to your hand?"

I thought about Audra's Prince, the dead escort, the choice to have only one tracker assist me.

"Fair enough," I gave up, deflecting his question. "I'll set out tonight."

Eliel's eyes lingered on my bandaged palm for a few more seconds.

"It was glass," I stated. "I was…not…fully alert," I fibbed. An easy enough lie to believe.

Eliel's focus travelled from my hand to my face.

"Report to me, when you return," he said.

"I will." I hesitated before leaving. "The other thing, which…" I coughed awkwardly.

"My sacrifice? Yes, I was wondering if anyone would mention it."

"Wh…" I sighed. "You know what I want to know."

"I have my reasons," was all he said.

"You're ending our bloodline. How does any reason make sense Eliel?"

Eliel looked slightly irritated. "You had no intention of prolonging it yourself. Why is it suddenly so concerning to you?"

I internally groaned. My reputation, my desire to take a step back from responsibilities, my enjoyment of…well, my reliance on alcohol, and revelry. It seemed it would constantly be brought up by everyone, very frequently, until the end of time, until my body lay cold in the ground. Fucking brilliant.

What a wonderful way for people to instantly discredit my words. The worst thing about it, was such a method had been provided to them by my own machinations, in part.

It was a foolish reason to discredit me, but most people here only needed foolish reasons, they didn't think, or look hard enough for valid ones.

Swallowing back my frustration I spoke, "It concerns your safety. Don't pretend you don't know what I refer to."

"I have my reasons," Eliel repeated.

Which, we just established, he would not be sharing.

Yes, he trusted me with his life, but not with information. What a strange sort of trust that was. How did that make me any better than the guards standing at his back?

"I'm worried about you," I admitted. "You know that."

Eliel smiled. "Yes, I know your questions come from a place of genuine concern. It is more than I can say for the others. It means…a great deal."

"What fucking good is that if you're out there putting your life in danger? I don't want it to mean a great deal. I want you to think about it and be careful. Far more careful."

Eliel rubbed his face. These gestures were things he did not permit himself in front of others, I had noticed. I had only ever seen him do this as a child, when we were alone, or when he had been in the company of his parents.

"It is your prerogative how you conduct yourself in your role and it is mine for my own," Eliel stated coolly.

"Why is everything so binary with you? So light and dark? So left and right? Why don't you let others help you?"

"Elias," he said abruptly. "I appreciate your concern, but I must ask you to let me carry out my plans. You will soon see their purpose."

I breathed out and stood. "That's what I'm concerned about. Your purpose."

Eliel clasped his hands together. "I have dreamt of it."

His voice was listless. I narrowed my eyes at him. Thoughts of my own dreams swarmed through my head. 'Dreams' was a generous description. Night terrors in fact.

"The sorcerers come to end us. We are powerless to stop it," he explained.

I took a slow breath in. I couldn't tell him they were just dreams. I knew better than anyone what power the tapestries of sleep held.

Though mine were memories, and Eliel's…

"You are working too hard," I replied. "Besides" —I scoffed —"there's not a person in Athlion who hasn't had such a dream."

Eliel's eyes flicked up. His gaze had always been probing, but now it was even worse, like he was searching for my own dreams, buried in my brain.

"What?" I asked, in an effort to end the analysis swirling in his eyes. "You know I'm not lying."

His gaze dropped, yet still he glanced at the table thoughtfully. Still he calculated and drew conclusions from thin air. How exhausting it must have been, for him to be constantly supposing something. I wouldn't wish to look at my own thoughts for long. They were hideous, fragmented, fucking chaos.

"In a few days," Eliel said quietly, "Come and inform me of your findings."

I pushed my chair back. "Get some rest, you look pale."

He nodded. I knew that nod meant nothing. He'd likely ignore my advice.

On my way back to my chambers, I found a servant, and instructed them to send word to the tracker that she was to meet me outside the Palace's Southern Gates tonight, at sundown.

Less than an hour later, that same servant returned to my room.

"My Lord, Shadae is currently not in the Palace. I was informed she is conducting a task with the Commander and some others at present."

"When will they return?" I asked, not looking up from the book I was reading. I was refamiliarizing myself with some military texts and records.

"It is not certain. The duration of their missions varies greatly. It could be hours or days."

I turned around "Where did you say they were?"

# CHAPTER 46- SHADAE

"Here you are," the waiter came over to us and placed four mugs of what looked like ale on our table. The Commander, Vykros, myself, and another tracker named Lideus were sitting around it, cramped into a corner of a small establishment, in the centre of Iloris.

I looked down. There were several strands of hair floating at the surface of the beverage. I grimaced.

"Uch-um, excuse me there's..." I pointed at the drink, trying to get the waiter's attention.

Vykros sighed as I opened my mouth.

"Yes?" the waiter said. His tanned skin cracked with lines as he narrowed his eyes.

The Commander looked at me and shook his head. *"No."*

My mouth remained wide open. I was confused.

"Is there something wrong with your drink, darling?" the waiter asked

I jumped as he slammed both his fists against the table and the cutlery on it rattled. I leant backwards. He moved closer to me.

"I...no, no." I raised my hands and waved them from side to side. "I wasn't—"

"Why don't you let me fix it for you?"

"I—"

I tried to protest, but ended up watching as the waiter picked up my drink, held it to his face, and spat in it, hacking up as much saliva as he could before-hand.

He slammed it down on the table, so hard, that part of the liquid spilt over the mug, and landed onto my hand.

I looked down at the drink in shock.

"Enjoy, little miss." He laughed to himself as he walked away, striding with thumping footsteps around the corner.

I turned to the others in disbelief. Vykros was shaking his head. Lideus was bowing his. He was quiet, and barely spoke in general. The Commander brought his own mug to his face.

"Couldn't you have warned me?" I said to them all.

"Warned you what? That they hate us and are just waiting for any excuse to do something? Are you completely dense?" Vykros said, looking at me disdainfully.

"I was thirsty," I complained.

Someone shoved their mug to me. It was Lideus from my right. He was still looking down.

"No, no, it's fine you're thirsty too, and it's not your fault," I told him, regretfully.

He didn't say anything, and just pulled back his drink immediately.

*What? No "I insist!" or "You should take it" or "Let's half it."*

*Well, I suppose that's my own fault too.*

"So today was useless," Vykros said.

We'd received a report about a suspected sorcerer duo in the far east of Vasara outside of the capital, in a town called Avaire. It turned out to be nothing more than someone's idea of petty revenge.

How much would you have to hate someone? To accuse them of being the very thing that was despised more than anything in this world. A sorcerer.

*What can I say? I would have been the one placing coils around their chest. How am I any better?*

*I have a reason? Is that it? Is that enough?*

"It happens a lot. You should know that by now," the Commander said wearily. "False reports are far more common than verified ones."

"I guess that's a good thing," I said quietly.

Vykros looked at me suspiciously, then nudged the Commander. "Did you recruit her or what? We must be getting desperate."

"I'm sorry, you're right. I'm oh so despaired we couldn't catch some sorcerers today. Happy?" I asked Vykros.

"Oh, fuck off," he said.

I couldn't help but think, that of all the trackers who had perished, why did it have to be Vykros who was spared?

I sighed. I didn't truthfully wish him ill, but still, he was like a thorn without any flower attached to his stem, all bite, no...emotion.

But maybe that made sense, that to survive this, to survive this job, you would have to rip your own petals off, tear the soft and gentle parts of yourself out.

The evening was approaching, and the dark orange glow of the sun setting cast circles of light on the wooden table.

It also made the thick transparent layer of saliva appear even clearer on the surface of my drink.

A few minutes passed, Vykros and Cheadd made some light conversation.

I was about to take off my jacket when a commotion was heard outside.

"...Sure...want...round....my..." someone said. That waiter. His footsteps were fast approaching around the corner.

"...Already...no...where..." another man's voice answered him.

The two of them appeared. The second man strode towards us briskly, stopping at the edge of the table.

Lord Elias. The second man was Lord Elias.

"You, come with me." He approached the table, looking in my direction.

I still had my jacket half off, having frozen when voices reached my ears. I looked up at him. From this angle he completely blocked out the sun with his broad frame. He glanced at my hands, clutched around the shoulders of my jacket.

"Put that on, we're leaving."

"My Lord," Cheadd addressed him.

"Who are you?" Lord Elias asked.

"The Commander... My Lord."

"Ah, yes, they said you were here as well." He scratched his brows quickly then looked around. His eyes scuttling about as if he were...nervous?

Why would the Lord be nervous around us? Here?

"My Lord," Cheadd said again. "We've been working all day, and Shadae has yet to fully recover from recent events and wounds. I'm not sure she would be of much help to you this evening."

Lord Elias narrowed his eyes at me. "She looks fine."

*What are you doing, Commander? Weren't you the one who said I should do as Lord Elias asks, without question, or hesitation?*

I stared at the Commander, as I slid my jacket back on.

Vkyros chimed in, "My Lord, if it is assistance you require, then I can—"

"Was it you who tracked down the group of sorcerers the other night?"

"Well, no, but I—"

"What is your ability?" Elias asked him.

"A Teleporter and a Navigator but—"

"I read the report," Elias said, "You were one of the Navigators who failed to pick up the traces she did." He pointed at me without looking in my direction. "Weren't you?"

"It was—"

"A what? It was your job, and you failed. So no, I don't wish for your assistance."

He turned back around to me, then glanced at the full mug on the table. "If you want that, drink it now, we're going."

I lowered my head to peer into the saliva and hair infested drink.

"Ummm, I...It's..." I was desperately trying to find an excuse to leave it here.

*Will it bother him? Will he think I'm wasting Vasara's resources? Will it offend him if I don't? Why is everything so complicated? Why do I have to think through every action and sentence I speak aloud around twenty times over before I decide upon it?*

As I was pondering this, a voice from my right spoke.

"They spat in it," Lideus said unfeelingly, speaking for the first time all day, still looking down.

Elias glanced at Lideus, then me. He stared at me for a few seconds. My mouth continued to open and close like a sea creature drowning for air on the shore.

Unexpectedly, he leant forwards, and picked up my drink, looking at it intently.

The waiter, who had begun slowly backing away as soon as Lideus had spoken, was stopped in his tracks when Elias, without turning around, reached behind him, and grabbed his wrist. He yanked him forwards with ease.

"Is this your doing?" he asked the man.

The man grimaced and had already begun to sweat.

"It's nothing." I stood, interrupting them. "It's nothing...it's my fault and I—"

Although I in no way believed it was my wrongdoings that led to this moment, I was willing to pretend I thought so, in order to avoid conflict. I would happily have watched as the waiter squirmed and shrieked under Elias' gaze, but we didn't need any more animosity from humans, the other trackers didn't. This would, as Vykros had put it, only give them an excuse to hate us more.

"I'm ready to go, My..." I was about to address Elias, by his title, when I remembered he didn't wish, or liked to be addressed that way. Did that only apply when he was alone or in front of others as well?

Once again, as my mind was flooded with questions, Lideus spoke.

"It was him."

I sharply turned to Lideus, but his dark blonde hair covered the side of his face.

*You refuse to speak all day but now? Now you're speaking?*

Elias needed no further confirmation. He pulled the waiter towards him then shoved the drink into his chest.

"You drink it."

"My...My Lord I—"

"What's the problem, it's your saliva, isn't it? Nobody else wants that in their mouth."

Vkyros looked utterly captivated by the scene. Cheadd looked thoroughly suspicious. I shared both their sentiments.

*Why would Elias do this? He has no cause to defend trackers, or sorcerers, or me.*

"Hurry up. I'm waiting," Elias said.

Seeing no other alternative, the man grabbed the mug with a shaky hand, and drank it in a few, thick gulps. He grimaced as he did, then coughed. That was probably the hair.

I couldn't help but smile a little, but quickly shook my head, and corrected my facial expression.

There were other people now, who had heard the commotion and come to watch, peering from around the corner.

This was bad.

The waiter was bent forwards, choking, placing his own fingers in his throat, trying to extract the strands of hair he had so considerately put in the drink from his gullet. Elias shoved him away.

"Follow me." He walked off without even glancing back at our table.

I turned to the Commander. He nodded for me to go.

I ran after Elias. He was already quite far ahead of me. His long legs allowed him to cross several metres each time he took a few bounding strides.

"So, you *can* talk," Vkyros said to Lideus as I moved away.

My hair was up in a small, but messy tie. I raised my arms to try and place some of the errant strands back within it as I rushed after Elias, but I could barely keep up the pace, and decided to stop trying.

He didn't halt until he reached a side street, where two horses were waiting. A young boy holding their reins was watching them.

"You may go," Elias said to the boy, placing a ray in his palm. The boy beamed at the money and scurried off, not before he caught eyes with me, and paled instantly. My uniform gave my tracker and sorcerer status away.

"Get on," Elias said. I looked at the horse, a grey steed, she was beautiful but…

Elias was about to ride off.

"I…" I had to raise my voice. "Don't know how to ride."

Elias turned around, stopped his horse, and lowered his head to meet my eyes. He appeared baffled.

*Why are you baffled? How is it that you thought a tracker who was locked up for near two years knows how to ride a horse? Even if I had learnt before I was captured, I'd be terrible at riding now. What? Did you think they let us ride horses in the draining centres? It seems as if you failed to ask about all of the recreational activities you imagined they allowed us to participate in when you were interrogating me.*

As much as I wanted to share my thoughts, I bit my tongue.

"We teleport…and walk, and I never learnt how to ride," I explained.

Elias rolled his eyes and closed them for a second.

Then he rode over beside me and got off his horse.

"Get on."

"I just said I—"

"You will sit. I will ride," he said. At this angle, he once again, blocked out the dim sunlight that had trickled down this alleyway.

I spun my head between him and the horse.

"But—"

"Are you always this...?" Elias appeared as if he didn't know how to finish his own question.

"No. I'm just surprised," I answered for him, prematurely, "And I've never been on a horse, so I don't know how." I examined the series of straps, buckles, and leather items atop the animal.

Elias pointed down at a stirrup. "Place your foot in there, I'll hold onto your arm, you use yours to grab onto the reins and hoist yourself up. If you need help, I'll push you."

I nodded, processing the information, and then did as he asked, clumsily. I managed to hoist myself up, sitting behind his saddle, after all, I would truly have preferred to minimise contact with Elias in general.

Seconds later, I realised that avoidance had been pointless.

Within the time it took me to let out one breath, Elias had mounted the horse, and was sitting in front of me, on his saddle. He reached out and grabbed the reins.

"Hold onto me," he said, sounding extremely reluctant.

"Ummm...Where?"

"What do you mean where? Where do you think?" His voice was sharp.

I very slowly placed my arms around his torso. I could have sworn Elias shuddered at my touch in discomfort, but behind his back, I had my lips pressed together in the same discomfort as well.

As soon as I had a loose grip on his abdomen, he rode off. I let out a little gasp and grabbed onto him tighter. My fingers dug into the fabric of the thin shirt escaping between his bronze plates of armour, at the top and bottom of his torso.

Elias rode with no reserve or consideration for anyone in his path. It was as if he knew they would hear him and disperse before he was too close. The wind slapped at my skin, and pulled more hair from my tie, pressing it across my face, and into my mouth. He was going so fast, the sounds around us were a blur, the sights equally distorted.

Sometime later, by which the sun had already begun to completely fade away, we were out of Iloris.

After it had quietened down, and there were only very few passers-by on the quiet roads, I spat some hair out from my lips and asked, "Where are we going?"

Elias ignored me.

I sighed. It was, unfortunately, loud enough for him to hear. That was the disadvantage that came with being on a road so quiet.

"I'm taking you to follow that trail again," he replied.

*Follow the trail? I've already explained that would be pointless, haven't I?*

I shook my head to myself. It didn't matter. If he wanted to prove that to himself, and take me along for the ride, I had no choice.

I'd been trying to distance myself from his body this whole time, so that although my arm was around his waist, our torsos and legs were not touching, and my face was not pressed against his back. I couldn't see anything over his wide frame at all.

As I was trying to decide whether it would be worth asking any more questions, Elias spoke.

"How come the other Navigator couldn't follow it, the trail?" He sounded suspicious.

"He..." How could I say that it was because he was arrogant and hadn't really tried to look? That would possibly get him into trouble, and as much as I disliked him, I didn't want him to be punished.

"He?" Elias repeated, waiting for my answer.

"It requires a lot of focus and concentration and—"

"So, he wasn't focusing?"

"No...no, it's just that it can be difficult to—"

"So, he isn't up to the task?"

I sighed again, more quietly this time. "He has successfully completed missions before. It's all just a matter of where you look and where the energy is concentrated and...exposure to...to...outside, to external influences."

Elias looked over his shoulder at me. It had been the first time he'd made eye contact since he'd lifted my drink off the table.

"You're making that up, aren't you?"

"No. No, I'm not. It really is different in different circumstances," I insisted.

"You're protecting him," he mumbled as he turned back around.

I laughed lightly. I couldn't help it. Elias turned slightly back to look at me, but seemed to change his mind halfway through, and looked straight ahead again.

"Is that amusing?" he asked.

"No. It's not."

"And yet you laughed." He sounded thoroughly displeased about the fact I had.

"Only because he would find it laughable to think I was protecting him," I explained.

"You are."

"I'm not."

Elias softly chuckled then. The vibration rippled across his torso and into my palms.

"Why?" he asked.

"I'm *not* protecting him," I tried to sound convincing.

Elias stopped riding. We were in the middle of a street. We certainly hadn't arrived anywhere.

"Why...Why have you stopped?" I asked, meekly.

"Get off."

"What?!" I couldn't hide the surprise in my voice, even though I know I should have made more effort to do so. He *was* a Lord, despite not wanting to be addressed as such. I would have done well to remember that more often.

And I, I was disposable.

"If you're going to lie to me, then I can't work with you. Get off and go back."

"You can't...I..." I stuttered in shock.

*Volatile? More like an arsehole.*

"I can't ride...I can't teleport."

"I'm sure you'll find a way," he took my wrists gently, and removed them from himself.

"I wasn't lying!" I protested.

"You've said that, get off."

My mind was blank.

"I...he—"

Elias fully turned his body towards me, his face in full view. His dark red hair had also suffered against the wind, but somehow it had fallen completely naturally around his shoulders. Meanwhile, mine was still stuck to my face and forehead in an erratic manner.

"I don't want to hear it. You're wasting my time," Elias told me.

How did I always end up in situations like these? Stay a Vessel or become a tracker. Stay loyal to the trackers or feed their every secret to someone else. I could never make a decision that felt as if it were right, that allowed me to retain a shred of dignity, to retain my soul. It was as if the world was determined to syphon it away, to chip at it and watch, laugh, and bet how long it would be before I shattered it myself before I became someone I could no longer recognise.

It was not dying that frightened me. But dying while I still lived and breathed. My soul withering with time until I was nothing but an empty shell. It was not the death of the body I feared, but of myself.

But Ava, Cheadd had told me to do as Elias asked, to live. To live for Ava.

But what would this life mould me into?

And when the time came, when I had become so irrevocably changed, would I care? Would I notice?

Elias' red eyes bore into mine. I didn't have time to think. I didn't have time.

I grabbed his waist again, his eyebrows shot up in alarm. He moved to grab my wrist, but I said, the words spilling out of my mouth in a rush, "I am protecting him."

Since I'd said it so quickly, and Elias looked so stunned, I repeated, "I am."

He searched my face from side to side. I was looking at him pleadingly. I could sense my face betrayed anxiety and doubt. After a few seconds, he turned around, and began to ride again.

"Why?" he asked in a low voice.

"Don't you know why?" I asked.

His horse slowed down again...

"Alright, alright. I don't know what they'll do to him," I confessed. The horse resumed its pace. "We don't get along, but I don't...want to see him suffer."

"Why should it matter to you if he suffers?"

"It just...does. We've suffered enough."

Elias tensed up underneath my hands. That was probably the wrong thing to say. I recalled what Cheadd had told me about how Elias had better reason than anyone to hate sorcerers. As if he would sympathise or care about our suffering. He would only champion it.

"Is that what you think?" Elias sounded on edge.

"You asked me to... tell you the truth. It is what I think. And truthfully, it wouldn't have mattered whether he was a sorcerer or human. I was only afraid for his punishment and for his mistake. I wanted to prevent him from...receiving one."

Elias scoffed. "Some people deserve to be punished."

"And some people don't. And they frequently get mistaken for one another," I said, without thinking.

Elias's eyes shifted ever so slightly to over his shoulder. "Mmmm."

*Back to the 'mmmh's' then.*

We rode in silence for another hour or so before we reached Vaden, near the Northern border. Elias dismounted. He turned around and made no effort to help me down.

I looked at the ground warily. He turned to me.

"Do you need help?" Once again, he sounded as if someone was forcing the words out of his mouth.

"Yes," I admitted. I mentally decided I would learn how to ride a horse tomorrow, so I would never need to go through this again.

He held out his hand, which I avoided touching, placing my hand instead on his bronze wrist cuffs. I could still see crumples from where my fingers had distorted the fabric of his dark red undershirt.

From here, I could lead Elias to the site. This was roughly around where we had teleported and set up camp initially.

"Do you want to see both camps, or the site of the fight, the second?" I asked as soon as I was set on the ground.

"Was there anything left behind at the first?" he inquired.

"No."

"Then the second."

I opened my mouth to talk but hesitated.

"Do you always do that?" Elias asked.

"Do...what?"

"Open your mouth for seconds before you actually speak?"

I closed it abruptly. "I...No, it's just that I'm never sure what I might be permitted to say."

"Permitted again." Elias rolled his eyes. "Just say whatever you like."

I couldn't help but think that was a lie. I could think of many things I wouldn't be permitted to say or ask.

*Why did you make the waiter drink that beverage?*

*What happened to make you hate sorcerers so much?*

*You're a hypocrite. Some people deserve to be punished, do they? Only if they're sorcerers? Right?*

"Go on." Elias raised his eyebrows.

I raised my head, trying to appear more confident as I said, "There's a chance I can teleport us there, but I've never tried it before."

"Then why would you even offer?" He scowled, the corner of his lips turning upwards.

"Because I'm...tired," I fumbled for an excuse.

"For someone who's so terrible at lying, you seem to do it a lot."

I scowled back now.

Elias continued, "I thought I told you to tell me the—"

I cut him off. "Because you're limping, and I noticed it a while ago. I was going to ask you if you were injured, or what happened, but I doubted you would appreciate it, and we're going to be walking for a while, so, I thought...I could try."

Elias was still for a few seconds and then suddenly, he doubled over, placing his hands on his chest, in the same place that I had been holding him minutes ago.

He started laughing. Hysterically. His laugh came out in stuttering low rumbles, then suddenly increased in pitch as he straightened up again, letting out one long sigh.

I peered at him, irritated. He probably mistook my speech for tender concern. It was only a matter of practicality for the both of us.

"You want to know what happened to my leg?" he asked me. "It's no longer there. That's because people like you ripped it off, and left me to fucking die, after killing all of the people I was travelling with, right in front of me." He gestured at the space in front of him.

I understood then what Cheadd had told me.

This explained why he hated sorcerers so much. Why he felt so justified in his hatred. Whether or not he was right or wrong about it wouldn't matter to him, not with a story like that. It didn't matter to most people once they had been wronged. I understood it, but I hated it.

I hated even more that I had felt that way, many times before.

"Then...I'll try to learn for next time," I said, glancing at the grass.

When I looked back up, Elias was regarding me as if I were some kind of living corpse.

"To teleport," I clarified. "I'll try to learn to teleport for next time."

Elias remained staring at me that way for a few seconds. Then he turned around sharply, shaking himself out of whatever trance he had found himself in. "Don't. I need you for your navigation skills. Don't waste time trying to hone others."

"It wouldn't be a waste...in fact, maybe we should just bring a Teleporter with us and—"

"No. No to both of those things."

*Why? Why wouldn't you bring a Teleporter with an injury like yours? You're a Lord, you could bring ten Teleporters with you if you wished.*

I closed my eyes again, shaking my head, and crouched. I touched the ground, tapping into my core. As suspected, the traces of sorcery had been long removed and were non-existent now.

"The traces are gone, as I suspected, but I can remember the way."

Elias nodded. I stood and began to walk.

We moved this way for around another hour. I could hear Elias struggling to maintain his balance, or traverse more difficult areas of land. As trackers, we had taken the darkest and most hidden paths in pursuit of our target, and they were always trickiest to cross.

But I said nothing, and I didn't turn around to acknowledge him. He would only laugh in my face once more or force me to walk all the way back to the Palace. If he wanted to prolong his pain, that was his choice. I wasn't about to sign myself up for anymore on his behalf.

*Anyway, apart from a slight limp, he looks completely unaffected.*

But...I knew all too well, how masterfully someone could hide pain. As a class four Darean, the drainings had been exhausting for me. Nauseating. Uncomfortable. But not agonising in the way it was for sorcerers of higher classes. When they'd arrived, their wails would bleed through the walkways loud enough to strip you of your senses, and they'd shuffle around after their drainings, wincing, tears in their eyes, doubled over.

And yet, as time went on, most would stop wailing. They'd get up from the drainings and move without grimacing, floating like pale and sullen statues, dull as stone. Their cries became grunts. Their tears dried up.

*I guess those who always walk through fire, stop screaming at the burns.*

Did they truly grow used to pain like that?

*No, not used to it...they just...learnt to live with the searing heat.*

Is the Lord Elias like that as well?

I glanced over my shoulder at him quickly. He still appeared unperturbed.

*I can't say. But... I suppose those in the worst agony...never have a tell.*

We reached it.

I stopped abruptly and Elias bumped into me.

"What are you—"

He stopped talking himself when he observed the scene before him. All of the bodies were still there. The bodies of the sorcerers had not been removed.

Normally, from what I was aware, when sorcerers from these camps returned to the site of a battle or fight, after removing traces of their energy, they would burn the bodies, or take them away via teleportation.

But not a single one had been taken or burnt.

Elias moved around me to stand by my right.

We both stood in silence for a few minutes.

"Why...Why didn't they retrieve their dead?" Elias asked, mumbling.

I couldn't answer. I didn't know.

"They had Elementalists, and Teleporters. I saw," I said.

"But they didn't use them," Elias stated.

"Is this a message?" I asked.

"Wouldn't you know better than me?" Elias said, without glancing in my direction.

"Do you know the motivations behind every human's actions?" I bit back. I abhorred the generalisation of every sorcerer as power hungry and evil, with a shared consciousness. It was what had created this hatred, this war.

Elias gave me a sidelong glance.

"Then no," I said, finishing my sentence before I could think to back out of it.

"Weren't you stuttering over your words only an hour ago? Now you're speaking to me this way?" Elias didn't sound angry, or authoritative at all, only confused and slightly curious.

*From what I've heard, you speak in far worse ways to others.*

"You asked me to be honest." I turned to face him. He repeated my movement.

"Honest. Not familiar."

*Familiar? Is this your idea of familiarity? How... disturbing.*

"Check the area," he instructed. "Alert me if you find anything that looks suspicious or different." He walked forwards examining the scene himself.

I walked in the direction away from where I knew Ava had died, from where Claus' body lay on the ground.

There were bodies that had their heads removed, that were lanced with swords and shot with arrows, arrows which rendered their healing ability null. The blood that surrounded them had darkened and dried. Their skin was grey. Maggots were making a feast of their flesh.

It was hard to look at. No, hard wasn't the word. It was painful. To know it was me who had led the trackers here, and led these people to their deaths, so undignified, so cruel. Guilt curdled in my stomach, festering at my insides. I was rotting slowly from within.

*Will I be able to free my brothers... before I become completely decayed?*

*Like these bodies.*

I walked between them, the debris, and the remnants of supplies that also, curiously, had not been retrieved. I had to press the back of my hand to my mouth to stop myself from gagging from the stench, which hung in the stale and unmoving air.

Elias was standing by a cart that had been left behind.

"Tracker," he called out to me. I crossed the field to him.

*I told you my name, didn't I?*

Although, it wasn't exactly shocking he had decided not to use it. No non-sorcerers ever did.

*When's the last time I heard someone say it? My name...*

"What is this?" Elias pulled me from my thoughts. He lifted up a pouch full of stones, each of them glowing, warm and bright with iridescent light. They were a variety of colours from orange, to blue, to violet, to crimson.

"They're enoliths," I answered. "They're stones imbued with sorcery that magic wielders use to communicate with one another. The light indicates the sorcerer from whom the pair of stones originates is still alive, and is in possession of their half. If it's dull, then the sorcerer is either dead, or no longer possesses their counterpart."

Elias peered at them curiously. There must have been around twenty of them in the pouch. The majority of them were alight.

Despite the fact my affinity for sorcery was poor, my abilities had emerged fairly early, and since my father had also been a sorcerer, he had taught me much about sorcery, magical artefacts, objects, spells, and classes. Enoliths were said to have come from an underwater cavern deep within the Ocean by Jurasa's lands, gifted by Sirens to a sorcerer.

*The Sirens. A gift. Right...*

But like all good myths, it was captivating in its possibility. Better to think those Sirens were our allies, than they'd beckon us to break our bones.

My father would in all likelihood, just as my brothers did, despise me for 'allying' with this red-haired Lord now, and sharing information he had passed down to me with him.

*I'm doing it to save them. I have to. I have to take care of them. The way you used to take care of us, for a time. Until you couldn't anymore. Until you stopped. Until you retreated into yourself, grew more distant, little by little, then left us alone. Where are you now? You disappeared one day and never came back. Some of them said you'd gone somewhere quiet to die. Some of them said you'd been taken. Some of them said you'd run. You never even said goodbye. So how could you judge me for this?*

"Can they be traced with these stones?" Elias asked, once again, anchoring me to the present.

I shook my head. "I've never heard of that happening."

"But if you could...if someone could, theoretically, it would be a Navigator, wouldn't it?" Elias dumped the pouch back down and turned around, leaning against the cart.

"Theoretically." nodded. "Or a Sense Transformer. They sense the core and energy of others far more powerfully, as in…" I searched for the right words to explain. "Navigators can traverse difficult land, and track things, including sorcerers down, but only because we can sense the echoes that sorcery has left in the earth, wherever it has crossed it. But we can't usually track down specific individuals, or specific energy. Sense transformers cannot find sorcerers or track them down, but… when they are in any sorcerer's close proximity, they can read their individual core, and tell immediately what class, abilities, and level of affinity for sorcery that individual has."

Elias looked slightly bewildered, but also nodded. "So, are you saying that it's possible or not?"

"I'm saying… it's unlikely, and it would be more likely to work if both a Navigator and a Sense Transformer were attempting this together. But even then, enoliths are powerful, and it's possible they're beyond such…things."

"But if it can be done, we can find these people and through them, find out where the others are…and put an end to this."

*An end to this?* I squinted. *We?*

"You disagree," he told me. It wasn't a question, he could simply tell.

I saw no reason to lie. "This was just one group, and they were very powerful. Even if by some small chance we found some of the owners of those enoliths, there's no guarantee they'd tell us anything, and…well… even if they did, there's no guarantee we'd find the group, or that if we *did* find them…we would succeed in taking them down, or that there wouldn't be survivors who would retaliate and join another group out there in existence to do so…and ….so on." I gestured with my hands to indicate there were an infinite number of flaws to his statement.

"Fuck," Elias said.

His response took me by surprise, not because he'd cursed, but because he'd done so in front of me.

"Did you see anything unusual?" he asked.

"No."

"I did." He motioned for me to follow him.

As we moved further and further away from the cart, my breath caught in my throat. My hands began to turn sticky with sweat, my limbs laden with the weight of dread.

We were moving closer and closer to that place.

Until we were right there.

Standing over Claus' body.

"This one." Elias pointed at him.

He didn't need to explain. Whereas everyone else's body was pale, mottled, and bloated, Claus' was black, and dark red in places. His skin looked dry, like it was stretched over his skeleton. He looked as if he had been thrown into the very depths of evil and resurfaced on this grass.

My body shook slightly. I swallowed, loudly. I had seen far too many dead bodies in the space of a few weeks.

Elias looked at me. "Do you have any ideas?"

"I...he's..."

But it was impossible, it couldn't be.

"Back to stuttering again," Elias groaned.

I got on the ground, and somehow found the will to crawl forwards towards the body. If I was right...

I reached out a shaking hand towards his forehead.

"What are you doing?" Elias demanded.

I didn't answer him. I used one finger to lift the still intact hair from it.

On it, a dark red insignia bore deep into his skull.

I drew in a sharp breath.

"What the fuck?" Elias said, quickly moving closer. "What is that?"

"It's...the mark of possession."

"What does that mean?" Elias sounded impatient.

The talisman around his neck. How hadn't I thought about this before? How hadn't I realised.

The mark had similarities, distant ones, but undeniable similarities to the one on his skin.

It had been holding his form, holding the illusion, and I took it off.

"Shadae?"

I blinked and turned over to look at him, surprised he had used my name. He was crouched on the other side of the body now, looking at me, waiting.

I pointed at Claus' forehead. "This man has been dead for a long time. Someone else...someone else was in possession of his body. That's wh..." my mouth was dry. "That's what this mark is."

"Who could do that?"

"A Necromancer," I told him.

"Accipereans," Elias muttered.

"Yes, Accipereans, class one. The only ability that is," I told him.

"These sorcerers...can possess a person? But this man is dead...does that mean—"

"No. Necromancers usually take control of recently deceased corpses, using these...marks to create the illusion of life and...undecayed flesh. They can also summon the dead from...the...afterlife," I wasn't sure what to call it, "to possess such corpses on their behalf, or do their bidding. Possessing the living is almost unheard of, it's harder to do. Either way, the mark on the shell is different, depending on the soul possessing it, unlike the marks for other curses, which remain the same, no matter who bears them," I answered.

"So the...original...owner"—Elias grimaced at his own description— "of this body is dead. The Necromancer isn't."

I nodded. "That's what I'd conclude, but I don't understand..."

"What?" Elias said.

"How I managed to...expel it?" I shook my head, my gaze darting around.

"You killed him? You killed...this thing?" Elias sounded shocked.

"Yes. But normally, the body of a possessed corpse is far stronger than a normal one, especially if that corpse belonged to a sorcerer. Even the arrows we use wouldn't have been enough to injure them."

"I see," Elias said. "They feigned death in this body."

"Meaning the sorcerers this person was with didn't know about his identity either," I stated.

We looked at each other. Elias looked troubled.

"So, they let themselves die. They left this body. Where could they have gone?" Elias asked me.

*How did you expect me to know that?*

"They would have to find another shell," I explained.

"Another corpse?"

"Or...not. It is rare, but they could possess the living, if they were powerful enough. If that's the case then this person would have marked some people ahead of time, probably without them realising, leaving them with the option to jump from one body to the next when necessary."

"So... they could be anywhere," Elias sounded exasperated.

"Yes. They could be anyone."

"How can someone check for these marks?"

"I don't know...I don't know enough about it."

Elias grunted in frustration. "The question is...what is this person's agenda? If they weren't working with these sorcerers, why? Were they working against them? And if so for..." Elias stopped himself, as he noticed me watching him, paying attention.

"This isn't meant for your ears." He sounded irritated.

My face fell. "You've already started speaking."

"Then pretend you didn't hear anything," he stood.

I stood too. "That would be lying, wouldn't it?"

"Very clever." He gave me a false smile. "Your task is to help me navigate and answer my questions, that's it."

"But you have more questions. Maybe I could help you with those."

"You're very keen to help me all of a sudden."

I gulped and glanced at Claus...at what was once Claus' body. "Whatever was inside this thing, killed my friend, the one who, the one...I was retrieving the body of when you found me at the gates of the draining centre. I want to find out what it is...who. I want to help you find them. I can navigate but I can do more than that too." I looked at him resolutely, my fists clenched as I lied.

I did want to know. But not for justice's sake. Not truly.

*If I help Elias, then maybe...freeing my brothers will be easier...if I get him to trust me...*

And Cheadd, he thought I'd brought Ava's soul some kind of peace by killing Claus, by ending her killer, but I hadn't. And I was only pursuing her killer selfishly.

*It's not my right to withhold this information from him...is it?*

But I couldn't bring myself to shatter whatever fragile closure was keeping the Commander together.

Or perhaps, whatever delicate illusions were keeping me from unravelling apart.

"I don't need you to do more than that," Elias said. "I don't need you to teleport or think. I need you to navigate and answer my questions. That's it. I will deal with the rest."

"I need to think to answer questions."

Elias huffed. "It's a shame you don't before you speak."

"I don't expect anything in return. I just want to know who did this myself."

"What a fucking pity." He threw his hands into the air. "You see I'd actually prepared a variety of gifts and favours to shower you with for doing all the things I've clearly asked you to refrain from doing."

I sighed and glared at him, not bothering to hide my annoyance.

"What about riding?"

"What?" Elias asked.

"Shouldn't I learn to ride a horse? That way you won't have to bear the horror that is my touch each time we work together?"

Elias appeared to be a mixture of stunned, irritated, and lost.

"You don't want a Teleporter, and you don't want me to ride with you. So, I should learn to ride a horse, shouldn't I?"

Elias let out a long sigh. "I thought learning to ride a horse was self-explanatory."

"I wouldn't want to presume."

"Presume to learn the most basic skill you will need in order to do as I ask?"

"Isn't thinking the most basic skill needed to do—"

"Enough, tracker."

Elias came around the other side of the body so that he was standing in front of me. "Unfortunately for the both of us, you seem to be the most proficient Navigator the trackers have, but my patience for your antics is not everlasting."

I looked down. I had probably already pushed him further than was intelligent to do so.

"Let me try and trace them," I murmured, looking at the body.

"What?" Elias was still looking directly at me.

"I can try and find out where the...possessor went, at least until they found their new body. They wouldn't have been able to return to conceal their energy, and whoever returned to conceal the others may not have been able to do so for theirs, since the energy of a possessor is different...they wouldn't have expected it to be amongst the energies here. It might not work but—"

Elias nodded. "Do it. Try."

"Will I be showered with some gifts?" I said, smiling sarcastically.

Elias didn't appreciate the joke. "You'll get the privilege of riding back with me rather than walking."

I snorted. "The privilege," I muttered under my breath. "The privilege that makes you shudder in disgust."

"I didn't say it was a privilege for me," Elias groaned.

I crouched beside the body once more.

I hadn't stopped shaking. My mouth still felt barren, and the smell drifting through the humid air was making my stomach turn, but I approached the corpse, and closed my eyes.

That was until, a piercing, unbearable, agonising pain shot through my skull.

And I started screaming.

## CHAPTER 47– NATHON

The Captain had never come to see me.

On the third night, he hadn't visited me, to ask for the Noxstone. There were three possible explanations for this. The first, was that he had taken some himself from Mathias. Although the Captain didn't strike me as the thieving kind, if he were truly desperate for the material, it was feasible that his morals could be bent somewhat.

The same kind of morals that made him strike me as the 'save a lone victim from assault' kind of person.

I chuckled to myself, throwing the enolith up and catching it in my palm, repeating this process over and over.

I caught it, and clenched my fist around it, sighing and leaning back into the pillows on my bed. My face fell, after all, this was what led me to ponder the second possibility, one that I had been pondering a few days.

That the Captain was still suffering from his wounds and had been too unwell to visit.

And there was a third possibility, that the Captain had never returned to the Palace at all.

But unlike with Jurasa's escort, where the candidate herself had been aware of the man's disappearance, if the Captain had not returned to the Palace for days, then the Lady who clung to him would already have alerted the entire Palace staff. In fact, it was likely that the entire population of Vasara would have heard about it by now.

Which made the third possibility impossible.

I had considered visiting the Captain to confirm which of the first two theories were correct, however, I could not think of any pretext on which to do so. Asking him why he had not arrived to ask for the Noxstone would have been completely out of my public character, after all, since the Captain retrieving it clearly did not benefit me in any way. The Captain was astute enough to understand this.

Yet still, it bothered me. I knew what would have transpired, what Mathias would have done, if the Captain had not intervened. I did not like to owe any debts. I was already roped into a large enough one with Sarlan. The Captain hadn't known who he had been saving and so, I technically owed him nothing.

But I knew, and remarkably, and inexplicably even to myself, I felt I owed the Captain. I would have preferred to know he was not mortally wounded. It bothered me that I was without this information.

It also bothered me that it had taken me far too long, longer than usual to deduce the information Mathias and Sarlan had ordered me to retrieve was, without a doubt...

In the Captain's possession.

My first impression of the Captain as 'not the thieving kind' was proving to be utterly incorrect.

It had struck me during Mathias' and I's alleyway conversation. Of course, I had said nothing, since it would have been unwise to inform Mathias of anything that was solely based on my suspicions alone. Both he and Sarlan would only accept facts and evidence.

But the Captain wanted access to Noxstone, and up until that moment, I hadn't been able to guess why. I hadn't believed that his request was connected to anything in Vasara, or the information that my father had lost. After all, there were hundreds of ways information could be transmitted and communicated, stored, and stolen.

Noxscroll was one of these methods, but it was even rarer than Noxstone and thus, was very rarely used. I had not seen or heard of Sarlan using it in at least a decade.

For a man who had never handled a Noxstone weapon before, who knew of the dangers of doing so, there was no reasonable explanation for his desire to possess some.

Other than to read something that had been written upon Noxscroll.

Why Mathias had withheld this information from me was not something I could currently comprehend and so, withholding my suspicions from him was entirely justifiable.

What had the Captain become embroiled in? I thought about Arton, about the men I had been ordered to kill just over one moon ago, about all of the people I had tortured, killed, and hunted because they had become embroiled in Sarlan's schemes.

I banged my head slightly against the back of the bed frame a few times.

I truly did not want to have to kill the Captain. I truly did not want to have to torture him. I...

I wanted to be wrong.

But I knew that I wasn't.

I had even contemplated warning him, or bargaining with him, asking him to hand over whatever information he had on his person in exchange for his life. But the Captain would not trust such a promise, and I could not blame him for his doubt. Which meant that if I confronted him, either with a bargain, or a warning, he would attack me, and I would invariably end up taking his life.

Perhaps I was simply putting off the inevitable, but against all logic, I felt I owed the Captain an opportunity to live. And so, I was opting for another alternative.

To steal the information back from him.

This would of course lead to questions regarding where I had found it and who I had stolen it from. Lying about this to Mathias and Sarlan was possible. Jurasa's escort would be a wonderful choice, since he was no longer breathing. However, that would lead to a chain of events which would most likely involve retaliation on Jurasa in some-way.

The only reason I could think to provide, was that it was a sorcerer whom I had found the information on, but the chances of me defeating a sorcerer who was not a Vessel were already questionable, and I still hadn't uncovered the draining centre's activities.

And finally, the reason why the Captain had stolen the information would remain unknown. That did not sit well with me, at all.

Still, I had decided that for now, I would steal the information from him, and consider the rest later.

Only, I could not steal it myself.

I smirked, gripping the stone tightly. "I was wondering when you would return."

The sorcerer was crouched in my window. I had left it open for several hours every night for the past few days, remaining awake during the duration that it was, waiting for her to come back.

"You have something that belongs to me." She sounded displeased and landed softly on the ground.

"Ahhh, yes." I was about to throw the stone into the air again, when I realised the sorcerer could easily enhance her speed, and grab it before it fell back into my hand.

"You failed to mention that you're a sorcerer." I gripped the stone tighter and swung my legs around, so that I was sitting on the edge of the bed.

"I fail to see why you needed to know," she said.

"To work together we need to trust one another, don't we?"

"It's because I don't trust you that I suggested our collaboration."

"A working relationship based on distrust will not work at all." I tutted.

"Give me the stone." She moved closer to me, stretching out her hand. Her outfit remained similar to the last one she'd worn when we'd spoken. Her shirt and hood were crimson, her bodice night black.

"I will, but you will do something for me in return."

"I won't kill anyone for you." She dropped her hand. The edge to her voice was clear.

I chuckled. "Of course not. If I wanted someone dead, I could easily kill them myself. What I need...is for you to watch someone."

"Who?" she said. She was very blunt, just as before. There were no fillers in any of her words. Her communication skills were...lacking. But it only made this exchange more efficient, so it suited me perfectly well.

"You watch this person for me and come back here, you will tell me what you have found, and during that conversation, I will give this *enolith* back to you."

Her lips parted as she let out a small sigh. I had made sure to let her know I was aware of what this object was. "Who?" she asked again.

"Do you know people by name here? Or should I describe them?"

"Describe them."

"He's Kalnasan, the escort for the candidate here—"

She raised her hand. "None of this means anything to me. Tell me what he looks like and where he resides."

I recalled the Captain's appearance in my mind. "He's around six foot. His skin is pale, sandy in tone. He has long hair which falls to his waist. It's silver, almost white, with some hues of blue. He usually has a… top knot, or a small bun tied at the back of his hair, held by an ornate pin of some kind."

"This isn't very relevant," the woman said.

"I'm trying to make sure you watch the right person," I protested.

"By telling me the way he styles his hair? Do you happen to know the colour of the pins?"

I squinted in irritation.

Describing the Captain in detail was easy, after all. In my experience, even the smallest and finest details of a person were important to take note of. And so, I had been inured to memorising characteristics and mannerisms. The Captain's were simply some of the most distinct I'd come across, and easiest to recall.

I supposed I did not usually need to describe them to this extent, it was only that this woman had no understanding or knowledge of any of the individuals who resided here, and I wanted to ensure she spied on the correct man.

Although…the Captain was the only man who looked remotely like what I had described within miles, most likely. This lengthy description was not truly necessary, and still, I continued…

"He is slightly broader than myself. He also wears rings, and his clothes are usually pale blue, white, or mint green, sometimes peach, or lilac. He wears garments which are typical for Kalnasa. Robes. Airy, long, and fluid."

"His eyes?" she asked.

"Violet," I told her.

"Where is he?"

"He's somewhere in this Wing if you…"

I then proceeded to give her directions from my chambers to his.

"When do I watch him?"

"As soon as possible."

"What am I watching him for?"

"He has a piece of Noxscroll in his room. I need you to retrieve it."

The woman stepped back and crossed her arms. "You said I was to watch him, not steal from him."

"Yes, well, I'd like you to do both. I'd like to know what he does with this paper, then I'd like you to take it."

"What is on this piece of paper? I've never heard of Noxscroll before. What does it look like?"

"It's dark, thick, calloused. I don't know what it contains. That is why I need it. You have the ability to remain in the shadows, to remain invisible. You will be able to do this undetected."

"I'm sure that is something you could also do."

"I'm asking you. A favour for a favour."

"You're asking me to steal something in return for something you have stolen." She sounded judgemental.

"You're a sorcerer. Before, informing anyone about your visit wasn't particularly beneficial to me. But now that I know you're a sorcerer, I could gain great favour in exposing you. As long as you remain useful to me, I will keep silent, but if not—"

"Ha." The woman stepped forwards again. "What are you implying?"

"You've already established that killing me isn't possible."

"That doesn't mean I can't do something else."

"What's your class?" I asked her. "You're ability?"

She only smiled in response.

"You won't tell me."

"As long as you do not betray me, I have no reason to, or to show you."

I tilted my head. "Very well. After this is done, we will help each other with our respective inquiries into those draining centres."

"Aren't you concerned?" she said, leaning on the large pillar by my bed.

"About?"

"Working with a sorcerer? About my objectives? My motives?"

"Aren't you concerned about mine?" I asked her.

"Not really."

"Then why should I be concerned about yours?"

"Because I'm a sorcerer. Aren't all humans terrified of us?"

"I don't know. I've not asked them."

She seemed to be studying me carefully, shaking her head. "You're either very foolish, or very reckless."

"I am neither," I assured her. "It's only that you and I currently have no reason to harm one another. Whatever your plans are, if helping you achieve your goals enables me to achieve mine, and it is the only way in which I can, the consequences can be dealt with later."

"You're selfish then?" she said.

I scoffed, although I did not disagree. "You're a fool if you think the only people who are worth fearing in this world are sorcerers."

"I definitely don't think that." She sounded disgusted.

"Then I'm sure you'll believe me when I tell you, I've dealt with dangerous humans several times in the past. The only difference between you and them is that your ability to enact your dangerous intentions is much more easily realised, and therefore, harder to control. You are harder to control, to manipulate, to deceive. That makes you more dangerous than some humans, yes, but not all."

She moved forwards, away from the pillar. "I'll watch him tonight."

"Tonight?" I leant forwards and stood.

"I need that enolith back as soon as possible."

"Ahh, yes. I suppose there's a poor sorcerer waiting at the other side who thinks you're dead. They won't be interfering now, will they?"

"The sooner I have the stone, the far less likely that is to happen."

"But it *is* a possibility?" That was a problem.

"If you're that concerned, you can return the stone to me now." She stepped forwards with her hand outstretched again.

"Tonight it is." I smiled and ignored her hand.

She closed her palm again. "And if he detects me?"

"That won't happen, will it?"

"It's not impossible. So, if he detects me? Do I kill him?"

"You told me that you wouldn't kill anyone."

"I would prefer not to, but if he sees me, then I don't see any other alternative."

"You did for me."

"That is because your disappearance would be too noticeable."

"So would this individual's, he is also an important person."

"How?"

"He is…you stated that such things meant nothing to you earlier. If I tried to explain his position or status you wouldn't comprehend it."

"So, if he detects me?" she repeated again.

I sighed and looked down at my leather boots. I hadn't thought too hard about this, since to my knowledge, a sorcerer could easily conceal themselves.

"I won't risk being exposed," the woman said. "You are one thing, you can be bargained with, but another individual? That is too much of a risk."

"If you kill him, you can forget about us working together." I had unconsciously ground my jaw.

The woman jerked her head back, observing me. "If he lives after seeing me, I won't be able to work with you regardless. Do you truly believe he would keep knowledge of a sorcerer in the Palace to himself?"

I pondered. I would previously have assumed not, but the Captain seemed to be more secretive than I had imagined.

"Even if you say that he would, I cannot guarantee it myself," she spoke. "So, if this man sees me, I will kill him, and you will not see me again."

I looked up and took several steps towards her, closing the distance between us.

"Yes. Yes, I *will* see you again, for if you kill this man"— I took a few steps towards her— "I will find you and kill you myself."

Her mouth twisted in suspicion. "You don't want this man to die," she murmured.

"I have already explained his status—"

"Yes, you have. But that doesn't explain why you would promise to kill me in return for his death."

I fell silent. It didn't. It didn't explain that.

"Is he a friend of yours?" she asked.

"No," I replied quickly.

"You need him for some reason then?"

Silence for a few moments.

"You could say that," I replied flatly, unsure.

The woman backed away towards the window. "It seems as if I'll need a list of all the people you need, so that I can make sure to avoid them, and their detection."

"There is no such list," I said with a blank expression.

"No list. Just one name then? What is this man's name?"

"You do not need his name. You have his information."

The woman let out a bemused and irritated sigh.

It didn't matter. I didn't need to convince her of anything, I only needed her to do as I wished.

"Keep your window open. I'll return later."

"I'll be waiting," I smiled.

"And all of your guards are asleep," she told me. "They don't appear to be, of course."

Interesting. "Corshick powder?" I asked.

"They'll remain that way for an hour or so," she confirmed.

Corshick powder was incredibly useful. And incredibly rare. If you could blow a small amount directly into someone's face, they would be rendered unconscious without appearing so. To all passersby, the guards that roamed the nearby hallways would appear dutiful and alert. It wouldn't have been hard for the sorcerer to do this undetected at all.

She had disappeared as I was contemplating the brilliance of this strategy.

I sat back down on the bed and placed my hands through my hair.

She would kill him, if he saw her, and there was nothing I could do about it. It seemed that the Captain was doomed to die as soon as he crossed my path.

An unfamiliar feeling settled in my abdomen, an unease, a restlessness.

This was generally why I preferred to conduct all tasks myself.

But I usually cared little about who lost their lives in the process, as long as it wasn't myself, or anyone Sarlan had ordered me to spare.

I didn't pray. I didn't believe. But, if there were any Gods, and they bore any favour towards me for whatever twisted and strange reason, I hoped they would intervene and allow this night to end smoothly.

No. That wasn't it. I hoped they would intervene and allow the Captain to live.

I laughed to myself, placing my head in my hands. I hadn't dared to hope for anything in years. Hope was dangerous. More dangerous than any human or sorcerer, and its lack of realisation was the most dangerous thing of all.

How could I dare to hope the Captain would live? Why? What purpose did hope in his survival have? Perhaps I was guided by an instinctual desire to keep him alive, knowing he might serve a purpose in the future.

I was usually sure of my own motivations, my own mind when it came to such things, but this task, this mission, ever since I had arrived in Vasara, I had felt increasingly less sure of myself.

I couldn't afford to feel that way.

This would work. This was the best method to apply to my current circumstances.

I lay back and closed my eyes, not falling asleep, but waiting, waiting for that statement to be proven right.

Waiting for the night to be over. Without any casualties.

Not waiting.

Hoping.

# CHAPTER 48 – HESTAN

One thing the young Princess Loria had not mentioned about Noxscroll, all those years ago, was that while it could be read under the light of Noxstone, it could not, it seemed, be read under the light of day.

I had considered there was simply nothing on this sheet of paper, that it was blank, but if that were the case, there would have been no reason to pass it onto me. Which led me to conclude that Noxscroll could only be read under moonlight.

The moon hadn't been out for days.

Days which I had spent in bed, sweating from fever and pain, exhausted from fatigue and blood loss. I had only just managed to return to the Palace before losing consciousness that night. Once I had come around, I had called for a healer, feigning the reasoning for such a deep cut on my shin. I had sensed the doubt in their eyes, but even if the truth was discovered, it wouldn't matter much. It was only that I didn't wish to be linked to the man who I had stolen the Noxstone blade from, if possible.

Each time I had lifted and examined the steel, I had done so with the utmost care. Touching it made me feel sick, both from the thought of potentially slicing off my own fingers, and from the memory of its previous owner, pressing that young man against a piss-stained wall.

It was a shame I hadn't been in a position to apprehend him, and hand him over to the authorities. Had I been an unknown man, with no responsibilities or status, I would have done so.

The blade truly was beautiful. It was dark and opaque, but under certain lights, indentions in its thick, yet light material glowed in faint indigo, dark green, and gold. The blade itself was curved at the point from outside to in, so that the tip was a precise and razor thin point. The handle was adorned with bronze symbols of bird wings, feathers, clouds, lightning, and serpents. I could have stared at it for hours, and still found new ways to admire it.

There had been no need for me to visit Audra's Prince after retrieving this, thankfully, but I would still have to come up with a reason for my sudden lack of interest in his blades. I hadn't managed to do so yet.

A silver streak of light penetrated through the glass of my window, casting a circular beam of it onto the dark ground of my chambers. They were usually orderly, but now appeared slightly littered. I'd been unable to maintain such cleanliness whilst injured.

I got up from the table I had been sitting at, waiting. I winced slightly as my leg took some weight. The site of the wound still stung tremendously, itched, and burnt. But I no longer had a fever, and the agony had turned into a bearable pain.

I stilled. The light that was on the floor for a brief moment darkened and shone brightly again within a second. I glanced at it, then at my window. I waited for a moment.

A bird flew by, and another. I let out a sigh of relief, having detected the reason for the lighting's flicker.

I knelt on the ground, with the knee from my uninjured leg. The Noxstone blade was in my right hand, and the paper in my left.

I took a deep breath. I was terrified of what this paper would reveal. All this time, I had been working tirelessly to find out what was written on it, without thinking of the moment when I would know. A part of me had believed this moment would never come, that I would never access a Noxstone weapon.

But I had suffered wounds for this, had put myself in danger for this. I knew the implications of what was written on this could, no, that they would be monumental, and the moon wouldn't remain cast on my floorboards for eternity.

I placed the paper on the ground slowly, as if I was afraid it would be blown away by the gentle breeze coming through the window. It remained in place.

I lifted the Noxstone blade gently. The moonlight struck it. At first the angle was off, the light reflected into my eyes, across the walls, but after an adjustment, and a turning of my wrist, the moonlight struck the paper and letters began to form.

Letters turned into words, words into sentences, sentences into a small paragraph.

*These ones are Accipereans, they're nearly drained. The others were partially successful attempts at assimilation. We continue our attempts, but the majority of humans reject the transference. Those that accept it are still insufficient. We continue to trade them with the others. The Vessels involved in the transference do not survive the experiments, but their absence remains unnoticed. Kalnasa's centre now consists solely of unsuccessful subjects and Vessels with little lifespans. It will be time soon. We have sent the others you requested for marking to the desired location.*

*N.A.*

N.A. Those initials.

*Nathon. Albarsan.*

I nearly dropped the blade onto my own leg.

I pressed my left palm down hard against the ground, my other leg gave way from under me, slamming my injury into the floor. My eyes remain fixed on the paper before me.

It couldn't be. It couldn't be.

It wasn't monumental.

It was devastating.

It was beyond the realm of anything I could have imagined would appear on this paper. It was beyond the realm of anything I could have imagined at all.

I somehow managed to remain alert enough, to place the blade next to the paper. I backed away from it slowly, sitting on the floor now. I placed my hands around my knees and stared, simply stared at that iridescent circle, at that focal point of moonlight, within which floated dust, within which was a secret that made me wish that I could tear my own eyes out.

I stood unsteadily, and walked into the washroom, leaving the objects on the floor. I gathered some cold water into my hand, splashing it relentlessly on my face and upper neck. It trickled down the pale blue undershirt I was wearing, onto my chest, over my heart, that was thudding and pounding, as fast as my thoughts were racing.

I needed to destroy that paper, I needed to get rid of it.

But how? How would I destroy it? Could it even be destroyed? I couldn't even think.

Minutes passed in this daze, minutes I did not have to waste.

I clutched at the doorframe of the washroom, and staggered out of it, still feeling lightheaded from the shock.

Someone was standing in my room.

With the paper and blade in their hands.

# CHAPTER 49 – NEMINA

The man closed the bathroom door behind him.

I glanced down at the scrap of paper he had pulled out from his pockets. The Prince had ordered for me to retrieve it, but I had seen, I had watched as this man examined its surface. I had seen the blood drain from his pale 'sandy' complexion, and his 'violet' eyes flutter in confusion and distress.

I waited for a minute or so. I had been concealing my appearance, shrouding it with the shadows. I was lucky I had mostly mastered translucency, one of the five basic spells. I had acquired mastery of them all, other than levitation. That would have been useful, considering how often I was climbing through windows recently.

I had been surprised the Captain had left his window open, but had figured out that was because he needed the moonlight to be able to read the paper, as well as the blade, and so, he had opened the window for maximum luminosity.

I didn't truly have the time to read this here, but I couldn't steal the blade myself. Theoretically, I could, but despite the fact I had handled these blades a few times, I still wasn't confident in their use. I would have preferred to leave it behind and get back to the Prince swiftly.

Besides, touching those blades brought back...difficult memories.

I needed to retrieve my enolith as soon as possible. I truly wished I hadn't needed to bring one in the first place.

Yaseer might assume I had lost the stone but Baz, against his better judgement, would assume that I was dead. I could not afford for them to follow me here. This task had already become far more complicated than I would have liked, and there were several days I had contemplated abandoning it all together, leaving as I had initially intended to.

My task, to infiltrate the draining centres, and put measures in place to facilitate the escape of a Vessel. A Vessel, Yaseer had stated, they desperately needed.

I could have been somewhere, in some quiet corner of the world, where people barely crossed. Tucked away, at peace.

Or maybe that wasn't true. How could I find peace, after all that had happened, after everything that continued to happen? How could I find anywhere, where people would not regard a newcomer with suspicion? It seemed that I had no choice but to stay, to fight, against my will.

I wanted to rest.

But I was here.

And I was walking towards the scrap of paper.

I lifted the blade slowly and stood, it only took seconds for the words to form on the paper. They were silver and bled onto the sheet like liquid ink.

I read it four times.

Over and over again, I took in these words, their weight, their meaning.

And still, air had become a foreign object to me, I could not grasp it with my lungs, I could not breathe.

Transference? They were attempting to transfer magical cores into human beings? They were conducting experiments on Vessels and humans. Which humans? How? How many had they done this with? Some of the Vessels, some of them were humans beforehand?

I'd heard screams. I'd heard so many…I never thought…

Kalnasa…why there? Who was betraying them there? Without Vessels Kalnasa would not survive for long. Who were these people they were marking? And what with? Kalnasa wouldn't last without the drainings. Neither would Athlion.

And that signature.

N.A.

The Prince knew. He knew about this torture. He'd in all likelihood sanctioned it, had allowed this to happen. Some of the sorcerers were the products of experiments, and they were being transferred, deliberately.

Was Baz? Did Baz…

There were footsteps. The man was standing across the room.

Staring straight at me.

He could see me. I had lost focus, in the midst of my emotion, I had dropped the invisibility, the translucency.

I didn't have time to deal with the man now. I had planned to kill him if he had detected me, despite the Prince's threats.

But now, now I had other plans.

The man charged towards me, grabbing a spear that leant against the wall. As he did, his hair flew behind him, caught in the wind.

Using speed enhancement, I spun around him, and reached behind his head, grabbing his hair pin.

The insignificant details had mattered after all.

The man's hair came undone, and I pressed his hairpin against his neck, nicking the blood slightly from a vein. He stilled. He'd realised by now I was a sorcerer.

I used his confusion and panic to grab the paper off the floor, and in one swift motion, imperceptible to the human eye, climbed out of the window.

There was another window, waiting for me, open.

And a man sitting behind it, who would not survive the night.

# CHAPTER 50- NATHON

There was a loud commotion at my door.

I sprung up from lying flat immediately and grabbed two blades from my belt. The guards were incapacitated, and the sorcerer would never have risked appearing at my door, not when the window was already open.

Someone was trying to force it down.

Who would be so utterly reckless as to try and knock my door down in the middle of the night?

The wood was strong, but after a few beatings from the assailant, it gave way, and fell to the ground. Dust from it blew up in the air. I remained still, waiting for it to cast away and reveal...

"Your...Your Highness." A ringed hand was gripping my door frame. It let go as the silhouette bent forwards at the waist and suddenly fell to his knees.

The Captain. The Captain was in my room, half dressed. The upper half of his chest was wet, and his hair was completely loose.

What had that sorcerer done to him?

I placed my daggers back into my belt and quickly ran over towards him.

"Captain? What are you—"

Before I finished my sentence, I sensed it.

I grabbed the Captain's shoulders and shoved him to the ground, just as I did, two blades soared over our heads. The Captain was still conscious but appeared unwell.

He propped up onto his elbows. Part of his hair was sticking to the wet skin on his collarbones. I looked at him searchingly. He met my eyes and opened his mouth to speak, but he had no time to talk.

"What is this?" the sorcerer's voice sounded from behind me.

I turned around. She held a piece of dark paper in her hands.

So, she had retrieved it, and I had been correct, the Captain had possessed it.

I stood in front of the Captain. He tried to move himself, but I placed a hand on his right shoulder, which was also wet, and shoved him as softly as possible to the floor.

"Stay there," I mumbled to him.

The Captain looked at me confused, and slightly disoriented. He truly did look sick, but he was still alert and conscious. He understood my instructions and my intentions.

"What did you do to him?" I asked the sorcerer. "I told you not—"

"Yes, you told me not to kill him. I didn't. His current state has nothing to do with me."

My fingers were still resting on the Captain's shoulder behind me. At this, I turned around and looked down at him. Why was he here?

"What is this, Prince?" the sorcerer repeated, bitingly.

I remained looking at the Captain for a few seconds. Was he here to help... or harm me? I turned around. "It's information I need."

"Information you need?" She chuckled slowly. "You mean it's information you didn't want anybody else to possess?"

"Most important information is the kind you don't wish for others to possess," I replied dryly.

The sorcerer pointed at the Captain with her other hand.

"Why don't you ask him why he's here?"

I was interested myself, but I replied, "Why don't you just say what you came here to say?"

"Don't play the fool with me Prince, not over this. If you think I'll work with you now, you're truly as insane as they say you are."

"You know this woman?" the Captain mumbled from behind me.

I ignored him. I lifted my hand off of his shoulder and stood fully in front of him now. "I don't know what you are referring to. I have no reason to lie." I tried to speak as calmly and confidently as possible.

"You have every reason to lie. How could I have expected anything different from the Vulture himself?" she spat.

I was not in the habit of placing myself in situations where I had the least amount of information. This was one of those.

It didn't seem as if she could be reasoned with.

"You've read it," I concluded. My eyes found their way to the paper in her hands.

"Yes, and so has your friend. You should have seen his reaction." She didn't sound as if she revelled in it, but it was clear by her tone the Captain had reacted poorly to its contents.

"Are you here to kill me then?" I lowered my head down slightly, and my voice.

The sorcerer didn't answer. But that was answer enough.

The Captain struggled behind me and pressed himself up against the wall. I kept my eyes on the woman.

"May I at least have the pleasure of knowing why?" I gritted my teeth as I tilted my head to the right.

She laughed coldly. "Why? *Why?* Because you're evil. I'd rather take my chances and kill you, than let you live for one more second in this world. I'm thinking your *friend* might be here for similar reasons."

I slowly turned around to the Captain who was now standing. He appeared sweaty and pale. I searched his body up and down.

"He doesn't have any weapons on him," I observed.

She winced at that, the bottom half of her face twisting in confusion.

I turned and stood back slightly, so that I was standing in between the Captain and the sorcerer, able to see them both by turning to the left and then right.

"You saw it, didn't you?" the sorcerer was addressing the Captain. "That's your Kingdom he's doomed to destruction."

I furrowed my brows deeply at that. "What?"

The sorcerer smiled. Her smile almost seemed manic, deranged. "You truly have no shame."

I looked at the Captain, but he only looked at me warily and said nothing.

I assumed the worst.

"I have no plans to harm Kalnasa," I told him firmly, meeting his eyes.

"And yet, it is your writing, your signature on this paper." The sorcerer drew my attention back to her.

I looked at Noxscroll as she waved it before her. Of course I couldn't see any text on it at all.

I tutted. "I signed no such thing."

"Is that what you were doing there, in Vasara's centre? Looking for more people to torture… to experiment on?" she said. Her voice was steely, but also full of abject despair.

This was becoming increasingly confusing and incriminating. The Captain gave me a quizzical look, his eyes betraying his doubt. His belief in whatever the sorcerer was implying was clearly becoming stronger at the revelation I had visited Vasara's draining centre.

"I was there because something is being hidden from me regarding those places and I want to know exactly what," I explained.

"From you?" the sorcerer said. Although she was employing no sorcery, there was an unmistakable air of danger all around her, a kind of destructive intent. "The orchestrator cannot also be oblivious."

"That is because I have not orchestrated anything," I said sharply. I wished now that I had worn my tunic, my jacket, which contained more hidden compartments and weapons. While I always kept my belt on for emergencies, I hadn't anticipated this turn of events, at all. All I was wearing was a thin, silky white undershirt, and the black pants and boots which had in total, five daggers attached to them.

I wasn't sure it would be enough. For me, perhaps, a very small chance, but if the Captain was attacked, he looked as if he would coil over instantly. Thinking this, I glanced at him anxiously.

"Why are you here?" I finally asked him, my voice becoming softer. The Captain looked as if he didn't know the answer himself.

"Because you signed this. A message that references the great and disturbing lengths you and your atrocious family have gone to, to make his people suffer."

I looked back at the Captain who remained silent.

"Captain...I did not—" I began.

"Who would be foolish enough to believe the words of someone like you?" the sorcerer interrupted.

Irked at her attempts to stop me from speaking to the Captain, I turned to her.

"Correct me if I'm wrong, but you yourself had done so up until a few hours ago."

"I never believed you, Prince. I only ever hoped I would survive long enough to outmanoeuvre you. But now... it seems that will be unnecessary."

"You were never this rash before," I said, taking one step forwards, to the right, towards the Captain.

"You know nothing about me, Prince."

"But you assume to know everything about me."

"Don't I? Don't I know? Wouldn't I know best?"

The woman was growing increasingly agitated, and the meaning behind her words increasingly difficult to discern.

"What are you talking about?" I asked.

The sorcerer huffed and threw the paper to the floor. "What's it to be, *Captain*...are you on his side or mine?"

I took one more step towards the Captain. "I know you have no reason to. But trust me. Please." I looked at him warily.

The sorcerer was amused. "That will be the biggest mistake he ever makes."

"You're the one who wished him dead."

"That was before I read this."

"Ahh, I see, now you wish him peace and longevity of life?"

"You have some nerve to talk about his peace, when it is you who has forced his homeland to the brink of destruction."

"I haven't." I raised my voice. The two words left my lips as sharply as the daggers at my hip might cut. "There's only so many times I can deny this."

"It doesn't matter how many times you do, I won't believe you. I won't let you hurt anymore people."

It struck me then, that I might really die here, tonight, in this room, in the dark. What a fitting end it would have been for my dark and brutal existence. What a shame, I had told Loria once, it would be, to have endured the dark all this time, only to never escape it. To have stumbled blindly through it, only to reach a dead end, to have never found a corner that was illuminated by some fleeting light.

But this was no fitting end for the Captain, and I had not yet assured Loria's safety.

"The Captain hasn't hurt anyone," I said, seriously.

"Captain?" she asked him. "What have you decided?"

The Captain didn't say anything, he only looked at me, then back at the sorcerer, but he did not move.

"I'm sorry but I can't in all good conscience, let you live now...nor you Captain, if you insist on remaining by his side."

"So, you're doing this for the greater good are you?" I snapped. "You'll only make things much worse for yourself, you won't realise that until it's too late."

"As I told you before...I'll take my chances."

I pulled the two daggers out of my belt, and swung in front of the Captain.

"Don't even think about intervening, you look terrible," I said quietly, speaking to him.

"It doesn't look like...she'll give me a choice," the Captain said coarsely.

I turned over my shoulder, "Ahh, so you can talk, I was beginning to think she—"

But before I could finish teasing the Captain, the sorcerer ran towards me. I twisted my left arm and aimed for her chest with my dagger but she, like a blur, spun around and grabbed my arm, placing it behind my back. I bent forwards and threw her over me.

As she rolled to get up, I flung a dagger at her neck. She dodged, although it scratched her ear. She used speed enhancement to rush towards me again and shove me to the floor. I grabbed a dagger from my boot and jabbed it aimlessly into the air at the blur of motion she had become. She evaded it and smacked my hand away.

I managed to hold onto the dagger and rolled to the side. She kicked me in the torso, then the face.

She was air, she was the wind that came through the window.

And how could you fight the wind?

You couldn't, but you could feel it, and you could, at times, see it.

I ran to the furnace opposite me, and grabbed a wooden log, just as a hand gripped my ankle, and swung me to the floor. I held the flame in front of me, standing up.

It blew towards the right.

I grabbed a dagger with my other hand, this time from my thigh, and jabbed to the left. I struck her in the knee.

She yelled and fell down, but very quickly regained composure, and disappeared again.

The flame flew towards me, I ducked. A blade swung over my head. But then, as I came up, an invisible gloved hand clutched at my throat. I used the arm with the dagger to stab at her hand, but I could barely move.

This was strength enhancement, her hand was squeezing my throat with a crushing power. I gasped for air, my vision was beginning to blur. It normally took around two minutes to strangle someone to death. Here, it would be a matter of a few more seconds.

The hand suddenly let go of my throat. I dropped to the ground instantly, and let out a hoarse cough, the air entering my trachea sounded like steel scraping against wood.

The Captain was standing in front of me. He had grabbed the log of fire and shoved it into the woman's face. She had raised her hand up just in time to take some of it to her palm. The glove on her right hand melted away.

Her skin bubbled and seared with burns. She yelled in intense pain, but within seconds, we watched as the skin on the bottom half of her face began to heal. The Captain staggered on his feet, looking weak.

Furious, the sorcerer sprung her hand forwards in the Captain's direction, and threw him at the back wall, beside the bed. His skull hit the bricks with a thud, and he slid downwards, blood dripping out of his mouth. His eyes were surprisingly still open, but they were dimming by the second.

I stood again. This time, stumbling towards the Captain. He looked at me drowsily, his head tilted up to do so.

"I told you not to intervene," I whispered angrily.

"You...." the Captain whispered even more quietly. "You're...welcome."

The Captain's eyelids began to close, his silver lashes brushing against his upper cheeks like a small bird's wings, fluttering in flight.

If he fell asleep, he might not wake up.

I could only think of one way to keep him awake.

This was far from ideal.

I placed my hand on his shin, where his wound was, from days ago, and squeezed down.

The Captain's eyes shot open instantly. "Agghhh," he flapped around on the ground like a dying fish. He looked at me irritated, and then...knowingly.

"I'm sorry Captain, I am, but you have to stay awake."

The sorcerer was still on the floor across from us, but she was getting up, already recovering from the singeing burns on her face and neck, the burns that would have been enough to sear the skin completely off a human being's face.

The Captain pressed his lips together and winced, clearly in pain. His eyes shot above my shoulder, and I turned around as the sorcerer approached us.

I turned to face the woman, "Look, I—"

But the sorcerer didn't let me finish. She lifted me by the arm and flung me to the right. I rolled backwards and landed in a somewhat crouched position, standing up straight afterwards.

She ran at me with the fire log and swung it at my face. I ducked backwards, and as I came back up, grabbed onto the log and shoved it to the ground. She backhanded my face with her strength enhancement, and I fell to the side, my ears ringing, and my vision blurring again.

She came up from behind me and grabbed my hair, pulling it hard so that I faced her. "I never saw you there," she said. "Why?"

"Saw...saw me where?" I asked, tasting blood in my mouth.

"Even now, in your last breaths, you lie," her voice was simmering with hatred.

"Even now, in my last breaths...I am nothing more than what people...believe me to be," I replied, laughing.

She held a blade to my neck. I grabbed the final dagger at my right hip and stabbed her in the foot.

"Aggghh," she yelled but didn't move. She simply lifted the foot up and used it to stand on the wrist I held the dagger in. The blood from the wound spurted onto my bare skin, but stopped, stopped within seconds.

How could I fight this? Fight wind that could...heal itself?

"I hope Noxos throws your soul into the deepest pits of suffering in Nevultus," she told me.

"If that's his goal, it would be more effective... if he let me live..."

"You think you have suffered? You," she spat.

She let go of my hair. The Captain was standing behind us. He'd stabbed her in the back with one of my daggers. He looked considerably worse than he had minutes ago. She reached with one hand behind her back and pulled the blade out. She swung at the Captain, but I turned, and grabbed her legs, dragging her back before she could reach him. She fell to the floor and dropped the dagger. She kicked me in the face.

She stood and with her ungloved hand, shoved the Captain hard in the chest.

But she froze, when she came into contact with his skin, the impetus behind her movements diminished.

I watched from the floor as the Captain let out a small gasp, pitiful yet painful. He clutched his head and sank to the floor. His eyes were wide, and brighter somehow, brighter than they had been moments ago, but they were full of fear, of terror.

"What have you..." I stood, beginning to address the sorcerer, but on reaching her, and grabbing her arm, she staggered back and fell to the floor. Her facial expression looked the exact same as the Captain's. The bottom half of it anyhow.

This was my chance.

I knelt on the floor and grabbed both of the woman's wrists.

"I didn't write that note. I didn't sign it. I don't know anything about experiments, or torture, or the draining centres at all. I had nothing to do with this. Which means that someone has implicated me in it. Remember. Remember this." I shook her slightly and she turned to me. I didn't know if she could fully hear or see me, but I continued.

"I could have killed you here and now, and if it is as you suspect, if I had signed that letter and committed those deeds, there would be absolutely no benefit or reason for me to let you live, but I am letting you live, because I am not responsible for these actions… and you are going to help me find out who is. You *will*." I shook her again.

She dropped back to the floor further when I let go of her wrists and looked around, but she appeared to have returned to full consciousness.

The Captain however had not.

"What did you do to him?"

She took in some shuddering breaths, then placed one hand over her mouth as if shocked. "I didn't…I didn't mean to—"

"You didn't mean to what? If he dies I—"

"I don't know…I don't…"

She stood and quickly rushed to the bed. Before I could process what she was doing, she grabbed the enolith stone I had set there and escaped out of the window.

I rushed to the Captain's side. He was still clutching his head. Sweat was now stuck to his forehead and his clothes. His body was clammy and cold.

"Captain. Captain, can you hear me?"

No response.

I grabbed one of his hands as gently as possible, but he quickly pushed it back against his temple.

"No…no…" he murmured to himself.

If this sorcerer had made the Captain lose his sanity, I would most certainly ensure she lost something in return. A finger, a hand, a leg, her tongue.

"Captain?" I addressed him again, although even I believed it was useless.

"Please…please…don't…" he whispered. He was staring at the floor as if the wood was a portal into a nightmare.

Was this an illusion? I had heard some sorcerers could conjure illusions, could conduct hypnosis, similar to that Telepath who had tried to kill the King.

If it was, there would be no way of breaking it, except possibly, for one.

"Captain, I truly am sorry…once again." My voice was still slightly hoarse from the choking.

I lifted my hand and struck him in the face, hard. He fell to the floor. His face was so pale now, that my strike had left a red print on his cheek.

I leant forwards, wrapped his left arm around my shoulder, and dragged him to my bed.

Once he was lying flat, I looked at him more carefully. I pressed the back of my hand to his forehead. It was hot. I did the same for his upper chest, which was also warm and clammy. I knelt beside the bed and slowly lifted the bottom of his pale blue trousers up, exposing his shin.

His wound was open, inflamed and healing very poorly. Someone had stitched it, but whoever had, had done a terrible job.

I sighed. My vision still hadn't fully restored, and my ears were still ringing, but even now, I could do a far better job at stitching this wound. I walked into the washroom and grabbed a towel, dousing it in cold water.

I returned and placed it on his forehead, slowly removing the errant strands of silver hair that were stuck to his face. His hair felt as silky as the garments I wore, more so. I rubbed it in between my fingers.

I shook my head and dropped the strands. I didn't have time to assess his hair's texture, or a reason to either. I still had to stitch his wound and find a way to repair the door. In hindsight, it was very impressive he had managed to kick it down in this state.

And I still hadn't figured out why he'd been so insistent on entering.

I returned to the bed and to the Captain's leg. Kneeling down beside it, I removed the stitches. The Captain, however, was a terrible patient and kept moving and jerking around in his unconscious state. It occurred to me that the illusion had in fact never ended at all, but at least he wasn't so fretful now.

Eventually, after much stopping and starting, I stitched his wound and dressed it. His wound was very warm and smelt dreadful. I'd make sure to ask the Captain who had seen to it when he awoke, so that I could have them dismissed. After all, any healer who worked this way would be better off never attending to any of the sick or poorly, ever again. It would be a service to humanity.

I chuckled to myself. It would probably be the first good thing I did for the human race.

I strode towards the door, and using the tools I had brought with me, repaired it within half an hour. I had learnt to do all manner of things as part of Sarlan's training as a child, including deconstructing and constructing a number of different objects, lock picking, cipher reading, and hinge fitting. This in particular was useful for when you needed to kick down a door that had no keyhole, but wanted to repair it before leaving, to make it seem as though you were never there at all.

Afterwards, I pulled the wide dark chair to the left side of the bed, facing the window which I left open. After all, although the room was cool, the Captain was not.

Sitting here this way, I could watch and wait to see if that woman returned.

I placed the golden cushion behind me and my feet up on the very edge of the bed. I glanced at the Captain. His pallor was still poor, his clothes still stuck to his skin with sweat, and his lips, which were normally slightly peach, were now as pale as his hair.

I leant forwards and lifting the cloth, felt his forehead again. Now, it was frozen cold.

I gathered some spare blankets the servants had left in the wardrobes and placed them on top of the Captain's body. He was shivering slightly. I walked over to the fire and rekindled it, allowing the flame to grow brighter and the room warmer. Eventually a faint orange glow from the fire cast itself across the darkened room. It struck the Captain's face softly, colouring it near gold. The sweat on it almost looked like stars.

I had done all I could.

Against all odds, the Captain and myself were still alive.

And now, I had to make sure that we remained that way.

## CHAPTER 51- HESTAN

I jerked awake. My face was turned to the right, my eyes quickly found a window.

This wasn't my window.

I propped myself up on my elbows but found it difficult to move. I looked down at myself. I was in a bed. I was covered in blankets, and near my feet there were two dark boots against the frame.

I sat up slightly, and as I did, turned to the left.

In a chair, with his eyes closed, was Audra's Prince.

He was clutching a dagger tightly to his chest. He was still wearing the white shirt, but now he had placed a dark jacket over his shoulders as well.

I...couldn't remember much. I tried to collect my thoughts, staring at the blankets as if they would provide me with the answers.

Fragments of memories returned to me. Fragments of the past.

She had touched my skin, and I had seen it, again, as if I were there, as if I were inside my body, all those years ago. I felt now, the way I had felt immediately afterwards, at the time my village had been attacked.

The years had passed, but the pain had not.

But I was still alive, and so was the Prince. Somehow, he had defeated her. I knew he was an impressive fighter, but still, that woman could have killed us both with ease. It had seemed to me, moments before I lost consciousness, that both mine, and the Prince's deaths were inevitable.

I turned around, expecting to see him asleep. But the Prince had one eye open, smiling slightly.

"You're awake."

I didn't see the point in confirming that. It seemed to me the Prince had most likely been awake this whole time himself.

He took his boots off the frame and sat forwards in his chair, pulling it closer towards the bed. He reached towards me. I backed away unconsciously.

"What are you so concerned about, Captain? If I'd wanted to kill or hurt you, why let you sleep here?"

"Why did you let me sleep here?" I asked, still keeping myself away from him slightly.

He reached out again insistently. "Because I do not want to kill or hurt you...evidently."

He pressed his hand against my forehead. It was surprisingly cold.

"You still have a mild fever, but it's better than before," he said thoughtfully, leaning back.

I swallowed. "I don't...understand..."

"The woman touched you, you...saw something, you couldn't move. That combined with the awful state you were in when you got here meant I had no choice but to let you stay."

That wasn't true. The Prince could easily have dragged me back to my room or let me die.

"Where did she go?"

"She left. It seems that touching you affected her as well," he looked at me cautiously, and I could see the hidden question in his eyes.

"Why did you come here, Captain?"

There it was.

"Why did you break my door down in the middle of the night, while you were clearly unwell, especially if what that woman said is true, and you possessed information that made it seem...as if I bore ill intent towards you?"

I shifted uncomfortably in the bed. It was strange to know I had been lying in the sheets the Prince had been. They even smelt like him faintly, an earthy musk, tinged with sweetness.

"It made no sense to me," I explained, "that you would sign something so secretive and important with your own initials. I do not know you well but...it struck me as...unlikely."

He raised an eyebrow. "So, you came here to...?"

"To warn you."

"You came here to warn me?"

"Yes." I recalled parts of the conversation between him and the sorcerer. "But it seems as if you already knew about this woman's...activities."

"I confess," the Prince said gently, "that I knew she would be visiting you. It was me who asked her to steal that paper from you. I knew that you had some. Your questions about Noxstone lead me to that conclusion. But I swear, I had no idea of its contents, nor did I ask her to harm you."

I nodded slowly, believing him for some reason. That did not explain how they had met, however.

"How do you know her, Your Highness?" I remembered to address him by his title, ashamed by the fact I had forgotten up until now, until I was fully awake.

"You're lying in my bed, in your underclothes. I've practically fussed over you like an adoring wife all night. Don't you think we're past *Your Highness*?" He smirked a little.

"You are still a Prince," I told him, frowning.

Fussing over me like an adoring wife all night? From a chair? With his eyes closed? Whether he was asleep or awake, that woman could have returned and slit my throat in an instant before he could even react. He hadn't even closed the window.

He shrugged. "As you wish." He crossed his left leg over his right knee. "So why did you want to warn me?"

I frowned again. I hadn't thought too much about that. I'd only had seconds to decide what to do. It was clear to me the sorcerer who had taken and read the message was greatly disturbed by its contents as well, and since anyone would be able to ascertain, or guess what 'N.A.' stood for, warning the Prince that someone might be coming to find or potentially harm him had seemed...

"It seemed like the right thing to do, Your Highness."

"Are you always guided by your morals, over intelligent reason?"

I said nothing. I was exhausted, from the fighting, and the visions I had seen, and the wound.

The wound.

I looked at him sharply. He raised his eyebrows interested in my sudden change of mood.

"It was you," I said.

"It was me?" He squinted and placed two hands behind his head.

"My leg," I replied. I was beginning to find talking more tiring by the minute.

"Yes, it was me that stitched your wound. Who stitched it before by the way? Was it a healer?"

"No," I spoke over him, raising my voice. "That is not what I meant, Your Highness."

I had only a faint suspicion before with the lunar, and the familiarity of that figure, but as soon as the Prince had squeezed my shin to keep me awake...it had been confirmed.

"In the alleyway...it was you," I finished, leaning my head back against the headboard as I did.

The Prince's face changed in an instant. I had never seen him look so...dejected.

He laughed lightly and closed his eyes, leaning his own head back against the chair. "I hoped that your spell of insanity and unconsciousness might eradicate that particular detail from your memory."

I said nothing.

The Prince licked his lips slowly, then let out a deep sigh. His eyes were still closed. "Let's not speak on it."

"But you—" I started.

"Captain—" he sighed.

"I do not understand, Your Highness. You...you could have stopped him easily yourself."

The Prince opened his eyes and shrugged, smiling, but there was no smile in his eyes. "Maybe I didn't want him to."

I looked at him incredulously. "I was there, Your Highness. I know what I saw."

The Prince licked his lips again. "Captain... I won't ask what you saw when that sorcerer touched you, and in return, you will ask me no more about this." He clasped his hands together in front of him and looked down at the floor.

I thought about it.

"I saw something from my past...but it was...different."

I had seen that day. The day my family and my village were butchered. I had tasted it, smelt it, felt it. But instead of being a child, I was an adult, as I was now, and as well as the bodies of my family, there had been other bodies as well, the faces of which I could not see.

The Prince laughed. "Captain, that's not fair."

"You do not have to tell me anything in return. But I saw some of what you wished to remain secret, Your Highness, and so..."

"So, in return you are offering me this piece of information?"

"Yes...if it will help you to feel less...exposed."

The Prince smiled genuinely this time and shook his head in surprise. Then he smiled with his lips closed. "Captain, for your own safety, you must pretend you did not see what was written on that piece of paper. I read it myself while you were sleeping. I can understand why you would wish to act upon it...but, whether you believe me or not, I had nothing to do with the events and actions that are written upon it and—"

"I do," I interrupted him.

The Prince looked up at me, in the middle of drawing breath.

"I do believe you, Your Highness," I told him.

The Prince's brows relaxed. "And I am grateful for that, but as I was saying, I do not know who is responsible. It is likely that if the person or people who are, discover you read this, you will die."

"And if I do nothing?" I shook my head, examining the rings on my hand. "I cannot stand by and watch these events unfold, knowing this information, even if it means risking my own life."

Kalnasa was a target, for something grander than I could probably understand. There were people there, good people, honest people, people I cared for, people I had grown up with. I had already lost so many of them in my youth, on that day. I could not do so again.

The Prince stood, looming over me now, coming closer to the bed. "You don't understand, Captain. You don't know these people like I do."

I thought of the man who had pressed him against that alleyway wall. What kind of people did this Prince know, was he forced to know?

"It doesn't matter, Your Highness, I must—"

"It doesn't matter?" He leant forwards, placing his palms on the sheets. "Your life, Captain, it doesn't matter?"

I gulped, suddenly, inexplicably, unsettled.

"In relation to this, if what is written on that piece of paper holds any truth, then no, my life cannot compare in terms of importance."

The Prince tutted and lifted his hands off the bed. "You're too stubborn, Captain. This will be the death of you."

"With respect, Your Highness, if Kalnasa falls, it will also be the death of me."

The Prince tilted his head to the window, sighing. "It's easy to watch those who are undeserving take a path that is damned. It's easy to turn away when it's a stranger, but when it's someone who is deserving, who is not a stranger, it is not..." He trailed off.

I frowned, peering at him curiously. How many people had the Prince watched walk to their own damnation, simply for the fact he had felt them deserving of it? How many had he stopped? Had he ever stood on that path, sheltering another from its cold clutches? What would it take for him to see someone as deserving of that intervention?

Was it not better to save a person, afford them another chance, than to forfeit their life? How many lives were wasted this way? Simply for the fact they had strayed, with no one to guide them back?

But... how many lives were lost, for the saving of those who had never deserved that chance? For the hope of redemption, crushed by the unrelenting nature of another's soul? A soul that would go forth to bring others pain?

It was up to ourselves, to find our way back when we were lost. Salvation in the form of intervention was never guaranteed. And to return, we must be willing to, to claw through the winds to reach the peak, shelter or no.

Could the Prince see then, what I could not? Could he sense whether that desire truly lay in another's heart? Had his time watching from the shadows of those roads, observing passersby, taught him how to notice?

Could anyone truly tell? Even of themselves?

Perhaps it was something one could only know after turning around, to find they were either climbing that mountain, or had slipped down the more alluring paths of darkness.

If I looked over my own shoulder, what would I find?

Did I even wish to look?

"You still look pale," the Prince declared. "You should rest some more. I'll find you something to eat. You should drink some water as well."

Fussing over me like an adoring wife now strangely felt like an accurate statement.

"Your Highness, I don't wish to trouble you any further, I—"

"Stop talking, Captain." He had his back turned to me, pouring water into a mug. "I can hear it's exhausting you. Your breathing has changed."

It was, and it had, but still, talking was the only thing keeping me from falling asleep, and falling asleep in the Prince's bed again, was not a part of my plans.

"Someone...ensured that I received the paper."

The Prince turned back around with the water. "What do you mean?"

"They made sure that only I would know, only I would see. I don't know who they were, they were cloaked"— I squinted thinking — "in the same way that woman was."

The Prince reached the chair and passed me the water. I took it from him. My smallest finger grazed his first as I did, where his grip encircled the bottom of the cup. I withdrew my hand quickly, wishing to avoid touching him further. My palms were clammy, I could feel.

The Prince noticed the rapidity of my action. It almost appeared as if he were about to smile but decided against it. His aurous eyes were distant and thoughtful as he leant back again, trained on my face with rapt regard. He sat back in the chair.

I turned away from him, sipping some of the drink, feeling unsettled once again.

The Prince was silent for a moment, before asking. "If it were sorcerers, then why didn't that one know?"

"She could be acting alone?"

"She definitely isn't. She had an enolith."

"An enolith, Your Highness?"

"So, you didn't know? It's—"

"No, Your Highness, I do. It's only that they're quite rare."

"Ah." He flicked his eyebrows up and down.

"You didn't know what an enolith was, Your Highness?"

The Prince turned to me with a look that said, "*Oh?*"

"It's stranger that you did, isn't it?" he asked, neither confirming nor denying his knowledge.

"I couldn't say, Your Highness," I replied.

"I'm not sure there's anything you couldn't do, Captain." He pointed to the entrance to his room. "How did you even manage to break that down?"

I looked up at the intact door. I'd assumed I'd imagined taking it off its hinges in my fever induced delirium.

"How did you repair it?"

The Prince winked at me, "I couldn't say." He grinned for a moment, watching my reaction, which was non-existent. His face resumed a more serious air as he asked, "So, do you think whoever passed that message onto you knew you?"

"Why do you ask... Your... Highness?" My drowsiness was beginning to increase.

"Because of your...nature." He waved at me. "The kind of person who won't give up on seeking justice."

"It's possible," I admitted.

"I think it's highly likely. Someone you knew, who intercepted this information, and believed you would have the means, and will, to act upon it. Somehow who knew you well, it seemed."

I shook my head in confusion. "I cannot think of anyone like that…Your Highness, and I didn't recognise her."

"It was a woman?" He shifted, turning in his seat slightly.

I nodded, to avoid speaking further.

"So, someone, or a group of people in Audra want Kalnasa to fall. I wonder if the riots were initiated by the same people." The Prince looked at the ceiling.

"The food shortage is real. The Hunt hasn't been able to find food sources for years." I thought about those mornings, those people who had fallen in the efforts to feed the hungry. I hadn't been able to stop thinking about them, since I'd heard of the riots.

"Is it?" the Prince asked. "What if…someone was taking that game first, before your Hunt could?" His golden eyes brimmed with thought.

"That…wouldn't be possible, the terrain is…brutal and difficult."

The Prince sighed. "Captain, it would not be hard… for people like me… to adapt to it." He paused between each part of his sentence, as if he regretted uttering the words. "Or sorcerers," he added.

"People like you, Your Highness?" I asked, but I knew what he meant. Assassins, spies, soldiers who worked in the shadows.

"Audra…Audra hones them, they are… instruments of death."

"Is that how you would describe yourself?" I peered at him.

The Prince laughed. "I'm the conductor, Captain, of the whole orchestra."

His nonchalance about the statement, made it far less convincing to me somehow.

"But you saved my life. You can pretend you did not…but" — I swallowed through my dry mouth — "you could easily have let me die. You haven't saved me for my utility, since you just tried to dissuade me from assisting you, or pursuing this further, Your…Highness." Breathing was becoming more difficult.

"Don't make the mistake of believing me a good person, Captain," the Prince grumbled.

"Not a good person, Your Highness, just… not an evil one," I sighed out the last words as a weak breath.

The Prince let out a soft huff, studying me carefully.

I had wondered, since the day I had first met the Prince on that riverbank, if he was as cruel, as cold hearted as people claimed. I had certainly received plenty of evidence that he was not a giving, generous, or selfless person. But I had not felt that he was cruel, or craven, or evil, that he enjoyed hurting others, or that he took pleasure in it.

I had sensed that he was dangerous, yes, but not malicious.

"You must be the only soul in Athlion, the Nine Divine Realms, and the Nevultus pits that thinks so." The Prince chuckled and looked at me again.

"Then I am the only person, Your Highness."

The Prince squinted then leant forwards again. "You're ill, I've heard that a fever and blood loss can make someone's cognitive reasoning poorer."

"My cognitive reasoning is intact."

"Evidently not," he replied.

"You restitched my wound—"

"I was the reason you acquired it, as well as the reason you have a fever, and are unwell in the first place," he said flatly.

"Would an evil person, a conductor of death, particularly care?" I asked, my eyes were growing heavy now.

"Captain?" The Prince noticed my eyes closing.

"Why…why did you want something green?" I asked quietly. I could barely hear my own voice. It was such an insignificant question. I would never have thought to ask it at another time, but now, half conscious, the question burst into my mind, and apparently, straight out of my mouth.

"Do you want it back?" the Prince's voice was teasing.

"It's not mine, Your…Highness." My eyes were fully closed now.

"The King told Loria it was his favourite colour," the Prince said with a mocking pride.

I laughed, my chest rising and falling in one quick motion.

I opened my eyes, startled. I hadn't laughed for…years.

The Prince seemed equally surprised. "I didn't know that you *could* smile, Captain."

"It's…I just suspected something more…interesting."

"It *is* interesting, isn't it? Do you remember when he asked her to stay behind at the ceremony? It was, in part, to look at that necklace. It might have seemed insignificant, but such things can capture the attention of others. Necklaces, clothes, bracelets," he paused. "Rings." I could hear the smile in his voice on the final word. "Don't you agree?" he asked.

"They hardly seem…the most interesting things about a person." I turned my head to face him, opening my eyes again with great effort.

"But they can enhance certain features. A neckline, a waist, legs, wrists… hands."

"I suppose I'll trust you, Your Highness."

"Why do you wear rings if not for that purpose, Captain?"

Is that what he assumed I wore them for?

"They…" I looked down at them. "They mean something. Each one. Some of them belonged to my family, others were gifts, Your Highness."

"Your family are—"

"Gone." I was still looking down at my hands.

"I see." He sounded thoughtful.

"Was it true...that story...about...the...time you...saw..."

I was growing increasingly fatigued, and apparently, increasingly unable to withhold my curiosity. The Prince was probably right, my cognitive reasoning must have been worsening.

"Yes, that was true, and my wish was fulfilled."

"Your wish? Your... Highness?"

"I got to see you fight, Captain, see how you move, how you wield your weapon, even if it was in that...location."

"I—" I started trying to speak.

"It was a sight to behold. I doubt I'll forget it."

"Your Highness...perhaps I... should return... to—"

"No, Captain. Sleep. Here."

My eyelids fluttered, desperately trying to remain open.

"I'll watch over you," the Prince said to me.

"And who...who... will watch... over you Your... Highness?"

The Prince ignored my question "If you insist on not forgetting what you saw, on taking action...what will you do, Captain?"

I could barely speak now. I was beginning to feel lightheaded and sweaty once again. I tried to formulate a sentence but only managed to blurt out one word.

"You."

A fragment of the statement I had intended to say.

"You will do...me?" the Prince said, sounding equally concerned and amused at my weak answer.

"Help...you."

"You want to help me?" he asked.

"Mmm-hmm." I nodded, closing my eyes again.

A shuffle of feet travelled through the air and then the Prince's hand was on my forehead. Again.

"It's getting worse," he muttered to himself.

His hand was so cool, and my forehead was so warm.

Without thinking, half delirious from the fever again, I raised my hand, and grabbed his wrist, holding his cold hand against my warm, burning skin.

I sighed as his ice-cold fingers touched my face. I could hear the faint sound of a voice in my head telling me I was being audacious and inappropriate. I shot my eyes open, realising my mistake.

I dropped my hand. "Apologies... I..."

But the Prince stayed where he was and left his hand on my forehead. He looked at me strangely, as if he were frightened of me.

"Does it... help?" he asked quietly.

"I..." I was too weak to formulate a reply.

In response, he pressed his hand tighter into my forehead, and placed another one, equally as cold, at the side of my neck. I, inadvertently, let out a relieved sigh. I could hear the blankets move and feel a weight next to me. The Prince had sat down.

"At least there are no rings on *my* hands." The voice was much closer to me now, rumbling in my left ear.

I was drifting into sleep.

"Rest, Captain. Nobody will touch you."

I leant, whether from the sickness, the fatigue, or the fever, into his cold hands, and did as he asked.

And I had a feeling, now that we had survived this night, that we had resolved to uncover the meaning behind those hidden words, that it would not be the last time I did.

As I sank deeper towards sleep, I felt the Prince use one of his hands to remove strands of hair from my face.

And as I slipped into unconsciousness, I heard him whisper, to me, or to himself, I could not tell.

"It *does* have hues of blue."

# CHAPTER 52- NEMINA

I recognised that face.

I recognised it, when I had touched the Captain's chest, when I had seen that death, those people cutting down those children, the smoke. I had recognised her face.

She was screaming, she was pleading, begging them for mercy, but they had been laughing, laughing as her blood splattered across their clothes, as her body was mutilated.

I didn't know how. I didn't remember how, but I recognised her face.

I had been staring at my own hand for the past hour.

I had made it back to my hideout. Somehow, I had stumbled, dragged myself, barely managing to maintain my translucency, all the way back here. The enolith was glowing again in my palm, red, dark crimson, the colour of blood.

I didn't even have the time to think about how I had left those two men alive. Perhaps it was good they were still breathing. Perhaps I had acted too impulsively but now, two people, two important people, if that Prince had been telling the truth, knew that I was here, in Vasara. They knew I was a sorcerer.

I had heard his words, as he gripped my wrists and shook them. I had heard them, and I could not, despite trying, formulate a reason why the Prince would spare my life, other than the possibility that he was actually innocent.

Had I been about to kill an innocent man?

I huffed and shook my head. No, the Prince may not have been responsible for that note, but he was far from an innocent man.

But I recalled, as I sat on the ground and time passed, I recalled that day when I had been selected for transfer from Audra, when that noble woman, cloaked in black and silver, had come to personally view me, as if I were an animal. I remembered she had reprimanded Marco for speaking to 'her son' who she said had known 'nothing.'

And it all seemed so obvious to me at that moment, how very wrong I had been.

But the thought that Baz, that people I had seen, had spoken to, even for a few moments, had suffered that way, made me sick, it made me...irrational.

There was a part of me that knew I was not well equipped to deal with these decisions, to deal with these revelations, but if not me...then who? Audra's Prince had not even known about this plot. If we did nothing, what hope did we have for survival? At all?

And what would come after that? If we should succeed? A life? I didn't know what that was. Learning to live, after years of just surviving would feel like learning to breathe after years of drowning. I knew the air would burn lungs used to water. That somehow, there was a bliss in the kiss of suffocation to me.

Was that why I had decided to fight in the end? Was my sense of justice truthfully a veil, for a deeper sense of fear? A fear of living. Fighting was all I knew. I'd turned fighting into my religion. Survival into my sanctuary, a siren I slowly got addicted to.

And now, I couldn't stop listening.

The revelation rose upon me with my energy. It was time, to discard these thoughts for now, and move. I had regained enough strength, enough power, to use the enolith. I clasped my hands around it and reached out.

But I didn't need to reach far.

Someone was close. Someone had already followed me here, and they were in possession of this stone's counterpart. I could feel it.

*Hello?* I said down the stone.

*Nemina? Is that you?*

It was Baz's voice.

*You shouldn't have come,* I said.

*You've been silent for over a week,* he replied.

*Where are you?* he asked.

*Go back.* I didn't answer his question.

*They want you to come back.*

I furrowed my brows, and stood, for no reason in particular.

*Why? It's not completely done yet.*

*They didn't expect it to be complete, but they want you to come back. It's too dangerous now. Things have changed since you left.*

I gripped the stone tighter.

*What things?*

*Just tell me where you are, then I'll tell you.*

As much as I wanted to stay here, and see this through, I'd already had my fill of impulsive decisions for one day, and I was exhausted, too exhausted to fight, or to talk, or to argue.

*Are you alone?* I put to him.

Silence for a few seconds.

*No. There's a Teleporter with me.*

A Teleporter? That was a massive risk. Despite teleportation's lower class, it was the ability that gave off the most energy, the most easily detectable energy. If trackers were around, and they sensed someone teleporting, that would not go unnoticed.

*You can't teleport here.*

*We have to.*

They were here for me. The longer they looked, the more at risk they would become.

*Use the stone as the location, a Teleporter can do it,* I instructed him. At least, I had been told this before, by Nyla.

Moments later, the air in front of me began to blur, similarly to the way the environment may look behind the distortion of a flame. Only then, a small, dark red light bloomed at its centre. It spread out further and further until the circle was a door, and through that door, stepped Baz...and a woman.

The portal closed behind them, and before I had the chance to ask who the woman was, Baz ran towards me and...hugged me.

I lifted my arms up in the air, uncomfortable. It wasn't Baz who made me uncomfortable, but the touching and the closeness he had thrown upon me.

"I thought...I was worried you might be dead," he said into my shoulder.

"You..." I was about to tell him that he was being ridiculous, then thought back to my actions a few hours ago.

That, and the woman watching us, made me play along.

"I'm not."

Baz let go of me and looked at me oddly. "I know that now but...still."

I patted his upper arm awkwardly. Having to pretend we were a couple in front of other people was draining. I smiled slightly at him, but he was too perceptive for me.

"What happened, Nemina?" He sounded upset.

"We need to leave first. We can't risk being found here."

Baz nodded and took my hand. It was an effort not to snatch it away, but the woman's gaze lingered on us.

"Who are you?" I asked her, frowning as I realised it had sounded cold.

"I'm Faina," she replied.

"She's nice," Baz said, trying to reassure me. Faina smiled slightly at his words.

She seemed the kind of person Baz should have been spending his time around, not me.

"Great," I said. "Thank you for the..." I made a circular motion in the air.

She nodded, meekly, then repeated the teleportation process.

This time we were shoved onto a pile of dark...sand, that seemed blacker than bronze under the night sky.

Sand. We were on sand.

There was only one Kingdom where sand existed.

I stood and looked down at my feet, my breathing quickened immediately.

Of all the draining centres I had been dragged to, Audra's had been the worst by far. Tapping into memories of the place felt like flicking thin ice layered over a frigid lake, ready to crack and swallow me at the slightest intrusion.

I could not go back there again.

I would not go back.

"Baz...?" I looked at him, pulling down my hood. I could see without it, but it suddenly felt stifling.

He came over to me and placed his hands on my shoulders. "Don't panic, we're not staying here for long. We aren't—"

"Why are we here at all?" I asked, fretfully.

"We're meeting someone."

Suddenly, an intense suspicion seized my thoughts. Was this really Baz? Was that woman really an ally? What if...they were illusions? What if, whatever had happened to me when I had touched that Captain was still affecting me?

I stepped back from him, my boots crunching into the golden grit beneath me.

"No...no, you...he wouldn't bring me here...he wouldn't."

"I'm sorry..." He sounded remorseful. "I didn't want to but—"

He reached out to me, but I pushed him away. The woman behind him, Faina, was watching us, wide eyed, and anxious.

"No. Don't touch me. Who are you?"

"Nemina...it's me."

"That's...no..." I sounded erratic, I could hear. It was difficult to, on one hand, be able to tell I was panicking, and on the other, believe the reason for my suspicion was justified.

That paper, that paper had come from here, that message.

I wouldn't go back. I wouldn't.

I lifted a blade out from my cloak and held it to my own throat.

"What?" His voice rose frantically "Nemina...what.... what are you doing, put...put it down! It's me! It's me!"

I looked at him, and at the woman, who was approaching me slowly as well.

"You're not taking me back there."

"I'm not! I...nobody's taking you back anywhere...I told you, it's me, and we're here to meet someone and talk, that's all, then we're going back."

"Back? Back where?"

"Remember...I said that something had changed? We were attacked on the border of Kalnasa. Vasara it's too dangerous, and Zeima... it's too far, and they're still searching Jurasa after last time, but...but we...we're in Kalnasa now. It's not good there. It's too crowded. We only came here to meet someone in private...and—"

"Meet who?"

Baz looked behind my shoulder and straightened up. "I'm sorry...she's..." he said to someone behind me.

I whipped around, dragging my hood over my face as I did. I stretched the blade out in front of me, wincing at the movement. The Captain's stab in the back hadn't fully healed, I hadn't been able to extract the fragmented parts of the blade out of my flesh.

"The same as usual," a displeased voice emerged from a blue wave. Ullna stepped out of the portal along with Yaseer and two figures behind them I did not recognise. One of them was the Teleporter, a tanned woman with a dark braid, who closed it behind her. The other was a tall figure, a man, heavily cloaked, his face hidden.

I squeezed the handle of the blade tighter and said nothing.

"She thinks that this is a trap," Baz explained quietly.

"If she were so particularly worried about a trap, she wouldn't have been so careless," Ullna replied.

I glanced at the four figures in front of me, trying to understand what was happening. Ullna's figure stepped forwards.

"We have a Navigator in Vasara, there for entirely different reasons. But, just hours ago, they communicated to us with their enolith, which *they* managed to keep on their person, that they had sensed a large wave of energy coming from the Palace. Acciperean energy."

I gulped.

"We've had to extract every agent from within the city, because of your stupidity." She came closer, completely undeterred by the dagger I was holding.

"Ullna," Yaseer said to her calmly, "This is not the time."

Ullna scoffed and pointed at me. "What did you do, girl?"

I kept my blade in my hand and remained silent...I wasn't even sure what it was I had done, how to answer that question.

"Please...she's—" Baz started.

"Quiet," Ullna said to him, "Answer me," she demanded.

My mind was both empty and addled. I still hadn't decided whether or not I trusted what I was seeing. The pain in my back was growing sharper, and memories of what I 'had done' were tormenting and confusing me, all at once.

"I...I don't know—"

"What do you mean you don't know? Any Navigator or Tracker could have sensed it, something that large and powerful and yet you...do...not...know?" She stepped closer to me again.

I stepped back.

Yaseer spoke softly. "This is not an illusion, Nemina."

I glanced at him. "Here...Here?"

"Nemina...please..." Baz approached me from the side.

I looked at him, through the cloak, still holding the blade in front of me.

"Nemina," he whispered.

I bit my lips so hard I could feel the skin begin to bleed.

"How am I supposed to know?" I asked.

"Why...is she like this?" the woman who teleported the others asked quietly.

"This is normal," Ullna sounded disappointed.

I turned to face her. My eyes darted between everyone. They were all looking at me cautiously, except for the cloaked man, who remained far behind, whose eyes I could not see.

"How else would we know all of this?" Ullna said.

"You just said it yourself, my...I...whatever I did set off an alarm. So, for all I know, this is an illusion, set by them...and I'm not going back there. I'm not."

"What is she talking about?" the woman with the braid said.

It seemed I was making less and less sense to people. And to myself.

"Don't you think a tracker would already have attempted to apprehend you? Employed the powers of several sorcerers to do so?" Ullna asked again.

"I wouldn't know, I can't remember the first time!" I shouted and jabbed my hand forwards to make my point.

I hissed through my teeth as I did, and bent forwards, winded.

"Nemina?" Baz came closer to me.

I stumbled back and stood again.

"We don't have time for this," Ullna said. "Do it," she said to Yaseer.

Yaseer sighed. "This is not the best course of action."

"We cannot linger." Ullna turned to look at him, her words snapped in the air.

Baz came closer to me now. "Nemina, I know you're frightened, and you don't want to be here. Neither do I, alright? But we need to hurry, otherwise we'll all end up dead, ok? Didn't we say that we were going to be allies? Come on, don't leave me here alone."

Each breath I took ached, causing a crushing sharp pain in the back of my lungs which was worsening with each inhale.

Baz's hands were in a pacifying position in the air. I looked at him and could feel my lips quivering slightly. This night had been too much. Too long. Too hard.

"Were you one of them?" I asked him suddenly.

"One..." Baz side eyed Ullna and Yaseer. "One of who?"

"One of the people...I heard screaming."

Baz's face fell, and became so serious, so cold, that I was almost sure in that moment I was in fact, in an illusion. It looked nothing like him at all.

"This is bad, Yaseer, her mind—" Ullna started.

"How did you know?" Baz asked, cutting her off.

Ullna stopped speaking, and I could see her shocked expression out of the corner of my eye.

It was so quiet here, so still. There was only a warm, musty breeze, drifting over the sand, scattering it against our clothes.

But in this moment, in this stillness, everything had shifted.

"So, it's true," I said, and put my arm down.

"What is true, boy? You had better explain," Ullna shouted.

But Baz and I were looking at each other, so intently, that her voice had blended into the breeze for us.

Only he and I knew, only he and I had memories that seemed to rest in the very sand beneath our feet, seemed to torment us from below, where Audra's draining centre lay.

Baz looked down at that sand, his eyes were so lifeless.

"Why didn't you—"

"Because I have nowhere else," he said.

Where else could an escaped Vessel go? Let alone one who was once human? He would be too dangerous for non-magic wielders. Too useless for the sorcerers. He had been afraid, I understood, that if this group discovered his truth, they would have discarded him. Perhaps they'd try to now.

Suddenly, I couldn't see.

I lifted my blade up again, gasping.

"What are you doing?" Baz asked someone.

Yaseer's voice rang out. "She is too unstable—"

I couldn't see. How couldn't I see?

"What have you done to me?" I waved my blade around in the air.

"It is only temporary Nemina. Please, relax," Yaseer replied.

*Relax? Fucking relax?*

"We cannot have you harm someone," Ullna said.

Is that what they thought? That I was dangerous? That I was some wild beast they had to cage. To chain like the creatures of sorcery bound to each Kingdom.

"No...let me see, don't—"

"Can't you see this is making it worse?!" Baz shouted.

The pain in my back throbbed, so intensely I let out a cry, and fell to the ground.

"Nemina!" Baz shouted.

"We don't have the time for this!" Ullna shouted again, "Baz...use your abilities, put her to sleep."

Ullna's voice became higher in pitch as she addressed someone. "What...where are you going?"

Someone's footsteps sounded from my right. They were quick and light, but purposeful.

Their owner knelt beside me. I tried to move away but they placed a hand on my shoulder. I jerked and slapped it away.

"Don't...don't touch me," I said to the mysterious figure in the air.

"Move away from her!" Ullna shouted at the person.

Completely ignoring her, the person spoke. "Where does it hurt?"

It was a man's voice, cool and soft. It was a voice I did not recognise.

Meaning, that it had to be the cloaked figure who until now, had been surveying this scene from a distance.

I didn't know whether to laugh or cry at his question.

*Where does it hurt? Everywhere. Every muscle, every bone, every tendon, every corner of my mind, my chest.*

I let out a weak laugh, that sounded as if it was brimming with the promise of tears.

"She's dangerous, can't you see!" Ullna said, coming closer.

The person sounded as if he rotated around. He didn't say anything, but for some unknown reason, Ullna became quiet, and backed away.

"Let her see," he said.

Yaseer sighed. In the next moment, my vision became clearer. The figure next to me was tall, and his cloak, now I could see it more clearly, was not black, but dark grey.

I looked up at him. He had a hood on near identical to mine, only darker. He reached out slowly towards my own.

I jerked away.

"Don't—" Ullna started, but the man turned around to face her. She swallowed and gritted her teeth, instantly silencing once again.

The man's hand was hovering by my face, "May I?" he asked.

Unfortunately, I could think of no-good reason to refuse, and I was keen to keep my five senses.

I didn't speak, and the man took that as confirmation.

His hand was ungloved, it was pale, slender, but muscular, and long. It was unadorned but looked smooth. He was probably not an ordinary member of this group, whose hands were all cut, bruised, calloused, and dirty.

As I was evaluating his origins, his hand made contact with the crimson fabric of my hood, and slowly drew it back.

Everyone gasped, except for the man, who remained silent.

I avoided looking at them and focused on the upper part of the man's chest, trying my best to avoid looking at his pointed chin.

"Your skin..." Baz said.

Yes, my skin was still healing from the burns I had suffered.

"It's..." I laughed and glanced at Baz's feet. "It's far from the worst thing I've experienced."

Baz's hand was over his mouth. I dreaded to think how I appeared. My eyes were cast down. I didn't wish to see the horror in their glances.

A hand came to rest at my chin. It was the man's hand. He held it with his index finger and thumb, and slowly, tried to tilt my face up. I tried to resist him.

"It's far from the worst thing I've seen," he said, echoing my words, in a tone that was only ever used when people were trying to comfort another person.

Not that I had heard such a tone very often.

I let out a shuddering breath, and let him guide my face upwards.

He stopped, his jaw clenched, his thumb pressed ever so slightly harder into my chin.

"Can you...?" Ullna said, directing her statement at the man.

*Can you what?*

I moved my eyes in her direction briefly, then looked back at the man, who still seemed tense. "So much for being 'not the worst thing you've ever seen'," I grumbled.

"It is not that," he said quietly.

He moved his hand up so that it came towards my cheek.

His hand had been on my face for a long time. I didn't have good experiences with people touching my face.

Unconsciously, I jerked away again.

"He's trying to help you," Ullna said, surprisingly softly.

"I'm..." I glanced back at him. His hand was hovering over the left side of my face now, which had been burnt.

He sat there patiently, not demanding anything, just waiting.

"I'm just not...I don't..." I stuttered.

Ullna scoffed. Again.

Baz tutted. "Is it so hard for you to guess why?" He sounded angry.

Ullna crossed her arms and said nothing.

The man moved so that he was fully in front of me now, blocking Ullna out of my view. He was crouching, his knees bent.

I didn't move. I examined his face, where his eyes might have been. I knew he was looking into mine, despite not being able to see his.

I nodded yes.

His fingers moved up my left jaw and rested there, his thumb softly pressed against my cheek, next to my nose. It was difficult for me not to shudder at the touch, from its unfamiliarity, and the pain it caused.

"I know," he said, "But it won't be long."

Within a few seconds, my face started to feel warm, but gently so. It prickled in the way the sun probably felt against people's skin, people who were used to its light, and could stand its heat. He withdrew his hand seconds later.

I reached up with my own and touched my face. It was completely smooth and healed. It hadn't just been my cheek, but my lips and the eyelids and the hair on that side too, that had been singed.

I understood then.

"Healer," I whispered.

He nodded.

"Where else?" he asked.

"Aren't we supposed to be discussing—" the woman with the braid said.

"That can wait," the man in front of me answered. Again, the woman was instantly silent.

I regarded him, squinting. How was it that he commanded so much authority?

"My back," I said quietly.

He moved around to my side and placed his hand on my shoulder blade.

After touching it, he drew it back almost instantly, and came to my side.

Without asking for permission this time, he grabbed my chin, and looked at my face much more deeply.

"What...let go of me," I said, but it wasn't his touch distressing me now, more his demeanour.

"What's the matter?" Ullna stepped closer to us.

"Who attacked you?" the man asked me, his voice was still soft, but now, it was pressing.

"I..." I hadn't planned on telling them.

"What is—" Ullna started.

But the man answered, his voice raised so everyone could hear.

"She has Noxstone in her back."

# CHAPTER 53- NEMINA

I didn't know what it meant, when Ullna and Yaseer looked at each other as if they had just heard the world was about to burn, when Baz, even Baz, looked mortified.

Noxstone. It must have been the material the Prince's daggers were made from, the ones that looked different from other blades. The same steel I had used to kill Karl.

That must have been why, why this wound couldn't heal, why the blade had broken into my skin.

That damned silver haired, sandy skin toned Captain.

"You must...be mistaken," Yaseer said, almost hopefully.

"I am not mistaken," the cloaked man replied.

"But there's no way—" Baz began.

"Anyone could survive," Yaseer finished.

"Noxstone in her back, severe burns to her face, a surge of powerful energy in the Palace," Ullna spat out each fact.

"There is only one individual who would own Noxstone in that Palace," the cloaked man said.

"The Vulture," the braided woman said. She hacked some saliva into her mouth and spat into the sand as she uttered the words.

Ullna came towards me with venomous intent. She had been warning the man to stay away from me, yet now, she charged towards me. I wasn't afraid of her, but I wasn't pleased at her approach.

"You foolish girl! You've risked everything. How did you manage to cross paths with that man? Does he know why you were there? What happened?"

The Prince was a 'man,' but I was a 'girl'? Weren't we around the same age?

As she grew closer, the cloaked man stood.

"Ullna. If she fought the Prince and lived, if she took a blow from Noxstone and lived—" Yaseer began.

"Then what? What does it matter if the Vulture is coming for us now?"

"It matters a great deal. I have never seen someone survive a blow from those blades. This is highly unusual," Yaseer insisted.

"This goes beyond your curiosity. Our safety and security are paramount. She is a liability."

"You were the one who sent her there, Ullna," the cloaked man said.

"No...that was Yaseer. I always said it was a mistake."

"Nevertheless, this is not something we can ignore," Yaseer ignored the accusation of his error.

"It is certainly something the Vulture will not ignore either."

"He doesn't know," I said. "He doesn't. He's still alive. It's only that I...found something."

They all turned to me.

I glanced at Baz, who understood immediately.

"What? What did you find?" Ullna asked.

Baz asked me. "You confronted him?"

I didn't answer.

"Deliberately?" Baz sounded alarmed.

"You sought him out?" Ullna asked, growing increasingly angry.

A deep shame sunk in my chest. I had acted on emotion, and I had not thought about these people's safety or security.

I had only thought about those guttural screams.

"He will not talk," I tried to reassure them.

Yaseer rubbed his forehead, exasperated.

"You...spoke to him?" Ullna sounded furious now.

The cloaked man sighed. "Perhaps you should let her explain, rather than asking her so many questions."

"Please...do. Explain," Ullna drew out her words.

"I found information about the draining centres in Audra."

I explained the contents of the message. It wasn't hard for the others to figure out what I had meant when I had asked Baz if 'it was true.' He was looking at the sand the whole time I spoke.

They were all startled, silent...waiting for me to finish. All of them were likely as nauseated, shocked, and terrified as I had been when I had first read the note myself.

"It was signed with the Prince's name. I went to confront him, thinking I could extract more information, but there was a complication...there was...another man."

Ullna interrupted, "Another man? Who? And you did this without informing us? Without asking?"

I continued the story regardless. "We fought and I...accidentally, touched the other man's skin and then—"

"The surge," the cloaked man stated. He and Ullna looked at each other. Ullna turned to Yaseer.

"What did you see?" Yaseer asked.

*How does he know...that I saw anything.*

"I...it was a battle. It was in Kalnasa, and it was a slaughter. There were people cutting down and killing the children, the adults, the animals, and laughing. They were..." I thought about the vision. "I couldn't see their faces. I didn't...know if it was real."

"It may be," the cloaked man said, "In the future."

"Divination," Yaseer said.

My ability, divination. That was, class two. I was...class two.

"So that was the future?" Baz asked.

"A version of it," Yaseer answered.

"That letter, it mentioned Kalnasa," I remembered.

"I should have anticipated this," the cloaked man said, sounding frustrated.

"The Vulture has always been beyond our understanding or surveillance," Ullna tried to reassure him.

"It's not him," I said, sure of that fact now.

"But you said it was signed with his name, you and he fought—" Baz asked.

"It's not him. Someone used his name purposefully."

"Of course, he would have you believe that. That man is a liar," Ullna stated, as if she knew him personally.

I shook my head. "After I saw that vision, I wasn't able to fight. He could have killed me then, but he didn't."

"He let you live?" Baz asked, surprised.

"How...bizarre," Yaseer said.

"He must be planning something," Ullna concluded.

"He was investigating the centres. While I was there, setting up those traps, I met him for the first time. He claims he discovered something was amiss about them and wanted to find out what it was. If..."

I suddenly stopped talking, grabbing my chest, the pain in my back grinding deeper.

The cloaked man fell to his knees in an instant. "She needs to be treated. Now."

"She hasn't finished explaining," Ullna said coldly.

"She will not be able to finish if she dies." The man placed his hand on my back and another on my arm, holding me up.

He turned towards me. "N...may I call you by your name?" he addressed me.

I could barely look up. I didn't answer his question.

"It...it's...it hurts." I was trying my best not to sob. How I had been able to speak up until this point was beyond my understanding.

"I can imagine so. Nobody has survived a strike from Noxstone, so the agony of that is...undocumented," he said.

"Please…get…it…out," I begged him. A moment ago, I had been asking him to remove his hands from me, now I was imploring him to place them wherever he needed, as long as the agony would stop.

"It will be painful."

"This is painful," I couldn't help but snap.

He didn't say anything, he only held his right hand out.

"Hold it."

I glanced at him questioningly.

Holding hands, touching my face. This was all becoming far too intimate.

"You'll need to hold onto something."

"I…agghhh." I bent forwards further as the pain intensified. It was as if the steel was digging deeper into my flesh by the second.

I grabbed his hand and squeezed it hard.

It was soft, and warm. A glow emitting from his palms radiated a soothing heat. It was green, and gold, like the colour of leaves in the morning.

I stared at that glow, I focused on that light, as he placed his left hand on my back and began to apply pressure.

I couldn't contain it.

The cries that escaped my lips sounded as if they had been choked out of my throat with a thousand clawed hands. I kept screaming.

Over and over again.

The sound of someone crying reached my ears like a distant echo. It was the woman Baz had come with, I realised.

Why the fuck was she crying? I was the one in agony.

My body trembled. I was sweating. My stomach was turning. I was squeezing the man's hand so tightly. I could hear, could feel, as I began to crunch at his bones.

And then, a wet crack. The sound of them breaking.

The man only took a sharper breath in and continued.

Ullna however, was not pleased. "Your hand!"

"Be…quiet," he grunted.

It felt as if it went on for an eternity, as the shards were dragged through muscle, sinew, blood, and tissue.

But eventually it was over and I, trembling, placed both my palms onto the sand, and hurled up the contents of my stomach.

Drips of water darkened the sand, falling one after the other. I had started crying.

The man's palm rested on my back still. He placed his arm around my shoulder slowly.

To heal an injury like that, must have been exhausting for him.

I couldn't help but think about the fact that if he hadn't been here, I would have died.

He must have been one of the only Darean Healers in existence, and yet he was here, now.

I looked over at his hand, which he had brought to his chest. I wiped the sick off the back of my chapped lips.

"Your hand—"

"It will heal." His voice sounded softer and weaker.

It wasn't healing.

"Healers cannot heal themselves," Ullna explained.

"Class one abilities are not without cost," Yaseer added.

"Why…didn't you say?" I looked up at him.

"We need you to live."

"Need me to live," I repeated his words in a mumble.

"We also need to discuss what we came here to," Ullna reminded the others.

The cloaked man whose hand was still around my shoulder, said, "I no longer have the time."

Ullna laughed bitterly. "Yes, well, that's hardly surprising." She glared at me.

"I'll return when I can."

"But that means—" Baz began.

"You will need to remain in Audra for a few days," the man confirmed.

"Is that…wise?" Baz said.

"We have no choice but to now," Ullna informed him. "Let's discuss." She motioned for the other two women to follow her. They did. Yaseer and Baz followed her slowly, but lingered behind, waiting for me, I presumed.

I turned to look at the man. His face was close to mine.

"Your…hand," I muttered, repeating myself again.

His lips stretched in a confused half smile. "You need rest."

"Why are your hands soft?" I asked him.

A frown replaced his tentative smile.

"Only the rich have soft hands," I spoke. "Who are you?"

"I'm a Healer," he said softly.

"No… you're"— I shuddered, suddenly feeling a deep chill — "someone important. You're someone powerful." Since the shards had been removed, I'd regained some of my strength, and my ability to think, and talk.

Yaseer was standing far away but frowned, as if he could hear our quiet voices.

Of course he could hear them. He had taken my sight.

He was a Sense Transformer, I realised.

I reached for the cloaked man's hand. He tried to pull away, but I grabbed his fingers.

"You won't see anything, if you touch my skin."

"How did you know I was trying to?"

"Why else would someone who dislikes being touched, touch someone?"

"Why can't I see anything if I touch you?" I asked him.

"Can you stand?" he answered with an unrelated question.

I tried to stand, but failed, miserably. My legs were still shaking.

"I...I'll wait a while."

"You cannot stay here," the man said, looking at me intently through his hood.

"Neither can you. You said so. Your disappearance might be noticed?"

He ignored my attempt at uncovering his identity.

"You are more than they said you were," he said, removing his hand from my arm.

"Than who said I was?"

"They're afraid of you," he told me.

That seemed obvious to me, but still I asked.

"How do you know?"

I moved my neck so that I could look at the bottom half of his face more clearly.

"Healers can sense the emotions of others."

I suppose that made sense, since Healers could mend the mind as well as the body. But it was only usually ever temporary when they soothed the mind, from what I had heard.

"So, you can sense mine then?" I looked at his chin.

"I can."

"What can you sense?"

He didn't answer.

I laughed, but I could hear the despair in it. "If you can sense my emotions, then you can sense...that I am afraid of myself."

His hand had fully moved away from me now, but he was still crouching beside me.

"I will return soon."

*Why is he telling me that?*

"I will try to return as soon as possible, so that you do not have to stay here for too long."

*That's why.*

"I was here for twenty years." I laughed. "What's another twenty days?"

"I know," he said.

My eyes searched his mouth and his neck, having nowhere else to focus. "They told you?"

He didn't answer.

"I need to go."

"Back to your Castle?" I remarked, sarcastically.

Why had I said that? This man had just saved my life.

Maybe that was exactly why.

He hesitated as he moved away from me, then chuckled. "If you say so."

He stood, then Baz, noticing that he was leaving, walked towards us. Yaseer had already disappeared.

"How long were you a Vessel?" the man asked Baz suddenly.

"Seven years but...I—"

"Have been assimilated?"

Baz nodded again.

"How long was she?" he asked him.

Baz looked at me confused. I didn't move. "Twenty..." he said warily.

The Healer was checking. He was checking to see who knew certain information.

Just as he was about to leave, the Healer crouched beside me one more time, and came very close to my ear. He spoke directly into it, "Do not tell anyone anything, apart from this man."

I looked up at him, eyes wide with confusion. "Why?"

He seemed to be smiling as he replied, "You broke my hand, you owe me this much."

I frowned. That had been unlike anything the man had previously said.

"You don't trust them," I realised out loud.

He remained bent forwards.

"Why should I trust you?"

The man reached out cautiously for my chin again, with his unbroken hand.

I didn't back away this time. What would have been the point? He'd already touched my face multiple times.

Witnessing the fact I remained still, the man leant forwards and put his first two index fingers very lightly under my chin, lifting it up slightly again.

"I already know you do," he said quietly.

I jerked my chin away and let out a sound of irritation.

He closed his two fingers into the palm of his hand, smiling slightly as he stood.

That was a lie. He couldn't tell something that wasn't true. I didn't trust him. At all.

"Distrust has a distinct feeling," he stated proudly.

"You mustn't be looking for it correctly."

He held his broken hand in the unbroken one.

"With you, there's plenty to see."

I stood very slowly and felt instantly dizzy. My ears rang, and my vision flickered. Baz grabbed my elbow.

"How are you going to explain that to your noble acquaintances?" I asked, nodding at his hand. I could feel Baz's eyes on me, probably wondering why I had assumed this man had any.

The man smiled softly. "Are you concerned?"

"Wouldn't you be able to 'see it' if I were?"

He tilted his head to the right. "You're concerned about much. It would be impossible for me to tell."

"And didn't you say you were in a hurry?"

Baz cleared his throat, sounding like he was hiding a laugh.

The man looked at Baz and me. "Are you together?"

"Are you leaving?" I replied.

Baz looked down, pressing his lips together harder. He obviously found this amusing.

The man pointed at Baz slowly. "He cares for you a great deal."

I was beginning to wish I had lost consciousness when I had been healed earlier, if only to avoid this conversation.

"I know that." I staggered, I needed to lie down.

The man took one step towards me. I held out my hand to stop him.

"Go. The sooner you leave, the sooner we can get out of this place," I said.

He nodded, beginning to turn around.

"And…thank you," I said, quickly, before I could change my mind.

The man turned around slightly and spoke, "It was nothing."

I broke his hand. I probably drained his energy enough that it wouldn't return for hours, maybe even days. How had it been nothing?

And knowing that, why had I been so insistent on speaking to him so harshly?

I knew, I realised, it was because I didn't trust good intentions without reason, without ulterior motives.

The man moved away and walked towards the Teleporter. He vanished with her, behind a blue wall.

I sank to my knees as soon as he left.

"Why did you stand up?" Baz asked.

"I don't know," I grumbled. "Who is he?"

Baz shook his head. "Only Ullna knows, apparently."

I huffed. "So, we'll never find out then."

"Not unless he takes that cloak off."

"We'll just have to come up with a scheme to make him."

It felt nice to speak with Baz again, I supposed, even if I was reluctant to admit it.

"I missed you." The words slipped out of my mouth. I turned away from him as I realised what I had said.

Baz appeared in front of me. His jaw dropped slightly, then he smiled brightly.

"Don't say anything," I tried to stop him.

"I *knew* you loved me."

"I'm just practicing for our act when we get back." I avoided eye contact with him.

He laughed and then, much to my surprise, picked me up.

"Ughhh…no…what—"

"I'm just trying to make sure the act is believable."

I was once again, too exhausted, and too tired to argue.

"Your gifts?" I said. "Put me to sleep?"

Baz nodded. "Yeah."

"Class two," I mumbled.

"So are you. Can't say I'm surprised."

"A Healer...they're class one, aren't they?" I asked.

"Uh-huh. I can't believe he actually exists." He sounded in awe of the man.

"He's not a God."

"He's the next best thing."

"Leaving me for him?"

He giggled. His laugh always sounded like a giggle. "First chance I get."

"That's it. You should use your telepathy to make him remove his hood, then you'll get to see his face."

"What do you think he looks like?"

I huffed. "I don't know. Normal."

"Normal?"

"What do you expect me to say?"

The Prince's in-depth description of the Captain suddenly came to mind, for no understandable reason.

"I bet he's beautiful. He has that...look," Baz said. We were getting closer to where Yaseer and Ullna were waiting now.

"What look? You can't even see his face?"

"A presence then?"

"A *presence*?" I rolled my eyes.

"Oh, come on. He's the tallest man I've ever seen. He's all smooth voice and long fingers."

I furrowed my brow and raised my upper lips in a scowl. "He's rich, whoever he is."

"Why *did* you say that thing...about noble acquaintances?"

"His hands were soft," I explained.

"Oh really?" He looked down and raised an eyebrow.

I tutted. "No. I mean...they weren't calloused."

Baz understood but still said, "Anything else about his hands?"

"You were the one analysing them."

"I can't see his face, what else am I supposed to do?"

"Avoid looking at him at all."

"It's impossible...it's his—"

"Presence?"

Baz nodded mockingly "I knew you'd understand."

I sighed. "He told me not to trust anyone but you."

Baz nodded and his voice became more serious. "He thinks there's a traitor here."

"How do you know?"

"He was here, after the attack. He told Yaseer, Ullna, and I."

"So why doesn't he want me to speak to them?"

Baz shrugged and I moved in his arms as he did. I winced in pain.

"Sorry! Sorry," He grimaced apologetically. "That Prince is a vicious shit, huh?"

I thought about the Prince and shook my head, "He's vicious, but he's—"

"He's what? You're not defending him, are you?"

"He was never there Baz. Not once." He was never in the draining centres.

"And? He can't have been completely unaware of what they were doing."

"I don't know. Maybe."

"I don't believe that."

"If you're a Telepath, can't you tell who the traitor is?" I asked him.

"Not yet." His voice dropped to a whisper as we approached the others.

He dropped me to the ground lightly. There in front of us stood Ullna, Yaseer, and Faina.

And there was another individual with them. Someone I didn't recognize.

He was slender, tall, his chestnut hair stood out from under a cap, a white one. In fact, he was dressed completely in white.

I recognised that uniform instantly.

He held out a tanned hand in introduction.

"The name's Vykros. You can leave your energy surge to me."

## CHAPTER 54- SHADAE

There was a fire burning in front of me. The ground was wet beneath my palms. This was soil. I was under a tree. The smacks against the earth and the coolness of the air were the next things that reached my semi-conscious mind.

It was raining.

I pressed my hands into the dirt and sat up.

Elias was sitting on the other side of the fire. He watched me push myself up, raggedly. I pressed my hand to my temple. My head was throbbing, the very front, sides, and back of my skull felt inflamed.

The faint sound of thunder sounded from above us. I couldn't help but look at the sky. It hardly ever rained in Vasara, let alone did it see thunderstorms.

"We shouldn't be sitting here," I said, as the rumble of the sound crackled in our ears.

Elias was eating something, tearing it apart with his hands. "You passed out. We couldn't leave."

*How about...how are you? What happened? Are you unwell? You passed out, that's probably not a good thing?*

No, of course, he wouldn't ask those kinds of questions. Not to me.

I stood, ignoring the stab at the base of my skull as I did.

"You shouldn't stay by the roots of a tree during a thunderstorm."

Elias looked up at me and said slowly. "It's raining."

*Great. I suppose staying dry is worth getting electrocuted. Am I supposed to thank you?*

I shook the urge to retort and walked towards Elias' horse.

He didn't move.

I stopped and turned around. My boots were squelching in the wet soil. I watched his back, he seemed completely comfortable, willing to sit here all night.

"Aren't we going back?"

"We can't. Not now. The weather isn't suitable for riding."

"So, we're staying here?"

Elias threw the remnants of whatever he had been eating into the fire, then stood, and stamped it out. "Not unless you pass out again."

I took a deep breath in and out.

*I didn't choose to pass out alright? Why are you acting like I did it deliberately?*

"What...happened?" I asked, avoiding eye contact with him. He strolled past me and took the reins of his horse. He started to walk. I followed him.

The chill of the air bit at my bones. I supposed staying dry had been better in the end. I put both my hands under the arms of my jacket and hunched over, starting to shiver.

"You touched that...thing, screamed, and lost consciousness," he answered me.

"For how long?"

"I didn't bring a fucking pocket watch with me," he grumbled.

*Of course not, what is your problem? But you can estimate a time roughly, surely?*

I decided to remain silent. Speaking to him was only going to end in a disagreement. But he spoke again, still facing forwards. "Do you remember anything?"

I thought about it. "No."

I didn't, only crushing, swelling pain in my skull, and darkness.

"Where's that body?" I asked.

"I'm not touching it. Are you?" He raised a brow, obviously understanding my answer would be no.

"But can we really just... leave it there?" My teeth chattered as the unfettered rain smacked against my clothes more strongly.

"It was lying there for a while already, what's the difference?" He sounded apathetic.

*Urrr...that we know the corpse is dangerous, and connected to a possibly imminent convoluted threat centred around the destruction and the death of more people? Why is this so hard for you to understand?*

I kept my thoughts to myself. I wasn't about to risk the consequences of voicing them out loud. I was cold, and tired.

After less than a quarter of an hour, Elias led us to an Inn at one of Vasara's Northern towns - Vaden. He must have known of a large number of Inns, and their locations, since he'd headed Vasara's military before.

Once we got into the Inn, Elias approached the woman in the entrance hall, asking for two rooms.

"Thirty rays each," the lady said.

*Thirty rays?! I don't have thirty rays.*

Elias turned to me with an expectant look on his face, waiting for me to take out that money.

"I don't have that on me," I replied guiltily.

Elias rolled his eyes and gave the woman sixty rays in tandem. "You're paying me back, tracker."

"I—"

He turned around, leaning one arm on the counter, and raised his eyebrows at me. He was challenging me to continue that sentence.

Challenge accepted. I was poor and a semi captive, what was his eyebrow raise?

"I don't have the money to pay you back," I spoke up.

Elias peered at me suspiciously, but before he could reply, the woman returned, handing us two keys. Elias strolled off towards the staircase that led to an upper floor. I followed him.

We approached two adjacent doors. He threw me one of the keys, which I caught. He turned to me again, this time leaning on the door frame of his rented room, with his right arm in the air, his hand in a fist.

"You just got paid, didn't you?" His unwavering gaze was demanding.

"Yes, but I...used that money," I looked at the ceiling and grimaced as I said it.

"You used all of that money...already?"

"Yes," I confirmed.

"What for?" He narrowed his eyes.

*What for? Since when did trackers have to report their monthly spendings? Do you want a breakdown of the food, toiletries, and medicines I purchase in the future? What about clothes?*

"You're thinking very hard about your answer," he remarked.

I sighed and rubbed my aching temples again. "It was her body. I paid them for her body."

Elias dropped his arm. "You paid those guards for a body?"

"I wanted to bury her." I tried not to let my voice waver.

"If you spend money every time you want to bury someone, you'll end up hungry and on the street within a month." He scowled.

I didn't look up, instead, I began to place the key into the door in front of me.

Elias was still watching me. "How much?"

My wrist froze in place. "One hundred rays."

"One hundred fucking rays?" He sounded angry. I closed my eyes in consternation, expecting a reprimand.

"It's just once. I'll...pay you back next month if you'll please... give me the time."

But Elias didn't seem interested.

"Who were they?" he asked.

I turned to the right, looking at him. I shrugged.

*I have no idea who they were. Do you think I'm intimately acquainted with guards who would spit at my feet?*

Elias frowned. "I think I remember from that day." He nodded to himself resolutely then said, "I'll get your money back."

"No please—"

He had just started to put the key into his door when he heard me pleading and glanced at me.

"It's done now. I don't want... to cause any trouble."

*I don't need that guard to beat the shit out of me for this, alright?*

Elias waved his key in the air. "You don't want to cause trouble, but you bribed the guards for a body."

"The body was worth it. But the money—"

"You won't last without the money, and I need my money back. Understood?"

I nodded, resigning myself to the fact that I had, once again, gotten myself into a less-than-ideal situation. I resolved not to do anything to or speak to the guards ever again.

At least, not until I wanted to get my brothers out.

Then I'd bribe, drug, or kill whichever one of them I needed to.

The thought made me shudder, but still, I knew I would do it.

Elias had already gone inside his room. I did the same.

It was larger than I had expected, and far more lavish than my own quarters back at the Palace.

*Of course, of all the places that he could choose to rest for the night, he, the Lord, would choose the most expensive and comfortable. He can afford thirty rays fine. I can't. In fact, why does he even need me to pay him back? Isn't he rich?*

I sat down on the large bed at the far-right wall. It was adorned with crimson, silk sheets and bounced under my weight. I threw back the blankets and huddled myself within them, still shaking slightly from my damp clothes.

I didn't realise I had fallen asleep.

I didn't even know if I was asleep.

But then, the pain, the pain as before, only more persistent, searing like a venom across the lining of my skull, crushing all its sides with a force so brutal, it stopped me from being able to think.

From the other side of the room, a voice emerged. "You're following me,"

The voice was so loud, so loud it thundered inside my ear drums, reverberated inside my head and my chest, but it was also quiet, a hushed whisper drowned out by a storm.

It was not a male or a female's voice. It sounded like knives scratching against steel, and the ripple of silk. It sounded like the screams of a burning village, and the choirs of divine beings.

I tried to get up. I tried to bend my head forwards to see the assailant, but I couldn't do anything, only move my eyes. I cast them downwards, my limbs vibrating with the effort of trying to move them.

I could only sense something, someone, like a mist so thick and foul, it made it hard to breath.

"You're following me," the voice repeated. It was in front of me, but behind me, it was in the furthest corner of the room, but next to my ear.

I tried to speak but could only manage a small squeal out of my mouth.

"Murderer of your own. Predator in white. I can smell it on you."

I could hear the distinct sound of someone sniffing my hair, my neck. The air next to my face became considerably colder. My lips began tingling from the change in temperature, my chest shuddering.

I was terrified and I was in so much pain, so much.

"You stole it," the voice sounded with the promise of more pain. "Bring it back."

I managed to move a finger. The index on my right hand twitched into the air.

In response, a force weighed down across my whole body, nullifying my attempts. The voice and the air became even colder. "Bring. It. Back."

I couldn't speak, and so I just thought, I yelled inside my mind.

*Stop. Stop. Stop.*

The voice didn't react, the pressure didn't change. "You will bring it back."

*What? Bring what back?*

In response, an image as vivid as the room around me flashed in front of my vision.

That talisman. It was on the body, steeped in blood. Then it was in my hand. Then it was around my neck.

"Bring it back," it repeated once again.

*When? H...how?*

"Retrieve it and I will retrieve it." It was getting closer.

How could I believe this force, this person, most likely a Necromancer, an Acciperean, would, after retrieving the talisman from my body, let me live?

As if this thing could sense my thoughts, the pressure on my body grew tighter. The bones inside my limbs felt as if they were being stretched, fissuring under the weight of a thousand people, a thousand deaths, a thousand lives.

A tear escaped my right eye, falling down my still paralysed face.

"Bring it back."

*What are you?*

The voice didn't reply and the pressure and pain both eased somewhat. I turned my neck, the slightest and smallest amount to the right.

Before me was...something I did not understand.

It was a person, but it was not, it was a form of a body, with legs and arms, and a face, but it sagged as if it was bound by fragile thread. It moved as if it were both liquid and air. There was a faint outline of hair, that fell like ink down its back.

"I can see your thoughts. I can feel your soul. I can taste your desires."

It wanted me to see its form, as it told me these words.

Had I been wrong? A sorcerer could have more than one ability, but usually, no more than two, and always within the same class.

I had thought this person a Necromancer, but here it was, in my sleep, a Dreamwalker, paralysing and reading me like a Telepath.

*How?* I squeezed the thought through the dread.

The pain came back tenfold. I didn't think it was possible for the torment to grow worse, but now, it had. I could taste something on my lips. I could feel something coming out of my ears, and my eyes. It was metallic.

It was my blood.

*Blood manipulation as well? No…it's not…possible…it's…*

The air grew so frosty I began to shiver violently. At the height of all these sensations, the voice grew louder and replied, "I drowned in blood and was born of blood."

This thing came closer, I could sense it in front of my face. Its own was grey and white, and where its eyes should have been, there were only holes. Where its lips should have moved, there was only the bare outline of teeth.

And then something dark, long, and icy, made contact with my face.

It was licking my cheek.

It was licking my blood.

I was howling, I was screeching, from the bottom of my lungs.

But no sound was coming out of my mouth.

Then as if it all had been an illusion, it stopped.

It ended.

I threw the blankets off myself and stumbled, without care or consequence, without any thought, towards the door.

I yanked it open so hard it slammed against the wall behind it. It was so dark, and the torches and candles that had been lit in the hallway were now out. I didn't realise so much time had passed. I didn't know I had been asleep for so long.

*Not asleep.*

*Not truly.*

How long did that last?

Was it truly over? Was I still in an illusion? I…I had to be sure.

I was shaking. I was tripping over my own feet, bent forwards running down the hallway, pressing my palms against the wall.

A door opened. A middle-aged man, who appeared wealthy, stepped out.

"Have you no consideration for anyone?" he hissed.

Another one. This time a man who looked like a merchant.

"Oi, bitch, some of us are trying to sleep." He paused and must have noticed my uniform before adding, "Of course, it's a fucking sorcerer."

"This one's probably deranged. I've heard of that happening you know," the other man replied to him. "Go and get the owner."

I could hear them, but I wasn't facing them, still stumbling towards the end of the hallway.

Another two doors opened.

A woman and a small child appeared in the entrance of one. "You've woken him up! Are you happy? You've woken us all up, you nasty girl!"

My breaths were exaggerated. I was still sweating and hunched over.

"Grab her," the first man said.

A large hand, belonging to the second man yanked my forearm roughly. I was already off balance and fell to the floor.

"Throw her out!" the fourth guest said, an elderly woman, it sounded like.

The second man reached for my arm again and pulled me up. He let go abruptly and stumbled back when he saw my face.

He pointed at me frantically. "She's fucking bleeding. What the fuck?"

I reached up with my hands and touched my face. I looked at my palm. It was streaked with red. There was blood on it.

So, it hadn't been an illusion, it hadn't been a figment of my dreams.

It had been real.

I looked at my palms wide eyed. I turned without thinking, and looked at the other guests, who all gasped, or shrieked at seeing me. The first man placed his hands over his mouth and walked back towards his doorway. The young child of the woman started wailing.

"I'm...I...no...it's not," I started, but I had no idea how to finish. What could I say to a group of human beings, who already hated, and were terrified of sorcerers, about seeing my face covered in blood, and watching me stumble around in the middle of the night?

*I was only visited by the epitome of darkness who drew blood from my orifices?*

I placed both my palms to my cheeks and wiped at them frantically, which probably, I realised too late, had made it worse.

I raised my palms in a pacifying gesture to the guests, which elicited a disgusted and frightened reaction. Of course, since they were covered in even more blood now.

"Please...I'm not—" I started.

"Get away! Get away from us!"

"Evil. These people are pure evil!"

"Abominations!"

"They shouldn't even let them out into society!"

I, realising there would be no appeasing these people, ran towards the stairs, down them, and outside, into the road.

A road was generous. It was one path, surrounded by a field of short grass.

The door to the Inn slammed behind me as I sprinted out. The clamouring of more guests being disturbed echoed from behind me. Lights blinked on, streaming through windows.

I had no plan, no idea of where to go, or what to do. I had no way of returning to Vasara. I had no way of travelling.

But I wasn't thinking about a plan, or thinking clearly at all. I simply continued to half-run, half-trip down a small segment of that path, and then cut around into the grass, stumbling down the side of the building, pressing my shoulder into the wall.

I fell to my knees, with one palm still on the wall, scraping it against the rocks and bricks as I did. A near full moon sat in the sky, peering down at me.

Shouts rattled from inside the building, and bashing around, something that sounded like an argument. I froze against the wall and waited.

And then, footsteps. A few people were leaving, coming out of the entrance.

They were coming to find me.

*Shit, shit. Where am I supposed to go? What am I supposed to do? I can't even defend myself with this cursed mark. Am I just supposed to let them kill me? Or beat me?*

No. My night had already gone terribly enough. I refused to end it with bruises, punches to the face or…dying.

I was probably deluding myself into thinking I had a choice in the matter.

Still, I pulled myself up and ran. I ran down the side of the building all the way to the back. I turned the corner. The voices were growing quieter.

But this was the back of the building. It was hardly a secure hiding location, or something completely unreachable, or unattainable. I had simply, only walked around the edges of the Inn. I'd have to hide somewhere else.

It was darker here. There were no lights coming out of the back windows.

*That might work to my advantage. Yes, alright. I can follow the back path and find a tree. I can climb it. Maybe that would work and then…*

Someone grabbed my wrist.

I startled, and tried to shake the person off, but it was a man, and they were significantly stronger than me. The voices were growing louder from the left and the right. That was hardly a surprise, all the guests would have to do is turn two corners to get here.

My heart was beating wildly. I was trapped, on all sides, I had nowhere to go.

I struggled again in vain, letting out a grunt of fear.

"Stop fucking squirming."

I did, stop fucking squirming.

Because, although I could not see him, his voice was unfortunately familiar.

"What did you do? What the fuck is wrong with you?" Elias asked, but quietly, as if he too, didn't want the others to find us.

I couldn't even see him, only the outline of him. The only thing I could clearly make out was his large hand around my wrist.

Before I could answer, a bunch of people emerged from both sides of us. A few in each group were holding flamed torches. I winced at the brightness of the light.

"There she is! It's that one!" a man said. Then he stopped, gasping, looking at Elias.

"My Lord, you've found her! Thank you! This sorcerer has been causing trouble!"

"She frightened us all!"

"She's clearly been possessed!"

One after another, accusations of an increasingly alarming nature were fired in my direction.

"Just look at her! She's clearly murdered someone!" a woman wailed.

*Murdered someone? What are you talking about? Since when did murdering someone involve blood coming out of your own eyes and ears?*

Elias pulled me towards him, turning so he could look at my face.

He paled.

"My Lord! Do you see? We're so glad you're here! You can take her to..."

But Elias wasn't listening. He was simply staring at my face, confused.

I felt like explaining what had happened, but who would believe me? Certainly not the guests, and knowing Elias's tendency to disregard everything I said, placing my hopes on him seemed pointless too.

"My Lord?" one of the guests asked, noticing Elias' inattention.

Elias, whose hand was still around my wrist, turned to look at the man who was speaking to him.

"She's dangerous! According to Vasara's decree, any sorcerer or tracker who is dangerous can be dealt with immediately! Please, Sir, protect us!"

Was he seriously asking Elias to...

"Asking the Lord to kill me? Don't you at least have the guts to do it yourself?" I spat, suddenly greatly irritated at the insinuation I had gone on a killing spree. I hadn't even touched any of these people.

"You! You vile little bitch!" the man said, reaching for me.

Elias used his other hand to smack the man across the back of the face.

I jerked back, surprised. The man grabbed his cheek and looked at Elias in pure shock.

"Do you take it upon yourself to enact the law over me?" Elias said to the man.

"My Lord...no. I...it's just...you heard her! She's a savage beast!"

"She's mine to deal with," Elias said loudly, raising his voice for all the guests to hear.

"My Lord...I...of course..." the man said nervously, still rubbing at his face. "You should be the one to deal the blow."

"That's right, My Lord!" a new man shouted. "You should take your revenge!"

Elias' grip tightened around my wrist very slightly as his muscles tensed up.

"Revenge?" Elias asked. "For what?"

I side-eyed him. Everyone went silent. It was very clear, even with the limited information that I had, what exactly it was the guests were implying Elias should take revenge for.

But to be asked directly what he meant. Would the man dare to answer?

"For all of us!" a woman blurted out. A collective sigh of relief could be felt amongst the people. "For all the lives that...that...those things have taken!"

"Who knows what she's been doing in the dark!"

I couldn't help but let out an exasperated sigh at that.

"She doesn't even bear any guilt," one sneered.

"That's because I didn't do anything!" I shouted. Elias squeezed my wrist, signalling for me to be silent.

"Yes! Yes, you did! You—"

"What? What did the tracker do?" Elias asked.

Everyone was quiet.

"My Lord, just look at her...she's clearly been...practising some foul evil, right under our noses! Right where we sleep!"

"Do you have any evidence?" Elias asked.

"But, My Lord, her appearance—"

"Do you have any evidence?" Elias repeated more harshly.

"My Lord, you know better than anyone we cannot wait for these...these *people* to unleash themselves!"

"That's right, My Lord, you've protected us before!"

*What does that mean? When?*

I glanced at Elias. Had he really killed sorcerers without any reason? Any...evidence before?

Of course he had. Why did I even doubt it?

"Is that a yes, or a no?" Elias asked.

"Well, no, My Lord but—"

"Then this conversation is finished," Elias said.

"My Lord! You cannot surely expect us to let her stay here!" the woman, the owner of the Inn yelled out from the back of the crowd.

"That is exactly what I expect you to do. You're all alive and breathing, and without evidence, so stop complaining and go back to your beds."

"My Lord!" several 'My Lords' sounded in protest.

"You cannot let her go unpunished!"

"This isn't right!"

Then some whispers about the Lord himself.

"He was always fickle!"

"He's probably drunk right now!"

"His mind's a wreck."

I looked at Elias again, but he remained focused, jaws-clenched. His red eyes seemed even darker in the obscurity of nightfall.

Elias let go of me, pushing me away. I lost my balance and reached out my palms just in time to soften my fall to the ground.

"Alright. How about this? You can have your justice if you take it yourself. Anyone who's willing to try, can try..."

Was he serious? I turned around and stared at him.

*What the fuck are you doing?!*

Elias glanced down at me, very quickly then looked back up.

How could I get out of this? If someone attacked me, I couldn't defend myself, perhaps to an extent, but I certainly couldn't kill them, not with this cursed mark.

And if I did manage to defend myself, the mark would certainly make me suffer for it. If, in the process, I hurt one of these people, so much as bent their index finger, I would be severely punished.

*First bleeding from my eyes and ears now this? Why did you have to find me outside those gates Lord Elias? My life has been significantly more perilous and disastrous since you entered it!*

But nobody moved, everyone just shifted on their feet, furtively glancing at one another.

"What happened to the laws that Vasara decreed? You were so eager to see them upheld?" Elias' voice boomed through the air.

I glared at him.

"Don't encourage them!" I half-whispered, half-shouted, only loud enough for him to hear.

Elias half-whispered back. "Stop speaking."

"My Lord...it is only....we dare not...infringe upon your authority."

Infringe upon his authority? These people, who just moments ago, were making cutting and undermining comments about him.

I huffed out a laugh in amusement.

"Something funny, bitch?" one of them asked.

"Just how fast people's minds can change," I replied, looking up at the questioner from under my brows.

"Minds can change! We haven't changed our minds about anything! You deserve to die! But that's...that's for our Lord to decide!"

"Didn't you just say the Lord was fickle?" I glared at the woman. "Who would let someone they thought fickle make a decision of life and death for them?"

Elias looked at me, squinting, bewildered.

"Pfff...we...we said no such thing, but of course a magic wielding piece of trash like you would fabricate such lies!"

I raised my eyebrows. "Are you going to attack me or not?"

"We're leaving you in the Lord's hands, he'll do far worse!"

"That's right. He'll know what to do with you!"

"That's if his mind isn't too 'wrecked', as you say." I took great pleasure in bringing up their comments and watching their reaction.

*Wait...what am I saying? Maybe I have been possessed. What's emboldening me to aggravate people already out for my blood?!*

*Both them and that...thing. Everyone is out for it, it seems.*

"My Lord, she's slandering us!"

I huffed again. "You were slandering him," I grumbled.

"Him? That's *My Lord* to you—"

I groaned.

*Why am I even defending this 'Lord?' Well, I suppose it's sensible. I have a far greater chance of surviving this night with him than with these people.*

"No respect at all!" one shouted.

I stood slowly, still feeling disorientated. "I'm waiting. Come on! Attack me! Aren't you angry that I urrr... let me see, what was it? Murdered someone? Made you look at some blood? Woke you up?"

Elias peered at me stolidly.

"My Lord, can't you see now, she's violent and aggressive and—"

"Yes. Very," Elias agreed. "And I'm giving you a chance to do something about that. Please go ahead." He gestured at me.

For the first time since I'd met Elias, he sounded as if he were smiling.

I turned around to check.

I hadn't been mistaken. He was smiling. I could see him more clearly in the light of the torches now. He was still wearing the dark crimson shirt, only without the armour.

He met my eyes briefly then returned his own to the guests.

"My Lord, we...believe this situation is best left to you."

"Yes, My Lord, we will...we'll let you deal with this!"

Mutterings of agreement, bows, and curtsies followed.

"Thank you for your trust, good Sirs and Madams," Elias said, cordially. "It's just a shame it took so fucking long to acquire."

The astonished expressions on the guest's faces were merged with increasingly angry whispers between them. But one by one, they disappeared, and scurried into the darkness.

My momentary relief was ruptured, as Elias grabbed my wrist again, and began dragging me behind him.

"Let me...let me go!" I said, with no expectation for that command to actually be answered.

"We can't stay here now."

"There's nowhere else for us to go!"

He stopped and turned around sharply, facing me. "You should have thought about that before you took a midnight stroll covered in blood."

"It—"

"It? It what?" Elias asked.

"It wasn't a stroll!"

"My apologies, what exactly would you call it then?"

"This is MY blood!" I yelled, feebly trying to pull my hand from his.

"Whose else would it be?" Elias said, completely unaffected by the revelation.

"I just meant...I didn't." I sighed looking at his chest, gulping as the memories of that figure returned to me. "I didn't know what I was doing."

"Do you ever know what you're doing?"

My head shot up and I narrowed my eyes. Elias used his other hand and flung something at me, it landed on the bottom half of my chin.

It was a handkerchief.

"Wipe it off."

I used my free hand to obey.

Elias sighed. I assumed it wasn't working. He let go of my wrist and grabbed the handkerchief from my hands. He paused for a moment, his eyes searching my face hesitantly.

But then, he reached forwards, and rubbed the material harshly against my chin, wiping some of the blood off. My eyes widened at the gesture, staring at his hands in disbelief.

*He'd come this close to a sorcerer, willingly?!*

I raised my gaze to find Elias peering at me.

"It's...coming...from your eyes," he said in a low voice.

I didn't reply.

His facial expression changed slowly, "I've seen this before."

I looked at him desperately. "What? When?"

Elias looked disturbed, his voice still sounding strangely, "A long time ago,"

He paused and then asked, his normal tone of voice returning "What happened? Tell me. Tell me right fucking now."

"I was sleeping, and then...that pain, the pain from before, when I touched that corpse, it returned, only there was someone there, and they were..." I swallowed. "They looked like...they were dead, but they moved like water and their eyes were gone, and it was so—"

"Cold," Elias finished, in a steely voice.

I met his eyes, startled. "Yes. Freezing."

I refrained from mentioning the talisman, and the debt I had to pay. I didn't need to give this Lord any more reasons to send me back to the draining chambers. Besides, did I really have a choice when it came to retrieving it? How could I explain that to Elias? If I told him about what had been demanded of me, he would make sure I couldn't deliver it, and I was...not keen on bleeding to death from my eyes.

But this thing, it had killed Ava. Could I really just hand over something it clearly needed?

Then again, what would be the point in me dying in refusal?

I could return the talisman first then deal with it later.

*Deal with it later. Pfft. I probably couldn't even deal with one of its eyelashes.*

*If it even has any eyelashes.*

Elias looked mortified, then turned around, and dragged me behind him again. I didn't say anything.

Eventually we reached his horse again, which was currently free of its saddle. I mounted the same way as before, but Elias climbed behind me this time. I turned behind me confused.

"I don't want blood on the back of my shirt," he said.

*And I don't want to be sat between your legs! And what about the saddle? Are we just leaving like that? Immediately?!*

"Here," Elias gave me the handkerchief again, only this time, he had poured some water on it.

I rubbed my face with it, and assuming he didn't want it back, placed it in a pocket in my pants.

We rode in silence for a little while before I blurted out, "It spoke to me."

I could feel Elias' harsh breath on my neck as he exhaled. I winced. It felt as if he was trying to compose himself. His breathing felt uneven behind my back. He squeezed the reins tighter.

"What did it say?" he finally asked, sounding apprehensive.

"It knows who I am, that I was trying to follow it."

"And?" Elias asked.

I hesitated before I answered. "It wants me to stop. It made itself... quite clear." I gestured to my eyes.

"You said it was a Necromancer,"

I nodded. "It must be but...it must be more."

"Did it do anything to you...beyond the...eyes?" Elias sounded uncharacteristically contrite.

"Beside the pain, and the intimidation...no. But..."

"But?"

"But...I don't think it will be so forgiving... if it returns."

"So, we'll have to be careful."

*We? This wasn't a one time venture?!*

I knew the Lord wouldn't want to give up the chase, but it wasn't him facing the threat of internal bleeding.

I pressed my lips together and looked ahead. "What do you plan on doing?" I asked.

Elias sounded curt when he said, "You'll know when I tell you."

*Yes, that's how knowledge usually works. I was just hoping you'd tell me now.*

But it was clear Elias didn't know himself.

The sun began to rise, casting a faint rosy hue on the edges of the grass. Petrichor drifted through the warm air. The paths grew more numerous and eventually, we reached the edge of Iloris.

"You said you'd seen it before?" I asked him. Despite my reservations about Elias, if he had, he was the only person who could give me any notion as to what I had just been tortured by.

"There's no being sure it's the same one."

"But they have to be similar. What happened to the last one?"

Elias' knuckles turned whiter around the reins. "I don't know."

My eyes darted from left to right. Then my brows evened out.

If he didn't know, they hadn't apprehended, killed, or caught this thing, but if he had seen it, he had survived the encounter, the chances of which, based on my experience, were almost non-existent...then...it had to be?

But I didn't know Elias well enough to ask the question on the tip of my tongue.

*Your leg? It took your leg? That time, your unit died. It was there. It was that?*

Some of the Palace's guards approached us and got on one knee.

"My Lord, we have been waiting for your return."

As they rose, they cast strange glances at me.

*I didn't want to be placed in this position on this horse either, alright? I would much rather have teleported or walked or... evaporated on the spot.*

Elias sounded alarmed as he asked, "What happened?"

"My Lord, there was an intrusion in the Palace..."

"Is Eliel—" Elias's voice rose.

"The King is safe, My Lord, the intrusion was detected by...trackers." The guard looked at me.

*Detected by trackers.*

"It was a sorcerer, My Lord."

"Have they been apprehended?" Elias asked urgently.

*Inside the Palace? A sorcerer?*

I couldn't help but glance back at Elias with a disbelieving look. But his eyes were firmly locked on the guard.

"Have they been apprehended?" Elias asked again, insistent.

"No, My Lord. They escaped. There were no casualties."

"Then why are you here?"

He was right, the news of there being a sorcerer in the Palace was greatly alarming, for the humans anyway, and it was also highly unusual, but still, since there were no casualties, and the King was safe, this news could have waited until Elias had returned.

The two guards glanced at each other before one of them said, "My Lord, one of the candidates is…" He paused, clearly nervous.

"Is what?" Elias pressed.

"One of the candidates is gravely ill, My Lord."

"Gravely ill?" Elias sounded distant. "How?"

The second one looked down before he said.

"One of the candidates has been poisoned."

# CHAPTER 55 – HESTAN

"Sir, we have tried all manners of concoctions, but the Lady will not wake, we cannot rouse her, and her pulse remains weak, her breathing erratic…I'm afraid all we can do is wait. We could try some other remedies, but they are…rather unconventional, and not so reliable."

Dyna was lying on her bed, her small chest shuddering, wheezing as she took in each breath.

I had been standing at the side of her bed, listening as the third healer told me his assessment.

I should have been here. I should have been nearby. But instead of protecting her, of doing my duty, of prioritising her safety, I had been in the Prince's chambers, warning him of danger, obsessed and preoccupied with this paper, sleeping in his bed.

My hands were trembling slightly in fists.

"Of course, it would cost extra to acquire such rare herbs—"

"Does money seem like an object in this instance?" I snapped.

"Well, of course not Sir, but …we have heard Kalnasans have fallen on hard times and—"

"Do what you are paid for by your King and I will pay for the rest," I told him. Although truthfully, I had no notion of how I would afford such an extortionate amount.

He bowed to me slightly mumbling, "Yes, Sir," and waddled out of the room. His golden healer garbs dragged behind him on the floor.

As soon as he left, I placed a hand over my mouth and closed my eyes. It was already an effort to keep them open. I was still weak and fatigued, and my wound, despite the Prince's efforts, had not fully healed. I reached out with my other hand and grabbed Dyna's.

I knelt beside her. Looking at her face, so innocent, so sickly now, pale, I felt a crushing weight in my chest.

They should never have sent her here, a mere child they had coddled, into a pit of vipers. There was no way she could comprehend or understand them.

The healers had told me that they remained unsure as to the method by which Dyna was poisoned. It could have been something she had eaten, drank, washed herself with, breathed in, been brushed, or scraped by.

No wonder they hadn't been able to heal the former King Elion if this was the extent of their skill. Thinking on it, as the Prince had declared, they had stitched my wound awfully too. How could it be that these were the best healers in this Kingdom?

I couldn't help but dwell upon the possibilities, of when she had been poisoned, on if she had known, or been afraid, if she had expected my help, or even called for it while it occurred.

I shook my head, angry, frustrated and loathing myself. I had failed her. It felt as though it was me who had poured the poison into her veins.

And of course, the one question that preoccupied my mind more than the others, was… who was responsible? Whoever it was, I would make sure that they suffered. But it could have been anyone. I couldn't even begin to draw up a concise list of the possibilities. There were too many people who could gain from Dyna's death.

But…the note on that Noxscroll. It could not have been a coincidence that Kalnasa was mentioned. Was it those who had written it who had struck Dyna in the dark? Or was it someone, something else?

Someone approached and entered the room, I turned around, anticipating the healer's return but instead, saw the King.

I bowed immediately.

"Your Majesty." My voice was hoarse and weaker than usual.

"Captain. I came to offer my…" His voice trailed off as he looked at Dyna. "I am truly sorry this has happened here, within these walls." The King's face was twisted in what I could only describe as discomfort.

I kept my head lowered as I said, "You honour us with your concern, Your Majesty." Although I knew perfectly well his not visiting would have been out of the question.

"Please know that any expenses for her treatment will be taken care of."

I raised my head to look at him. He was dressed in bright red, the precise shade of his hair, which was braided slightly at the sides now. His long jacket reached his knees, and he was wearing his crown.

I glanced up at his head, then back to his face.

"Thank you, Your Majesty, we are most grateful."

"It is the least I can offer you." The King's eyes reached Dyna again and he tightened his mouth slightly.

"What is her condition?" he asked me, gently.

I looked at Dyna as I replied, "She is weak. They say her chances of survival are slim, Your Majesty." My voice sounded detached.

"But not non-existent," the King said, offering me a small smile. "We will be holding an assembly to announce this development."

"Your Majesty?" I asked, assuming he would have wanted to keep this affair quiet. It would not be good for the King's reputation if people learnt that one of his candidates had been attacked during his Courting Season. Of course, it had happened in the past, but one of the candidates dying, or being this close to death, hadn't happened for centuries.

"We must find those who would seek to harm us, Captain. They will be expecting our silence. I would rather not indulge their assumptions."

I looked at him, slightly confused. First, this man sacrificed his fertility, now he was openly admitting and announcing to the world, that which would scandalise him. It was almost as if he did not want to be the King at all.

But his poise, the manner in which he held himself and spoke, the way he looked each and every person he addressed in the eye. It all spoke to the contrary.

"Please come to the main hall shortly. The announcement will be made in half an hour's time."

"Yes, Your Majesty," I bowed again.

The King turned and left the room, his guards following him out.

A short time later, I returned to my own room to get fully dressed. I had still been wearing the light and loose pale blue garments I'd had on from the night before.

I removed them, and instead, placed a pair of brighter blue pants on, and a white upper robe. It was decorated with silver leaves, fine and small, along the shoulders and the edges, where the robe cut across a white undershirt, the collar of which sat high upon my neck. I raised my arms to pin my hair back, but they began to shake, and so I let it hang, loosely.

I was exhausted.

The wound, the vision from last night, the note, the riots, Dyna.

It was unlike me to feel emotional, or feel inclined to weep, but in this instance, whether from sheer exhaustion or overwhelm, the urge to do so prickled behind my eyes more powerfully than ever.

But still, no tears came, only a heavy weight of foreboding dread and sadness that lingered in my heart.

My eyes found the Noxstone blade still strewn on the floor of my chambers. I lifted it up carefully and returned it to its hiding place. Then, grabbing my spear, and placing it on my back, made for the hall.

It was almost as full as the day the King was crowned.

It was a sight to behold, for then, there had been silence, and now, there was noise across this vast space, whispers of speculation and quiet conversations merged together as a roar. All the words were to the same effect. People were speculating as to why had the King suddenly called for this meeting, with this many attendees.

"It's the Courting Season. He must be announcing the chosen candidate!"

"It's too early for that, it must be something else, those riots in Kalnasa are..."

"Sorcerers have been causing trouble again, I heard that..."

I made my way through the thronging crowds, to where, I knew, I would be allocated to stand, near the other candidates.

As I arrived, I stood next to Zeima's Princess and her escort, who were, unlike the majority of the attendees, standing quietly, looking around with interest and suspicion. Maiwen was next to them, with, it appeared, a member of the King's Royal guard, who must have been standing in for her escort. A partition separated us and the others, Vasara's candidate, and Audra's.

Audra's Prince was looking at me. His arms were crossed. His sister was speaking to him quietly, but he appeared to be unfocused on her words. He ever so slightly narrowed his eyes in my direction, then looked around me, behind me, from where I had come. His eyes found mine again, and I could tell he was wondering where Lady Dyna was.

I turned away, unable to bear the question in his eyes.

The King stepped forth, followed by his guards. A few members of his Council and Lord Elias were also there. They hovered behind him as he approached and stood in front of the throne. It felt as if an invisible force swept over the space.

Silence fell.

Everyone got on their knees. "All hail the King!" they repeated, I repeated, three times.

We rose and the King spoke.

"Thank you all for coming at such short notice. I am truly grateful and blessed to have so many loyal subjects within this city, these walls."

A suffocating tension sat in the air, growing heavier with each passing second.

"However," he paused on the word. The power of his pause was so great. Only I knew what was to come next, the others would be wondering.

"It is with great regret and despair, that I must announce a tragedy has befallen us, within the same walls of which I speak."

Some whispers then, spreading across the hall, bouncing, and leaping between lips.

The King waited for them to quieten.

"Let it be known that anyone who attacks an ally of mine, a guest..." His voice lowered with his gaze. He paused again before he said, "...Will not go unpunished."

The trepidation from the crowd was tangible.

"The Lady Dyna has been poisoned," he said, his voice rising in volume.

The silence was broken immediately. A flurry and urgency in all the murmurs sprouted to life. Zeima's Princess glanced at me, and I could feel the force of a hundred judging gazes in my direction. I could hear the disdain in their voices.

"What of her escort?"

"Wasn't he supposed to protect her?"

"He's the Captain, isn't he..."

"How did he..."

"He's never..."

I tried to block their voices, their stares out. I focused on the floor, the white and golden stone, the flecks, the splatters of colours in the marble.

It was endless, the speculation and shock from this announcement was still ongoing. Zeima's Princess placed her hand gently on my forearm.

"I am most sorry, Captain, I will pray for her."

I closed my eyes slowly, then opened them, turning to her. "Thank you, Your Highness."

On turning to my left, my plan on avoiding eye contact with the others was nullified.

Maiwen was looking at me sorrowfully, Vasara's candidate suspiciously.

I avoided the Prince's gaze. I did not wish to know how it appeared.

The King spoke again. "The Lady is alive, for now."

The crowd began to speak again, but abruptly stopped as he continued. "However, her condition is critical. This attack is of the highest severity. It is an offence to both myself, our people, and our Kingdom. Whoever committed this vile act of treachery will be found. Please, investigate, and report to my Council." He gestured behind him, "If there is anything that you know which could help us find this assailant."

He was silent for a few seconds before he said, "That is not all. The Lady was likely poisoned sometime during the night. However, our trackers have reported that during those same hours, there was a powerful surge of energy, magical in origin, within the Palace, the kind which could only emerge from an active sorcerer."

The crowd erupted into chaotic conversation.

My eyes glazed over, and I stared in front of me at my feet. There was only one explanation for such a surge. I had no idea such a thing was possible. This was...

"It is, therefore, highly possible, that this deed was committed by a sorcerer."

The crowd grew even more frantic, as did my mind.

Both myself and the Prince were the only two people who knew that was not the case. But how could we declare that? Our silence would mean Dyna's poisoner would invariably remain undetected, and the direction of this investigation would remain incorrect, so fundamentally and devastatingly wrong.

But to reveal it would mean our certain deaths.

"Before this tragedy, I had planned to keep the following information from you, at least for a time. I am sure you will understand why. We live in fragile and complicated times. But now, it is more relevant than ever." The King's voice was soft. He spoke unhurriedly, but there was a sense of eminent importance to his words that silenced the audience again.

He took in a deep breath and spoke, "My father and mother were victims of sorcery. They died by the hands of sorcerers."

Not a single sound, or breath, or whisper met his statement. Shock had stolen them all.

This information, combined with all the rest. The threads and fates of all the individuals I had come across were linked, but in a way I could not see, could not grasp at.

"For twenty years, we have lived in peace. But it has been a false peace. Sorcerers continue to commit acts of violence and sabotage. They plot against us almost daily. This cannot be allowed to continue. Not when they seek to tear down the very structures, the very history on which humankind has been built. Not when they murder our families, our allies, and our leaders. We can no longer stand by and accept the inevitable destruction we invite upon ourselves if we do nothing. This latest act is tantamount to a declaration of war."

The crowd began to speak again, this time their voices almost becoming shouts. Lord Elias looked at the King with concern, I noticed. His Council members however, seemed unperturbed.

"People of Athlion. It is my greatest wish to see you live, to see you thrive, to see you prosper, and survive in this world. To watch as you grow old and bear children, who are free to laugh, and play, and roam anywhere in these lands, without the threat of harm. It is my greatest wish to protect you. I will dedicate my life to this goal. In return, I ask you to assist me in doing so. Some of you here may remember the war, some of you may even have survived it…lost those you loved to it. We cannot and *will* not wait for the sorcerers to rise again, to burn and devastate our lands, and our homes, as they did once before."

The King's voice, although as smooth, graceful, and cold as before, was different now. It was forceful, powerful, the weight of his words could be felt keenly with every sentence.

Murmurs of assent emerged from the attendees.

"Our trackers are in pursuit as we speak. Please assist them in any way you are able, and please, protect yourselves and your loved ones. Keep them safe. We must band together, in times of calamity and doubt, to be each other's security and strength."

The crowd were staring at him in awe and reverence.

"That is all. You may go."

People began leaving, speaking amongst themselves. I turned around to do the same when the King called out.

"Not you, Captain." He turned to my left. "Nor you, Prince."

I finally looked at Audra's Prince, who was slightly turned towards the door. He stopped and spun on his heel when he realised he was being addressed.

He quirked a brow. "Me? Your Majesty?"

"If you would."

The Prince's sister glanced at him worriedly.

"You are the King," the Prince said. "So, I undoubtedly will." He smiled, tightly.

Much faster than I would have anticipated, the hall was emptied. Zeima's and Jurasa's candidates cast me sympathetic glances on their way out.

Left behind were myself, a far distance to my left, the Prince, and in front of us, the King, flanked by his guards, and his Council members.

"Please, come forth." The King gestured with one hand for us to come closer. He then sat on his throne.

I did as he asked immediately. The Prince was slower to respond but followed, coming up to stand at my left, an arm's length away.

We didn't look at each other.

"Prince," the King started. He stopped, pondering his next words. "The trackers have informed me that the surge of energy came from the West Wing of the Palace,"

They knew.

"There is a North, East, West, and South within each Wing, including the West Wing," the King explained. "Since the Courting Season began, we have always stationed candidates in the West Wing based on their geography in relation to Vasara. North for Kalnasa's candidate, East for Zeima's, West for Jurasa's, and South…for Audra's."

The Prince remained silent. I remained silent.

"I'm quite sure you're astute enough to understand what I am about to say. The trackers have informed me that the surge came from the South of the West Wing, where you reside." The King clasped his hands in front of him on his lap as he finished speaking.

I had not been sure, but now I was. This was my doing. When that woman had touched my skin, I had felt such a strong force enter my body, my chest, my mind. I had been the source of the surge, from the Prince's room. There was no question that the Prince too, had come to this conclusion by now.

The gravity of this situation was undeniable, the risk, the implications, the potential consequences, were all insurmountably devastating.

But the Prince…the Prince laughed, lightly, as if a silver chime had sounded.

"Your Majesty. Are you asking if I am a sorcerer? If you are, couldn't you get one of your trackers to…sniff me? Or whatever it is that they do." He waved his hand over himself.

He gave a polite but entirely false smile. I was looking at him now, marvelled at his ability to act so blithely in this situation.

But the Prince's gaze remained forwards, not meeting mine.

The King narrowed his eyes and returned a similar smile in kind. It was like watching two snakes tilted up on their bellies thrusting their necks forwards, hissing at one another, waiting for the other to strike.

"If I believed you were the culprit, you would not be standing here now."

The Prince jerked his head back and raised his eyebrows. He clearly didn't believe that was true. "So, what is it you wish to know, Your Majesty?"

"Such a powerful surge must, undoubtedly, have come from a powerful sorcerer. You are a man who possesses astute and great observation skills, it is well documented and rumoured. I wish to know if you noticed anything Prince." The King's words were languid.

"You flatter me, but even I cannot employ such skills while sleeping, Your Majesty."

The King remained silent for a few moments.

"The Captain has suffered a great deal from this incident." The King turned to look at me. "Is there anything you wish to ask the Prince in relation to the disturbance?"

I couldn't shake the feeling the King knew something about the interactions the Prince and I had experienced. However, if so, as he said, why would he not apprehend us immediately, and how would he have gathered such proof?

It had not escaped me that the guards outside the Prince's room had not noticed the disturbance. The Prince had later explained to me that a powder had been responsible for that. Was it possible that the King had become aware of its use on his Palace staff? Even so, the powder rendered those guards unconscious and therefore, they would have been unable to recall any information.

The Prince looked at me then, placing his hands behind his back, and tilting his head to the left. I did not meet his eye, but instead, looked at the King as I said, "If the Prince was sleeping, it seems futile, Your Majesty."

"If... the Prince...was sleeping," the King repeated, slowly, as if he were savouring every word. He looked at the ground in thought. "Do you suspect anyone, Captain?" he asked, slowly looking up again.

Answering this question was dangerous, and so I only replied, "Nobody in particular."

"Do you believe a sorcerer did this?" the King asked.

I frowned slightly. "I would not presume to know. But if Your Majesty believes it possible, then I believe it is a strong possibility as well."

"I do not believe in coincidences...that is all." He looked at the Prince as he said it.

"Your Majesty, may I ask...if the sorcerer's trail has been caught?" the Prince asked.

The King looked behind him at Lord Elias.

Elias stepped forwards and spoke, unusually tense. "The trackers found two places in Iloris where teleports were used. The intruders were probably the source, teleporting out of Vasara to escape. The trackers are currently trying to find out where those teleports led to."

"I see." Audra's Prince nodded, "Thank you, My Lord." He bowed to Lord Elias, in what felt like a mocking gesture.

"Captain, did you notice anything?" the King asked.

"Your Majesty?"

"Anything unusual? Your quarters are next to the Lady Dyna's are they not?"

I steadied myself. I knew my facial expression remained blank, but my mind was a torrent of anxiety and desperation.

"Unfortunately not, Your Majesty. It grieves me that I was not...able to protect her."

I could feel the Prince's eyes on me then. Again.

Fargreaves grumbled from behind the Prince. "Why exactly was it, that you weren't able to do so, Captain? It strikes me as highly unusual. Since when were you so careless?"

My jaw muscles twitched as I met the man's eyes. But before I could answer him, the Prince doubled over next to me.

He was laughing.

"Forgive me, forgive me, My Lord." He waved his hand back and forth in front of his face as he straightened up. "But since when did you protect anything... other than your own self interest?" He placed his hand on his abdomen as he let out a sigh. I looked at him, internally shocked, but externally unaffected.

"The question is for the Captain, not for you, Prince," Fargreaves replied, looking at the Prince with contempt. "Unless you would like us to return to the question regarding the South Wing?"

The Prince clicked his tongue.

"The fault lies with me, not with the Prince," I said. "You are right, I failed to be diligent and protect her, that is my burden to bear, and my shame. I cannot answer your question. I can only promise not to repeat my errors and commit myself to finding the culprit."

"And how do you intend on doing that?" Fargreaves asked me.

"However necessary," I replied.

The Prince interjected again. "The fault cannot lie with both the Captain and the sorcerer, so which is it, Sir?" He looked at Fargreaves.

"That is something only time can determine, Your Highness," Fargreaves spat back.

The Prince nodded. "Yes, yes, I agree. That is usually the case. The truth has an interesting way of making itself known."

"Indeed," the King replied. The King's voice snapped Fargreaves out of his temperament and he bit his tongue, not replying to the Prince this time.

"Your parents, Your Majesty, for example. The truth of their death was *certainly* unexpected." The Prince glanced at him.

The King simply sat there, clearly assuming the Prince had not finished, waiting for him to do so.

But the Prince said nothing else.

Lord Elias replied, "The King has been working to uncover the culprits of his parents' death for a while."

"Ahh, I see, so His Majesty believed it best to conduct that investigation in secret."

"Exactly," Elias replied gruffly.

"But not this investigation," the Prince added, inclining his head in Lord Elias' direction.

"It's not for you to question His Majesty's actions. Your involvement in this affair is still questionable. Your deeds have not yet come to light," Fargreaves said.

"*My* deeds?" The Prince's voice changed so suddenly I couldn't help but turn to look at him. He sounded as if he was circling Fargreaves, watching, enjoying his oblivion before he pounced.

The Prince took one step forwards. One step. That was all. Now he was in front of me, his fingers fiddling behind his back, his thumb running along the edge of his fingers.

One step, and everyone had held their breaths.

The Prince smiled at him sweetly. "I thought I recognised you, ever since you approached my sister and I at the opening ceremony, but I couldn't quite remember. And then—" he clicked his fingers— "it came to me."

Fargreaves' mouth twisted as if he had just swallowed something sour.

"I remember your visits to Audra. I remember…" His voice grew quieter and more drawn out, "…What they were for."

Fargreaves puffed his chest out and laughed sardonically. "I made no such visits."

"Didn't you just hear His Majesty?" He pointed at the King without taking his eyes off Fargreaves. "I am a man in possession of astute observation skills. Are you denying His Majesty's judgement?"

"As His Majesty said, such skills are based on rumour alone."

"And documentation." The Prince held one finger in the air.

The King watched the two of them patiently, his chin was propped up by his right hand, his elbow resting on the arm of his throne. He made no sign he was bothered by this diversion in conversation, in fact, he appeared interested in it.

I, however, felt uneasy.

"Documentation likely based on rumour," Fargreaves retorted.

"If that's the case, then why do you remain so suspicious about my activities? If my skills of observation are pure speculation, then why would you have expected me to witness anything at all?"

Fargreaves stilled, like a fly caught in a spider's web.

One more step forwards from the Prince. I watched him move. I waited, I wondered what he would do next, how he would go in for the kill.

I found myself almost tantalised by it.

"You're becoming confused, Sir. You don't even remember the points you yourself made mere minutes ago." The Prince tutted, then let out a mocking and exaggerated sigh. "How can you serve His Majesty like this?"

"That's enough, Prince," Lord Elias said.

The Prince ignored him, taking another step forwards.

"But… my memory is impeccable. Most unfortunately. You were there. You did visit. You may not remember, but I do. *Very* well."

"This is conjecture, Fargreaves does not like to venture far from Vasara," a dark-haired man cut in. Trenton, I recalled his name.

"Then he must have liked the reason for his visit far more than he disliked the travel."

"Prince," Lord Elias cut in again, a warning sound in his tone.

"Which was it...the young girls or the young boys that you favoured? That, I can't quite recall."

The King raised one eyebrow behind his hand, and side-eyed Fargreaves. Lord Elias, who had been about to warn the Prince again, left his mouth open.

*Young girls and young boys...*

Fargreaves scowled. "Your lies will not save you from suspicion."

The Prince placed one hand on his upper chest, removing it from behind his back. "Oh Fargreaves, come now, you don't remember? Don't—" he started laughing — "Don't you remember when you mistakenly thought I was for sale? The first time we met? You looked so mortified when he told you who I was."

*Thought he was for sale.*

My heart sank.

"Although I confess, I *had* half-forgotten it myself. You were one man in a sea of nefarious men I would prefer... to have forgotten." The Prince's voice grew quieter towards the end of his sentence.

Lord Elias was looking at Fargreaves with undisguised contempt. The King was watching the Prince fascinated.

"Your Majesty," Fargreaves addressed the King. "He is lying, this is an unacceptable attempt to divert attention from this inquiry. I recommend that we detain him now." Fargreaves stepped towards the Prince, his eyes glowering with anger.

I, without contemplating or thinking, stepped forwards as well, so that I was in front of the Prince.

The King's eyebrows raised even higher at that.

My movement had been a mistake.

If I hadn't visited the Prince, that surge might never have occurred. If I had never stolen that paper, he would never have attempted to retrieve it here, and the sorcerer would not have read its contents and attacked him. I felt not only responsible for Dyna's condition, but for the danger and suspicion the Prince was now under.

But still, these were feelings based on events which I knew to have occurred. To the others present, there would be no reason, no understandable reason for me to defend the Prince, at all.

"What are you doing, Captain? He is likely responsible for the Lady's demise, and you stand there and defend him?!" Fargreaves spat.

"He is not responsible," I replied, calmly.

"How can you be so certain of that?" the King asked, removing his hand from his chin, and draping it over his legs.

I looked slightly over my shoulder and met eyes with the Prince for the first time during this audience. His eyes betrayed nothing, but the slight tightening of his lips, the tug at their corner, which I had witnessed many times now, told me he was pleased with this development.

I turned back around before I could react to his facial expression, and addressed the King, "He is not a sorcerer, as you know. I agree with Your Majesty that a sorcerer was the likely culprit. After all, your healers have not been able to understand or uncover how the Lady was poisoned in the first place. That strikes me as the work of sorcery, Your Majesty."

I had no choice. If the Prince and I were to avoid suspicion, I had to use the incorrect presumptions these men were making against them.

I had chosen our safety over Dyna's justice. A deep disdain for myself enveloped me, so consuming, that it was hard to hide as I spoke.

"I wish for the real culprit to be brought to justice." The disdain grew more intense. "Your Majesty, the Prince saved your life, and he, I believe, is not careless, nor reckless enough to murder a candidate while he is here, and certainly not by poisoning them, or by working with a sorcerer. I agree that there are several…threads and points of information which may cast suspicion over him, but they are not evidential. They are simply circumstantial, and weakly so. It must also be recognised that anyone who was planning to undertake this attack, would have done well to cast suspicion on the Prince, in light of his reputation."

My words had a dual meaning. One, to the men in front of me, about my thoughts and declaration of the Prince's innocence with regards to Dyna, and another, to the Prince himself, reaffirming my belief he was innocent of the crimes the note on that Noxscroll mentioned.

Reaffirming I believed he was framed, that I would defend him, until the last.

I glanced back at the Prince as I finished speaking. His facial features had become more relaxed, his smile softer. His grin seemed to communicate he had expected I'd turn to look at him.

The King stood. "You make some excellent points, Captain, I confess. Though I am surprised to hear you voice them, since you seemed so reluctant to share your suspicions and thoughts before."

"While I will not condemn an individual I suspect to be guilty without evidence, I will defend one I believe to be innocent."

"How touching," Fargreaves said smugly.

I stared at him, making no effort to hide my disgust at his existence.

"That's lovely, but the most guilty often appear most innocent, Captain. We must consider all possibilities," Lord Elias said flatly.

"Here's a possibility that could prove to be informative." The Prince stood by my side again. "Where is Jurasa's escort? He's been missing for days. Perhaps you should look into that, My Lord?"

I tensed up beside the Prince. After the great efforts I had just gone to defend him, he was actively mentioning something dubious which he and I were directly involved in. Regardless of whether this was to deter Elias, the King would not dismiss this point so easily.

Elias furrowed his brows and stared at the Prince.

"We agree that it is rather suspicious," the King said coolly.

"Who knows? Perhaps the culprit is the same as the one who poisoned the Lady?" the Prince speculated, knowing full well that was incorrect.

"We do not know if the escort is dead or is simply missing. Furthermore, if he was murdered, the motive for his killing is very much unclear," the King replied.

The Prince shrugged. "Yes, that's true, but still, I just thought I should mention it."

"We thank you for your cooperation, Prince," the King said.

"Of course," the Prince looked at Fargreaves.

"You may return. We will keep you informed of any developments. If you do learn anything, please, share it with us." The King nodded to his guards, dismissing us.

"Most definitely," the Prince said cheerfully. I nodded.

We bowed and turned to leave. The Prince followed behind me by several steps and the guards behind him some more.

Once I had left the hall, I did not turn around to look at the Prince, for there were guards who had been sent with us to escort us to our rooms. It was of course, an act which was labelled something in the interest of our safety, but it was most certainly an act to keep us under watch.

I made my way immediately to Dyna's room. The guard left me at the entrance of the North of the West Wing.

I had taken a few steps down it when a hand on my wrist pulled me down a narrower walkway.

"Ssshhh." The Prince put his finger to his lips. I stared at him, looking down at his face, which was far too close to mine. I stepped back. He abruptly let go of my arm and stepped back as well.

"What are you doing?!" I whispered, panicked. "Are you completely..."

The Prince crossed his arms, and his left leg over his right, leaning back against the wall. He raised his eyebrows and smiled with his mouth open slightly.

Seeing his amused expression, I composed myself. "Your Highness, you shouldn't be here," I whispered again.

"Since when I have done what should be done, Captain?" he whispered back.

"I need to go back, Your Highness." Our conversation continued to be spoken in hushed tones.

The Prince looked me once over and said, "How are you feeling?"

I startled, how was I feeling?

"What does it matter? I am not the one lying prostrate in my bed, Your Highness."

The Prince appeared unimpressed. "You were... yesterday." He sounded irritated at his own reminder.

"I am well, Your Highness."

The Prince tilted his head. "But... your hair is different."

"What?" The bite in my tone was clear and so I quickly added, "That's not connected."

"Yes, it is," he argued, looking delighted with himself.

"Your Highness, I am grateful you asked over my welfare, but I must go." I started to move, but hesitated as the Prince, I had noticed, was looking down at his shoes, appearing troubled.

I knew I should leave, but instead I found myself speaking, "Your Highness?"

He sighed and with one press, pushed himself off the wall. "I can imagine your thoughts, Captain. That it was because of your decision to warn me last night, that you were neglectful of your duties etcetera etcetera that the Lady is ill."

I was silent, he turned to me. "Am I correct?"

"Your Highness—"

The Prince held up a hand. "Don't bother answering that. I know that I'm correct." His every movement, the pinch of his brow, the fiddling of his fingers, exuded unease.

I shifted back to my original position and said quietly, "Why are you here, Your Highness?"

He shrugged. "To thank you."

I couldn't help but shake my head. "You do not seem to be someone who is prone to gratitude."

"That is because I have rarely met a person I had good reason to be thankful for," he sounded pensive. "Or to."

I said nothing. The more I learnt about the Prince, the more I realised that was likely accurate.

"And I came to offer you my help."

That was suspicious.

"You? Offer me help? Your Highness?"

"You help me, and I'll help you," he said casually. He pointed in the direction around the corner, towards Dyna's room. Then he folded his hand back under his arm.

"You are already under suspicion. It is not wise—"

The Prince stepped towards me. "The time for making wise decisions has long since passed, don't you think, Captain?"

"No..." I let the word linger. "I do not think so, Your Highness."

"Don't you want to find out who was responsible?" Another step towards me.

"We should not be having this conversation."

"We've had plenty of conversations two people shouldn't have, Captain."

"Your Highness," I protested. The closer the Prince grew, the stranger I felt.

"Captain," he repeated in the same pressing tone.

"The choices I made, which led to these events, and to the crossing of our paths were mine to make, alone. I did so without any incentive, or bribe, or the promise of a favour. When I"— I looked around to make sure there were no guards close by — "helped you, I did so with no expectation of help in return. Any danger I faced in doing so was the result of my own decisions. You do not need to place yourself in this predicament. I want nothing and expect nothing from you."

The Prince let out a long breath. "But I want something from you, Captain."

I waited and let those words sink in. I couldn't understand which emotion was dominating my mind. Confusion? Anticipation? Surprise?

"Your Highness, I apologise but I must do what I have failed to do thus far. I have been preoccupied with—"

"With things which have led you to uncover vital information regarding the welfare of your people."

I looked down and placed one hand through my hair quickly, the Prince watched my movement and then continued. "I would like your help, Captain. You may accept, or you may refuse. You may also accept or refuse my offer to help you but..."

He came very close to me then, lowering his voice to the quietest level I had heard him speak, "You are *one* of those people, Captain, I have reason to be grateful for, that I so rarely meet. It would be unfortunate... if we were to part ways... after only having just crossed paths."

My entire body was raked with tension. My breath stuck in my lungs. I couldn't see any reason why or how crossing paths with this Prince had been a good thing.

But...I could not deny, to part ways now would feel...an error.

I composed myself, shaking my head before replying, "Perhaps it would be for the best, Your Highness."

"Do you really think so?" He leant his face forwards slightly.

I didn't know. Yes, no. I could not decide.

I took a deep breath in and turned to the left to avoid his gaze. As I did so, the brush of a hand, his hand, slipped against my right cheek.

It was the back of his fingers. So fast, so light, like the touch of the wind, come and gone in an instant.

I reached for that cheek myself automatically, but the Prince's hand had already been drawn away, hovering in the air near my neck.

"You're a liar, Captain. I should have known, after the performance you put on back there."

I lowered my hand. He did the same.

"You still have a fever."

"It will pass."

"Will it? Hasn't it been days now?" He took a step back, glancing at me reproachfully.

"I cannot ask the healers for their attention, not now, Your Highness."

The Prince snorted softly. "Why would you? They're dreadful."

Yes, the hope for Dyna was already slim, and with this fact, even slimmer.

I sighed and looked dejectedly at the floor, the Prince, who must have realised my thoughts said, "Do you think it is deliberate?"

I knew what he was referring to, for I had already wondered so myself. "The quality of the healers?"

"So, you thought so too."

"I cannot say."

"You cannot say who was the culprit of this affair yet proclaimed me innocent in front of His Majesty himself." He chuckled lightly.

I looked at him sharply. "That is because you are innocent."

"Only to you. To the others, I am…" He thought for a moment, searching for a word but only ended with, "…Not."

I looked at him, trying to think of a way to end this encounter.

The Prince got on his knees suddenly.

"Your Highness?!" Even when whispering, the anxiety in my tone was obvious.

The Prince raised his head and looked up at me from the floor. "I only want to see the wound."

I moved my leg away. "That's not necessary, Your Highness."

He placed his palm on the tip of my shoe. "You don't want to call the healers away. Do you wish to die instead?"

I didn't reply, glancing around nervously, my fists clenched tightly.

The Prince was still looking up at me from the floor. Here, the shadows of the narrow walkway struck his jaw, underneath his neck, his hair, making his every line look more defined.

The darkness, it suited him somehow, I found myself thinking.

The Prince narrowed his eyes, then moved his hand, still looking at me.

I didn't move.

He was still looking at me when his hand made contact with the bottom of my shin and slid underneath my pants.

His fingers were cold. Their light touch sent rivulets of faint chills up my leg.

I turned away, suddenly feeling strange.

The Prince lowered his head and placed his other hand on my leg. After a few minutes, during which I was holding my breath, anxiously anticipating what might happen if a guard came down the walkway.

The Prince stood up and back. "It looks better."

I cleared my throat and nodded, still facing towards the main corridor.

Instantly, the Prince was in front of me, having come around to my left.

"What are you looking for, Captain? Nobody will see us. The guards are just as inept as the healers."

"I…" I cleared my throat again. "…Was only being cautious, Your Highness."

The Prince pointed at my leg. "You're not cautious. And I am glad of that. I thank you for it."

I turned away down at the floor again, unable to meet his gaze still. I couldn't say why, but the Prince's visit here had made me feel much more restless and uneasy than his presence had done so before. The events of the last few days had altered my mindset. Perhaps he was right, I had not been cautious before and this was the result.

"Do you still have his blade?" the Prince whispered.

I nodded. "Yes, Your Highness."

"Keep it."

"You do not…wish to have it back, Your Highness?" I looked at him cautiously.

A pained expression crossed his face for a brief moment, before it resumed its normal countenance. "No, Captain, I do not wish to possess that weapon."

Of course not, why would he have wanted anything of his?

"Of course, Your Highness, forgive me, I should have realised that—"

"I have enough of my own." He smiled, "I do not need another. But it may be helpful to you, in the future."

"I still cannot wield such a blade."

"You will learn, I have no doubt. Keep it, Captain. It will be better if you have it. You are after all, a more deserving owner."

"Thank you… Your Highness."

The Prince laughed again, lightly, but very quietly. "You are such an interesting man, Captain. Thanking me for a blade you rightfully took for yourself, for a blade I just declared I did not want. Why thank me for such things?"

It did not take me a second to reply. "Because I know you are capable of taking it from me, should you so wish, Your Highness."

"So, you are thankful I have not forcibly retrieved it from you?" Disappointment coloured his voice.

I frowned. I didn't know how to tactfully respond to that. I could only think to say the truth which I found escaping my lips before I could stop myself talking.

"No."

"No?"

"I suppose it is more"— I leant my head against the wall slightly, glancing at the Prince from the side — "that I am pleasantly surprised, Your Highness,"

The Prince's eyes brightened in shock, and he opened his mouth in a wide, amused smile "Pleasantly surprised?"

I nodded. "I am thankful to be pleasantly surprised by you, rather than—"

"Bitterly disappointed?" He came closer to my side, his right arm was at a ninety-degree angle next to him, leaning against the wall.

"No."

"No again?" the Prince said, teasingly.

"If you would let me finish Your Highness," I said flatly.

"Ahh, please do." He leant fully against the wall standing to my left.

"You continue to do and say things which I do not expect, or which go against that which others say about you. I am thankful the things they say are not entirely true, or that if they are, for whatever reason, you choose to refrain from exacting such behaviour towards me, Your Highness."

The Prince smiled and turned to look up at the ceiling too, wide, and white, and arched, like all the ceilings here.

"I remember when we met Captain, that you told me you didn't pay attention to rumours."

"But I am aware of them, Your Highness."

"I told you then, and I'll tell you again, that some rumours are true, Captain." He sounded insistent about the fact.

"Some are not."

We stood in silence for a few seconds.

"Do you know what my favourite rumour is? About myself?"

I had the feeling this conversation had already gone on for too long. As inept as the guards were, they would soon notice we had not yet returned to our allocated rooms.

But still, I couldn't help asking, "Which, Your Highness?"

"There are some which are…really quite awful. But they're all very creative, I will say. Still, there's one rumour, that people truly believe, even now. It's that I"— he paused and laughed with his mouth closed — "that I was blessed by the Gods." He laughed some more, the sound rumbling next to me. "That I was bestowed a 'gift' and that I must have sacrificed something in return for it. Some say it was my life span, or my soul, my emotions. Others say my memories, my rank, my…humanity."

He turned around and looked me in the eye. "Can you believe that? People truly believe I was blessed, that I was touched by the Gods, that I was…lucky."

"Some would say you are fortunate, simply for being a Prince, Your Highness."

"Then they would be wrong."

"Would they?" I asked, thinking on how I had grown up, on the starvation I had witnessed in Kalnasa.

The Prince was gazing at me openly and curiously. He seemed in that moment, not a Prince, or an assassin. Not a warrior, or a spy, or a Vulture. Not confident, or proud, or skilled. He only seemed a young man, blessed only with the one thing all were afforded – a life raked with struggle.

I met his gaze. "People will believe whatever makes them feel most comfortable about something, Your Highness. You are…renowned, your deadliness is a source of fear for many. Perhaps by believing your activities have a point, a purpose, a divine source, they feel they can rest easier."

The Prince smiled softly. "Captain, you cannot begin to know what is right or wrong about me."

I swallowed, in silence, perhaps that was true, but, somewhere, somehow, I felt that it was not.

"Perhaps that is what it means to know a person," I said, turning to face forwards, and looking at my shin. "To learn all that is right and wrong about them, both in rumour, and in self, and be able to tell which is which, which is real."

"Your Highness," I added, realising that I had omitted it from the end of that sentence.

"Two words…which are not," the Prince said.

"You are a Prince."

The Prince raised one eyebrow.

"Unless of course, you did sacrifice your rank, in return for your blessings, Your Highness," I found myself adding, and smiling.

The Prince tutted. "Ahhh, now you know my darkest secret, Captain."

"So, I have begun…to know what is right and what is wrong about you then, Your Highness."

The Prince turned to me, and we looked at each other once again. "Are you sure that's something you'd want?"

Our gazes remained fixed upon one another. The words we had spoken, the question he had asked growing further away, sinking into the distance, the longer we stood here.

What was I doing? I had spent far too much time here.

I moved away from the wall. "We can never be sure of anything. Your Highness, I really must—"

The Prince moved away from the wall and nodded understandingly. "Go."

Before I did, I asked, "Will you come back, Your Highness?"

The Prince looked at my hair then at my face. "Would you like me to?"

The Prince's help would make a large difference, and if he was willing to offer it, then I would be a fool to refuse it.

Perhaps I was a fool to desire it.

"Yes, Your Highness. I accept your offer."

The Prince nodded, smiling slightly. He crossed his arms again. "To be quite honest, regardless of what you had said, I would have attempted to help you, and inform you of my findings. Whoever harmed Dyna, may well intend to harm Loria."

I understood then, his true motivations. They made far more sense than the vague conclusions I had been beginning to draw.

"Of course. I understand," I said.

I moved towards the exit of the hallway, then found myself hesitating, for the third time.

"Fargreaves," I said quietly.

The Prince sighed. "Do not trouble yourself. He will be dealt with."

I didn't know whether to be reassured or concerned.

"What does that mean?" I pressed.

The Prince walked past me, cautiously heading towards the exit himself. "That you do not need to trouble yourself," he repeated.

"I am already troubled by it...amongst other things, Your Highness," I said, thinking of the alleyway incident again.

The Prince turned around in surprise, just after peering around the corner.

"Why?" He sounded confused.

"Do you truly not understand why, Your Highness?" I repeated questioningly.

The Prince shook his head casually. "No, not really."

Wouldn't the information trouble others? I thought of Lord Elias' face, he certainly had been, but I supposed, the others had seemed impartial to it.

"He does not deserve to be in his position, with his past."

The Prince chuckled. "Most people in such positions have such pasts." Then he looked at me. "Except for you."

He peered at me thoughtfully then quietly turned and disappeared around the corner.

But I did have a past, a past he was simply unaware of.

Minutes later I returned to Dyna's room, she looked much the same as before.

Only now, there was someone by her bedside.

In front of me was a man, clad fully in black and cloaked. The bottom half of his chin was visible from under the hood, pointed and pale.

"If you wish to live, then you will stay silent."

I was speechless, not from the threat of death, but from his figure. He was tall, taller than me even.

I glanced at Dyna worriedly.

The man noticed.

"Tell me what I want to know, and I will save her."

*Save her?*

In response to the quizzical expression on my face, he removed one glove to reveal a hand, long, and lithe.

A hand on which a warm golden glow was pooling in his palm.

I had thought them all dead.

I had believed them a myth.

But here before me, here and now, stood a Healer.

## CHAPTER 56- NEMINA

I hated to admit it to myself, but the night sky in Audra was the most wondrous thing I'd ever seen. I'd heard the skies were even more beautiful in Kalnasa. I couldn't remember if that was true. The last time I'd been there, I was a small child.

Then again, I'd forgotten the sight of night skies altogether. I'd been in Audra's draining centre for years, tucked far under layers of sand and stone. No sky. No stars. Nothing.

Hiding our tracks in the sand was almost impossible, so we'd levitated to a location the female Teleporter had found. Since Baz and I could not levitate, we'd been carried by the others here, by Yaseer and Ullna.

We had landed by a darkened alcove, surrounded by mountains and cliffs which jutted up at sharp, almost threatening angles. There were trees here, but they were barren, only littered slightly with few golden leaves, their branches were dark and twisted, as twisted as the paths around these peaks. Sand still dominated the landscape. A golden sea of grain.

Baz approached me. "I can't believe you!"

I turned towards him, facing away from the sky. I had been lost in its purple and black hues for the past few minutes.

"You just let her carry me! Just like that. You ran straight over to him when we heard we'd have to be carried." He pointed behind him to Yaseer.

There had been no way, after my injuries, that I would have let Ullna near me, or had the strength to let her touch me.

"You're alive, aren't you?" I asked him, exhaustedly.

"She carried me like this." Baz tugged at the back of his shirt upwards, reaching one hand over his back. "Like I was some prey she'd picked up from the ground."

I smirked slightly witnessing his demonstration.

"Oh, I see. You find this funny." He placed his hands on his hips, smiling as well.

"She hates me far more than she dislikes you."

"That's debatable."

I looked at him with an eyebrow raised.

"Alright, it's not really debatable but still." He pointed at me, smiling a little.

"Thank you for your sacrifice," I said, half serious, half not.

"What do I get in return?"

"Stop being ridiculous," I mumbled.

"Not even a kiss from my beloved?" He approached me with his arms outstretched.

I narrowed my eyes at him and lent back slightly. "Please no."

He chuckled, giggled again, and put his arms down. He sighed. "They've made food. Come and have some."

I shook my head. I had no appetite after having blades pulled from my back.

"You just purged up your stomach contents, you need to replace them," Baz said seriously.

"I will, just not now. I'd probably just purge them again if I tried."

Baz twisted his mouth in understanding, then nodded, and left in the direction of the food.

I sat down on the ground, pulling my knees towards myself.

Someone came up beside me.

It was the female Teleporter. She held something out to me.

"They said you won't eat, but at least take this." She handed me a flask of water.

The thought of liquid sloshing around my stomach made me internally retch, but I took it from her, and replied, "Thank you."

She hovered there.

I looked up at her. "Yes?"

She was staring at me liberally, as if I were a strange exotic animal, or an unusual plant she had come across on the road.

"Do you want something?" I asked, sipping at the water. As much as drinking made me feel nauseous, dehydration would be worse. I remembered all too well what being deprived of water felt like.

The woman nodded yes slowly, then spoke, "My sister she...she's a Vessel in Audra."

The flask I was bringing towards my face stopped halfway.

I gave her a sidelong glance. "What are you asking?"

Although this conversation was clearly a difficult one, the woman seemed almost calm.

"I want to ask if you'd seen her or...whether you know if she's alive." She stopped for a moment then added, "Or dead."

I returned the drink to my lips and took another small sip. "You're asking the wrong person. You should ask him." I nodded in Baz's direction.

"I've already asked him."

I exhaled deeply. "I wasn't...with the others for a long time."

"I know. But if there's a chance you know, I need to ask." Her voice remained resolute, but there was also a hint of desperation in her tone.

I didn't reply, only rubbed my thumb along the edge of the rust-coloured flask.

"She's younger than me, prettier. Her skin was lighter too. She had long hair and pale brown eyes."

This could have been a number of the Vessels.

I shook my head no.

"She had a birthmark on her chin."

*Her chin.*

The flask shattered between my hands.

The water soaked through the fabric of my pants.

My hands were bleeding, but I wasn't looking at them, I was only looking forwards, at the landscape, at the ground far below this jutted out stone and the sky in front of me.

The others overheard the shattering. Baz ran over, and Yaseer stood, glancing over at us. With his senses he didn't need to move to understand anything.

Baz ran between us. "I told you not to ask her!"

The woman tried to cut around him, but he blocked her path.

"Why did you do that? Do you know her? Do you know someone with a birthmark?" The woman sounded persistent.

Baz tried to hold her back.

"Do you know her?" she repeated, from behind him.

"Aeesha, go back, can't you see she's not able—"

"Yes," I let out in one raspy breath.

Baz turned around instantly, both he and Aeesha were staring at me.

"She's dead," I uttered.

Amali was dead.

Aeesha's lips quivered. "Oh," she said quietly.

Baz looked at her pitifully. "Aeesha—"

"I know now. It's alright. I know. I just…just… wanted to know."

Seconds later she shouted. "She's…oh Gods…she's…. she's…"

Little by little, Aeesha broke down. She began to let out choked sobs and grabbed Baz's arms.

Ullna came over in a few quick strides. "What have you done?" she said to me "Why are you upsetting her? This noise will attract attention."

I didn't look at her. "Her sister is dead. She died in the same draining centres we are camping above."

Ullna went quiet, then she placed her arms around Aeesha's shoulders, and led her away.

Baz remained behind. "I didn't know…you knew anyone there."

I placed my now healing finger on the ground, stroking patterns between the small, gravelled stones. "I did, before."

"She's been asking everyone for years."

I laughed bitterly. "Of course, I would be the one who knew, the one to tell her."

"Maybe it's… better… that she knows," Baz said quietly.

Listening to Aeesha's wails, it was hard to convince myself that was the case.

"She used to give me some of her rations," I murmured. "I was thirteen then, she was the same age. They'd taken mine away because I..."

I paused as I remembered the reason. Not one I could utter aloud. Not one they could know.

Baz was silent, patiently waiting.

"Anyway. She gave me half of hers. We spoke a few times afterwards. I vowed I'd pay her back in some way. But—"

"That's not possible anymore," Baz finished my sentence.

"Not in life, no."

"Not in life?" Baz sounded concerned.

"In death though, it is."

Baz snorted, "You say the weirdest shit."

"I mean it." I met his eyes. "Even if it's the only thing I do. Even if it's the only reason I'm here, if I die, I don't care...as long as they all do too."

"Don't...Don't say things like that," Baz sounded offended.

"Don't pretend you don't know," I replied. "That's what they want me for." I nodded in Ullna, Yaseer's, and Aeesha's direction.

"But you don't have to."

"I want to," I said, forcefully.

"Not when you first arrived there, remember? You wanted to leave. You wanted peace."

I rubbed my forehead. "I still do, but"— I chuckled — "I want them to pay as well."

"You can't have both. Peace and revenge." Baz told me.

"I can't have the first, without the second."

Baz sounded regretful when he replied. "You won't find any solace in vengeance."

"Maybe that's true for some people, but I won't be able to rest until they're had their retribution."

"This isn't the right way, Nemina."

I crossed my legs and spun around on my hips to face him. "Do you know which is? Do they?" I gestured behind me.

Baz didn't say anything.

"I don't care what you think. I don't care if you hate me. If they all hate me. Since nobody has been able to tell us the right way, I think it's time to stop looking. We don't have the time to look anymore."

Aeesha's sobs sounded in the background, even louder.

Baz sat down in front of me, crossing his legs too. "I understand—"

"No—"

"No?" Baz sounded so furious I jumped slightly.

He spoke again. "I've spared you the details because who would want to hear them? Because they'd probably upset you. But..." He pulled both his sleeves up.

His arms were covered in scars.

"We can't heal like you. Those of us who weren't born sorcerers, we can't. I spent my whole life hearing about how cruel sorcerers were, how evil and then...humans came to our town, it was more like a shack. They came for us because we were poor and who would notice we were dead and gone? Who would question it? They'd just say we died of hunger."

He held his forearms up. "I had a mother you know. They took her as well. I don't even know where she is. And they took me, and they did this. They didn't explain why. They didn't say anything. We all had to figure it out for ourselves. I was fifteen, Nemina." He rubbed the tip of his nose with his thumb and let out a sad laugh. "Do you know why I didn't tell you about this?"

I looked at him and very slightly shook my head.

"It's because I was afraid you'd hate me." He began tapping his fingers restlessly against his knees. "I'm not a human, but I'm not a sorcerer either. I'm just floating around somewhere between the two." He waved his hand from left to right. "I was afraid the people here, back there, that they would despise me for that. That you would."

He searched my face, when I didn't speak, he continued, "You say I don't understand, and maybe I don't, not like you do, but" — he looked at his arms — "does it really matter? Whether I was born a sorcerer or I was made one? Does it really matter?"

His brown eyes seemed larger than normal as they found mine. "Does it? Tell me, how is it that I don't understand?"

I maintained eye contact with him. "Who do you think did this to you?"

He frowned "What? What do you mean *think*?"

"I mean. Do you think it was those humans, who took you away, who gave you those scars? Or do you think it was the sorcerers, who because of their actions in the past, gave the humans a reason to hunt us, to drain us, and that because of that hunt, the balance of the world was thrown into disarray, and people like you needed to replace those who had died? Was it the humans or the sorcerers who did this to you?"

Baz stood quickly, his sleeves falling down his arms. "That's the problem. You think it's all sorcerers and humans and a large line down the middle."

"Isn't it?"

"No!" Baz shouted. "No," he said more quietly. "It's about the people in the world who want to hurt others, who want to beat them into submission, who want to dominate, who want to kill." His words were hurried and frantic.

"You mean like me?" I asked, tilting my head up.

Baz froze. The finger he had been pointing at the ground stilled in place.

"I said you didn't understand because you don't. It has nothing to do with the fact that you were born a human, and nothing to do with what you've been through. You just listed several things, that as of now, all humans are doing to all sorcerers, either born or made, and still, you act as if there is a complexity to this situation."

"I don't want to become like them Nemina."

"That's your decision."

"You act like kindness is the weakness." He sounded mournful. "But the real weakness is hate. That's a cheap thing for those afraid to pay."

"Pay?" I looked straight ahead.

"Being kind costs," he said quietly. "Empathy too. But there's a power in that. It's a cost only the strong can endure...I think."

I glanced up at him, my brows creased. I didn't know what to say. What to make of his words. Weren't there plenty of people in this world deprived of love? Those who had to survive without it? Weren't they strong when all they had to rely on was themselves?

But...I knew that was not what he meant.

He did not mean that receiving love was the strength.

But giving it.

I shook my head. "I've endured enough."

"People always call it righteous..." he trailed off. I raised my eyes to him. He met my glance sidelong.

"Anger," he explained. "That's what they say, isn't it? Righteous anger."

"Sometimes it is," I answered flatly.

"Most of the time it isn't. Most of the time it's an excuse. People like to look for someone to blame. For something to hate. It makes them feel...powerful." He let out a mournful chuckle. "But...where's the justice in that? How many people are angry at others, not because they deserve it...but because it's better than the alternative. Better than accepting life is cruel to everyone."

I scoffed. "Life is cruel because people are. And those people deserve to choke on wrath."

"If you spend your life, making it your mission to rid this world of cruelty, you're going to end up bitter. There's no ridding it from the world, Nemina. It's not your responsibility to—"

"That's what people say to themselves so they can sleep at night, knowing those people are breathing the same air."

"Or revenge is what people cling on to, to make it all seem sensical. There's no sense in trying to understand bad people. Or killing them. It's like trying to swallow the ocean. You'll never be fast enough. It will only fill up again."

I shook my head, scoffing. "With water. Not with filth."

"Nemina—"

"I thought you wanted to fight?" I turned to him.

"No," he said firmly. "I wanted to help."

I was quiet. So was he. We stared at each other at an impasse.

This was pointless. Baz saw the good in people.

It was not that I did not, only that I saw it in the people with the chains around their ankles, their necks.

And I could not stand it any longer.

I had lied to myself, when I told myself I could run, that I could leave it all behind, that I wanted to.

I knew I could not rest unchained, while those chains still existed.

I turned away and asked Baz something I had been wondering about. "What did that man mean? When he said that he'd take care of the energy surge? That tracker?"

Baz seemed grateful for the change in topic. He sighed. "He works for us. With Yaseer. He helps to divert the trackers away from us when he can."

I thought about what Baz had told me about the attacks. "Then I'm not sure I have much confidence in his promise."

"He can't possibly do it every time."

"I suppose. When did—"

Aeesha ran over towards us, Ullna and Yaseer bounding behind her. I stood immediately but before I could regain my balance, a hand grabbed me, and a bright blue circle surrounded us all.

When we came through the other end of the teleport, we were falling.

We were still in Audra, that much I could tell from the sky, from the cliffs, but now we were in a completely different location, somewhere high above a large building.

"Ullna!" Yaseer shouted.

Ullna dove in my direction and grabbed onto me by the cloak I was wearing. Yaseer lunged towards Baz, doing the same.

We began to levitate, but somewhere, from the edge of our vision, a dark shadow appeared.

"Riders!" Yaseer shouted. "Riders are here!"

# CHAPTER 57- NEMINA

Before us was a man, straddling across the back of a bird. An Erebask so magnificent its wingspan could have enfolded a group ten times our size. Its feathers were dark inky blue, but in the light of the moon, they appeared silver.

I'd heard of these birds.

The man was clad in an outfit that seemed to be a direct copy of his Erebask's colouring. He pressed down, and the creature soared towards us, its talons outstretched and open. Even from here I could tell one slash of its claws would rip clean through an abdomen.

Ullna, Yaseer, and Aeesha began moving, trying to fly away from the clutches of all the riders. One cut across from the left striking at Yaseer, but he avoided it easily, his senses heightened.

Another went for Aeesha, she used her powers to teleport in various places across the sky, evading capture.

A third rider appeared and headed straight towards Ullna and I. She gripped the back of my cloak tighter with her left hand, then with her other, reached forwards, and tore part of the cliff edge from itself. She flung the debris in the rider's direction, who yelled out and pivoted.

*She's a Telekinetic. Darean. Class Two.*

The first man flew towards us.

On the back of his Erebask, was Aeesha's unconscious body.

He lifted something from his clothing, a dark blade, and flung it in our direction. Ullna twisted and the blade swung past us.

I needed to levitate. I needed to do it now.

I reached above me and grabbed Ullna by the wrist. She looked down at me distressed as she realised what I was doing. I pushed her wrist off mine.

"NEMINA!" Baz screamed.

I tumbled down through the sky. The weightlessness of the air was stark, the speed at which I fell even starker. I closed my eyes. I tried to focus. I had mastered the other basic skills, and so this one should be possible, under this stress, here and now, to acquire.

But I was still falling, faster and faster. I spun around so I was facing the ground but couldn't hold my position, and flipped over in the air.

Someone grabbed my arm and yanked me up.

His tied-up hair had come loose, flowing past his shoulders, onto his lilac shirt.

Baz. Baz had actually levitated.

"What are you doing?!" he exclaimed, gripping my wrist so tightly it felt as if it would bruise.

Another rider came towards us. There were more now. Seven of them.

Baz threw me into the air.

I rose above him and floated, staring at him confused. I wasn't moving.

Ullna was next to me, her hand outstretched in my direction.

Telekinetics could move people as well as objects?

Baz frowned, seemingly concentrating ferociously. In the next instant, one rider began to fly into the other. The two Erebasks yelled fretfully, clawing at one another, and tumbled down to the ground.

Baz was doing it. He was using his abilities as a Telepath.

Another rider approached us from behind. Yaseer appeared and outstretched his hand, taking the rider's sight.

But the man atop the Erebask only laughed. "You think blinding me will work?" He laughed again and flung his dagger towards Ullna. She turned around and stopped the blade in its tracks, inches before her face. I began falling again, before Yaseer grabbed me.

This wasn't enough. I had to do something. I was currently being flung around like dead weight.

The rider pressed forwards towards Ullna. He had just been about to throw another blade, when I struck Yaseer's wrist using strength enhancement, and using speed enhancement, leapt across the sky a short distance.

I landed on top of the Erebask's back.

The bird shrieked and the rider turned around. He lunged with a blade at my chest, but I stopped him, grabbing his wrist and breaking it within a second.

"Fuckkkk!" he wailed, sounding terrified.

I grabbed him by the neck. He tried to remove my hands, but before he could place any real effort into the attempt, I threw him off the Erebask.

The bird screeched, clearly attached to its owner, and plunged down towards him.

"No!" I yelled at the Erebask, knowing it was futile.

In seconds, Ullna was by my side, reaching her hand out towards me.

I readied myself to jump, when at the corner of my eye, a dark blade pierced through the sky, heading towards Ulna's skull.

I made the jump, but instead of grabbing Ullna's hand, I shoved her forwards.

The blade plunged into the side of my left thigh. I yelled out. The pain was intense, ravaging at my flesh instantly. Ullna tumbled, confused as I fell.

Understanding what had happened, she flew towards me, but was stopped by another rider.

The pain from the blade was infinitely worse than last time. The force had been stronger, the speed of the blade immeasurable, and the wielder of the weapon clearly trained in a way the Captain had not been.

The man who had thrown it, his eyes were glazed over too. He couldn't even see. But it didn't matter to these men, these people. No matter what senses Yaseer took, it seemed they could work without them, that they could kill without them.

The rider who had thrown the blade, flew towards me. In the next second, the talons of his Erebask circled my torso, curling around my back. He was laughing, crazed, directing his Erebask as far away from the others as possible.

The blade was still in my leg.

I pulled it out, unable to avoid screaming as I did. The man looked down, the laugh from his face wiped away instantly. Evidently, he was still able to hear.

I stabbed the bird with all the strength I had left in its underbelly.

Its cries were so loud and so piercing, that I covered my ears as it dropped me, the other Erebasks around us cried out in a similar manner, a symphony of suffering playing through the stars.

The rider was thrown from the Erebask. Both he and I were falling adjacent to one another, tumbling towards the ground.

Above me, I could see the vague silhouettes of Yaseer and Ullna, both occupied in combat, and Baz, under Yaseer's arm, who looked unconscious. Baz was probably unused to exercising as much power as he had. After all, the vision the Captain had created, the first one I'd experienced and triggered, had completely disorientated me.

I had just been about to accept my fate, when the man falling beside me grabbed my arm, and yanked me towards him.

He spun in the air, and drew another blade from his belt, submerging it into the stone we were falling beside. It slowed our fall, not much, but enough.

Enough for us to somehow both be breathing when we landed on the ground, strewn with sand and stone, surrounded on all sides by towering buttes. The moonlight had weaved around them at just the right angle. There was a small pond, a basin, in the centre, reflecting its glow.

I had fallen on one side of the pond, the man on the other.

I could hear the sound of several of my bones breaking as I landed.

And the man, laughing again, manically.

There was no way he too hadn't suffered grievous injuries.

To the tune of his delirious laughter, I lay there on the ground, grunting and wheezing, in searing pain.

It had only been hours since I had been in agony, and here I was, writhing in it once more.

I was beginning to understand why the man was laughing.

But I could not understand why he had bothered to try and capture me. He would have had a better chance of survival had he tried to slow his fall alone.

We should never have come here, no matter the desperation, no matter the situation. Vasara's trackers were the largest unit hunting down our kind, but Audra's warriors were trained like no other, this even I knew.

And I would not, under any circumstances, return to those draining centres.

I turned onto my back, there it was again, that night sky.

Not even that could maintain its beauty now. Now this sky would forever be a reminder of this night, those screams.

I reached down to my left thigh. It was bleeding profusely, barely slowing from my healing capabilities.

I moaned from pain as I touched it.

If only the Healer could show up now. Where was he, I found myself wondering? Lounging in a lavish castle, dining in a great banquet hall, dressed in the finest silks.

As I lay here, broken and bleeding on the ground.

I turned back onto my front, with great effort, and intense pain. I dragged myself forwards, on my elbows towards the water. I sniffed it, it seemed fine. I placed a small amount on my finger, then licked it. It tasted normal. I waited a few minutes and felt nothing so, assuming I would be here for a while, and that I would die without water with this much blood loss, drank some, cupping it in my palm.

One drip had tasted adequate, but the cup tasted stale.

I raised my head to look at the man lying across from me. His hair was long and dark, now covered in dirt, and strewn across his cheeks. His features were sharp and angular. One half of his face was covered in blood, and his eye was completely swollen over, forming a purple against his brown skin. His shoulder looked as if it had dislocated, and one of his legs was clearly broken.

He slowly turned his head towards me, noticing my presence. He looked down at my hands which were cupping some water.

If he expected me to satiate his thirst, then he was even more insane than I had thought.

"Kkk, crrr..." He made some gurgling noises and began coughing up blood.

I returned to drinking the water, ignoring him.

At some point I passed out.

Hours later I regained consciousness. The sky was becoming brighter, but it was still dark, so I figured, I couldn't have been unconscious for long.

I reached down to my thigh again. The bleeding had stopped but not completely. The places where my bones had ached and broken, were still throbbing, but less forcefully.

I got up on my elbows and managed to get into a seated position.

My vision turned blue immediately as I did, the blood loss must have been greater than I had thought.

I forced myself to drink some more of the disgusting water again and pressed some of it into my wound.

"Aggggghhhhhhh, FUCK!" I screamed as I did. What was it in Noxstone that could cause such intense and prolonged torment? I'd have to ask that arrogant Prince about it the next time I saw him.

I lifted up the brown bodice of my clothing and tore off a piece of the dark undershirt. I tied it around my thigh, half sobbing as I did.

I turned towards the man, who wasn't moving.

I should let him die there.

But not before asking him some questions.

I dragged myself backwards, half upright, my legs in front of me, until I was sitting beside the man.

Up close, his condition looked even worse.

I reached forwards and placed my fingers on his neck. He still had a pulse. I double checked to be sure since I was wearing leather gloves. The fact he was still alive was miraculous.

I leant back, against the dark stone his body was lying by, taking deep breaths, exhausted from having dragged myself here.

I opened my eyes slowly to find his unswollen one, small and dark, looking at me.

"Haven't"—he choked in between his words — "killed me yet?"

I looked at the state of him. "What would be the point? You're dead soon anyway."

"Hahahaha." He choked on more blood again. "You sound ... crrrr...like someone I know."

"You're going to answer" — I took a breath, needing a break between talking — "some questions."

"Some... caaa... kkrccc" —he continued to cough up blood, which dribbled down his chin — "you really do...sound like... him."

I stretched out my uninjured leg, and pushed my foot down on his broken one, hard. He screamed. It was deep and throaty and drew up more blood from his lungs.

"Why did you take me here? Your fall would have broken far easier if you hadn't," I questioned him.

The man laughed again, in the same crazed way as before. "I'm sorry.... but...torture isn't...going to...crrr ksfsss... work.... on me."

"Oh really?" I spoke.

I did the only thing I could think to do.

I pulled off my glove, reached forwards, and touched his skin.

I could hear the faint sound of his deep howl of pain as I was plunged into a vision with him.

*A room. Large. A seat. A throne. A man on it, tanned skin, golden eyes, an unkind grin plastered across his face.*

*"You really think so?" the man on the throne says to the other.*

*It is him. The man at the bottom of the steps. The same as the half dead man on the ground. Only now he is clean, dressed in a dark robe. His hair is tied back in a long, tight ponytail.*

*"There's no other explanation Your Majesty, it grieves me to say so," he says.*

*The man's grin remains unchanged. "Do not lie to me, Silus."*

*"Your Majesty, I would not dare," Silus bows his head slightly.*

*"He has never disobeyed me before," the man on the throne says.*

*"I do not understand it myself, Your Majesty,"*

*"You will complete the task in his stead."*

*"Yes, Your Majesty."*

*"I don't want a trace of that family left alive."*

*"Yes, Your Majesty,"*

*The 'Majesty' stands up. "Since when did he develop such morals?" He clicks his tongue. "When did he grow so insolent?"*

*Silus does not reply.*

*"Watch him, every second of every hour."*

*"He will know, Your Majesty,"*

*"It doesn't matter. As long as he is reminded of who he serves."*

*"And if he disobeys again, Your Majesty?"*

*"You know what to do."*

The vision before me blurred, like the water of a lake, the images merging together, until I was thrown into another.

*Silus is on a roof, a hood over his head. He is crouching, looking down at the scene below. Kalnasa.*

*A large training ground, surrounded by short buildings, and trees dotted with pale flowers. Their scent suffuses with the night breeze. The roofs of the buildings are curved and mint green. People are training, a few left in the late hours of the night. The last one places his spear down and retreats inside the building.*

*Silus does not wait. He moves, silently across the roof. He curves between and around the edges of the balconies and upper walls, tiptoeing across them as if he walks on air.*

*He throws himself through a window and lands soundlessly on the ground.*

*Inside, a large office. A cool blue carpet below his feet. The walls are sage in colour and there are straw mats placed in front of a pale wooden desk. Behind the desk is a stack of shelves, occupied by various books and scrolls.*

*Silus looks around briefly, then tucks himself into a corner, behind one of those bookshelves, blending in with the shadows.*

*A woman walks in. She turns around and strolls towards the desk. A bright pink robe floats behind her. She's placing a hand on her outstretched belly as she sits down.*

*A man follows her shortly afterwards. He leans forwards and kisses her on the forehead. He is wrapped in a navy robe, his hair in a top knot. He smiles as he looks at her.*

"My love, you should be sleeping."

*She groans in response and bats his hand away.* "I can't sleep, the baby kicks too much."

*He pats her hair.* "Let me make something for you, to calm you a little."

*She looks up at him and smiles.* "If it will make you feel better."

"It makes me feel better to make you feel better." *He kisses her forehead again.*

*The navy clad man disappears to a back room. The woman leans on her desk, reading something before her.*

*But the man from the shadows emerges. She opens her mouth to scream.*

*But silence.*

*Silus slits her throat.*

*She falls back onto the floor, gasping, her eyes wide, looking up at him. She clutches at her neck as she reaches up and knocks over a bookshelf behind her. A loud crash. Silus stands there and waits.*

*The man from the back room runs out and takes in the sight. He draws a spear from an adjacent wall. Silus throws a dagger at him, but the man in blue avoids it and leaps over the table plunging for him. Silus darts to the side but not fast enough to avoid a strike of the spear. The two men stand facing each other. The resolve in the dark blue eyes of the navy clad man is strong, but it fades as he sees his dead beloved on the ground, slumped against the wall.*

*He charges towards Silus. They fight, like two dancers against the darkness. They dodge one another's blows, their feet light, at one with their legs and their arms. Silus trips the man in blue, who stumbles, but twists his spear to strike Silus' back. He does. The impact is forceful and demanding. The man in blue regains his composure.*

"Who are you? Who sent you?" *the man in blue asks.*

*Silus does not respond.*

*The man in blue looks him up and down.* "You're one of his, aren't you?"

*Silus attacks. The man in blue evades.*

"He knows, doesn't he?"

*Silus ignores him and fires another dagger through the air. The man in blue somersaults over it and lands on the ground.*

*Somehow, apart from the bookshelf the woman pulled over, not a single thing in the room has been touched, or disturbed.*

*The man turns and sprints into an adjacent room. Silus follows him, but too late. A bell, a large bell in the room, which the man in blue rings.*

*All around, the hallways and corridors come to life.*

*But the man in blue cannot do both, he cannot ring the bell and defend himself from the dagger that flies through the air. He knows this. It lands in his chest.*

*Silus waits for the man in blue to fall, waits until he is sure he will die. He makes for the exit, the window, but pauses.*

*He pauses in front of the woman, slumped on the ground. He looks at her. He knows he has no time. He knows that any second now, the other Kalnasan warriors will come, will enter the rooms of their leader, their mentor, and find him, and his beloved dead. He can take on one, three, eight, perhaps ten, but more than that, he isn't sure.*

*No trace left behind he had said.*

*He doesn't know if she's far enough along. He doesn't know.*

*He closes his eyes and looks away, swallowing and wincing, as he flings a dagger at her stomach.*

*He was meant to kill the others too. He knows that he has failed.*

*But he has no time. He has done what the other man could not, he has completed the main task.*

*It will have to be enough.*

*He jumps out of the window and into the dark.*

The images blurred again, merging like the ocean with a cloudy sky, drifting further away like a thick dark fog, until they were gone.

My hand drew away from his skin. I was sweating. The man on the ground was staring up in front of him, confused, not truly alert.

It would be pointless to use this method of torture, if it not only caused me anguish, but rendered the person I was questioning unable to speak.

"How...crrr... my... skscrr... memories," the man spat out. He had come around much faster than I had anticipated.

His memories? I had thought divination was only about predicting the future, not witnessing the past.

Had I seen the Captain's past or future then?

I placed the question to the side.

"I'm sure you have many more you'd prefer not to relive," I said, coldly.

He didn't know it was painful for me to watch them too, that it disorientated me, and made me feel even weaker. Let him think I would be unaffected. Let him think I had something of an upper hand.

He choked. "Those.... are... nothing."

"We can always dig around" — I took a breath— "until we find something."

He turned towards me. "Please...crrrr.... help...yourself."

This wasn't working and I was too exhausted to reattempt a method with a low chance of success.

Physical torture was ineffective. Emotional torture was ineffective.

There was therefore, only one thing I could offer him, in return for answers.

"Answer me, and I'll save your life."

He chuckled. "And how do you...crr.... cuggrr... plan on saving me?"

Blood was still coming out of his mouth. He had little time left.

"I know a Healer."

He stilled. His non swollen eye widened.

"And if that isn't enough, I know your name, I heard it there, in your head, and if you die, I'll make sure everyone knows it. I'll tell them all you caved at the first instance, that you gave up every ounce of information you could possibly offer. You'll be gone, but those you care for will not."

I took a deep breath. I was taking a risk. Who was to say a man like this cared for anyone? But still, I persisted, "What will *His Majesty* do about that?"

He remained quiet, his one eye looking at me with dread.

*The risk paid off. He does care. For one person at least.*

To prove my point, I leant forwards and whispered, directly in his ear.

"Silus."

# CHAPTER 58 – HESTAN

"You encountered an acquaintance of mine last night. Is that correct?" the Healer asked.

I took one look at his cloak. The top half of his face was covered. "Yes."

"What is your name?"

"Will you tell me yours?"

The man smiled, understanding I would not give it to him.

"I wish to know what you saw."

My facial expression remained blank. "Why?"

Of course, I was willing to do anything to save Dyna, who lay unconscious and unaware beneath us. But the woman's touch, its impact, had not escaped my mind, I doubted that it ever would. It also did not escape me that these people were dangerous and powerful. Handing information to them freely, would not be wise.

"You do not need to hide anything from me. I know about the note you worked so ardently to read."

"The note and the vision are different," I asserted.

"But they may be connected." Although he had said 'may' he had spoken as if this was not a possibility but an irrefutable fact.

I looked over at Dyna and clenched my fists, unsure of what to do, or say.

The man watched me silently. His unnatural level of patience was probably meant to be calming, but I only found it deeply unnerving.

"Sir," he finally broke the silence. "Do you not wish to assist us?"

Assist them? This sorcerer wanted, expected me to assist them?

"I would never work with someone like you." My palms became clammy, the images from that day blazing through my mind.

"That is disappointing." He lowered his head, "Since the person behind this plot to ruin your home, and to do more damage to our kind are one and the same, we could help each other a great deal."

"There's no way for me to trust your intentions, or the sincerity of your words."

The man raised his head. His lips parted as he let out a small breath. "As things currently stand, you have little choice but to."

"I would rather exhaust every possibility first."

"You do not have the time. We do not have the time."

He raised a long and lithe finger, pointing to Dyna. "She does not."

"She is a child." My voice was rough, "And you would use her in your bargains."

The man was calm and collected. "Someone is using her already. Only they are using her death, and I am offering her life."

"In return for my loyalty, which I do not offer so freely."

I could not offer it. I could not risk the consequences. It was not because he was a sorcerer, although that did form part of my reluctance to make a deal with him. It was the fact that he, as many sorcerers were, was unpredictable.

But then again, so was the Prince.

The man, as if reading my exact thoughts, spoke, "Do you believe Audra's Prince to be any less dangerous?"

I gave him a hostile look. "Of course not."

The man tilted his head with a gesture that implied the question, *So what is the problem?*

"Audra's heir is already in collusion with one of our own, if you are working with him, you are already by extension, working with us."

"The Prince and I—"

"I personally removed the steel you plunged into a sorcerer's back while defending him. Why go to such great lengths if not for the existence of an understanding between you?"

I could not think of a reply for that.

"What do you want?" The pain in my shin began to worsen. I had been standing for too long.

"I have already explained."

"Not that, afterwards." I placed more weight onto the other leg.

The Healer's eyes moved down to my legs. "You are injured."

"Answer my question."

Clearly not concerned by my injury, the man did as he was asked. "Whatever will be necessary, to achieve our goals."

"And what are... your *goals*?"

"For now, at least, they align with yours, finding the author or authors of that note."

"What will you do once you've found them?"

The twist of the man's lips was accompanied by the words, "What do you suppose?"

*Kill them, then.*

"I agree on one condition."

The man didn't respond, anticipating my next words.

"Once those people are found, you will hand them to me and allow them to be tried and sentenced under law."

The man had been holding his hands together in front of him. At these words he dropped them.

"No."

I furrowed my brows.

"There is no justice for sorcerers under your law. If anything, the culprits will be rewarded."

"So, you simply mean to find these people and kill them, without any evidence?"

"We will have evidence. We will find it, hopefully, with your help."

"What if you kill someone who was forced into these actions, who was unaware of their purpose?"

These were the kind of questions that plagued me still, when I thought about lives, I myself had taken.

The sorcerer joined his hands together again. "You have an unshakeable morality, Sir. That is admirable. But such a trait is not something those who must fight to survive can uphold. Currently, the Kalnasans fall under such a category, without even being aware of that fact."

He stepped forwards, closer to the bed, and to me. "We will deal with them ourselves. We would prefer if you assisted us, since you are Kalnasan, and have knowledge of the Kingdom's inner workings we do not possess. However, even if you refuse, the Prince will not. We will be working to find this culprit. It is up to you whether you are involved in the process or abstain."

"You hardly offer me much choice," I said irately.

The man didn't disagree, but said, resolutely, "Choice, the ability to choose, is what we are fighting for. To have it is freedom, to be without it is imprisonment."

The man walked towards Dyna and outstretched his hand. I stepped forwards out of instinct to stop him, but he had removed his gloves, and his palms were glowing, warmly.

Golden orange threads emerged from his hands and travelled towards Dyna's chest. A light entered her and shimmered, glowed underneath her skin, spreading out, down her limbs, and into her face.

I watched, mesmerised as her breathing became easier, and the colour in her face brighter.

After a brief time, the man closed his fingers over and stepped back. He began to put his glove back on silently.

I thought of the conversation that had just passed in the main hall, what Lord Elias had said about teleportation. How had we been able to have this conversation uninterrupted?

"How did you get in here?" The question I realised I probably should have asked immediately escaped my lips.

The man faced me. "Through the door."

*Through the door?*

"I did not teleport here," he added.

So, this man simply walked into the Palace freely?

I supposed, that as a class one Darean, he was highly powerful, and his ability to maintain translucency was probably heightened.

Dyna's eyelashes fluttered. I rushed to her side, but she remained asleep.

"Do you know"— I glanced at the Healer hopefully— "what happened to her?"

The Healer apologetically replied, "No more than you do. Poison."

"Can you tell the kind?"

"Not without time."

Dyna groaned in her slumber.

What was her life over my pride and doubts? Why had I even thought to prioritise them?

"It was..."

But the Healer wasn't listening. His hands were once again glowing with a deep light.

Only now, it was green, and it wasn't coming from his palms. He was clutching something tightly within them.

His mouth straightened into a tense line and his breathing quickened. He didn't move or speak.

"I must leave. Now."

Even though he remained in place, waiting for my reply, his words betrayed an urgency and distress.

"It is up to you. Farewell."

I was so startled by his immediate change that I didn't speak as I watched him make for the door, the outlines of his person becoming faintly invisible as he moved.

"My past," I spoke to his blurry silhouette.

He stopped walking.

"I saw my past."

He regained his full form and turned. "Your... past?" Those two words sounded strained. "You recognised what you saw?"

"Yes," I confirmed. "It was different somewhat... but it was my past."

His chin turned sharply to the right. He glared at a small, non-important point on the floor.

"Thank you," he said quietly.

Before me, the door opened on its own, and closed behind it in kind.

Dyna stirred in her bed, her eyelashes beginning to flutter once again.

I knelt by her side. "My Lady?"

She opened her eyes unfocused. "Hestan?" she whispered.

"Yes, My Lady, I am here."

"I.... I was...." She lifted her hand and gripped the bottom of my arm. Her eyes were wild and frightened.

"It's alright...You are safe now. You are well." I tried to reassure her.

"No." Her voice was pleading. "You don't understand."

"My Lady?" I searched her face with a furrowed brow.

"He told me to drink it. He promised"—tears fell down her face — "he promised that he would let them go. But he told me if I lived..." She choked on her sobs.

"Told you...what?" I whispered.

"That he would kill them all."

# CHAPTER 59- BAZ

The distant sound of arguing woke me up.

"She is gone, there is no use in..." A male's voice said.

"Without her we are trapped here!" A woman's voice, Ullna's voice.

"We need to focus."

I sat up. We were situated in a similar place as before we were attacked, only it was smaller, and less well hidden.

I stood. Yaseer turned towards me, instantly aware of my movements.

Ullna followed his gaze. She strode in my direction.

"Use your enolith, find her," she ordered.

"Find...." I was about to ask who when it dawned on me.

Nemina wasn't here.

"Where is she?!" I asked, in a hushed, but frantic tone.

Beside us, a green light emerged, through it stepped Vykros, and the man, the beautiful Healer, clad in black.

Vykros winked, saluted, and then returned through the teleport he had created.

The man in black remained in place.

Ullna gave Yaseer a look that promised him great pain. "You called for him?"

"This situation is unprecedented."

"He cannot be here now!"

"What happened?" the Healer asked coolly.

He strode towards Ullna and through his hooded cloak, glared at the wound on her face. "This cut is not healing."

Ullna jerked her face away, avoiding his touch.

"Noxstone. Again." The Healer sounded woeful.

"It would have been much worse than this if not for..." Yaseer glanced at me anxiously.

Ullna tutted again and a troubled expression flashed in her gaze.

"If not for what?" I asked.

Ullna was clearly reluctant to answer and so, Yaseer did instead, "Nemina."

"Nemina?" I repeated. "But her powers aren't even..."

Yaseer winced slightly, watching me with a pained look.

My face fell, turning very slowly to Ullna.

Ullna met my eyes. "The girl took the blow."

I raised my eyebrows.

"Deliberately?" the cloaked man asked, his voice tinted with concern.

Ullna nodded in response, frustrated.

"She saved your life," the man concluded.

Ullna was obviously unhappy about this fact.

I was unhappy about the sour expression plastered across her face.

"All the time, you've been berating her, scolding her, blaming her, doubting her. The least you could do is look grateful that she saved you…not…disgusted," I blurted out.

Ullna for once, didn't reply.

"She could be dead!" I failed to keep the emotional strain out of my voice.

"That is why we must look for her swiftly, and why I have called the Healer." Yaseer looked at the man. "I am sorry to—"

The Healer interjected. "No, I would have been displeased had you not called upon me."

The Healer looked at Ullna intently as he spoke. He was clearly displeased Ullna had not informed him of the situation herself.

Yaseer smiled tightly at his response.

"Your enolith," Ullna stated to me.

I felt around for it. "I…it's not…I don't have it anymore. It must have fallen when—"

"Fuck," Ullna cursed. I couldn't help but widen my eyes at hearing her swear.

"I didn't realise it was so difficult to keep a hold of these things for *some people*," Ullna hissed.

"One of *those people* stopped you from getting killed by a lethal blade," I snapped.

The cloaked man smiled. The bottom half of his face the only part exposed once again.

"He is right. It is no surprise the stone was lost, or that the young woman saved your life," the Healer said.

Ullna looked at him doubtfully.

"She knew that she alone had a chance at surviving a blow from those weapons," he explained.

Ullna's hand hovered over the cut on her face. "She may not survive this one. It was…clean and direct."

"Where was she hit?" the Healer asked solemnly.

"I am not sure, but I saw a lot of blood as she fell."

"She fell?" the Healer sounded confused.

"We were airborne. Riders attacked us. Nemina cannot levitate," Yaseer stated.

"She was already weakened by her previous injuries." The Healer's voice was grave. "Where did she fall?"

Yaseer and Ullna looked at each other.

"Near the Citadel."

I could not see the Healer's eyes, but from the way his body language changed, I could imagine they were currently filled with intense discontent. "What were you doing near the Citadel?"

All three of us shifted anxiously on our feet at the Healer's slightly enraged tone.

For me, that was because it had been completely unlike the previous manner in which he had spoken. But for Ullna and Yaseer…I wondered if they had seen the Healer in this mood before, and if they had seen the consequences.

"Our Teleporter made an error," Ullna sighed.

"And our Teleporter has been taken," Yaseer added.

"Aeesha's been taken?" I asked.

Yaseer nodded regretfully.

"That building? That tall, dark structure, with the domed—" I began to ask.

"Yes, that is the Citadel's centre," Ullna confirmed.

"Then we have no choice but to go there ourselves," the Healer said.

"She wasn't alone," Ullna said solemnly. "When she fell, one of the riders, I saw him grab her."

"One of their riders?" The Healer's voice was even more gritty and demanding now.

"Why would he do that? He was falling himself," I pondered out loud.

"Perhaps he thought he could survive the fall, and bring her back," Yaseer speculated.

"Those warriors are trained to estimate every variable with utter precision. He would have known what he was doing, the risk to his own life when he reached for her," the Healer dismissed Yaseer's guess.

"So, they know who she is?" I remarked.

"There is no other explanation," the Healer said confidently.

"But how?" Ullna sounded doubtful.

"She was…well known here," I mumbled.

"Why?" Ullna looked baffled.

"She…had a habit of…" I tried to find the words, "Not being as obedient as they would have liked."

The corner of Yaseer's mouth turned up. "That does sound like her."

"They kept her separate from us, for years. So, they always recognised her as distinctly separate from the rest of us."

The Healer sounded unsettled when he asked. "Where did they keep her?"

I nodded my head. "Deeper underground, but other than that…I really don't know anything."

"It will not be the only reason she is so easily recognisable," Yaseer murmured. The other two nodded in agreement.

I frowned. "What's the other reason?"

Yaseer stopped Ullna from answering, she had probably been about to berate me for my lack of understanding.

"He wouldn't know," Yaseer reminded her.

"Know what? What wouldn't I know? Why do you always take so long to answer questions? It's always staring at each other for twenty seconds at the minimum before you speak!"

Ullna scowled, Yaseer ignored my outburst.

The Healer said. "It's her eyes."

"Her eyes?"

"And her hair," he added.

I placed my hands on the sides of my head and shook it, letting out a laugh. "What? Her eyes and hair? What does that have to do with anything?"

"You were still free when they made the decree, weren't you?" Ullna sounded suspicious.

"Just tell me!"

"After the war, a decree was issued that restricted it. They believed, and still do, that it contributes to the development of the birth of sorcerers."

"What does?"

I decided if they didn't actually explain what they were speaking about in the next five seconds, I would infiltrate their minds and find out, even if I lost consciousness again.

"Cross breeding… between the Kingdoms," Yaseer answered.

"Does it? Actually contribute to it?" I looked at the three of them in turn.

"Of course not," Ullna spat.

"But what do you mean…how can you tell?"

"Don't you know anything?" Ullna said.

"Can't you just answer a question normally?" I bit back.

Ullna was about to reply bitterly, when Yaseer spoke up, "The people from each Kingdom possess distinct physical features. Skin, eyes, and hair colours that are characteristic of each territory. You're aware of the brown or bronze skin, dark hair, dark or golden eyes those from Audra possess. You're probably also aware that in Vasara, many have red, or auburn hair, sometimes brown."

"Like Nemina," I said slowly. Her hair was a searing flame, tinted with gold, a burning copper.

"Yes, but, in Vasara, the people have eyes which are usually red, brown, or rarely, blue in colour, but Nemina's are—" Yaseer started.

"None of those," I finished his sentence.

"Exactly."

"In Jurasa their eyes are blue, or green," Yaseer continued, "In Zeima, pale blue, or brown, and in Kalnasa they are either violet, dark blue, or—"

"Grey," I whispered.

"Your friend is half Kalnasan, and half Vasaran," the Healer confirmed. "And she's likely one of the only people left in this world whose heritage is mixed in such a way."

"So, her features would be easy to remember," I understood.

"But...that Season they hold—" I started.

"It is restricted, not banned," the Healer stated. "Political alliances come before their theories and principles."

Ullna scoffed. I sighed. That was to be expected, I supposed.

The Healer spoke again, "Ullna and I will search for Nemina. She witnessed her fall. Both of you should remain here."

"But I—"

"Acciperean." Although the Healer's eyes were covered, he seemed to look at me earnestly. "I will find your friend. I will bring her back."

It was hard not to be distracted by the grace of his movements, his mouth, his voice.

My eyes shuffled around his form, not knowing where to rest. "You can't know that for sure, just let me—"

"No. Your emotional attachment to her will only cloud your judgement, and being so near to the Citadel is extremely dangerous."

Ullna cleared her throat and eyed the Healer with clear disagreement.

Was Ullna actually on my side for once? It seemed impossible.

"That's exactly my concern," I stressed. "The fact you have no emotional attachment to her at all and she"— I pointed at Ullna— "probably wouldn't bat an eyelid if she died."

Ullna took several steps towards me. "That girl is impulsive and reckless. She is dangerous and often foolish. She has no sense of reason or ability to compromise. But...if you think I do not care whether she lives or dies, or the fact she is the reason I am still breathing, then you are wrong."

"You only care because you want to use her...both of you." I looked at the Healer.

"Be that as it may, it is reason enough," Ullna replied.

"No, it isn't! Reason enough for how long? How long would you fight for someone who is simply a means to an end for you?"

"Until that end is reached, which it is not. You are currently wasting our time and hers."

No, she was most definitely not on my side.

"If she dies...it will be because she saved your life."

"I am aware of that, which is why I would like to hurry."

"So that you can maintain a clear conscience?"

"Ha." Ullna's laugh was short and clipped. "My conscience hasn't been clear for years."

She strode away and the Healer, before following her, said, "Reach into my mind." He commanded me so flippantly as if he were asking for a cup of water.

"W...what?" I mumbled. I wasn't sure I wanted to. "I'm not sure I can. I just used my...and well, now it's been too soon since—"

"Do it. It will be easy. I'm letting you in."

"Why are you hovering there?" Ullna shouted at the Healer from behind him.

Sensing I had little time to do so, I complied with the Healer's request. I was drained but I managed to reach into the Healer's mind swiftly. He had been right. It was far easier than the times I had done so before. A willing participant made a difference it seemed.

He was thinking of something. At first, I couldn't understand it, couldn't make sense of the images, or sounds or words.

But then it became clearer.

It was a memory. He was showing me a memory.

It was brief, but vivid, almost as detailed as reality, as if he had been clinging onto it, thinking on it, making sure each colour and shape remained intact.

It was him...and...

I withdrew from his mind.

In my stupor at the shock at what I had seen, I was silent, looking around the space for a point of refuge, feeling disorientated.

"She is not a means to an end," the Healer insisted softly.

Then he vanished behind his translucency.

Yaseer was standing to the side, he had obviously been able to hear what had just transpired, but he said nothing, and sat on the ground.

I stood in place, trying to process what I had just seen.

But I couldn't, I simply gazed at the ground and murmured.

"Shit."

# CHAPTER 60 - NEMINA

I dragged myself over to the pool of putrid water, and cupped some into my palm, returning to Silus' lips.

"No...no—"

"Drink it, or you'll die." Though I hadn't wished to satiate Silus' thirst, I needed him to live a while longer.

He had stopped coughing up blood now, but his voice was still weak and quiet. "It's not...drink...able."

I threw the water onto his face.

"You saw me drinking it!" I snapped.

"Did you...think...I'd tell you?" He chuckled through coughs.

"Why bother saving me then?"

"It won't...kill you...just.... make you feel—"

I'd placed it on my wound. I put my head in my hands. It was as if I unconsciously sought out and ended up in situations which would harm me.

Maybe I was some kind of demented masochist.

"Where's...this...Healer of yours?"

I had no way of knowing.

"He'll come."

"You're...crrr...lying..."

I took my head off my hands and looked at him, debating whether it really was worth leaving him alive.

"I can...we can...tell."

"Well, just shut up and die then," I groaned.

"How...lovely."

"Lovely? You killed a pregnant woman, and Gods know who else."

Silus let out a sudden groan of pain. I didn't spare him a glance. I was sure I'd hear him moan that way for a while yet.

"I...didn't...have a...crrrgeerkk... choice..." He was back to gagging on blood.

"Oh really? Only the man who refused then."

"He...he's different...he would.... he could do anything...not me."

"Spare me the speech. Do you expect me to pity a piece of shit like you?"

"Why...not?"

"Why not? Fuck, you really are the worst of humanity." I spoke looking forwards, not at the man. "You killed a pregnant woman and play the victim. Who cares if you were given an ultimatum? If it was your life versus hers, you should have sacrificed your own worthless one."

I was not in the mood to filter my words, and especially not for the benefit of this man.

"And don't get confused, I'm sparing your life so I can ask you questions. If I thought you didn't possess any information, I'd have killed you already."

"You're...just...like they say..."

"What are you talking about?"

"The...Acciperean...they kept...with the dogs."

He recognised me. I couldn't decide whether that surprised me or not. Perhaps I simply didn't have the energy to feel any particular emotions about it at that moment.

"Don't ...you...want...to know what...they...gcrrkkk... said...about you?"

"Do I want to know what a bunch of sadistic torturers said about me?" I asked sarcastically. "No."

"They said—"

"I just said no."

"You were...brash...and vicious."

My lips quivered and I began to laugh, placing my hand over my mouth. I felt woozy at the deep intake of break that the laughter stimulated.

"And...terrifying...and...beautiful."

Beautiful? I looked at him with contempt.

"They...they did," he insisted weakly.

The thought made me physically more unwell than I already was.

Or perhaps that was the water.

Or the blood loss.

Or the fall.

Or the wounds from earlier.

Or the divination I just performed.

Or the fact I hadn't eaten.

A noise. I couldn't see its origins, but it was nearby us, and then it stopped.

"What...was..." Silus began asking.

I grabbed his hips, and pulled a dagger from his belt, holding it close. He yelled as I did. It probably aggravated the pain from his extremely broken leg.

"If someone is there...you may as well show yourselves. I'm not going anywhere... clearly," I spoke into the air.

"Why...would you..." Silus spoke.

"Sshhh," I hushed him.

Someone stepped from the shadows. It was a man, dressed in similar clothes to Silus, only his jacket was longer and was lined with silver instead of gold. Also, unlike Silus, his head was clean shaven, cropped very close to his skin. His golden eyes regarded me with...amusement?

"Look at you. You managed to throw Julios off his rider, and you've practically finished him off." He pointed at Silus.

"Alijah," Silus groaned.

Alijah sauntered over towards us, stopping a few steps away. The closer he grew, the further I had to tilt my neck upwards.

"You're coming with me, leave him there."

Silus didn't react, he'd clearly expected such an outcome.

I narrowed my eyes. "I'd rather die."

"They said you'd say that."

Alijah reached from behind him and withdrew a pair of cursed shackles. From another pocket deep in his pants, a bunch of binding coils.

"Remember these?" He shook the shackles in his hands, smiling. They jingled.

I looked down at Silus, who was watching me out of one eye.

I was still bleeding and unable to stand, so speed enhancement was useless. I didn't have a combative ability that would allow me to attack Alijah, and I could barely defend myself. I didn't even have the energy to maintain translucency either.

But I did have one option.

It would have to do.

I took both hands around the dagger and pointed it towards my heart.

Alijah, who had been coming towards me with the binding materials, stopped.

"You won't do it," he squinted.

I wouldn't until the last moment. It wasn't as if I'd stab myself right now before I could be sure there was no way I could render him unconscious.

He came closer. I held the blade in place, in response to my stillness, he moved faster.

I reached one arm forwards, keeping the other hand around the dagger, and gripped his wrist, hard.

But Alijah was faster. Before I could apply any level of force to crush it, he knocked me backwards. My head slammed against the ground. The dagger I had been holding easily fell out of my hands.

He pinned them to my sides.

I leant forwards and headbutted him, using my non injured leg to knee him in between the thighs.

Alijah barely reacted, and only let out a slight grunt, before he pressed down on my wrists harder, and dug his right knee into my left thigh.

Exactly where my wound was.

I howled in pain. The bleeding returned with full force, and my vision blurred, a wave of nausea accompanying my agony, churning through my abdomen like a blazing furnace.

I couldn't react or move as Alijah slipped one of the shackles around my wrist.

"No...no..." I said pathetically, barely able to form words. I struggled but Alijah easily prevented me from moving. I kicked my feet out from in-between his legs, wailing weakly, as the movements tore my wound open even further.

As he reached to place the shackle on the other wrist, I lifted the already shackled one and reached for a dagger at his belt.

His eyes widened in alarm. I held the dagger to my throat.

Then there was blood everywhere.

All over my neck, my chest, my torso, spilling like a relentless rainfall across my skin.

A blade was lodged right in the centre of Alijah's neck, its tip skimming my chin.

Alijah removed his hands from my wrists and clutched at his throat. He looked at me with rage.

Knowing he would die, Alijah pulled out a weapon and raised it, ready to plunge it into my chest.

I barely saw it as his body blurred before me, and was launched to the right, so forcefully, that it flew over Silus, and landed a far distance away.

I was still holding the dagger at my throat, my movements halted in confusion when a familiar voice reached my ears.

"You don't need that anymore." His voice was quiet and soothing.

I didn't have the energy to move much. I tried to bend my neck to see what was in front of me but there was no need. Within seconds the Healer was at my side. His cloak draped half-over my body as he gently reached for my hand.

His gloved one covered the back of my own and stayed there for a moment. He gently pulled my own away from my neck and removed the blade from it. Then he removed the shackle from my wrist since it hadn't yet been locked.

I didn't say anything, I only stared at him, at the bottom half of his face. His head turned to the side as he examined my body. His lips twisted as he saw my thigh.

"Can you stand?"

The same question he had asked me less than a day before.

I closed my eyes and moved my head very slightly from the left to the right, feeling weaker with each passing moment.

He took off his gloves, and with his right hand, reached for my leg.

I grabbed his wrist.

His face sharply turned back towards my own.

I shook my head no, very slightly again, then with my left hand, raised a finger, and pointed in Silus' direction.

*Heal him first. He won't last for much longer. You can't heal two people at once.*
The Healer's head followed the direction of my finger. His lips curved downwards.

"No." He understood my request and denied it.

He reached for my leg again, but I gripped his wrist harder. He could easily have resisted me. I was frail and slightly shaking at the effort now.

But he stopped again. I pointed towards Silus more insistently.

"I'm sorry," he said, then reached for my leg.

I made some weak sounds in protest.

Part of me was dreading the agony he was about to unleash. It had been horrendous when he had pulled some shards out of my back, when I could still walk and talk and hadn't been bleeding. Now?

"I know. I know." He offered me his other hand, just like the last time.

I looked at it. It had healed.

*Healers can't heal themselves, so how...how has his hand mended?*

"It's alright," he insisted.

I shook my head no. I'd definitely break it again. There was a chance I'd break his whole arm this time.

He seemed to change his mind and moved towards my chest. He placed his hand on my collarbones. His fingers were freezing, I couldn't help but jerk at his touch.

He removed his hand immediately and seemed concerned.

I nodded yes.

He repeated the movement, and I could feel, as my broken bones began to fuse back together, as my other injuries slowly began to heal, as I regained some energy.

Enough to speak. He was trying to make sure I could speak. He wanted to hear what I had to say.

Once he had finished, he whispered. "I am here for you, not him."

"We need him,"

"We need you."

"We need him," I insisted, but despite the fact I could now speak, it was still difficult and tiring.

"Please," I whispered.

The Healer sighed roughly, then stood, and walked towards Silus.

I heard another voice.

Ullna's voice.

I pushed myself up on my elbows, still mostly lying down, so I could witness the scene.

Alijah's head was a bloody pulp, smashed against the stone wall.

Silus was still alive it seemed, Ullna was standing beside him.

The Healer must have been explaining my request, Ullna glanced confusedly at Silus' body, then at me.

After we made eye contact, she turned back to the Healer and nodded.

He bent forwards and spent some time over Silus' body. The warm glow of his abilities cast a light over the bottom half of his face.

It took longer than I had anticipated. Silus must truly have been minutes away from death.

The Healer returned to my side after muttering something to Ullna.

He wordlessly stretched out and reached for my thigh. His hand hovered over it. He seemed unsure of where to place it or what to do. I was still pressed up on my elbows watching him as he was distracted.

"Can't?" I said through an exhale, breathing deeply, either from the nerves of anticipating his healing, or exhaustion, or both.

The Healer, still looking at my thigh replied, "Not here, we should—"

A large length of coil wrapped around the Healer's body.

From above, a rider soared and began landing. The binding coils she had curled around the Healer tightened. They were so light, like cobwebs, the fine promise of death.

She dragged him away from me.

I tried to prop up on my elbows but instantly became lightheaded.

The rider dismounted from her Erebask and purposefully strode towards Ullna.

Ullna, who was lying unconscious next to Silus.

Silus who was standing, hunched over her, unsteadily on his feet.

Had I saved Ullna, simply to be the reason for her death as well?

The rider who had just arrived looked over at Alijah's corpse.

"Leave him. He's not important now," Silus told her.

The rider then looked at the ground. At Ullna.

"Take her. She won't be a problem," Silus ordered.

For whatever reason, the rider obeyed Silus, and walked around him to lift Ullna's body, which she did so with ease, as if it weighed nothing.

Silus turned his attention towards me. He grinned, the swelling on his eye had completely disappeared now, along with all his other wounds and so, his face was clear. His two dark small eyes drilled into me. His sharp features looked even more angular than the buttes around us.

When he reached me, he kicked me hard in the face. The effort I had been maintaining to keep myself elevated was eradicated instantly.

"You really did know a Healer. Ha. Thanks for that."

My mouth tasted of blood.

"Did you think once you'd fulfilled your promise to heal me, that I'd come with you willingly? That I'd sit around with you all, wagging my tongue? They said a lot about you, but they never said you were so *utterly* stupid."

He lifted me up by the hair, then threw my body forwards, so I was forced to kneel in front of him. He dragged me across the space, my injured legs making full contact with the ground. The feeling of it, when one was all but cut to ribbons at the thigh, was so excruciating I began screaming.

Only I had been screaming so often over the past few hours, that my voice was cracked, and my screams now sounded like raspy groans.

He was dragging me in the direction the Healer had been thrown in, but his steps halted, and I, finding the will to lift my head and eyes, noticed the Healer was nowhere to be seen.

Silus crouched beside me, and his hand shifted from the top of my hair to the back of my neck. He whispered in my ear. "Where has your Healer gone? Mmmmm?"

He raised his voice significantly. "Is he lingering somewhere in the shadows? What does he plan on doing, I wonder? Those coils mean he's nothing more than an ordinary person now." Silus' eyes searched the area. "If he comes out, I'll take both him and you back without breaking any of your bones."

Silus laughed. He was genuinely finding this whole situation exciting.

"Oh, come on! It was you who saved my life wasn't it, Healer? At least let me thank you in person!"

Silence.

He turned his head towards me, his breath hitting my face. "Look at that, sorcerer. Your Healer isn't truly *'your'* anything. It appears he's run off and left you here. Isn't that sad?" He frowned mockingly.

I tried to turn but only managed to move my eyes in his direction.

"Good," I grunted.

The female rider had put Ullna on the back of the Erebask, and was standing to the side quietly, obediently waiting instruction.

"Find him," Silus said to the woman without looking away from me. "He can't have gone far."

She nodded and began to move, but before she could take more than two steps, a voice sounded from behind us.

"Didn't you say you wished to thank me? Why then, send someone after me with such ill intentions?"

Silus spun around, pulling me with him as he did, so forcefully that I half yelled again, as my leg was twisted.

Silus guffawed. It was tinted with shock. I looked up to see the Healer standing before us, with no coils around him at all.

"Now how did you manage that?" Silus' voice rose in pitch.

"Your subordinate did a poor job at sealing them."

Silus grimaced and with a tight smile, turned to face the 'subordinate.' I couldn't see her face, but judging by her previous actions, she was probably terrified by that smile.

"That's no matter. She can make up for it right now." Silus flicked his head in the Healer's direction. The woman emerged, running towards him.

As she did, she drew two blades from her belt. The Healer stood there doing nothing, patiently waiting for her to close the distance.

As she did, he held out one hand and clicked his fingers.

He disappeared.

"Shit!" the woman shouted.

In the next instant, she had lunged to the side, somehow anticipating his attack even when it was unseen. That made sense, considering how the other riders had fought when blinded.

Unlike the time it had taken the rest of us to deduce this, the Healer seemed to realise it in an instant, and dropped his translucency. Employing it when it was useless would be a waste of energy. Instead, he used two fingers to press into the woman's shoulder. The movement looked like a flick but behind it was enough force to send her flying backwards several metres.

*Just how strong...is his strength enhancement?*

The rider rolled over and stood, lunging for the Healer with her daggers. She feigned several lefts and rights. The movements of her arms were so rapid they blurred. But the Healer still hadn't drawn one weapon, and was simply turning, twisting, and ducking, avoiding all her blows. Down, to the side, a spin to the right.

The woman grunted in frustration and went for him once more. This time he grabbed her forearm, lifted her, and smashed her body into the ground. She coughed. He bent forwards to reach for her, but she rolled over, and jumped onto his back. He reached behind him and flung her off, over his head, as if she were a fly.

She landed crouched, her back to him. She dodged as the Healer tried to grab her and turned around to face him once more.

"Hurry up!" Silus shouted.

The woman, hearing him, frantically attacked, but this time, the Healer used speed enhancement to whirl around and disarm her within less than half a second. She appeared stunned. The Healer didn't do or say anything.

The woman tried to kick him in the abdomen, but he jumped back. She took out another weapon and went to stab him in the foot. A strange move considering it was clear he would see it coming and avoid it. He did, and reached forwards to grab her by the collar.

But with her other hand, she reached up and placed a chain around his wrist. Although she had not been able to attach the chains to the other, the cursed shackles would have weakened him instantly. In that instant of drainage and shock, the woman grabbed the Healer's cuffed wrist, and twisted it behind his back, ready to link it to the other.

*Not him.*

He could save countless lives. He could do so much more for the sorcerers than I ever could.

Let him live in his Castle, let him sleep in beds clad in silk and fur, let him never go hungry or thirsty. I didn't care. Not truly. So long as he would not go there, as long as he would not be locked behind those walls, deep beneath the ground.

He could not go there.

He could not.

"No," I mouthed into the air.

The thought took over my very being. A starving despair sequestered in my soul erupted through my veins.

All of a sudden, the woman backed away from the Healer. He took advantage of her hesitation, and moved away, turning to look at her.

Blood was coming out of her nose.

More like pouring. Pouring until it fell like a torrential storm down her neck, her chest.

Then it began coming out of her eyes.

Her ears.

She began to scream, pausing between each outburst in shock. She almost sounded like a child.

The blood kept coming, as if her body had been a cage for it, and now, it was trying to get out.

Now it was coming out of her mouth.

The spaces under her fingernails.

She howled and clutched at her face, which grew paler and paler by the second. The whites of her eyes turned red, the veins under her now much paler skin began to burst.

She looked at Silus pleadingly.

As if he could help her.

"What the fuck?" he muttered, half baffled, half disgusted.

She screamed desperately and so loudly that Silus flinched.

She dropped dead to the ground, blood continuing to flow, bubbling out of her crevices, even afterwards.

Silus let go of my neck and left me kneeling. He stood and took his own weapons out. "As rare as a Healer is, I'm not going to let you turn me into bloody broth," he asserted.

The Healer was still staring at the woman's body, he didn't even acknowledge that Silus had moved or spoken.

But Silus, determined to ensure he fulfilled his declaration, went for the Healer, who hadn't yet had time to take his shackle off.

They fought much in the same way, only Silus was faster than the woman had been, and within less than a minute, had already cut the Healer in several places, his clothes being torn and scratched apart.

The next time Silus went to strike, the Healer manipulated his shackle, pulling the chains taught and raising them above him, to parry Silus' blow.

Silus's blade cut the shackles off the Healer's wrist.

Silus' eyes widened and his mouth twitched up in annoyance. The Healer's demeanour changed. He appeared and gave off an aura I had not recognised on him before. Silus noticed the change as well.

The Healer became invisible again. Somehow, Silus anticipated his movement and rushed towards me, slashing out with his dagger as he did.

The Healer reappeared with his back to me. His arms and legs spread slightly, as if that would shield me further.

As Silus slashed out his dagger, the Healer made a sweeping movement and disarmed him. Silus had no other weapons on him now. I had removed them all earlier.

But Silus didn't seem to care about his lack of blades, or anything at all.

Because the strike of Silus' dagger through the air had achieved what he had wanted.

The hood the Healer was wearing fell backwards, and a black piece of thread that had bound it around his shoulders, floated to the ground.

Silus was staring at the Healer's face. His mouth was widened, his eyebrows raised. His expression was full of so much astonishment and horror, you would have imagined he was looking at a mountain of rotting corpses.

For someone who had just watched his comrade die in a sea of her own blood, who had only reacted with mild disgust, a reaction like this...

Silus didn't make another move to attack. He didn't make a move at all.

Before me, the Healer placed his hand over his back and drew a longsword. It rang through the air as he did so. He stretched it out by his side.

Silus laughed in disbelief and only uttered one word.

"You."

He looked over the man's shoulder at me briefly, then back at the Healer's face. He observed his stance, his sword.

As if someone had possessed him, Silus' facial expression completely changed. He smiled widely, shaking his head in a resigned manner, looking up at the sky.

He tutted. "How disappointing." He let out a small laugh.

"I really, *really*... would like to have known what happened next."

He made eye contact with the Healer, who without any reservation or hesitation, lifted his sword, and took Silus' head off his body.

# CHAPTER 61- ELIEL

The early morning sun from the stained-glass windows cast the Jurasan King's cloak in a variety of colours.

We had met after all, in a shrine.

Meeting in the Palace was too dangerous and something the King would not have agreed to. Elementas shrines were in several places throughout Iloris, often dedicated to each one of the Gods. This one was dedicated to the God of Thunder - Tundros, but owing to his lack of popularity in Vasara, his shrine was small. It was the Patron Gods of Vasara, Furos and Terros, who were subjects of the largest shrines here. The smaller ones were often deserted, especially this early in the day, when the darkness of the night had only just melted into a sunrise.

"Your Majesty," the Jurasan King said, withdrawing his hood.

I had never seen this man before. It was said very few had. Elias, who was sitting next to me, sucked in a breath as his face was exposed. He made eye contact with me and raised his eyebrows. In this light, in this setting, with his appearance, the Jurasan could rival any statue of the Nine Gods, including the one of Tundros behind him. His ash blonde hair was so long, it skimmed the edge of the table, despite his towering height.

"Your Majesty," I replied, smiling.

It would have been customary for the Jurasan King to bow, since while he too was a King, Vasara was still the ruling Kingdom. But he remained straightened, showing no signs he would perform such an action.

"Please, sit." With one finger, I gestured to the chair at the opposite end of the table.

The Jurasan King used his left hand to draw back the chair. He flicked his cloak up from behind him, which was a dark green velvet, and sat down.

The rest of his outfit was a similar colour, although it was mostly hidden. The stark contrast of the dark clothing to his hair was striking. After seeing this man once, it would be easy to identify him once more. Even in attempting to describe him, only few details would be needed, since all of his features were unique.

It was hard not to ponder on the significance of the fact he'd managed to hide the details of his appearance for so long.

I rested my hand on the table, my fingertips poised on the wood.

"You've shown us your face." I needed to understand.

"I would prefer to do so, rather than wait for your inevitable attempts to discover its appearance."

Elias scoffed. The Jurasan King ignored him.

"I would not be the first to try," I pointed out. "Yet you do not reveal your face to the other curious parties."

"The other curious parties have no chance at success," the King responded. He clasped his hands, lacing his fingers over each other. "I am sure I can count on your discretion." He looked at Elias, "And yours."

"Of course," I confirmed. "I am grateful for your trust."

The King smiled. Seeing his face fully, and seeing it with this expression, it was hard not to feel a sense of wonder. This man had only ever been spoken of as an entity, a force, someone people admired, respected, and feared. A man loved by his people. A sort of divinity surrounded his existence, a reverence.

And yet, his smile made him appear youthful, carefree, as if no such burdens plagued him. Only it was accompanied by the words, "I hope that is reciprocated."

He was smiling, his words were polite, but behind them, a warning was clear.

Elias leant forwards with one arm on the table. "How did you get out of there?" he asked.

He was speaking of Liquanon, the attack.

The Jurasan King's gaze shifted towards him, glinting in the sunlight. "When you are able to answer that question... then I shall answer that question."

Elias squinted and tilted his head in an expression that said, *Really?*

The King, who had clearly felt that matter was dealt with, looked back at me. "You summoned me."

"I did." I nodded. "You will have heard of the attack on one of the candidates by now."

"It would be difficult not to hear of it. I am assuming that was your intention." He sounded disapproving.

"A sorcerer has not once infiltrated this Palace, not since the war," I stated.

"I am aware," he replied.

"Then I am sure you will agree, that in light of the situation, the need to deal with these groups has starkly increased."

"With all due respect Your Majesty, the act of a lone sorcerer cannot be immediately connected to a whole group."

"That is why dealing with them all is the best option," I asserted, lowering my head, placing my palm flat on the table.

"War... is never the best option." The King sounded disdainful, but relaxed at the same time, as if he were sharing an opinion about a meal he disliked. "Once you make efforts to eradicate these groups, and I am sure that with your resources, you will undoubtedly succeed, you will only incite the sorcerers remaining to attack. Would it not be better to investigate this matter first?"

"It's too late for that," Elias said from the side. He sounded dismayed. "Once that announcement was made—"

I interrupted Elias, "It would be foolish to wait for the sorcerers' actions to grow more dangerous. Investigating would only give them the time and opportunity to become so."

The Jurasan King didn't reply, but he looked disappointed. Still, I did not need his full approval, as long as I could persuade him helping me was in his interests, that would suffice.

"Elias," I said.

Elias spoke up. "The sorcerer who was here used teleportation. You may or may not be aware of this, but teleportation, although employed by sorcerers of a lower class, gives off a large surge of energy, and Navigators can, with time and focus, trace their coordinates."

"Yes," the Jurasan King replied bluntly, "I was aware."

"The teleportation coordinates were within Jurasa, meaning that the sorcerer teleported to and from your Kingdom," Elias reached the point.

I added more, leaning forwards. "This is the *second* time sorcerers who have proven themselves to be dangerous were found to have been based in Jurasa."

"There have been countless sorcerer bases over the past decades, all over Athlion, so what is the relevance of this information?" The defensive tone in his voice did not escape me.

"The relevance is that now, such sorcerers have managed to infiltrate these walls. Once just days ago, and once before that"— I paused and ground my teeth slightly— "when my parents were murdered."

The King's eyelids fluttered. "Yes. I heard of that as well."

"Then you understand my concern."

"Understand, yes. Agree with, no."

"Is it—"

But the King interrupted me, Elias frowned as he did.

"Being the King of Jurasa does not make me able to survey every inch of its soil, nor does it make me responsible for those who come and go, crossing its borders freely."

"But, if not you, then who do you propose should take responsibility in apprehending and detaining these sorcerers? They are after all, residing in your Kingdom, Your Majesty," I asked.

The Jurasan King sneered silently, through his eyes. "Residing, are they? So, the Navigators tracked them to their precise location?"

It was not for nothing, I could begin to see, that this man had become a King of great renown, when he was but a child.

He continued, "And since when were Vasara's trackers restricted by the borders of different Kingdoms? Those borders haven't stopped them taking that *responsibility* upon themselves in the past."

Elias shifted in his seat.

"I cannot ignore this coincidence, Your Majesty," I addressed him.

"And I am not ignoring it either. Since our last conversation I have, as you requested, been surveying my Kingdom more thoroughly for any sign of sorcerers. As the Lord just stated, teleportation would be difficult to miss."

"Are you saying our trackers have been misinforming us?" Elias asked, sounding half-interested, half-frustrated at the implication.

The King looked at him calmly. "Or that they have been fooled. All I can say is that there have been no such signs of sorcerers in Jurasa."

"Could it not have been you, that was fooled, Your Majesty?" I put it to him.

The King didn't seem convinced of that possibility at all. "If that is the case, then I fail to see how I can assist you any further."

Such reluctance to cooperate. Such abrasiveness in his furrowed brow.

"Then please. Let me enlighten you," I began. "Allow the trackers to take up residence in your Castle. Allow them to operate from within your quarters and conduct their duties from there, for a short time."

"No," the King replied. He said it without force, easily, as if he were refusing a drink. He clearly did not deem an explanation necessary.

I had expected this refusal, since there was much secrecy surrounding not only the King's appearance, but also his home. Nevertheless, I pressed on.

"Then another residence near your location. Give them somewhere to work from."

The Jurasan King tapped his index finger on the wooden table four times.

He stopped. "That can be arranged."

"And you will allow them to examine your draining centres since—"

"That. Cannot." The Jurasan King enunciated each word.

I coughed slightly before speaking again, shifting the shoulder of my still healing left arm. "If it is indeed your Kingdom these sorcerers are originating from, it may be the case that those in your draining centres are aware of their movements, perhaps even some of the members of these groups."

The King clasped his hands together again, leaning forwards, so that his forearms were pressed into the table. "You wish to enter my home. You wish to examine my draining centres. Your Majesty, if you suspect me, then why not simply say so?"

I leant back in my chair. "Because I do not suspect you."

The King breathed out loudly through his nose in a half chuckle. "Then you will not be so aggrieved at my denial of this particular request. Our draining centres are not to be tampered with. They are operating under strict guidance. I will not have your trackers interfere with that."

A thought struck me. "Could it be...that you lack Vessels?"

The Jurasan King frowned as if he did not understand my question. "Doesn't everyone?"

It was not surprising that the King was aware of this information, as was I, as any ruler of the Kingdoms would be. But Elias turned between the King and I, confused.

"Everyone?" Elias whispered to me.

The Jurasan King heard but ignored him. "You will understand then that such an interference and delay is not possible."

"Our trackers can easily ask questions without interrupting the drainings," I argued.

"Since I do not have proof that is the case, they will be asking no questions at all." He was insistent, but not aggressive.

"By not asking your Vessels such questions, we may be missing a vital piece of information," I stated.

"Then I will ask them myself."

Elias and I looked at each other. Imagining that this King would interrogate his own Vessels seemed preposterous.

Then again, I had recently done the same.

"Please. Do that," I spoke. "I will be most intrigued to find out what you have discovered. Perhaps while you are asking, you can make inquiries about Lord Beckett."

The Jurasan King straightened slightly "Why would I do that?"

"Your sister's escort has been missing for over a week," I informed him.

The Jurasan King blinked hard and stared at the table. His eyes moved to the side, he frowned, clearly puzzled.

Elias watched him warily.

The King's eyes returned to mine. "Why was I not alerted previously? The Princess' security is dependent on his presence."

"I would gladly have alerted you, however, the Princess herself did not report his absence initially. She stated she believed his absence was only temporary and that he would soon return. But given how ardently Lord Beckett stayed by your sister's side, that possibility, even to me, would have seemed unlikely."

Elias cleared his throat and looked up at me from his brows. His gaze seemed to be warning me not to aggravate the King too much on this matter. He was clearly wary of this man, as he had been the first time we had crossed his paths.

"You may send another escort in his stead. I am sure you are keen to be sure of her security, after this recent attack. Even if your sister is only here for appearance's sake, it is only you, I, and Lord Elias who are aware of that."

"Has there been a search?" the King questioned.

"Yes, and he is nowhere to be found. Nobody has seen him. If you wish, you may speak to your sister and—"

"No," the King interjected. "I cannot stay for long."

I peered at the statue of Tundros over the King's shoulder. "Do you believe in the Gods, Your Majesty?"

"Of course," he replied.

It was hard to tell whether his response was genuine.

"Then I will pray for you, that you succeed in this endeavour."

The Jurasan King looked directly at me. The light from the stained-glass window coloured his ash blonde hair rust and maple red. "Would a prayer from a man of no faith truly work?"

Elias stiffened up. I smiled, meaningfully. It was surprising the King could deduce information so well, it was almost refreshing to be in his company, to be around someone with a like mind.

"Who knows? One can only try."

"Spare yourself the effort," the King said, bluntly, but neutrally. He had an interesting way of making everything he said sound authoritative without sounding judgemental.

The King's attention was drawn to Elias. "What are your thoughts?"

Elias was visibly startled at being asked so openly. "About what, Your Majesty?"

"About a war."

Elias stopped breathing for an instant. My eyes were fixed upon the King. If he was trying to sow discord between us, then it was a futile attempt. I already knew Elias disapproved of war, but he disapproved of sorcery even more.

"I think the King is—" Elias started.

"I am not asking His Majesty, I am already aware of his opinion, and his is not the only one that matters. I am asking for yours."

"Right," Elias said gruffly. He side-eyed me before answering. "I don't want war, but it seems inevitable, doesn't it?"

"Is that what you think?"

"I just said…" Elias stopped, and cleared his throat, likely remembering who he was speaking to. "Yes, that is what I think."

The King's eyes flitted between both of us quickly. "Your father did not want a war," he said to me.

Elias intervened. "His father was—"

The King spoke over him. "He instigated the last one. He was heavily involved in it. But there was a reason, that despite these groups you mention, he never declared a full-out war again. There was a reason he only ever dealt with the groups when the need arose. Did he not discuss it with you?"

I looked down at the wooden table. My father had discussed little with me.

"I know my father's attitude towards sorcerers was…complex."

"He was afraid of them," the King said.

"Fear is never a good reason to make a choice," I rebuked.

"Unless it is founded. People speak of fear as if it is a sin, a weakness." The King looked almost despaired as he spoke. "But some things are worth fearing. Some people are worth being careful of."

I sat up straighter. "If we remain only in fear of the sorcerers, they will one day, very soon, exploit that fear. They will drag our world from the ground by its roots."

"Your father knew that to survive, to win the last war, was nothing short of a miracle, and that it had only been because the sorcerers had not expected such a campaign. This time, they are ready, and if you strike first, they will strike back with a force we may not survive," the King was speaking quickly, but clearly.

"If they strike first? Have they not already done so?" I put to him.

"The Lord could tell you, that what they have done so far, is nothing near close to what they are capable of." The ominous tone in the King's voice was overwhelming. His speech was intended to deter me from my course, but if anything, it only made me surer of it.

"Perhaps you are right," he continued, "And they are planning something, but if you strike first, you eliminate any possibility of solving this peacefully."

Elias laughed. It was hard for me not to do the same. The King looked at him unimpressed.

"Your Majesty… that time has long since passed," I said softly.

The King shook his head, dismayed. "If you should pray for anything, you should pray for this…that if this war you are so desperate for begins, you will be killed early in its course—"

Elias's eyes glimmered with rage. "You dare—"

"Because if you are not," the King spoke over him, "You will watch as your mistakes manifest as destruction and death, and they will make you watch."

I lowered my head and my voice. "I am not perfect, nor am I unflawed, but I know this will not be a mistake."

The King clearly disagreed but changed the topic, asking. "The candidate? Is she alive?"

"Just." I thought of the Kalnasan girl lying on her bed, frail and feeble, and felt a pang of dread, anticipation.

The King nodded. "One sorcerer, one attack, discreet and quiet, and the girl is left clinging to life. Imagine hundreds, using the full force of their abilities against us. You believe you are protecting your people, but you are only dooming them to the fate of this girl, or a fate far worse."

"Thank you…for sharing your opinion, Your Majesty."

"False gratitude is not necessary. I do not share it for your thanks. I share it so that on the day you realise you made this mistake, you will remember this conversation, and that if fate is kind to you, you will live to never forget it." His voice was sharper now.

The King stood. "I will send another escort here within the next few days. If the Princess is harmed in the meantime, then our arrangement is void."

"She will not be harmed," I assured him.

"That, I am sure, is what you told King Dunlan about his niece."

His attitude had become significantly more hostile over the past few minutes.

"It's hardly as if he'd tell the candidates otherwise. Each one knows the position carries risks," Elias defended me.

The King looked at Elias regretfully. "You're right, of course, it is only a shame that the promise of their safety cannot be guaranteed."

"That is the sorcerers' doing, not his," Elias snapped.

"Is it?" the King asked, not expecting an answer. "How far back does the chain of cause and effect go?"

"You're overcomplicating things, Your Majesty." Elias sounded frustrated.

"Oversimplifying them is for people who do not wish to face difficult truths."

Elias opened his mouth again, but before he could refute that point, I spoke, "Which difficult truth do you refer to?"

The King raised his hood, preparing to leave. "That we are no different from them. We are fighting for this world. We are fighting to live. Somewhere along the passage of time, we decided it was impossible for both humans and sorcerers to do so, and ever since then, every act by either side has been fuelled by that same motivation. It is easier to vilify the sorcerers when they possess certain abilities, and easier to victimise ourselves when we do not. But who is the true evil and who is the true victim?"

The question hung in the air as the King finished by saying, "The difficult truth is we are each both, and we are no more deserving of this world than they are."

Elias frowned thoughtfully.

"You certainly have sympathies for their cause." I tilted my head.

"Not sympathies, only the ability to see the obvious similarities, and the ability to admit it to myself," the King corrected me.

Elias was quiet, still, thoughtful.

"I can admit the similarities, but I have no need or time to appreciate them. What good will that do?" I asked, casually.

The King smiled tightly, not truly.

"How well you manage to summarise, the very core of the issue," he said bitterly.

He turned and strode out of the door.

As soon as the door had closed, Elias turned to me. "There's a shortage of Vessels?"

"You cannot speak of that to anyone."

Elias waved his hand. "I know that."

"Not even when you're drunk."

Elias raised a brow. "Right... because I thought that rule didn't apply when I was drunk."

"It would be best if you did not drink in public at all."

"I don't..." Elias sounded defensive. "I don't drink in public...most of the time."

I looked at him concerned. As if he had realised what he had said, he shrugged, crossed his arms, and added, "It tastes better alone."

I continued to look at him worriedly. "You should truly...try to..."

I found myself surprised. It was the first time in a long while I was lamenting over my own words, unsure of what to say.

"I am trying," Elias' voice cracked a little. "I am."

I nodded. "I am glad."

Then wiping the small smile off my face, I said firmly. "If anyone hears of that information, there will be mass panic."

"How long has there been a shortage?"

"Nearly a decade."

"A fucking decade?!" Elias raised his voice. I turned to him slowly.

He calmed down instantly and suddenly seemed in deep thought.

"What is it?"

"It's nothing."

But he scratched his stubble with the back of his hand, something he only ever did when he was troubled.

"No, it isn't," I observed.

Elias ignored my probing and asked. "How is it being dealt with?"

I peered at him. He seemed consumed in his own thoughts, too preoccupied to notice my inquisitive gaze. What lingered through his mind?

After a few moments, during which my gaze was not returned, I sighed. "As of now, it isn't. We simply have to find more to drain, that is all. Mostly that is easy enough."

"But this ...war"— he gulped —"you're so sure is coming, won't it wipe them all out?"

"I do not plan to wipe them out at all."

Elias frowned. "Then what are you planning?"

"You're working with a tracker, aren't you?" I asked, evading his question.

"Yes but—"

"Bring her to the festival, there's someone I need her to meet."

## CHAPTER 62- SHADAE

Couldn't they have designed better outfits for this weather?

I twisted my neck, trying to separate my skin from my collar. The jacket was a light material and cropped, but the under shirt, which was white, and embellished with gold buttons, stuck to my body, as did my dark red pants.

All around, the festival was in full swing. People passed by. Their eyes were bright with wonder as they gazed at the stalls, the games, the show. They were laughing, revelling in the atmosphere, strolling past in loose crimson pants, airy golden skirts, and short amber vests.

I felt a tug on my thigh.

I looked down, a young child, no older than six had his small fingers gripped in the folds of my pants. His wide brown eyes stared up at me, his curly brown locks falling in front of them slightly.

I immediately raised my head and looked around, trying to see where the child had come from, failing to see anyone who appeared as if they had just lost one.

I moved my leg, trying to shake myself from the child's clutches, but he only clung on more stubbornly.

"Go," I whispered. "Go back."

"My mama says you can help," he said blankly.

"Your mama is wrong, go back to her," I insisted, glancing around nervously.

"Mama is sick," he insisted.

*So? I'm not a healer? Do I look like one?*

"Then you should find her a healer," I replied.

"No!" The child screeched so loudly, that the people strolling past overheard, and looked in our direction.

"Is that a tracker?"

"What's she doing with that boy?"

I swallowed anxiously and looked back at the child. "I'm not a doctor alright? I can't help your mama. I'm sorry."

The child shook his head so viciously he was probably hurting his own neck. Tears started to pool in his eyes.

I crouched. The child's hand didn't move. "What's wrong with your mama?" I asked.

This child clearly wasn't going to leave, better to amuse him and avoid another outburst.

"Mama has a baby."

*Ha. You're right. That is terrible.*

"What's wrong with that?" I said, trying to soothe him.

"Mama has a bad baby."

I understood then. The baby was a sorcerer.

Was it possible for a baby to exhibit signs of sorcery? That early? The mother probably thought I could take her baby away and get rid of it.

Its own mother.

Did she really expect a baby to be drained?

This boy would be better off running away from home. What would happen if he showed signs of possessing certain abilities in a few years? How long did he have before he could no longer walk these streets freely? Before his own mother turned him in?

But what could I do? Even if I saved the baby from its fate before another tracker heard about this, I couldn't take care of a child.

Still, could I really let a baby be apprehended?

"Where's your mother?"

The boy began hauling me by the arm, I followed him, street after street. Flags were stretched, banners decorated with intricate symbols, the dark red ink shining bright against gold in honour of the celebration. Bunting hung over us, it stretched from window to window, from post to pillar. Most people were too busy immersing themselves in the festivities to afford us a second glance.

We reached a quieter road. The boy let go of my arm instantly. He ran up ahead and around a corner.

I followed him, slowly.

"Thank you," I could just about make out a voice.

A man placed a lunar coin into the little boy's palm. The child beamed widely then ran off.

*You little shit! Mama needs help. She certainly does if she has a devious little child like you! Ugh.*

The man was leaning against a wall, his side facing me. A dark crimson cloak, almost brown, and tattered, covered him.

"I knew that would work."

Elias removed his hood, turning towards me. He looked neither happy nor delighted about the fact it had.

I sighed, looking down.

"What were you going to do?" he asked me.

"About what?" I pretended to play ignorant.

Elias snorted. "I told that boy exactly what to say. He's run errands for me before, I know for a fact he would have recited every single word correctly."

"I didn't really hear much of what he said, because of the crowds and…"

I looked off to the side, remembering Elias' previous commands not to lie to him.

Still, if it meant surviving, I would lie, many times.

The power of a well told lie was like birdsong. Deceitful in its decorations. A threat passing as a pleasing melody. I was surrounded by such chirping here. I could learn to mimic the warbling.

I had to.

"You would have tried to save the baby. Wouldn't you?" Elias said.

"No," I replied quickly, realising in that instant, I had just revealed, that I had in fact, heard what the boy had said.

Elias raised an eyebrow.

"I would have brought it back," I insisted.

"Even I wouldn't have brought a fucking baby back."

*Well, aren't you a hero.*

"What would you have done? Waited till he was four or five and then took him?" I met his eyes.

He didn't respond.

It was so easy for him and all the others to overlook that place, those centres, to convince themselves as they fell into sleep it was for the greater good. But they didn't see the children crying and begging for it to stop when they were drained, or the parents being pulled apart from them as they were ripped away from their homes, the only evidence they were ever there an unused bed, a bowl in the cupboard never touched. Though some families got rid of those. Some burnt the wood and the sheets, smashed the ceramic into pieces.

"It's your job, not mine after all," Elias muttered.

"You should be thankful about that." Normally, I would have schooled my tongue around him, but this trick, and his unbothered attitude about the apprehension of small children loosened it easily.

"Oh, I am," he huffed.

"Why couldn't you have told the child to say it was you who sent him?" I demanded.

"Because I couldn't risk any unwanted parties overhearing and following you…Do you want to be killed on one of these back streets?"

*As if you care. Being a tracker dooms me to die in Vasara, so the likelihood of dying on one of these streets is already high, isn't it?*

I had received a message this morning, that 'His Honourable Lord Elias' had requested my presence at the festival. The presence of trackers wasn't unusual at such events, they were designed to deter any sorcerers from potentially causing trouble, but I had not initially been scheduled to attend. I had been looking forward to the quiet.

Lord Elias was dressed the complete opposite to how you would expect someone of his stature to be. While all the other nobles would later undoubtedly appear in some of their most extravagant attire, underneath Lord Elias' dark crimson cloak was a plain white tunic, laced with a ruby coloured thread near the top of his chest, forming a loose collar around his neck.

*Like that. How hard would it be to design a collar like that?*

Lord Elias caught my eye, glaring at his collar with jealousy. He frowned, clearly baffled by my intense stare.

He looked down at his collar and shirt, finding nothing there of interest, then glanced at me again.

"You need to change."

"Why?"

Elias stood forwards and revealed that he was in fact, standing in front of a small wooden door. He opened it. Behind it was some kind of abandoned shop, which appeared to once possess jewels, the majority of which had been stolen.

"In there, there's a bundle on the floor." He nodded inside.

"But...where do I leave these?" I gestured to the clothes I was wearing.

"Leave them there, we'll come back after."

*We?*

I went inside the door, having to walk closely to Elias' outstretched arm and chest as I did.

He was so tall and broad it was like walking past a fortress.

Inside on the floor was a long linen dress, amber in colour, and a cloak.

*A cloak? Just when I thought I'd finally be able to breathe today. I have to wear this. This is even worse.*

But, I decided, being dressed in this outfit was still far better than having to deal with a sorcerer fresh from the womb.

Elias closed the door behind him. I hurriedly got dressed. It had been a long time since I'd worn a dress, so the sensation felt foreign, the air slipping between my shins strange. The dress was just as plain and simple as Elias' shirt, with similar lacing near the top, only in white, and the cloak was a slightly darker shade of amber than the dress was.

Just before my fingers touched the handle, a voice outside reached my ears.

"My Lord! What are you doing here -ey? The festival's that way!"

"I'm coming later," Elias replied to the unexpected guests.

"Ahhh, with His Majesty?"

"That's right." Elias sounded slightly tense, but perhaps that was because I knew the circumstances. In reality the tone of his voice probably sounded friendly and jovial.

"Is it true, My Lord? That you've been appointed again!" The two voices of these people sounded like those of young, and excitable men, perhaps even adolescents.

"I hope it is!" the second one exclaimed. "My Lord, they say there was never another General like you! They say you were the best! I hope I'll get to serve under you one day."

Now there could be no mistaking the slight twang in Elias' voice when he replied, "I hope so too."

"So, it *is* true!" the first one said, sounding as if he was bouncing on his feet. "I can't wait to tell the others!"

"Yeah, they'll be delighted! Some of them served under you, you know? They'll be so pleased to hear—"

"Wasn't it Zarlon?"

"Yeah him! Do you remember him, My Lord, oh and there was Yvina too!"

Elias cleared his throat. "I remember them."

"You do! Yvina had a thing for you, you know—"

"Oi, don't say that to him!"

I let out a groan so loud I was surprised nobody overheard.

*Yvina avoided misery. I hope she's happily married to someone else now...*

"Well, she did! She still does ...probably, even after everything!"

*No. There's no hope for the woman.*

The man tried to correct himself, presumably after alluding to 'everything.'

"I mean...urrr...it's just that—"

Elias interrupted their frantic warbling. "Go and tell them, please, I'd be happy to see them later at the festival."

"Really? We will, My Lord, we'll go now!"

The sounds of their footsteps scurrying off became quieter, as did their excited chatter.

I had only ever come across people speaking of Elias with disdain, sometimes respect, but I hadn't realised the Lord had been, and was also loved.

Gods knew why. Had they actually met him?

I opened the door. Elias turned around, looking me up and down.

"Let your hair down," he said immediately.

*It's not enough that you have to cover me in this cloak, now you want my hair covering my neck too? Do you want me to die from heat sickness?*

He did in fact, probably wish for it to some degree.

I reached up and did as he asked, not bothering to verbalise my arguments once again.

"Good," he said sternly.

He began walking down the alleyway he had been leaning in. He put his hood up. I did the same.

"We're meeting someone," he finally told me.

"Who?"

"I don't know yet."

I frowned and looked at him. The fabric of our hoods slightly covered our face, but he could still sense my mood.

"The King requested this meeting. He asked me to bring you along. He wants us to meet this person."

I decided it was best not to say anymore after that.

"Are you...going to the festival?" I asked.

"Why? Did you want to go back?"

I snorted. "Gods, no."

I could see the corner of Elias' lips twitch up slightly into a smile, for a brief moment. Very brief.

"Why?"

*Because it's not a festival I can enjoy, is it? Just one I have to stand around for, waiting and hoping no sorcerers expose themselves, so that I won't have to attack, apprehend, or kill them.*

"I don't like crowds," I replied. That was true at least.

"Mmmm," was all I received in response. A few seconds passed before he added, "We may not have the time."

"Yvina will be disappointed," I said flatly.

My eyes widened at my own comment, and I hastily looked away, hiding my face under my hood further.

But Lord Elias didn't scold me, or remind me of his title, or my place, he simply said, "It's better she doesn't see me."

*Well, on one thing we can agree at least.*

"Here." Elias threw a pouch at me, which I only just managed to catch, blinking several times as I did.

I looked down at it, feeling its hefty weight in my palm.

"That's the money you gave those guards. Don't give it away anymore."

*He actually...got my money back? That's...*

*Well, I'll be able to afford to eat more but...those guards...they're going to truly hate me now.*

After some time walking in silence, we reached a modest, and comfortably sized house at the edge of the city centre. Elias knocked on the door, but it opened of its own accord. He turned back to look at me, then beckoned me to follow him inside.

"Come up," a muffled voice from somewhere atop a wooden staircase called out.

Elias went in first. I trailed behind him, up the stairs. Eventually we reached the source, the room the voice had come from, and stepped inside.

I recognised him instantly.

Elias, however, didn't seem to know who he was speaking to. He withdrew his hood and looked at the man, but when he noticed I had frozen, he turned in my direction.

The man in front of us was staring at me as well. He was middle aged, bald, his tanned skin lined with age. His eyes were red, the same colour as Elias', only much darker compared to Elias' more ruby coloured ones.

Elias' eyes shifted between us.

"You know her?" he asked the man.

The man's eyes glimmered as he stood and came towards me. He was slightly shorter than I was, but still, it was hard not to be intimidated by his presence.

"Of course, My Lord. I remember each and every tracker I mark."

It would be difficult to forget the face that branded me with the Curse. The Curse of Servitude, one of the fifteen grand curses, he had explained to me.

And one of the most difficult to break.

Breaking it was only possible through three means.

One, through death, as all curses were. Not ideal.

Two, the constant renewal of healing magic being streamed into your blood on a regular basis. Essentially impossible since Darean Healers were virtually non-existent.

And then there was the third option, cutting it out of your skin, or cutting the limb it was attached to off.

Only there was no guarantee it would work. Often the Curse of Servitude recognised the intention of its removal and immediately spread its poison through your veins as a consequence of disobedience.

There were many trackers who had tried the third option and failed, many times.

This Curser hadn't explained the pain though.

The pain the branding of the mark caused was forever etched into my memory, and unfortunately, this man's face now was as well.

I looked down and away from the man, unable to maintain eye contact.

"She screamed a lot, this one."

I immediately locked eyes with him again. He seemed pleased about that.

"But she didn't pass out. That's quite rare in fact."

Elias was stunned speechless.

*That's right Lord, be thankful my job isn't yours.*

"My name is Narvo. The King has told me you have some inquiries regarding a marked corpse. I am at your service, Sir." Narvo bowed to Elias.

So, Elias must have told him about that body, Claus' body.

I wondered if he had told him about my bloodied overnight torture as well.

*Or what was it he called it? My 'midnight stroll.'*

Elias nodded. He withdrew a sheet of paper, which had some drawings upon it, and gave it to Narvo. Narvo raised his eyebrows immediately, looking at Elias as if he had handed something to him mistakenly.

"You know these marks?" Elias asked.

"The marks of possession. The marks of necromancy," Narvo explained.

I had told Elias all of this already. Didn't he believe me?

"That's what she said," Elias looked at me.

"Then your tracker is knowledgeable—"

"She's not my..." Elias rolled his eyes, seeing no point in finishing that sentence.

*Gods. Is that what they'll call me now? The Lord's tracker? Like I'm his pet?*

Clearly the idea revolted him as much as it did me.

*That's two things we've been able to agree on today. Ha. Unusual.*

"Of course, My Lord, apologies. But the tracker is correct. There is no doubt."

Elias snatched the piece of paper from the man's hands and walked over to Narvo's desk. He took out a quill dipped in ink and passed them both to me.

"Draw what you saw," he instructed me.

I stared at the paper as if it were poisonous. "I can't...draw that thing."

"Try," Elias looked at me insistently, but also apologetically. His face tightened uncomfortably at his own request.

My hand shook slightly as I took the paper and sat down at the desk, trying my best to depict what I had seen.

Elias' breath hitched as he watched the lines I drew merge together.

"It looks much the same as what they described," Narvo said thoughtfully.

I had already told Elias this too. What was the meeting? A design to make sure everything I said hadn't been a fabrication?

"Could it be the same one?" Elias looked at Narvo with apprehension.

"I am not sure. We have no way of comparing, since the bodies from the past, should they have possessed marks, are long since gone."

I remained seated, absorbed in the horror of my own drawing. It was so hauntingly disgusting to look at. I was surprised I'd been able to depict it at all.

"And the marks on the King's parents?" Elias said.

The man hummed. "They were not the same as these."

"The girl? Did you examine her?"

Elias must have been talking about the candidate. The announcement the King had made about both his parents and the attack had spread throughout the trackers like a wild flame.

"I did, but there were no marks." Narvo shook his head.

I could, perhaps should, tell them about the talisman.

But the thought of dying in a bloody pool was sobering enough.

Elias sighed loudly. I turned in my chair to face them both.

"Is there a way to navigate, to track the person who is leaving these marks behind, and trace their energy?" Elias inquired.

Narvo shrugged. "Possibly but wouldn't your…" He stopped and corrected himself. "Wouldn't the Navigator here know more about that."

"You're a Curse user, so your knowledge is also helpful."

A Curse user, or a Curser, a class four Acciperean, and he here was, working for the King.

Narvo thought on the question for a few moments. "Have you tried?"

So, Elias hadn't told the King, otherwise Narvo would have already been informed, and known the answer to that question.

I couldn't help but look up at Elias, he didn't meet my gaze, but the man noticed.

"You have tried," he murmured, fascinated. "What happened?" he asked.

Elias looked at me warily. If I didn't know my own situation better, I'd assume he was asking me for permission to tell Narvo.

I found myself nodding slightly.

Elias spoke, only then. "The Navigator became unwell. She was bleeding and confused."

"Bleeding?" Narvo sounded surprised.

I didn't know whether that question was addressed to me or Elias, so I remained silent.

Elias confirmed. "Yes, and it seemed to enter her dreams as well."

"Impossible," Narvo whispered, he sounded equally appalled and enthralled by the discovery.

"Clearly not," Elias muttered.

"There could be more than one of them," Narvo posed.

"It's the same person," I blurted out.

"How are you so sure?" Narvo asked me.

*Because the talisman clearly belonged to a Necromancer, and the person walking my dreams demanded I return it and called it something of theirs, and during that conversation, well, more like interrogation, I started bleeding and couldn't move.*

Which reminded me of the fact I had omitted that detail before.

"I couldn't move either, in the dream. I was bleeding, and I was dreaming all at once, and the figure alluded to the fact it was the Necromancer who had possessed the corpse we found."

"This is…concerning," was all Narvo could say.

"Concerning?" Elias asked disapprovingly, clearly implying the word was not sufficient to describe the situation.

Narvo averted his eyes.

"Do you know of a way we can identify these marks on a person, search for them?" Elias asked.

Narvo frowned. "I will think of a way. I will mull it over, My Lord."

"Do it fast," Elias instructed.

It was only then that still at seat level, I looked at the man's hands and arms.

There was no Cursed mark on his skin.

He saw me watching him, saw where I was looking.

"Yes," he answered my silent question. "I do this willingly."

*Why? How can you live with yourself?*

I just stared at him.

He asked. "How old are you?"

"Twenty-five," I answered in a quiet voice.

"Just as old as I was, at the start."

He looked over my face then said, "You think me evil, don't you?"

"I—"

"No, no, don't answer that. The Lord is here, you cannot speak your mind, I know."

"Sir—" Elias interrupted him.

"Apologies, My Lord. It's only that these young ones don't know. They haven't seen what you and I have seen."

*Young ones? I'm hardly any younger than the Lord here.*

With a pause of silence in the room, Narvo continued, "Yes, I am a sorcerer, but the things I saw them do, the devastation I saw them unleash, I could not stand by and watch. I would prefer if such measures were not necessary." He pointed at my wrist, "But alas, the sorcerers grew entitled and greedy, grew unaware of their actions and their wrongs."

"They were not my wrongs," I said sorrowfully, pitifully. My voice sounded pathetic at that moment, like a desperate child's begging for love.

"But who's to say they won't be? You? Who can truly predict where their life will lead, what doors their pain will open? The past is written so we can learn from it."

*Written by who? If the killers have the pen, the legends will always praise the murderers.*

I did not say this aloud. Elias was standing behind me after all. Perhaps he'd even written some of that past down.

"It is better this way," Narvo nodded.

*Mass suffering inflicted on all sorcerers? A deep-rooted pain that you yourself have cast upon us? How naïve are you to think such a pain will not manifest into something far worse with time?*

My voice changed then, gritty with anger and disgust. "Better to make sure pain is all we know? That we can only hope for a bit of relief and nothing more?"

Elias spun his head towards me, but the man replied before he could say anything. "No. It would be better if you ceased to exist, but such a thing is not possible."

"Then you too, would cease to exist."

The man shrugged slightly, unbothered. "I only live to atone for the sins of my brothers and sisters, those I once called my friends. If I could die with all sorcerers. knowing this was no longer necessary, I would gladly tie a noose around my own neck."

*What? What is wrong with you?*

He saw my reaction. "You think me mad."

Was he the mad one, or was I? To move and breath and know each step would be saturated with suffering anyway, in a world where I was condemned for breathing, punished for pursuing life. How absurd. What an infinitely formidable and unbreakable absurdity.

But Elias. Didn't he too possess it? Didn't everyone who chose to live? The humans spent so much time dwelling upon *our* abilities, they forgot true power lay elsewhere. The power of persistence in the face of pain. The power of fingers clawing deep on the very edge, their muscles summoning a strength never known before. They were so afraid of us, of sorcery wiping them out, that they didn't see it. Their fear was stronger than their ability to see this shared truth weaving between us. This shared gift.

Narvo was wrong.

No sorcerer could take that gift from a human.

And no human could take it from a sorcerer, with a shackle.

Or a curse.

*You're not ridiculous to want death, but we are, to choose life, in this world.*

*But I would rather be ridiculous, than be nothing.*

*If I'm to die, I'll die for a dream, foolish I know that may be. I'll take these chains to the grave. Better to try, and be taken early, than slip away life's prisoner. I'd rather go yanking at the steel, than forget how to feel alive.*

*You're not mad Narvo. You're a shell.*

"That's enough, we're leaving," Elias cut in.

"Come back anytime, My Lord, and feel free to bring the Navigator."

"Pppfff," I let loose from my lips.

Elias didn't thank Narvo and just left the room, expecting me to follow. I hurried to follow but was stopped by Narvo's voice.

"Can't you sense it on him?" he asked.

I turned around, at the doorway now.

"He reeks of it."

I was already sure Narvo was out of his mind, and this only seemed proof of that.

"What are you talking about?" I asked in a low voice.

Elias' footsteps stopped as soon as he realised I wasn't behind him.

Narvo shook his head and grinned. "Never mind girl, never mind."

*Never mind? You can't just turn around and say something as ominous and foreboding as that and then drop your point halfway through?!*

Elias's voice called out from below. "Come."

I looked at the man one last time and reluctantly, exited the room.

Elias and I traversed the streets back towards the centre of the city. On the way back, we stopped by the same store, and I changed back into my clothes. I handed the dress and cloak to him. He tossed it behind my shoulder onto the floor and shut the door behind me.

Once we reached the centre of the festivities, Elias spoke again. "Go back to work."

"So, you'll stay?" I gestured around me at the festival.

"What concern is it of yours?"

*Do you have to be so abrasive about everything? I'm asking you a question, not pulling out your teeth.*

*Although, they're starting to feel like one and the same thing.*

Three guards from the Palace approached Elias. Their gold armour clunked with their heavy steps.

*At least I don't have to wear that.*

Elias turned around, I stood behind him, blocked off from their view.

"My Lord!" They sounded distressed.

"What is it?" Elias sounded bored.

"My Lord, there's been an emergency!"

Elias looked at the man as if he did not believe, for one moment, that there had been an emergency.

"What's wrong?" he asked out of politeness, it felt.

"It's one of the guards, My Lord! They've fallen dead!"

*Oh no. What...a...shame. Truly heart wrenching.*

"Why is that my concern?" Elias asked.

"My Lord, it was...it was a sorcerer!"

"That's right, My Lord. His skin turned foul and there was a great cloud of smoke—"

"It wasn't smoke! It was...it was—"

"It killed him, My Lord! He was clutching at his chest, and he had something in his hand! It was a necklace of some kind—"

*Oh.... oh no.*

"A necklace?" Elias stepped forwards.

But in that instant, I became visible to the guards. The one furthest to the left made eye contact with me.

"It was her!" He yelled. "She gave it to him! She killed him!"

## CHAPTER 63- HESTAN

"You don't have to be here," I reassured Dyna as I glanced at the festival's attractions.

It had only just been over a day since Dyna had awoken. She had recovered much faster than I had anticipated, most likely due to the Healer's capabilities. The Palace's own healers were stumped at the revelation that she had miraculously awoken from her slumber.

I, of course, had acted the same way, professing I had simply been sitting by her bedside when she had done so.

"It's fine! It's fine." Dyna laughed nervously, twisting a lock of her hair with her right hand, her left arm locked into mine. "I'm feeling well," she insisted.

"It's not that," I said under my breath.

Dyna gulped and looked away.

After she had awoken, she had been delirious with fright. She hadn't been able to identify the figure who had threatened her. No matter how much, or what I questioned her, she simply replied with the same three phrases.

*"I don't know."*

*"I didn't see."*

*"I can't remember."*

But what she did remember, was that this person had stated it was her, or the lives of her siblings.

Dyna had seven siblings.

At first, she had insisted on fulfilling her side of the bargain with her own death. She had even got on her knees and begged me to kill her myself.

Seeing her that way, filled me with rage. Whoever had made her this afraid, this desperate, was utterly despicable.

What's more, he would now know she was alive, and so Dyna was, despite acting boisterous, occupied with the thought her siblings were unsafe, and that she was the cause.

Once she had come to her senses, she had suggested she play dead, but such a scenario would be impossible with the frequency the healers of the Palace were coming to check in on her. If she simply disappeared, where would she go alone? If I went with her, it would be very obvious she had escaped and was thus, not dead at all.

And so, after some deliberation, and a long few hours spent trying to calm her, we agreed the best course of action was to wait, be cautious, to keep Dyna heavily watched, and guarded, and to alert King Dunlan of the threat. The latter I had done this morning.

I could only hope my letter would not be intercepted. There was a chance of that happening, but what choice did I have?

As much as Dyna wished to resume her normal activities, appearing in public like this, so soon after the incident, was a direct and blatant demonstration to her attacker that he had failed. I wasn't sure if that was information we should be revealing so soon, so openly.

"You're with me. As the Princess said, I'm lucky to have you. You'll protect me."

She sounded as if she were reciting a prayer to herself.

"I will, My Lady, but still, I could protect you from within the Palace walls as well."

"Yes but...but...I don't want to be there, for now."

It was understandable. It was obvious now that she had said it. Nobody would enjoy lingering around the area they had been near-killed in.

"Besides, everyone's been talking about the festival for weeks! The games, the parade, I want to see it all!"

"Very well, then I shall be beside you."

"No! You must enjoy the festival as well!" Dyna insisted stubbornly.

I looked around. There were stalls everywhere. In front of us, villagers were throwing small chips into cups, competing for prizes. To the right, there were several stalls selling luxurious jewels, clothing, armour, and even weaponry. The best and finest merchants from across the Kingdom had all collated here.

Down a street to the left, there was a similar scene, only with a variety of stalls selling food, the rarest delicacies, and the largest cuts of meat. The aroma of their juices wafted through the air. The smell of cinnamon cut through that, insistently sweet, warring with the scent of spices. Stacks and trays of it all sat on silver and golden platters, glistening in the sunlight.

It was nothing like Kalnasa. In truth, I had never seen anything quite like it in my life. As much as I could appreciate and admire it, immersing myself in it was another matter altogether.

Soon there would be a Parade. The candidates as well as a variety of dancers, musicians, Chimeras, and the King himself would ride the streets atop adorned chariots.

But before that, at the very centre of Iloris, the area having been cleared out for the occasion, there would be the conduction of a tradition that had occurred at every Courting Season for centuries.

Dice of Desire, that is what the people called it here, but it was officially titled 'Thrice Dice.'

Dyna and I were heading to the centre of the city now, where we would take our space at the table for the game. The closer we got, the denser the crowd grew, they parted for us. It was easy to identify us by the outfits we wore.

Dyna and I had arrived wearing a matching colour -mint green. Dyna's dress was made from fine silk and near her abdomen, a dense sewing of silver thread formed swirls around her waist. I, meanwhile, wore a vest, its v line and lack of sleeves exposing my upper chest and arms. The heat was far too stifling to wear anything else. My hair was held in a top knot bun with a pin. Dyna's was braided.

The crowd cast us glances as we walked by.

"The ladies are staring at you!" Dyna said joyfully.

There were, in fact, several women staring in my direction and whispering, some even laughing.

"Mm," I replied.

"Oh, don't be like that! My mother said she's tried to arrange a marriage for you several times and you always refuse. Don't you want a wife?" Dyna nudged me, urging me to glance in the women's direction.

"No. I have no wish for a wife," I said flatly, consciously looking in any direction not in line of sight of those women.

"No wish for a wife?" Dyna's eyes were blank. She sounded as if I had declared myself to be a mass murderer.

"No."

"Why?"

"I...I just don't."

"You're strange," Dyna sounded suspicious.

It was those who clamoured and rushed to get married to the first woman they met who had always seemed strange to me. Not that I would tell Dyna that, she was currently desperate to marry a man she barely knew.

The path cleared. In front of us was a large, hexagonal shaped table, lined with crimson velvet. The top of the shape was currently unoccupied, where the King would stand.

We walked to where we had been placed, which, if you were to stand in the King's position, would be the top left edge of the hexagon, our sides to the crowd.

To our left, and at the base of the hexagon, completely facing away from the people, stood Maiwen and a new individual, who appeared to be a replacement for her escort. Jurasa must have known about the old one's disappearance by now. I glanced away from him hurriedly. I had no intention of making eye contact with him again.

To our right stood Rhana and her escort Jayli, both of them were dressed in bright blue. Opposite them, stood Tarren and her escort dressed in blood red, and opposite us, there was an empty space, where Audra's Prince and Princess would stand.

The crowd spoke in excitable whispers, in amongst them were those placing bets on the winners. Dyna gripped my arm tighter as we took in the scene.

The volume of the crowd's whispers shifted, decreasing. At this change, everyone stilled, the crowd once again parted.

Opposite us, Audra's Prince and Princess approached the table.

Each and every person who laid eyes on them was left speechless, unable to utter any words, incapable of looking away, but appearing as if they desperately wanted to. Loria arrived at the table first. Her dress was inky black, shaped in a vest that formed a high collar around her neck, clasped with a silver ornament. There were two slits at the dress's waist, exposing her skin.

The Prince followed closely behind her.

He was wearing what resembled a jacket with no sleeves, it was black and had a stiff collar, but it dipped sharply into an almost straight line that exposed his bronze skin all the way to his waist. There were silver clasps near its bottom, and around his neck was a choker of a similar colour, the shape of a serpent, its head and tail at the edge of his collarbones.

The crowd slowly resumed talking once the two had reached the table.

"My Lady, I'm glad to see you well," Loria addressed her. The table was wide, but the Albarsans were no further than three arms breadths away from us, and so could easily be heard, even over the noise.

Dyna stammered, staring at the Prince and Princess, the Prince in particular. "I...thank you, Your Highness." She sounded nervous. She suspected everyone responsible for her most recent attack, especially the other candidates.

It dawned on me then, that I hadn't even considered the Prince or Princess of Audra would be the responsible parties and that truthfully, I had no reason to absolve them of suspicion so quickly.

"Captain, you look different today."

I looked up to see the Prince, staring at me.

His sister let out a small laugh. "Doesn't everyone? We're meant to adorn ourselves with the best attire for this occasion, aren't we?" She raised one eyebrow at him, and the Prince furrowed his, looking down at her from the side, seemingly irritated.

"It's because he normally looks boring," Dyna interjected.

I slightly pulled away and looked down at her in shock.

The Prince's laugh interrupted my state of confusion. He had his hand on his half bare abdomen.

I sighed and schooled my face back into blankness.

Dyna tried to soften her words. "No, not boring, I mean...it's just that...he doesn't like extravagant things."

The Prince had stopped laughing now and replied, "Not boring, just—"

"Poor," Tarren inserted herself into the conversation.

The Prince's face fell, and he clicked his tongue, not hiding the scowl he threw her way. Loria cleared her throat, trying to get his attention, but the Prince paid her no mind.

"Weren't you the very person in doubt of Kalnasa's dire financial situation during our last conversation? But now the Captain of the Hunt himself is poor?" He tutted. "If you're going to spout nonsense, at least keep it consistent. How embarrassing for you."

Tarren's face flushed red, and she remained silent after that.

I couldn't stop myself from watching the Prince, waiting for his gaze to return our way. As it did, I found him smiling at me. The sight stirred something strange in my chest.

His sister watched us silently. Dyna too.

"May I introduce myself to your esteemed selves?" Maiwen's new escort spoke. "Lord Parlin, member of the King's Royal guard."

It seemed I wouldn't be able to avoid his gaze after all. He looked at us all in turn, for a long time.

"It's a pleasure to meet you, Sir," Loria replied on our behalf.

"The honour of meeting you all, as well as being here, is entirely my own," he replied.

"It's a shame the last one didn't share your sentiments," the Prince said, wholeheartedly.

Maiwen who had been looking down, fidgeting with her hands, stopped doing so.

It was difficult not to make eye contact with the Prince at that moment, for the same reason Maiwen had stilled.

"Alas, Lord Beckett was an honourable man. His disappearance is truly a great pity." Fortunately, Lord Parlin didn't seem to be able to sense the awkward air hanging around us.

"So why didn't you look for him, instead of taking his place at the first chance you received?" the Prince asked.

This time I couldn't help but make eye contact with the Prince and tighten my jaw. The Prince noticed, and a grin graced the edges of his lips.

The man seemed horrified. "Your Highness, I would never...He...Lord Beckett was a friend. I am but doing my duty as requested by the King and I would never—"

The Prince waved his hand in the air. "Alright, alright."

Just at that moment, a chariot approached from our right.

The King was seated in a sedan, its dark red curtains semi-transparent, and moving in a gentle breeze. It was carried atop some horses, and the Palace servants who were riding them. The crowd grew even more agitated at seeing it approach.

Once it stopped, one of the Palace servants went to draw its curtain back, but before they could, the King stepped out.

Dyna gasped and the face of Audra's Princess became awe stricken.

The King somehow managed to appear even more ethereal and God like each time he showed his face. He was dressed in resplendent gold, the sleeves of his upper clothing were long, but they were ballooned and cuffed at his wrists. The rest of the blouse-like garment wrapped around his body and stopped at his hip trailing down like a river across his darkened gold pants. His hair was for the first time I had seen it, tied into a small knot at the centre of the back of his head. It made all of his features look even stronger.

Behind him trailed Lord Elias. His brow was knitted, and he was dressed far more simply, in a dark red jacket, and pants.

Someone else stepped up behind us, grinning at the crowd. He raised his voice. "People of Athlion. Fair folk of this Kingdom. Welcome! To the ninety-eighth annual game of Dice of Desire!"

The crowd yelled in response, cheering, and waving flags, smiling at one another, shouting in each other's ears.

"Here are the rules!" the man continued, his hands dancing, his mannerisms animated and theatrical. "One representative per Kingdom shall play. Before these noble competitors, are a set of two dice. The dice have six sides. Five of these sides contain the numbers one to five, the sixth side, however, contains a cross."

He leant forwards, his finger outstretched.

"Each round, the players will agree on a number on which to bet. The player the furthest away from the number is last, the player the closest is first. In the event there is a tie, the players will roll until a winner is established. If, however, a player should roll a cross, they will automatically be eliminated from the entire game."

The man lowered his voice for the final sentence, his every word sounding more dramatic than the last. I cast a glance over the others at the table. They were all watching him attentively.

"Round one is called 'Ask that which I dare not answer.' The winner of the round can ask the player who came last any question, and they must answer honestly!"

The crowd whispered at that, likely speculating, or discussing which answers they wished to hear. This round didn't seem troublesome. Lying was the simple way around it, and there was no way in which to prove, in most cases, that the truth had not been told.

The man lifted up two fingers. "Round two is called 'Give that which I dare not part with.' The winner may ask the player in last place to give them something of theirs, which they desire."

That round was worse.

"The final round!" The man paused, his head moving from side to side, making eye contact with several members of the crowd. "Is called…'Grant that which I dare not offer.' The winner of the round can ask any wish of the player in last place, and they *must* fulfil it. The only wishes that cannot be granted is marriage to the King, or anything in violation of Athlion's laws."

That round was certainly the worst. Who knew what those around this table may ask of others, what positions they could place them in?

"And so! Keep your eyes open and your breathing quiet. For dice shall be rolled, desires shall be granted, and the deepest ones...revealed."

The man slid away to the side, and the silence that dropped over the large space was filled by the King saying, "Who will play?"

Tarren stepped forwards, Maiwen also, Rhana too.

Dyna whispered to me. "You do it. Please?"

I looked at her. She appeared unnerved, still ill at ease with her surroundings. I nodded and stepped forwards closer to the table.

At that precise moment, Audra's Prince did the same. When he saw that I too, had joined the game, he smirked. He spread both his arms out and held the edges of the table, leaning forwards.

"Who would like to choose the number?" the King asked.

"Five, Your Highness!" Tarren shouted, before anyone else could volunteer.

The King nodded. He reached forwards with his long fingers and grabbed the two dice in the crimson cup. He shook them.

We all followed his action. Each of our cups were a separate colour, corresponding to our Kingdoms. Vasara's red, Zeima's grey, Kalnasa's blue, Jurasa's green, and Audra's gold.

The King lifted his cup first.

A three.

The crowd murmured a little but were silent swiftly after.

The dice were to be revealed in a clockwise direction to the King.

Next Rhana revealed...a seven.

It was my turn to lift the cup then. I placed my hand around the pale blue clay, my rings clanking against it sounding loudly in the quiet.

A six.

The crowd became more excited.

I hadn't thought about what I might ask if I won any of these rounds, as I had assumed Dyna would play.

Maiwen was next, she lifted up her cups to reveal a two. One dot on each dice.

The Prince came after, he leant his head forwards, lifted one arm off the table from the leaning position it was in. Some of his dark tousled hair fell over his forehead. He lifted his golden cup very slightly and laughed a little.

A ten.

He looked up at me and seemed to say with his eyes, *You better think about what you'll ask me.*

Tarren didn't even spare a second before she yanked the lid of her cup up.

A five.

The crowd, clearly having waited until this round was over, began speaking to one another. Their lips rapidly moved as they glanced at the Prince and Tarren.

The Prince leant back and crossed his arms. He turned to his left slightly looking at Tarren, waiting.

The crowd, noticing he had changed position, hushed at once.

"Congratulations, ask away," the Prince tilted his head at her.

Tarren turned to him and straightened her head exaggeratedly. She cleared her throat.

"Your Highness. I would like to know…" She paused, but it was clear she'd had a question in mind. The crowd held their breaths. The Prince looked unamused.

"If it's true…" she continued.

The Prince raised his eyebrows nonchalantly.

"Whether or not you are betrothed!"

The wind, the slight breeze, felt suffocatingly loud at that moment.

"Surely not," Dyna whispered, standing slightly behind me.

I furrowed my brow, the stretched-out silence, the lack of the Prince's answer felt uncomfortable.

The Prince licked his lips and let out a light laugh once more. He tilted his head further to the side and raised his eyes for a second, in a gesture that looked as if he were contemplating his response.

Then he shrugged, his right arm escaped its crossed position to lean on the table again.

"Yes. That is true."

The crowd exploded in a frenzy of shock.

The Prince was betrothed?

It seemed…impossible.

His blithe mannerisms in response to the question, his body language, his grin, all felt antagonistic.

How could the Prince have been betrothed without anyone knowing? Or was he lying about it? Was this a game to him?

It was a game, I had to remind myself. Not only these dice, but this whole Season.

Even the King seemed surprised, one of his eyebrows darting up quickly. The Prince's sister was the most shocked however, her eyes wide.

Tarren clearly hadn't expected that response, her mouth half open. "To whom?" she let out inadvertently.

The Prince wagged his finger from side to side. "One question. If you'd been clever, you could have asked me 'To whom are you betrothed Your Highness.' But you didn't." He shrugged again. "Hardly surprising though."

Tarren was stunned and turned back to her escort, looking at him with confusion.

The Prince also turned back to the table. Loria tugged at his sleeve slightly as he did. They shared a silent look.

After which, the Prince met my eyes again. He didn't grin, or smile however, he only examined my face thoughtfully for a moment.

"I'll go next," he announced, looking at me still. Then he turned to the King. "If you'll allow me, Your Majesty."

The King nodded slightly in response.

"A three," the Prince said.

The King rolled…a seven.

Then Rhana… an eight.

I rolled. My mouth instantly dried.

A nine.

Maiwen rolled. She clasped her hand over her mouth as she saw her dice. She lifted it in the air and held it forwards to reveal that one of them had rolled to a cross.

So now, Maiwen could no longer benefit from this game, but she could no longer be exploited from it either.

A cross didn't seem too awful.

The Prince rolled. He lifted his cup swiftly this time. His eyes glinted as it revealed one dot on each dice.

A two.

Dyna' worried gaze settled on my face.

Tarren rolled, looking very intense as she shook her cup. She slowly and dramatically lifted her lid to reveal…a five.

Dyna murmured. "Doesn't that mean?"

Yes. Yes, it did.

I had already given the Prince a great deal. My time, my health, risks to my own life, honour, position, and reputation.

But here I was, giving him something else.

A knot in my stomach was beginning to form, anticipation, nerves, uncertainty.

And yet, it was because of everything the Prince and I had already experienced, and exchanged, I did not feel particularly concerned.

Was it right to feel that way? The audience were all casting me sympathetic glances, as if they supposed the Prince might ask for my head.

He wouldn't need to ask. He could easily take it himself.

"Captain…" the Prince began. He placed his hands behind his back and stepped even closer to the table. "What can you offer me?"

What did he expect me to say in response? I had nothing of value. I certainly didn't have any money.

I placed my hands behind my back as well. "What is it that you want?"

The Prince's mouth twitched.

The crowd began to shout out suggestions.

"His money!"

"His sword!"

"He doesn't have a sword you dipshit...His spear!"

"His most prized possession!"

"A night with his wife!"

I flinched at that suggestion, and couldn't help but look out towards the crowd, in search of the person who'd yelled it.

"His shield!"

"His horses!"

I didn't have any horses.

The Prince's eyes remained fixed on me. He seemed to be enjoying watching my increased perplexed reactions to their hollers, judging by the slight smile he wore.

Dyna said from behind me. "What are you going to—"

She stopped speaking as she overheard another audience member scream. "HIS HOUSE!"

"I don't know," I whispered very quietly, barely moving my lips.

"Captain, there must be something you're willing to give me?" The Prince glanced at me expectantly.

I smiled tightly, politely. "I'm afraid not, Your Highness. I do not—"

"This!" Dyna exclaimed from behind me.

I turned over my shoulder, to see Dyna's hand, high in the air, her fingers pointing at ...my head?

The Prince's eyes followed her hand.

"His pin!" she said proudly. "It's made from the finest silver and...and..." She thought hard, scrunching her facial features up. "It has gems embellished on it which are only mined in Kalnasa like..." She looked up at the pin, standing on her toes. "It has amethysts and diamonds...yes!"

She smiled brightly, returned to the soles of her feet, and put her hand back down.

She looked at me as if expecting praise. She had suggested it because I had nothing else, suggested it to avoid the possibility of me needing to offer up something far worse or more valuable.

But it was a pin, and while it was true it was likely one of the only things of monetary value I owned, this game only happened once in a generation. The Prince was one of the only winners of one of these rounds in history. He could ask for anything, and I would be obliged to give it to him, without any question or escape. A pin would hardly suffice in this...

"Perfect," the Prince said, smiling widely.

I jerked my head around and squinted at him incredulously.

The crowd seemed as confused as I was.

"A pin? He actually accepted a pin?"

"Is that it?"

"He could have asked for anything!"

"Fucking boring! Why don't you –" a crowd member began.

At this, the Prince sharply turned towards the throng, his lips curling in a scowl. He was glaring at an individual, he must have met the man's eyes instantly, as if he had been able to tell which lips each and every sentence had escaped from previously.

The man stopped speaking instantly, as did everyone else.

He turned back to me, his facial features returning to normal. I was still watching him with suspicion.

"Didn't you hear her? Amethysts," he said, smiling widely.

Deciding I didn't wish to drag this out further, I replied, "Very well. If that is what you wish for."

"It is. What I wish for," the Prince replied, looking at me intently.

I turned sharply away, glancing at the King. "If you will, Your Majesty. A ten."

The King nodded. "A ten," he repeated.

He rolled first.

A three.

Rhana rolled.

A six. She let out a sigh of relief, knowing she was now guaranteed not to be the loser. This was after all, the round with the most to lose.

I took a deep breath, placed my hands around the top and bottom of the cup and shook, rolling the dice within.

I lifted it, my heart suddenly increasing in rate.

A nine.

I sucked in a breath.

The Prince rolled next, quickly, and casually as if he didn't care about the game at all.

A four. Unlike Rhana, he didn't seem to be so relieved at his safety.

Tarren rolled last, closing her eyes, and seeming to pray as she shook her cup.

She lifted her cup and let out a gasp of joy, slapping her hand against her chest.

A seven.

My body felt stiff, stuck. I stared down at the table, my gaze plastered to the nine I had rolled. The crowd perked up once more.

"Captain," the King said. "You have won."

I could ask the King anything. Anything of him I wanted.

I slowly turned to him. He was utterly calm, at least outwardly. He even looked a little riveted.

Dyna was still, quiet.

For she and I both knew what I would ask, what this opportunity could offer, one we could not ignore.

"Your Majesty," I started, raising my voice as confidently as I could manage. "I request you form a new trade agreement with Kalnasa, that pertains to the supplies of food, medicine, crops, and water, in light of their...of our current situation."

The crowd whispered softly, but they were tense. As was I.

The King didn't speak for a few seconds. He frowned slightly. This game was a tradition in his Kingdom. By his own customs, he could not refuse, he could not go back on his word.

But that, I knew, was only in public. I had no idea what the King may, or may not do, when it came to this wish in private.

Still, I had to try.

Lord Elias seemed fretful and restless. He kept glancing at the King as if wishing he would turn around and speak to him.

"That is a very honourable request, Captain. One for your people, and not yourself. I should have expected it," the King stated.

"Will you grant it, Your Majesty?" I asked.

The King smiled softly. "While such an arrangement will by no means, be born swiftly, and will be difficult, and arduous to settle, it is my duty, not only to abide by the traditions of this season, but also to help others in Athlion in time of need."

And yet, Kalnasa was currently in crisis. Where was this help of which he spoke?

"I will fulfil your wish, Captain, but please, be mindful you will not see its fulfilment for quite some time."

"I understand, Your Majesty. I am grateful."

The crowd breathed out collectively, speaking to one another in hushed tones.

"The game is concluded!" The man who had introduced it returned to his position. "But that is not all! Fair folk go forth and enjoy all this festival has to offer and remember...today is a day where desire is yours to fulfil, and...reveal!"

The crowd cheered and clapped, whistled, and eventually dispersed.

The King was the first to leave, turning away, with Lord Elias following at his heels.

The others around the table began to leave with their escorts. I turned to Dyna and offered her my arm, stepping down from the platform.

"How are you feeling?" I asked in a quiet voice.

"I can't believe the King agreed," she muttered.

I, however, couldn't believe he had *truly* agreed. Not just yet.

We walked through the thronging crowd, finding it difficult to get through. As before, many watched as we passed, commenting to one another, their eyes sweeping over our figures.

The crowd instantly stopped speaking and backed away. Naturally, Dyna and I halted, slowing our step in bafflement.

"Captain!" a voice called out from behind me.

I turned to find the Prince approaching. The crowd parted from him as if he were a river passing through a glen. Princess Loria strolled behind him with ease.

"Your Highness," I addressed him cautiously.

The Prince stopped a few steps in front of us. "Where are you going?"

I side-eyed Dyna, who also looked at my face. "We were...going to explore the festival, Your Highness."

"But you still haven't granted me my wish."

Ah. That. I didn't think he would actually come to claim it. I had simply thought he had been amusing himself and the crowd with his declaration.

"You didn't think I'd come for my reward?" he inquired.

"The reward is...poor, Your Highness. I am sure I can offer you something far more suitable in time, if you are willing to be patient."

"I am not," the Prince said, taking one step towards me.

Dyna let go of my arm, as if she were frightened of his closeness and presence, backing away.

I turned to her, then back to the Prince.

"Can I?" he asked.

He had his hands raised in the air, near my face.

I could easily remove the pin myself if he were so keen to possess it. But it was hardly as if I could refuse him with all of these people watching us.

During my silence, the Prince's hand edged forwards slightly. It found its way around the back of my head. To reach, he had to move slightly closer. He pulled the pin out of my hair, which fell loosely at its undoing.

The Prince's hand hovered there for a while. Too long. He watched as my hair escaped its former position, as the strands fell in front of my face. My eyes.

The crowd didn't dare speak. Neither did I.

The Prince's fingers clasped around the metal. He withdrew his hand then took several steps back. Slowly.

He spun the pin between his fingers. It danced between his digits as if he were flipping a blade threateningly. The purple amethysts caught the light of the sun, casting his fingers in fleeting sparks.

He threw it in the air. It twirled several times against the bright blue sky before it fell back into his palms. He didn't look as he threw it, and caught it, again and again, grinning at me instead as he backed away. He let out a small laugh and turned around, still tossing the hairpin in the sky several times as he walked off.

Dyna came back to my side again, and gradually, the crowd began to resume a normal level of chatter and movement.

We remained in place as she said, "It doesn't even have diamonds...what if he's angry?"

"He knows that already," I reassured her.

"What? Does he?" she said cluelessly.

Of course he knew. There were no diamonds, and the amethysts on that pin were of poor quality, and very small, very few. There was no true reason to wish for that pin.

"Yes, don't be alarmed. The Prince is only—"

"Only what?" she asked, interested.

I shook my head, unable to finish my thought.

"It doesn't matter. The pin doesn't matter."

"But...he came back and asked for it," she protested, bewildered.

We spun around and began to stroll again.

"He had to. Those are the rules."

"Oh." Dyna didn't sound convinced.

Truthfully, neither was I. The Prince didn't seem someone who respected or followed rules, hence why I had assumed my exit would have been of little consequence.

"He's betrothed! Can you believe it!" she hissed.

"It does not matter whether I believe it," I replied with restraint.

But honestly, no I could not.

"That poor woman...having to marry...*him*." Dyna's eyes darted from left to right, she continued to whisper. "He's terrifying."

It was precisely for that reason it was difficult to imagine the Prince with someone. To imagine him being tender and caring towards them. Could hands that had been coated in blood touch another with reverence and softness? Could someone become a corpse or lover, under the same palms? Did he wear a smile when he killed? Was it the same as the one he'd worn pulling the pin from my hair? How would one sit upon his face, should it look upon someone he loved, I wondered...

Pictures of him tending to my wounds flashed before my eyes.

"Perhaps not always..." I spoke my thoughts aloud.

Dyna snorted. "When then?"

I turned away from her. It was hardly as if I could reply. "*When I was in his bed, and he put a cold compress to my forehead.*"

Dyna mused aloud. "I wonder who she is. Probably one of the noblewomen from Audra. I wonder which one. There are a few his age. There's Theadra, she's supposedly very beautiful... oh and there's also Lilian, she's apparently the heir to a large fortune."

Most likely Lilian then, considering the political benefits.

"There's no use speculating, who can say, My Lady, why don't we—"

"No!" Dyna blurted out before I could finish. "I don't want to go back."

I sighed. "I know, I wasn't going to suggest that."

"Alright…then let's…" She turned around searching the streets. "Let's eat something."

I nodded. We made our way over to the food stalls.

Dyna froze as we grew closer.

She was afraid.

"We do not have to," I told her.

She was afraid it was poisoned.

"Let's do something else." She sounded disappointed.

We turned in search of another activity when a woman approached us.

"My Lady! Sir! Thank you!"

Dyna was too stunned to respond. "For what Madam?" I asked her.

"Your wish, Captain!" The woman standing before us was Kalnasan. She must have travelled here specifically for the festival, to sell her merchandise, most likely.

"Thank you," she repeated.

"It was the Captain's idea!" Dyna insisted.

"My Lady would have asked the same."

Dyna didn't disagree with that.

"How…How is it there?" Dyna asked the woman wearily.

"Oh, My Lady, it's…" Her voice quivered but she quickly composed herself. "Would you like to look at my stall?" She pointed over to a table with lush fabrics and clothes.

Dyna was about to protest. We didn't have much money after all.

"Free! For you! As a thanks, to both of you."

"Of course!" Dyna replied excitedly then. "The Captain needs some new clothes."

I smiled at her encouragingly. I had no wish or desire for new garments but if this endeavour would ease her mind, I was willing to indulge her.

Dyna ran over to the stall, clutching at the fabric. The woman and I followed behind.

"Please madam," I said. "Finish your sentence."

The woman cleared her throat and tucked some of her long dark hair behind her ear.

"It's…the most horrifying thing I've ever seen." Her voice was quiet and full of raw despair.

I had expected an answer that was negative, but not to this degree.

"What do you mean?" I rushed to ask before we reached Dyna.

"There's no words that can describe the horror."

"What horror?"

Her voice was distant. "They're eating the children now."

I stopped walking. I was normally remarkably controlled in my outward expression of shock, emotion, or displeasure, but I, with one foot in front of the other, stopped walking, and clenched my hands, which were clasped behind my back tighter together. I was staring at the woman with no reserve.

"The—" I started, my voice barely audible.

Dyna bounded over to us, holding a white robe. "This one, Captain! It would go so well with your hair!"

I was still stunned into a stupor. The woman had stopped walking as well and was watching me guiltily.

"Yes, Captain, it would suit you well," she said.

It took a while before I looked at the garment. Dyna noticed something was amiss immediately and appeared anxious.

"What's wrong? Did you see something? Is someone—"

"No, My Lady, you are safe, I apologise. It is only...the garment...I've not owned something like this for some time. I'm not...accustomed to it." It was indeed very fine material, expensive.

When I was a child, living in squalor, I had not owned anything at all. Even when I did begin to own such extravagant and expensive items at around the age of eighteen, it had felt unusual. I had lost them all in recent years, but in truth I had not particularly missed them since I had grown accustomed to doing without them for over a decade.

Dyna frowned but quickly smiled again. "Oh! Then you must have it! Is that alright?" She turned to ask the woman. The woman seemed surprised to be asked for permission.

"Of course, My Lady, it's yours." She smiled warmly at her but sadly as well.

I understood. Watching Dyna, her brightness, her joy, her warmth, knowing those her age, or younger were possibly being offered up as food by their own people, their own families. It was enough to crush your soul as you regarded her.

Dyna threw the garment at me. I caught it. She ran back over to the stall again to select something for herself.

I looked at it mystified. I was still processing the woman's words.

"Since when?" I asked her quietly.

"A month now."

*A month?*

"The King, he's—"

Her voice was full of disdain as she replied.

"The King hasn't been seen since you left."

## CHAPTER 64- NATHON

From up here, the number of people who had come to this festival was even clearer. They stretched out for miles, down every street, every alleyway.

But I was only searching for one person.

"Why are you still holding that?" Loria murmured. She waved at the exultant crowds atop our black chariot, adorned with golden birds and silver engravings. The parade had us flaunting our existence as if we were figurines.

My hand came to a halt. The Captain's pin balanced between the two fingers I had been twirling it around.

"Why not?" I smiled and waved at the crowd as well. They appeared both terrified and enamoured by any direct eye contact I made with them.

Loria's soft smile was still plastered on her face as she turned towards me and spoke. "Because it's a pin."

I shrugged and propelled it into the air once again, catching it. "And?"

"Why are you so occupied with it?" Loria sounded cynical, but her face remained blissfully serene.

"I won it," I said nonchalantly.

"You could have asked him for anything." Loria diverted her attention to the crowd again, who soaked up her glances with longing.

"I don't need anything," I replied.

Not anything the Captain could provide, at least.

Loria glanced at me with doubt.

"Plus, this is sharp. I could easily use it as a weapon." I lightly tapped the tip with my finger, holding it up to the sunlight. It glinted as the rays struck the metal.

Loria followed my movement then her eyes returned to my face. "How come I'm the one telling you? That was an opportunity we should not have wasted." Her voice sounded slightly bitter.

I frowned, my eyebrows furrowing at her. It was unlike her to make such comments. After all, she was right, it was usually me who reminded her of such things.

"What's the matter?" I asked casually.

Loria didn't reply.

From up here, nobody could hear us, or see our lips moving. This was possibly one of the only times Loria and I would be able to speak this openly.

"If you want to speak, do it now. We won't get this chance again." I grinned at more crowd members, my words escaping through my teeth.

"Did you poison that girl?" she asked sadly, bluntly.

I had expected that.

"Absolutely not," I replied instantly.

Loria's shoulders sank in what seemed like relief.

"Do you know who did?"

"No," I told her.

"Does the Captain?"

"No," I repeated.

"Does the Captain suspect you?"

Without even thinking I replied, "He doesn't."

Loria faced me again, her expression puzzled. "Really?"

It made sense she would ask. It would have been perfectly reasonable for the Captain to suspect I had poisoned Dyna, under the majority of circumstances.

But we were no longer under such a majority.

"Really," I reassured her grinning.

"How? Why?" She was bewildered at the thought.

"We have an understanding," I informed her.

Loria blinked slowly and opened her eyes to look at the crowds once again. "You're toying with him," she let out in one breath.

"No," I replied adamantly. "I am not."

Loria didn't seem to believe that. She only looked at the pin in my hand and raised a brow as if it proved her point.

"This has nothing to do with…"

I stopped speaking and turned away. Defending myself against such accusations wasn't something I ever usually felt the need to do. I was confused at my own attempt.

Why did it matter whether she believed so? Why did it matter if I wasn't?

"You're betrothed?" Loria added after a few seconds, putting an end to my internal battle.

I laughed slightly. "My betrothal is not the one we should be occupied with."

"Since when?" She ignored my attempt to avoid the question.

"How would I know? I probably found out after everyone else," I said huffing out another laugh.

"Who is it?" she asked the questions rapidly, one after another.

"Why? Would you like to congratulate the bride to be? Send her a gift basket?"

Loria let out an exasperated sigh, without changing her facial expression. "I just want to know."

I didn't enjoy speaking about this subject, hence why nobody knew about this betrothal. I had no intention of following through with it, but I did not have the means or plan to escape from it either. That bothered me. Immensely.

"Who?" she pressed.

"Wouldn't that ruin the surprise?" I squinted at her as we turned a corner, and the sun hit my eyes.

She didn't speak at first, staring at my sun-stricken face with sympathy.

"I'm sorry," she said seriously.

My betrothal was at the bottom of the list of unwelcome things I'd been dragged through in recent years, in terms of difficulty. It bothered me, but in considering events higher up on that list, it became diluted, something I had no time to dwell upon.

"Sorry for what? Your betrothal is far more complicated," I snickered. But there was a part of me that absorbed her condolences and felt strangely grateful for them.

The Parade came to an end as the afternoon did, and although the festival was still in full swing, each of the candidates and their escorts began to leave.

Loria and I did the same. I walked her to the Palace gates and stopped.

She froze mid-step as she noticed. She turned over her shoulder. I smiled and nodded. She understood, I had somewhere to go.

Less than an hour later, I reached my destination. As much as I loathed the very thought of seeing Mathias' face again, and had already decided after he injured the Captain, that I would make him die far more slowly than I had previously planned one day…for now, I had little choice but to answer his summons.

I had seen him in the crowd. I had expected to. Nobody else would recognise him of course, but he had subtly held up four fingers across his crossed arms.

In four hours, he had indicated. Meet in four hours.

Then he had held up two fingers, one being his thumb.

That indicated we were to meet in the second, alternative location. Not the Solar Inn. Usually this was because it was deduced the first location had become insecure or compromised.

And so, I strolled into the second establishment on time, titled the dreadful 'Vasaran Vine,' and found him instantly, standing at the bar.

I perched myself on a vacant stool next to him.

"Recovered then?" I smiled into the drink I ordered for myself. Mathias' hand tightened around the handle.

He forgot himself, his purpose, the secrecy we were meant to maintain as he grumbled, "That Kalnasan is dead when this is over."

I placed my drink down on the counter.

"Are you sure about that? He's bested you once before," I reminded him.

Mathias turned red with anger. "He's dead," he spat viciously.

*No... that will be you.*

He had likely already expected the Captain to die of that wound. Little did he know I had tended to it myself. The thought filled me with an unfamiliar sense of satisfaction.

"Afraid of bumping into him again?"

Mathias was silent, only scoffing, which meant he was. That must have been the reason he'd wanted to meet here instead.

I had never met anyone other than Sarlan that Mathias was wary of.

"Enjoying the festival?" I asked an alternate question. I leant my left elbow on the counter as I turned towards him, perching my cheek on my fist.

Without replying, Mathias placed his right fist on the counter, turning as well.

On his middle finger was a dark ring, engraved with the letter "A."

My eyes rested on it for a moment, then found his face, self-satisfied and smug.

To any outsider it would appear as if nothing had happened.

But that ring, that ring was a command, a call.

To return to Sarlan.

Immediately.

I stared at Mathias for a second or two, then averted my gaze back to my drink. My mind was full of endless speculation as to the reasons behind this sudden change in plan.

"The festival is fine, but I must return to work soon," Mathias spoke.

I looked at him once more. "I for one am enjoying it, I hope to stay until the end of the festivities." *Why have I been summoned?*

"Alas, sometimes we must forgo such things, for the sake of work." *You're not permitted to ask questions.*

"In such instances, I tend to ask others to cover for me, perhaps you should try that." *Why does he need me? He can use the others.*

Mathias's face grew grim. "I can't. There are too few of us. They've even lost some lately."

*Lost some?*

Mathias took advantage of my confusion. "There used to be more. But four have left recently. Tumultuous times." His voice was the perfect display of dismay, tinged with the tone of idle gossip.

*Four?*

I couldn't comprehend it. How were four of Audra's unit, Sarlan's human embodiment of weaponry, taken out, at once?

My brow relaxed as I realised the only possible way, the only possible adversary who could succeed in such an endeavour.

Sorcerers.

My mind wandered to the cloaked woman. Had she been involved in this?

And how could I leave Loria alone? Especially after the incident that had just occurred with the Kalnasan candidate.

"I have to go back in three hours," Mathias spoke up. *You have three days.*

"What about your friends? Won't they miss you?" I grinned. *What about Loria?*

"My friends aren't alone. They'll be fine." *We're watching her.*

This felt inherently wrong, as if I were being propelled into flames. I knew there was no way I could refuse this summons, but every part of me was protesting, writhing at the sound of its call.

Mathias stood. Placing a few rays down on the countertop. "Drinks on me."

I regarded the coins with disdain. "Are you sure? After all, don't you need money for medicine?"

Mathias' hand rested on the coins he had just placed down. He grinned falsely.

"There won't be any medicine. I'm perfectly fine," he bit.

*For now.*

He leant forwards. "You won't be so lucky next time." His voice dropped, blending into the cacophony of noise around us.

"There won't be a next time." I side-eyed him. "I'm perfectly fine."

He jerked away, an expression of fury plastered across his face, and all but bashed his way through the stools towards the door.

Mathias, who had always been completely discreet, had now been utterly unnerved by a defeat to the Captain.

The Captain didn't even realise how much power he had.

At the thought, I dug into my pants and pulled out the pin.

There were amethysts on it, that was true, but they were dull. It would probably only sell for one lunar, maybe two.

I pricked my finger on the edge of the pin once more, the tip causing an indentation into my skin.

But it was sharp. Yes. Very.

*For now, Mathias, perfectly fine, for now.*

# CHAPTER 65 - NATHON

"Where is he?" I asked a guard standing outside my father's office. I had barged in, expecting to see him sitting there, waiting for me.

The guard opened his mouth in shock, as if he hadn't expected me to speak to him at all, or anyone to speak to him, ever.

I raised my eyebrows.

"Where…is…he?" I repeated.

"He's not receiving you here, Your Highness."

"Couldn't you have told me that before I walked in?" I grumbled.

"I'm not permitted to speak to Your Highness."

"You're speaking to me now," I alerted him to the obvious.

The man seemed absolutely stunned by this revelation and opened and closed his mouth a few more times before shutting it for good.

Asking him any more would be pointless, and cruel. If it had been Sarlan who had given him the order to keep quiet, then I was risking his tongue, and perhaps his life.

I was exhausted. I had left instantly after the festival and ridden here as fast as possible. I had only just made it on time within the three-day window, mostly due to the fact I had only slept three or four hours each day, and travelled for the remaining hours at full speed. I had debated leaving Loria a note, but my disappearance would probably have only made her slightly suspicious, not enough to cause alarm. And truthfully, I hadn't had the time.

Just as I was about to traverse the dark hallways to look for the man, a voice emerged from behind me.

"Come. He's waiting."

I turned around to find my mother, standing at the very end of the corridor. She had her hands clasped in front of her. Her face was stoney and full of undisguised contempt.

I strutted towards her, my steps fast and clipped. "Mother. It's been so long. Did you miss me?"

My mother said nothing, but her face contorted even more painfully.

Of course, she hadn't been bothered by my absence. In fact, there had, not in my memory, ever been a time when my mother had loved, cared for, missed, or worried about myself, or Loria. To her, we were Sarlan's possessions. It was as if she saw us as a gift she had promised him, and handed over, and now that she had, she was devoid of any responsibility towards us, any relation.

It was honestly baffling how easily she had been able to achieve such a distance.

She walked onwards and I followed her. We came to a set of stairs I was unfamiliar with, that led deep underground.

She stopped and outstretched an arm in a dismissive gesture towards the stairs.

"Go," was all she said.

I glanced at the passageway leading into darkness. Although it would theoretically make no sense for my father to end my life at this stage, I could not rule out the possibility.

"Don't be impertinent. He is waiting. He does not have all day."

I smiled tightly. "I rode three days and nights here with hardly any sleep to arrive on time, so you'd think that—"

"Stop whining," my mother cut me off. "That is your duty."

I clicked my tongue.

Why had I even opened my mouth? Arguing with her was pointless. My father could slit her throat, and she'd likely gargle out a choked 'thank you' as she died.

I licked my lips and smiled tightly at her once again. I began to descend the stairs. Her gaze from behind felt tangible. I was almost glad when I was swallowed by the darkness and could no longer feel it on my back.

That was until the screaming reached me.

I had heard screaming several times before. I had even sometimes, been the one to induce such noises. But, these screams, they were…not the same.

I slowed my steps. Gradually, light emerged in the form of candles and torches adorning sandy walls of stone.

The screams grew louder. I turned a corner.

Three people were standing there. They were slim and dressed in rags.

One of them ran towards me and fell to his knees, gripping at me with his hands.

His chained hands.

"Sir, Sir…do you…do you have any…water…"

I couldn't move. My muscles had tensed up at the sight.

The second person, a woman, followed. She had been holding a tool. So had the first man, but he had discarded it before falling at my feet. By the looks of it, they had been fixing some part of this wall.

"Water…water…" the woman chanted moving towards me as well.

The only one who wasn't speaking, who didn't move, was the third person.

It was a young boy, about twelve, who looked at me with hatred.

He glared at me for a while, then shouted at the two adults. "Get away from him. He won't help you. They'll be coming back soon."

The woman turned slowly towards him, as if she were caught in a trance. The man was still plastering himself to my shin.

"Do you want to die?!" the boy shouted angrily. He rushed towards the man and yanked him off me. He took several hasty steps away, watching me as if I were about to pounce on him.

"Don't punish them for this. We haven't had water for nearly a day," he said to me.

"Water...water...water..." the woman continued to chant, her voice raspy.

I was utterly perplexed, I couldn't gather myself or understand anything that was happening around me. I watched the scene as if in some kind of hypnosis.

Two voices came around the corner, one of them instantly recognisable.

They both stopped speaking when they saw me.

"Good. You're here," Sarlan said.

"That one, Your Majesty, one of the assimilated," the other man, presumably an overseer, pointed to the child.

The boy stiffened up and let go of the man's arm. "I haven't done anything," the boy protested.

My father smiled at him. "I believe you."

The man with my father came towards the boy, and roughly dragged him away. The boy tried to loosen himself from his grip. "Get your fucking hands off me!" he screamed.

Something switched inside my mind.

I stepped forwards and pulled the boy towards me.

"What are you doing?" I addressed Sarlan and not the other man, who looked at me with shock as I took the boy from him. The boy continued to look at me with loathing.

Sarlan chuckled with his mouth closed. "It's no matter, we are going in the same direction. Bring him." He turned around and walked off. The man followed him.

The boy squirmed under my grip.

I let him go.

He grabbed his upper arm and looked at me under furrowed brows.

"Leave," I told him.

The boy laughed brokenly. "And go fucking where?"

I couldn't help but raise my brows. Nobody ever spoke to me that way, not because I forbade it, but because they were far too afraid of me.

"*Your father* is waiting," he said sarcastically.

I couldn't process anything that had happened within the last few minutes. This boy knew who I was, and still.

I debated what to do, but I truly had no idea or inclination. This place, this situation, was far too unfamiliar.

I followed where my father had walked off to. It took me several minutes to find him.

He was standing in the centre of a rectangular hall. It was a dull brown, and its base was stone, the four narrow walls around it made from dark brick.

To the left, right, north, and south, several rows of stone narrow benches were lined up against one another. In the centre stood my father, and the man who had been accompanying him.

And I counted instantly, sixty-seven people.

Sixty-seven terrified looking people.

They all looked at me as I entered, some pleadingly, some with detestation, some blankly.

The sixty-seven people were surrounded by around thirty or so people, many of whom carried weapons of Noxstone. There was a boundary drawn on the ground in front of them, a partition separating them from the rest of us. They were huddled and squashed together.

Sarlan outstretched his hand to the space next to him, indicating I should stand there. He frowned as he realised the boy was not with me. He whispered something to the man next to him, giving him an instruction. That man disappeared.

I didn't move. Sarlan came towards me instead. Unlike my mother, he didn't seem to care much for shows of winning or losing. He knew after all that such gestures and actions meant nothing in truth.

He sighed as he looked me up and down.

"Why am I here?" I asked him pointedly.

My father chuckled again. "Here in Audra or…" He pointed behind him "Here?"

"Both," I replied.

"Because you answer when I call. Because…" Sarlan didn't offer an end to the sentence.

"Very elaborate," I said.

The people behind my father watched our conversation tensely, their eyes switching between our two faces.

"I would like to show you something." He came closer and stood at my side. He let out a loud sigh as if he had just breathed in fresh air.

Moments later, the boy was dragged in, kicking, and screaming. "Fucking pig! You piece of shit! Let fucking go of me!" he cursed.

I stepped forwards. My father's arm came out in front of my torso instantly.

I looked at the scene around me. Thirty, no I counted, thirty-four men were ready to attack me, some with Noxstone, if I so much as moved another finger.

I looked at my father from the side to find him watching me, smirking.

He dropped his arm, after all, he knew that I understood.

I could defeat a large number of people in hand-to-hand combat at once, but not when they were trained in a similar manner to myself. Not these soldiers. Not alone.

"I heard you were asking about this place," he stated.

"I was curious," I lied. I had asked because of Arton's dying words.

"It would have been better for Marco had you curbed your curiosity."

I squinted and side-eyed him.

"He told you little. He is a loyal servant." Sarlan almost sounded as if he admired the man.

It was true, Marco had barely told me anything. All Sarlan's subjects were circumspect about speaking openly. Attempting to extract information from Marco had been like trying to draw blood from a corpse.

"But still...he told you too much."

I swallowed. In the silence, it echoed as a loud gulp.

"Your mother dealt with him. I'm sure you can imagine what that entailed." Even without looking at him, I could hear the smile in my father's voice.

If it was my mother who'd dealt with him, then I would have preferred to not dwell upon it. Either way the result was the same. Marco was dead.

Another life, ended by my hands.

"Why kill him, only to bring me here now?" I asked the obvious question.

"Because only I decide what you know, and when."

This place, this draining centre, I had figured out, it was why Arton had run. And standing here now, his naïve, desperate bravery seemed, I could finally decide... not ridiculous in the slightest.

"And what...is that?" I asked, glancing around the room.

"Mathias has told me you have failed to ascertain who the thief of our intelligence is."

I tried my best to remain composed, to think of anything other than the Captain as I replied, "That's true."

My father spun on his heel and came to stand in front of me. "I don't believe you. I think you do know, and that you are withholding information from me. You've gotten into a habit of doing that lately." He smiled very slightly then said, "Before, Silus would have been able to confirm such suspicions, but... no more."

I couldn't withhold my shock. I hadn't liked Silus, but I could admit that he was skilled to almost the same degree as myself.

"Silus?" I couldn't help but ask.

"And not just him." My father seemed to delight in delivering the news. "Alijah, Julios. *Rina*."

He exaggerated Rina's name. There had been a time, many years ago when she and I had been engaged in a strange and altogether empty relationship. I supposed he thought her name would hurt me somewhat.

But the truth was that each name, including hers, was like a jolt to my system, and not for emotive reasons. It was simply for the fact that these people had been some of the most loyal and skilled warriors that had worked under Sarlan. If they had died, then...

"You feel sorry for the boy?" my father asked, pointing at him. The boy's face was twisted in anger.

I was distracted by his expression of fierce determination and the information I had just received.

"It was *his* kind that ended their lives." Sarlan's voice rumbled with aggression.

I had been right. It was unsurprising and baffling simultaneously. Which sorcerers would dare to fight Audra's legion head on? Why take that risk?

My father continued. "The information that has been taken is in relation to our activities here." He pointed out around him "Activities you understand, which are for the good of our people, to protect them against the devastation these sorcerers can unleash."

I remembered the note, I remembered what it had described in relation to experiments...assimilations?

Were all these individuals a product of such tests? I stared at them all helplessly.

My eyes found their way back to Sarlan's again. Despite their gold colouring, they were darkened by the shadows. It made his face appear even more brutal.

"You say you have not found the culprit. We cannot afford for the information to fall into the wrong hands, and so..."

My father spun back to my side and nodded at the black clad guards.

In an instant, they stepped backwards in unison. Each of them raised a crossbow.

The people behind the partition began to scream, their voice curdled with unhinged levels of panic and fear. A few attempted to run but were hit by an invisible barrier as they tried to cross the partition line.

The boy stood there, his eyes, his facial expression hadn't changed once, still full of unrestrained fury.

Despite my father's previous warnings, I made a move to step forwards.

But the guards were faster.

They fired. Their dark and thick arrows were enough to skewer a bear, some went through two people at once. Some landed in the neck, the abdomen, the face.

The screaming intensified. In less than a second the bowmen fired again.

I jumped forwards and disarmed two of them. I knew it was useless, and yet I dared. For as soon as I did so, another arrow flew past me, taking the place of the one I had prevented firing.

The screaming stopped, replaced by the groans of the dying noises of sixty-seven people.

No. Sixty eight.

The boy was on his knees clasping at his stomach. One of his hands was on the floor in front of him. He coughed up blood and spat it out of his mouth. I stared at him wide-eyed. He stared back at me.

He didn't look sad, he only looked enraged.

Then he fell forwards, his face smacked against the cold hard stone.

Their bodies were piled on top of one another. The smell of blood was pungent. It reeked of it. It reeked of urine. Some had soiled themselves through sheer terror before they had been killed.

I had seen things, things I could not forget, things I could not forgive both myself, and others for, things I hoped I would never need lay eyes on again.

And yet somehow, this was the worst of them all.

My father placed his hand on my shoulder softly and whispered in my ear, "This is for the best. They cannot be allowed to live, with such information out there, unacquired. If you had found the offending party this could have been avoided but..."

I smacked his hand off my shoulder and glared at him. He professed the death of these Vessels was for the greater good, that these sorcerers were a stain on society, but he massacred them in front of me, because he knew I would shoulder the memory, the guilt.

Guilt was something I had grown numb to with time. Through necessity. Through the inevitable change that had occurred in me as I had grown, been honed as an instrument of death.

The Bird of Death.

But this...this...

He could always see, always see the parts of me that ached, and fired directly at them when he wanted to win.

And it almost, always guaranteed he did.

He knew I could not bear to witness it, that I had refused to take on such tasks in the past. I had been punished for those refusals then, and I had accepted that, I had taken that pain gladly.

But this, I could not stomach.

"You act as if they would have lived regardless," I spat.

My father chuckled once. "You're right, but they would have served their purpose. They would have lived for longer. Especially the children."

My eyes were drawn to the boy.

"He reminded me of you that one," my father said, following my gaze. "Just like you at that age."

My throat felt tight. I swallowed the urge to scream.

After all, as he had yelled 'Get your fucking hands of me,' I had thought the exact same.

Sarlan took one step towards me. "Kill the thief. You have three more days. I know you know who it is."

"I don't," I insisted.

Sarlan smiled, coldly. "Three days, Nathon. Three days. If it is not done, then I will have to devise a way to loosen your lips. I'm sure you'd prefer that didn't happen. After it is done, you will inform me of their identity. After the Season is over, you will return here immediately, since I am short on weapons now."

My father approached and softly patted my upper arm. He said in a calm voice, "If I find out you have been protecting the culprit, I will make sure they suffer immensely for your attempt at heroism."

I thought of the Captain, of him being subject to some of the methods of torture I knew Sarlan was capable of.

That I had experienced.

I shuddered slightly at the thought. My father, with his hand resting on my arm, noticed.

He looked at my arm with fascination then back at my face. "I must admit, I'm most curious to find out who this person is."

I shook my arm out of his grasp. "As am I."

"Ha. Truly, they must be an incredible individual. Do not forget however, it is I you obey."

"You can make me suffer," I bit. "But you cannot make me kneel."

Sarlan's smile was predatory as he replied. "Kneeling means nothing. You would kneel to Vasara's King, would you not?"

"He is more worthy of it than you," I spat.

Sarlan laughed then. "I am sure your high opinion of His Majesty will reassure him greatly as he lies in a grave."

"Is that not what you chase?" I huffed. "The empty adoration of thousands, praising your name."

Sarlan chuckled. "Mass hatred. Mass love. They are unshakeable forces of cultivated truth. One you yourself, have experienced."

My brows flattened.

"And cultivated truth... is often more powerful than any reality," he added.

"And more convenient," I spat.

They called me the Bird of Death, then hid behind my wings. The more feathers they gave me, the more shade I cast over their own foul deeds. Including Sarlan's.

But that was fine. If that shade protected Loria from the blinding heat of the sun, of our father.

And I would not shield the rest forever, despite what Sarlan thought.

"But I do not seek praise for praise's sake," he stated.

"How noble of you," I smiled falsely.

"Your Kazal has recovered, you should know. Ride the Erebask back if you wish."

I had only been gone a little over a month, that injury would only just have healed.

"I'll use a horse," I said.

"Are you sure? You have three days. It will take you that time to get to Vasara on horseback. You'll effectively have to kill the culprit on sight as soon as you return." A slow grin spread across Sarlan's face as he spoke.

"I'll have to find out who they are first," I maintained my lie.

"So, you have no intention of meeting the deadline?"

I didn't reply.

"I'll be generous. Four days. You have no excuses after four days." His tone of voice was teasing almost.

I fiddled with my fingers.

"How's your sister? Is she doing well?"

"Yes," I replied gruffly.

My father raised his brows at my answer, then turned to the guards.

"Clean this up," he ordered.

Sarlan's face settled into something of a calm expression as he turned to leave, the guards following him. A face of falsified warmth, ready to meet those beyond these chambers.

I stood there for a moment, looking at the pile of bodies in front of me.

No wonder that cloaked woman had tried to kill me. In fact, it was a wonder she hadn't tried to kill me beforehand, knowing my identity.

I quickly left soon after, desperate to get out of that place, desperate to return to Vasara.

After all, once I'd arrived, I'd have one day.

One day to produce a plan I had never tried to enact before.

To save my target's life.

# CHAPTER 66 – THE HEALER

This corpse made the last one look beautiful.

My boot was on its back. More like through it. Through the withered ribcage, the skin turned grey that had been stretched over the bones so tightly, that it puckered at the places where it met the skeleton.

"How long will this go on?" Ullna pleaded to my right. Her face curled in disdain as she took in the scene.

I brought my foot forwards, bringing it over the corpse. I rested it in front of its torso and turned it face up.

I sighed, closing my eyes.

"It's not this one," I confirmed.

"Did you really think that it would be?" She gestured at the body reluctantly. "This is the seventeenth. How many more will you... personally examine?"

I glanced at her from the side, unbidden strands of hair slapped my cheeks as the wind surged.

"We cannot afford to be careless." My tone was flat.

"This isn't being meticulous, this is..." Her steely eyes softened slightly, and she restarted her sentence. "You must let this go."

I turned back to stare at the corpse.

This was not the one, no. But the one I was searching for, they had not made their promise lightly. I remembered the resolution on their face when they'd sworn to return.

I unconsciously swallowed, for I remembered as well, word for word, what exactly it was they'd vowed.

"What are you trying to find, to prepare for?" she asked imploringly, a hint of irritation in her voice.

I raised my chin, finally taking my foot off the body.

"There is no preparing for this," I replied in resignation.

"Then why? Why do this?"

"I would like to know...when my end is near."

Her face froze over with confusion and doubt, with shock and disbelief.

"Your...end?"

"If we are fortunate."

"Fortunate?" She repeated the word as if disgusted by it.

"If we are fortunate then it will be my end."

She was still frowning, attempting to process my words as I clarified.

"Only mine."

# CHAPTER 67- SHADAE

I'd lost count of the number of days I'd been in Vasara's prison cells. Going by the sunrises and sunsets, it had been two, or three, perhaps. But I had fallen asleep for a large amount of that time, drifting in and out of consciousness.

Despite their discomfort, they were still a far cry from the quarters I'd had as a Vessel. Here at least, I had a makeshift bed to sleep on, the floor was covered in straw, and we were even fed, and given water, at regular intervals.

It seemed like a luxury to me.

But not to the others I was locked up with.

To my right, a middle-aged woman was behind bars. She had been yelling and protesting her innocence every hour of every day, even in the middle of the night.

I'd just woken up to her attempts at garnering sympathy from the guards once again.

"Please! Pleasssseeeee, I tell ya, I didn't do anything! Listen here! Please, I have children! I have...I have four children!"

"You ain't got children you hag! Shut it!" The prisoner locked up to her right shouted, an older man.

"I do! I do have children! Who are you, heh? How would you know? You following me you fucking creep? I bet that's what you're here for, you fucking pervert!"

"As if I'd want the likes of you, you deluded bitch!" the man retorted.

I refrained from commenting. Even here, I got far more sleep than I ever did as a Vessel.

A young man was locked up to my left, his long dark hair skimming the ground he sat on. "Can't you tell her to be quiet?" he hissed at me.

I sat up slowly and turned to him. The gaps between the bars were slimmer at the sides than the front, but still large enough to look through.

"You think that would work, do you?" I said, not hiding the irritation in my voice.

"You haven't spoken once. It's worth a try, who knows, maybe she'll listen to another woman."

I snorted and tutted at the same time.

*And maybe we'll all be released tomorrow and there'll be no more poverty or war or ridiculous suggestions in the world.*

"What? Too good to get involved with the rest of us?" the man spat.

"Too tired," I replied.

"That's because we're not getting any fucking sleep thanks to that bitch."

"You tell her then," I insisted.

"I've already tried! Are you stupid or something?"

"That's a sure good way to get me to do you a favour." I smiled at him sarcastically.

I hadn't meant to engage in conversation with any of these people, but this man was starting to press on a nerve I didn't know was irritated.

"What do you want me to kiss your ass now?" he asked.

"I just want you to leave me alone."

"Selfish bitch," the man mumbled under his breath.

*Selfish? Are you the stupid one? I'm in the cell adjacent to this woman. I'm locked up here with the rest of you.*

"Scum like you should stay where they belong," he added proudly.

*And...there it is.*

I laughed, "Congratulations!"

"What? What are you going on about?" The man sounded baffled.

"You lasted for longer than most people when it comes to bringing up the fact that I'm a sorcerer." I gestured to my tattered and dirtied tracker uniform.

"That's because..." But the man stopped speaking as the sound of the gates opening at the end of the corridor travelled with a large creak to our ears.

A few sets of footsteps could be heard, traversing the hallway.

"Your Majesty!" the woman in the adjacent cell squealed. "I'm innocent! Please! Please, I have children! Five children!"

I rolled my eyes.

Seconds later, the gates to my cell swung open, and three people stepped inside it.

The King, the guard who'd accused me of murder, and Lord Elias.

The man to my left sat forwards watching the scene with interest. The King heard his scuffling and turned to look at him. He backed away instantly.

I sympathised with him on that at least. There was something dreadfully disturbing about the King's cold eyes.

Which were now fixed upon my face.

"It's her." The guard nodded enthusiastically. "She gave him that thing!"

I glanced at Elias, he was watching me quietly. He looked me up and down. I turned away, feeling conscious under his gaze.

The King took a few steps forwards. An overwhelming unease overcame me, and I instinctively backed away, pressing my back to the wall.

"Did you?" the King asked.

I glanced at Elias again, as if he were some sort of focal point, but his face was unreadable.

I found the courage to look into the King's pale eyes.

"It's not like that...I—"

"Don't try to get around it! You gave it to him! I was there you—"

The King turned over his shoulder and silenced the man instantly with one glance. He looked back at me.

"It's not like what?" the King inquired.

"Please, Your Majesty let me explain." I held up my palm in a pacifying gesture.

"I am waiting for you to begin," he said softly.

I dropped my palm and placed both of them on my thighs, rubbing them anxiously.

I looked at my legs as I spoke. "I did give it to him, but only because he..." I lost my words "It's like this...I took the thing from the body of a sorcerer I'd killed because..."

*Because I what? Felt guilty about his death? That sounds terrible. But I can hardly say I took it as a keepsake. Now I'm being silent, and it looks even more suspicious. Say something! That man was right, I am stupid!*

"Because?" the King urged me on.

I looked up, I may as well tell the truth, I decided, since no other explanation made sense.

"I felt guilty, Your Majesty, for killing him. I know that I'm not supposed to, and it won't...it doesn't affect my ability to do my job. I mean...I killed him anyway and I'd...I'd do it again but, I'd never killed before, and I felt...unusual about it, so I took his necklace, but I swear, I didn't know what it was." I rushed the words out.

The King watched me as if I were a deeply ancient and interesting artefact.

"And then"— I tore my eyes away from his studious glare — "after that mission, I went to the draining centre. I wanted to bargain for the body of one of the trackers so I could bury her. That's not unpermitted, is it? I mean not officially."

I didn't wait for him to answer that question as I blurted out, "But since I didn't have any money at the time, they asked me to hand over a treasured possession of mine to keep hold of, until I could return, and pay them the money they requested for her corpse."

"That's not true!" the guard interrupted. "I...we never asked you for any money! You...you stole that body!"

"She didn't," Elias said languidly. "I was there afterwards. I saw her with it. She'd clearly just been given it."

The King glanced at his cousin and nodded, trusting his words.

I glanced at Elias, once again. I tried to convey my gratitude with my eyes, but he appeared almost bored.

I continued. "It's not... that it was a treasured possession, the necklace, I didn't even know what it was...it's just, it's the only thing I had on me that meant anything in particular. I didn't know what else to give them, and her body was about to go...there, and I wanted to get it before it decayed because I knew I'd have to carry it...somewhere..." My voice trailed off as I realised my explanation was beginning to sound chaotic.

The King was silent, processing my words for a moment, then he said, "Lord Elias has told me you are quite knowledgeable about sorcery."

*Do I...confirm or deny that? Which is worse?*

"Therefore, I find it difficult to believe you had no notion of the nature of the object you took from the body of that sorcerer."

*Lord Elias, you've dropped me in shit... once again.*

"It's true, Your Majesty, I know... a fair amount, but I was not able to gather the relevance behind that object until we..." I looked at Elias. Did the King know we had gone there for a second time?

But the King seemed to gather my meaning regardless. "It is also suspicious that you gave the object to an overseer."

My heart started to beat faster, as if wishing to escape my ribs, my fate. This was not how any of this had meant to go. I had formed a plan, to get my brothers out, albeit a loose plan. But I had never meant to be roped into Elias' quests or...jail.

"Your Majesty...respectfully, and if you'll permit me to say... if I'd wanted to kill an overseer what would be the point?" I laughed nervously.

"Perhaps he wronged you."

*In that case I would have killed them all.*

*Don't say that. That definitely won't help.*

"Even if that were the case, why would I give him this object in the presence of another guard who could easily identify me?" I gestured at the other guard.

"Perhaps you had planned to end his life as well but were stopped from doing so."

My lips parted in surprise. He was so suspicious of me. Of us.

"But... if that had been my plan, why would I risk ending their lives separately?"

"Perhaps such objects take time to create or acquire." Each of his proposals was said with leisure, simplistically, as if they were basic facts like *water is a drink*, not attempts to accuse me of murder.

"I only acquired the first one by chance, Your Majesty, how would I have been able to acquire a second?"

"Perhaps you planned to end his life in a different way."

*Perhaps, perhaps, perhaps. Perhaps I'm actually innocent!*

*Gods, if I say that, I'll sound like that woman with an ever-increasing number of children.*

"Your Majesty...it would not be worth the risk."

"I do not know what you deem to be worth the risk. I do not know what value you place on your own life."

"If I placed little value on it, why would I attempt to protest my innocence at all, Your Majesty?"

The King seemed to dwell on this for a second.

"I didn't intend to kill him. I didn't," I pleaded. "And...and if by your suppositions I had planned to kill the witness, then why would I wait so long? Why wouldn't I make sure he was dead immediately after the first man had died?"

"You were called to the festival at short notice, but initially, you were scheduled to have that day to yourself. It would have been the perfect opportunity for you to end the witnesses' life."

*Wonderful. It all matches up, timing, motive, tools. Just brilliant.*

But still I grasped at whatever thread of reason I could.

"How? Your Majesty.... Even if you're right and the timing matched up, I still would have had to actually kill him, and if my intention was to cover my tracks, then I would also have.... needed to hide any evidence and...get away with the crime. Also... since the schedule of the overseers changes so often, from what I recall, I wouldn't have been able to... guarantee he wouldn't be working that day, and even if he hadn't been, how would I have known where to find him? I haven't had the time or ability to follow him or his movements."

My words were both fretful and confident at the same time. I raised my head, trying to appear self-assured, but I was trembling slightly.

"You may have. How am I to know?" the King asked.

*Why do you look like you're enjoying this interrogation?*

"The Commander. You can ask him. He has been with me most of the time, Your Majesty."

"But not all of the time."

"The rest of the time I have been with Lord Elias," I said.

"But not all of the time," the King repeated.

He seemed adamant that I was guilty already.

"But... the rest of that time would have been during sleeping hours. Even if I had been able to follow the...witness, what use would there have been in knowing where he slept, if I planned to kill him during the day?"

The King, to my surprise, smiled. He held his right elbow with his left hand and grabbed his chin with his right.

"That is true." His eyes flickered with an almost mad satisfaction.

"Your Majesty she's lying! She's deceiving you! You can't trust these people!" the guard exclaimed.

The King was still looking at me. "It has nothing to do with trust. Only logic."

He moved his chin away from his hand and looked over his shoulder at Elias.

"I believe her," Elias said.

I raised my eyebrows at him. He met my eyes briefly then returned them to the King's.

The King nodded slowly. "As do I."

The King faced me again. "However, regardless of whether or not your crime was intentional, it was still a crime. A man is dead because of your actions. You are not devoid of punishment."

Just then, a fourth man stepped into the cell, and my heart rate increased even more.

Parthias, one of the worst of the overseers.

*It's hardly as if there's a pristine collection to choose from.*

"Sorry I'm late, Your Highness." His serpent-like voice made me shudder.

The King waved over his shoulder in a gesture of ease. "Lord Elias needs you for now, and so your punishment will be delayed."

I outstretched my palms against my thighs. "What punishment, Your Majesty?"

"If you were a human, it would be incarceration, but you are a sorcerer, and we cannot waste your core, and so, you will return to being a Vessel once—"

I stood sharply. "No!"

Lord Elias looked at me not entirely surprised. The King raised his eyebrows very slightly.

I shook my head. "Your Majesty, please…"

"It is not for you to decide what His Majesty does." Parthias' sleazy voice cut through the air.

The King turned to Elias.

"Let her try," Elias said.

*Try what? You better not have agreed to something awful on my behalf again. Although, what could be worse than being a Vessel? No, don't think about that, there are probably worse things.*

"Lord Elias seems to have faith in your ability as a tracker," the King said. He didn't sound bothered about my interruption at all. "However, you will still need to be punished, and so, we will have to think of an alternative way to do so, should you prove capable."

Parthias chuckled. "There are a few people I can think of who can take any punishment in her place."

I couldn't see my own face, but I could imagine I had paled at that statement.

Just as swiftly as I had stood, I dropped to my feet, prostrating in front of the King at the lowest ground level possible. My forehead made contact with the floor, as did my palms.

"Please, Your Majesty, I beg you, don't…don't…Let me accept punishment now, whatever that may be, I can be…whipped or hurt or…take an eye or an ear…but please…please…" I could hear tears starting to form at the back of my throat, stinging it, scratching at it. I cleared it in an attempt to quell them.

The King's voice came from above my head. "Please what?"

*Please don't touch my brothers. Please do not involve them in this. Do whatever you want to me but don't hurt them. I beg you.*

The King didn't seem to know what I was talking about. If I told him of my brothers, wouldn't it only give him the idea to use them in my stead?

Lord Elias however, understood somehow, and spoke.

"Nobody will take your punishment but you. The King's justice does not operate that way and can only be enacted by the King alone. Anyone who is willing to take or give the punishment to another on your behalf will be punished themselves. You will take the punishment, you can be sure of that, so there's no need to rush."

His tone was forceful, and his words had been disguised as a semi-threat, but he hadn't been speaking to me, those words had undoubtedly been directed at Parthias.

I gingerly slid upwards into a kneeled position and looked at him.

"The King will decide when he decides, no sooner," Elias' voice became calmer.

I nodded slowly.

The King and Elias looked at each other and nodded. The King turned to leave with Parthias and the guard. Elias remained in place as the gate closed behind him.

He crouched in front of me. "Who's worth an eye?" He sounded sceptical.

I was too afraid to tell him.

I looked away at the ground.

He sighed loudly. "You need to stop protecting people, and burying people, and giving people deadly cursed objects."

*Why again must you act as if I deliberately immerse myself into these situations?*

I turned towards him. "Why..."

*Why do you care?* Was on the tip of my tongue, but I didn't, for some reason, have the heart to finish the question.

"Why do I care?" Elias finished it for me. "Because we have a task to do, and we can't do it when you're sitting in your shit in this cell."

"I'm not!" I looked around and pointed defensively at the makeshift toilet. "Sitting in my own shit!"

Elias smiled slightly. I suddenly felt ridiculous at having had an impulse to prove that point.

The woman from the cell to my right took the silence as an opportunity to plead her case again.

"Sir! Sir! I'm innocent, please My Lord! I have six children!"

Elias turned over his shoulder to look through the bars. "Wasn't it five? Did you have another one in your cell just now?"

I chuckled under my breath, then quickly stopped.

*Laughing at a joke he made? The intensity of that interrogation and the fear of imminent death must have damaged my mind.*

The woman gulped. "It's six! It's six! I'm just...I'm delirious from the hunger!"

"You're just plain delirious," the man to the cell on her right shouted.

"No! No! Sir, I'm innocent, please! You...you helped that girl just now, so please help me! You can ask the King on my behalf!"

Elias scowled. "Ask the King on your behalf? You're here because you gouged your own husband's eyes out. I saw it in the records before I came here. There were four witnesses."

Even the man to her right was silent about that.

"He! He was looking at another woman! It's his own fault!"

"I'm not surprised," I mumbled.

Elias side-eyed me and smirked. "Besides this woman helped herself, it had nothing to do with me."

He stood and opened the gate to my cell.

"Let's go."

The woman continued to protest as I followed him. Her pleas gradually ebbed in volume as we walked down towards the main gate.

"Where are we going this time?"

*This time...that sounded...far too, how was it the Lord described it? Familiar?*

But Elias did not answer. He waited until we got further away from the cells and were walking down passageways which were quiet and unoccupied before he spoke.

He stopped and turned to me, but he looked at the ground, crossing his arms as he replied.

"We're going to visit my mother."

*I was right. There are things worse than being a Vessel.*

# CHAPTER 68 – LORIA

It was hardly as if I could say I was surprised that Nathon had disappeared, again. Only it had been seven days, and people were starting to notice his absence.

After all, the ball had just begun, and Nathon was nowhere to be seen.

I entered not entirely alone, but with the other candidates who were all dressed in clothes both lavish and eloquent. Their escorts were dressed equally beautifully. Just as with the opening ceremony, the games, this whole affair, a chance to make a lasting impression was grasped at eagerly by everyone.

I made myself scarce and went to find some drinks at a table far across the room. All around people chatted, danced, and laughed. Some falsely, some joyfully, some heartily. The atmosphere here was at complete odds with my sense of unease, and with the true nature of this place, these people.

The King was already sitting at the centre of a banquet table at the front of the room, surrounded by other high-ranking officials, his Council members, and his cousin. His arm was out of a sling now.

"You look beautiful, Your Highness." Princess Rhana approached me.

I looked over her form. She wore a dress, a stunning grey, with a tight bodice and large bottom which trailed behind her, and gloves that extended to her elbow. The sleeves of her dress skimmed their edges. Those sleeves were laced with silver, dusted over the fabric like frost, similar to the decorations interwoven into her curls.

"You far outshine us all, Your Highness," I replied.

She gestured at my dress. "Coming from the one who wears gold so well."

The gold silk draped over my form like a curtain. Its back was bare to the hips and its front was pinched under the breasts. It left me feeling as if I were scintillating, but glaringly so, in the way the sun might, when it strikes your eyes at an uncomfortable angle.

"I'm not sure that's…" I started.

But Rhana's eyes widened, observing something over my shoulder. She didn't say anything, only took one step back and curtsied.

I braced myself for the inevitable.

Turning around slowly, I replicated her action.

"Your Majesty," I said.

The King watched me as I sank and rose, his dark red eyelashes fluttering.

"No cloak this time." He smiled amusedly.

Against my better judgement, I smiled back, surprised by his statement.

"Unfortunately not," I said, only half truthfully.

"I would say it's rather fortunate," he stated, regarding me keenly.

I averted my gaze and gracelessly reached over for my drink, knocking it over in the process. I hurriedly picked it up and went to clean up the stain it had left behind.

"It's alright," the King said. A servant had stepped in to erase my mess as I turned towards him.

"Are you nervous?" he asked.

"I've never been to a ball before," I admitted.

"Oh?" The King's voice raised his eyebrows.

I cleared my throat, with no real need to clear it. "So, Your Majesty will have to forgive me for any"— I glanced over to the servant who was still cleaning up the stain— "mishaps."

The King stepped closer to me. He reached out his hand.

"Will you dance with me, Princess?"

I stared at his open palm, his fingers pale and long.

The moment he had asked, the moment he had reached out his hand, a stillness had settled throughout the hall, sticking to everyone. It had lifted the voices and conversations from their lips, and held onto them tightly, keeping them at bay.

I could feel Rhana and her escort watching with shock, could see from behind the King's shoulder, Dyna and the Captain staring at me.

They weren't the only ones.

"I thought…Your Majesty, that it wasn't permitted for the King to dance at this ball."

The King's hand remained where it was. "Then…would you like to be the first to change that… with me?"

Where was Nathon now? When I needed him, at this critical moment.

I found myself surprised at the thought. What did I truly need Nathon for now?

I placed my palm in the King's. Small gasps, both delighted and disgusted, scattered throughout the four corners of the room.

We had touched.

It wasn't the first time, but it was the first time we had truly touched, and everyone was watching.

His palm was unexpectedly cold, not overly, but invitingly so against my own warm one. We made our way to the centre of the hall, where others were dancing. They cleared a path for us, many of them stopped momentarily. The musicians stopped playing, waiting for the King to be ready.

For us to dance.

The music began. The King's hand found its way to the small of my back, sliding there carefully and gently. He was far taller than I was, and to look at his face, this close, I had to tilt my neck back quite an amount. As we began to move, his fingers clasped around my own and he gazed at me with no small amount of interest.

Or was it something else behind his eyes? Something worse? Something more? Something better? Something deeper?

I couldn't tell.

He leant forwards to speak directly at the side of my face, next to my ear. "You've never been to a ball, yet you dance so well. How is that?"

I swallowed nervously. I could feel my palm clamming up against his steady hand, which meant he could as well. I supposed if he sensed I was nervous, it wouldn't arouse any suspicion, so as long as the true reason for my nerves remained concealed…

Which were…what exactly? That I was standing this close, whispering and dancing with a man I was destined to kill.

Or that…I was beginning to doubt I even could.

Would it be like this? If I could make him choose me? Would it be a night where he lay by my side, as he whispered, joked, and smiled, as he looked at me with hope and wonder? Would it be a night like this when I killed him? What would his face look like? What would his eyes say then, at that betrayal?

"I learnt to dance when I was young, Your Majesty, but I never used…my lessons. Until now."

"What else have you learnt?"

What did that mean?

"Your Majesty?" I replied, confused.

"What do you do when nobody is looking? When they aren't all watching like they are now? When you're alone? Do you dance then?" His voice floated, intertwining with the music swelling around us.

I laughed, my voice quivering with anxiety, "No."

"Then?" the King asked. Our exchange was largely inaudible, as the sound of strings moved through the air, but there were plenty of people, I assumed, who would be able to lip read in the crowd.

"I…read much. I used to spend much time in the library at the Citadel as a child. I would always trouble my guards to accompany me there. I think"— I smiled at the memory a little — "they grew tired of the books but…I never could."

"You have a favourite?" the King asked.

My mouth twisted into an awkward smile. "I do but it's rather—"

"Tell me," the King's voice dropped even quieter. "What is it?"

"It's…a fable. The Arrow," but I'm not sure Your Majesty would enjoy it."

"Why not?" He sounded almost offended.

I turned my head to look up at him. He was smiling, enjoying this back and forth.

"It's a children's tale, Your Majesty," I lied. That was not the reason.

"And yet," his words were slow, "It's your favourite. You must have read several books since then, and still, it remains the closest to your heart."

"That's true but...I fear I may raise your expectations too much, Your Majesty." I laughed unsteadily again.

"You could never fail to meet the expectations I have of you, Princess."

At this comment, my hand unconsciously stiffened up and tightened around his, which I realised, in a state of panic, only seemed to appear as some sort of whimsical and pathetic longing for his compliments.

But the King only returned the tightening of my hands with a soft squeeze of his own as he replied, "Not that you should seek to meet them."

"Isn't that what we're here for, Your Majesty?" I raised my eyes at him confidently.

"Officially,"

Only that wasn't what I was here for.

"And unofficially?" I dared to ask.

"Unofficially, it is the sovereign who must hope to win over their chosen one. The candidate cannot refuse in name, but they can in heart."

I chuckled at his statement. "Your Majesty, I do not think that is something you need trouble yourself with. At least half of the candidates are already..."

I stopped speaking as I realised the ease at which I had slipped into more casual conversation.

The King and I spun around, weaving between other couples, our steps light and sure, unlike my words.

"Already?" the King urged me to finish.

"Devoted to you, Your Majesty." I flattened the tone of my voice, trying to resume the formal demeanour, which was slipping from my grasp the longer we danced.

"Are you one of those?" The King's lip curved upwards, and his eyes searched my face.

I blinked several times before answering. "I admire you but I..." I hesitated.

The King's smile began to show his teeth. "That is good."

"Your Majesty?"

The King dipped my back during a portion of the dance.

"I can't win over a heart that's already been given," he whispered.

I rose back up.

"But you could take one of those so easily," I answered, softly.

I do not know what part of me was lured into his words, was always tempted by the desire to counter, and challenge them, but it was awakened now, it was alive, as it had been each time we had spoken.

"I do not wish to take it...but to earn it," the King said earnestly and quietly, as he looked into my eyes.

The dance ended, yet we were still locked in a hold.

The musicians began to prepare for the next dance, shuffling parchment on their stands. Some couples left the floor and others joined, but the King and I still hadn't moved. His fingers sprawled out across the small of my back.

They dropped in an instant as the crowd went quiet.

As the doors to the hall opened.

Unlike the doors to the throne room, and to many others in the Palace, these were located high above the ground, with several stairs leading down to the bottom, lined with gold and crimson carpets that shimmered in the light.

Beaming as brightly as that gold, and walking through those doors alone.

Was Nathon.

## CHAPTER 69 - HESTAN

Dyna gripped onto my arm so tightly her knuckles paled, near matching the shade of the white robe I wore.

I looked at her startled. She appeared shocked, glancing in the direction of the hall's entrance.

Had she seen something? Someone from that night? Was someone dangerous here, someone she recognised?

But, as I asked myself these questions, I realised the hall had become utterly soundless, even more so than when the King had asked Audra's Princess to dance.

I followed Dyna's gaze to the door.

And I understood immediately.

Standing at the top of the stairs was Audra's Prince. Audra's Prince who was universally feared, notoriously lethal, whose name was tarnished in darkness and in death, defiled and drowned in slaughter and blood.

And there he stood, looking…

Like that.

His light brown skin glittered in the dwindling sunlight, as if it were made to be illuminated by a sunset. His chest was almost completely visible. He wore a chemise that was black but transparent. It covered his arms and only the outer part of his chest, sliding down his torso to meet a dark belt at his hips. His pants were made of a similar, but much opaquer version of the material, decorated with the same golden patterns interwoven into the thin, and curtain-like fabric of his upper clothing. The chemise's back, however, was long, and fluttered behind him down to his shins. He walked down the stairs slowly, one by one.

His dark golden eyes searched the hundreds of faces in the hall with speed. He was clearly looking for his sister.

"My gosh," Dyna whispered under her breath.

"He's half naked!" A woman exclaimed to her partner.

"Disgusting! Absolutely disgraceful!" another said, fanning herself.

"To think he'd have the nerve to show up, late, wearing…this!" a man stuttered.

Several voices began to make their displeasure known, but the truth of the matter was easy to discern.

The Prince looked far more beautiful than any of the attendees.

I had not cared for such things. I still did not see the use, in either possessing or seeking them. Such superficial splendour came and went. Trying to hold it, like trying to preserve the petal of a blossom tree, destined to wither and fall.

But beauty. No. Beauty was no fitting word for what he was. It felt too empty to describe him. Too shallow.

Dyna's hand let go of my arm. "He's actually handsome!"

My head turned sharply to meet hers.

"Wasn't he always?" I asked her, confused, glancing at the Prince again.

Dyna giggled, covering her hand with her mouth. "I suppose, only it's his…"

But the rest of Dyna's words were drowned out, as I returned to watch the Prince, and found him staring at me.

Dyna and I were at the furthest point at the back of the room, the Prince the furthest to the front, and still, from the distance, I could feel his gaze, fixed in my direction.

He stopped walking, and several people turned towards us, wondering what it was the Prince's attention had been caught by.

Dyna spoke in a hushed manner, "Why are all these people looking at us?"

But before I could answer, she had noticed.

"Why is *he* looking at us?"

But before I could answer that, she inquired again, "At…at you?" She sounded uncertain.

"I don't know." I glanced around the curious faces with discomfort.

The Prince began descending again, his eyes now fixed elsewhere.

"That was so strange! What does he want?" Dyna exclaimed.

She was doing an incredible job of acting well, appearing joyous and normal, of shoving her fears to the back of her mind, of speaking on, talking about, and filling the silence with activities, or conversation. She had always been that way, but it had been even more obvious since her poisoning, and perhaps, since the culprit remained unfound, even more necessary.

She squeezed the folds of her lilac dress tightly. We both wore the garments we had acquired from the Kalnasan merchant, whose words I had not soon forgotten.

Whose words I had been dwelling on every hour of every day since.

The Season would soon be over, I told myself, and soon, I would be able to answer the questions burrowing into my mind about Kalnasa's state, to see it for myself.

Several minutes passed. Dyna and I spent them politely conversing with others, wandering around, observing the various statues and ornaments that had been brought here for this occasion. Some were made of glass, others marble, others water and ice.

It was hard not to glance around at the food wasted, at the sculptures that could be melted down into water for cooking, and for heating meals, at the platters that remained untouched and not think of...it.

I frowned deeply at the thought.

"Did my entrance offend you as well?" The Prince's voice crooned from my left. He tilted his head, standing at my side, watching me frown. I fixed my face into a neutral expression. Dyna stood next to me, her large dark blue eyes watching me closely.

"No, Your Highness."

Loria stood next to the Prince, her arm in his.

"It's nothing, Your Highness, he's just...not a ball person," Dyna hurriedly said, probably believing she was saving me from genuine suspicion.

I side-eyed her, trying to silently convey that was not in fact, necessary.

"I would never have supposed," the Prince said ironically.

"Nor I, that you would arrive in such a manner...Your Highness," I returned his sarcasm.

Dyna tensed up. Loria blinked hard. The two of them seemed deeply surprised by my statement. It was enough to make me question what had given me the audacity to say it.

But the Prince only seemed entertained.

"How little we know of one another, Captain. Isn't it shameful?"

We knew far more about one another than we should have.

Loria, who always seemed to interject when her brother spoke in this way, interceded.

"My Lady" — she looked down at Dyna — "the other candidates and I have arranged ...a get together of sorts after the ball. We would be very happy if you could join us. I know the past few weeks have been trying for you, and it would please me to see you smile, and enjoy yourself."

Loria's invitation sounded genuine, but still, I could not help but glance at the Prince during its delivery.

He had been watching me the whole time.

"Can he come?" Dyna pointed at me.

The Prince answered. "I am going to be rather selfish and request I have the Captain all to myself for a short time. I'd like to...rectify that issue of our lack of acquaintance somewhat. Especially since he seems to be the only person within this hall who wasn't mortally offended by my arrival."

"I wasn't!" Dyna said defensively, then she frowned and looked at me, realising what the Prince had said.

I too was struggling to comprehend his words. His sister, however, seemed as if she had expected them.

"The other escorts will be there, as will we, and all the guards of the Palace will be present, so, you will be safe, I promise," Loria reassured her.

Dyna looked unconvinced. I shared her sentiment.

"I'm sorry, Your Highness, but I should stay by the Lady's side." I met the Prince's eyes.

He scratched the back of his head then turned to Dyna. "My Lady, do you think you could spare him for an hour or so?" He clasped his hands in a pleading gesture. "I'd be most grateful."

She looked at him with an unabashed level of shock, then at me.

"Your Highness...I'm sorry but—" I started.

"You were staring at him when you came in...is this why?" Dyna blurted out, too loudly. Some people even turned their heads at her urgent tone.

I side-eyed her again. Her youth was at times like this, inconvenient.

The Prince laughed. "That, and the fact he's the only person wearing white in the whole room." He appraised me slowly. "Combined with his hair he looks like—"

"A Celestial!" Dyna blurted out. "That's what I said! I chose it for him, you know!"

Celestials, it was said, were servants of the Nine Divine Gods, crafted and made by them, and that only Noxos refused to craft any. The accounts of people who claimed to have seen them were all the same. That they were resplendent, grand in stature, larger than any creature in Athlion, and that they appeared bathed in white, silver or gold.

I blinked slowly and my lips tightened.

The Prince crossed his arms and made a sound that was difficult to distinguish between agreement or disapproval.

"So, do you think you could spare your glorious companion for a few hours?" he asked Dyna. Her turbulent eyes found my face once again.

In the end, despite my reservations, meeting with the Prince, I knew, was something I could not refuse. If he wished to speak to me, there must have been a reason.

I nodded at her and smiled, very slightly, to the point where it resembled more of a wince.

Dyna gulped and forcefully nodded. "Very well."

"Wonderful. I'll find you later, Captain." The Prince's eyes glittered with intent. He strolled towards us, placing his palm over the upper half of his torso.

He bowed in Dyna's direction. After he rose, he reached out to me with his other hand.

His fingers brushed against my shoulder fleetingly. I flinched at the action but took care not to follow my instinct of brushing his hand away.

As they did, his fingers made contact with the hair draped over it.

He peered at it with great focus, then his face relaxed.

"You had something in your hair...Captain."

From around us, a few whispers could be heard. Fortunately, it didn't seem completely out of character for the Prince to do something so presumptuous or unusual, so they quietened down rather swiftly.

The Prince lingered for a few moments, then stepped back, and walked away.

The remaining hours of the ball passed by in what felt like a vacuum where time ceased to move. It consisted of endless dances, conversation, and idle gossip rippling around the room like a polluted river. It took everything I had to muster the strength to withstand it. Not because I was unable to tolerate events like this. In fact, I was rather indifferent to them, they neither excited nor bothered me, but because the Prince's invitation had occupied and oppressed all other thoughts within my mind.

Eventually, however, it was over. Dyna came to bid her farewells and left with Loria, Princess Rhana, and Jayli at their heels like a shadow.

Audra's Prince, however, had vanished.

It did not surprise me however, that he had done so. It was hardly as if he and I could be seen parting together, if we wished to discuss sensitive matters.

Once I'd returned to my room, I entered the washroom and stood in front of the mirror. My fingers angrily and hurriedly tore through my hair.

Until I found it.

It was so small, almost invisible, but as my hair had been laced with several small braids tonight, within one slot between the grooves, an almost identical colour to my own hair, was a piece of silk.

I yanked it out, suddenly realising I was beginning to collect strange and unknown materials with hidden messages.

It took great effort to unfold the tiny piece of silk, and an even greater effort to read the message inside.

Directions.

I memorised them, then pocketed the silk. I waited for a short time, then carefully made my way around the Palace, taking care to avoid being witnessed by too many as I made my way to the described destination.

The Prince was sitting on the ledge of an alcove, looking outwards at the night sky.

One push was all it would take to kill him. One stumble for him to fall to an early grave. But he sat on it, utterly calm, one leg perched up, his right arm resting on his knee.

He was closer to death than any man in Athlion perhaps, to the backdrop of both screams and starlight.

I braced myself. I hadn't fully approached him, but he heard me instantly, turning around. He didn't move. The alcove was fairly small, it could probably only fit a handful of people. And yet, with only the Prince and I in it, the space felt crowded somehow.

I glanced over the edge, frowning.

The Prince watched me for a moment. "I would have thought you were quite used to heights, Captain, being in the Hunt."

I regarded his stance, his imperviousness.

"You certainly are, Your Highness."

The Prince shifted slightly but didn't come off the ledge. His clothes rustled with the movement. He was still wearing the same ones. The light from the moon illuminated the fabric in tones of silver as well as grey and black.

"You came faster than I expected," the Prince stated.

"Your directions are to thank, Your Highness," I said coolly, but internally I was tense, waiting for the Prince to reveal his reasons for this rendezvous.

The Prince beckoned me closer to the ledge. I eyed it suspiciously. He clearly found my reluctance amusing. After a few moments of debate, I carefully approached it.

The Prince pointed at the sky, the moon more precisely, which tonight was full, and illustrious.

"Like that," the Prince said softly. "With your clothes and white hair... I was going to say... you looked like that."

I wasn't sure how to respond, I only watched him in a daze.

The Prince dropped his hand and stood. He took a step closer to me again. I watched him cautiously. A silver sheen suffused over the edge of his neck as he walked through the moonlight, his sleeves billowing in the soft breeze like the petals of a flower.

He looked down and licked his lips briefly. He almost appeared uneasy.

"You need to leave, Captain."

His admonishment baffled me. The placid expression on my face was completely nullified by his statement.

"They know. About what you stole," he explained.

It wasn't as if I hadn't anticipated this risk, but it was one thing to be aware of its existence, and another for it to come to fruition. It felt as if a wave had engulfed me, pulling me underneath its weight.

The Prince watched me with a regretful look in his eyes as I took in his words.

"You...told them, Your Highness?" I concluded.

The Prince frowned deeply. "No, Captain, I did not tell them."

Now I was utterly baffled.

"Then...how?"

"They know what was stolen, and they..." The Prince seemed to be pondering how to explain. He fiddled with his fingers and thumb slightly. "They will find out your identity soon. Regardless of what I say. There are others they can use."

"I cannot leave the Lady now."

"Then take her with you."

"That...is not possible. And if I leave, would that only make me appear guilty to these people?"

"No. Your Kingdom is in a dire state. Leaving now to return there wouldn't seem particularly suspicious."

"I cannot, Your Highness."

The Prince sighed, exasperated.

"I had a feeling you might refuse, Captain. Your removal from Vasara would have been preferable. Nevertheless, it doesn't change the second part of my plan. We must give them another individual."

My face did not betray my disapproval. "Condemn another person for my actions, that is not—"

The Prince raised his hand to stop me speaking. My gaze fell to the silver light of the moon, rippling against the surface of his palm.

"Captain. I understand you are someone to whom morality and integrity are important. But these things matter little when you are being hunted by these individuals, for they possess none." He placed his palm back on his chest and with a mocking smile, added, "I would know."

He brought both his hands behind his back as he spoke again, "The only way to cease their hunt and therefore, prevent them from discovering the truth, is ending the hunt for them first, and the only way to do so... is this."

I understood his words, but I could not accept them. I shook my head. "No, Your Highness."

The Prince chuckled in a fatigued manner. "Well, in all honesty, Captain, I am enacting this plan anyway, your approval isn't necessary. I am simply informing you of the danger you are in."

"I do not wish for you to do this, Your Highness."

"No? You wish to be taken and apprehended by these people?"

"No, but—"

"It will not happen, Captain. While I have the ability to turn their attention elsewhere, I will," he declared adamantly.

A light breeze drifted through the open space, caressing his hair, sending some of his locks across his forehead lazily.

"Why, Your Highness? Why tell me at all?"

The Prince's light laugh was carried by the wind. "When I offer to work with someone, that doesn't *usually* involve me placing a blade in their back, and burying their body in the ground."

My voice was crisp and unwaning as I replied. "Surely the trouble saving my life is worth, far exceeds any benefit our alliance may have to you. I am quite sure you could complete the mission of discovering the authors of that note on your own, or at least with the help of...other parties. To be frank, you do not need me. This, we both know."

The Prince remained silent for a long time. The breeze continued to play with his clothes.

"Normally, in these situations, a person would agree, and offer up several reasons why their life should be spared. It's almost as if... you're asking me to kill you," the Prince remarked, his voice expressionless.

The remote possibility struck me then, that he was here to do just that.

I stepped back, once, twice. I looked around, unbidden fists forming at my sides.

"This would be the perfect place to do so," I commented, slowly.

The Prince looked over the ledge. "Is that what you think?" He gave a cold laugh, as lifeless as his previous words.

"Is it not so?" I challenged him. "Perhaps there is a reason you wish for me to live I do not know of, but you could also end my life, here and now."

The Prince was still looking out over the ledge, he huffed out a weak laugh again.

"I have no intention of killing you, Captain. I never did. If I had done, I would have killed you a long time ago."

That statement did nothing to placate me.

"Then what are your intentions... Your Highness?" My voice was thin and steely.

The Prince moved away from the ledge, and regarded me carefully, as if he were thinking of his answer while looking at my face.

He pinched his brows with his thumb and forefingers, looking down.

"You truly have complicated things, Captain." He laughed and shook his head.

I waited, watching him. For some reason, I believed his words. I believed if he had wanted to kill me, he would have already done so. He and I were aware that when it came to combat abilities, he was far superior.

He clapped his hands together softly. "Since you have removed all other options only one remains."

"And which is that?" I asked warily.

The Prince wearily closed his eyes and shook his head again, exhaling loudly through his nose.

"It won't concern you." He opened his eyes and smiled tightly. He turned around, ready to leave.

It is difficult to say what possessed me in that moment to step forwards, and stop him with my arm, which I stuck in front of his chest.

Although I moved swiftly, the Prince's agility prevented his skin from coming into contact with my robes. He backed away, blinking hard and jerking his head in my direction.

"And you?" I said quietly. "Will it concern you?"

Surprise flashed through the Prince's eyes, but it was quickly replaced by a wave of irritation.

The Prince, without answering, side-stepped my arm, and attempted to move around it.

I blocked his path again, with my body.

This time, he tutted and glanced up at my face. "No, Captain. It will not. Now, let me pass."

I didn't move.

"I do not believe you, Your Highness."

"Why should that matter?" He frowned.

"What will happen if the culprit is not found?"

The Prince shrugged, "They'll look for—"

"No," I interrupted him. "What will happen to *you*?"

The Prince sucked in a breath, then released it slowly. His voice was low when he answered.

"Nothing."

"You said to yourself, how can we work together if one of us is incapacitated?" I reminded him.

"No, no, they won't incapacitate me just…" The Prince laughed, but then his face froze over, shifting in a fraction of a second, as if he had just realised his words.

"Just what…Your Highness?"

The Prince licked his lip then cleared his throat. "Goodnight, Captain."

The Prince tried to leave for a third time.

"We're not finished," I said to his back, sternly.

The Prince moved his head over his shoulder. "Oh? Aren't we? What is it… that we have left unfinished?"

"Is this why you were gone for days?" I asked him. My voice was betraying signs of agitation now, disquiet.

The Prince turned back to face me, so that our positions were reversed from just minutes ago. At this angle, the moonlight struck his face rather than his back.

"I didn't realise you'd noticed."

My brows dropped. "That is not an answer, Your Highness."

"So many dances tonight, Captain, and here we are, having one of our own. Questions, answers, no answers, accusations, self-sabotage, secrets." He huffed. "Do you truly expect me to give you everything?"

"It's one question, Your Highness."

"No, Captain, that is most certainly not what it is."

I took a few steps towards him, the shadow of my own body falling over him. He glanced at me up and down as I came closer. "If you will not answer then let me speculate. You were gone for days because of this. You have been ordered to kill me, for some reason, you do not wish to do so. You therefore decided you must offer up another in my place, to take the blame. If you do not do that, then it will be you that suffers…am I correct?"

The Prince smacked his lips together, and looked over my shoulder at the sky, laughing. "You should really stop thinking so much, Captain, I—"

"Am I correct?" I insisted.

The Prince's eyes very slowly slid towards my face. "Of course not."

I shook my head in disbelief. "Perhaps others would believe that because of your status, such a thing would not be possible. I would have believed that too once, until..." I lifted my finger and pointed down towards the wound on my shin. The Prince's eyes followed the movement.

"Now, I am not so sure. In fact," I hastily added, "I am almost certain that is not the case."

"Your confidence is admirable." The Prince raised a brow.

"As is your insistence on denial," I retorted instantly.

The Prince grinned at that, appearing both irked and gratified. Astonished and offended.

"Ha." He fiddled with his fingers behind his back.

We stared this way at each other, frustrated and unrelenting. The Prince made it clear he would not be confirming or denying anything.

I took a step back. "There was a man," I remembered. "A sorcerer. He healed Dyna."

The Prince raised his eyebrows.

"I can ask him. For assistance."

The Prince squinted. "And what would be the difference between asking him and me? Of him framing another and me framing another?"

The question threw me off guard.

"None, Captain," the Prince answered for me.

"Still, it would be better if you were less involved, Your Highness."

The Prince looked at me smugly. "It's about ten years too late for that."

I frowned.

*Ten years? Too late for what?*

The Prince cleared his throat and clasped his hands behind his back.

"Ask him. If you wish. Since you are so stubborn regarding your own life, I will not stop you preserving it using the means you see fit. I only hope he's as competent as you imply."

"I believe he is."

The Prince smiled with sarcasm. "So, you believe in his capabilities, but not mine?"

"It's not that."

"It is. Although I can't say that I blame you for your distrust."

Then why was he asking?

The Prince pointed at me. "But you should know that I trust you, Captain. Not with everything, but with a small amount." He dropped his hand. "Which is far more than I usually offer."

Knowing the Prince trusted me felt unusually gratifying, but also unnerving, since I could not understand why a man of his background, his position, would trust me at all.

"I am grateful for your trust, Your Highness...and for the warning."

The Prince nodded. "This man, will he help us with other matters?"

"He will."

"So, you have decided to agree then? To our...alliance?"

"Yes, Your Highness," I replied frankly. "I have."

He smiled slightly at that, then turned to the side.

"This man will help us, but at what cost, I wonder," he mused aloud.

"I asked him the same."

"Directly?" The Prince raised a brow.

I nodded in confirmation.

The Prince seemed impressed at that. Not that it was particularly impressive.

"And what did he say?"

"That our interests aligned in such a way the cost was irrelevant."

The Prince huffed in clear disagreement.

"Who is he?"

"I don't know, Your Highness, he was disguised."

"Like that woman."

I nodded in confirmation once again.

"There's something else."

"You really weren't finished with me." The Prince laughed. "I didn't realise you had so much to share. How come I had to approach you, Captain?"

"You have been gone for days," I reminded him.

The Prince's face dropped at that. He resumed a serious air. "What is it?"

I proceeded to tell him of the words that Dyna's attacker had uttered.

"That...tells us little."

"Other than his gender," I stated.

"Not even that. There are plenty of ways to make yourself appear and sound like a man or a woman, even a child, if you are young, or small enough."

"So, it truly does tell us nothing." I sighed.

The Prince waved casually. "It's no matter. We will discover their identity soon, and they'll be dead soon afterwards."

"Dead?" I said flatly.

The Prince squinted in confusion. "Do you suggest we...let them live?"

"We could detain them."

The Prince smirked. "This person was connected enough to enter the Palace and poison that girl. I am not quite sure detaining them will prove effective."

I breathed in and out quickly, casting my eyes to the ground in frustration.

"You're too just, Captain," the Prince remarked gently.

I looked up at him, he had his head tilted, observing me.

"Not resorting to death as the first option for all things hardly qualifies as just, Your Highness," I replied.

"It counts as believing that others are, which...is usually something only just people can do."

"But you do not."

"I do not," the Prince sighed out.

I uttered the first question that came to my mind without thinking on it.

"You think yourself an unjust person, Your Highness?"

"Oh, Captain." The Prince shook his head. "There you go again."

He stroked the side of his own jaw quickly, outlining its cut. "But it's alright. It means that during our allyship, I can do whatever it is you cannot, and you can maintain your" — he waved his hand around in a circle— "purity of soul."

"Purity of soul?" I repeated the words bitterly.

"Good faith in others? Sturdy reputation? Nobility? Morality? Place in the Divine Halls? Choose one," the Prince said teasingly. "The blood is already on my hands, Captain, why stain yours with it also?"

I couldn't help but chuckle weakly, shaking my head. The Prince was startled by it. That was understandable. I had not yet appeared truly amused in front of him.

"Your Highness, you accused me just now of seeing the good in others far too often, or too easily, but...you are assuming much about me now, much which is not true. If your statement earlier this evening was right, there is still much that we do not know about one another. If you truly believe me the pinnacle of righteousness, you will invariably end up disappointed."

The Prince smiled the whole time I spoke.

"Captain, I've been disappointed by the majority of people. I know you aren't someone who is inclined to believe me, but I hope you will this once, when I tell you, that there is no future I can envisage where you will be added to that list."

We stood in silence for a few seconds.

"You should wear white more. It suits you," the Prince said, looking me up and down.

I looked at his attire in kind.

The Prince smiled and looked at his own clothing. "Mmmm. It's rather revolting, isn't it?"

"No," I replied instantly.

Did he really believe that?

The Prince raised his brows and looked at me.

"It's too your taste then? Should I lend it to you?" He stroked one of the transparent sleeves mockingly.

"No," I said, only this time in a disgruntled manner.

He laughed, openly and lightly. "You can't refuse. You like it, you just said so. I'll give it to you."

"Please do not," I grumbled.

He laughed again and I found myself smiling slightly as I watched him appearing so genuinely delighted.

Our eyes met, and I shook my head, looking away, wiping the smile from my face.

"You need a reason, there you are, I wish for you to live, simply so I can see you in this." He gestured to himself.

"Then you should kill me now, Your Highness," I retorted dryly.

The Prince laughed again. His laugh rang across the space like chiming silver bells. He shook his head.

"No. I don't think I will. In fact, I'm even more determined to ensure you live now."

I let out a groan.

The Prince clearly enjoyed mocking me. He watched me react to every word with a glint in his eyes.

He held out his hand. "Give me the message, I'll dispose of it."

I took out the silk and handed it to him, placing it in his palm, quickly withdrawing my arm.

But the Prince grabbed my wrist before I could fully do so. His fingers were insistent but not painfully. They held my wrist like a bird perching quietly on a branch. Just with the time his fingers had met my leg, their touch was insistent, demanding, a focal point of gentle force. I furrowed my brow at his fingers, then at his face.

He placed something else inside my palm. It was a balm of some kind.

"For your wound," he whispered.

My wound was much improved, but still not fully healed.

"Thank you, Your Highness." I glanced down at him, this close together, I was taller than him, but only slightly.

His fingers brushed against mine rapidly as he nodded, took his hands away, and left.

In the moonlight, the balm, which was golden in colour, looked white. I opened its lid and smelt it.

It smelt…slightly sweet, woody, and musky.

It was a familiar scent, I realised, although I hadn't known its true origins before.

It was the exact scent the Prince always carried.

# CHAPTER 70 -SHADAE

It was no wonder Lord Elias looked half alive. Last night had been that grand ball, and he had most certainly, been drinking.

We had walked a fair distance away from town, on our way to meet his mother. Elias had initially suggested we ride, but I still hadn't been able to learn how to ride a horse well enough.

Which was probably part of the reason why the scowl on his face was so deeply etched into it.

In all honesty, I was surprised Elias had even managed to awaken this early to take me here.

Unless of course, he hadn't slept.

I peered at him cautiously...maybe he really hadn't.

Elias noticed me watching him.

"Do you have something to say?" His voice was dull.

*Please don't fall asleep halfway through a conversation with your own mother and leave me as the only conscious one in the room.*

"No, no," I replied casually.

Elias turned away imperviously.

Sometime later, we reached a house. It was large and appeared to be stately, situated not right at the outskirts, but not too deeply within the city of Iloris either.

Elias stopped at the door and spun towards me. "She's not entirely coherent," he stated flatly, his eyes blank.

"Oh..." I glanced at the windows.

*Then why are we here? Is she coherent enough to...help us?*

But that question was pointless. We were here now, and that meant for whatever reason, Elias believed the answer to be yes.

"And don't..." Elias started to speak again, sighing through his words.

The door swung open.

"Is it you?"

Elias' mother was a head shorter than me. Her light brown hair was tied up, and her eyes, a bright red, glimmered with joy as they fell upon her son's face.

"It *is* you." She smiled, brightly.

Elias smiled too, but with more restraint. "It is."

The woman grasped his hand, clutching it tightly, then used the other to cover it.

Then, as if she had only just sensed my presence, she turned her head in a staggered way towards me.

The quizzical look in her eyes quickly disappeared.

She reached out and grabbed my hand instead.

I couldn't hide my bafflement, staring at her hands as if they were coating mine in acid.

"Hello," she said to me, staring at me with wonder. "Don't you look wonderful?" She eyed me up and down.

I opened my mouth and looked to Elias for salvation, but he only watched impassively, feeling, of course, that he had already explained.

*She wasn't entirely coherent.*

Did she even recognise my uniform? Did she even know I was a sorcerer?

His mother was still staring at me.

"I'm Erilia," she beamed.

"Shadae," I said uncertainly, as if I was unsure of my own name.

It was her family, her kin, who were responsible for the fact my brothers were in chains, but here she was, holding my hand, stroking it tenderly as if I were her own child.

She grabbed Elias' hand with one of hers and mine with the other. She pulled us towards the entrance.

"Come, come, I've just cooked something."

Snatching my hand away would be rude, but being dragged along like this by her, side by side with Elias felt so unnatural, that the discomfort on my face couldn't be hidden.

Elias didn't seem to notice, that or anything else.

We reached a kitchen. It was small, a long narrow rectangle engulfed by white tiling. A pure ivory table sat at the centre surrounded by several chairs.

"Sit...sit." She grinned at us brightly and hurried over towards the various pots and pans she was attending to.

Elias sat down instantly. There were only four seats around the table. Two were facing towards the woman, and the countertops, one of which Elias had placed himself in. The other two were facing away from her, towards the entrance we had come through.

I wasn't keen to keep my eyes off Erilia, and so I sat next to Elias.

He frowned as I sat down, as if he had expected me to stand, sit on the floor, or even run out of the house.

*Why are you looking at me like that, huh? She said sit, so I'm sitting.*

But I realised, it wasn't me he was frowning at.

It was the smell.

Of the food.

I squinted at Erilia, busying herself over a half-prepared meal. I couldn't identify any ingredients that would smell...like that.

"She can't cook," Elias muttered under his breath.

Just as he had done so, his mother spun around, and placed two bowls in front of us of.... something.

Bits floated around in sand thin brown water, pieces of what appeared like meat and hard uncooked vegetables. Part of it was thick and sludgy, sticking to the sides of the bowl relentlessly. The rest had a sheen of oily bubbles, reflecting my widened eyes back at me.

"Oh, oh! I'll get some drinks," Erilia moved away again.

I slowly and subtly glanced at Elias from the side.

"Just eat it," he whispered.

"Eat it?!" I whispered back angrily.

Elias looked up from under his brows, slightly hunched over the table.

"Look at it!" I hissed.

Elias furrowed his brows. "I can see it," he snapped in a hushed voice.

"It's...what even is it?"

Erilia remained completely oblivious a few metres away.

"Just do it," he grumbled.

Before I could respond, Erilia returned. She placed a jug of water and some wine on the table. Elias reached for the wine immediately, pouring himself a glass. His mother watched him grab it eagerly and frowned, puzzled.

*Don't you know your own son drinks? Why would you even offer up wine for breakfast?*

Although, as I glanced back down at the watery concoction, I concluded that I was in fact, grateful for that wine, and poured myself a glass.

Elias's glass froze halfway up to his lips as he watched me do so. I only widened my eyes in response and lowered them to the bowl.

*You think I can get through eating this without the wine?*

Elias continued to drink, understanding.

Erilia sat opposite us and dug into her own creation, sipping it off the spoon, seemingly delighted.

I looked over at Elias again and found him watching me.

*Not entirely coherent and no taste buds either.*

Elias picked up the spoon and began to eat, I tentatively did so, raising it to my mouth. It slid down my throat like congealed milk.

I placed my hand over my mouth instantly. It was an effort not to spit it out.

Elias coughed as he swallowed. He clutched at his glass of wine and drank some more. I did the same.

Erilia watched us silently, her gaze full of innocence and unbridled joy.

"Do you like it?" she asked, directing the question at me.

*Why ask me? Ask your son!*

But her large eyes watched me expectantly.

Elias swallowed another spoon, half gagging as he did. Erilia, who was still waiting for my judgement, didn't notice.

"It's..." I stared. "I don't recognise the ingredients...they're not common, where I'm from."

Erilia looked slightly dejected.

"But it's..."

*Likely to give me food poisoning, disgusting, genuinely unfathomable, indescribably horrendous.*

"Lovely," I finished.

"Oh! I have more!" Erilia exclaimed gleefully, rushing back to the kitchen.

I stared after her, my jaw dropped.

Elias' concerned expression told me that he too, was dreading the extras. He glared at me.

"What?" I whispered harshly. "You told me to eat it!"

"To eat it, not... to beg for more," he grunted.

"I didn't!" I turned around to make sure Erilia was still occupied, then faced Elias again. "What was I supposed to say, that it's horrible?"

"That you weren't hungry," Elias gave me a wonderful alternative, much to my irritation.

"I don't think I'll be hungry for *days* now," I whispered through gritted teeth, gesturing at my bowl.

Elias sipped some wine, watching me over the glass.

"It's bearable," he said as he pulled the cup away.

"You're practically choking on it!" I retorted.

"Alright, so you're doing a better job then," Elias remarked sarcastically, still whispering.

"Well, I'm used to eating shit," I spat back, thinking of the food I'd eaten at the draining centres.

Elias raised his brows. My face fell.

*What is wrong with me?! Does this soup have an ingredient in it so poisonous it loosened my tongue? Why did I just say that?*

"I mean..." I began.

But Erilia returned.

"Here!" She placed the whole pot on the table. A variety of herbs and leaves which had just been added, were floating on top, swimming in the sea of sludge.

"I'll have it," Elias said suddenly, "If that's alright with you," he directed to me.

*None of this is alright with me.*

"Elias!" his mother reprimanded him. "It's impolite to take a lady's food!"

"No…it's alright," I faced his mother, "I'm not very hungry anyway." I glanced at Elias as I used his excuse, but he was already facing back into his bowl.

His mother shrugged and poured the remaining contents of the pot into it. Elias slowly blinked and sighed as it filled up.

*Can you really eat all of that?*

But Elias dug in, seeming to have mastered hiding his cough more easily.

I still hadn't finished my portion, so I returned to it. I could feel myself sweating with every mouthful.

"So…how's your unit?" she asked Elias.

Elias sighed. "Mother…I don't… have a unit anymore."

I watched as Erilia furrowed her brow and scratched her head, after which, she brought her palm back down to the table.

"No…you…you do," she insisted quietly.

"No, I don't. That was years ago. Remember?"

Erilia's eyelashes and lips quivered. She placed her hand over her mouth, but she quickly dropped it away again. All her movements seemed erratic and fuelled by confusion.

"I'm…forgetting things again…aren't I?"

Elias winced, but gently. Pity and concern were in his eyes. "It's alright."

Erilia cleared her throat then looked up at me, smiling suddenly. "You're…you…work for him?" she asked, her tone becoming more uncertain at the end of her sentence, as she realised she may be wrong.

"We work together," Elias answered.

"Oh…Oh…I…but…" she shook her head, "You're not from here." She squinted at me.

"That's because I—" I began explaining.

"She moved here some time ago."

I frowned slightly but was astute enough not to look at Elias.

"Oh," his mother said. "Do you… like it here?" Do you like working with my son?"

*No and definitely no.*

"Yes," I lied, smiling.

"Ahhh, of course. They all like him!" She reached out and stroked Elias's upper arm. Then she frowned. "Liked…liked him," she corrected herself. Her facial expression was changing every second.

It brightened again, "He's always made people feel at home, welcome, he's always—"

"Stop," Elias met his mother's eyes. His tone was serious enough for her to cease speaking immediately. An awkward air passed through the room.

"Yes…he…treats us well," I said hesitantly.

Elias's head rotated in my direction.

*You're… welcome?*

"He's always so busy! Never comes to visit his parents anymore!" She turned to Elias, "Just the other day your father was asking about you."

Elias leant back in his chair and closed his eyes.

Somehow, without knowing, without him saying anything, I understood.

Elias' father couldn't have asked that.

Elias didn't have a father.

Not anymore.

"Mother –" Elias tried to speak. A forlorn look clouded his eyes.

"He's always so proud of you! He is!" She nodded at me.

I pressed my lips together.

"Mother," Elias repeated, slowly opening his eyes. His glance was so pained, so drawn out, that even I empathised with him in that moment.

"He's not here anymore," he said softly.

"Oh, I know but he's coming back soon and—"

"No, mother. That's not what I mean. You're…forgetting again."

Erilia rubbed her forehead. Her mouth twisted within the space of several seconds from a frown to a laugh, to a smile, to a frustrated grimace.

Then a quivering lips once more.

"Oh…oh…" She looked up at Elias, "I'm so sorry…I…. oh. Gods you must—"

Elias shook his head slowly as if to say, *It's alright.*

She remained silent for a few moments then poured herself a glass of water.

"So…why…have you come?"

"Where's Harlin?"

"Oh…she's urrr…she's outside."

At my confused look, Erilia explained, "She's my friend. Well, she was…my husband's sister…she…lives here too. She…helps."

I nodded.

"I need to ask you something. If you don't remember that's…it doesn't matter." Elias said. "But I need to know…if you know."

Elias had never sounded this unsure before. It was strange.

"Of course, anything to help my boy." She watched him tenderly.

"I need the sword."

His mother's face fell instantly.

"Mother, I know that—"

"No!" She shot up, it was so unlike her previous actions that Elias and I jumped.

"No! That sword is evil! That…that *thing*! He was never the same after holding that! Never the same!"

"I know…" Elias said, "But I need it." Elias tried to make his words sound gentle, but his voice was unmistakably tense.

I remained silent, but internally, I was trying to make sense of the situation.
*This must be his father's sword.*
"Years he had that thing! You know what he did with it! And still...you.... you...how could you!"
*What he did with it?*
"I do know," Elias sounded a mix of impatient and sorrowful, "That is why I need it."
"No! I don't want to see it...to think about it! Ever! You come here! You...ask this! You...you!" Tears spilt from Erilia's face frantically.
"Mother...please," Elias stood, trying to comfort her.
"Don't!" She jerked away. "Don't!"
After hearing the commotion, a woman entered the room.
"What's wrong?" Harlin, it must have been, asked. Her dark brown eyes were tarred with restrained anger.
"He..." but Erilia couldn't finish the sentence, sobbing between her words.
"I need the sword," Elias explained. Harlin whose hands were around Erilia's shoulders now, glowered at him.
"Why?" she asked bitterly. Then she noticed me, "And why is a tracker here?"
Erilia stopped sobbing at that. She stared at me, understanding flashing across her eyes. "You...you brought one of them here!" she yelled.
I stood and took several steps back, naturally preparing to be attacked. Since I couldn't defend myself fully with the cursed brand upon my wrist, I needed to create some distance.
But Erilia lunged, slipping out of Harlin's hold. Her fingers were outstretched, clawing forwards.
Elias stood in front of me.
Erilia's nails landed on his face, slashing across his cheek. Elias flinched slightly but barely acknowledged the injury.
Erilia, realising what had happened, shook her head violently, and began trembling. She watched her son, her eyes full of disdain and confusion.
Small trickles of blood escaped from the scratch marks on Elias' face.
*The same colour as his eyes.*
I shifted on my feet behind him, looking up at the back of his neck, the side of his face.
"After what they did to him! You...brought one here!" Erilia glared at me angrily, "I even fed her!"
*Unfortunately.*
"I asked her to be here." Elias's voice remained, as it had done since we arrived, vacant and tired.
"She!" Erilia spat. "You're..."

Harlin gently moved Erilia away, who apparently, had lost all resolve once she'd discovered she had been hosting a sorcerer.

Harlin glared at Elias, "That thing was destroyed along with the rest."

"No, it wasn't. He never handed it over," Elias replied confidently, "Neither did you."

Harlin raised her brows in surprise. "How did you know that?"

"So, you're lying," Elias said, not answering.

Harlin laughed coldly. "Why don't you ask your sorcerer to find it for you?"

*'Your' sorcerer...Ugh...*

"That's not how it works," Elias retorted.

*You really didn't need to clarify that.*

"Where is it...*aunt*?" Elias dragged out the final word.

"Aunt now? You don't even come to visit, but I'm your aunt, when you want something."

"And when I don't," he replied, smiling falsely.

"You're just as bad as he was."

Erilia blinked hard several times, staring into space, not seeming to register the insult directed at her dead husband.

"Will you tell me?" Elias ignored her statement as well.

"What do you even want it for?"

"What do you think?" Elias asked.

*There's no way she'd be able to know. Even I don't know what you want it for.*

"The fact I have no idea is what concerns me," Harlin continued to look at Elias with apprehension.

"Don't worry, I won't be doing what he did with it," Elias' voice was bitter.

"How have you got the gall to—" Harlin started.

Elias' voice rose. "You don't own that blade. It was his, and by rights, it is now mine. Tell me where it is, and I'll leave. You don't have to worry about me visiting again for a while."

"That blade shouldn't belong to anyone," Harlin snapped.

"Which is all the more reason why you should have handed it in, but you didn't. Why didn't you?" Elias tilted his head and raised his brows.

"You know why," Harlin hissed.

Elias stood patiently. I was behind him still.

"It's at the lodge."

Elias nodded and took a few steps towards his mother. She was on the ground now, crouching. She gradually raised her head as he approached.

"I'm sorry I upset you, but I'm doing..." Elias halted then laughed and shook his head. "It doesn't matter," he said quietly.

He spun around and walked away, striding past me swiftly. I followed hurriedly, I didn't want to be left alone in a room with those two women, even for a moment. They clearly wanted me dead.

Elias walked as he always did, in long strides, so that it was an effort for me to catch up to him.

When I finally did, I stood to his left.

His face was still bleeding.

"Ur...your..."

Elias kept walking but bit out a, "What?"

"Your face...It's still—"

Elias rolled his eyes. "It's nothing."

He began walking faster.

"Can you...slow...down."

Elias didn't slow down, instead, he came to an abrupt halt.

I hadn't expected that, so I walked a few steps ahead of him and turned around.

"You wanted to walk," Elias reminded me.

"Yes, but...I can't..." I waved my hand around in the air, trying to find the words.

Elias' eyes flattened, as if he had expected, and grown accustomed to how long it took me to form sentences.

"We didn't get to exercise much," I explained.

Elias moved his head to the side, glancing at the ground, then continued to walk. Slowly this time.

"So...this sword..." I put to him.

He sighed deeply. "I've long suspected something about it. I want to confirm it."

I hesitated to ask the next question. Normally, I wouldn't have but...he had stood in front of me.

*He also made you eat that...concoction.*

"Why...didn't you do it...before?" I asked tentatively.

"Do you need to know that?"

"No but—"

"Then stop asking questions. I'll tell you what you need to know, that's all you need to remember."

*Can you really blame me? The intensity of that conversation with your family about that blade would make anyone with a brain cell curious.*

I was about to thank him then, for defending me, when I realised he was part of the reason I wasn't even fully free.

*Thank you? No, that's ridiculous. Besides, he doesn't seem like he'd be in the mood to accept thanks, or even expect it at all. But then...shouldn't I try to make sure he has a favourable impression towards me? I suppose the only reason I'm out of that cell is because of his favourable impression of me. Wait...Is it favourable? Or just not...unfavourable?*

I changed my mind, I faced him, opening my mouth to speak. He was watching me.

"What are you thinking so deeply about?"

"I...wasn't—"

"You're terrible at controlling your facial expressions," Elias said bluntly, looking away.

*How would you know about that? You never even try! Not that you'd need to, you can get away with whatever you want to, 'Lord' Elias.*

"I was just going to say...thank you...for...getting me out of the cell and for the..." I gestured to the left side of my own face.

Elias's face twisted in a complicated mixture of emotions I couldn't understand.

"It took you that long to think of that?" Elias said, suspiciously.

I frowned and turned away. "I didn't know if I should, or if you'd want me to."

"I don't want you to."

"So, you can understand my dilemma." I gave him a side glance.

"There is no dilemma. I don't want you to thank me, from this point onwards."

I shrugged.

*Easier for me. I didn't even want to thank you anyway.*

"Are we...going there now?" I inquired.

"Not now, later." Elias replied.

"Oh..."

"What is it?" Elias asked reluctantly.

"No, it's only that...you...look..."

Elias abruptly stopped walking again and faced me.

"Stop being so petrified to speak around me. You can say whatever you have to say. I've already told you that."

"I..." I glanced at his dark boots. "It's hard for me to believe you."

"What exactly is it you'd think I'd do if you said something I disagreed with?"

*Anything? I don't know.*

"Do you think I'd kill you? Is that what you're worried about?"

I faced him, lifting my chin up. "No."

"No, you're not worried about that, or no, you don't think I'd kill you."

"I don't think...that you'd kill me. But I...can't be sure."

Elias took a step towards me. "I'm not going to kill you. I don't just kill people because of something they said for fuck's sake. I also have no intention of sending you back to the draining centres, even if you do start to become a problem, I'll just use another Navigator. So, say what you want to say."

"As long as it isn't 'thank you'..." I replied.

Elias squinted and huffed a dry laugh out, although there was little humour in it.

"As long as it isn't that," he drawled.

I nodded then. I closed my eyes as I told him. "You look...terrible. You look as if you might fall asleep on our way...there."

Elias started laughing. "That's it? That's all you were going to say? Gods, I thought it was something awful."

"That would have been enough to get me killed as a Vessel," I retorted dryly.

Elias peered at me. "You're not a Vessel anymore."

*It's not as if I'm much better off.*

But no, despite his promise, I wouldn't say that.

"In here" — I tapped the side of my temple— "I am."

Elias's expression grew thoughtful. He shook himself out of it and reassured me, "I'm capable of the journey. You won't need to carry me back."

I grimaced slightly.

*How would I even carry you? You look as if you'd weigh five of me.*

"Was it the ball?" I asked as we began to walk again.

Elias grunted in confirmation.

"What was that like?"

"Awful," Elias replied.

*Oh sure. Dancing, lavish costumes, food, and wine. Terrible.*

"It was," Elias insisted as he noticed my doubtful expression.

"It's for the Courting Season?"

*Wait, wait, this is strange, I'm making casual conversation with you, I should stop.*

"Fucking joke," Elias rolled his eyes again.

"Why do they still hold it then? Didn't they limit cross breeding between the Kingdoms several years ago?" The questions slipped out, despite my previous resolution to stop talking.

*Wait... Asking him questions about Vasara's decrees, this is a bad idea, I—*

But Elias only spat out, "Politics, alliances, money." Each word festered with contempt.

I raised my eyebrows in quick flicker as if to say, *That makes sense.*

We continued onwards, back into the town centre and the Palace, the rest of the way in silence.

Elias approached some of the guards and returned to me.

"We're taking a carriage, follow me."

And so, minutes later, the two of us sat face to face inside a ruby decorated, golden, lavish carriage, drawn by two horses, and two coachmen.

It was cramped but spaced out enough our feet weren't touching.

"What is it? That you suspected about it...the sword?" I decided to ask.

Elias, who had been looking out of the small window in the carriage, turned towards me slowly.

"That's relevant, isn't it?" I challenged him before he could try and tell me it wasn't.

Not disagreeing, Elias faced out the window again as he replied, "My father wasn't...well. He never had been. His moods were...erratic. He was prone to...Anyway, that's why I wasn't sure, after what happened with that blade, but..."

I waited patiently for him to finish. My fists clenched tightly on my thighs.

"After you got yourself arrested..."

*Got myself arrested? Seriously? You think I went up to the guards and begged them to cuff me and throw me in a cell?*

But Elias didn't notice my irritation. "After that, they showed us the talisman on that guard's body, and I recognised the mark. I'd never seen it at any other point, nothing like it. It made sense, even you didn't recognise it as a cursed mark, not the way you did on that corpse we found."

That was true, the mark on the talisman and on the corpse had been different. Although there were vague similarities, it was as if the mark on the talisman was a small fragment of a larger whole. The one on the talisman had almost looked decorative, floral, like a leaf vine.

Its design was undoubtedly a deliberate attempt to disguise its true purpose.

Elias faced me again, his eyes flickering with an inner frustration as he spoke.

"That mark. It was on my father's sword."

# CHAPTER 71 – BAZ

I waved my hands frantically in front of the Healer.

"You can't...go in there!" I half-yelled, half-whispered at him.

We were standing outside Nemina's tent.

Although his face was covered, I could see the frown at the corner of his lips. "Why?" he asked.

"She doesn't like visitors. Or anyone to be quite honest. But that's...I mean...she doesn't want you in there."

The Healer stood there like a tree, its leaves gently blowing in the wind, calm and rooted, firm and unperturbed.

"She requested that?" he sounded indifferent.

"Yes...yes," I replied regretfully.

The Healer glanced at the tent's entrance for a moment then turned around and leisurely walked away.

"Where are you...is that it? Are you leaving?" I called out after him.

"Where's your tent?" he asked me.

"My...my tent?" I replied. "It's next to hers...you're walking the wrong way, if that's where you want to go."

He only nodded.

I gestured for him to come towards me, then strolled into my tent with him.

We had long since left Audra and were now hiding within Kalnasa. Despite our reservations about being here, there was no way we could linger in Audra after what had happened.

Going to Audra had been a mistake. Nemina had been very right about that. All we'd managed to do was to nearly get ourselves killed, alert Audra to our existence, and get Nemina badly wounded.

But here, in Kalnasa, it was only a matter of time before we had to leave.

Although we were staying in the outer plains, and had even scaled up Kalnasa's mountains to find shelter, the brief moments we did spend in and around the larger villages, were horrific.

There was no way to find food here, no way to sustain our survival.

It honestly felt as if we were jumping from one disaster to the next. I wasn't even sure Yaseer had a plan anymore.

I settled down. A chill breeze slapped against the tent's fabric. The Healer sat opposite me.

"So...you wanted to talk?" I put to him.

The Healer nodded again. Not the speaking type, I had noticed, which wasn't exactly ideal.

"About....?" my voice rose in pitch.

"How far along are you, in mastering your abilities?" His voice was deep, but cool, and gentle.

I puffed out my lips, the air escaping them in a sigh. "Not far. I mean what happened in Audra was just desperation, I guess, but then, you know, I passed out afterwards, so I'd not exactly say I'm very good at it."

The Healer had one of his legs crossed over the other, looking down at his own legs as I spoke.

"What you saw..." he started.

I tensed up.

Yes, what I saw, what he showed me.

"I won't tell anyone." The words tumbled from my lips.

The man only nodded again.

I wanted to, I wanted to tell her but...

I didn't even fully understand what I had seen...only...partially.

"Will you?" I asked him, "Tell her?"

The man shook his head.

"But—"

The harsh slap of the tent opening sounded from behind me.

"I need some of your—"

I spun around. The Healer looked up over my shoulder.

Nemina had entered the tent.

Well, hobbled in.

Her hand was over her abdomen, her face pale, a purple smudge under both her eyes. She slowly turned towards me, her eyes filled with confusion.

"What? You said I shouldn't let him in your tent, not mine!" I protested.

The Healer stood as I defended myself.

"You are ill," he stated.

Nemina straightened up, but it was obvious she found it difficult to do so.

"I'm not ill."

I winced at Nemina. "You do...look ill."

She looked at me in vexation.

"Your injuries have not healed?" the Healer asked.

"Wasn't it you who healed them?" she replied, raising an eyebrow.

The Healer remained silent.

"I can't sleep, that's all," Nemina explained, casually.

Seeing an opportunity to divert the topic in the silence, I turned back to the Healer.

"Have you seen Yaseer?"

"I have not."

I stood. "I'll get him for you."

"Don't"

"No."

Nemina and the Healer both spoke at the same time, looking at each other after they did.

I stood between them, my head turning from side to side, unsure of who to direct my question to.

"Why?" I ended up saying to the air.

The Healer and Nemina both glanced at each other, wondering who would answer.

"I'd prefer to keep this between us," the Healer explained.

I sank back down.

"What about Ullna, she knows who you are doesn't she?" I peered at the Healer.

The Healer didn't deem my question worth answering.

"Why did you kill him?"

"How did you do that?"

Nemina and the Healer both asked each other a question at the same time, again.

They stared at each other.

"Don't you two know how to have a conversation?" I asked them.

I raised my eyes to meet theirs. Looking at them both, I realised, the answer to that question was obviously no.

"Wait," I realised what they had both said, "What did you do?" I turned to Nemina.

But it was the Healer who answered. "She manipulated blood."

Nemina's jaw clenched, and she gulped slightly. "I thought that was you."

"It was not," the Healer stated.

Nemina let out a slow breath. Her eyes fell to the ground, but her face was still tense, her eyes shifted around as if trying to make sense of everything.

"I don't know how," the fatigue in her voice was clear. "I don't even know how I used divination. I don't know anything."

The Healer tilted his head watching her. "Have you told them?"

"If he doesn't know," she pointed at me, "Do you think they do? Besides, I just said... I thought it was you."

"Blood manipulation is an Acciperean ability, not a Darean one."

Nemina seemed unbothered, "I didn't know that either."

"Seriously?" I looked at her. "I mean...it's manipulating blood."

Nemina gave me a displeased look. "Right, thanks."

"But you can manipulate blood, I mean that's..."

Nemina looked at my face, clearly wishing for me to stop talking about the blood.

"Anyway...you killed someone?" I squinted at the Healer.

But Nemina answered for him.

Speaking over each other, answering each other's questions. These two were beyond help.

"One of those soldiers," she added, "As soon as they saw his face."

"Then you know why I killed him," the Healer said sedately. "It is the way it has to be."

Nemina frowned, but she knew he was right. So did I.

"So...urrr...does that mean, if we see your face, you'll kill us instantly too?" I asked.

The Healer was silent.

"Really?!" I sputtered out.

"It is the way it has to be," Nemina repeated his words, imitating the unfeeling way in which the Healer had uttered them.

The Healer's mouth twisted into a mixture of a smile and a sneer.

"If you are going to do it, make it as quick as you made it for him," she requested.

I raised my hand tentatively. "I'd truly prefer you didn't do it at all. I mean, you know I can keep my mouth shut so..."

Even though I couldn't see his face fully, the demeanour and body language of the Healer warned me to shut my mouth, now.

Nemina didn't notice anything strange, fortunately.

"What did you need?" I asked her, trying to alter the topic.

"Leave it," Nemina said dismissively.

"So...is that why you didn't want to see him?" I asked Nemina, pointing at the Healer. "Because he killed someone? I really didn't think that you, of all people, would have a problem with that so..."

Nemina let out a sharp sigh and turned to me.

I raised my hands up. "I just think that if we're going to work together that we should... you know...get everything out there and...you know...be honest with each other."

The Healer was watching me confusedly.

"He's like this, just ignore it," Nemina told him.

"That's not fair! It worked on you, didn't it?" I smiled and raised an eyebrow.

Nemina tutted and looked away.

"You didn't say no!" I laughed.

She shook her head, but the corner of her lips turned up slightly.

"My thigh," she said softly. "It's not fully healed."

"Is that it? You didn't want him to know? Seriously? He can heal it for you and—"

Nemina shook her head. "It will heal itself eventually...but..." She looked up at the Healer. "If he tries to heal it again, he'll use all his energy. I'm sure he's already exhausted it the first two times without saying anything. He can't just keep doing that over and over again. I can't take it all for myself."

A long stretch of silence passed, during which the Healer and Nemina stared at one another.

"You think I would have given it all to you?" the Healer asked, his voice tinged with genuine curiosity.

"I don't know."

"Ah, yes...you don't know anything," he smiled.

"That's a really ridiculous reason for—" I started.

Nemina side-eyed me.

"Why were you even standing all this time?"

"I get it! Alright!" she exclaimed.

"Don't know anything. That's true," I mumbled. "You don't know how to be sensible either."

"I'll leave now," she said, moving away.

The Healer stepped forwards. Nemina noticed and turned around.

*Will he? Tell her?*

She searched his half-covered face from side to side. "Yes?" She pressed.

He took something out of a place deep inside his cloak and held it out to her.

Green, glowing, bright, two of them,

Enoliths.

Nemina glared openly at his gloved hand.

"Why?" She sounded truly taken aback.

"In case a situation like Audra repeats itself."

"What... and you're going to stop whatever it is you're doing and answer my call instantly?" She smiled to herself, eyeing the Healer curiously.

The Healer was silent a moment before he replied.

"Take it."

Nemina wasn't foolish, she would, I knew now, do whatever she needed to do to increase her chances of survival. She didn't care about pride and so, she gently took the stone from his palms. Then without sparing him a second glance, walked out of the tent.

"Don't I get one?" I asked the Healer once she left.

He looked over his shoulder at me.

"Forget I asked, forget it," I cleared my throat. "I get it...she's...you're..."

The Healer said nothing.

"You know...I already know—"

"I do," he said before I could finish.

I already had a very vague sense of his appearance. I had seen parts of it when he had shown me his memories. But since they were from his perspective, I hadn't actually seen his face, only his hair, or his reflection in a sword.

But here I was, still alive.

"You just said you'd kill anyone who saw your face."

"Did I?" The corner of his lips curled up.

I frowned and thought back on the conversation. He was right. He hadn't. Nemina had just assumed it and he had...remained silent.

"You didn't correct her though. Why? Don't you want her to see your face?"

"No."

"Really...but—"

"It is not necessary," the Healer stated.

"Not sure that makes any sense...it feels...very important to me."

The Healer took a breath in and returned to his original position, sitting down.

Then, he raised both his hands to the sides of his face, to his hood. They halted there for a moment, as if he were unsure.

And then, he drew it back.

It was one thing to see glimpses of his appearance in vague and hazy memories and another to behold his face in reality.

He didn't even look human. If the Gods did exist, I imagined they would look exactly like him.

No, they definitely would.

The same colour as the enolith he had just given to Nemina, two large but slightly slanted green eyes met mine, framed by hair that had been hidden away.

Hair so long that it touched the floor.

Hair, tinged with a hint of gold, but so pale.

His face so delicate and long, just as his hands were.

*He does have a presence. Even Nemina wouldn't be able to deny it.*

But I couldn't even tell her.

And he didn't want to show her.

He took off one of his gloves and held his hand out to me.

I was still stupefied by his beauty and didn't even spare his hand a glance.

"Who are you? I mean...I don't recognise you...so... who?"

He chuckled and drew it back. Then, with his iridescent gemlike eyes still fixed upon my dazed ones, he replied.

"My name is Raviel."

## CHAPTER 72- ELIEL

Lady Dyna swallowed the food cautiously, taking small pieces at a time.

"Is it not to your tastes, My Lady?" I asked her.

Her cutlery clanked hard against her dish as she jerked her hand up in a defensive gesture. "No, Your Majesty, it's lovely, I just…I…" She looked down then back up at me quickly. "Apologies. You've set out such fine food…I just don't have much of an appetite."

I nodded with understanding. Neither did I.

This was the fourth person I had dined with in the space of less than two hours.

This was the final stage of the Courting Season. I would dine with each of the candidates one at a time, unaccompanied by their escorts. The idea was to permit the King or Queen a chance to converse with, and better understand the candidates before they made their final decision.

One meal, as if that would be enough. It wouldn't have surprised me if the truth behind the Lady's loss of appetite was nervousness. Not, due to my own presence, but because this meal was her final chance to make an impression on me.

It felt almost malicious to feign these interactions, to raise the Lady's hopes not high, but to any level at all, considering that as far as I was concerned, her age had automatically made her an unsuitable choice.

Not that this was the attitude of the nobles of the Court, or the Council. Some of them held the view that the Kalnasan Lady would be a good Queen, an ideal one.

By that, they meant that because of her age, she would be docile, easy to command and easier for them to influence.

But I had no interest in influencing any of these candidates, at all.

The Lady and I had already passed several minutes in conversation. Our time was nearly at an end.

As with all the candidates, the time of their meal was limited to half of an hour.

Dyna placed her cutlery down, wiping at her face with a handkerchief softly and hesitantly. She cleared her throat before speaking.

"Your Majesty. Regardless of the outcome I…wanted to thank you."

My face remained impassive, save for the slight arch of one eyebrow.

"Thank me?" I inquired.

She nodded. "For helping me, when I was sick, and for your promise."

I smiled at her gently.

"Your Majesty, I hope that you will allow me to ask, has there been any...progress?"

"On which matter, My Lady?" I placed my own drink down and shifted in my seat slightly.

"Both matters, Your Majesty," she half-whispered.

I sighed regretfully. The promise the Captain had requested had not been unexpected, considering Kalnasa's state, however, enacting it was another matter altogether. To provide that much aid to one Kingdom would take much time, and resources, and it would also be an issue with several nobles.

After the festival, I had heard many had spoken about the results of Thrice Dice, and that several were unhappy with the promise I had made. How, they had asked, would we afford it? Why should we save Kalnasa from their own destruction?

But not once had a wish granted through Thrice Dice been refused.

"With regards to the promise I made to the Captain," I started. "Such a request will take time. Trade has been blocked by...those protesting in Kalnasa's outer cities. We will need to negotiate with these groups and convey our intentions to them. Then, for such a large number of provisions to be gathered, agreed upon, and transported, a large meeting of the nobility across Vasara will need to take place first. It is being planned as we speak, but even then, My Lady, I cannot say how long that will take. In the meantime, I have instructed many merchants and suppliers to put aside at least five percent of their stores to be sent to the Palace, which I intend to pay for, and send onto Kalnasa, but until the grand meeting is held...it will likely not be enough. The instauration of Kalnasa will be...difficult."

I leant forwards, elbows on the table. Dyna blinked several times, clearly, she had not anticipated I would answer at such length.

While she was in a state of confusion, I continued, "Unfortunately, those searching have not found the culprit of your poisoning, but I am confident that matter will be resolved. And soon."

The Lady nodded. "Thank you, your Majesty. I understand that the promise you made is...challenging and that the Captain asked for much but, I hope you understand his reasons."

"I do, My Lady. You and he care greatly for your people. It was wise for the Captain to use such a chance to ask for something so ambitious."

Dyna smiled, chuckled slightly, and swallowed some of her drink. "Unlike Audra's Prince. I can't *believe* he only asked for a hairpin," she mumbled into her glass as she continued to sip.

I frowned in thought.

"It is certainly unusual," I replied.

"I—" Dyna opened her mouth to respond.

But the doors to our left opened. "Your Majesty, the time is up. The final candidate awaits."

Dyna rose and curtsied, spreading out the bottom half of her wine red dress. I nodded in acknowledgement. She swiftly drifted towards the doors which closed behind her.

Moments later they opened once again. I rose.

Loria stood unmoving, in front of the doors which had closed behind her. The dark dress which covered her arms but exposed her shoulders, only made her blend in with the shadows even more.

"Please, Your Highness…sit." I gestured at the seat opposite the table.

Loria smiled, half-heartedly. She walked out of the shade, wincing a little as the sun struck her, and shrouded the vision across her dark golden eyes, before regaining her composure, and sitting down.

I too sat down, once she was settled.

"You look wonderful," I stated.

Loria sat up straighter as some servants plated her food. I raised the fingers on my left hand from the table to refuse any more. Despite the fact I had eaten only minimal quantities with each meal, I was already full, overly so.

"As do you, Your Majesty," she returned the compliment.

"You'll have to forgive my impudence. Please feel free to enjoy whichever of the dishes you like. I've had my fill of them unfortunately." I glanced at the food.

Loria shook her head. "You are the King, you may do as you please, Your Majesty."

*You may do as you please.*

Many of the things I wished to do, things that might please me, were completely outside the capabilities of someone who occupied a throne.

At the thought, my lips curled up slightly.

"Do you truly believe so?" I asked her.

Loria's hand froze as she reached for her glass, her eyes meeting mine in the same instant.

She looked away and grabbed her drink hurriedly.

"You are right," she said after a long moment of silence, "Being a King has its limitations as well."

"As does being a Queen," I added.

Loria searched my face, as if looking for a hidden meaning behind my words.

"Yes… that is true," she said after a pause.

I watched her mannerisms, the way in which she slid her fingers around the chalice, the way she held the gold metal to her lips and cast her eyes downwards into the wine. Was she calm? Was she terrified? There was no way of knowing. She was like her brother in that regard, her emotions hidden too well.

"Have you enjoyed the season?"

"It has been…" she searched for a word, "Eventful."

I thought about her statement, the opening ceremony with Elias' arrival, the Coronation with the Vessel's assassination attempt, Lady Dyna's poisoning.

"You are right. My question was in poor taste. Considering everything that has happened, it would be impossible to enjoy it," I said thoughtfully.

She remained silent for some moments, not contradicting but not affirming the statement.

"It will be over soon, Your Majesty," she stated gently. Her voice was soothing, her attempt to console me obvious.

"I'm sure you are glad of that."

Loria smiled softly. "Whatever the outcome, you shall have a Queen. It is cause to celebrate."

"Especially if that Queen is not you?" I rested my chin upon my right hand.

Loria squinted. "You jest surely?" Her brows evened out. "I would be honoured, but I would be equally pleased for you, should you choose another, Your Majesty."

"I jest?" I raised an eyebrow. "Then what is it…that you are doing?"

A slight line between Loria's eyebrows formed. "What is it… you would like me to do?"

"This may be our last conversation. Wouldn't it be simpler if we could speak freely?"

"*Can* we speak freely?" Loria retorted instantly, almost reflexively.

I gestured around the room. "We are the only one's here."

Loria glanced around it doubtfully, as if she truly wondered whether that were the case, as if she expected someone to emerge from behind the curtains, at the edges of the windows.

"I asked you once, but you did not answer. Given the choice…would you have come here at all?" I asked.

Loria's eyes returned to mine. Her lips parted then closed.

She shrugged. "I cannot truly say what it is I wish for and what it is I feel compelled to do. I do not know which is obligation and which is want."

"What about the things you do not wish for? Surely you must know those?"

Loria's eyelashes flickered, "I suppose."

"And what… are they?" I leant further into my right hand.

Loria watched my movement, which must have appeared flippant and casual in manner to her.

"To be…confined, or…used."

"It could be argued that being a Queen involves both of those things."

"Not necessarily," Loria stated, "It depends on the King, does it not?"

"On a great deal more, unfortunately," I replied softly.

"You ask me difficult questions, Your Majesty." Loria looked down at her food, cutting it as she spoke. "If my answers are...vague, it is not because I do not wish to speak freely with you, but because I am unsure of their answer."

I watched her wrists and fingers move across the silverware.

"I think there is a great deal you are sure about. Why do you pretend otherwise?"

Loria's knife froze on her plate, but her wrists resumed their movements in less than a fraction of a second. "You think too highly of me, Your Majesty."

"It is not that I think too highly of you, only that others think too little."

Loria finished slicing the food on her plate into portions. However, instead of placing any in her mouth, she placed her cutlery crossed atop it, and looked up.

"It is easier that way, Your Majesty. I am sure you understand."

I raised my brows. I was surprised to hear her admit it.

"I imagine you think you are protecting yourself, by deceiving others as to your true level of comprehension and knowledge. Or that you believe if the expectations from others towards you are low, that you can never fail to meet them." My voice rose questioningly.

"Something akin to that," Loria subtly nodded.

"But if everyone constantly maintains low expectations of you, then you will begin to expect little of yourself, demand little, convince yourself you are no more than that which others have deemed you." I leant forwards deeply into the table. "Why would someone such as yourself wish to do that for the remainder of their existence? Wouldn't it be"— I paused, unintentionally, watching her apprehensive expression before finishing— "a waste?"

Loria smiled genuinely, blinking a few times. She seemed to have found my insinuation that such a way of life would be a 'waste' amusing.

"But I digress," I leant back. "It is our choice alone how we live with the circumstances we find ourselves in."

Loria was silent for a moment. "Your Majesty, I do not...mind if others believe it is a waste. Is it not better to live a life you choose, regardless of what others may believe of its value, than one which others deem worthy, but which you do not care for? Would the latter not be the *true* waste?"

The way she answered questions, the way she wove words had, from the first moment I had spoken with her, fascinated me, impressed me even.

"And is being Queen...one of those scenarios...that you would not care for?"

"No," Loria shook her head. "Not your Queen."

My lips parted in surprised at her response.

Loria noticed. "You said...that we could speak freely, Your Majesty."

I felt myself grin. "Yes, but I did not truly expect you to do so."

Loria smiled as well. "Such *low expectations* you have of me, Your Majesty."

I chuckled a little. "I already told you my expectations of you are not ones which you could fail to meet, but that is not because they are low."

"Then why, Your Majesty?" Loria pressed.

I watched her torso rise and fall in sharp breaths as she waited for my reply.

"Because...I feel I do not truly understand you. That makes you...interesting."

Loria frowned. "Can we truly understand anyone?"

I took a deep breath, narrowing my eyes and smiling slightly before I spoke. "Lady Dyna believes being Queen to be the salvation for her people, but she is wrong. Princess Maiwen, it is clear, has no interest in being Queen, nor does she seem to possess the temperament suitable for it. Princess Rhana is in love with someone else. I cannot say who, but it is obvious her heart lies elsewhere. While that doesn't seem to deter her from taking the throne by my side, it will invariably become a problem. The Lady Tarren is only interested in the idea of what being Queen could be, the title, the riches, the jewels, she has no knowledge of what it will truly entail. That is likely because her father, who was friends with my own, has no intention of informing her, lest that ruin the ardency at which she pursues this marriage. But you"—I breathed out slowly— "I do not truly understand."

"Some would say that is not a good thing, Your Majesty," she replied warily.

"Perhaps you are right. But it is...intriguing, and it means that any expectations I have had of you have constantly shifted, and risen."

"And what expectations are those, Your Majesty?"

I stood. Loria's head rose to meet my eyes and followed them as I walked down the length of the table and over to her seat.

I reached out my hand. It hovered near her cheek, not touching her, only tracing the outline of her oval shaped face through the air. The space between our skin prickled with an insistent energy. Wild and impatient. Persistent yet delicate. A charge, I knew, she too could feel, by the widening of her eyes.

Those eyes were fixed upon me, wondering, waiting, expectant.

My hand stilled before I answered.

"I expect you to say yes."

# CHAPTER 73- NATHON

The hall burst into a rapturous frenzy as the announcement was made, although I had already known the outcome.

Immediately after the final dinners had been conducted, Loria had told me we had succeeded. The King was to choose her to be his wife.

Her breathing had been rushed, but her face flushed with relief and satisfaction.

I could not, however, find it within myself to share her sense of fulfilment.

I could not quieten that part of me that wished we had failed. Our success only meant Sarlan's plan was one step further towards completion.

From our backs, we could feel all eyes upon us, more specifically, on Loria, who, despite knowing she was the subject of their curiosity, jealousy, and perhaps in the rare instance, congratulations, did not turn to acknowledge them at all. It was only when she met eyes with the King before us, that the corners of her lips turned upwards slightly, as did his.

To Loria's left was Princess Rhana, to my right the Lady Dyna. All the escorts and candidates stood in a line at the foot of the throne's platform.

The King rose from that seat. He took some steps forwards, still maintaining eye contact with Loria for a few moments. My eyes found her face again. She truly did look…pleased.

The King glanced over our heads at the audience. "The Courting Season has concluded. However, as you all know and remember, it has not been devoid of incident or danger. We thank the Gods that each candidate and escort remain alive and well."

"And His Majesty!" Someone from the crowd yelled.

"Aye! Thank the Gods!"

"Aye, aye!" a few more voices muttered.

Unlike Loria, the King seemed to meet all their eyes, and acknowledge them with light smiles.

"I am most grateful to those who have cooperated with us on this matter, and I am pleased to say" — the King looked down to my right — "that we have found the culprit responsible for the Lady's poisoning."

The Lady stiffened up beside me, taking in a sharp and high-pitched breath. Even without looking at her, I could sense her trembling, and could see, from the corner of my eye, the Captain's hand reaching out to steady her.

The King turned very slightly over his left shoulder and nodded. Moments later, a man was dragged out onto the platform on the space between the King and the candidates.

There was a sack over his head, dark red and silken, hiding his face, but it did not matter. The crowd gasped collectively. The identity of the man was already half revealed.

His uniform was as white as the marble stone of the steps the King descended. The King paused on them.

He reached forwards and pulled the sack off.

Beneath it, was the face of a young man, one of Vasara's trackers. His short brown hair was tousled in spikes, disorganised by the material that had been shoved over his head. His eyes darted around the room as he quickly ascertained where he was. He looked up and met eyes with the King who was regarding him coldly and unkindly.

The King's hand gently cupped the back of his head, leaving it there as he faced the audience again.

The tenderness of his hand's movement combined with the disdain in his eyes was...disturbing.

"We have discovered that this tracker, who calls himself Vykros, was working with rebel sorcerer groups. He has confessed to his crimes, including the attempted assassination of Lady Dyna."

*Confessed?*

This Vykros had likely been tortured for such information. Who knows what he might have 'confessed' under such circumstances?

I knew how easy it was to loosen the lips through such methods, not just in search of the truth, but of lies as well.

The man shook his head, his mouth agape. He took in the audience's judging, disgusted, and frightful glares. He appeared as if overcome by a sudden fit of fear, and interrupted the King as he attempted to speak again.

"NO! IT'S NOT TRUE!"

The King's jaw clenched as he slowly cast his head back down. "The things we found upon this tracker's person, and in his quarters, were clear evidence of his collusion. It pains me we have been betrayed. You are aware we go to great lengths to prevent such measures."

The King yanked the man's right arm up and pulled his sleeve down revealing the cursed mark I had heard bound trackers to their role.

"However, on closer inspection, we found that this tracker had nullified his curse. Only the sorcery of Healers can achieve such an effect, and only with great amounts of power."

*Healers?*

The Captain and I both remained facing forwards, but I had no doubt he and I were sharing the same thoughts.

The Healer the Captain had mentioned, the one who had cured Dyna.

This confirmed it. The man had actually been colluding with those sorcerers, but if they were truly responsible for Dyna's attempted assassination, why would the Healer have arrived to save her life?

It was possible, of course, that it had been part of the ploy, to gain the Captain's gratitude and trust, and that their intention had not been to kill the Lady, only to use her.

The crowd remained aghast, but there was the unmistakable feel of awe and delight in the air as well. Many people would revel in such a display.

And they called me a psychopath.

The tracker on the ground turned to the Lady, "It wasn't us. It wasn't!"

He must have known it was in the sorcerers interests to ally with the Captain. But whether his protestation of innocence was genuine, could not be determined by that goal of allyship at all. If they had done it, they would want to maintain the pretence they had not. If they hadn't, then they would wish to make that known.

In short, the man's declarations amounted to nothing.

The King pulled the man's arm back as he tried to inch forwards towards Dyna on his knees. "The punishment for this betrayal is death. The punishment for the attempted murder of a human is death."

While it was obvious the man was genuinely afraid, he only maintained his innocence. "I promise, I swear, My Lady, it wasn't me, it wasn't us!"

Dyna's eyes were wide with panic, she continued to shake beside me. The Captain remained unmoving, but I could only imagine the anger he felt at the possibility of the assailant being in front of him, and the confusion at whether he should believe his protestations of innocence.

"I, King Eliel Solisan, declare that you…"

As the King delivered his judgement, Lady Dyna mumbled under her breath, so softly, it was only possible for both the Captain and I, the two people directly beside her, to hear it.

"It wasn't him," the thin wisp of her voice travelled to our ears.

"It wasn't him," she said slightly louder this time.

She stood straighter, and I could tell from her body language, she meant to defend the man's innocence.

She made to move.

Without looking at her, I grabbed her wrist.

The Lady Dyna's age meant she wasn't well versed in the art of subtly. She opened her mouth confused and looked down at where my hand had grabbed her arm. I could feel the Captain's eyes on me as well. I didn't move.

Fortunately, the audience was in a state of confusion, distracted by the King's speech and this turn of events. Even if any of them were to notice my gesture, it could be anticipated as a way for me to prevent the Lady from acting rashly towards her perpetrator, letting the King's justice be done.

"What are you—" she began to say.

"Don't move." I barely parted my lips or made a sound as I instructed her, continuing to look forwards at the King.

The Lady, I could feel, turned to the Captain, who was no doubt aware of my actions. She looked at him questioningly. I could not see him fully, but whatever he did, gestured, or said to her, made her turn back to face me, and say even more quietly.

"Why?"

I only gave her a quick side glance which communicated the words.

*Don't speak anymore. Just do as I say.*

There were two reasons for this.

Firstly, a reason which the Captain would undoubtedly not care about, was that I was already under suspicion for Lady Dyna's poisoning. The death of another, even if he were innocent, would clear my name. Now, more than ever, I needed to remain under as little scrutiny as possible.

But the second reason, which had likely struck the Captain as well... was this. If this man had not committed this crime, if he truly were innocent, then the real culprit had likely been instrumental in framing him, perhaps even handed him over to the King, created false information regarding his involvement, or been the one to torture the 'confession' out of him.

If this death sentence were stopped, the culprit would only frame another, and his alertness, his guard would go up significantly, having had his first attempt at clearing his name fail.

But if this man were to die for his crimes, then the real culprit would believe himself free from suspicion, making it far easier for us to detect them, and discover their true identity.

Better to let them think they had succeeded and catch them in the midst of their delusion, than know they had failed and chase them through the shadows. After all, the more you tried to swat a flea, the more it leapt around. It was only if you approached it carefully and quietly, that you could convince it of safety, before you crushed it with your palm.

Many who operated this way were nothing more than those fleas, jumping from one carcass to the next. They branded me the Bird of Death while they lay eggs amongst the ruins, running at the first sight of danger. They believed this protected them. But I had seen enough of their like to know it only made them predictable.

However, while this thought had come to me instantly, and it was not beyond the Captain's capabilities for it to arrive to him at once as well, I was surprised he would also be willing to let this man die for the sake of our plans.

The Captain, who seemed the very embodiment of morality.

The Captain, who had implored me just days ago, not to frame an innocent for his own actions.

The Captain, who had also told me there was much I did not know about him, that he was not the pillar of righteousness I implied him to be.

"Let it be known," the King's voice rang out, pulling me from my thoughts, "That such crimes will never be allowed to transpire without consequence. That we protect our people from those who would harbour us ill will. Let it be known" — the King took some more steps forwards, so that he was even closer to the man kneeling on the ground— "that we will not fall."

The King raised one finger on his left hand, a signal to someone.

Within seconds, the mark on the man's arm, which had clearly been re-applied, began to move under his skin. Its dark black ink turned into a scorching red. It bled into his wrist and sprawled rapidly through his veins.

He wailed and clutched at his right arm with his left hand. The intensity of the spread grew, and his skin began to wither away, along with bone, simply disappearing into the air. At first one finger, then another, the remnants floating before him, landing on the white ground like dark ash.

The King watched, not a trace of emotion or discomfort in his eyes. There was not the perverse fascination the crowd held. There was not the discomfort the other candidates displayed, shifting anxiously on their feet, or the terror in Dyna's eyes…there was simply nothing.

Both he and I…did not react at all.

I, because I had seen far worse.

He…I could not say.

As the man's arm began to shatter in the same way, he stumbled forwards towards Dyna. The King did not intervene, he only watched. The tracker barely made it two steps before his right leg also began to disintegrate into nothing as well.

"It wasn't me…it…" The right side of his face began to disappear.

Dyna's breaths had turned rapid, shuddering in and out.

The man grew closer, reaching out his last remaining arm. It was now only metres away from the Lady's own.

"I…I…" Dyna started, "This…isn't…"

I gripped her wrist slightly harder, reminding her she should remain quiet.

"I'm…I…I'm sorry," she said, as he was now only inches away.

"It…wasn't…nghh…m…mee," he garbled.

Tears fell down Dyna's cheeks.

The man was now directly in front of us, almost translucent.

"I know," Dyna whispered in that same quiet voice.

But it was enough for the man to hear.

He dropped his arm. His brow, or what was left of it, relaxed, and then, he instantaneously became dust at our feet.

We stared at the remnants of the once living man. Dyna's tears fell into the pile of ash, wetting it, darkening it even further.

My hand remained on her wrist.

"I…know…" she mumbled again.

Weeks ago, this platform had been tainted in blood.

Now it was tarnished in ash, and in tears.

*"Let it be known,"* he had said.

I looked up and found the King watching us.

And for the first time since I had arrived, I felt it keenly and undeniably. That of all the things my father had been wrong about, and they were numerous and many, that calling this man conceited and inexperienced, an easy target…

Was perhaps the grandest lapse of judgement he had ever made.

# CHAPTER 74 - SHADAE

Lord Elias hadn't shown up.

It hadn't been 'later' our trip to retrieve the sword had been planned. It had been days later.

Only now, Elias wasn't coming.

Well, it didn't matter to me. Not having to spend another moment around him was hardly distressing.

Still, I had received a note that I was to go to the forge and retrieve this blade for him, alone. I was in all honesty, stunned he had trusted me with the task.

Only then I had remembered, that if I decided to inform anyone about it, it would benefit me in no way whatsoever.

I scowled to myself at the thought, as the carriage he had left me rode along. There was nothing he could instruct me to do that I could disobey, and he'd even had the audacity to let me do a task alone. His confidence in his authority was so strong he didn't even feel the need to accompany me anywhere.

*Wonderful. It's not as if I've been attacked numerous times for being a sorcerer whenever we've ventured anywhere together. Journeying alone is completely safe no doubt.*

I tutted and frowned again. The fact Elias had needed to intervene during any of those instances irked me. I wanted to be able to defend myself.

*Why get picky about my defences? If the Lord is willing to stop someone from punching me in the face, why should I get stubborn about that?*

*But still, I can do this. Perhaps he's expecting me to return from this trip on my knees, humbly thanking him for his company, making grand declarations about how ill-advised I was to take it for granted.*

*So, I can't defend myself, but I can...run away if I need to.*

I grunted out loud, remembering the times Elias had been walking so fast I hadn't been able to keep up with him.

*Alright so what if I'm not fast at running? I'll manage. I'll figure it out. Don't be expecting me to come grovelling, Lord who wishes not to be called Lord, Elias.*

I sighed, it was hopeless. I was probably going to get mortally wounded on this trip.

*All that talk about not doing anything if I said something you disagreed with...it's as easy as sending me on an errand alone...you wouldn't even have to lift a finger to kill me. Coward.*

I stopped myself. Why was I getting so irritated about this?

Fundamentally, going in search of a sword alone was still more preferable to working in a large group of other trackers with the likes of Vykros. I hadn't seen him for days which meant the next time I was working with the trackers again, we would definitely be scheduled to work together.

The carriage stopped outside a small, forested area. A place of such dense greenery was incredibly rare in Vasara. Then again, knowing this little piece of land belonged to Elias' family, made it understandable.

I got out, glancing around at the paths. They were slightly gravelled, the sun forming incandescent spots along them as it pierced through the leaves of the trees.

An older woman shuffled towards me. "You're Shadae?"

She was dressed in unassuming clothing, and covered with a dark red, slightly rose-coloured shawl.

"I am," I replied. Since I was wearing my uniform, there was absolutely no purpose to denying my identity.

"He told me you'd be coming."

*I see, not entirely alone then. At least, not in the sense where I'm trusted to fulfil a task without betraying you, only still in the sense that if I were attacked, I'd end up a bloody heap amongst this gravel. It's not as if this old woman can defend me, unless she was secretly a trained warrior in her youth.*

"I'm Agnesa. I used to serve the Lord Gillion."

I nodded, understanding that Lord Gillion must have been Elias' father.

"I've kept the house ever since and the surrounding properties." She smiled proudly to herself.

*Looking after the house of a dead person...why?*

The woman must have noticed the expression on my face and furrowed her brows slightly. "It's an honour for me and Lady Erilia pays me well."

*Well, now it makes sense. If you offered me money to look after the house of a dead person nobody was occupying, I'd agree instantly.*

I smiled and nodded. "Of course, I'm sure she is glad that you stayed."

Agnesa, who was clearly both easily flattered and offended smiled again, the wrinkles around her eyes tightening, her brown hair tinged with grey bouncing in the bun she'd placed it in.

"It's this way." She walked forwards, slowly.

*At least I can keep up with you.*

*No, in fact, you're probably fitter than I am, I'll probably still struggle.*

"I've prepared a room."

I side-eyed her, my eyebrows flattening.

"A room?"

She nodded without looking at me. "Two actually, I thought the Lord might be coming as well but—"

"I didn't realise that...I'd be staying."

The woman smiled at me gently, her small eyes closing over as she did. "Usually, the Lord likes to stay here for a while when he comes, so I just assumed."

"Oh...well, if it's alright with you, I'll probably leave once I've finished here."

The woman's face fell.

*Offended again? How come when people spit at my feet, and call me a slut, and a piece of trash, I have to remain impassive? But you get to be throwing around facial expressions like that because I don't want to sleep under this roof?*

"If you wish," the woman replied in a clipped tone.

*Maybe she's lonely, but no, even if she were, she wouldn't view a sorcerer's lack of company as a loss, would she?*

We approached a small wooden structure, the door of which was tall and sturdy. A dark thick keyhole made of metal lay at its centre. The woman took out a chunk of keys, and placed one in the lock, opening it.

Inside, dust floated through the air, catching colours under the sunlight. The wooden slats on the floor were coated in it. All around the tables, the walls and the shelves, were a variety of weapons, and papers strewn about.

As I examined my surroundings, the woman walked over to a box, and took out another key. Once I realised what she was doing, I joined her at her side, just in time for its lid to open.

The blade inside was the largest and longest I had ever seen. It reflected the sunlight so harshly it seemed to radiate. The handle was long, golden, and decorated in a winding vine like pattern. The engraving was scarlet and travelled along the sword's face.

And there it was...the mark, small, but branded into the blade clearly, the dark red standing out against the bright silver.

"How is it...this clean?" Was my first thought. "Have you—"

"No," the woman anticipated my question. "This is the first time it's been open in...years."

"How many?"

"Since he died. Twelve."

Twelve years. That would have made Elias surely no older than fifteen? Sixteen? when his father died, judging by his appearance.

"How is that possible?" I murmured to myself.

"Mmmmm," the woman hummed. It instantly reminded me of Elias.

*So that's where he got his hmmming from.*

I reached out to touch the blade, the mark more precisely, but my hand hovered above it cautiously. I frowned, disturbed.

"You've seen it before?" the woman asked curiously.

I didn't know if this woman was someone deemed worthy of possessing the knowledge around Elias and I's activities. I remained silent.

"I haven't," she told me. "I thought it was just an emblem of some kind. But...then Harlin told me about Elias' request."

"Most people would think that. It looks harmless," I told her.

"Still, I should have known," the woman murmured to herself bitterly.

"How could you have?" I turned to the left, looking at her.

She sighed, placing one hand in front of the other, and faced me.

She pulled up her sleeve.

The Curse of Servitude. The Tracker's mark.

My eyes widened and returned to her face instantly.

"You—"

She nodded. "For fifteen years."

"Then...how did you...end up here?"

"A long time ago. I saved his son's life. He thanked me by offering me this position."

I looked from side to side, my mind was engulfed with endless thoughts.

"You...saved Lord Elias's life?"

She nodded.

"Does he know that?"

She shook her head.

"Why?"

"It was a condition. I was not to tell him, at all costs."

I furrowed my brow. Why thank someone by stripping them of their responsibilities as a tracker, actively acknowledging the weight of their deed if...

I realised.

"He didn't want anyone to know why—"

She smiled tightly and raised her eyebrows, nodding yes again.

"Officially, I was Lord Gillion's 'Guardian' they called it," she explained. "It is permissible, in rare instances, for those nobles who wish to have a tracker follow them at all times, ready to defend them against any sorcerers who may attack."

"I've never heard of that...of a Guardian," I said quietly.

"That's because they're very rarely appointed. Most wouldn't trust a tracker to live by their side."

"What's your class?" I asked her, changing the topic.

In response the woman closed her eyes. The soil beneath us trembled, parts spouted through the floorboards, rolling across the floor, scuttling.

Then, the shaking abated in an instant.

Darean. Class three.

Elementalist.

"Only earth?" I asked. I knew most Elementalists could control two elements at least.

"Fire and wood are a poor match," she explained, gesturing to the wooden structures around us.

I huffed in agreement. I would prefer she didn't burn us alive.

On second thought, staying here, and spending an evening speaking with this woman, didn't seem so torturous after all.

I reached for the sword's hilt and grabbed it out of the box.

My arm fell to the ground instantly.

"Shit!" I swore under my breath.

The woman watched me amused. "You're not used to handling weapons? How long have you been a tracker for?"

"Not long," I muttered, wincing at the pain in my wrist. "I *have* handled weapons just not one this...heavy."

With great effort, I placed it back in the box, and lifted it up, a sheen of sweat forming on my forehead.

I held it across my chest, manoeuvring it many times before it lay across my arms in a way that was at least, somewhat manageable.

The woman was frowning in my direction. "What class are you, dear?"

"Four. I'm a..." the box shifted in my arms again. "Navigator."

The woman chuckled. "That makes sense. That boy is terrified of us. A Navigator seems harmless enough to him."

I had already guessed the reasoning behind my selection. But I had thought Elias was suspicious of, untrusting of sorcerers.

Not, that he was terrified of them.

"But he...lived...with you?" I was still struggling under the weight of the blade, breathing heavily.

"Yes. But it wasn't just the fact I saved his life he was unaware of. He never knew who I was. His father never told him."

*Did his father tell him anything?*

But then I recalled what Elias had said. His father was unwell, erratic, his moods unstable.

But his father had saved, or at least, helped this sorcerer before me, given her a better life...

I mentally decided that such a man was worth having faith in, at least...for now.

"Why are you telling me?" I realised the weight of her revelation.

She sighed slowly and shrugged. "The Lord Gillion is dead now and, well, you won't tell Lord Elias, will you?"

*How do you know? I just might.*

She scanned my face and chuckled without mirth, "He wouldn't believe you, child."

*Well, that's probably true. His faith in me is hardly absolute.*

During my silence, Agnesa spoke again. "Elias loved him very much. He was devastated when he died." She looked at the ground sadly. "And his mother...she hasn't been the same since."

"I...met her," I said. "She...wasn't too happy with my...presence."

The woman laughed coldly. "Yes, that woman already bore a deep hatred for sorcerers while her husband lived, let alone after he died."

I weighed the advantages and disadvantages of asking the next question.

I glanced down at the box. "How did...he die? What is it that he did...with this?"

The woman squinted, but then sighed, sitting down at the table a few steps away.

"He was stationed at a fortress on the outskirts of Vasara." Her voice was both flat yet full of melancholy as she answered. "It was during a time where the activities of the rebel sorcerers were much more widespread and public. You must understand that he had done this *thing* many times before and he was not...entirely well."

She gulped before continuing. "He was meant to defend them, the humans who were living behind that fortress...but in the end...he...with that" — she nodded in the direction of the box — "he slaughtered an endless number of people. In a fit of madness, they say. Some suggested a Telepath forced him to do it, but...there were no traces of sorcery or its energy anywhere on his body afterwards."

She rubbed her hand over her mouth, clearly finding it difficult to discuss this subject. A pang of guilt pressed on my chest for asking.

"Then, he stabbed himself in the chest. They found him at the fortress, surrounded by all the bodies, pierced on his own blade, kneeling on the ground."

Newly horrified by the object in my arm, I grimaced, and looked back down at it.

A newfound understanding of Elias' words dawned upon me. He had believed, or at least, most had believed that his father's nature simply leant itself to a breakdown which culminated in him taking his own life, and the lives of countless others.

Nobody suspected anything else, not after no traces of sorcery were found on his body.

But, if this sword did bear this mark, then it was possible that somehow, the influence of this figure, this person, whoever it was, had seeped into his mind, in a way which had not been detectable.

"His wife blamed it on sorcerers, of course." Agnesa sighed. "According to her, it was the deeds he had witnessed sorcerers do, that drove him to insanity. Elias he...well, he was never one to go along with what others said but...what other explanation was there?"

She glanced at me hopefully. "You think it's the sword, don't you?"

I nodded slightly, it felt wrong to refuse her the confirmation, after she had just told me so much.

She smiled, her lips wobbling slightly. "I hope you're right. I never believed it when...I never believed it."

*You don't know what you're saying. If we're right, and this blade is cursed, if Gillion's actions were the result of this...thing, then it's far worse than you could imagine.*

"I need to take it to him now," I said.

Agnesa stood. Her body brushed against some papers on the table as she extended her hand out towards me, and patted my upper arm.

"Be careful, girl and...look after him, will you?"

*What? I absolutely will not look after him! He'll probably kill me the first chance he gets no matter what he says. It would be like looking after your own executioner, making sure their blade is sharp enough to slit your throat. I'm not completely foolish!*

I opened my mouth to speak, but decided against it, she was looking at me so optimistically.

*You're a sorcerer and you're asking me to look after him? Gillion's generosity has made you too hopeful...*

"He's a good man you know," she stated, looking to the side.

*If you say so...*

But, despite my internal scrutiny, I couldn't find any mental evidence to suggest he was a bad one either.

Was he wrong for not doing more for sorcerers? For us?

Was I lying to myself about the ease at which he could lift a hand to change it all?

Was he simply as stuck as I was?

I shook my head suddenly. Too many questions. Too confusing. But still one escaped my lips.

"How...did you save his life?"

Agnesa let out a small chuckle. "That...is too long a story for us to discuss here and now. You must get back to the Lord."

I nodded, as I did, my eyes fell on the table, at the papers on it.

"What...are those?" I gestured at the symbols sprawled across the paper, stepping closer to the table. I leant forwards, although the box limited my movement.

Agnesa came to my side. "The marks they found on their bodies."

"Whose bodies?" I continued to examine the drawings carefully.

"The King's and the Queen's," she answered as if it were completely obvious. "The former...King. Elias saw them. He came back here and drew them, I think he hoped that they"— she waved her hands over the papers — "would help in the search for their killers, the sorcerers who did this."

"They're…" I leant forwards further, to be sure.
The woman leant forwards too, to glance at my face.
"They're what? Do you know which curse this is?" Her voice rose expectantly.
"That's just it," I turned to meet her eyes. "This isn't a curse at all."
The woman's eyes widened frantically.
My voice dropped. "This isn't sorcery."

# CHAPTER 75 – HESTAN

"It looks the same," Dyna observed as we approached the border.

"There is no way to tell from here," I reminded her.

Her face twisted painfully. "But surely," she cut herself off, grabbing her reins tighter. "You're right," she whispered, "I only wish we could have returned sooner. All of this has been for nothing."

I thought about the note, the Healer, the Prince.

It had not all been for nothing, far from it.

But it had nearly cost us both our lives, at one time or another.

"We came as soon as we could. Your father and your uncle will know of your efforts." I smiled at her.

It was true, we had left before sunrise this morning, when the Palace was hushed, the air still cool.

Dyna pursed her lips, her eyelids lowering.

"I...hope so." She sighed deeply. "I wish I'd had the opportunity to say farewell. To some of the others, I mean."

"They won't be aggrieved, My Lady. I am sure several of them have departed as well."

"Some will stay for the wedding, will they not?"

I nodded. "Some."

Dyna shuddered. "On second thought... Perhaps it is for the best. I'm not sure I could have stood to see the look on that Prince's face as he bid us farewell."

I chuckled under my breath.

I thought about how the Prince might have looked, what he might have said. A teasing smile, a probing remark. A parting gift perhaps. Something ridiculous.

I would see the Prince again. Of this, I had no doubt. There was no need for farewells between us.

We came closer to the gates of the outer city. Some of the armed guards who had arrived to accompany us back began to ride ahead.

"My Lady, Sir, it will be better if we ride ahead of you as well."

Dyna and I cast a glance at once another.

"Why, may I ask?" I said.

The guard hovered near us as the others got into formation.

"For your safety, Sir. You will see."

With that, he jolted his horse forwards, joining the others.

Dyna's face was cast with fear.

"Ride closer to me, My Lady." I gestured for her to close the gap between our horses some more.

She did as I asked, peering anxiously around her.

Moments later the gates opened.

Nothing.

It was not that there was nothing which amounted to the threat to our safety the guard had alluded to. It was that there was nothing at all.

It was utterly silent. Normally, there would have been people bustling around, even this close to the gates at the outer border. But there was only the howl of eerie silence, carried by the breeze, and the rustle of stones and leaves, being pushed along the ground.

"Where is everyone?" Dyna mumbled.

I took in the scene around me, the grey cobbled road, the small and inexpensive houses, the alleyways the...

The bodies.

A family of four had hung themselves outside of their home.

A couple, huddled in an alleyway, dead in each other's grip.

A young man, who could be hardly older than Dyna, collapsed outside his front door, his face grey, his lips blue.

Disjointed sobs escaped Dyna's lips.

"Get those bodies down! Don't you have a brain? The Lady is here you fool!" One of the guards shouted to the gate's attendants, some of whom were now escorting us as well.

The man nodded and agreed meekly, shuffling over to scale the roof of the family's home, and cut down their bodies with his blade.

Dyna watched as he did.

"My Lady, look away." I tried to get her attention.

But she didn't turn around, only replied, facing away from me.

"What would be the use now?" Her broken voice was shattering.

I couldn't think. It was as if her question had wiped my grasp of vocabulary from my mind.

What would be the use? Such images, once seen, could not be wiped away by the closure of your eyes.

At times, closing them only made them even brighter, clearer.

Dyna had already seen far too much for someone of her age.

I frowned, recalling the scenes I myself had witnessed, six years her junior.

And all the scenes since.

"Oi! You little brat...get back here!"

My head snapped around. One of the guard's fists was clenched tightly around the collar of a figure standing by his horse.

The figure was a child.

The child's jade pale skin looked even more stark against his slit dark blue eyes, which he averted, refusing to make any eye contact. Some of his dark matted hair was also caught in the guard's clutch.

In response to the boy's silence, the guard jerked his collar even harder. The child let out a small yell, and tripped over his own feet, falling to the ground, his palms scraping against the stone.

A small coin pouch emerged from the boy's right hand.

The boy trembled, his face pressed into the dirt, but still, he gripped that coin pouch as tightly as possible.

The guard dismounted, he raised his foot and went to kick the boy away. The boy curled up into himself, anticipating the strike.

But it never came.

The guard drew his foot back and narrowed his eyes at me.

"Captain. You're not defending this thief, are you?" His words were laced with disdain.

I smiled tightly. "Sir, you're not assaulting a child a fraction of your size...are you?"

The guard huffed and spat on the ground at my feet.

"Captain, maybe the rumours are true? The Hunt was keeping all the goods for themselves"—he eyed the boy behind me — "and the coin."

"This child is not part of the Hunt."

"Ha. That's right. That would be impossible." He grinned unkindly.

"Sir?" I asked.

"The Hunt no longer exists...and you're no longer a Captain."

I made no sign this revelation disturbed me. It most certainly did, but there was a part of me that had predicted this outcome.

I swallowed and cast a brief glance at my feet before meeting the guard's eyes again.

"This child is only hungry," I stated.

The guard turned to look at another two men behind him. Slowly, one by one, they all cast glances at one other.

And erupted into laughter.

I clenched my fists behind my back, watching them. I did not turn around, but I could feel the boy behind me approaching, growing closer to my back.

The boy grabbed one of my clenched fists with his own small hand. I swivelled my head over my shoulder, looking down, but the boy did not meet my eye, only glared at the guards with disapproval.

This close, I could see just how small he was, but because of his state of starvation, it was hard to estimate his age. He could have been five, or ten.

The guard finally spoke again. "Hungry, is he?" He jabbed a finger in the boy's direction. "What right does a skinny mutt like him have to take our money? What about our bellies? Our hunger? Huh? The blight in this place doesn't exclusively apply to children. There's no time for charity here." He spat the words out aggressively, spittle jumping through his teeth.

"What did *time* ever have to do with it?" I asked flatly.

The man clapped his hands together as if amused. "I get it. You're one of those. Feel free to starve to death after giving all your money and food to the little ones then. Ha."

"If everyone thought the same way you do Sir, your gold pouch wouldn't exist at all. After all, somebody still pays you," I reminded him.

"That's because I earned it!" The guard stepped closer to me. At this, Dyna, who had been watching from a distance atop her horse, got off it.

I shook my head no. She should stay where she was.

"This brat, what did he do, huh? Nothing!"

"He's a child. What is it that you *expect* him to do, Sir?" My irritation grew every time he spoke, rekindled anew with his obtuse selfishness.

"Give me my money back, that's what!" He half-jumped on the spot, pressing his heels up off the ground, "And receive the punishment that he deserves."

"There will be no punishment." I iterated every word clearly, enunciated them precisely.

The guard raised his brows. "Won't there now?" He turned around to his men. "You hear that lads, no punishment!"

Some of the men laughed along with him, a minority looked slightly uncomfortable.

"How about you take it for him then?" the guard said.

Dyna strode forwards then, purposefully, her face twisted in determination.

"Sir! Have you forgotten who you are speaking with? Even if the Hunt is no more, the Captain has been the reason you have filled your own stomach for years! Have some respect!" Her nostrils flared from anger, but I could see the trembling of her arms as well.

The guard, faced with a descendant of the King, seemed a little less agitated suddenly.

"My Lady, I respect him very much." He eyed me mockingly, "But also I respect the King's justice…your uncle's justice."

The false demureness in his voice was so painfully obvious that even Dyna, who was usually oblivious to such things, noticed it.

"My Uncle would be appalled if he heard of your actions! The boy will give you your money and that will be the end of it."

The guard thought for a few moments then bowed. "Yes, My Lady."

Dyna turned to me and the boy. I faced the child, he glared at me imploringly, silently begging for my intervention.

"It's alright," I said quietly so that only he could hear. "I'll give you some of my money later."

The boy blinked multiple times but still refused to let go of the pouch.

"And some food," I added.

The boy's brows loosened at that promise.

I reached over and gently removed the pouch from his grasp.

I stretched out my arm, the guard came and snatched the pouch from my palm. Dyna nodded and walked away.

"And the boy is travelling with me," I called out.

The guard laughed, pocketing the pouch deeper within his clothing.

"You can't be serious. You wish for us to travel with a thief?"

"Sir, you have my word, should the boy attempt to steal from another, then I will take his punishment in full."

The man's eyes glittered with satisfaction.

In my haste, I had spoken too rashly. That statement, I now realised, was a mistake. It would be easy for any one of the guards to feign a lost object, some stolen money. It would be easy for them to create an excuse to punish me now.

"Oh really? And what if he does, what then?" The guard arched a brow.

"Then he and I will travel the rest of the way alone."

"What about the Lady?"

"I trust you will bring her to safety."

There was no way they could not. Despicable as they were, they had been tasked with Dyna's safe arrival, and they could not risk the King's wrath should they fail.

The guard tilted his head looking down at the boy. The boy drew closer to me as he did, now clutching my entire forearm.

"He's very attached to you, isn't he?" The guard probed.

I didn't reply.

"I wonder how long it will be before he's just meat in someone else's stew."

Without taking my eyes off the guard, I reached out and placed my hand over the boy's ears drawing him closer to my side.

"Yours perhaps, Captain?" His suggestive voice drifted as he walked away, chuckling to himself.

I removed my hand and looked down at the boy.

"No more stealing, or I'll be punished," I said.

He nodded enthusiastically.

I took his hand and led him to my horse, placing him in front of me and my saddle, before I mounted it as well.

The boy said nothing, he had bandages around his wrists, which were dirtied and frayed. He rubbed at them silently, peering around him nervously.

The company grew quiet, and combined with the barren nature of our surroundings, an illusion of calm was in the air. But it was only that.

I wondered who the boy was, what his name was, what had happened to him, where his family were. But it was clear he was in no mood to speak, and I didn't wish to pry his worst memories from him.

We rode for a while longer. At some point, noises stretched towards us. Clamouring and brittle in nature, urgent and aggressive.

After the outer city and its villages, came the Central City, Celion.

Normally there would be guards here, soldiers that the King had deployed to keep watch at the gates.

Now, there were indeed individuals standing at the gates, but they were not the King's guards.

Three men and one woman, all armed with a variety of weapons approached us. Behind them, a mob of people hovered, outside their homes, around posts and pillars, watching us with darkened expressions.

"Let us pass, woman," the lead guard spoke again, addressing the female at the front of the group.

The woman quirked a brow, her eyes flicking over our company quickly. They rested upon me and the boy for a brief second, her mouth twitching slightly.

"I don't think so," one of the men from behind her said.

"It's been too long since we've seen you lot out of that Palace," a second one replied, his long dark hair tied back.

"You must have seen us leave," the guard replied angrily.

The woman at the front of the group shrugged, narrowing her silver eyes. "There was no reason for us to stop you from leaving. You could have left at any time, we couldn't predict that."

She took a step closer.

"But we could predict your return. Easier to greet you that way." She batted her eyelashes mockingly.

"I won't warn you again, woman. Let us pass or I'll cut you and your friends down."

The woman pressed her tongue against her lower lip and raised her eyebrows disbelievingly. "You won't have the chance."

The horses became uneasy, as if sensing the danger, the imminent threat all around us.

"What is it you want?" I asked the woman.

She drew her eyes away from the guard and towards me.

"I recognise you."

"He was the Hunt's Captain, most people recognise him," the guard interjected.

"Isn't it obvious what we want?" The woman ignored him. "We want to eat. We want what her uncle has." She pointed exaggeratedly at Dyna.

"We don't have much food on us," I replied warily.

The woman waltzed towards my horse with confidence. "You misunderstand me. You and your envoy will stay here. We're taking you, holding you hostage if you will. One of you can go and report the incident to the King. And they'll tell him" — she rested her elbow on my saddle. The boy in front of me flinched away from her slightly— "that either he releases some of his food stores, that he meets with us to discuss our *starvation,* or we will start sending him a fresh corpse each day. And once we get to his niece, we'll start with her fingers, then her toes, then—"

A sword was plunged straight through her mouth. She choked on her own blood and coughed it up, straight onto my leg, and onto the boy's side.

I yanked at the reins, and pulled the horse to the side. My face contorted in horror. The boy's eyes were wide with terror.

The guard she had been conversing with just seconds before, wiped blood off the back of his face as he yanked his sword out.

Chaos erupted within seconds.

The villagers were plunging toward us, loathing in their eyes.

I frantically swivelled my head around in search of Dyna. She had already begun to ride ferociously into the distance, a few of the guards following her.

But it wasn't long before several of them fell to the ground, with arrows and knives in their backs.

Amidst the confusion, my horse gave out from under me, and threw myself and the boy forwards. I reached out and grabbed my arms around him, twisting in the air to land on my back, and cushion his fall.

The horse partially landed on top of my lower legs, I let out a groan at the pain, which was especially piercing in the leg that had already been injured, the one that was already scarred.

The horse's legs had been slit, and approaching me now, was a man, a sword hung by his side, covered in thick blood.

I shoved the boy to the side and dragged myself from out under the horse's legs. I just managed to grab my spear on time to block the blow the man had directed at my head.

I had barely stood on aching legs before he attacked again. I spun the spear in front of me, defending myself once more.

I had no interest in killing these people.

But as the man charged at me for a third time, unbridled rage in his reddened face, I realised with crushing clarity, that I may not have a choice.

The boy stood behind me, crouching as if ready to attack someone, watching and waiting.

The man before us yelled and lunged forwards for my head again. I ducked and rose, thrusting my spear forwards, intending to disarm him.

Instead, he produced another sword and trapped my spear between it. It wobbled and vibrated under the strain of two blades crushing it from each side.

At that moment, my gaze scurried around. All before me, a flurry of people, even children were fighting. Several villagers were dead. Several guards were dead. There was the distinct smell of guts, and the iron tang of blood in the air. The sound of metal clashing on metal, of the wild screams of those intent to kill, and the agonised ones of the mortally wounded and dying. The cries of the mothers who knelt by their children's bodies, of the children who knelt by their fathers.

The man pressed down further, intending to break my spear in half. I freed myself by jumping off the ground, spinning in the air to the side, and landing on my feet, crouched.

I got up. He went for my torso. I blocked his strike and hit him in the face with my other hand, now clenched into a fist. He grabbed his bleeding nose and looked up at me, shocked. With his bloodied fingers, he reached for my neck. I jerked back and swung my spear from top to bottom diagonally, striking at his legs. He fell to the ground.

I kicked him back and rested my foot on his chest. He struggled, and attempted to get up, but I struck him hard in the face with my heel. He fell unconscious.

The boy was watching me in half-awe, half-petrification. I ran over and grabbed his hand, pulling him with me as I said, "You need to hide! Go!"

I let go, but the boy refused to do the same.

"You'd be safer with them not us," I insisted urgently, having to raise my voice over all the noise.

The boy still gripped me tightly. Then his eyes widened, looking over my shoulder.

I turned, a woman, who was also wielding a spear, had been inches from piercing me through the neck. I smacked her weapon away with my own. She tried to raise it back up again, but before she could, someone, another villager ran into her, making her lose her balance. She fell onto her face.

I stepped back, pressing the boy back as well. We watched on as the villager who had knocked my attacker to the ground, was followed by many others, who all snapped, and grabbed at his clothing.

He was pressing something close to his chest.

"I found it! It's mine!"

"We've got children! We all need to eat!"

"That's right you have to share some!"

"Why should I? WHY SHOULD I? HAHAHAHA." The man's wide eyes were fixed on the bundle in his arms.

Another woman stepped forwards. A baby was cradled in her left arm. She lifted her fist, and with a kitchen knife, stabbed the man in the eye.

He wailed, he screamed incorrigibly, but still with one hand, he gripped the bundle ardently, only using the other to stop his bleeding.

He was still screaming as he tried to run away.

The woman who had been holding her baby, a vacant look in her eyes, a hollowness to her cheeks, reached out and grabbed his hair, pulling him back.

Someone else standing in front of the man reached out, ready to take the bundle from his arms. The woman's eyes widened as she watched, as she realised her perceived prize would go to someone else. But she only had one hand.

She discarded her baby, practically threw it to the ground.

Within seconds, its muffled cries were halted as it was trampled over.

Not one person stopped. Not one person spared a second thought for the new-born.

I instinctively pressed the boy and myself further back, my eyes widening, but we couldn't escape this place, this scene.

The woman gritted her teeth and grabbed the package from his hands. The now half-blinded man reached out screaming, trying to retrieve the food back, but he couldn't see. The woman tried to run away, but the villagers followed her still, fighting amongst themselves. Some drawing weapons.

They grabbed at her skirts and she fell to the ground, the food leaping from her palms.

Still, she didn't make a sound as they walked over her back and crushed her skull, as they clawed at the small package, huddling over it, stretching it, grabbing as much as they could from its meagre contents.

In the distance, the small figures of Dyna and one guard could be made out, higher up in the village. They were heading towards the Palace. They had gotten away it seemed. Just one of them. Just her.

I let out a sigh of relief and turned, intending to find a place to lie low.

The boy followed me.

"Stay with them...they..."

But I frowned and glanced over my shoulder at the trampled baby on the ground, the trampled mother just metres ahead of it, at the ongoing brutality all around us.

I had been wrong. He was most certainly not safer here, with these people.

The boy watched my face almost sympathetically, as if he were waiting for me to realise something he had known all this time. As if I were the child and he the grown man.

"Come with me." I grabbed his hand. The slight smile in the boy's eyes was evident. Even now, he could smile. Even now, he was glad.

But he had probably been alone for weeks, perhaps months now, and there was no way of knowing what had happened to him before then.

I ran with him, weaving through the disarray, leaping over the corpses. I found it, a small dark road, one I had used before, we could go down there and...

"Stop!"

I pressed my feet firmly in place. Before us was a much larger group of villagers this time.

"He'll do nicely," one of the men said, eyeing the boy hungrily.

"Mmmmm..." another woman said beside him. "He's a little thin but...meatier than the one from last week."

I frowned, trying to conceive of a plan.

There was no way I could envisage escaping this alive without killing now.

My fingers twitched. I reached behind me, for my spear.

"Not this one," a voice commanded the herd of people.

Upon hearing it, the air felt like lead in my lungs.

With my hand still on my weapon, over my shoulder, I slowly pivoted around, to face the source of the voice behind me.

Kaspian. The man I had discharged from the Hunt just a day before leaving for Vasara, was standing before me, seemingly the leader of his own kind of unit now. His hair was longer and his grey clothes more worn, but he still had that steely presence, that determined air.

He didn't move. He eyed the child beside me, then the people behind us, who had quailed at his glare, before he spoke.

"As you can see, Captain, I didn't need that medallion after all."

# CHAPTER 76 – NATHON

I fastened the buttons on my sleeves, reflecting on the fact Loria's wedding would be the first I'd been to as a guest. Not as a spy, or an assassin, or a means to an end. Not to watch and hover over the celebration in the shadows, waiting until one of said guests was alone.

Weddings were something I associated then with death, rather than life or…love.

But although I was a guest at this wedding, could I truly say this one was any different? This wedding itself was nothing more than a means to an end. A pathway, laden with golden silk and robes, with vows and rings, with the promise of eternity.

But it was a pathway to death.

The deepest, darkest, blood red was the colour of Vasara's funeral attire. For weddings, it was the brightest and most piercing gold, and unlike in other Kingdoms, where guests were encouraged to don a different shade to the bride and groom, in Vasara, guests were expected to mirror them. I'd never cared much for clothing. After all, I could only ever associate it with those times I'd been ordered to dress in a certain way, to please the eye of a certain person. But I had no desire to catch the eye of anyone at this wedding, only to use my own eyes, to watch, to observe.

If anyone were to make an attempt on Loria's life, it would be today. Once she was married to the King, that would be it. It would be far harder for someone to try and kill her once she was the Queen.

I left my room and walked towards the chamber that had been allocated to her. The place where the King's servants would attend to, and dress her for the occasion. I knocked on the door once I arrived.

"It's me," I called through the wood.

"Come in," Loria's soft voice sounded through the door.

I tentatively pressed my palm against the handle and pushed down.

Inside, Loria was surrounded by several people, who were weaving golden ornaments through her hair, through the braided crowns they had created. Her dress ruffled as she shifted in her seat to meet my eyes. Its train was so long it nearly reached the other side of the room. It appeared transparent without actually being so. It glittered but not offensively, only subtly, golden beams of thread catching the light, dancing in it.

My head travelled the length of it, before turning back to her face. She looked like a statue. The magnificent kind in Elementas shrines. Reverential, glorious, yet lifeless somehow.

We said nothing.

It felt for the first time, that we understood each other without words. It felt now, we understood each other far more than any of the times that we had used them.

Loria's fingers flung behind her. She placed them on the wrist of the attendant whose hands currently hovered above her head. "Please, leave us for a moment." She gave the woman a closed lip smile.

The attendants, after bowing and curtseying appropriately, left the room.

Loria was sitting in front of a mirror, but she hadn't been looking in it. She was only staring at her hands, which were cushioned in the fabric of her dress.

I stood behind her. She glanced up then, at the mirror, staring at me through it.

"How...do you feel?" I asked, uncertainly.

Loria frowned at me. "Does it matter?"

Our eyes were fixed upon each other.

"Yes."

Loria let out a hushed laugh. "To you?"

"To me," I replied seriously.

She placed her arm on the back of her chair, swivelling around to face me directly. "I'm"— she laughed, smiling softly — "afraid."

I took a few steps forwards, her neck craned up as I did.

She was smiling, but her fingers were gripped tightly around her chair. I could see the muscles on her face tightening, her teeth grinding behind closed lips. She was afraid.

I had wanted to protect her from this feeling. I had wanted to make sure she would never feel scared, fearful, or uneasy.

I had known, perhaps, that it was impossible in this life, to make sure someone would never feel those things at all. I had known and yet I had hoped to change it.

Even if it took everything I had. Even if I had to face the worst terrors this word had to offer, and even if it were not avoidable she should face the remnants of them, I would face them anyway.

I would do whatever I could. I would take what little power I had, to take as much of it away from her as possible.

"It will be over soon," I told her.

"Not truly."

Not truly. Once Loria married, our father would arrive.

And who knew what it was, that he had planned.

"But you'll have me by your side the whole time, won't you?" I grinned.

Her face flattened. "That's even more terrifying." A shadow of a smile played at her mouth.

"For those who try anything while I am...yes...it's very terrifying."

She gulped and didn't respond.

I crouched in front of her, meeting her eye level.

"Don't think about it now." My voice grew significantly quieter for no particular reason. "I'll think about it. I'll do the thinking for us. You just..." I gestured at her outfit.

"Get married," she finished my sentence, sarcastically.

"Exactly, it's such a small thing after all...isn't it?" I tilted my head, smiling widely.

Her fingers loosened around the chair, and before I could stand, they were wrapped around my own.

I stared down at our hands in shock. Her touch was considerate, light and careful. I couldn't remember the last time she and I had shared affection. I didn't know what to do.

She placed her palm over my knuckles.

"You don't understand," she whispered. "These things are second nature to you. You're used to them. They don't scare you. You are the source of people's fear, nobody would dare touch you. But I...I am not like you."

She withdrew her hand.

*You're used to them.*

*They don't scare you.*

*Nobody would dare touch you.*

It was hardly as if I could blame her for her feelings towards me.

I felt like a fool. For a moment I had thought...

I shot up on my feet, clearing my throat.

"That's why you should leave the thinking to me...see?" I gave her a grin. "When the time comes. You won't need to act."

Her eyelashes fluttered. She turned back around wordlessly.

Our conversation was finished.

The wedding itself was as lavish and long as I had anticipated.

Loria and the King joined hands as they made their vows, a transparent veil still over her face, only afterwards was it lifted by the King's hands. Loria's back was facing us, those candidates and escorts who had remained for the wedding, being situated directly at the front of the hall.

I watched the King's face, his eyes as he took in Loria's appearance. Celebratory music and a choir sounded as they were pronounced married, as the King leant forwards and placed a kiss, so light it barely even seemed to touch Loria, on her cheek.

As the music continued to sound, Tarren mused to my right. "Where's the crown? Aren't they going to crown her?"

I closed my eyes, shaking my head.

Princess Rhana answered from my left. "Her Coronation will occur later."

"Oh," Tarren furrowed her brow, "When?"

I took my chance to leave the exchange and follow the guests who were making their way to an adjacent hall, the same one the ball had taken place in. Grabbing a drink off a passing tray a servant was carrying, I leant against a table, watching the scene before me.

"Enjoying the show?"

My lips formed into a smile as I turned to my left. The same words he had spoken the first time we had met.

"Lord Elias, surely you're aware by now that I love a grand spectacle?"

Elias stood next to me, leaning on the table as well.

"I thought that was only when you were at the centre of it." He swallowed some of his drink.

"Of course not. It's far more interesting to watch from the side-lines."

Elias laughed into his cup, then he drew it away from his face. "I suppose I should congratulate you. You must be pleased with this result," He pointed at Loria and the King who were standing together, greeting, and conversing with the guests.

"Congratulations?" I crossed my arms and turned to face him slightly. "Weren't you the one who implied this marriage was the worst kind of cage for the winner?"

"Just because I think so, doesn't mean you do, Prince." He gave me a false, tight smile and drank again.

"Well, I suppose you must be pleased, at least a little. You must have been terrified your cousin would marry someone unsuitable…like that child, or…that golden haired woman."

Elias side-eyed me.

"It would have been hard for you, to look upon the sight of his marriage to such a woman every day, and be constantly reminded of what could have been. What…could be." I side-eyed him back.

How awful he would have found it, should that golden haired woman have been crowned. A walking, breathing reminder of his undiscovered deed. A living embodiment of how close it was to being revealed. He would have watched her sit by his cousin's side and garner his favour, his trust.

"I've made it no secret I think this Season is ridiculous, or that I would be glad to witness its abolition," Elias mumbled.

"*No* secret?" I squinted at him.

Elias was silent for a moment, then laughed bitterly. "How fortunate you are. Your reputation is already so horrendous that nothing you could do would ever cast a shadow over you," he muttered.

"I'd hardly say yours is glorious." I crossed one leg over the other at my ankle. "But I suppose, being in an important position now, you'll have to make great efforts to revive it. It will be difficult…*almost* as difficult as reviving a corpse."

Elias rolled his eyes. He placed his empty goblet on the table behind us and turned fully to face me. "Or as difficult as climbing over an eight-foot barbed gate."

I clicked my tongue. "That sounds impossible."

"Sounds," Elias replied.

He went back to his drink. I watched him, a half-smile dancing across my lips.

"What do the Council think of it?" I asked, peering over Elias' shoulder at Loria again.

"They wanted him to marry the child or the golden-haired woman."

"An infertile King who married the wrong woman. They must be delighted," I remarked, grinning.

"The King is not a man who can be easily swayed by their opinions or suffer for them."

I faced Elias, "I know."

I did. I knew. I agreed. This King was not to be underestimated.

"Enjoy the rest of the spectacle." Elias strolled away.

The rest of the spectacle passed as the light grew lesser and the darkness of the night permeated the space, the sun replaced by candles and the heat of small flames. I picked an appropriate moment to make my exit, wandering, not back to my allocated room, but into the city, Iloris. I made my way through the hallways which I had now memorised and...

I stopped. A wave of nausea roiled through my stomach.

I blinked hard. My vision blurred.

My palms began to sweat.

I spun around, attempting to drag myself back to my room.

My mind was swarming with a thick and dense cloud, my thoughts, my confusion struggling to pierce through.

*What's happening?*

*I...I've been careful...*

*How...*

*I need to get back...*

*There are...supplies there...that...could...*

*Stop this...*

But I had only made it through several corridors, before a heavy, crushing drowsiness washed over me.

I remained standing, my eyelids fluttering, begging to close.

I took several more steps forwards sluggishly, my feet dragging behind me. But I fell to my knees. The impact of my bones hitting the floor echoed through the narrow space.

As did the footsteps that approached me.

I had no energy, no ability to engage the muscles in my neck to look up, to see who it was.

That placed a sack over my head as I fell into the dark.

# CHAPTER 77- LORIA

Eliel's room was at least three times the size of any I had ever seen.

Not his, it was our room now.

He came around to stand in front of me, as I observed the furniture, the curtains, the bedsheets red as blood.

If one night, I slit his throat, it would only blend in with the material.

"Loria." The King's voice shook me from my dark thoughts.

I watched him curiously. I realised it was the first time he had said my name, without any titles or addresses. My name. Alone.

"Your..." I stopped myself. "Eliel," I said instead.

He smiled, his face becoming even more beautiful as he did.

"It pleases me to hear you say that."

"It pleases me to hear you say my name as well."

The unspoken assumption of the night hung in the air.

Eliel turned around, and removed some of his outer clothing, placing it neatly folded on a table. He was left in a golden undershirt, against which his pale skin looked utterly white. It was like regarding the sun embracing the moon.

As his long fingers lifted from the final garment he placed down, he turned to me, his back to the window.

"For this night at least, I have no expectations of you."

But I had expectations, of myself, and perhaps, a curiosity about this man I loathed. It hurt me that I had wondered about him as a person far too often. It frightened me. I knew it was foolish. I knew it was wrong.

"Loria?" His voice lilted in a questioning tone as I fell silent.

"Which night?" I asked.

Eliel tilted his head. "This—"

"Which night will you?"

Eliel, understanding my meaning, raised his chin and sighed, looking over to the side of the vast space.

"Only when you wish for it."

I wished for it. I wished for this to be over, as Nathon had said it would be.

Father would not be satisfied until this had been done. Sacrifice or no, he would expect me to be sure. He would expect me to do this. He would wish for it.

There was a fragment of my soul, quiet and persistent I knew, that wished for it myself, because there was perhaps, a small part of me that wanted to.

But a larger part that did not wish for it, because as soon as it was done, Eliel's death would follow.

I wasn't sure, as I had told Eliel, what I wanted, what I desired. I had never had the chance to think about it.

If in another time, in another life, if I had been sent here, under different circumstances would I wish for it? Would I wish for him?

"And if…I do not," I uttered.

Eliel laughed. It was the first time I had heard him genuinely do so. His laugh was airy and light, as if it were the embodiment of a fresh breeze, of cool raindrops that slid along the leaves of the tree, falling onto your face, and trickling down your skin.

He shrugged. "No-one would know."

"You're not…displeased?"

Eliel shook his head and took several steps towards me. He cautiously reached out for my arm, but his hand hovered in the air, unsure. I didn't move. He took that as a sign to place his hand on my shoulder, the thumb and forefinger of it slightly cupping my neck.

His thumb moved back and forth, tracing slow and careful lines along my collar bone. "How could I be displeased?"

My mouth felt dry, I swallowed to no avail.

"But I—"

"The sacrifice served several purposes. One would be that no-one would know…if you did not wish it."

"But don't you want—"

"Very much so." His voice had dropped. "But not when someone is unwilling. Never then."

The brush of his finger sent ripples of tingling currents down my arms, into my neck.

"And if that means never…then it shall be never," he finished.

"I do not…wish for it…to be never," I whispered.

I placed my hand over his, gently holding it. His thumb stopped moving.

His hand travelled up my neck and rested on my jaw, his thumb on my chin.

He came closer, towering over me, looking down at me tenderly.

Our chests were pressed together. I could feel my heart slamming against my ribcage, his ribcage as well. He must have felt it too.

His right hand reached out, brushing strands of hair away from my face, and as he did, with his left, he brought my face to his.

I let him place his right arm around my back and draw me even closer still.

He enfolded me into himself, into his embrace and I sunk into it, like a waterfall that had reached its brink. Like one that had been waiting for the edge with nervous anticipation, only to plunge off it so ferociously, to fall so fast nothing could stop it.

And then there was a touch against my lips. Barely perceptible, like the whisper of air against water of a lake. His mouth had met mine with painfully soft tenderness.

And yet, with that touch as light as a breeze, was a flame, was a fire that seared with an insistent, yet tender urgency.

There was no time. There was nothing but this. Everything around had melted under that blaze, reduced to ash at my feet. And I was basking in it, the flames crashing in my lungs, screaming at the seams, ready to burst, to come undone. I let the heat through my veins, I let it be my blood. His hands became my home. His faintest touch became my harbour, vanquishing all storms. A flickering light in a dark tempest of a world.

It was the first time I had felt adequate.

The first time I was *something*. The first time I had longed to be anything at all.

It would be tonight. It would have to be.

And then I could say that I had done my part.

But I could not say that I had hated it.

That I hated him.

I made to move into him, but just as I did, he pulled away, the echoes of his weightless touch still lingering on my lips. His hands were still around my face, his gaze still full of softness as he spoke.

"But it will be."

I frowned, confused, slowly recalling the words I had uttered before that fire had lit. I was still locked in a trance, dazed by the brightness of those flames.

He moved forwards. His lips hovered at my ear, his hushed voice sounding inside it. "It will be never." His left hand trailed down my arm, stroking the skin as he spoke.

Until he reached my fingers and grasped at the ring placed around one. The ring he had wedded me with.

My eyes travelled towards my hand. The ring was alight, engraved with a mark brandished into the band. I did not recognise, only for one thing.

That it was sorcery.

Like the shackles used to bind Vessels, the ones used to subdue creatures of magic.

Eliel had seen to it, that this ring would be imbued with a curse.

I couldn't move.

He backed away from me but remained close. He watched the ring do its work as his gaze trailed up and down my body.

"I did not lie, when I said I wished for it."

My lips quivered. My eyes were wide.

"That I wished for you…" he continued, his tone tinged with regret.

"I..." I tried to speak but only a small crackle emerged from my lips.

"I wish..." Eliel shook his head and looked down at his feet. "I wish I had been wrong."

He met my eyes again, my eyes full of bewilderment.

"There were several purposes to my sacrifice. But the main purpose was to ensure that nobody could achieve what they wanted. What you wanted."

"I...didn't..." I managed to croak out the two words.

Eliel sighed, disappointed.

"An heir that bore my blood, and the blood of another, that child could be a weapon. I would rather have no children, than one that was to be used in that regard." His voice grew colder, more certain.

"I wasn't sure at first, if my assumptions were correct, but I received the confirmation that I needed not too long ago."

I trembled.

"Better to let you believe you had fulfilled your plan, to bind and keep you here, than let you go."

Tears pooled in my eyes. I wanted to explain I had not wished for this, that I had only agreed to it in fear of my own life, that I too wished things could be different. That the conversations we had shared, had not meant nothing, they had not left me untouched.

But I could feel, could sense, that it would be pointless.

I managed to shake my head slightly.

"I do not know what the nature of your plan is," Eliel resumed, "But there are several who plot against me, who wish to take my life, and replace me with another."

Eliel's eyelids flickered to the ground. "I am sorry Loria...but I cannot let that happen. I cannot let you, or anyone else succeed."

A tear escaped my right eye, instantly dropping to the floor.

Eliel watched me shed it and winced.

"I have no intention of harming you."

I thought about the entirety of events that had transpired over the past few weeks. How many of them had been influenced by Eliel's manoeuvres? By his assumptions. By his dedication to survive?

Eliel noticed my expression of thought.

"You may or may not have come to suspect it...but there is no reason to withhold it from you now." His eyes flickered to my ring. "The poisoning of Kalnasa's candidate was my doing."

If I had not already been utterly still, I would have been rendered immobile at his confession.

My eyebrows raised, my jaw tightened, my fingers shook even more violently.

"It had to be done."

*It had to be done? Why?*

My mind was a torrent of a thousand thoughts.

Nathon and the Captain, had their collusion been related to this?

Had the Captain, had Kalnasa designed similar attempts on Eliel's life?

But Dyna, she had wanted to marry him, I was sure, she had known nothing.

Nathon would not have revealed our plans to anyone, there was no possibility, no circumstance where he would have done so.

Nathon.

What...what would happen to him now?

"Her death had never been my intention," Eliel was gazing at the floor, brows furrowed. His voice was distant, as if he were not here but far away, retreated somewhere inside himself. "I needed to see how Kalnasa would react, and..."

He cut himself off. He raised his head suddenly, meeting my eyes directly. "So many times I have been let down, by the base selfishness of others. It is...the only thing I have found reliable, in all the years I have lived."

Silence brewed between us, a thick and vicious tension, tangible. Ossifying in my bones.

"I truly hoped you would be...an exception."

Inside, desperation sweltered within me. I wanted to respond but I could not speak.

He came towards me and crouched. With one arm under my legs, and another behind my shoulders, he carried me in his arms, and placed me on the bed, his bed, horizontally.

As he placed me down, my hair slapped against my face. He leant forwards and gently brushed it to the side. Tears still fell from my eyes. He wiped them away from my cheeks softly. His eyes searched my face.

"Foolish," he whispered.

The word mingled in the air between us. Was it I he called foolish?

Or himself?

I tried to speak, to tell him he was no fool. But it was only a small breathy noise that emerged from my lips.

Eliel watched my efforts. His face a picture of reluctant sorrow. He bit the inside of his own cheek, then sighed deeply, lowering his own head, glancing at the bedding.

He hovered there for a few moments, before standing up, turning away, and leaving me immobilised in the room.

# CHAPTER 78- HESTAN

The house that was once mine, was now Kaspian's.

I stood in my own sitting room, surrounded by several people I did not know. They were scattered across my furniture, sprawled across the countertops, leaning against the walls.

And at the centre, settled down into a large seat by a log fire, Kaspian sat, staring now, at the child beside me.

"Is he yours?" Kaspian asked.

I gritted my teeth, "Of course not."

Kaspian twisted his lips. "How would I know? Look at him. He's clinging to you."

"That's because I saved his life."

Kaspian laughed. "I see. So exactly like with you and Our Majesty then. No wonder you think it's normal."

"It is generally normal to have positive feelings towards someone when they prevent you from dying," I replied starkly.

"Positive feelings," Kaspian nodded yes. "But that?" he pointed at the child whose fingers were so tightly clenched into my clothing his knuckles whitened.

"He's a child," I pointed out.

"You aren't."

"I was."

"*Was*," Kaspian emphasised.

"What do you want?" I bit.

"It's actually good for us that you possess such a strong attachment to the King. You're going to stay here. No doubt that niece of his will reach the Palace and tell him all about your predicament. Then, assuming the King won't want you to be dismembered, he'll finally feed us."

"You think you can keep me as a hostage?" I asked. "You think that will work?"

"I'm sorry but there's no *think* about it Captain. You *are* our hostage. Look around you." He gestured at the several people occupying my house. "Where is it you think you can go? You'd have to kill every single last one of these people to escape. You could probably do it, but your conscience wouldn't allow it."

I huffed. "If you're going to start removing my fingers and toes, my conscience won't be a problem."

"Then let's hope it doesn't come to that."

Kaspian stroked his chin with the back of his knuckles. "I'll let you keep the child...as a gesture of goodwill."

"The child isn't something to be kept," I replied irritated.

"It's only a phrase," he replied defensively. "Anyway, if you refuse and decide to try and fight your way out of this, then you won't be able to prevent that boy from death this time."

My facial expression, which I normally could keep utterly unaffected by my emotions, warped in disgust.

"You...you were never this way," I remarked. It's true that Kaspian had always been brash, honest, and at times insensitive, but he had also been idealistic, brave, and selfless.

"Perhaps I always was, and you just never stopped to look?"

"No. You're threatening children now. The very children you made your speech about when—"

"When you dismissed me, yes, I remember it well." Kaspian tilted his head.

I clenched my fists. "Kaspian. No matter the situation. This is wrong."

"The situation?" He laughed. "It must have been lovely for you in Vasara, all that food, that wine, those refreshments." His lips parted, the tip of his tongue tracing his canine tooth. "But here Captain...here we are starving. And a starving person doesn't care much for how they fill their stomachs. Hunger can do things to you. It doesn't come from here, no." He placed his hand on his abdomen. "But here." He pointed at his head. "It's this maddening living thing, an itch you can't scratch, ricocheting through every fibre of your body. It forces you to be alert, while you weaken and tremble. It screams at you to eat, its hands around your throat, threatening to choke you, laughing and yelling its taunts, driving you to the edge, loosening your tongue, and clouding your thoughts. At first, perhaps, you can ignore it, but after a while, those thoughts grow more fragmented, your mood more erratic, who you are lost to those hands around your neck. *Nobody*, I have come to understand, can stay noble while hungry. And not even because they choose to commit sin, or do wrong, but because hunger worms its way inside their heads. If it can't have food, it will have you mind. If it can't eat bread, it will eat your heart, until nothing is left inside you chest. Until its as hollow as your stomach. That is what hunger is. It is not a growl in your core but a grip on your soul."

I had stiffened up. I remembered, I too, had once felt this hungry. But as with any physical sensations, they were dulled by time, replaced with others. With a blade tearing the muscles in my leg, with another pressed to my neck, with fingers brushed against my face, or fear, or unease, or confusion.

"You don't believe me, Captain?" Kaspian watched my reaction. I didn't respond. All knew I had been born in one of Kalnasa's poorest villages, Shinoba, but none knew the true extent of my family's poverty.

Kaspian continued. "I've seen it…I've seen people lose their minds, I've seen them eat their own children, I've seen them eat their own flesh. I've seen…" he trailed off for a moment. "How easy it is to say this is wrong. How easy to look at those of us on the ground, clawing and fighting for the scraps, and regard us with disgust…and yet you would turn and look up at your King, praise him, glorify him, when he is the reason we are driven to such depravity."

I shook my head. "People are pushed into situations which they cannot fathom or imagine," I spoke. "They are faced with choices others may never have to endure. But what they do when they are faced with them is entirely their decision. They cannot blame others for their actions."

"You haven't changed at all, Captain, and here I thought Vasara might expose you to some difficult realities."

My brow dropped. *Expose me to some difficult realities?*

"You are wrong," I replied. Too often people believe that someone who endeavours to make moral, or just decisions, must do so simply because they have not been exposed to those difficult realities, to the harsh truth of the world, and too often we wash away the deeds of those who do not, with the reason they were exposed to them too much, and for too long. But it is far more often that those who endeavour to give this cruel, cold world a slither of warmth, do so, because they know its worth far more than the rest. It is not because they are naïve, but because they are not."

The room fell quiet, those who had been picking at their fingers, or playing with their weapons, or sipping from my cups, stopped moving.

Kaspian sighed. "I was wrong. You have changed. You're even more ridiculous than you were—"

The house shook.

The smash of objects falling to the floor and breaking, the half-yells, half-mutterings of people in the room, all sounded at once.

"What the fuck was—" Kaspian started.

But the house shook again, this time rumbling far more violently. The boy clung to my leg even tighter. I took several steps forwards to grab onto a beam from the floor to the ceiling.

Kaspian turned to me, a suspicious look in his eyes.

"I've only just arrived. How would this be my doing?" I snarled.

Screams sounded from outside. Screams of agony and of terror. Toe curling ones.

I moved towards the door.

"Where are you—" Kaspian tried to grab my arm.

"Do you really think you can keep me hostage now?" I retorted, shaking free from his grasp.

I swung the door open and ran out into the street. Kaspian, several of the other individuals, and the boy followed me.

We turned to the right, where the wails were coming from.

"It's not coming from the Palace," a woman behind me remarked.

"It could still be the King!" a man said, "Kaspian, I told you that he'd—"

"Shut up!" Kaspian barked without turning around.

A cloud of darkened dust travelled up the road towards us, the distinct sound of pounding against the ground.

"Horses...that many..." the woman said.

"What's...that smell?" the man asked.

As if in response to the question, a screeching sound, high pitched and ringing, followed by a thick and booming explosion of flames.

"Grenades! Fuck! Those are grenades!" the man wailed.

Another one, closer to us now, the smell of burning wood, of charred flesh curled all around us. Dark, smoky tendrils that travelled up our nostrils and slid into our mouths.

"We have to go!" Several of the people started running, in the direction of the Palace, the only direction in which they could go.

Kaspian and I didn't move, staring at the incoming sea of smoke, fire, and dust.

"Why aren't you going with them?" I asked him.

"Why aren't you...and him...?" He pointed down at the boy who was still by my side, trembling.

The next explosion was so close we could feel the heat.

Kaspian and I didn't think for another second. We both spun around, he with his grey jacket trailing behind him, I with the boy under one of my arms, and ran.

As if those fires had been waiting for our attempt to flee, they flared all at once, chasing at our heels. Kaspian jerked back, his eyes widening as some began to swarm in through the side, wood flying into the air, howls with them. He ran into my side accidentally, then glanced behind him over his shoulder.

I was running alone.

I stopped.

"Kaspian! What are you—"

"It was the King," Kaspian muttered ahead of me. He was staring into the distance, his expression blank and distant, resigned and lost.

Hope bloomed in my chest. In the distance, a blurred image of a crown of dark red hair and pale eyes emerged.

Vasara's King was here.

"He's come to—"

But my voice was strangled by the look plastered across the King's face, miring that hope.

Vasara's King had not come to our aid.

For around him, were hundreds of soldiers, some atop horses, some on foot, glistening in golden and blood red armour.

Cutting down everything in their path.

## CHAPTER 79- NEMINA

Yaseer's eyes flickered frantically over the scene in Kalnasa. They glazed over cloudily as he enhanced his sight.

"They're being attacked," Yaseer said softly.

Baz threw his hands into the air, exasperatedly, "That much is obvious, isn't it?"

I watched Yaseer's face keenly, his eyeballs moving swiftly.

"Who's attacking them?" I moved closer and asked.

Yaseer's eyes resumed their normal appearance as he drew back to our surroundings. "It would seem...that it is the King."

Baz frowned. "His own people? I can't believe it's come to this."

"No," Yaseer said. "*The* King."

"What...why?" Baz blurted out.

"How would we know?" Ullna replied, her arms crossed, standing on the edge of the mountain, peering down at the clouds of smoke.

"We have to leave," Yaseer turned, his cloak flapping behind him. Ullna followed him.

Baz and I made eye contact.

"You...we're just going to...to...to... leave these people...like this?" Baz stuttered.

Yaseer spun around. "We cannot risk being caught. We cannot even say why the King is here. He may know of our location. This may be an attempt to draw us out."

"So what? We should use the lives of these innocent people as our cover?" I asked.

Yaseer sighed, he and Ullna looked at each other.

"We have no choice," he insisted.

"We do. We have a choice and the ability to help these people—"

"An ability they would kill you for," Ullna reminded me.

"If they were all sorcerers down there, would you do this?" I pointed behind me and turned between their faces. "Would you let them all die?"

Ullna and Yaseer didn't respond.

"How are we any better? If we let humans die for our cause, and we see that sacrifice as necessary, as if they owe us—"

"Weren't you the one desperate for revenge?" Ullna asked.

"Revenge on those who deserve it," I reminded her, "These people have nothing to do with—"

"They have everything to do with it," Ullna snapped. "Regardless of whether they were the ones to commit such crimes directly, they have all stood by while they occurred. Why should we risk our lives for theirs? For what? Will they thank us for it? If we want a future where sorcerers are not hunted for their cores, we must ensure that there are sorcerers left, and there won't be, if each time a human needs help, we jump to their rescue. Even if we could help these people…what then? What afterwards? If you're still there when the dust settles, you'll be chained and bound."

"I understand." I turned away.

Baz remained flustered. "That…that's it?"

I avoided his gaze, staring down over the precipice. The smoke was hazy, but through it, even without sense enhancement, the buildings, and houses from below could be made out, some crumbled black and into dust.

Yaseer stepped forwards, patting Baz's shoulder. "This is not our fight. We have our own, and we must live, if we are to win it."

He removed his arm. Baz's dejected and bemused expression followed him as he trailed off. He and Ullna sped away.

I raised my head, facing Baz, who sensing my look, returned it.

"I can't—" he began.

"Then come with me," I said.

Before he could act, before Yaseer, who had inevitably heard what I had said, could turn around, I ran at Baz, embracing him in my arms.

And pushed us both off the precipice.

The air around us howled as we shot through it.

There was still one of the five basic skills I had not yet accomplished. I knew Baz himself hadn't acquired them all either.

But he had accomplished the one we needed now.

My arms were still wrapped around his upper shoulders. We had spun around in the air several times, leaving my back to the ground and his to the sky. He pushed his torso up slightly, and wrapped his right arm around my shoulders, as we levitated through the clouds.

Clouds which slowly became lighter, and less dense as we pivoted, as our direction changed. I opened my eyes, having had them closed, and turned to see Baz make for a rooftop.

We stumbled as we found our footing, clutching at one another frantically, tripping over our feet.

We parted and heaving out deep breaths, took in the anarchy around us. The heat from the fires smacked against our faces immediately. The foul stench of death, smoke, and blood plunged into our noses and mouths in the same instant.

We had landed on a building. The rooftop of the adjacent one was no more, the bricks had crumbled into a concave pile, sinking into a hole in the ground.

There were people trapped under the rubble. There were hands emerging from the layers of collapsed brick and dust.

Down below on the ground, people ran, some fought, some stood in place crying. Soldiers adorned in gold and scarlet were cutting them down.

I had spent some of the first years of my life here. I could hardly remember it. All I had were glimpses, small snippets of the past. But they were filled with gentle peach tinted skies, smooth lined streets, small villages, beige houses, curved roofs, smiling faces.

Now, those same streets were lined with ash and corpses. Those same faces were cut to pieces, frozen in a scream as they formed an expression for the last time.

Baz let out a shuddering breath, "What do we do?"

"Whatever we can," I replied.

"But he was right, they can't see us."

"And what if they do?" My words were as lifeless as the bodies on the ground.

Baz didn't reply.

"If they see us...I'll kill them," I resolved.

"That's the soldiers, what about the people?" he asked.

I didn't say anything.

"Nemina...what about the people?" Baz spat urgently.

"You'll have to wipe their memory—"

"But I can't. I can barely use this." He tapped his forehead. "I wouldn't know how, Nemina."

"Then you stay here. I'll go and I'll cover my face. If anyone sees it, we'll find them afterwards, and you can try to...use your abilities then."

Baz took my upper arm and pulled me away from the edge of the roof, hard.

"No. This won't work, and you can't go down there alone."

"Yes, I can."

"Look what happened when you went to Vasara alone. When you were in Audra, with that man...alone."

"I can," I repeated.

"But you can't even levitate, how will you—"

I shook myself out of his grasp, "Please stay here."

I raised my hood, pressed my heels off the edge of the roof, and jumped.

My landing was terrible. In fact, I most certainly dislocated or fractured my ankle.

I took in a high pitched, pained breath, standing up and avoiding placing weight onto my foot.

I glanced up. Baz was glaring down at me, concerned.

I moved, half-hobbled away from the building, towards the throng of soldiers at the centre of a large square. But even as I moved, I could feel my ankle bone stitching back together slowly.

I didn't even know how I had manipulated blood before.

It was the only capability I had that would be particularly useful.

I blended in, bumped through the crowds of terrified people, running, bashing past me, vying for a way out, looking for a street or an alley with no soldier at the end of it.

But no such place existed.

A soldier came for me, swinging his sword at my head.

I lifted my hand, and using enhanced speed, swerved around his strike, punching him in the throat. He choked up, unable to breathe. I took the moment to use my own knife to stab him in the same spot.

He fell to the ground. I stepped over his body. I would have preferred to use translucency, but I couldn't afford to expend my energy on anything else.

It only took a few more minutes before I was at the heart of the bloodshed. By now, my breathing was hurried and deep. The soldiers had cornered most of the villagers into the square, surrounding them from all sides. They closed in, cutting them down like blades of grass.

It wasn't difficult for me to get swept into the sea of frightened faces, of children clutching at their mother's skirts, of men brandishing weapons that looked old enough to cut bread at best. Everyone was so tightly compressed together, the scent of sweat mingled with blood, the swell of quivering voices weaving through all the heads.

I shoved through to the front of the crowd, which wasn't challenging either. Nobody wanted to be the closest to death.

As soon as I was there, a soldier came for me. She yelled as she thrust her sword forwards towards my chest.

I disappeared.

The woman paused, the villagers who had been close enough behind me shared her expression of fear and confusion. All around the massacre continued. It continued as I reappeared and shoved a blade into the back of the woman's skull.

She fell to the ground.

I turned over my shoulder as another soldier approached me. The villagers before me looked on, unsure of who they should be more terrified of.

I threw the same knife I had been holding at him, directly at his eye. My aim wasn't superior, but by enhancing the speed of my throw, and at this close a distance, it found its mark.

The man grabbed his eye, dropping his sword.

In the split few seconds his hesitation afforded me, I took several steps forwards, and kicked him backwards.

And stood on his skull.

A child behind me screamed, several of the soldiers turned around at the high-pitched wail, to find me standing with the bodies of two soldiers at my feet. The man's brain matter was stuck to the side of my boot.

A Vasaran soldier took several steps forwards, signalling behind him for others to follow. The villagers nearby trembled.

The man's auburn hair was tied back, his expression harsh.

"Kill this one now," he commanded the soldiers behind him.

He stood and watched as two soldiers approached me at once.

But they were still several steps away from me, when each of them fell to their knees, clutching at their throats.

I lowered my eyes, and sighed in relief, as they choked on their own blood.

The man who previously had been so sure of his command, raised a hand in the air. More soldiers came to him.

"This one's a sorcerer," his voice bellowed, "Get the cuffs."

They shuffled away behind him, obeying his command.

At this, the remaining soldiers, who had successfully backed the villagers into a submissive huddle, turned their attention to the scene.

"Don't you think we anticipated finding the likes of you here?" the man said, reaching from behind him.

A crackle on the ground, a snap, as he pulled out a binding coil, fashioned as a whip.

He spun it around in his hands a few times, curling the ends around his fingers.

"It's hardly as if I was hiding," I responded.

The man strode forwards purposefully. I concentrated, I furrowed my brow, clenched my jaw.

Before it had only been born of necessity, of perhaps fear or urgency.

I had to command it now, I needed to...

I stumbled backwards, falling onto my hips, my palms pressed against the ground as several of the villagers swarmed in from behind me, full of anger and resentment, charging at the man with bloodthirsty yells, and vicious intention.

They trod on my legs, my hands. I cowered into myself, raising my arms above my head, taking hit after hit, desperately trying to crawl through their legs, and away.

"Fuck!"

"By the Gods what!"

The cries of the soldiers sounded all around. The villagers still standing in a huddle to the right didn't move, only watched as their fellow neighbours tore the soldiers to pieces with their weapons and their...

With their...

Teeth?

I backed away, losing my balance. My ankle was still not fully healed, my limbs were bruised, my face swollen. I staggered down a side road, bent over, clutching at my ribs. A sharp crushing pain crawled through my core.

I was sweating as I coughed up blood onto the pavement.

A soldier was there, watching. He came towards me. I could barely stand, my energy was depleted, I hadn't yet learnt how to conserve it properly, and especially not when injured.

I swerved backwards, only just avoiding his blow to my upper chest. He aimed again. I thrust forwards with my foot, kicking him in the abdomen. He wobbled, minimally.

The kick had been done with the wrong ankle.

I let out a high-pitched moan of pain, and fell to my side, holding out my hand to slow my fall.

I turned to find the man, a dark silhouette against the blue sky, his sword above his head, ready to plunge down into my flesh.

I had no choice.

I raised my arm, I'd have to take the blow, he might even cut it off, but I had no time, no ability to rise.

My palm remained outstretched over my face.

But the sword never fell.

Instead, the man did, to his knees, and onto the ground.

I gradually withdrew my palm from my face, the gaps between my fingers revealing the soldier, his face greying, paling, his skin drying.

But there was no blood this time...there was nothing.

He collapsed, his face pressed into the ground, directly before my knees. I stared down at him, an expression of deep confusion and concern etched on my face.

"You haven't really gotten any better at this since we last saw each other."

My facial expression shifted into one of recognition, and then, horror. I steadily raised my eyes, one was slightly swollen, obscuring my vision, blurring it slightly.

Just as his had been in Audra. On the night I had leapt through the sky, and he had dragged me with him to the ground. His head had been separated from his neck by the Healer's sword. His body had keeled forwards before me, lifeless.

Only now, Silus was here.

Yet he appeared translucent, with hues of blue and grey rather than the tan and peach that had once coloured his complexion.

"Hahahahaha." He leant forwards, placing his pale hand across his stomach. "Look at your face!"

I was still shocked, blinking hard, making sure what I was seeing, was indeed real, and not a figment of my injured mind.

"Aren't you fucking happy? Aren't you going to thank me?" He came closer.

I was sure then. Those eyes, small and dark, they were still the same.

"You're dead," I said, looking up at him. "He killed you."

He laughed, but he didn't appear entertained, only indignant, and utterly resentful.

"Yes," Silus spat. "And I'm going to make sure you wish he never had."

# CHAPTER 80- HESTAN

We had made it to the Palace gates.

So had hundreds of other people.

Kaspian and I tirelessly shoved through the throng, several of them allowed us to pass, simply for his presence.

Or that they thought we could do something about the closed gates before us.

There were hundreds of people at them, at least three dozen at the front, banging on the thick wood with their fists, begging, making pleas through sobs to be let in.

"I have children!"

"You can't do this! They'll slaughter us!"

"OI, CAN'T YOU SEE WHAT'S GOING ON DOWN HERE?"

They blended into a cacophony of mournful beseeching, a chorus of sorrow.

The boy, who was now half perched on my left shoulder, as my arm rested under his legs, stared around warily. He tugged at my hair.

He pointed towards the top of the gate.

Dyna was standing there.

My face hardened. What was she doing? Why had she been sent here? Had she been forced, or had she come of her own free will? If so...why her? Where was the King?

I pressed through the crowd to get closer.

"My Lady!" I yelled at her.

She turned to the sound of my voice. Her face momentarily relaxed in relief. She wouldn't have known if I'd survived.

I hadn't known if she had survived either, seeing her alive brought me a small piece of calm.

She faced away from me and turned the crowd.

"The King has sent me here to tell you he cannot open the gates. There are people here in Reyaru as well, and if these gates are opened, their lives will be—"

"What about our lives?!" someone screamed.

"Why should they get shelter and not us?"

"Just because they could afford to live behind the gates! Is that what makes them worth saving?"

"Please…please!" Dyna raised her palms, attempting to quieten the crowd. "The King cannot open the gates, but he intends to send out warriors to help defend you, and give you weapons to help you defend yourselves!"

I frowned, it was unlike Dunlan to hide behind walls and gates, to ask others to fight on his behalf.

"So, the King wants us to do his fighting for him!" someone protested.

"His quarrel with Vasara wasn't our doing!" someone else exclaimed.

"Please understand!" Dyna sighed. She still appeared weathered and worn from the journey to the Palace. "We cannot allow them to breach these gates."

"What about the outer gates? They've already breached those! Both of them!"

"Wake up, girl! They're already inside!"

"If these gates are stronger…why not let us in! What are we out here dying for?"

Jeers of agreement spread throughout the space. People raised their fists, their words and voices blurring into indiscernible sentences.

Kaspian hollered to me over the noise. "Still believe your King gives a shit about us now?"

"He's your King too," I reminded him.

"What kind of King lets his people die for nothing?"

"Everyone! Please stay calm!" Dyna fumbled, turning from left to right. "The King will—"

Silence.

I felt myself shatter into a thousand pieces.

No angry words of protest. Not a single remark of disdain. No cries, not even from the children. Nothing.

No sound, save for the impact of the arrow that protruded from Dyna's chest. She opened her mouth silently, glaring at her torso as a red sea grew and grew and grew underneath her pale clothing.

She tumbled forwards, clutching at her chest.

And fell two feet away from me to the ground.

I didn't realise I was shaking until the boy in my arms placed his hands on my shoulders to steady himself.

The crowd erupted into wild chaos.

Screaming, so violent and loud swarmed all around us. The villagers became frantic, spinning around. They knew the attackers had caught up, that there was nowhere left to go.

Several of them resumed their pleas for mercy, clutching at the wood, scratching at it, their nails leaving marks, but their fists denting nothing.

Their feet paid no heed to Dyna's corpse.

I stepped forwards reaching out to her lifeless form on the ground, my hand trembling.

Someone grabbed my clothes from the back and yanked me away.

Another arrow, this time in the nape of a man whose profile I had just been covering.

Kaspian let go of my clothing. "Are you trying to get killed?"

I lunged forwards. "Dyna—"

"Is dead. What's the use in you dying too?"

Dyna...was dead.

The screams that moments ago had been so loud were instantly drowned out.

I was instantly immersed in a hollow empty blankness...

Until Kaspian yanked me backwards again.

The same noise we had heard less than an hour ago had returned. A herd of horses blazed towards us.

Blazed towards a crowd, standing on their feet.

People sensing the inevitable, grew even more frightened. Their shrieks increased in volume, some piercing, some howling, some heavy, some raked with tears.

The smell of smoke and fire surrounded us, the shadows of the oncoming army, crossbows in hand, cast over us. There was no light, there was no wind, only stale darkness, thick with terror.

I grabbed the spear from behind my back, and pushed through the crowd, with great difficulty. Everyone was trying to get as far to the edge of the horde as possible. Kaspian followed, without it seemed, really understanding why.

Just as the horses began to flatten and crush those at the very edge of the mass, I moved forwards and threw my spear at a point along the outer edge of the gate. It embedded itself in the wood. I flung myself upwards and grabbed it, climbing onto it, balancing whilst holding the boy in my arms.

"Hurry!" I yelled at Kaspian. There was enough room for two on the length of it, and it was sturdy enough to carry us both.

Kaspian did as I asked and thrust himself up. Several people around us, who wielded swords or spears, found points along the outer gate to do the same.

But the majority had no time, weren't near enough, or did not carry an adequate weapon.

The horses flew through the crowd of several hundred within the space of seconds.

Within those seconds, the soldiers atop them had pounded countless lives into the ground, their bodies into pulp.

He sat at the front of the troop, and just as he approached the centre of the gate, he raised a crossbow, and fired at its centre, with perfect aim.

Vasara's King.

Athlion's King.

An explosion raged through the atmosphere. The noise smothering out all other sounds. A gigantic hole was blasted through the thick and sturdy material, a material nobody had yet been able to breach. How had he done it? The gate had been impenetrable, the people's assuredness in its strength absolute. But now, it had fallen as if it had been nothing more than a silken veil.

The impact of the blow vibrated through the wood, and threw several who were standing on their weapons off them. Myself included.

I grabbed it as I fell, the boy and I hanging from it. The fall wouldn't kill us due to its height, but should we fall to the ground, we would be trampled to death within seconds. I glanced down briefly, to see exactly that happening to some who hadn't managed to stay atop their makeshift perches.

With my right arm around the spear, and my left still around the boy, I ground my teeth and raised the boy up.

"Take...him..." I told Kaspian. I was beginning to sweat profusely from the effort.

Kaspian hesitated for a moment, then did so. He reached out his right hand to help me up moments later.

From up here, and now the horses had passed, the devastation they had created, the death, was even more visible.

But Dyna's body no longer was.

# CHAPTER 81- HESTAN

"Give me your spear," I said to Kaspian, outstretching my hand.

He narrowed his eyes but did so.

On my toes, I pivoted to face the Palace, looking up at the height of the gate.

"You're not going up there, are you?"

"I can't go through the crowd," I replied, still glancing up, mentally calculating how I could thrust myself over.

"What are you doing this for? You think he'd do the same for you?"

"It doesn't matter. I must try."

The boy was staring at me, I faced him. "Stay with this man. He'll protect you."

Kaspian didn't look convinced.

"I'm not your Captain anymore, perhaps I was never fit to be. But will you do as I ask? One final time?"

Kaspian snarled at the boy slightly. "You do remember I threatened to kill him, don't you?"

But he hadn't truly, only informed me that had I tried to escape, the boy might have died in the ensuing conflict.

"Please don't," I smiled tightly.

"Then make sure you come out of there."

I nodded. Then, repeating my actions from before, I aimed Kaspian's spear high and threw it at an upper part of the gate. I used the slight momentum from the small amount of length I had from my own spear to jump upwards, and grab onto Kaspian's, hanging from it. I swung myself up onto its base.

It would have to be left here. I would have to enter the Palace without a weapon, I would have to find another one along the way.

I thrust myself upwards once more, this time, gripping onto the top edge of the gate, that met with the stone walkway lining it.

The guards had long since dispersed, likely to the Palace, in an attempt to defend the King.

Some had likely dispersed away from it, in an attempt to escape.

There was nobody here.

The villagers of the Inner City, of Reyaru, were not in their houses. They were not on the streets.

Where were they? Had they fled? Was Dunlan's unwillingness to open the gates a chance for the residents to evacuate? Hadn't he thought those living outside it deserved a chance at evading death as well?

I skipped down the stone stairwell of the wall, peering around at the landscape, quiet and dull. It was as if the wall partitioned two completely different realities, on one side, death and devastation, bloodshed and pain, fear, and desolation.

On this side, it was almost peaceful, serene.

I waded through the empty pavements, up the incline, turning my head down each corner to ensure that I was correct.

Nobody was here.

The Palace gates themselves were open, blasted so, likely by the same mechanism the other gates had just been forced down.

I stepped in softly.

There were no guards, no staff, once again the space was utterly devoid of any signs of existence.

I made my way through the hallways punctuated by towering pillars of pale blue and white. They met a ceiling painted with a rendition of a sky, coloured with the first glimpses of a sunrise. The circular and arched windows let in the dull light of a day clouded by smoke, casting weak silver iridescent patterns on the floor.

I halted.

Voices.

I made my way towards them, high upon a balcony, and curled around the corners.

To the throne room.

It was practically empty, the pale blue of the floor shone brightly without many occupants to cover its colour. A peach and rose-coloured depiction of clouds acted as a backdrop to King Dunlan, not sitting, but kneeling before his throne. His hand was clutched at one of the arm rails. His sapphire and silver crown curled over his forehead and long dark hair. His brown eyes were slit in tension and anticipation.

Vasara's King stood before him, his sword at his back. A whip was clasped in his left hand. Its length and his face were smeared in dirt and blood. Several soldiers stood behind him quietly.

I regarded the scene, keeping to the shadows the pillars cast from high above, crouching, peering through the railings.

There was an air about the Vasara's King that was unavoidable, easily felt by all who were in his presence. It was one I had detected on several occasions while I had been in Vasara. But now, it was as if a veneer had been peeled off, and only a sharp and cold blade, removed from its sheath remained.

"There is no use in begging for your life," the King said unfeelingly.

Dunlan lifted his chin slightly. "It is not my life I beg you for, Your Majesty."

"The Lady Dyna is already dead," the King stated, completely unmoved by the words he had just uttered.

Dunlan's entire face seemed to tremble, his eyelashes, his lips, his cheeks. "She was…your blood."

My hands tightened around the railings I had clasped them around.

"Yes, and yet you sent her to Vasara."

"She didn't know…your father…he…"

"Did he? Did he know?" The King asked.

Dunlan nodded yes.

*She was your blood.*

Vasara's King, had his father been…Dyna's father as well?

Had the King come all this way, simply to end Dyna's life?

It struck me then. That it had, in all likelihood been him, that Vasara's King had been the one to poison her.

I ground my teeth so hard I tasted blood where I had bit into my own cheek.

"The others will not get far. Pegasi or no," the King remarked.

So, he had not only come for Dyna then. He intended to hunt the others as well.

"Your Majesty…I can only assume your reasons for your grievances with me," Dunlan said. "But my wife, my children, my people…it has nothing to do with them." He spoke carefully and unhurriedly.

"Your people?" The King looked at Dunlan with dismay.

Dunlan drew back, standing to his full height, flicking his dark blue tunic behind him as he did. He was just as tall as the King and broader, but he cowered before him now.

"I thought so," Dunlan said dejectedly.

I flitted my eyes between the two crowned men. There were unspoken words between them only they understood.

There was indeed another reason Vasara's King was here.

That note, that Noxscroll, it had spoken of a design to bring Kalnasa to its knees. Was it Vasara's King who had orchestrated it?

I couldn't decide, couldn't fathom whether the two were correlated or connected.

A moment, exactly as this flashed before my mind.

Only I had been ten.

The sorcerers had swarmed into our village, our house, and killed my parents, my brothers before my eyes.

And I had been too frightened, too young, unlearned in fighting and the cruelty of the world, too weak to do anything but watch.

It would not be so this time.

I straightened up, resolving to somehow, without a weapon, do whatever it was I could to protect the man who had found me, in that cupboard all those years ago, who had offered me shelter, who had given me a place to feel safe, to call home.

But Dunlan spoke again.

"How did you know?"

Vasara's King's face remained impassive as he replied. "Your crimes remain the same, no matter how they were uncovered."

"But they were *my* crimes Your Majesty. They were no-one else's."

*Crimes? What crimes?*

The King blinked slowly. "Do you expect me to take *your* word as truth?"

"If you do this, there is no turning back, you cannot wipe an entire Kingdom from existence and expect the others to stand and watch, to do nothing. You are starting a war."

The King shook his head calmly. "I expect them to do no such thing. But you can rest assured, I have no desire to start a war amongst humans."

Dunlan laughed, deeply. "You truly expect this to go unanswered?" His attitude had changed from pliant to furious within minutes.

"And who will answer?" Vasara's King replied confidently.

Dunlan didn't respond.

"War or no war. Your Kingdom's very existence cannot be tolerated any longer."

"Cannot be tolerated?" Dunlan spat, stepping forwards, his long dark hair swaying behind him. "These are people's lives you speak of."

"The same people you have been watching starve to death?"

"Only because we did not receive the appropriate assistance from—"

"The other Kingdoms? Yet you expect them to act after you are gone."

Vasara's King shifted his whip from his left hand to right, then drew his sword, ready to fulfil his promise. I fully straightened now, and leapt over the balcony, landing on my feet clumsily, behind Dunlan's throne.

The eyes of Vasara's King lit up. Dunlan spun around at the sound. His eyes widened.

Vasara's King held his sword by his side. He drew his head back slightly, his chin up.

"I should have expected you to survive, Captain," he remarked with a closed lipped smile.

"What is this, Your Majesty?" I spat through gritted teeth.

Vasara's King turned his head to glance at Dunlan, then back at me.

"Your King would have been able to inform you, I am assuming he has not yet done so. However, I am here to take his life and since you have no weapon, I am not particularly concerned about your ability to stop me."

Dunlan however, reached into his robes, while still looking at me.

He pulled out a dagger.

And slit his own throat.

Even Vasara's King, who always appeared as if nothing could surprise him, furrowed his brow in shock, stepping back, frowning.

I rushed over to Dunlan, catching him before he fell forwards, holding him by the shoulders.

He appeared as if he wished he could speak, but he could not. Blood was spilling from his throat, a waterfall of ruby against a sapphire lake. It spilled onto my pale clothing, coating it with yet more blood.

Dunlan only reached for his hand and removed a ring. He pressed it into my palm and clutched my shoulders, his mouth bubbling with blood as his head fell onto my knees.

With his face up in my lap, his eyes travelled over the angles of my own before they stopped moving.

Before he stopped breathing.

His body lay drenched in blood on my legs.

I glared down at his corpse.

My father.

My mother.

All three of my brothers.

My mentor.

Dyna.

Dunlan.

Was Kaspian still alive? The boy?

Zain?

Purcell?

How many more?

How much longer?

I gripped the ring tightly into my hands, slipping it onto my thumb. It slid over blood.

I could hear the King take several steps forwards.

I didn't meet his eyes. They were still fixed on the King's body.

The King I had served since I was a child. The King who had shown me a new purpose, a new life. The King who was the first to offer me a warm smile after it had happened.

"It's good you survived, Captain," Vasara's King spoke.

Something hit me hard at the back of my skull. My ears rang, but I could still hear the King's voice, soft and purposeful as he spoke.

"I'd like to test a theory."

## CHAPTER 82- ELIAS

The sun stung as it forced its way through the curtains, offending my skin, my eyes, my skull.

That dreadful Season was finally fucking finished.

I hadn't intended to consume as much alcohol at the end as I had at the start, but the conversation with Audra's Prince had been enough to break my resolve on that promise.

I stumbled from my bed, fumbling for my clothes, eventually making my way into the hallway.

I went to his room, he wasn't there.

The Council chambers, he wasn't there.

The library, he wasn't there.

The throne room.

Eliel was nowhere to be seen.

I went out to the training grounds, a daily occurrence now since I'd taken on my new role.

I stopped in my tracks, spinning around frantically, groaning as I did it too quickly, and a wave of dizziness washed over me. I kept to the shadows as I approached an attendant.

"Where are all the horses?" I asked him.

The boy gaped at me, as if he had seen a walking corpse. Although truthfully, that was probably exactly how I appeared.

"The horses?" I repeated.

"They went with the army, My Lord…"

"You're telling me, that the army, which I am in charge of, left, without my knowing?"

"I…I thought you were with them, My Lord."

"With whom?" I asked, growing more irritated, and confused.

"The…soldiers, My Lord."

I waved my hand in the air, slapping it against my leg in exasperation.

"Where did they go?"

"I…I'm not sure, My Lord."

"Was the King with them?"

"Yes, My Lord?" the boy said questioningly, as if it were the most obvious fact known to humankind.

Eliel had left with an army? I frowned so deeply that my vision blurred. What the fuck was going on?

"Is anyone still here?"

The boy frowned. "Anyone?"

"Fargreaves, Trenton, Raynard...?"

"Trenton is, My Lord...but he left the Palace earlier."

"Where the fuck is everybody?" I murmured to myself. Realising the boy was still watching, I turned to him.

"Thank you, you can go."

"But...I work here...My Lord..."

"There's nothing much to work on here today. Here." I pressed a lunar into his hand. "Go."

The boy glared down at the coin and smiled very briefly.

"Yes, My Lord..."

"Wait!" I called after him.

The boy, still reeling from our serendipitous encounter, stiffened up unnaturally.

"Can you find someone for me?"

The boy nodded yes, slowly.

"I need to speak to a tracker. Her name is Shadae, bring her to..." I paused in thought. "Tell her to come to my chambers as soon as she's able."

"Yes, My Lord," the boy repeated.

After he had left, I stormed back into the Palace immediately and headed for Eliel's room.

I had forgotten he was married. It was one thing that he wasn't in his room, but where was his new wife?

I banged on the door with my fist. "My Queen?" I spoke.

Nothing.

I grunted and walked away.

Eliel had left in the early hours of the morning with an army, without informing me.

What exactly was the point, or the purpose in my position, if he were just to do these things without my knowledge?

I was furious. I was beyond consoling or reassurance. Where would he have taken such a large force? What had he been planning all this time?

All the events that had occurred over these past few weeks, I should have pursued. I should have pursued all the threads of suspicion much more strongly.

But I had been preoccupied.

I made my way down to the underground levels of the Palace, each step sending a sharp pain through my head and my hip, but I ignored it. I rushed frantically until I reached the correct level, the correct door.

I took out the key, which was hanging around my neck, under my shirt, and opened it.

I fell to my knees, my head in my hands, half weeping in relief.

I was afraid he had found this. I was afraid he had taken these, to fight those against whom normal steel did nothing.

And he couldn't use them.

He didn't know what these blades could do.

Nobody did.

Not truly.

I glanced up.

Rows upon rows, stacked into the walls and shelves, crushed into corners.

The collection I had been gathering for years, sequestering behind these doors.

Noxstone looked even darker underground.

# CHAPTER 83- NATHON

My arms were chained above my head.

I crooned my neck forwards and groaned as my eyes slowly began to open.

This position was uncomfortable, but I had been in it many times before.

Still, judging by how dry my mouth was, how painful my knees were, it had been at least a day, possibly more.

I bent my neck up, glancing at the cuffs.

Were they...cursed cuffs?

Did my abductor think that I was a sorcerer?

I laughed out loud, my throat cracking hoarsely as I did.

As if summoned by my laughter, a figure emerged from the corner of the room.

The King. The King stood in front of me.

I was still drowsy, else I would have noticed his presence instantly.

He was alone.

I raised my head to meet him, licking my cracked lips before talking.

"So... it was you?" My voice was raspy as I spoke.

The King dragged out a chair that must have been pushed up against the back wall and sat on it.

I sighed deeply. A dark curl of hair fell over my forehead.

"Where's Loria?" The edge to my voice was clear.

"She is safe."

I pulled slightly on both my chains, they rattled loudly.

"Do you mean this kind of safe?" I smiled coldly.

The King was silent, half his face was cast in darkness, the other in semi-light.

"So, what, Your Majesty...you really *do* think that I'm a sorcerer?" I asked.

The King raised his eyes at the cuffs. "It is only a precaution."

"This feels as if it's rather more than that," I replied.

The King said nothing, he simply observed me closely.

I needed to pry more from him.

"This is hardly a way to thank me after saving your life, is it?" I put it to him.

"The very life you hoped to take?"

I stilled.

So, he knew.

The King tilted his head to the side, parting his lips slightly. His wine red doublet almost looked black in the dark.

I maintained my smile, but truthfully, I was at a loss as to how to escape from the one situation I had so desperately hoped to avoid, on how to ensure Loria and I could emerge from it alive.

I raised my head up slightly. "You'd already be dead if that had been my intention."

The King smiled softly to himself. "I think your design is far grander than that."

*My* design?

I licked my dry lips again, huffing out a laugh as I looked to the side. "I see, do you think I was responsible for your parents' deaths as well?"

"No. I do not."

I met his eyes.

"I know who was responsible for their deaths," he stated.

"Ahhh yes, you seem to know everything. Sorcerers too, wasn't it?" I raised a brow.

The King took in a deep breath and held it, peering at a spot on the ground by my knees. He met my eyes, they glittered with distinct knowing.

The smile I had been maintaining dissolved into nothing.

I laughed in disbelief.

"It wasn't sorcerers," I said.

"No," the King said, his voice ringing clearly and calmly. "It was not."

I swallowed. He had started a war. He had placed the blame for his parents' death at the feet of those who wielded magic.

And yet, here, and now, he claimed to know who was truly responsible.

It was difficult for me to be horrified. After all, my father, my mother, Mathias, the people they associated with, the things I had done, all possessed horrors enough for me to have become impartial to any other.

But as the King sat before me, uttering these facts unemotionally and plainly, facts he knew I could separate, could draw the inevitable conclusions from, complete and utter dread undulated through my veins.

Enough for me to hesitate before I whispered, "It was you."

The King only lowered his eyes.

A thousand theories as to why the King had ended the life of his own parents fumbled through my mind.

The King almost sounded aggrieved as he spoke. "It was necessary."

I stared at him.

"They would have seen Athlion ruined," he said more quietly. Seriously.

I had decided that this man was dangerous, was powerful, was cunning, but I had not believed him to be ruthless, or to be a killer.

My father had been wrong about this man.

But I, I had been grievously wrong as well.

"Do you not wish to know?" the King asked, folding his hands over his knees, leaning forwards, "How it was that I managed to detain you?"

I had indeed wondered, but dwelling on how you were detained, while you were detained, was simply a waste of mental capacity, the kind that should be utilised to plan your escape.

The King didn't wait for my answer.

"You are right, I do know much. I know that the Princess visited our apothecary to acquire medicinal ingredients, the kind only used for wounds, and that she visited your chambers just a day afterwards, to deliver a balm to you."

My face stiffened.

I had given that same balm to another.

"It acts slowly, in truth I had expected for you to fall ill far sooner, but I suppose you have your unnatural tolerance to poisons to thank for the delay. You need not be concerned. I have already given you the antidote."

It wasn't myself I was concerned about.

"At that time, I was unsure whether you were guilty of the offences I suspected. It wasn't until your three-day absence, that I became certain. I know your father's troop of spies suffered some large losses. You stated your presence in Vasara was based purely on your own whim. If that truly were the case, then your father's summons would have resulted in your permanent stay in Audra, since your presence there would be even more vital after such losses. And yet…you returned. There is only one discernible reason for such an illogical decision, and that is simply that your purpose here was entirely intentional…and not at all innocent."

I tilted my head back. "This is all conjecture, Your Majesty, you have no real proof."

The gall I had to declare that the truth he had pronounced so accurately was nothing more than a theory, was difficult for even me to employ.

"I will obtain it," the King stated.

I smiled and shook my head. "You can try, but I would have thought that all knowing mind of yours would have deduced that these methods"— I rattled my chains again— "will prove rather ineffective…and my sister, she doesn't know anything."

The King stood. He signalled behind him, a man stepped into the room, his short dark hair casting shadows over his face. Trenton.

The King only made a nodding motion and Trenton, who had clearly been nearby this whole time, left.

The King came closer and bent forwards so that our faces were at eye level.

Then he said, through the quietest exhale I had perhaps ever heard.

"You may have underestimated me, Prince, but I have not underestimated you. I believe you when you say you can withstand agony others cannot."

He stood to his full height.

"But can you withstand another's?"

I struggled forwards bashing against the shackles. "You said that she was—"

"Not her," the King interrupted.

The doors opened, Trenton walked in, followed by another man, huge and burly in form. He dragged someone behind him, someone I could not see.

He threw the individual to the floor.

His silver hair spilled over the black floor like light on the surface of a dark ocean at night. His clothes were covered, woven with dark blood.

My limbs felt heavy, my mind desolate.

The burly man who had dragged the Captain in, reached forwards and gripped him by the back of the head. A fistful of his silver hair was in his palm as he yanked the Captain's neck back, forcing him onto his knees.

Forcing him to face me.

The Captain's eyes, although hazy, flickered with alarm as he met mine.

The King watched our silent exchange from the side.

He pointed at the Captain.

"Him."

# THE END...

*F*ate of the Five will return with the second part in the series in 2026!

# GLOSSARY OF LORE

## Sorcery System

There are two types of sorcerers. Dareans (Darr-ee-uns) whose sorcery gives back to the world in kind, and Accipereans (Accip-eerie-uns) whose sorcery utilises more of the world's energy. Both Dareans and Accipereans are required for balance and the world's survival. Sorcery in Athlion can be thought of like the water in an Ocean. When a Darean uses sorcery, it fills up the Ocean with water, but when an Accipereans uses it, it takes water away. This is why the usage of both is required to maintain a balance, and a steady level for the world to function. The Vessels are drained for their sorcery, so that it can be released into the world unnaturally/indirectly instead.

There are four classes of sorcerer within each type, class four is the weakest, class one is the strongest.

All sorcerers can master five basic abilities: Translucency, Levitation, Enhanced Speed, Enhanced Strength and Enhanced Healing. The remaining abilities are entirely dependent on the individual.

Of these five, only translucency can be extended to things other than the self. To an entire group of people, rendering them all invisible, to an object, or to clothing which can be worn, yet seen through by the wearer e.g. hooded cloaks.

Sorcerers can have more than one ability but a maximum of two, within the same class.

## Dareans -(Dar-ee-uns)

Class four: Navigator, Shielder (can also create shields which stand in their absence), Nourisher, Teleporter
    Class three: Elementalist
    Class two: Telekinetic, Sense Transformer
    Class one: Healer

## Accipereans -(Accip-eerie-uns)

Class four: Dream walker, Illusionist, Curser,
    Class three: Sound manipulation
    Class two: Divinator, Blood Manipulation, Telepathy
    Class one: Necromancer

## Curses

Curses are wielded and applied by Cursers (Class Four Accipereans), apart from the curse of possession, which only Necromancers can wield. There are known to Athlion, fifteen grand curses and three minor curses. The effects of the grand curses are permanent unless broken. The effects of the minor curses can be temporary or permanent.

The three minor curses are often applied to objects. The fifteen grand curses more often operate by marking the flesh. All curses bear a mark of a different symbol, which only Curse users (or Necromancers) can inscribe properly. The grand curses are also ranked by their strength and their difficulty to break. 1 being the weakest, 5 being the strongest.

**The three minor curses:**
***Curses of subjugation***
Subdues the cores of sorcerers/ their abilities (for instance with the trackers' arrows and the Vessels' shackles)
***Curse of ownership***
Prevent weapons from being wielded, either by anyone or allowing the weapon to be wielded only by a specific individual
***Curse of sight***
Allows someone to see their true nature, usually applied to mirrors and is rarely used

**The fifteen grand curses:**
***Curse of Servitude (this is the curse used to bind trackers to their role)*-** Strength: 4
Nature: Bound to serve someone, will die if do not.
How to break: Strong healing magic to nullify the spread from disobedience or cutting off the limb/skin where the curse mark is. (However cutting is not always a guaranteed method, as the curse may begin to spread as you cut).
***Curse of Memories*-** Strength: 2
Nature: Forget several of your own memories.
How to break: Be moved to tears by recalling one.
***Curse of Oblivion*-** Strength 4

Nature: The memory of your existence is obliterated from everyone's minds across the world, except for those who cursed you/were present when you were cursed.

How to break: Someone dreams about you or kills the one who cursed you.

**Curse of Touch**- Strength: 2

Nature: People are pained by your touch.

How to break: Bathe in a river of fresh blood that has come from great suffering or fear/pain (e.g. bathing in a river after a battle).

**Curse of Solitude**- Strength: 5

Nature: Anyone who loves you will come to great misfortune and be cursed themselves (randomly by one of the fifteen curses).

How to break: Unknown.

**Curse of Enchantment**- Strength: 2

Nature: Obsessed with/love someone against your will.

How to break: Their death.

**Curse of Disease**- Strength: 1

Nature: Constant sickness and pain.

How to break: Drink the venom from a Vilkan's fang.

**Curse of Decay**- Strength: 1

Nature: Flesh slowly rotting/turning into tree bark.

How to break: Drink the venom from a Larlynx's fang.

**Curse of Daylight**- Strength: 4

Nature: Sun burns your skin.

How to break: You must burn someone you care about to death.

**Curse of Nourishment**- Strength: 4

Nature: Cannot eat normal food, the only way to sustain life is to eat the dead.

How to break: Eat the eggs of an Erebask (they only lay eggs once every five years and are very protective of them).

**Curse of Misfortune**- Strength: 3

Nature: Unfortunate in all areas of life.

How to break: Kill someone who is very fortunate and successful.

**Curse of Possession**- Strength: 4

Nature: Allows a Necromancer to possess the marked person either themselves or with the dead. It is also a mark of ownership over that body. If the original owner of the body is still alive, or recently deceased, an object is often worn to tether the possessed soul to that shell more strongly (like a talisman). A body can bare the mark, without a Necromancer ever using or possessing it, but the mark indicates they usually have the capacity to possess that body.

How to break: Give your heart wholly and purely to another without expecting anything in return. They will then possess your essence and soul over the necromancer (this is rare).

***Curse of Confinement*** - Strength: 1

Only allowed to travel within a very small certain area e.g. a town, often paralyses the user at onset.

How to break: Usually done by a piece of jewellery...usually a ring of bracelet that binds itself to skin, must cut the digit/limb off with a blade.

***Curse of Truth*** - Strength: 3

Nature: Unable to lie, and others around you are unable to lie in your vicinity.

How to break: Meet someone with whom you can be wholly truthful without reserve, in this instance, the curse will break entirely.

***Curse of Immortality*** - Strength: 5

Nature: Live forever, often in exchange for something. If the exchange is not provided, then suffering will be brought to the victim's life. This suffering can take any form e.g. crippling pain, sickness, the suffering of those around them etc.

How to break: Unknown

## Creatures of Sorcery

There are fifteen creatures of Sorcery known to Athlion. Each creature is ranked in strength from 1 to 5 and rarity from 1 to 5. Five indicates the strongest/rarest creatures.

After the Wielders War, a decree was issued by which, magic creatures native to each Kingdom were assigned as creatures of servitude, to regulate their activity. These creatures were those most common in those lands. The others are rarer, more difficult to find, or are astute enough to evade capture. The creatures of servitude are:

- Erebasks (Air-y-basks): giant eagle like birds, usually dark blue or black in colouring with golden eyes. Ability to discharge lightning. Native creature of servitude in Audra. Strength 4, rarity 3.

- Chimeras: half lion, half goat, and with a serpentine tail. Their tail may sting another, causing the victim to die a slow death from venom (up to 7 days). Golden, amber, or white in colour. Native creature of servitude in Vasara. Strength 2, rarity 4.

- Vilkans: large wolves, with two tails rather than one, larger fangs and claws both capable of seeping lethal, very slow acting venom into someone's flesh. (Up to 28 days). The only time this is not the case is if the venom is drunk by someone with the Curse of Disease. White, grey, or black in colour. Bright blue or grey eyes. Native creature of servitude in Zeima. Strength 3, rarity 3.

- Larlynx's: large lynxes, feline like. Usually golden in colour, sometimes brown. Eyes are golden or green. Fangs capable of secreting lethal fast acting venom. Can also employ translucency and are experts at camouflage. Native creature of servitude in Jurasa. Strength 2, rarity 3.

- Pegasi: Winged horses, larger steeds than normal. White or grey. Eyes are usually pale blue or silver. Native creature of servitude in Kalnasa. Strength 3, rarity 3.

## Other creatures of sorcery, known to exist in Athlion are:

- Banshees (also referred to as Witches): They can take three forms. One human, one of the death of a person they are predicting, and their true form. Their skin is lined with indiscernible symbols, their hair silver, and dark, their eyes shut. They can foretell the death of others, and their scream can render others weaker. Strength 3, rarity 5 (most believe they are extinct). Mostly dwelt in Zeima. Also found in Kalnasa.

- Pixies: Green, blue, or purple in colouring, with bright eyes and transparent opulent wings. Small, but able to induce different human emotion/action by whispering into one's ear. They also feed off human tears, both of suffering and joy. Strength 3, rarity, 3. Mostly dwell in Jurasa. Also found in Kalnasa.

- Centaurs: Half-horse half-human, extremely strong, fast, and lethal if combatted. Brown, black or auburn in colouring. Strength 5, rarity, 3. Mostly dwell in Kalnasa. Also found in Jurasa.

- Mermaids: Sea creatures, half human, half fish. They are scaled across their arms, and their hair usually resembles sea foliage. Their hair, scales and tail are of the same colour. Usually gold, blue or green. They are able to control water should they wish. Strength, 3, rarity 4. Mostly dwell in Jurasa.

- Sea Serpents: Usually white, blue, or purple. These reptilian like creatures are extremely strong, fast, and agile. They are able to spit water. Strength 5, rarity 5. Dwell in oceanic parts around Jurasa and Audra.

- Sirens: Sea creatures half-human and half sea-serpents Unlike mermaids, Sirens appear extremely "beautiful" to the human eye. They possess no scales on their arms and can change their tails to legs for a several days at a time. All have tails of dark colouring like black, grey, or navy blue, but their eyes and hair colour are usually bright such as golden, silver or auburn. Their skin tone can be a variety of shades. They are capable of channelling power into their voice to lure humans to do as they say. Strength 4, rarity 4. Mostly dwell in Jurasa.

- Salaths: Large scorpion with three heads. One of their heads is blind with heightened hearing, one is deaf with heightened sight, the is both death and blind but with heightened sense of smell. Their sting will not kill, or cause pain, but wipe someone's memories entirely – Strength 5, rarity 5. Mostly dwell in Audra.

- Perins: Large stags and deer with horns containing healing elixir. White, golden, or brown in colour. Strength 3, rarity 5. Mostly dwell in Vasara and Jurasa.

- Gargoyles: Batlike creatures with wings and sharp teeth that can induce agonising pain. Strength 2, rarity 3. Mostly dwell in Vasara and Jurasa.

- Krakens: Large squid like creatures that dwell in large bodies of water. They can generate sound waves from water that can cause fatal eruptions and decompress the skulls and internal organs of humans. Mostly dwell in Jurasa.

## Elementas

Elementas is the religious system that is widespread across Athlion. It involves worshipping nine Gods and Goddesses of the elements. Each Kingdom has two Patron Gods, other than Noxos (the God of Darkness/Death) and Lumos (the God of Light/Life). But each Kingdom practises the worship of all Gods. Celestials are Divine beings, created by the Gods to act as their servants within their realm. The only God said not to create Celestials is Noxos.

It is said that if someone dies by sacrificing their life for another, or if their soul is pure at death, that they will rest in the Divine Halls of the Gods. Some may gain partial reverential status. The Divine Halls are the territory of the God of Light – Luxos. It is said that those who have grievously sinned, and whose souls are tarred with evil will descend into the Nevultus Pits after death, where eternal torment awaits them. The Nevultus Pits are the territory of Noxos.

## The Nine Gods

- Aquos: Female, Goddess of Water and Emotions

- Arkos: Male, God of Wood, and Tranquillity

- Glacios (Glass-ee-os): Male, God Ice of Intelligence
- Furos (Few-ros): Male, God of Fire and Perseverance
- Terros (Tair-os): Female, Goddess of Earth, and Wisdom
- Tundros (Tun-dros): Male, God of Thunder, and Courage
- Ventos: Female, Goddess of Air and Freedom
- Noxos: No fixed or known form, God of Darkness and death
- Luxos (Loox-os): No fixed or known form, God of Light and life

## Which characters believe in the Gods?

Characters that do: Elias, The Healer, Baz, Dyna, Yaseer, Rhana, Sarlan, Jarian
Characters that are unsure: Hestan, Nemina, Shadae, Ullna, Fargreaves, Cheadd, Strava, Nyla
Characters that don't: Eliel, Loria, Nathon, Silus, Mathias, Kaspian, Trenton

## The Wielders War

*Fate of the Five: Veil of Vasara* is set in the Year 1118
The Wielders War began 19 years earlier in the year 1099.

## Currency

- 100 **rims** are equivalent to one **ray**
- Ten rays are equivalent to one **lunar**
- Ten lunars are equivalent to one **soler**

## Rare Plants, herbs and creatures

There are several unique species of plant and herb existing throughout Athlion. Some can act as recreational drugs, some as tea leaves, spices, healing remedies or poison.
Those mentioned in Fate of the Five: Veil of Vasara and relevant to its timeline include:

1. Riggon: A herb that can be used for seasoning, where it will add a spicy, tangy taste. It is also used in herbal remedies to help wounds heal faster, or ease pain. Dark green with a pale green border, extremely spiky edges. Found in Kalnasa.

2. Tuspian Leaf: A leaf from the rare Tuspian flower. The flower itself is rare, but even when it blooms, it rarely grows leaves on its stem. The flowers are deep amber with stiff upright peals, their colouring grows more intense the closer to the centre of the flower they become. The leaves are similarly amber, soft and rubbery. The leaves can be crushed and used as a deadly and slow acting poison. The antidote can be produced from extracts of nectar from the flower, which is difficult to collect, since the flower only produces nectar every few months, in small quantities, rather than continuously. Found in Vasara.

3. Papaver: A powder produced from grinding the leaves of the Papaver plant. The plant is flowerless and grows easily under most conditions. It is considered a 'weed' by most farmers and landowners. However, its adaptability and widespread habitation means that it has become the most popular recreational drug in Athlion. It is illegal to use in Kalnasa, Zeima and Jurasa, but not in Vasara or Audra.

4. Pitho: A small and deadly bird, that can unleash toxins into the bloodstream of anyone who touches it, even for a brief moment. The toxins are odourless and undetectable on release. They permeate through the skin of those who touched the Pitho and can even penetrate the majority of fabrics. On entering the bloodstream, the toxin kills its victim over a period of 48-72 hours. The final stage involves the appearance of a characteristic amber rash across the body, vine like, crusted and bright. There is no known antidote. Found in Jurasa and Kalnasa.

5. Ardicum: A fruit used to make Ardica wine. This wine is known as the strongest in Athlion. The fruit is a fleshy, deep crimson, soft berry. It is circular and striped bright red. It can be eaten as a fruit, with minimal intoxication effects. It is the fermentation/aging process that turns the juice into an alcoholic beverage. The beverage is legal across all Athlion. It is most expensive wine available. The fruit is found in Jurasa and Vasara.

6. Corshick powder: A sedative which when blown in the face, renders the victim unconscious of mind, while still appearing alert and awake from a distance. The effects last from thirty to ninety minutes. The powder is orange in colour, produced from concentrated domes of sand in Audra.

## Social and political structure

All Five Kingdoms are ruled by a monarchy. Various people rule over large towns, cities, and provinces within each Kingdom, as well as lead special units of warriors. Titles of relevance in order of importance are as follows, (from most to least important):

King/Queen, Prince/Princess. Duke/Duchess, Earl/Countess, Viscount/ Viscountess, Baron/ Baroness, Lord/Lady (note, Lord Elias initially inherited the title of Duke, but was stripped of it years ago), General, Captain, Knight

## Measurement of time

Days of the week: Lunday, Torday, Airday, Tierday, Farday, Sairday, Solday

The twelve month year is measured in quarters, based on the Patron festival of the Gods.

**The quarter of Aquos**: Janaire, Foraire, Malaire
**The quarter of Arkos and Tundros**: Avraire, Meelaire, Junaire
**The quarter of Furos and Ventos**: Julaire, Auvaire, Setaire
**The quarter of Glacios:** Ovraire, Novaire, Delaire

**Athlion's lore is very extensive! A full glossary will be available on Fate of the Five's official website soon!**

# ACKNOWLEDGEMENTS

Thank you to the readers! Thank you from the bottom of my heart for reading *Fate of the Five* and for coming on this journey with Nathon, Hestan, Nemina, Baz, Raviel, Loria, Eliel, Elias, and Shadae.

The bare bones of this story were created when I was just sixteen. You should have seen the first draft. It was horrendous. None of the characters that exist now, existed then. In fact, if you had read that, this end note would have been a profuse apology.

The story has changed a lot with time, and characters I never intended to be instrumental became main characters. (Nathon I'm looking at you). Characters I never intended to have chemistry, well...I ran with their chemistry. (You can guess).

One thing I knew I wanted to depict with this story for a long time was the challenges of living in a difficult and cruel world, which in ways, reflects many parts of our own. I wanted characters that had gone through difficult things, who had needed to make difficult decisions and choices, even if that meant that their flaws were obvious. I hope you have grown to love some of *Fate of the Five's* characters, as I have. Either way, thank you for reading. Thank you for your energy and time. And thank you for supporting me, an indie

I want to acknowledge the many countries that inspired world building elements of Athlion. These ranged from Morocco, India, Bulgaria, Egypt, (Audra). Ghana, Switzerland, Scotland, Ukraine, Czech Republic, Canada, (Zeima). Japan, China, Korea, Romania, Bavaria, Greece, (Kalnasa). Italy, France, Germany, Croatia, (Vasara), Ireland, England, Iceland, Indonesia, Peru, Costa Rica, Norway (Jurasa)! It is from our own world that the richest ones can be created in books, I think. The architecture, fashion, food, and scenery of these places helped me build Fate of the Five's world. *(Please note that the Five Kingdoms are not intended to represent these cultures themselves, but that the landscapes, buildings, and stylistic elements of these countries informed the book's own visual world!)*

I also must thank all my beta and ARC readers, who gave me the confidence to publish this. Especially Kishakori, Daella, Jules, Esmée, and Kate Kauri. Kishakori, thank you for designing the cover. When I was on the verge of giving up due to agent rejections, you gave me faith and memes. (Check out her Webtoon *Awakened by Shadow*, it's amazing!) Kate, thank you for all the writing rants and cheering me on through the months-long writer's blocks. For the joy and laughter. For all the voice notes. Daella, you were the first person to ever read the entire book, other than myself. Thank you for being the first person who made me feel this book was worthy of being printed. I will never forget that. Jules, for your enthusiasm, excitement, hilarity, and Reddit expertise -you're a bright light! Esmée, thank you for making this story your personality (which was already amazing), and convincing me Fate of the Five has hyperfixation potential. I appreciate you always!

Thank you to my map designer Danny! Working with you helped me consolidate the world of Athlion into something even more tangible (considering where the rain flows and where crops are farmed, you know – things I should have thought about at the beginning). Thank you to my proof readers – Daisy, Lex, Spanishbruja, Aneeka, A.J, Book_dragon1112, Anoko, Anoko's mother, (basically Anoko's family) for picking out my hilarious typos. (Pushing through the CROWS, and an arm's BREATH, using some tea LIVES).

I want to thank from the bottom of my feral fan fuelled heart, every artist I worked with to bring Fate of the Five characters to life and help me market this book! Zai, Dunken, Roser, Alice, and Akito,– you five in particular, are never leaving my basement, we're working together for life now. A big shoutout to all my writing and book friends who have encouraged me throughout this journey. You don't know how much you salvaged me from giving up. Big shoutout to Carren, Rebecca, A.J, Eli, Jules, Miki, and Sim. To every reader who ever sent me a kind message before the book released or told me they were looking forward to reading it – I am eternally grateful to you, for always. Especially to my street team – thank you for being the hype squad an author could only dream of.

Thank you to my mum – thank you for inspiring me, even when you do not know it. Thank you for encouraging me to write this book, and follow my dreams, to try and make a living from them. Thank you for pushing me to publish this on my own.

Thank you to my sister, who is the best example I know of someone who is always trying to be the best version of herself. Kind, brave, intelligent, empathetic, funny, loyal, trusting...even when the world did not always give her reasons to be so. That villain arc ain't getting to us! (TBC).

Finally, thank you to my best friend Mercedez.

Without whom, I would not have survived to write this book.

With whom, I learnt to write about friendship and love.

# ABOUT THE AUTHOR

Niamh Rose is a British author of fantasy novels. Her fixation on Dr. Who aged eight and on Lord of the Rings aged twelve set off a lifelong love of the fantasy and supernatural genres. Niamh's adoration of all things mythological, and magical goes into everything that she writes, as well as influences from her favourite shows, anime, manga, and books.

Some of her favourite reads are *Heaven's Official Blessing, Grandmaster of Demonic Cultivation, All for the Game, Circe,* and *Infernal Devices.* Some of her favourite shows include *Merlin, Interview with the Vampire, Alchemy of Souls, Game of Thrones, Attack on Titan,* and *Fleabag.*

When she's not writing, Niamh enjoys playing musical instruments, reading, drawing fanart, and scrolling through Pinterest (for character inspiration!) Niamh is currently working on three different book series; *Fate of the Five, To Forge A Sinner,* and *We Who Dwell in Dreams* and three standalone books; *The Notes of No-one, The Stars that Bleed* and *The Last of their Craft.* You can find more about her projects on social media @niamhrosewrites.

That's the official version. Unofficially, Niamh is a fictional simp who writes her maladaptive daydreams down. If they're going to be that detailed, she may as well flesh them out, right?

Printed in Great Britain
by Amazon